IN THE
LIGHT OF
WHAT WE
KNOW

IN THE LIGHT OF WHAT WE KNOW

0 Miles   1   2

0 Kilometers   2

ZIA HAIDER RAHMAN

FARRAR, STRAUS AND GIROUX   NEW YORK

Farrar, Straus and Giroux
18 West 18th Street, New York 10011

Grateful acknowledgment is made for permission to reprint the following material:
Excerpt from the poem "Home Burial" from *The Poetry of Robert Frost*, edited by Edward
Connery Lathem. Copyright © 1930, 1939, 1969 by Henry Holt and Company, copyright ©
1958 by Robert Frost, copyright © 1967 by Lesley Frost Ballantine. Permission granted by
Henry Holt and Company, LLC. All rights reserved.
Excerpt from "Little Gidding" from *Four Quartets* by T. S. Eliot. Copyright 1942 by
T. S. Eliot. Copyright © renewed 1970 by Esme Valerie Eliot. Reprinted by permission of
Houghton Mifflin Harcourt Publishing Company. All rights reserved.
Two lines from *Rabindranath Tagore: Selected Poems*, translated by William Radice
(Penguin, 1985). Copyright © William Radice, 1985.
Image on page 496 © Time & Life Pictures / Getty Images.

Library of Congress Cataloging-in-Publication Data
Rahman, Zia Haider, [date]
    In the light of what we know : a novel / Zia Haider Rahman. — First edition.
        pages   cm
    ISBN 978-0-374-17562-7 (hardback)
    1. Male friendship—Fiction.   2. Investment banking—Fiction.
3. Missing persons—Fiction.   4. Global Financial Crisis, 2008–2009—
Fiction.   5. World politics—21st century—Fiction.   I. Title.

PS3618.A3835 I53 2014
813'.6—dc23

                                                    2013038711

Designed by Abby Kagan

www.fsgbooks.com
www.twitter.com/fsgbooks • www.facebook.com/fsgbooks

1   3   5   7   9   10   8   6   4   2

To Lily

Our concern with history, so Hilary's thesis ran, is a concern with preformed images already imprinted on our brains, images at which we keep staring while the truth lies elsewhere, away from it all, somewhere as yet undiscovered. —W. G. Sebald, *Austerlitz*

IN THE
LIGHT OF
WHAT WE
KNOW

1

Arrival or Wrong Beginnings

Exile is strangely compelling to think about but terrible to experience. It is the unhealable rift forced between a human being and a native place, between the self and its true home: its essential sadness can never be surmounted. And while it is true that literature and history contain heroic, romantic, glorious, even triumphant episodes in an exile's life, these are no more than efforts meant to overcome the crippling sorrow of estrangement. The achievements of exile are permanently undermined by the loss of something left behind forever. —Edward W. Said, "Reflections on Exile"

Now when I was a little chap I had a passion for maps. I would look for hours at South America, or Africa, or Australia, and lose myself in all the glories of exploration. At that time there were many blank spaces on the earth, and when I saw one that looked particularly inviting on a map (but they all look like that) I would put my finger on it and say, "When I grow up I will go there."
—Joseph Conrad, *Heart of Darkness*

It is not down in any map; true places never are.
—Herman Melville, *Moby-Dick*

In the early hours of one September morning in 2008, there appeared on the doorstep of our home in South Kensington a brown-skinned man, haggard and gaunt, the ridges of his cheekbones set above an unkempt beard. He was in his late forties or early fifties, I thought, and stood at six foot or so, about an inch shorter than me. He wore a Berghaus jacket whose Velcro straps hung about unclasped and whose sleeves stopped short of his wrists, revealing a strip of paler skin above his right hand where he might once have worn a watch. His weathered hiking boots were fastened with unmatching laces, and from the bulging pockets of his cargo pants, the edges of unidentifiable objects peeked out. He wore a small backpack, and a canvas duffel bag rested on one end against the doorway.

The man appeared to be in a state of some agitation, speaking, as he was, not incoherently but with a strident earnestness and evidently without regard for introductions, as if he were resuming a broken conversation. Moments passed without my interruption as I struggled to place something in his aspect that seemed familiar, but what seized me suddenly was a German name I had not heard in nearly two decades.

At the time, the details of those moments did not impress themselves individually upon my consciousness; only later, when I started to put things down on paper, did they give themselves up to the effort of recollection. My professional life has been spent in finance, a business concerned with fine points, such as the small movement in exchange rates on which the fate of millions of dollars or pounds or yen could hang. But I think it is fair to say that whatever professional success I have had—whatever professional success I *had*—owes less to an eye for detail, which is common enough in the financial sector, than it does to a grasp of the broad picture in which wide patterns emerge and altogether new business opportunities become visible. Yet in taking on the task of reporting my conversations with Zafar, of collating and presenting all the material he provided, including volumes of rich and extensive notebooks, and of following up with my own research where necessary, it is the matter of representing details that has most occupied me, the details, to be precise, of his story, which is—to risk putting it in such dramatic terms as Zafar would deprecate—the story of the breaking of nations, war in the twenty-first century, marriage into the English aristocracy, and the mathematics of love.

I had not heard the name of the twentieth-century Austrian American mathematician Kurt Gödel since a July weekend in New York, in the early 1990s, when I was visiting from London for a month of induction at the head offices of an investment bank into which I had recently been recruited. In some part I owe my recruitment to the firm, of which I later became a partner, to Zafar, who was already a derivatives trader in the bank's Wall Street offices and who had quickly established a reputation as a bright though erratic financial wizard.

Like Zafar, I was a student of mathematics at Oxford, but that, to put it imprecisely, was the beginning and the end of what we had in common. Mine was a privileged background. My father was born into a well-known landed family in Pakistan, where he met and married my mother. From there, the newlyweds went to Princeton, where they had me, making me an American citizen, and where my father obtained his doctorate before moving to Oxford so that he could take up a chair in physics. I am no genius and I know that without the best English schooling, I would not have been able to make as much as I have of the opportunities that came my way.

Zafar, however, arrived at Oxford in 1987 with a peculiar education, largely cobbled together by his own efforts, having been bored, when not bullied, out of one school after another. His family moved to Britain when he was no more than five years old, but then, at the age of twelve, or ten, by the new reckoning, he returned from Britain to rural Bangladesh for an interval of some years.

To him, Oxford must have seemed, as the expression goes, a long way to come. In our first term there, as we lounged in the Junior Common Room beside windows that gave out onto the garden quad, I observed that Zafar's pronunciation of the names of various Continental mathematicians—Lebesgue, Gauss, Cauchy, Legendre, and Euler—was grotesquely inaccurate. Though my first reaction, I am a little ashamed to say, was to find this rather amusing, I soon grasped that Zafar's errors marked his learning as his own, unlike mine, which carried the imprint of excellent schoolmasters. I must confess to a certain envy at the time.

The greatest difference between us, however, the significance of which I did not begin to ascertain until two years after our first meeting, lay in our social classes. As I mentioned, my father was an academic at Oxford, and my mother, after seeing off her only child to university, had returned to practicing as a psychotherapist, throwing herself into the retraining necessary to make up ground lost while raising me. My maternal grandfather had been Pakistan's ambassador to the United States and had moved in that country's elite internationalist circles; his closest friend had been Mohammad Asad, Pakistani ambassador to the UN shortly after 1947, a man who had begun life as Leopold Weiss, an

Austro-Hungarian Jew born in what is now Ukraine. On the paternal side, my grandfather was an industrialist whose fortune, based on landholdings and tenancies, he augmented with the profits of shipping enterprises.

More than once during term time, Zafar came with me to lunch at my parents' home, a large double-fronted, three-story Victorian house like many in that part of Oxford, though somewhat more capacious than the homes of most academics. To this day, whenever I return there, I feel an ease and lightness suffuse my being as I tread across the sweeping arc of the driveway, the gravel crunching underfoot, up to the stained glass of the wide front door.

On his first visit, Zafar stood at the threshold, wiping his feet over and over, his eyes darting about the large hall, his mouth slightly open. Evidently, he was, as people often are, astonished by the books, which were everywhere: shelves hanging wherever a wall would allow, books overflowing onto the floors, even leaning accordion-like on the staircase along the wall. In the family room, old issues of science magazines and journals, my father's subscriptions, sat in box files on shelves that scored the walls like lines on a writing pad. More recent issues lay about in small piles on a sideboard and on the floor. Zafar surveyed all this, but his eyes settled on the far wall that was covered with my father's collection of old maps, mounted and framed, of the Indian subcontinent under the British Raj, an area that today stretches from Pakistan across India to Bangladesh. Zafar drew up to the maps and it was apparent that his focus had fixed on one in particular, a map of the northeast corner of the subcontinent. Minutes passed as he stood silently gazing at it. Only when the time came to move to the summer room for lunch, and my father rested his hand on Zafar's shoulder, was my friend roused from his intense study.

When we left, Zafar suggested that we walk back to college, rather than take a bus, and I agreed, assuming that he wanted to discuss something. The mathematician Kurt Gödel used to walk, setting off at sunset and returning after midnight, and found that his best ideas came to him in this stretch of time. Albert Einstein, who was deeply fond of Gödel, and who was also at the Institute for Advanced Study in Princeton, used to say in his later years, when he no longer engaged in much research, that he went to the institute daily only for the privilege of walking home with Kurt.

I thought Zafar wanted to talk, but in fact he was silent all the way down the Banbury Road. I sensed that he was searching not so much for a form of words but for clarity of thought. I recalled the map to which my friend was obviously drawn, and though I wanted to ask him what it was that had held his attention, I was reluctant to break the contemplative silence. On reaching Broad Street, as we approached the college gates, he spoke. You must meet my parents, he said, and that is where he left it.

More than a year passed before I did. On the day Zafar finished his final exams, in two years rather than three, when my own were still one year off, he informed me that his parents were to arrive at seven thirty the following morning. He asked me to meet him at the college's north entrance, to help him load his things, after which I was most welcome, he said, to come with them to a café in Headington for some breakfast, before the three of them, he and his parents, set off on the journey back to London.

At seven thirty on Saturday, Oxford was, and I expect it still is on every Saturday morning, perfectly quiet. It was odd that his parents should arrive so early; after all, the trip from London would have taken only an hour or thereabouts. The only explanation I could imagine was that Zafar was ashamed of his parents and did not want others to meet them, and that it was for this reason he had arranged to be collected at such an hour.

I found Zafar and his father already loading bags and boxes into a Datsun Sunny. His father had a beard and was wearing a skullcap. Standing in gray trousers, Hush Puppies, and a green V-neck sweater, he greeted me with a smile, tilting his head in what seemed a rather deferential way. *Asalaam-u-alaikum*, he said, before breaking into Urdu, a language that I know Bangladeshis of a certain age could speak but that is today, in the main, the language of Pakistanis. I supposed that Zafar had mentioned to him that my family was Pakistani originally. When I responded that my Urdu was very poor, Zafar's father looked disappointed, but then he took my hand into both of his and, rather unconfidently, repeated hello a few times.

Zafar's mother, standing by the car in an indigo sari that was pulled over her head, also greeted me with *Asalaam-u-alaikum*, but she bore herself with a self-assurance I did not see in his father. Pointing to the sandstone buildings around us, some of which had stood there for several hundreds of years, she commented on how old everything in Oxford looked. Can't they afford anything new? she asked earnestly. I looked at Zafar, who I am quite sure had heard this, but his eyes avoided mine. I understood then that in the two years he had spent at Oxford, a town less than sixty miles from London, this was the first time they had visited him, and this only as he was leaving the place stealthily one morning.

His parents' pronunciation of *Asalaam-u-alaikum* seemed rather affected, although I was able to recognize it as the one adopted by certain pious Muslims, particularly by many of those who have undertaken the pilgrimage, the tour of duty, to the holy city of Mecca. There, amid the throng of thousands of Muslims from across the world, this greeting presumably acquires a special significance as mediator in a Babel of languages, the Nigerian greeting the Malaysian and the Bangladeshi greeting the Uzbek. Perhaps an Arab pronunciation of the phrase proclaims the spirit of brotherhood. Standing there, as he and his father finished loading the last of the boxes, I wondered if it was his parents' religiosity of which Zafar was ashamed, though I understand now, having learned something of Zafar's own religious turn, that this was unlikely. I believe that while he was ashamed of his parents, he was more ashamed of being ashamed.

My own father had encouraged in me a sympathy toward the numinous claims of faith without ever surrendering the authority of science. He is a Muslim, my father; not a zealot but a quiet believer. He has always attended Friday prayers, which to him serve a social function, helping him to retain a link with his roots. While some connections gave in to the attrition of time and distance, others he deliberately let go because, as he explained, he was keen to see his son set his feet in the West. Apart from the Friday ritual, my father does not pray, not even once a day, let alone the five times ordained by Sunni Islam. He has never worn a skullcap, my father, and has never shown a drop of guilt for drinking alcohol. He drinks only on occasion, "certainly at christenings and bar mitzvahs," he likes to say. "Oh, look," he will remark, as he takes a bottle of fifteen-year-old single malt from the cabinet, "this whisky has certainly come of age. Let us baptize it in the name of the father and the son."

Despite these impieties, which, it is fair to say, stand in the lee of a great Pakistani tradition, going back even to the country's founder, Jinnah, who was known to be rather partial to whisky, my father described himself then and does so now as a follower of the faith. When I once asked him how a physicist could believe in God, his answer was that physics did not explain everything and it did not answer the question, Why these laws and not others? For him, it was not enough to regard the world as being simply as it is. I would have to decide, he told me, whether science was enough for me.

My mother, on the other hand, had only disdain for religion. Islam, she said, oppressed women and encouraged people to accept their abysmal lot in this world in exchange for the promise of some fanciful happily ever afterlife. Not for her such opiates.

Zafar's mother interested me more than his father did. As I write this, I remember an intriguing article, which I came across in a journal in my parents' home and which is now easily obtainable on the Internet. The article, written by the primatologist Frans de Waal, concerns his studies of kinship recognition among chimpanzees. De Waal and his colleague Lisa Parr, the article stated, presented their subject chimpanzees with the task of matching digitized portraits of unfamiliar female chimpanzees with portraits of their offspring. Astonishingly, they found that chimpanzees could match the faces of mothers and sons, thereby establishing kin recognition independent of previous experience with the individuals in question.

Had I been set the same task, I'm quite sure I would have failed to match Zafar to his mother, for I saw no resemblance between them. In his father's aspect, a softness of the eyes, a roundness of face, and a tilting of the head—all of these I recognized in Zafar. But his mother seemed entirely alien to my friend, her eyes sharp and determined, the face long and thin, and the mouth tense.

When we encounter a face, we view it as a whole, by a process of integration of the parts, which takes place, as some scientists and physicians understand it, in the optic nerves long before any transmission reaches the brain. The otherwise dizzying abundance of information that hits the retina is distilled in this tract of fibers behind the eye into a sign that our intelligence can absorb. When we see a strip of letters, a billboard slogan, for example, we cannot help but read the word; we do not see each letter separately, but rather, instantly, we grasp the whole word and, moreover, its meaning. As I stood there, on that June morning in Oxford, my friend's mother's face offered no sign of resemblance to Zafar, as if their respective faces were words written in different languages.

My lasting regret is that I made my excuses and did not go with them to Headington for breakfast. At the time, and immediately afterward, I told myself that I had sensed that in his heart my friend did not want me to. But the truth is that I myself, to my own shame, felt embarrassed for my friend. Sharper still was the disconcerting feeling I had in those few minutes that a distance had opened up between him and me for reasons I did not grasp in their full subtleties. After that day, Zafar did not mention his parents again. If friendship has a cost, then perhaps it is that at its heart there is always a burden of guilt. I don't deny that I've failed to do certain things, failed, for instance, to provide support in the hour of need, or step in when that's what a friend should do, failed as a friend. But my regrets for the things I did not do pale against the guilt I bear for an act of commission and its consequences.

All the same, it is not guilt alone that brings me to my desk to put pen to paper and reckon with Zafar's story, my role, and our friendship. Rather, it is something that no single word can begin to describe but which, I hope, will take form as I carry on. All this is quite fitting, really—how it ought to be—when I call to mind the subject of my friend's long-standing obsession. Described as the greatest mathematical discovery of the last century, it is a theorem with the simple message that the farthest reaches of what we can ever know fall short of the limits of what is true, even in mathematics. In a sense, then, I have sat down to venture somewhere undiscovered, without the certainty that it is discoverable.

When he stood before me on the doorstep of our home, my disheveled friend uttered the name of Gödel clearly and correctly, and I recalled instantly the bright afternoon of a Sunday in New York when I suggested to Zafar that I had caught up with him mathematically. I had assumed that Zafar's grasp of mathematics must have slipped, for after taking a first-class degree at Oxford, he left the study of mathematics entirely, quite to everyone's surprise, to study law at Harvard, while I, on the other hand, after completing my third year and then taking a year off, continued with graduate studies in economics and applied mathematics.

My suggestion to him, as we walked along a tree-lined street in Greenwich Village on that Sunday all those years ago, invited from him what seemed then the cryptic response that mathematics was full of beauty. I felt compelled to ask what he considered the most beautiful mathematics he had come across, and perhaps that is what he had intended, that I ask this question—I cannot tell. Gödel's Incompleteness Theorem was his unhesitating answer, and though I remembered the statement of the theorem well enough, I nevertheless failed to perceive why he regarded it as particularly beautiful. Within any given system, there are claims which are true but which cannot be proven to be true. So states the theorem. So simple. In its implications, it is a shocking theorem, granted, and some time later, that is to say in the weeks following his sudden reappearance on our doorstep, years after that July day in New York, Zafar would explain to me in simple terms why Gödel's Incompleteness Theorem mattered so much to him and why, if I may be allowed to interpose my own view, the world was foolish to ignore it in an age of dogma.

Walking with him down that New York street, I thought to myself that perhaps such beauty, as he perceived, might lie in the theorem's proof rather than in the statement itself. Yet I could not recall the proof of Gödel's disturbing result—I am not sure I ever knew—and I assumed that after his departure from mathematics some years before, Zafar would also have lost all memory of it. I was wrong, of course, for when I prompted him, he began in the manner of an excited child to describe an argument, setting down apparently irrelevant pieces of the puzzle in all its corners. Barely a few such pieces had been laid, before the fragmentary image of a proof reared up toward me. I caught something then of beauty, unfortunately a beauty so nascent that I cannot tell if I had truly seen it or if I had merely been carried away on my friend's euphoria. Presently his animated exposition was interrupted when we ran into a colleague and, so to speak, lost our way.

We had many walks on the streets of New York, a city to which I returned on business nearly every month, and in the streets of London later. Many of those walks abide in the memory, but if any of them stand out from the rest, then a good claim may be made by two others.

The first was near Wall Street, and, while arguably of little consequence insofar as Zafar's story goes, it remains a fond memory for me, despite present circumstances. For the better part of the walk, my friend coached me, helping me to commit to memory a poem by e. e. cummings, *somewhere i have never travelled*, as he discussed its rhythms and cadences and parsed its images into a sequence. His memory held a prodigious store of poetry, and this poem was his answer to my request for something with which I could woo the woman who was to become my wife.

The second was of an altogether different kind, disconcerting, for it revealed a side of Zafar that I had not the slightest knowledge of until then, when I had known him already for close to a decade. It was 1996, and my wife and I were settled into our new home in South Kensington, while Zafar had returned from New York and was living in London. At the end of the working day, our ties slack around our necks, the two of us met for a quick drink at a pub in Notting Hill, though our meeting up was by then less and less frequent. I had a few beers, and Zafar, as always, ordered one glass of champagne. His choice might have seemed rather pretentious but for the fact that Zafar could not hold his drink, did not much like alcohol, and, moreover, as he once explained to me, found champagne agreeable because it had all the fun of fizzy lemonade without the latter's unsettling effects on the stomach. At college, as was to be expected, his predilection attracted some mocking, but I like to think that over time his habit was seen as an endearing quirk.

After an hour, we set off on Portobello Road toward the crossroads where we were to part, I to catch a cab home and he to join Emily. I later learned that the troubles with Emily were already in full throe by this time, and I marvel now to think that as we sat in the pub and talked, he had disclosed nothing of those difficulties.

We were walking along the road when a voice boomed: Oi, mate. Zafar and I turned to see two men leaning against a railing, looking at us. Both had closely shaved heads and wore jeans, and both had a certain barbell muscularity. The first man, the one who had apparently spoken, was several inches taller than the other and wore only a white T-shirt despite the time of year, while the second wore an open leather jacket, ineffectively obscuring some of the excess weight around his torso. The tall man in the white T-shirt, so obviously the alpha male of the pair, fixed his attention on my friend. A quizzical expression spread across the man's face.

Do you speak English? he asked Zafar.

Zafar looked at him, turned his head toward the shorter man, and then turned back to the alpha male, before replying in the haughtiest Englishman's accent, affected to perfection: Terribly sorry. Not a word. Good day.

Zafar touched my elbow and we both turned and walked on. After a few steps, I asked him under my breath, What the hell was that about? When Zafar replied, he told me that from where I had been standing, I could not have seen what he saw.

Which was? I asked.

The shoulder of the man in the T-shirt, he said.

What? That the sleeves had been rolled up to the shoulder?

Revealing the tattoo of a swastika and beneath it the characters *C18*, he added.

I knew what a swastika meant but I had no idea about *C18*.

C18, explained Zafar, stands for *Combat 18*. The 1 corresponds to the first letter of the alphabet and the 8 to the eighth.

So what? I asked.

AH are the initials of Adolf Hitler and Combat 18 is a notoriously violent neo-Nazi group.

Oh, I said limply.

After three blocks, Zafar turned sharply into a mews leading us away from Portobello Road, saying that he wanted to take a detour. This seemed odd to me, given that he was already running a little late for supper with Emily.

Halfway down the empty mews, I heard the sound of footsteps on the cobblestones, and I turned to see the two skinheads now following. Zafar told me not to say a word and pulled to a stop. The men came up to us.

You being funny? said the man in the white T-shirt to Zafar. Bit of a smart aleck, eh? You dirty little Paki.

Are you a racist? Zafar asked the man.

Bit lippy, aren't we?

Zafar didn't reply but turned to me and said, Do you see this gentleman's shoulder? I looked at the man's shoulder, as did this man, the alpha male. He looked at his own shoulder.

And then suddenly the man was on the ground. He was choking and coughing and clutching at his throat, the most hellish, rasping sound coming from his mouth.

The man in the leather jacket stood stunned. Zafar told him to listen.

I punched your friend in the throat, said Zafar. You can pick a fight with me or you can call for help and save your friend.

The man did not move.

Do you have a phone? he asked him.

The man nodded.

Zafar then touched my elbow and we carried on down the mews, at our backs the dreadful gasps of the man on the ground and his friend's gabbling into the phone. I was stunned.

Back on Portobello Road, I asked him if he thought they'd go to the police.

In court, it would be the word of two suits, two meek South Asians, against the word of bullyboy skinheads, one with a swastika and Combat 18 tattoos. What would they say? That we picked a fight?

We parted ways then. Only later, as images of that evening came back to me, certain questions presented themselves. Had Zafar sought to avoid the two men or had he in fact picked a fight? Had he turned into the quiet mews in order to evade the skinheads or to confront them?

That evening in 1996, I saw an aspect of Zafar that was new to me. But I didn't know what to make of it. What had happened seemed almost ridiculous, but it was real. If anyone had told me about it, I would have disbelieved him.*

As I write this, I see that Zafar's return on that September morning in 2008 was welcome not only because it stirred the embers of our early friendship, which had never ceased to glow, but also because it afforded me a chance to shift the focus of my own thoughts. Habits of mind are not easily broken from within. His arrival coincided with a time of reflection in my life, precipitated in some measure by the turmoil in the financial markets and the looming prospect of being called before a congressional or parliamentary committee, all of which had left me, as a junior partner in the firm, with feelings of helplessness. Such feelings are, I am sure, foreign to many men and women in my business, who, like

---

*The following year, I read in the press of the arrest and conviction of a number of members of Combat 18, although two of its ringleaders absconded to the United States, where, curiously, they claimed political asylum.

matadors, acquire enormous self-belief from subduing the great beast, the bull or bear, that is the market. Yet in 2008, my dreams were not for greater wealth but for the recovery of a sense of control in my personal life.

To a large degree, my introspection grew with the increasing distance between me and my wife, a woman for whom I no longer felt any passion and for whom, at bottom, I struggled to find respect. When I met her, she had come to finance after a year of teaching in a school in a Kenyan township near Kisumu, by Lake Victoria. She spoke then of the children, whom she obviously loved. She told me of eight-year-old Oneka, who would valiantly thrust up his hand to answer a question put to the class, and when my wife acknowledged him with a nod, little Oneka would say, *I don't know.* She spoke of the children by name, she sent them cards, and she would tell me how much she wanted to go back and spend more time there, that she was going to squirrel away her earnings in finance for the freedom to do so soon. As our love blossomed, she became certain that when the day came, she would persuade me to go with her. But fifteen years later, with her idealism faded, she approached finance with the vigor of the convert. The last time our conversation had alighted on the topic of her days in Africa, of her dreams then, I caught in her eye the look of embarrassment. If that embarrassment had been for her failure to return to those children, I would have comforted her tenderly: Don't they say that when mortals make plans, the gods laugh? I saw instead that her embarrassment was for having ever felt so idealistic; it was scorn for her own naïveté.

Cold, unfeeling statistics tell us that marriages are now about as likely as not to end in divorce. Many of our friends were separating or had already divorced, but my wife and I had long regarded ourselves as shielded against whatever foul wind was driving apart so many couples around us. We even comforted ourselves with invented true stories of how those failed marriages had been doomed from the start, that this divorced couple had not had sufficiently similar interests, or that another had been doomed by a rivalry we believed we could detect from the very beginning.

The seat of our faith in the endurance of our life together, it is plainly visible to me now, was the store we set in the similarity of our cultural backgrounds. My wife and I were both the children of Pakistanis, immigrants, Muslims, and we had faith that our union was of things greater than ourselves, that it would survive, even flourish, because of a history of generations that intertwined in us. We could never imagine that the strength of our faith might merely have been conjured from longing.

Weeks of such rumination had fed a growing fear of what the future held, when Zafar's reappearance came as a relief and diversion, though later it would come to mean much more than that. Seeing him again restored in me a sense of continuity with something older than my marriage, older than my work—a period of limitless possibility. There was the revival of things forgotten over years of pounding the professional treadmill while watching life ebb away from the home. Seeing him was enough to set off in me an electrical firestorm of associations that had lain dormant for years, and I felt a renewed sense of the timeless beauty I had known during my studies. Mathematics, as Zafar had said many moons ago in New York, cannot contain its own beauty.

It had seemed extraordinary to me in those days that my brilliant friend had ever chosen to give up a career in mathematics to study law, and when I once asked him why he had switched gears so sharply, he replied merely that it could be an interesting thing to do. Kurt Gödel had edged toward madness over the course of his life, near the end relying on his forbearing wife to taste his food first, for fear that it might be poisoned, so that when she herself was taken gravely ill and was unable to perform this function, Gödel starved to death. I think that Zafar had some premonition of the madness that might await him in mathematics, though this danger, I see now, never actually left his side. This, then, is how I understand him now: a human being fleeing ghosts while chasing shadows. This also accounts for the twists and turns in his working life, changes of direction that I came to observe largely from afar, as in time our friendship lost its moorings, in the way perhaps of many college friendships.

Through a web of friends and acquaintances, I maintained some notion of Zafar's path, but even before he disappeared there seemed curiously little known about him. Sometime in 2001, Zafar vanished from sight altogether, thereafter to become, from time to time, the subject of rumors, some apparently preposterous, that he had converted to Roman Catholicism and married an English aristocrat, that he had been spotted in Damascus, Tunis, or Islamabad, and that he had killed a man, fathered a child, and, absurdly it seemed, spied for British intelligence.

That day in 2008, when Zafar resurfaced on my doorstep, he stood there, for one hovering moment of stillness, waiting to be let in, and I perceived the spark of recognition in his eye. The house had not changed much since he had last set foot in it nearly a decade before. He asked me if I had fixed the leg of the ottoman in the study. I laughed. One corner of the ottoman was still propped up by books.

Do you have the leg?

It's still there under the desk, I replied.

I'll mend it—but not today. I have to sleep.

An hour after I left him in the guest room, I went back to collect his clothes and found a small pile beside the duffel bag. Zafar was murmuring in his sleep. For a minute, I tried to decipher his words but I couldn't.

I took his laundry to the cleaners, where I noted the sizes of his pants and shirt (I wish now that I had checked the pockets but I didn't). Then, before heading to the office to put in a few perfunctory hours, I stopped off at the Gap intending to buy some new clothes for him, like the ones he was wearing, cargo pants and flannel shirts. I'd got as far as the checkout before realizing I'd absentmindedly picked up a pair of khaki trousers and a blue cotton shirt. A banker's taste in clothes is about the only thing predictable in banking.

That first day he slept late into the afternoon and then took a long bath. Sitting at the kitchen table, clean-shaven and dressed in a bathrobe, he ate a ham-and-mushroom omelet I had prepared, washing it down with coffee and orange juice. He ate slowly, even carefully. He still looked older than his years, though now younger than he had appeared standing on our doorstep. Lines radiated from his eyes, and his jowls hung from his jaw like the worn-out saddlebags on an old horse, and I wondered what, in the matter of a decade, had come to pass in the life of the man I once knew that he should look so used up. When he finished eating, he brought together the knife and the fork, pushed the plate forward, and began his story.

2

The General Welfare of Our Eastern Empire

The subject of our policy on the North-West frontier of India is one of great importance, as affecting the general welfare of our Eastern Empire, and is especially interesting at the present time, when military operations on a considerable scale are being conducted against a combination of the independent tribes along the frontier.

It must be understood that the present condition of affairs is no mere sudden outbreak on the part of our turbulent neighbors. Its causes lie far deeper, and are the consequences of events in bygone years.

In the following pages I have attempted to give a short historical summary of its varying phases, in the hope that I may thus assist the public in some degree to understand its general bearings, and to form a correct opinion of the policy which should be pursued in the future.

—General Sir John Adye, *Indian Frontier Policy:*
An Historical Sketch, 1897

When Mahmoud Wad Ahmed was brought in shackles to Kitchener after his defeat at the Battle of Atbara, Kitchener said to him, Why have you come to my country to lay waste and plunder? It was the intruder who said this to the person whose land it was, and the owner of the land bowed his head and said nothing. So let it be with me . . . Yes, my dear sirs, I came as an invader into your very homes: a drop of the poison which you have injected into the veins of history. "I am no Othello. Othello was a lie."

—Tayeb Salih, *Season of Migration to the North*,
translated by Denys Johnson-Davis

On Friday, March 22, 2002, I climbed aboard a twin-engined Cessna at an airfield outside Islamabad. Already settled in were three passengers and, separated by a curtain still tied back, two flight crew. Mary Robinson, the UN high commissioner for human rights, sat with a thick file on her lap, her precarious coiffure touching the curved hull of the plane. Sila Jalaluddin, wife of Mohammed Jalaluddin, was seated facing her, and as I climbed aboard she nodded her recognition but after that there was no engagement. Just beyond them was another pair of seats. In one was a young man I did not recognize, dressed in a suit and tie, with a metal briefcase against his lower leg. The other seat was empty for me. I was on my way to Kabul, still with only a vague purpose. I had been asked to go by the UN rapporteur for Afghanistan, and by Emily, who was working for Jalaluddin in the new reconstruction agency he headed. But my commissions had been so lacking in detail that I could not avoid the thought that I was coming so as to meet Emily. My stated business, at least as documented, was to act as adviser to a department of the new Afghani administration. Advisers were numberless in Kabul, like stray dogs in Mumbai; even the advisers had advisers, and none of them were less than "special advisers" or "senior advisers."

Shortly after we took off, a U.S. Air Force jet rose up alongside us. A bolt of sunlight glanced off the glass dome of its cockpit and flamed out before shriveling away. The plane was to escort us throughout the journey. An F-15 Eagle, I want to say—but what do I know? It was a fighter plane. It was a perfectly familiar sight. Yes, it rose up alongside us exactly as those fighter jets do in movie after movie. You experience the power not through the moment but through the focused light of umpteen filmic depictions of U.S. military might. What smart senator doesn't know he can marshal the support of a people primed to believe they can do the things their boys, their heroic selves, do on the big screen? Reality is no match for the fantasy. But don't suppose the senators and congressmen know any better; how many of these same senators, themselves reared on a diet of satellite images of laser-red targeting crosses hovering over enemy bases, of crouching silhouettes of special ops entering enemy tents in the desert, a diet of stealth and victory, how many senators have taken their conception of what America can do from what they've seen on the American movie screen?

I love America for an idea. The reality is important but ambiguous. In Senegal, there stands a building where slaves were stored before they were sent on to the New World. It was built in the same year as the

American Declaration of Independence. I love America for the clear idea behind the cloudy reality. Without the idea, the joys of America would be mere accident, the ephemera tossed up by the hand of fate, to disappear in the wind. And what is that idea? It is the idea of hope, that grand, audacious idea that makes the Britisher blush with embarrassment. It may be an idea not everyone cares for, but it is one I need, I want. I love her for her thought, first, of where you're going, not where you're from; for her majestic optimism against the gray resistances of Europe, most pure in Britain, so that in America I feel like—I am—a sexual being. Before 9/11, I was invisible, unsexed. How is it that after 9/11 suddenly I was noticed—not just noticed, but attractive, given the second look, sized up, even winked at? Was that the incidental effect of no longer being of a piece with the background, of being noticed, or was it sicker than that? Was this person among us no longer the meek Indian, the meek Pakistani, the sepoy, but fully man? Before 9/11, I was hidden behind the wall of colonial guilt after having been emasculated by a history of subjugation.

Zafar seemed rather carried away with his praise of America, and it's quite possible that I let out a smile. After a few moments, he picked up his story.

With the F-15 Eagle at our side, he continued, we flew over some of the most dramatic terrain I had ever seen. Small aircraft do not generally fly at high altitudes, and the shadows of the morning's slanting sun accentuated the relief of the land, the two planes casting darting shadows over the landscape, so that it was hardly a stretch to imagine us wefting and warping between the mountains and hills of northeast Afghanistan. Somewhere not far away in the vastness of the Tora Bora mountains, we were told in those days, was Osama Bin Laden, a hunted man even before his proud claim of responsibility and, we thought, soon to be found. As I looked out the window, I saw a land bleaker and more beautiful than anything I had seen in Bangladesh, and I could see how this place of hard habitation bloomed a romance that condemned it to Western intrigue. The Afghanistan below me was austere—there was no grass, not the least blade; it was neither lush and verdant nor wet, as Bangladesh was, but instead it was a land of dusty, earthy tones. Whereas my beautiful Sylhet sang the song of seasons, of a yearly cycle, Afghanistan's barren, ragged desolation moaned a long dirge of ancient wonder, the earth's broken features ready to receive fallen horsemen, the lost traveler, and all the butchered tribes. I understood why the European was drawn to such a place, saw why he would want to walk the numberless silk roads that crisscrossed this stretch of Central Asia, and, in my mind's ear, I heard the homilies of British colonials and postcolonials who broke bread with the natives to return home with wondrous stories of having survived the mountains and the Muslim horde, or to proclaim the Afghan's humanity and to stress with limitless piety the need to build bridges across cultures.

At a safe distance, the plane followed the line of an escarpment, broken here and there by the odd craggy outcrop, and I imagined that if I closed one eye, I could extend my finger and run it along the sharp edge. I thought of the contour maps that mountaineers and orienteers use, maps that by means of lines joining points of the same height gave you a feel in two dimensions for the three-dimensional relief of the known world. There was a time when you saw the same idea on weather maps on television, isobars, those curved lines of equal air pressure, before everything became simpler still with bright petaled suns, such as a child might paint, and bubbly clouds. Maps, contour maps and all maps, intrigue us for the metaphors that they are: tools to give us a sense of something whose truth is far richer but without which we would perceive nothing and never find our bearings. That's what maps mysteriously do: They obliterate information to provide some information at all.

Like the London Underground map, I said.

It never tells you, said Zafar, where on earth any given station is. In one sense, it's no map at all but a diagram; it's not topographical but topological, and the question is always: What use is imagined for the map? Harry Beck, the man who designed it, must have realized that when you're riding an underground train, you don't really care about geographical location or distances. Famously, if you kept to the map, to get from Bank Station to Mansion House you would take the Central Line train to Liverpool Street, change onto the Circle Line, and get off five stops later, at Mansion House. But when you got to street level you would look down the road and discover that you'd traveled barely four hundred yards. The map helps you navigate your way around its own schematic world and requires you to abandon the reality of tarmac and buildings and parks. Only afterward do you step out and again find London.*

---

*Zafar's discussion of maps continued, but I have chosen to include it here as a footnote. I am reminded of a passage in *The Razor's Edge* by Somerset Maugham (an author I rather liked as a boy), in which the narrator states: *I feel it right to warn the reader that he can very well skip this chapter without losing the thread of such story as I have to tell, since for the most part it is nothing more than the account of a conversation that I had with Larry.* Having dismissed the passage thus, the narrator goes on, preposterously I think, to state: *I should add, however, that except for this conversation I should perhaps not have thought it worth while to write this book.*

I will forgo Maugham's addendum but include here Zafar's discussion of map projections. I have added two diagrams culled from the Internet, which correspond to diagrams that Zafar himself sketched very crudely in the course of the discussion.

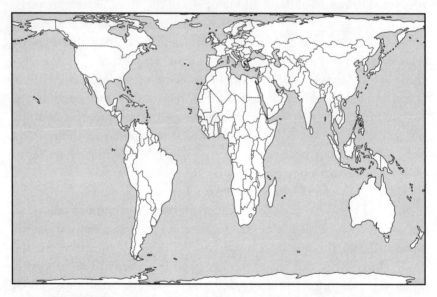

Have you, Zafar asked me, ever seen the Peters projection?

I've heard of it.

Have you seen it?

I don't think so.

It's a version of the map of the world in which areas of landmasses are shown proportionately, said Zafar.

It's the one, I interjected, where Africa looks vast. I do remember it.

Africa looks vast because it *is* vast. In fact, on Mercator's projection, which is the

Thoughts of topographic maps visited me in that cabin as I looked over the vales below. I didn't speak to the other passengers, exchanged not so much as one pleasantry, and when the bright sun rushed out from behind a cloud, I hid my face in a copy of Dante's *Inferno*, which Emily had sent to me when I was in hospital. I was once the patient of a psychiatric hospital.

If Zafar's eyes contained a confirmation of the accusation I felt in his words, I did not see it. I remembered, of course. But it was an unpleasant

---

most widely used, the one everyone's familiar with, the one that everyone remembers, Greenland appears bigger than Africa, when in reality you could get fourteen Greenlands into the whole of Africa.

I had no idea.

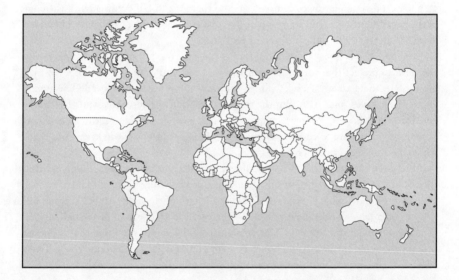

It gets better, said Zafar. In Mercator's projection, Brazil looks roughly the same size as Alaska, when it's actually five times bigger. Another odd thing is that Finland looks longer, from north to south, than India. In actual fact, it's the other way around.

When it first came out in the 1980s, continued my friend, the Peters projection set the cat among the pigeons, precisely because it was obvious that the choice of map projection had political implications for how we see the world. Critics of Mercator's projection had pointed out its flaws, and they did have something; after all, how many schoolchildren have looked at maps and asked, Which is the biggest country in the world?

The basic problem of mapping the globe is how to transfer the curved surface of the memory, for a number of reasons, and I'm ashamed to say that between Zafar's landing on my doorstep and his reminding me then, I had not once recalled any aspect of that episode. If anything, I'd suppressed it.

We arrived, he continued, at Bagram air base outside Kabul. The line of mountains rose beneath the sun, but it was an impotent sun, bright but without heat, so that when the door of the aircraft opened and I stepped out behind Mary Robinson and Sila Jalaluddin, the cold March air came as a cracking slap across the face. That is how Afghanistan greeted me.

———————

earth, an oblate spheroid, onto a flat surface. And there's another complication: If you stand on the earth and start walking in any direction and just keep walking, you'll never hit any kind of boundary. You can just keep on going around the world. But if you stand on a map, a rectangular piece of paper, and do the same, you'll eventually hit the edge of the paper. Getting a representation of the curved surface of the earth onto a bounded piece of flat paper, that's the business of projection.

You have the same problem in translating poetry. You start off in one language and you have to project the work onto another. And the similarity is even closer. In map projections, there are a variety of things you want to preserve, such as area, distances, angles in triangles, and so on. But the trouble is you can't preserve them all. The mathematics won't allow it. Your flat map can't reflect every one of these things even approximately. You have to choose among them which ones you want to keep. And that's where the choice of projection comes in.

There's an easy way to show how you arrive at Mercator's projection. Take a ball and slice off the very top and the bottom. Then imagine stretching it out so that the surface looks like a hollow tube. Now cut a slit along a length of the hollow tube. You can roll this out on a table. Notice how you've lost the very top and bottom of the ball and, in fact, if you look at the common Mercator's map of the world, you'll see that it doesn't actually show you the North and South Poles or even small regions around them. That's Mercator's projection, but there are different ways of projecting the world.

And the similarity with poetry? I asked.

The cartographer's job is to take the material on the surface of the globe—lakes, mountains, and cities—and represent these on a flat surface. The translator takes a poem, a piece of text, in one language and has the task of trying to represent aspects of the poem—rhyme, meter, rhythm, metaphor, and meaning—in another language. A cartographer doesn't give you a miniature globe with all the same details on it as the globe of the world itself has. Nor does the translator simply give you the poem in the original language along with a Hungarian dictionary.

Both of them face the same problem, namely, that they cannot capture everything exactly and they have to give up some things in order to convey anything at all. In going from the curved surface of the earth to the flat surface of a map, the cartographer

A Land Rover drove me to AfDARI, the Afghan Development, Aid, and Reconstruction Institute, near Shar-e-Naw, an organization that I came to understand had yet to earn its grand name. The vehicle tore through every crossroad; at that time, ISAF* soldiers had been instructed never to stop on their routes, so mayhem ensued in a city now overrun by Land Rovers, Pajeros, Land Cruisers, and monster Humvees. At AfDARI, I was taken to the guesthouse by an orderly, who motioned directions to me. We passed a shared washroom outside the bedroom, with a toilet and a large bucket of water in which a tin cup floated on the surface. The room was bare apart from a single bed, a pile of blankets, and a small table beside the bed, with three legs, though one, I noticed, appeared to

---

would ideally want to preserve a number of aspects such as relative distances (so that the distance between Islamabad and Kabul should be in the same proportion to the distance between London and Dhaka on the map as it is in the real world); relative areas (so that the ratio of the area of Nigeria to that of the borough of Brooklyn is the same on the map as it is in the real world); angles (so that the angle subtended at Bagram air base outside Kabul by the lines to that air base from the island of Diego Garcia in the Indian Ocean, home to an American air base, and from RAF Brize Norton in the Royal County of Oxfordshire is the same on the map as it is in the world); and so on. There are a number of such aspects, more than these few that I mention, but the fact is that the cartographer can't preserve them all.

It all depends on what you want the map to show and what use you have for it. People talk about things being lost in translation, but things can, of course, be gained in translation, too. A cartographer might add things, such as borders, which may or may not have some physical manifestation on the earth. But even if there is a fence to mark the border in the world, that fence is not the same as the political border represented on the map: A break in the fence doesn't vitiate the political border. After all, the red line on the map doesn't represent the fence and, in fact, the fence itself only represents the border.

But the point of all this is that all these representations or translations begin from needs. Consequently, the loss of information and understanding that every act of representation involves is the effect of an act of destruction that serves a need. We might appear to have taken a step forward, but in fact we took one step back and two steps forward. Every time we want to understand anything, we have to simplify and reduce and, importantly, give up the prospect of understanding it all, in order to clear the way to understanding something at all. This, I think, is true of all human inquiry.

*Zafar is referring to the International Security Assistance Force.

have come from another table, its color and shape quite different, and its length, too, giving the table a slight tilt. Paint flaking away from the walls suggested another history, and already I felt that this place contained an allegation against someone. The orderly pointed to an electrical outlet near the door, waved his hand, and shook his head. Either it didn't work or I was not to use it; I supposed it was the latter, since if it didn't work, I'd have found that out myself, and he needn't be fussing. In the opposing corner, a *bukhari*, the kerosene heater that I would see everywhere, had yet to be turned on. Behind me, I noticed that the door to the room had a lock and key. There were windows facing onto the courtyard, with curtains partially drawn. On the other side of the room, there was what appeared to be another window, looking out the back. When I took a step closer to it, I saw that the bedside cabinet, a veneered chipboard thing, was wedged under a door handle and that the cabinet itself stood on some pieces of wood, presumably to bring it up to the right height. What looked first like a window was actually the upper part of a door, with the cabinet acting as makeshift lock. It was, I noted, an exit route. Through the glass pane, I saw the outline of a leafless tree, its branches dividing endlessly and dark as if dipped in pitch, and I thought of the X-ray image of a blackened, cancerous lung, the image intended to frighten us.

What I first learned about AfDARI came from the program manager, Suleiman, who visited me in my room shortly after my arrival late in the afternoon. AfDARI had been established by Australia's overseas aid agency, with Taliban acquiescence, a few years after the Soviet withdrawal in the early 1990s, though its funding had come from a variety of sources. It was involved in a number of small aid and development activities primarily focused on Mazar-e-Sharif, Kandahar, and, of course, Kabul, but was now being sidelined by UNAMA,* he explained. Suleiman was a tall young man, without a beard and dressed in Western clothes, which raised the obvious question of whether his appearance had been different in Taliban days, which is to say only a few months before. He had, he would explain, spent two years at Indiana University in the U.S., which suggested that he came from a well-connected family, and he was now second in command at the institute. Suleiman's most distinctive

---

*United Nations Assistance Mission in Afghanistan.

feature by far was his eyes, not their color, a tepid gray, nor their great arching eyelashes, but the manner of their movement, the intermittent darting here and there, toward the door, the windows, and later, outside, around about him. They called to mind small mammals, mice or rabbits, the kind that share their habitat with predators and know their only advantages are their alertness and nimble feet, advantages that could win them a few decisive seconds. If there had been any hint of darkness about him, I would have taken it then for evidence of fear.

That evening, after Suleiman left, I ventured out into the streets looking for a bite to eat before turning in for the night. I introduced myself to the guard, Suaif, whose English was more proficient than he first let on. He reminded me to make curfew and pointed me in the direction of somewhere I could get a meal. Dusk had settled on the roads and kerosene lanterns had been lit here and there. Suaif called after me as I crossed the road and handed me a shawl. March is cold, when dusk bites deeper, so that those who remained in the streets were swaddled in shawls or, in some cases, ill-fitting Western coats, with dull, lifeless synthetic fur trim. I walked a little in the neighborhood. In a nearby canteen, sitting with my back safely in the corner, I ate a meal of kebab and a vast stretch of warm bread. On the wall to the side, a tessellation of mirrors gave me a view of myself and of men, young and old, some bearded, their heads covered in lungees or pawkuls, another old man reminding me of my father, all eyeing me suspiciously, my black shoes shining, and the defiant, sharp crease of my trousers sliding down from under my shawl like the blade of a sword. Now there's a metaphor to arouse the orientalist—so trite, so damn obvious, so journalistic, so crude, and, in the face of ignorance, so damn effective. I ate my meal and I thought perhaps Suaif had given me the shawl for protection against more than the weather, a shield to blunt a few of those suspicious looks.

The next morning at seven o'clock there came a knock on the door. I was already awake. I had made the bed, washed and dressed, and had been writing in my notebook for an hour. This was always the best time to write, to reflect and consider the previous day, to discover what I thought after a night of letting the unconscious brain, the better brain, sift through the impressions. Mathematics was like that, wasn't it? Amazing that you could go to bed with a problem, the hardest problem in the world, something you'd been banging your head against all the previous day. But you might wake up in the morning with the answer all laid out. You might even remember a point in your dream when you worked it out, when you even said, in your coma, *Eureka!* and after waking, for a moment you wonder if it's make-believe, if you've concocted the fiction of having solved it only for the somnial satisfaction, but you know it's real because when you race through this newfound solution, now raised into your conscious mind, when you scramble for a pencil and a piece of paper to jot things down, you see that it works, you confirm the dream.

At the knock, I slipped my notebook into a pocket and opened the door. A boy of ten or eleven came in carrying a tray with a cup of tea and what looked like a biscuit. He glanced at the rickety table before setting everything down on the bed.

He asked me if tomorrow I wanted a bigger breakfast. The boy's English was strong, simple, and clear, with the exuberant confidence of the young, free of the self-consciousness that comes later. He explained that he would clean my room when I went out. I smiled at him but I don't think he would have noticed my embarrassment. What's there to clean? I thought.

I am always embarrassed in the presence of cleaners, never able to shake off the thought that I ought to get up and help. I once admitted this at a dinner party hosted by friends of Emily, a soiree of young professionals preening and posing. One of the party was looking for a new housekeeper, which gave rise to a conversation about that old cliché, the difficulties of finding help these days, although this particular formula was conspicuously avoided. When I offered my comment—that I'd always felt embarrassed when the cleaner appeared—there was a quick response from a lawyer straight out of the Home Counties, a young man who wore a silk handkerchief in his breast pocket.

But everyone has servants in India. See it on television all the time.

Even the servants have servants, I said.

Really?

But who cuts the barber's hair?

I beg your pardon?

In the village with one barber, I explained.

Quite so, said the young man, looking around the table.

In his mind, I was Indian and my frame of reference for such domestic things must be India. Fair enough, I thought, making excuses for him. How is he to know? For a certain kind of Englishman, the subcontinent remains India. Yet I didn't get a single knowing look from anyone around the table, a glance to say that I was British, too. But there was another presumption that was harder to bear, one of class.

There are, of course, cleaners in the service of affluent households in the cities and towns of India and South Asia, cleaners and cooks and guards and gardeners and other staff. But the root of the embarrassment I have in the presence of cleaners has nothing to do with India, nothing to do with ethnicity or heritage, the things they used to call culture, as if that was the beginning and end of culture. For wherever in the world we had lived, London or the village in Bangladesh, my own family never had staff, never had servants; other families did. My family *were* the staff.

As the Afghani boy retreated from the room, he smiled with an insincerity that left me with a surprising sense of sorrow. Alone in my room, as the day opened outside, my thoughts settled on these three men I'd met, Suaif, Suleiman, and this boy, three generations of Afghans now in the service of their saviors. Everywhere in South Asia is a class of men, and in some parts more and more women, working for the white man, to carry his load and do his bidding in these troublesome corners. They spring from the ground where wars are fought as if the shelling and mortars have fertilized the soil to cultivate this corps of agents, from a cadre of peons to offices of administrative assistants. There will always be locals to buy the foreign peace, and who can blame fathers whose children are dying of war? Sound markets, including financial markets, promote the allocation of resources—in the language of economists. That's mother's milk to the world's affluent. But here it operates in its state of nature. The Toyota Land Cruisers pour in, sacks of treasure in tow, and the rebuilding needs builders and men have families to feed. Belief in the grand project isn't just about choosing one idea over another: The difference, everyone is told, is food and security. What's there not to believe? So that necessity mothers the buffer class of native informants as urgently as a mother will kill to save her child. Will that boy with the tea, or that young man Suleiman, grow up to demand his inheritance, and what will he regard that to be? Will he seek to restore everything he shares with his countrymen or, in his obeisance, has he come to despise himself so much that all he can think to acquire is the authority of his masters, retaining all the same structures, the same commercial contracts, the same foisted governance and culture of power, while hating every man who reminds him of his own vulgar self?

Not five minutes after the boy left, Suleiman showed up bearing yet more tea. He set the two cups down on the bedside table, in a patch of morning light, and insisted that I take the bed, the only place to sit, while he remained standing.

I told him that something about the name of the institute had troubled me.

You mean the Dari in AfDARI? It's clever, isn't it? asked Suleiman.

Cute. But Dari is only one of the languages spoken in Afghanistan.

Indeed, replied Suleiman.

Not exactly inclusive.

I wasn't here when the institute was formed, Suleiman said, but I expect the Australians were pleased with themselves when they thought of the name.

Didn't anyone say anything? I asked.

You mean Afghans?

Yes.

I'm sure they did, he said. Something like: *Well done, a very clever name. Now please give us the money.* We can discuss this as we go.

Go where?

I want to show you the city.

Outside in the courtyard, Suleiman introduced me to Suaif, the guard. I did not mention that I'd already made his acquaintance. Class and status evidently trumped the seniority of age, but I found it impossible to address Suaif by his first name; I hesitate ever so slightly even now. He reminded me of my father. There was that same lost look my father had, out of place, as if waiting for something. Suaif had been an engineering professor, he explained, at Kabul University.

What happened to your job? I asked.

Oh, it's still there, but it isn't worth the money. I am paid more by the UN and these NGOs.

Had I heard distaste in those words, *the UN and these NGOs*? So it was with the drivers I came across and with staff generally; the aid agencies had put a bounty on the heads of locals who could speak English. The professional classes had been taken down from university chairs, schools, and offices, and conscripted into the menial service of the newcomers. Wages rose, production did not, so prices had nowhere to go but up.

Suleiman and I took one of the NGO's Land Cruisers, along with a driver, and drove to a hilltop where the battered Intercontinental Hotel looked out over the city. Outside, we slung the shawls around our necks, puffing condensation from our mouths, moisture that now clung to the cindery dust enveloping everything.

I hear the Four Seasons is coming, said Suleiman.

The hotel?

Yes, replied Suleiman.

How many seasons does Afghanistan have, by the way—or this part of it?

Four.

No less from a long view than at close quarters, fractal-like, Kabul was the picture of a city scarred by war. I had seen many South Asian cities from an elevation, from flat roofs over an undulating ocean of roof-top after rooftop, where sheaves of steel reinforcements still stand, embedded in the protrusions of supporting columns that run the heights of the buildings. Such excess reinforcement, along with foundations of superfluous depth, measures of apparent redundancy, signaled the hope of later adding to the height of a building with time, money, and a growing economy. The books will tell you of Kabul's storied history; it might even once have had a future. But if the buildings were anything to go by, its recent past was inhabited by a beaten people possessed of the knowledge that the future was not to be trusted.

For crying out loud, what was I doing in Kabul? I was in Dhaka when Emily called. I was practicing law, trying to sue multinationals and public officials for corruption; I was trying to bring about reforms in the procedures of government institutions, such as the Bureau of NGO Affairs. At the moment Emily called, I was in a meeting with a former finance minister of Bangladesh and a senior British government official, the latter flying in from London solely to finalize the British government's commitment—money—to a project whose purpose was to develop the small business sector, SMEs as they called them, small and medium enterprises. The British government official had felt the two-day trip necessary in order, as was intimated to me, to ensure I would co-head the project; they didn't trust the ex-politician. The parking bay of the premises of the NGO, an NGO that the ex-politician had set up *to give something back to the people*, he had said to me, leaving me wondering what on earth he'd have said his political career had been about—that parking bay came up more than once in tales of fat brown envelopes handed over by men stepping out from Land Cruisers just long enough to seal a deal. I took Emily's call in the parking bay.

I was in the meeting and it was an important meeting—are we not required to think something is important when everyone else seems to think it's important?—and yet I took the call and stepped out. I never turned the cell phone off. Did I so need to hear from her that I always left it on in case she called? And when she called, I made my excuses— It's a call from Afghanistan, I remember saying to them, to the sound of oohs and knowing aahs, for that's all you had to say in 2002: *Afghanistan*, and the word alone was a conclusive argument. I stepped out into that sullied parking bay of favors bought and sold, and I listened to her voice.

You must come here, she said. You could make such a difference to the lives of twenty-five million people.

Did she think that Afghanistan was the only place that mattered? And did she think that I might be flattered into coming? Worse still, did she believe that anyone could make *such a difference*? She did. They all did, this invading force of new missionaries. They were an army in all but name, not the army carrying guns that cleared their path, nor one carrying food or medicine. But they came bearing advice and with the arrogance to believe that they could make all the difference. Yes, they mean well, but the only good that an absence of malice guarantees is a clear conscience. I knew Emily believed in their creed, and when I saw that she did, when I understood that she did, suddenly, as if a wire had been cut inside, I had in me a thought, not yet an intention but a question, one set out in the languages of my childhood and in the perfectly clean lines of mathematics. I had a thought as powerful as an idea born in oppression: Who will stop these people?

I'm in the middle of trying to make some difference, I replied, to a population of one hundred and twenty million, give or take. If you're telling me, I continued, that I can make five times the difference per person, then I suppose I can't argue with that.

This was the woman whose call I awaited every moment and yet, on that call, as I stood in the parking bay of an NGO located in Dhaka's

Gulshan diplomatic area, as I listened to the voice of my beloved, I began to feel the heave of something inside me turning over, deep within me, and larger than us, the trifling matter of *us*. That was why a month later I was in Afghanistan, no more or less clear an answer than the gut opening.

This part of the world was just another chessboard, as I would be just another piece, but that is the way of this history, from one dark stretch of road onto another. Kabul, a city of war, had had its part of British blood and more. There was the First Anglo-Afghan War, itself just one step in the long march of British military colonial hubris—and by British I mean that the officer classes were British; the rank and file were drawn from the Indian populations. On New Year's Day 1842, at the war's end, General Elphinstone surrendered to the natives despite the protestations of his officers. Having secured guarantees of safety for the sick and wounded, who were to remain in Kabul, Elphinstone set off on the journey back to India with the rest. But no sooner had the last British soldier left the city than the sick and wounded were slaughtered. As for the departed British soldiers, worn down first by battle and now by the arduous passage in the dead of winter, those sad men were picked off at narrow passes as they staggered knee-deep in snow. Sixteen thousand died. General Elphinstone, in a shamefully un-British display of cowardice, surrendered himself to the Afghans, even as he well knew that none of the soldiers would be spared. One man who managed to reach safety was the surgeon William Brydon, who remarkably survived after having part of his skull shorn off by a sword. Upon arriving in the safety of Jalalabad, when asked where the army was, he famously replied, *I am the army.* When Elphinstone died in captivity a few months later, his body was sent back to the British garrison in Jalalabad, where he was buried in an unmarked grave.

Laid out below us was the ramshackle city in dusty morning light. Coming up the Upper Garden Road, the same winding road that we'd taken to gain this hilly vantage, an old man pulled himself, one leg in front of the other, until a detail came into view. He was missing a foot.

Suleiman, too, was looking that way, though I wonder now if he had followed *my* eye, for the image, so commonplace, I would have thought, cannot have been one to have caught his attention.

This is what war has given us, he said.

I asked Suleiman if there was any reason to be hopeful.

For myself I could be, he replied with brutal selfishness.

I am as impressed by honesty as anyone, but when there is a hint that a man is taking me into his confidence, my first instinct is to suspect him. Am I to be flattered? And is he about to break another's confidence? I think Suleiman noticed my unease. He smiled incongruously. Two ways he could go, I thought, both qualifications to what he said: either undercut or extend. He did neither, instead making an observation that might have raised a flag, had I considered more carefully its rather rehearsed, even scripted, language.

Afghanistan doesn't have the oil of the Khazars, he said, and we're not ready to prostitute our women like the Thais. Unlike the Westerner's, ours is not a spiritual poverty but a material one. When our needs in that area are met, we will not have the dilemma or crisis of Western man.

At length, we climbed again into the Land Cruiser and descended back into the city, where Suleiman was eager to take me through Wazir Akbar Khan, an area where foreigners, NGOs, and crooks had already starting buying property. Every so often, he'd bid the driver slow down but not stop as we passed homes that, he explained, were known to be owned by Talibs, even if title was held by Pakistanis who disavowed any connections.

It must be quite easy to get a message to them, I said.

A message? asked Suleiman.

With the Taliban everywhere, even in Kabul, it must be quite easy to get a message to them, no?

Suleiman looked at me as if calculating something before resuming his role as guide. He pointed out other houses, formerly belonging to Talibs but that had been acquired by Westerners for their rocketing market value, including diplomatic missions and their staff, whose real estate purchases had boosted Taliban funding. Property in 2002, even in Kabul, was booming, as it was the world over.

There's a saying on Wall Street, I said. When there's blood on the streets, buy property.

I like that. Yes, that's exactly right. Now all these foreigners own property here and they have a double reason for wanting ISAF to stay. This is what it is about, isn't it? Breaking eggs to make an omelet.

I glanced toward the driver.

What? You don't think he agrees? asked Suleiman. And what does my view matter? I'm a threat to no one. You see, I'm powerless.

But you're number two at AfDARI, I said.

Well, we'll have to discuss AfDARI, he replied, glancing up at the driver, whose eyes flashed across the rearview mirror.

3

The Point of Departure
or The House of Mourning

In March of 1971, the Bengal state—at that time officially East Pakistan—declared its independence as Bangladesh. West Pakistan imported troops to put down the rebellion. Until India's armed intervention in December 1971, Pakistani troops waged war against the Bengalis. Estimates place the death toll at 3 million, the refugees into India at 10 million, the number of women raped at over 200,000 and their resultant pregnancies at 25,000.

> —Dorothy Q. Thomas and Regan E. Ralph, "Rape in War: Challenging the Tradition of Impunity"

We Americans are aware of what is happening in Cambodia and South Vietnam because this country has a big stake there. But Bangladesh is a different case. There is no major American involvement or commitment there, nothing which approaches the needs of that young, impoverished nation. And so, the memory of what happened there may already be growing dim in many of us. But what did happen there will never be forgotten by the people of Bangladesh, especially the women. —Garrick Utley, NBC News, February 1972

So began Zafar's exposition of the events in Afghanistan, and even though I could not have imagined then where it would ultimately go, it had become clear that he had a story to tell, a disclosure by parts. There were the digressions, the tangents, the close analyses, and broad reflections—all deviations from a central line. I am convinced now that nothing in his account was out of place, nothing extraneous, even if at times it seemed incomplete and obtuse. If I am left with the sensation of being manipulated, then it also appears to me that there was a method and, behind that, a purpose.

I won't deny that I have already altered his narrative, not the details of each episode, to be sure, nor the order in which things happened, but the order in which he recounted them. While I am keen to preserve the sense of his design and purpose, I cannot but wonder if Zafar's own ordering of his exposition, which began so very far back, with a childhood journey, and which left the start of the story of Afghanistan to much later on, might actually have been driven by a wish—a wish unseen, as he might have said—a wish to delay broaching the matter of Kabul and all that came with it. Though, as for that, I suppose it could equally be said that I'm bringing forward Zafar's Afghan story so as to put off the things that I myself fear to confront.

If I were putting together an ordinary biography, I would proceed chronologically, taking the subject from the earliest record all the way through to the documented end. Moreover, if I were writing about someone famous or even merely known, someone with a standing in some quarter, a great German composer, say, then I could fairly claim that with the bare reminder of the subject's significance in his field, I would discharge any obligation to explain my motive for undertaking a study.

Anyone who met me a decade ago—who met me a year ago—would not have taken me for a philosopher. But though I am no Socrates now, this mind of mine tends toward great questions of life and meaning when I try to consider what it is that moves me enough to undertake the task of writing this, this thing, something that already promises to occupy a considerable portion of my time and that will ask me in due course not to flinch when flinching is demonstrably in my character.

Heroes of one kind or another—that's the stuff of biography. Yet I'm not breaking any news if I say that our interest in the lives of heroes is not just because of the impact they made on history but also, more personally, because there is a hope to learn something for ourselves. What is the good life? How to live? This ancient question of philosophy can remain academic to a man only until the day it comes at him in the form: How am *I* to live? To say that an unexamined life is not worth living is, in my mind, putting things a tad too strongly. What I know now, however, is that an untested life can lead some people into a kind of moribund discontent that cannot easily be shaken off. Zafar would say that no one is the author of his own life. He may be right. But though I have thought otherwise, I now believe that for some of us, it is essential to keep intact the illusion that authorship is possible. This means a heroic life. How it is writ, small or large, is another matter, but it must be a life tested and strained and overcome. I have never had such a life.

Still. Let's be clear. Zafar is not the natural figure of biography and, in the end, the reason for my current enterprise has no footing in proper biographical inquiry. Rather, its basis is in the private and intimate connection between two people, so that the field upon which his life has had significance and impact, the field that now draws my interest is, egocentrically, the field of my own self. That conclusion seems unavoidable, all the more so when confronted by this question: How far into the consequences of an act does one hold oneself responsible?

There's an old joke about guilt: The Catholics believe that God invented guilt for them, but the Jews maintain that they're the ones who deserve it. Guilt is a feature of Catholic theology and is something of a touchstone of Jewish humor. But as far as I can tell, guilt does not have the same stature in Islam as it has in Judeo-Christianity, and it certainly did not feature in my family life growing up. No weekly repentance of sins.

I feel no guilt for what I did in finance. There's little doubt that the financial crisis will translate into an economic one and that recession will likely follow. People will lose their homes, their jobs. But tell me how I can feel guilt for doing something that was not only legal but actively encouraged by governments everywhere. I never sold mortgages to house buyers; I bought large bundles of them from commercial banks and apportioned the packages into parcels that were sold on to investment firms, all of it done aboveboard and without so much as a quizzical look from regulators. If am to feel guilt, then surely it is for something that I should not have done, when I knew I shouldn't do it, and when that something harmed others. But even then, how can I be responsible for all the consequences?

The analogy with biography lends itself, if not because of the subject, then because of the process. There is something like an archive from which I'm drawing. There are my own memories of conversations and events, and then there are the recordings I myself made of talking to him. But there's something more personal. Coming down for breakfast one morning, I found a plastic bag on the kitchen table full of them, dozens and dozens, notebooks of all kinds, bound in leather or cloth or glued, most of them no thicker than a checkbook, each of them small enough to have been tucked into the pocket of a coat or cargo pants. They were numbered, though not by the same writing implement, some by pencil and others by blue or black ballpoint. I took them into the study, where slowly I began to read them. Slowly, I say, because they were not easy reading. They were dense, not merely accounts of events but also the record of ideas and thoughts and readings, excerpts from books and annotations to excerpts. Coming back to them, again and again, I found descriptions of incidents interlacing the ideas, connecting one idea to another. Strikingly, I saw only fully formed and complete sentences, no orphaned phrases or even scratch marks, no crossings out.

I have absorbed more of them than I was aware of doing so at the time, their content and form so fused that their influence on my reading self, long after I had laid them down, was to direct me toward their subject matter and, moreover, to condition my mind to look for the kind of questions that Zafar's own had asked. They are lessons, though nothing in them shows any intention to be regarded as such, unless they were intended as lessons to himself. In particular, his notebooks contain certain long, freestanding passages, and in trying to find a way to characterize those passages, I am sent to the dictionary, where I am reminded that the word *essay* connotes such words as *effort* and *attempt* and it is therefore all the more apposite to consider here one such essay, on the subject of the influence of one writer on another, which begins with an observation Zafar evidently had while reading an interview with a writer. My friend observes that when a writer is asked which authors have most influenced her, it's often another question that she answers: Who are her favorite authors? (Zafar referred to the writer as *she*.) The implicit overarching question is: What or whose books is your book like? The writer's answer is of course limited to the influences she perceives, but there are problems in the way influence itself is measured or understood. Imitation or similarities in style or even content may be how influence is perceived by a reader, but such things may not capture the greatest influence one writer has on another. When Dick Fosbury introduced his flop, he was imitating no one. Until then, a high jumper would not have survived a Fosbury flop because raised soft landing areas were yet to be introduced and a Fosbury flop would have ended in a broken neck. The influence of former jumpers on Fosbury could not be found in Fosbury's imitation of anyone. Zafar argues that the greatest influence on a writer may be on her psychic dispositions as a writer. Reading Philip Roth, writes Zafar, might clear the way of inhibitions that held you back from writing about reckless desire, the temptations of power, and the immanence of rage, or reading Naipaul might convince you to seize the ego that so wants to be loved, drag it outside, put it up against a wall, and shoot it. One writer can change another writer's writing self. Such influences are perhaps harder to measure, but surely they have much greater impact and, in Zafar's opinion, are much more interesting.

My license to order his account according to my own design comes indirectly from Zafar himself. In his notebooks, in a passage reflecting on the narratives we impose on our lives, he writes that when the ancients saw clusters of stars in the sky, they joined them up in an order that evoked a shape they already recognized, something that held a meaning for them, and into this configuration they read properties of the celestial night. Our memories do not visit us in chronology, and the story we form by joining up the memories involves choices with the purpose of making a whole and finding a pattern.

Perhaps I write then with some vague aspiration that the process can illuminate me to me, a kind of eavesdropping on oneself, eavesdropping in the way Zafar might have meant, as if writing is the manifesting of a hope to catch oneself in the middle of things. But even in making this observation I am already giving in to a tendency to get ahead of myself, for it was only afterward, only after reviewing everything, including my conversations with Zafar and certain conversations with my father—much of which will surely find its way onto these pages—that I have felt moved to begin the present undertaking.

The foregoing, this little reflection of mine, has swelled to excess and yet I feel it is only the beginning of something, something shorter, I hope. What I am saying is that my friend has had a great influence on me, in the mind and therefore on the page, the measure of which may yet grow, I think.

Where, then, did Zafar begin, if not in Kabul? His account started out on something much earlier, another journey, one in his boyhood, a horrifying journey by train returning to Sylhet, the area of Bangladesh where he was born. My friend's account began at the very root—that I do understand—of what was to come much later.

In my childhood, said Zafar, there were small signs along the way, which I only dimly perceived without ever understanding, that the people whom I called my mother and my father were not my biological parents. I have always sensed that in the emotional gulf between me and my parents there lay some or other meaning, but a more refined concept than that remained beyond reach for some time. I acquired the belief that the feeling had something to do with the huge cultural and social leap I had made in one generation, away from my father's life—that of a peasant as a young man, then bus conductor in London, then waiter. I had moved away from a life with few choices into my own life, one that was breaking loose with unimagined possibility, even in my boyhood.

Wresting myself from the given order of things, I was engaged in something unnatural and subversive, not merely against my parents but also against the expectations of the world, which were apparent to me as clues left by adults to be pieced together. I saw one mother who made a point of talking to my teacher, Miss Turner, when collecting her blue-eyed boy at the end of the day. The two women might laugh about something or other, or Miss Turner might ask how the boy's piano lessons were coming along. And then the following day, when Miss Turner spoke to the boy in the classroom, I heard in her voice the subtle note of deference that told me everything I needed to know about the world and its expectations.

There was comfort in mathematics, which teased my mind, drew it in and emptied it of everything. I caught glimpses of a kind of truth. I remember first encountering long division, which was set out in a book as a mere process—something to be done, if not understood. But I could not stop asking myself why it worked. We take much for granted, much that is granted by others, and we're told to do as we're told, and we agree. And we must agree. I haven't the time or, for that matter, the inclination to work out that the earth is basically spherical, but when I see the curve of the horizon from a plane, I believe I have seen something that is consistent with what I have been told is the truth, that the planet is curved like a ball. But how can we know that we're accepting something that we ought not to accept, without knowledge of the why? In mathematics, the why is everything. How, or rather, why, did this mechanical process of long division work, calculating how many times one number goes into another, working out the remainder, and then the carrying over. Why did someone think it would always work? What was going on?

On my way to school one dreary morning, a realization blossomed in my mind: the idea of a number base. The idea was never contained in such words, and only later did I learn about other bases such as binary and hexadecimal. I see the connection, but what still eludes me is how the mind can make the journey, how it covers the ground between two ideas; what I do not understand is how contemplation of long division led this organ in the skull to an understanding of number bases. I grasped that when we add, subtract, multiply, and divide numbers, we are relying on a base of ten to represent them, but this base is entirely arbitrary, of our own choosing. The numbers themselves do not care.

This was the kind of thinking I had settled into even as a boy and, at the time, I saw in such tendencies of my mind the root of all strife between me and my parents. For a long time I felt, which is to say I consciously thought, that our difficulties were of my doing, my fault, that I had brought upon my parents some grief to warrant their treatment of me—to warrant the violence. I know now, of course, that self-blame is rather common among children in such circumstances as mine.

There comes a day for most people, I think, when they see their parents through the same lens as they see others, as human beings who stand alone and apart with aspirations for their own lives, and with all the flaws that are laid bare by defeated hopes. Such an epiphany can come in a moment, in a fraction of a second, in which everything is compressed and laid out at once. When it comes, it could, I suppose, be unsettling, as if heaven lifted its veil. I remember learning what Islam teaches: that on the day of judgment no family ties are recognized and that each of us stands apart before the maker, only for himself.

One such moment that I can remember, though not the first, was on the day I learned I had a place at university.

In the week before that day, Mrs. Fraenkel tapped me on the shoulder in a busy corridor at school. Mrs. Fraenkel was a history teacher, whose physical appearance always warranted a pause. She seemed forever weighed down by the same gray-and-brown wool pullover, her mauve hair an abandoned nest and so dry it could burst into flames at any moment. Her wrecked teeth, like a mouthful of broken cigarettes, denied her the self-confidence to smile for longer than an instant.

She never actually taught me, but since candidates for Oxford entrance were a rarity in my school, word of my application must have reached her in the staff room. As pupils filed past on their way to other classrooms, Mrs. Fraenkel, whose fingers and face bore chalk marks, asked me how I intended to get to Oxford for interview. I could hitch a ride with a family friend of hers, she suggested, and explained that her friend's son, a pupil at a school whose name meant nothing to me then, was also trying for Oxford entrance. I later learned that Mrs. Fraenkel had moonlighted as a private tutor, and I speculated that this might be how she knew this family.

He's bright enough but not in your league, she said.

Perhaps this was the kindest remark anyone could make, anticipating as I now believe it did the anxiety I would feel on meeting these magnificent people, the sort of thing that should be said even if you don't believe it to be true. In those days, I knew nothing of what I've come to know of the upper classes, who seemed to my mind then either fat people in dusty wigs, half recumbent or mounted upon some unfortunate horse, in paintings with gilded frames, or thin people who stalked the globe, gathered loot, and discovered the sources of rivers already long known to unimportant people. With such ideas in my mind, it was easy to dismiss them. But the middle classes—that is to say the intelligentsia, the writers, academics, doctors, and lawyers, and all those whose labor is framed by the transmission of words, written or spoken, but only after years of study—to me these people were forbidding in the particular power they held. They seemed to have a natural, ordained intimacy with what I loved, the world where I was safe, the world of imagination, books, and ideas. When I looked closely at people in the public library, none of them conformed to my idea of the intellectual elite, who never came to the library but had, I believed, shelves and shelves of books at home.

At seven o'clock on the morning of my interview, I took an hour-long bus journey from Willesden Green to High Street Kensington. At the appointed place, I was picked up by Mrs. Fraenkel's friend. Inside the car, in the driving seat, was a middle-aged woman who spoke to me in a rich French accent. I smelled perfume. Her short hair followed the line of her white neck, a string of pearls straddled the collar of her blouse, and the slender fingers of one hand held the steering wheel while those of the other rested on her thigh, the tips of the fingers just below the line of her skirt. I cannot remember her name. In the front passenger seat sat her boy, Laurent, I was told. As I settled in, Laurent crooked his head toward me, flashed me a confident and utterly disarming smile, and resumed his conversation with his mother. The car seemed to move without any sound, like mercury over steel, but what I remember most vividly is that I was able to cross my legs.

I did not have much to say to these people, and they seemed busy discussing arrangements for coaching Laurent. I was informed that he was "a fencer," not merely that he liked fencing. As we broke free of the suburbs of London, I lost myself in the book I had brought with me, volume one of *Mechanisms in Modern Engineering Design* by Ivan Artobolevsky, translated from Russian into English in 1975. Some years before I had come across the single volume in a poky secondhand bookshop in Marylebone for the price of two bottles of milk. It was an utter delight, a compendium of designs of lever mechanisms with page after page of beautiful diagrams. The elderly bookseller, who in my imagination was the same Ezra Cohen whose name was etched into the storefront, explained to me that the book had been distributed by the Soviet Union throughout the third world, at knockdown prices as part of their propaganda efforts. When I expressed surprise at how well informed he was, Mr. Cohen shrugged his shoulders. I'm an old socialist and I like books, he said.

An old socialist who called the Russian effort propaganda, including this, a collection of mechanical-engineering diagrams for building bridges and machines to raise water and irrigate land. I did not stay and talk to Mr. Cohen, for already I was dreading returning home with, instead of milk, a book written originally in Russian and in symbols and diagrams. I have since imagined a conversation in which I stand silently and listen to Mr. Cohen, with all his books around him, talking to me, not about the building of bridges, not about breaking the chains that bind the poor, but instead explaining to me what I have since come to understand, that the idea is the thing and that words can do only so much.

After the interview, I decided to give myself some time before rejoining Laurent and his mother, and so I took a walk through Oxford, around the Radcliffe Camera (twice), under the Bridge of Sighs, down to Magdalen Deer Park. Everything was as I had seen it in the books at the public library near my home in London, yet now a future at Oxford was more than an idle dream. But there was something new and unexpected.

As I walked through the streets, one thought returned to me over and over. One thought kept surprising me, springing at me from behind walls and at corners, like some trickster; one thought followed me around the city as I walked through its cobbled streets and along its sandstone walls: I would never again be destitute.

It was early December, and by midafternoon the light was retreating. I made my way back to the Eastgate Hotel, where Laurent's mother had ensconced herself for the day. When I arrived, she and Laurent were taking tea by the fireside in the hotel drawing room.

How did it go? she asked me, as Laurent bit into a scone.

They've given me a place, I said.

What do you mean? asked Laurent, through a mouthful of scone. His mother looked at him sharply.

I think the college offered me a place, I said.

No, said Laurent, they don't tell you until later by post. First you take the entrance exam, which you did last month, right?

Right, I replied.

Then they interview you and after that they let you know by letter.

One of the fellows—are they called fellows?

Yes.

One of the fellows said they looked forward to seeing me next autumn.

What exactly did he say? asked Laurent.

Well, she said—she was a woman—that they were pleased to inform me that I had a place to read mathematics at the college and they hoped I would accept, and they looked forward to seeing me next autumn.

There was then an odd silence as the information seemed to take root. I am not so naïve now, nor perhaps was I so naïve then, as to remain blind to their incredulity, though at that moment I, too, felt my own disbelief, as I heard myself.

You must feel overjoyed, said Laurent's mother.

I'm happy, I said, but mainly I feel hungry.

I wasn't sure I had enough loose change to buy anything to eat in this expensive hotel.

When I arrived back in London in the early evening, my father opened the door. It was a Tuesday, which was my father's one day of rest from waiting tables. As a child I walked home on Tuesdays with the thought that my father would be there and that I would probably do something to make him angry. Years into adulthood, I have felt a recurrent anxiety on Tuesdays, which did not ease until these last few years, when I slipped from the cycles of the working world so that one day ran into the next, the weekends ceased to frame the week, and each day became nameless over time.

At the door, my father said nothing about the interview. I thought then that perhaps he had simply forgotten about it, or that he had not grasped how much turned on that interview. In the kitchen, my mother was chopping coriander leaves while the lid on the rice pan rattled, letting off bursts of steam. She asked me how the interview had gone, to which I replied that the college had offered me a place to study there. She smiled, and in a turn of phrase that I have never forgotten, and whose translation into English I think preserves the sense very well, she said: Good. This will vindicate me in the eyes of the extended family. I sensed that behind this remark lay some vast story and one I already suspected my mind was not equipped to hear without cost. My father simply said: That's very good. Have you eaten?

It struck me then that my father might not have forgotten about the interview and that he might indeed have grasped its significance, and that perhaps this was why, at the front door, he could not bring himself to ask me about it.

I don't know if it was merely the fact of listening to Zafar again after all those years, but I have to confess that his voice and his language sounded beautiful to me. Reading his notebooks and reviewing the recordings have been a pleasure, even lulling me here and there into a state of hypnotic calm, notwithstanding the knowledge of what came to pass and that everything was circling toward violence. In writing this account, I can't deny that my own language, on the page, beats in places to the rhythm of his, rather like—I don't mind admitting—the movement synchrony and posture mirroring of couples. Zafar spoke in balanced sentences, apparently crafted, on occasion perhaps sounding rehearsed, though this should not be regarded as a criticism, bearing in mind that he had probably spent most of his life considering the matters he was now setting out.

At times the composition of his speech evidenced a South Asian sensibility, as if he had learned English grammar from Victorian textbooks. There was no reason to expect his command of English to be anything other than fluent. But I always believed that I could detect an occasional unruly inflection of accent and, moreover, I perceived in some aspect of his composition—its occasional verging on the stilted, perhaps—that English was his second language, though I daresay he'd long outgrown use of his childhood language, Sylheti, a language related to Assamese and Bengali yet with its own script, he told me.

I remember asking him in college if Sylheti was another language altogether or merely a dialect of Bengali. Max Weinreich, the linguist of Yiddish, writing about the difference, replied Zafar, said that a language was a dialect with an army and a navy. Zafar is not quite right: I have discovered that Weinreich himself actually attributes the remark to a student of his. What I have been unable to trace, however, is the origin of something my friend said to me later, at the very end of the same conversation, when we parted. An exile, said Zafar, is a refugee with a library.

My search of the Internet and books of quotations yielded no source for this. I like to think that this was Zafar's own observation, not so much because it offers a penetrating insight—like many quotations, it teases but does not satisfy, yet it is enough—but because the words seem so appropriate as applied to him. Zafar was an exile, a refugee, if not from war, then of war, but also an exile from blood. He was driven, I think, to find a home in the world of books, a world peopled with ideas, whose companionship is offered free and clear, and with the promise that questions would never long be without answers or better questions.

This was not the first occasion, I said to Zafar. You said that this was not the first occasion you saw your parents as individuals, individuals with their own hopes for themselves.

Indeed it was not, said Zafar.

I poured him more coffee. He took a sip, set down the mug, and continued his story.

The first occasion, he said, was some years earlier, before I was sent back to Bangladesh. On Saturdays, my father would go to work at one o'clock in the afternoon, not as he usually did at nine o'clock. The Governor, which is how my father always referred to the proprietor, recognized the extra demands placed on staff on Saturdays. The restaurant, in the heart of London's West End, remained open until much later on Saturday, into the small hours of Sunday, in fact, in order to serve nightclubbers and pubgoers staggering in for a curry.

On Saturday mornings, continued Zafar, my father and I marked a routine of visiting the library. On the way, he would buy the *Daily Mirror* and the *Sun*, which he would read in the children's library while I leafed through the books. Many librarians in those days refused to stock some papers because the Page 3 girls fell foul of library dress codes, so to speak.

I'd take out my little notebook and research the things I had noted in it during the week. I'd look up the unfamiliar words I'd come across that had defied my palm-sized, well-worn Collins dictionary, and I'd browse the shelves and pick out another set of books to take home. Sometimes my inquiries would send the librarians retrieving books from the adults' section, a large and separate room on the other side of the entrance foyer. My father would sit and read silently while all this happened around him. I have happy memories of these hours. But things changed on a day that was to be the last on which we walked together to the library.

At the desk in the foyer, I handed back the books I had finished reading over the preceding week. The librarian always mispronounced my name, saying Zay-far rather than Zaff-far. I did not correct her mispronunciation on the first occasion because I was so grateful that she had remembered my name at all. After that, of course, it became impossible to call attention to the error.

She said, Hello, Zay-far, and I acknowledged her, but then as I turned toward the children's library there came a new thought, as if unannounced. I was nine years old then.

I thought that I ought to go into the adults' library, not the children's. Even though the prohibition against under-sixteens seemed to be strictly enforced in that library—maybe in all public libraries in those days—something told me that the staff would not stop me. Don't get me wrong. I have come across anti-intellectuals in the most unlikely quarters, people who unpredictably bay at the whiff of aspiration, some because they can't stand an uppity nigger, as it were, and some because love of learning visibly pains them. And in Britain in those days, of course, knowing your station was demanded not just by the superior classes but by every class. Yet I was sure this librarian would not stop me. I think my father had already sensed that something was afoot. Certainly, he did not meet my eyes. Later, whenever I thought about why I was sent back to Bangladesh, I would recall this moment, even if I could not find a direct connection.

I think I'll go to the other library today, I said. There's something I need to look up.

Everything happened slowly. My father did not lift his eyes from the floor.

Well, come and get me when you're done, he said.

He turned and I watched him enter the children's library with the two newspapers rolled up, wedged under the arm, his head down. I saw a man who might have thought his life insufficient, amounting to little more than a handful of routines marking his time on earth. If there was drama in the lonely heroism of a workingman, he did not know it. I have thought my father believed he had no entitlement to his anger at life's inequities, since his life was the envy of many of those he had left behind in Bengal. I see now that he also carried enormous guilt for having survived the atrocities of the 1971 war. But that Saturday morning, as he walked into the children's library, what I believe I felt was his heart breaking. Watching a door close that can never be opened again is, I am sure, enough to break a heart.

Zafar had fallen silent, and I believed I saw sadness in his face, but I thought that this was just as likely to be my own reaction, projecting my own sadness onto him, as psychotherapists would say. All of it is hard for me to imagine, so far are his circumstances beyond my own experience, but perhaps the longing for a certainty in the love of one's parents never dims with time.

Something he said raised a question in my mind. Zafar had twice referred to being sent back to Bangladesh, sometime after his twelfth birthday, he had said, and I wondered whether he had mentioned that fact in order to open up this topic, perhaps even to draw questions from me.

At college and through the years of our friendship before he disappeared, I could never bring myself to ask him directly about his family or his childhood. We never, for that matter, talked about that day his parents came to Oxford. It was not that I had limited interest—my interest had always grown. In fact, I am inclined to think that a mark of a developing friendship is that one's solicitousness extends further back and deeper, no longer content with asking merely how the friend is doing but developing interest and concern in all the things and people, the workplace, love, and family, that stand and have stood as influences upon the life of the person one cares about more and more. I never did ask him how his parents were, how they were doing, even though he asked me the same on many occasions.

There was an invisible barrier in the way, and Zafar had put it there. I don't know when it came up, but it was there already at college, erected under cover of darkness. He never volunteered information, and perhaps that stark absence had built the invisible wall. Even when I hadn't known not to ask about his childhood, I had learned not to do so. And yet here was my friend twice referring to being sent away.

If I have already altered the order of his account by bringing forward the thread leading to the events in Kabul, then it is in part because that is what Zafar's story ultimately came to. That would be reason enough, but the fact is that I myself am tied to those same events—I almost added *in ways I could not foresee*.

Even if that were true—that I could not foresee my ties to what he would eventually come to—it would not be *right*. For what is the place of obligation and duty? How much *should* one foresee the consequences of one's own actions? And how much do other causes that combine with one's own actions, and thereby muddy one's role, exonerate one? If Zafar began with childhood, was he signaling a greater class of causes, the beginning of every thread? I have an aversion toward drawing links between boyhood and the grown man; when I have seen it done it has all too often felt specious and self-serving, not to mention un-proven and unprovable. What did my friend intend? What did he mean?

At first I was reluctant to intervene in his narrative. But as I listened to his stories of childhood unfold, to the theme of a gulf between himself and his family and the world about him, it seemed to me that this epi-sode of being sent back as a child was vital. It was evidence of the gulf, before or afterward, between him and his parents and, indeed, it might have widened that gulf. I convinced myself that since Zafar appeared to have stalled I could jump-start his storytelling again by prompting him about this. I wanted to know more about his parents' reasons for sending him to Bangladesh and about his experiences there, and so I asked: Why did they send you back?

When he looked at me, I felt, as I have often felt in his company, that he was searching me, as if he were tracing out the context from which my question had emerged. His head was tilted and his eyes flickered over the corners of my face before again fixing on my own.

Mine were not the sort of parents that believe children are owed reasons, he said.

But they must have given some explanation.

That it would be good for me, perhaps, to know something of my roots, he said.

What's so funny? I asked. Zafar was chuckling.

That's a translation of what they said, and the translation allows spec-ulation that there might be something specific I should know.

Why is that funny?

Because the original Bengali doesn't contain any such suggestion.

I'm not sure I follow.

I was a child. It was not a happy home. Asking questions was an act of aggression.

So you don't know why they sent you.

It only came to me much, much later, as I learned more, that perhaps they had wanted me to spend time with someone in particular. In their way, I think that sending me to Bangladesh was their greatest act of kindness toward me. Shall I tell you about the journey?

At the airport in Dhaka, said Zafar, I was met by a distant uncle, an edgy young man, whose head glistened in oil and whose forefinger and thumb seemed permanently engaged in parting a tuft of mustache. The man hailed a rickshaw and haggled with the driver, while I heaved my bag onto the foot ledge and struggled to pull myself up onto the seat; I was not tall then, my height below average for a twelve-year-old in Britain and about average for a ten-year-old. My new uncle jumped in beside me, and fumes from the mustard oil in his hair seized my nostrils.

Today the highway from the airport into the city is called Airport Road. In 1981, the Mymensingh-Dhaka Road was already laid in asphalt, but it was covered in potholes collecting water. I had arrived at the peak of the rainy season, and though the clouds had peeled back in that hour, their effects were visible. Everywhere the roads had been churned up by the surging water, and even short trips across the capital would be uncomfortable, even dangerous.

The uncle seemed pleased to see me. You've become quite the Londoni sahib, he said, pinching my shirt and tie. I held on tightly to the clattering rickshaw, convinced that either my bag or my body would be thrown from the bone-shaking cage of steel and tin. His hand came to rest on my knee as he nattered away through irrepressible chortles, his eyes dancing with apparent delight, before asking me if my parents had sent anything for him. They had not. I wanted to say sorry, but his face bore so much defeated expectation that my voice failed me. The remainder of the journey passed in silence.

At the train station he went off to buy a ticket, while I waited on the platform. A clump of boys, about my own age, appeared to be taunting a fruit seller, who tried vainly to shoo them away, as if they were pigeons.

Ahead of me there lay a long journey across half a country. I think now of my parents sending me through all of that, of them standing at London Heathrow waving at me as I passed through the departure gates, their earnest looks in which I searched for a smile. Could they have predicted how fraught the journey might be?

An hour later, the uncle returned and handed me the ticket, and I did not ask if there was any change from the cash I had given him. The Sylhet-bound train would leave at around four in the afternoon, he said, and I should follow the other passengers. Then he disappeared into the crowds without looking back. Watching him vanishing into the multitude, I had the impression that this is what adult life consists of, encounters with people who are impermanent and want something, and that I, like everyone else, am only a cameo in the lives of others. There was more than one way to consider my uncle's bearing, but what was clear to me was that this man had helped me yet I had done nothing to earn or repay his help.

I waited for the train and watched the people around me. A few had begun to eye me, to them an object of curiosity; my jacket and tie (fitting neither me nor the scene), my polished shoes, the starched collar, everything about me calling attention.

At four o'clock, I boarded the train. As I reached the highest step, I turned. Spread along the platform was a mass of bobbing black hair like a long wave of silk. Suddenly I felt the first stirrings of what I would later come to recognize as kinship, a feeling that alarmed me, a sense that I was of a piece with a group of people for the most basic reasons, simple to the senses and irrational. They all looked like me. But this alone was not adequate reason for disquiet on my part.

Years later I would see a similar sight, a heaving mass of heads, some with turbans and others with caps, surrounding a white Toyota Land Cruiser with United Nations markings on its sides, in the heart of Kabul in Afghanistan, and I would recall this moment at the train station in Dhaka.

For now, I was on my way back to the place where I spent my earliest days. I still had dim memories of the village. Sitting with you, here and now, my uncertain friend, I cannot recall those memories themselves, the ripples on the surface of a young child's mind, but I am able to see that those early days set in motion deep currents coming down over the years, even to today, here and now. At twelve, I had still retained from my first few years a schematic sense of where things were, but only by their relations to others: the pond out at the front, the crisscrossing trunks of coconut trees stretched over it, the forest behind the kitchen hut, the pomelo tree growing over the roof of another hut, a tin roof, so lavish. But we know today that a young child's brain doesn't have the tools to form durable memories; its memories are unfixed, like impressions in sodden clay. And while some memories accumulate, others displace. Today, the young child's memories have been overwritten by memories set down in my teens.

There are also the notebooks I have kept since my boyhood. Contained in them is a record of things, some settled and others only incipient, all of them bearing signs shimmering with intangible meaning, like strange markings left on the vestments of the dead. Those years in Bangladesh were all in all years of tranquility. They did indeed begin with horror and end with pain—I will come to that—but in between they were peaceful years, and there is nothing to say about them except this: Peace, day in, day out, does not make for memories but collapses into a haze of warm feeling, like long summers of play and plenty. Yet can there be any doubt that peace and stability are what a child needs most? If you ask someone what kind of childhood he had, you don't have to wait for an answer to tell if it was a happy one, because in the moment that he considers the question, his pause shows that he has nothing to say, that he has only a general impression without specific events, as if to say it was just fine, a happy one. But for those whose childhood was unhappy, their faces always give the game away; their faces always have something to say, because something happened, things happened, something remembered or to be forgotten, even if they choose not to speak about it.

I was twelve years old and traveling alone across a country that was neither home nor foreign to me, a traveler whose world moved about him. Are we not, as those children's books tell you, traveling through space at thousands of miles each second, still flying outward because of that first centrifugal bang? My passage to the northeast seemed to me free of any conscious direction, not of my own, in any event, so that sitting on the train I acquired the notion that my body had come under the mediation of an energy in the land, borne across miles and miles of fields of rice, from the unfamiliar forests and hills, from the tea gardens and waterfalls, breath rising from the green and the red earth, across lakes and ponds and a labyrinth of waterways. I became convinced that there was meaning here, awaiting my return, meaning in the way that mathematics can disclose its secrets in the unlikeliest places, when, for a moment, you feel as if light is pouring over everything, not because you've found a solution, but because what puzzled you for so long, for days or maybe only hours, suddenly makes sense.

Meena, when did you get back?

My wife was standing in the kitchen doorway, tall, beautiful, film-actress looks, without her coat, barefoot. She could have been there for a while. I had sent her an email earlier in the day letting her know that Zafar had appeared not a moment after she'd left for work. (As I consider this now, it is entirely plausible that Zafar watched and waited for Meena to leave before ringing the bell.)

Hello, boys, she said, smiling. My goodness, where have you been? She skipped across the kitchen and leaned over to kiss him on the cheek.

For the first time I saw Zafar smile, for the first time since he had appeared on my doorstep in the morning, so many hours earlier. Most faces are transformed by smiling. Some become beautiful. Some even lose their menace, a menace that suddenly seems implausible in the first place. It was as if every trace had been removed from my mind of the unrecognizable human being that had first appeared at the doorstep. More remarkable still is the degree to which our regard for a person is transformed by his or her smile. We are defenseless against ourselves, against an instinct that is the opposite of the flight instinct, as if we have been overcome by a flood of endorphins leaving us craving more, the particular effect of which in Zafar's smile, I should say, was to make you complicit in his toying with you.

I've been here and there, Zafar replied.

That's not like you, Zafar, so vague. I'd expect that from Emily but not from you. Where was your last stop? Somewhere exotic, I hope.

This was Meena, Meena who knew what she wanted, sometimes only what she wanted. I had been sitting with Zafar, listening for hours, if not for years, to a story unfolding, and in comes Meena, jumping to chapter ten, cutting to the chase, the film-actress drama junkie, and lo she brings up the name of Emily. In the years I have known her, a dozen years in which she was shaped by the rigors of investment banking—or i-banking as she now calls it—Meena has gone from a tenderhearted and generous spirit to a maestro in making the inappropriate sound merely careless. I can hear him now, for I'm sure Zafar would remind me of what I myself have said: They were the same years she was married to me.

Afghanistan, replied Zafar.

How thrilling!

Yet even as she said this something in her voice expressed no surprise at all.

What took you there? Or should I say who? Come. Tell all.

Watching the two of them, I was reminded of that charm my friend had, charm that one could not easily describe as boyish because of the sense one had that there was some deft control behind it. Women liked him. I remember now a walk in Central Park years ago, when I was in New York for work—the same walk, in fact, during which he suggested the poem that I would later recite to Meena. I remember that we were stopped by two people, a handsome young man and a beautiful young woman, coasting along on bicycles. They looked only a few years younger than us, perhaps college students, but at that time of life a few years' seniority is taken for a world of experience. The two had lost their way and wanted directions, yet before I could respond to the woman, Zafar interrupted.

Forgive me, but I have one question, he said, looking at the woman.

He and I stood in our sharp suits, collars open, while the young woman, dressed in Lycra, stood astride the crossbar of her bicycle. She had a face and figure that Zafar would later describe as unbearable.

The clip you're wearing, said Zafar, in your long brown hair—do you always wear it so, or are you wearing it like that now in order to keep the hair from falling across your face while you ride your bike?

You're right, she said, nodding and smiling. It's to keep the hair out of my eyes.

The young man was also smiling. I'm sure Zafar noticed that. How, I thought, could he bring himself to say *long brown hair*? I gave her the directions she'd asked for, but even as she listened to me she glanced at Zafar and continued smiling at him.

As they were about to turn to go, Zafar spoke up again.

I have one more thing I'd like to say.

Oh, yes? said the young woman.

If this man is your boyfriend, then he's very lucky indeed.

I don't think I've ever understood how Zafar managed either to bring

himself to say such things or to get away with them. Perhaps it's the former that compels the latter.

The young woman smiled and let her weight fall on the pedal of her
bicycle. As she moved off, her back to us, she said: He's not my boyfriend.

My name is Zafar. What's yours?

She stopped, as then did her friend, and the two of them pushed back
toward us.

My name is Eva, said the young woman.

I'm pleased to meet you, Eva.

Zafar introduced me and continued: You could follow the directions
my friend gave you, or you could walk with us a little before carrying on
with your journey.

The young man was chuckling. I don't know if you're interested, he
said, but my name is Bruce.

Hello, Bruce, said Zafar, beaming at the young man. Of course I'm
interested. Without you, Eva might not have stopped two young men for
directions.

At those words, laughter tipped out over the group of us.

Meena wanted details about Afghanistan.

How are you, my dear? asked Zafar.

You dreadful tease. You can't throw such words around willy-nilly,
she said.

What words? I asked her.

Afghanistan, she said, shooting me a dismissive look.

Tell all and tell it now, she said, as she made her way toward the drinks
cupboard.

Still impatient, I see, said my friend.

Life is short, Zafar—

And patience comes to those who wait, said Zafar.

Meena, I interjected, why don't you pour one for Zafar?

Whisky? she asked Zafar, who nodded.

Meena caught my eye then, and though Zafar was not looking at either of us at that moment, I had the thought that I have often had in
Zafar's company, that he was nevertheless aware of being watched. Meena's
brow was furrowed with unmistakably genuine concern, as if to say, My

God, he looks dreadful. I thought to myself, If only she had seen him before he'd slept, before he'd washed and shaved.

As I think now of that moment, all those months ago, of Meena's searching look to me to corroborate her concern for Zafar, I am struck not just by its tenderness but by the instant bond between her and me, if only briefly, forged by the sincerity of her plea. I think now that perhaps this is what we had lacked by never having had children, a common enterprise of concern and love beyond ourselves or each other, whose effect might have been to bring us closer together. Of course I know that the facts speak against such a romanticized view of family, I know that many marriages fail in the year following the birth of the first child, but because Meena and I had never had children, a vacuum was left for such speculation.

Has he told you yet? They're going to fire him, she said to Zafar.

She set down a tumbler of whisky in front of him.

We don't know that, I said.

Wake up and smell the whisky, said Meena. You saw the email today? I saw several emails.

The badly drafted email about badly drafted emails?

The message about using profanities in emails—I did, I replied.

Meena gave no response. The firm had issued a warning against the use of obscene language in emails, and the warning had made it onto the financial news wires, which, I imagine, is how Meena had heard about it.

Are you still doing MBSs? asked my friend.

To the extent that anyone is, which is pretty much not at all. The business is dead in the water. Now it's all about unwinding trades that everyone thinks should never have taken place. But where were they in the heydays, banging on the phone for more, screaming across the trading floors for more and more? They couldn't get enough of the stuff. Where were the fuckers then?

When you say they, asked Zafar, which they are you talking about?

All of them—bankers, investors, consumers, even the brainless bloody regulators—the whole world was gorging itself.

But you're not thinking of all of them, are you? Who is *they*?

He was right, of course. There was one group I hated above all others, one group that drew most of my fury. I was a new partner in the firm. Last in, first out. My career had been built on mortgage-backed securities, collateralized debt obligations, credit derivatives, and everything else that was now being laid for a bonfire, while my own firm was readying to tie me to the stake to satisfy a public's lust for blood. This was a temporary discipline, the villagers running amok at night to purge their own souls, only to return at daybreak to the old ways in the perverse belief that they had been cleansed by sacrifice.

At work, I would come upon groups of partners huddled in conversation that would break up on my appearance. My team's trading books had been taken over and parceled out to traders on the fixed-income derivatives desk. Half my team had been fired, and I'd been told to lie low, take a vacation even. I knew where it was heading: an email from the senior partner suggesting that we talk, and of course he would do all the talking.

In a way, it was my fury that had complicated my decision. And what a decision it was that lay before me: to leak to the regulator information about wrongdoing at the firm or not. What happens in the firm stays in the firm. Or so the convention went. But it was not my convention, not when it immunized the firm from warranted scrutiny, when it provided the veil of secrecy behind which rogue bankers went about their sordid business, shielded by a wider circle of bankers who, if not active in the furtherance of shady dealings, were complicit through their knowing failure to call a halt. I do not exempt myself. I knew, for instance, of a program of deals that were plain wrong, and I had been part of that wide circle that averted its collective eye at the appropriate moment.

The United Kingdom's Financial Services Authority was privately the laughingstock of bankers. They advocated a principles-based regulation, they said, with a light touch they proudly touted at every conference, in every press release, but they were useless and we knew it. We hired the regulator's own former supervisors to head up our in-house compliance departments. We lured them away from government service with lucrative private-sector salaries. And because they knew that that was the sort of future awaiting the favored, they were *compliant* with us long before they ever set foot in our offices. In 2000, there were fifty-nine criminal convictions for insider dealing in the United States. Meanwhile, in the U.K. there were none. It's all there on the Internet, if you look for it. But that was the point. No one did. Everyone in finance relied on the yawning indifference of the public and the press to what was really going on.

The regular Joe doesn't care so long as he gets his mortgage or loan. Don't they say that all that evil needs is for good people to do nothing?

And now I was in a position to leak something to the regulators, who never had the means or the skill to detect these things in the first place. I did not need to wait for the letter from the congressional committee. I did not need a venue, because I could inform the regulators directly. I could tell them a thing or two that would earn more than a few column inches in the papers, now that people are cottoning on to how much their personal lives hang by the threads of finance and how vulnerable they are to its fortunes.

Some leaks take courage. There are the leaks by junior civil servants in the planning departments of African governments, men struggling to make ends meet and feed their families, who face penury, or worse, if they're identified. But as I hide behind anonymity, when there is no prospect of my livelihood being destroyed, no prospect of being reduced to destitution, a leak is cowardly. I never needed the money of finance.

By which I do not mean that for some noble reason money held no power over me. Nothing fine owned my allegiance. I was never the artist or mendicant of a Somerset Maugham novel, never the pilgrim of Art or God obsessed with a journey foreswearing material concern.

The partners made a killing from me, I explained to Zafar. We made them hundreds of millions, me and my team. That's much, much more than they're losing now. I built up this business when it was nothing more than an idea, when Wall Street was still struggling to figure out how to price these things. You were there at the beginning, for God's sake. Do you remember me dragging you out to a pitch at Lehman, when I was getting the Street on board? You showed them the mathematics and they lapped it up. And now my firm, your old firm, is treating me like dirt even though not one of them had a bad thing to say when they were rolling it in, hand over fist. Do you think they're going to return the money they made? Who would they return it to? Everyone made money through those trades. Everyone.

Did you think they were your friends? asked Zafar.

I didn't think they were hypocrites.

And some of them were your friends?

Some of them were my friends.

With friends like that, said Meena. You think there are friends in finance?

Why not? I asked.

And what about lady friends? asked Meena, turning back to Zafar.

My friend smiled, and despite the talk of workplace treachery and double-dealing, I recognized how much I had missed that smile. What was contained in that countenance of his? How many times had he deflected and disarmed another with that smile? It was an answer to questions whose answers would otherwise be insufficient, and in that smile, in the large eyes and the tilt of the head, there was the reflection of an inner quality of which today it seems so anachronistic to speak, but there it was, a goodness of spirit. If I risk taking it too far, I might say that it was compassion.

Are you seeing anyone? she asked.

She'd have to squeeze into my backpack.

Meena let out a laugh.

Zafar had always had an easy way with her, and she with him. There had always been a sibling quality in their affectionate familiarity. And I suppose the two of them had more in common, in their social backgrounds, that is, than she and I did.

You'll be staying, won't you, Zafar? she said.

My friend nodded and thanked my wife.

Stay for a while, she said. Stay as long as you want, of course, but stay for a bit.

Zafar did not look to me for agreement or encouragement to stay, and I supposed he knew that my welcome was always there. What he might not have known was that a tide of emotion had swept over me—the memory of the intensity of affection I had felt for this man came ringing back across the years, no less soundly for all the discomfort in discussing my circumstances at work. I had missed him, particularly so in the past year. I had heard rumors about him from here and there, some even from Meena's acquaintances, but I had no solid idea what had become of him lately, as if in traveling the map of the world he had found its edge and crossed it. I did want to know what had happened, but I understand only now where much of the intensity of my curiosity came from. I cared for him, of course, and I do not think I ever properly grasped that nettle.

But if you had asked me then, as I sat in the kitchen that day with these two people to whom life had brought me closest—if you had asked what it was that aroused my desperate *interest*, I would have told you this: Having seen that my own choices had taken me into a loveless, childless marriage, not to mention the materialism that never seemed enough, having made choices that mysteriously failed to express my innermost longings, I believed that in Zafar's life I might learn something of how things could have been, for worse, if not better. On some crude social-psychological level, is that not one of the ancient functions of friends and peers: to show us the way, or warn us of roads that lead nowhere, and always to reassure us through their errors, which we never made? There but for the grace of God go we. I would have said something like that, and it would have been a lie, a well-spoken lie of the most stubborn kind, the lie that we tell ourselves.

I've never claimed to be a master of self-knowledge, and perhaps such a thing is illusory if, as Zafar said, there is no path from the self to the self, but what I would say now is that my friend had acquired a totemic place in my imagination, an emblem of an idea I have wanted to believe to be true, whether or not he himself did so. Zafar was to me proof that we are not prisoners in the lives we lead, that though with each choice we might break away from lives unlived, we are not condemned by circumstance or chance to the here and now and this. The irony is that he himself denigrated the will and its role in charting our way in the world. But irony, such as it is, only sharpens our interest.

That's very kind, Meena, said my friend.

Excellent, she announced. You should take notes, she said, turning to me. Get a recorder even, one of those Dictaphone things—I bet Zafar has some stories to tell, don't you, Zafar?

She smiled at him again.

But now, she continued, I have to love you and leave you. I need to make some calls to New York. See you boys in the morning.

Meena took the bottle of whisky with her.

The kitchen seemed empty. Zafar played with the glass in front of him. I got up to get another bottle of whisky from the back of the cupboard.

Are you under investigation? asked Zafar.

What makes you think that?

The email Meena mentioned.

That was a firm-wide email sent out today reminding staff not to use swearwords in emails.

We both know that's not what emails like that are about.

Tell me, Zafar. Tell me what they're about.

They're reminders to thousands of employees that their emails might fall within disclosure in the course of legal proceedings. They're a reminder not to put things down in writing and on the record. But you know that: Meena wouldn't have left her comment about the email where she did if she didn't think you knew what it actually meant. Does she think proceedings of some kind are on the way? Investigations?

You'd have to ask her.

The conversation stopped. I know he was staring at me, and I imagine he understood I did not want to go into it all, not yet. It was too soon, too quick.

She's right, you know, I said, pouring myself a whisky. Where the hell have you been, Zafar? For pity's sake, you just disappeared. I heard all sorts of things. Goodness knows if one-tenth of them are true.

As I sat down at the table, Zafar pulled out what looked like a cell phone.

It's a DVR, a digital voice recorder, he said. You can listen to the conversations on it. Take it. In fact, keep it.

Zafar looked at his glass and moved it forward by an inch. The whisky rippled back and forth.

It was, of course, an odd thing to do—bring out this DVR and give it to me—but even if I was intrigued to know what was on it, I was struck more by the fact of Zafar volunteering something that must surely have been private. Conversations, he said. Which meant other people besides himself. It was so out of keeping with my idea of the man. But I don't think the weight of that moment really bore down until later, when I came to understand that he had wanted to unburden himself of something, and that this physical gesture, this divestment, was a sign, a way of defining the beginning.

Do you have anything else to drink?

I smiled then for what must have been the first time since seeing him again. There was a bottle of champagne in the fridge, which had been sitting there for a year, waiting for something. I popped it open, set two flutes on the table, and poured.

Zafar was caressing a button on the voice recorder with his forefinger, apparently lost in thought, before pressing it. A tiny red light came on. One tiny light.

The kitchen was vast, far too big for a couple. Meena and I could each move in this house virtually unnoticed by the other, a freedom earned by affluence. We were free to ignore each other most of the time, which made all the more difficult the minutes when we couldn't. The kitchen had become a room to leave when it had served whatever function had warranted your visit. It was sterile, inert. There were no signs of breakfast or meals cooked regularly, or even merely eaten, in it, no greasy-capped bottles of olive oil on the counter by the stove. In the cupboard sat Le Creuset pans whose insides were as free of blemish as newly fallen snow is without children. It was in every way unlike the cluttered, warm, and fragrant kitchen of my parents' home, not the fire around which a family eats. There were no children and therefore no stray pieces of paper with crayon spirals, circles, and scrawls, no trophies of a child's efforts pinned to the fridge door by magnets. Indeed, there were no magnets, no magnetism. Now the dirty crockery from Zafar's supper sat in the sink, the handle of an abandoned pan rising above the top like the handle of a bayonet, the only sign of life in this room. Here was clean steel, marble, and granite, and perfect lighting for perfect dinner parties for perfect couples. And I was sitting with an old friend—I laugh to think this—the strangest man I ever knew, as my career crumbled into pieces, my wife laughed, and life slipped ever more from my purchase. That's how it felt then, life slipping away. If I had been asked to characterize the feeling, I would have said that professional progress had given me direction and purpose, and now, with its slow-motion collapse, I would have spoken of the loss of a sense of control. But that would have been off the mark: You don't have to wait until you lose something to ask if it was ever worth having. Little wonder that I didn't author those words but found them in my friend's notebooks.

Does your job mean more to you than you thought it did? asked Zafar.

Is that what you think?

It's a question.

It's always meant a lot to me.

You never needed the money, did you?

Money's useful.

I remember you bought this house before you even started work.

Zafar looked around the kitchen. The big house had been bought with my grandfather's money.

Was it prestige? asked Zafar. Respect of one's peers? The chance to make your own money? Or maybe it was the mathematics? That's fun, isn't it?

I felt uncomfortable, but even now I'm not sure quite why. Behind his probing there was sometimes the sharp edge of a threat; perhaps that was the trial lawyer in him.

We've always been open with each other, haven't we? said Zafar.

I glanced at him. Was there irony there?

It was all those things, I replied, but that's not wrong, is it? It's what everyone wants, I said.

Challenge, prestige, something difficult, a bit of mathematics, and some pocket money to boot—those are the things you got out of finance, but they're not why you're still in it.

Go on.

The mistake you make is the same mistake everyone makes about finance, continued Zafar.

Which is?

They don't see that finance changes people. Everyone thinks that the guy madly making big bucks, that master of the universe, actually wants the big bucks, when in fact the money itself means nothing to him. Very soon he doesn't even want what the big bucks can buy, but wants what they represent, what they stand for.

Zafar stopped there, in the middle of expressing an idea, it seemed to me, and I saw, for the first time since his reappearance, that old sudden stillness in his eyes when he was taken away on his thoughts.

Everyone, he continued, wants his life to stand for something other than what it would, which is about eighty years—in the West, at any rate—eighty years of working, eating, sleeping, shitting, breeding, and dying. Lives of buttoning and unbuttoning—who said that?

Don't know. Tell me, why is finance so different from anything else?

It isn't all that different, but it's easier to see what's really going on because money attracts power over others, the greatest power being to provoke envy, and the envy of others affirms one's own choices. Other walks of life can do that too.

All this is a little too New Age for me. Even a bit facile.

But as I said this, the brusqueness of my language only confirmed to both of us my discomfort with the conversation.

My friend topped up the champagne flutes.

Think of those numbers and base ten, said my friend.

Yes, exactly. I'd like to get back to the story you were telling. See. The red light is on, I said, nodding toward the DVR on the table.

We choose markings for numbers, on a screen or a page, continued Zafar, because we need something we can contain in our perception. The base is not relevant to the nature of the numbers but is relevant to us only because it gives us icons for numbers.* We need icons even if they hide the truth of the number—*because* they hide the truth of the number. That truth would exceed our intelligence. If I ask you to think of an elephant—in fact, let's run an experiment. Think of an elephant. What do you see? What do you have in your head?

An elephant. I have an elephant in my head, I replied.

Now think of the number fifteen.

He paused, then: What are you thinking of?

The number fifteen.

Wrong. You have the image in your head of the numerals one and five, of fifteen, don't you?

True.

That's not the number fifteen but a representation of it.

But isn't every word just a representation of the thing itself?

Yes, but I'm not asking you to think of the words; I'm asking you to think of things—an elephant and the number fifteen. And when you thought of fifteen, one-five, you didn't think of the number—you thought of a representation of it. In other words, you think of something that requires you to invoke an entirely separate code in order to break its

---

*Zafar is referring to the decimal representation of numbers: The number 2,743, for example, means three 1s, four 10s, seven 100s, and two 1,000s, each position indicating a successively higher power of 10.

mystery—in this case the code is base ten. Again, you thought of a one followed by a five. That makes sense only as a representation of the number fifteen and only if you have a base ten. But where's the code in the picture of an elephant? None. You were thinking of one particular elephant, the elephant in your head. But for the number fifteen, you had to settle for the numerals one and five. It's as if numbers are saying: In order to see me at all, in order even to meet some visage of me, you have to make a choice.

And what's this got to do with the price of oranges? I asked. I was irritated.

The whole thing is too abstract, continued Zafar, this business of our lives standing for something else. All we know is that we don't want it to stand for nothing. So we dive headlong into becoming heroes, becoming the big swinging dick on Wall Street or the rock star or the hot-shot human rights lawyer. Which is about making our lives stand for something that our intelligence can grasp, saving us from confronting what we fear might be true—or what we would fear if we gave ourselves the chance—namely, that we're accidental pieces of flesh, mutton without meaning.

You're losing your job, your career, and something's going on between you and Meena. You must be losing that sense of control you always had, or thought you had.

Very profound. I'm feeling much better already, thanks. But you're right. It's too abstract. I want to go back to the story *you* were telling. Tell me about Bangladesh, about those years you were there as a boy. Please.

Zafar took a sip of champagne before continuing with the story. He could never be hurried—at least not by me.

Bangladesh, or Bangla-desh, he said, means Bengali-land. The nation borders the Indian state of West Bengal, whose people also speak Bengali, who *are* also Bengali. And yet there is no state of East Bengal. Indeed, the national anthems of both India and Bangladesh were written by one Bengali, the poet Rabindranath Tagore, who, as Bengalis never tire of reminding Westerners, won the Nobel Prize for literature in 1913. Bengali-ness, then, is not a feature that singles out Bangladesh.

If you were to search for anything distinctive about Bangladesh, you would not have to look far, for the place is covered in water, its surface fully one-third aquatic during the rains. Imagine that! Every third step you take is a watery one. The land is a vast confluence of rivers, the silty, sodden soil where the deltas of three great rivers of the world interlace. And if this were not enough water, every year the monsoon rushes in from the Indian Ocean and tips the sky over the whole country, swelling the rivers until brimful they snap like a whip and gouge out new routes around hills and through the earth.

Land of Three Rivers might have been more distinctive as a name for the country, a name richer with meaning. These are no ordinary rivers. They are not settled. Their courses are ever shifting, their tributaries twist and turn like the tail of a dragon in ecstasy, sweeping over the bank and into the makeshift homes of fishermen and their families. The Brahmaputra starts out north of the Himalayas, in China, curling itself around the eastern edge of the mountain range, through Tibet, before bursting upon Bangladesh, where its name changes to Jamuna.

The holy Ganges begins in the Gangotri Glacier in the central Himalayas and carves out a route across the north Indian plains and into Bangladesh, where it divides into many branches and where the locals give it other names, many names, as if the changes of name will bring the rivers home.

The third river, the most Bengali of all, goes through several names before uncoiling into the Indian Ocean. The Barak gathers itself from the corners of the northeastern Indian states, from Assam, Manipur, and Mizoram, and as it enters Bangladesh it divides in two to become the Surma and Kushiyara. These two rivers are reunited farther downstream, after receiving tributes from legions of lesser ones, to form the mighty Meghna, a beast of a river.

I was on a train moving over a network of bridges and railways superimposed upon this vast lattice of rivers and tributaries. We crossed many bridges. Most creaked painfully as the train slowly ground over them before picking up speed on reaching the other side. As we crossed one bridge, I peered below and saw the rusted carcass of a train carriage jutting out of the brown river, as if pointing a crooked finger toward the offending bridge.

Sometimes, the train came to a stop to wait for the tracks to be cleared of livestock. The herdsmen made no haste in moving their cattle, and the train driver sometimes climbed off and walked the length of the carriages, inspecting the chassis of the train, as if it needed monitoring. Once or twice, he and a herdsman shared a biri, a local cigarette.

Sometimes the train would slow to a crawl before entering a sharp bend, where it would tilt precariously into the curve so that you could see the iron rails on the sleepers directly below the window. It seemed that at these sharp bends the outer track had been laid higher than the inner track, and I wondered if it would be safer if the train were to speed around these bends rather than slow down. Indeed, it seemed to me that the engineers (of the Victorian era, though I would not have known that then) must have had it in mind that trains would come into the bend at great speed and had accordingly laid the outer rail higher than the inner. At sufficient speed, the force of being thrown outward by the centrifuge of turning a bend would equal the force of being drawn downward because of the tilt from the uneven rails, thereby resulting in a smooth ride, as on the high-speed trains throughout continental Europe today.

For an hour, I drew schematic diagrams in my little notebook of a carriage that would tilt inward, rather than outward, under the impulse of the centrifugal force as it came into a bend by means of holding the carriage in a brace that allowed it to roll, and weighting it along the bottom. At the time, I had no need for or knowledge of such words as I use now in describing what I did. But even as I drew my diagrams, whenever the train crawled into a bend, I would get up and take five steps to the other side of the carriage, on the off chance that my own weight might make the tiniest difference that could save the train from tilting over entirely.

I performed this righting maneuver twice before noticing another boy in the carriage doing the same. He seemed about my own age, though I now think he might have been a little older. The boy appeared to be traveling with his parents, both of whom looked elderly, thin, dark as night, their leather skin pulled onto their bones, giving the impression of bags stuffed with coat hangers. I could not tell if the boy was merely imitating me or if he had reached the same conclusion regarding the need to act as counterweight to the tilt of the train. His mother and father watched him, and when their eyes met mine they smiled at each other.

The boy came up to me and held out a mango. It was smaller than the mangoes I had seen in the Indian grocery stores in London, and it was yellow, without any of their unripe shades of red and green. The boy was so close that I could see the meniscus-like impressions in the fruit where his fingertips held it. I could even smell the mango's sweetness.

Reaching into the pocket of my trousers, I took out an unopened tube of Polo mints that my parents had given me in London and I offered it to him. He shook his head, but I insisted, taking his left hand and levering apart his fingers with mine. He smiled and returned to his parents, straightaway offering the Polos to them.

I pulled out my pocketknife and carefully peeled the mango, making nicks in its surface before pulling off the skin in strips, which I held between my thumb and the flat of the blade.

When we arrived in Srimangal, most of the carriage emptied out. The town was a major commercial center of the Sylhet region, and it was evidently the nearest stop to the ultimate destinations of many of the passengers. As we left Srimangal, we passed through vast orchards of pineapples and also what I now suppose were orange groves. The pineapples were ripe and ready for harvesting, or nearly so, but the oranges were fledgling and green.

The first time I met Emily's grandfather, the old man regaled me with a story about his war years in the Burma campaign. Emily and her mother rolled their eyes, having heard this story more than a few times. In his own estimation, the war was Sir Hugh's finest hour. He had plodded through much of the five decades since as a jobbing barrister, the honor of Queen's Counsel eluding him (the style *Sir* deriving from an unearned baronetcy). His wife, a severe woman with a fearsome reputation, had risen through the political classes, helped along by a jolly good start in the social classes, and, as a vocal baroness in the House of Lords, she had held fast the Tory line on social issues—defending the family, for example, when it was under threat from the permissive society.

The Burma campaign! I restrained myself—I was one snort from laughing uncontrollably. This is not real. These people are not real. They're caricatures. With those three words, the Burma campaign, I had instantly forgotten what I already knew of the private lives of these people, the hidden lives that made them real, disastrously so.

Sir Hugh told me his story about the oranges of Sylhet that saved his life. It was simply that. While garrisoned in Sylhet, just across the border with Burma and then part of British India, the young soldier took gravely ill. The father-to-be of Emily's mother was nursed back to health by a steady intake of the juice of oranges from Sylhet. Sir Hugh looked cheered by the retelling of this story, and I wondered if he thought the oranges of Sylhet brought us closer together.

Zafar then came to a stop. He appeared distracted and leaned back in his seat. I wanted to hear the story and hoped he would not break off his narrative and risk losing his thread. I could never tell at the outset of his digressions whether he had simply thought of something irrelevant but interesting and wanted to share it, or whether, as in the proof of a larger mathematical theorem, he had merely stepped aside to establish a lemma or minor proposition, before returning to the proof of the main theorem, where he would apply the lemma or proposition.

Time appears to slow down, said Zafar, at moments of crisis, stress, or anxiety. Time slows down, we think, during a car crash or when a person falls from a great height into a net, the latter being the setting for certain scientific experiments conducted to explore this experience of the slowing of time. The experience of time slowing down is now understood as a function of the creation of memories. According to the science, it seems that during stress, groups of neurons known as amygdalae are engaged into activity. Associated with this is a spiked increase in the number of memories recorded by the brain in every tiny interval of time—in every instant, you might say. The sensation of how much time passed during an event is dependent on the number of memories associated with the event by the brain; the more memories, however instantaneous, the greater the length of time that is perceived to have passed. That is why we think time slowed down, when in fact we captured an album of photographs in the blink of an eye.

In the early evening, as the light was retreating and monsoon clouds colluded behind the hills, we came to a bridge where the train ground to a complete stop. An hour passed—or perhaps it was ten minutes—and being somewhat irritated by the persistent halting, I decided to leave the carriage to stretch my legs and see things for myself.

We had stopped by a town strewn along the banks of the river from where the train tracks rose up toward the bridge, beneath a visible moon, free of the distant clouds, nearly full, in fact, and phosphorescent. As I climbed off the train, I took into view the town's main thoroughfare, two hundred yards or so of a wide dirt road. The rains had polished it, raising the edges of bricks that had been set into the dirt road, not in any tessellated order but laid here and there to supply traction to rickshaws and carts. In the failing light, kerosene lamps were being lit in the tin-roofed shacks on both sides of the street, while men squatted beside baskets of fish and vegetables.

Some way off, at the front of the train, the driver and his junior were locked in animated discussion with a throng of men. Something was happening. As I drew closer I found to my astonishment that I understood what was being discussed. I should have expected to hear Sylheti at some point, but I was not ready for it. Evidently, we were in Sylhet, nearing the end of the journey, having passed the trading center of Srimangal and now deep into the province. The boy from my carriage who had presented me with the mango was standing at the edge of the throng, his back to me. I stepped close to him and asked, in Sylheti, what was going on. He turned and smiled at me, perhaps pleased that I spoke Sylheti, and explained that the townsfolk thought the bridge was unsafe. They say, explained the boy, that an hour before we arrived an iron beam fell from the bridge, so it is now weakened.

A few villagers were standing close to the bank side and I approached them to see what it was that they saw. The river below me was wide, several times wider than the train was long, and was running fast. In the monsoon season, the rivers are swollen, many to bursting point, and some flow so fast they are impossible to navigate by boat. Above the river, stretching all the way across it, supported on several pillars was an iron truss bridge. It was, I remember thinking, as high as the blocks of flats in London where we lived—where I used to live.

I remember the height of those flats. I remember hearing that Joya had died. Joya visited my mother often, her two little children with her, though I never sensed any strong connection between her and my mother. After my mother first met Joya, she said that Joya's children were mixed race. I knew what that meant as a matter of fact, yet what saddened me was the note of disdain I heard in my mother's voice. But I was always glad for any visitor who would draw the attention of my mother and, on Tuesdays, my father. Sometimes, when Joya left our home late, she would promise to switch the lights on and off in her living room, whose window we could see from our flat, to let us know she'd crossed the housing estate safely. It was Joya's idea. My mother didn't seem to care to look, or perhaps she knew that I would look. Joya jumped from a window in her flat one day and landed on the chain-link fence that marked the concrete play area. My mother told me this and seemed troubled by it on the evening she told me. On the following Saturday, as my father and I crossed the housing estate on our way to the library, I counted the eleven floors to her living-room window.

The small crowd of townsfolk, the driver, and the assistant were walking onto the bridge. I joined the boy, my new friend, and we moved with the group onto the tracks and toward the river. As we walked along the tracks, the train driver periodically peered over the handrails and shone a flashlight down the side of the bridge, while his assistant brought a hammer down hard onto the rails. The bridge reverberated sounds that seemed to come from the iron upper framework, not from the deep underbelly of girders and I-beams. We reached a third of the way across when one of the townsmen called out the point where the girder had fallen away. A discussion followed, most of which I did not catch. On the other side of the river, there was a coil of flickering lights, where the bridge landed on the riverbank. I asked a man standing at the edge of the crowd whether the train would stop there. There was another town at that end, he explained, and, because it had a telephone, the train driver stopped there to collect messages.

I told the boy, in my awkward Sylheti, that I would carry on walking across the bridge to the other side of the river and catch the train there.

It would be nice to walk with you, he said. But I have to go back to my parents. Where is your family?

In Bilaath, I said. *Bilaath*, or *Vilayet* as it has otherwise been transcribed into English, derives from Persian and Ottoman Turkish, in which the word meant governorate or district. In Bengali, the word is used to refer to Britain. In fact, one English colloquial name for Britain, Blighty, somewhat archaic these days and mainly reserved for comedy, is derived from the word *Bilaath*, which was current in India in the time of the British Raj.

Do you have any brothers?

I suppose now this seems like a curious question, but at the time, it did not. Friendship is one of life's mysteries.

No, I replied.

The boy smiled and set off for the train.

Could you keep an eye on my bag? I asked.

Of course. Don't worry.

I walked farther onto the bridge, the first town receding behind me, into an unlit region between two hives of human activity. Beneath me, the swollen river thrashed about in the dark, throwing up white arcs of reflected moonlight. Deep from within it there seemed to rise a growl.

I wasn't far from my ultimate destination. The plan was that I would be met at the station by another uncle, my father's brother.

At the other side of the river, I came upon a second hub of human life, a few shacks and stallholders. Kerosene lanterns left a shuddering glow on surfaces. I smelled the sting of mustard oil and heard its crackle.

The stallholder was frying a mixture of onions and chickpeas with some spices, and the smell was, as Brits would say, terrific. I had eaten nothing more all day than the mango the boy had given me. I gestured to the old man behind the stall that I would like some of what he was cooking. He took my money and wrapped up a portion in a small cone of newspaper. Across the bridge, the train blew its whistle and I could hear the intermittent chug of the pistons heaving the wheels. All the smells, sights, and sounds, from the pan in front of me, from the train across the water, from the river's moan, from the string of glowing lanterns, from the solitary moon—all claims on the senses came to me as one, as if merged into the entire night.

The snack was delicious and I asked for four more: another for me and three for the boy and his parents.

If I close my eyes, I can hear the sounds again: the groan, the creak and snap of girders buckling, the high-pitched whistle of wires flying, the crash of a carriage hitting the tower, of another hitting the pier at the base, and then the sound of water, not a splash but as if the growling torrent had leaped up and crunched the falling carriage in its teeth. Halfway along the bridge was a splay of girders, their edges picked out by the moonlight. The river had taken the train, separating the carriages into prongs in the water.

The townspeople on both sides rushed to assist, launching their skinny boats into the river. I climbed down to the riverside, almost losing my foothold in the mud and loose earth. It seemed to take forever, and by the time I reached the riverbank, bodies and all sorts of articles were already visible in the gray waves under the light of the moon.

I wanted to help and clambered onto a boat with two others. But everyone must have known that the passengers had had little chance against the enormous impact.

Of course I waited for my new friend and his parents, but I never saw them again. Perhaps they survived, perhaps they were rescued by another boat and taken ashore, but they had been sitting in the front carriage, as I had been, and that carriage would have taken blows from the front and behind, between river and train.

Zafar poured us both some more champagne.

We drank silently.

You never told me about all this, I said to my friend.

Should I have? he replied. There's a lot we haven't talked about, isn't there?

I know that I looked down when he said this. I know that I reached for the stem of the glass, lifted it, and drank. Was that shame?

Did you get home that night? I asked him. It was home you were going to, wasn't it?

My friend, you know me well enough to know that I couldn't possibly use the word *home* without couching it in so many caveats as to make it useless. I was going back to my father's village, the family homestead, the place where I had lived as an infant, the place where I believe I was born.

After the train crash, I spent a few hours trying to help, but I was an outsider, a small boy from Bilaath, who didn't know how to steer a boat, who couldn't pull a body out of water. When I began to feel I was getting in the way, I stepped back from it all. The townspeople were incredible; they'd quickly taken control of the situation and seemed to know exactly what to do, as if their collective consciousness preserved the means to meet such adversity.

I started walking along the railway track toward Kulaura station, where I was supposed to meet my uncle, my father's brother. I did of course look for the rumored telephone, but when I found it, a man was busy trying to get through to Sylhet city to inform the authorities of the disaster, and my own needs seemed to me petty. My bag was gone, of course. I had nothing other than a wad of cash in my pocket, a penknife, passport, notebook, and a pencil.

I pushed what I had seen out of my mind because it was so big and I did not know how to think about it. The pure night was rolling in, and though it would not be cold, I knew that I would be afraid of the dark.

The clouds had now dispersed, revealing the blue night that kept the stars apart. There were so many stars. City dwellers see this rarely, on vacations when their senses are addled by many new things at once. They cannot dream of the clear darkness, how the stars emerge only when everything else in the world is held at bay.

I remember it all so well, but I also know that I cannot recall the memory with the character of perception I had then, the way we see things as children. I saw the moon in its near-fullness and understood that though we call it moonlight, it is, after all, only sunlight and that we're always living in the glare of one star, reflected or not. Don't they say that even the oil in the ground is just the compressed energy of the sun?

Two people can see the same thing differently—that is obvious—but the notion that the same person can see the same thing utterly differently, something about it unsettles me, leaving a vacancy between me and those days, like an empty chair between two people.

An hour or so later, I came to a level crossing, a patch of crumbling tarmac. In the distance, on a ribbon of mauve hemming a hill against the edge of the sky, I saw a light moving at the pace of a star. It grew brighter before dividing in two. The car was a white Land Rover, which, I would learn, was in the service of the UN, much like the Land Cruisers and Pajeros so ubiquitous among aid organizations in the third world today. As it drew near, I waved it down and, after explaining my predicament to the driver and offering to pay him something, I jumped in. He'd take me to the village, which involved a considerable detour, he explained, and his employers would not be happy if they knew. I understood what he was saying.

It was a terrible ride, the roads entirely unsuitable for cars, made worse by the rains.

The driver dropped me off about a mile from the village. He'd not heard of it but he did know the post office station that I was able to name, and that is where he set me down, before turning back. As I watched him drive off, I was startled by the oddity of a large white car in an area of the world that I knew was without electricity, without running water, without decent roads, generations away from modernity.

There was only one route ahead, past the brick and tin-roofed hut of the post office, down the road of broken earth, which narrowed into barely more than a footpath. This eventually led into a forest of bamboo thickets, in which the path became more solid, being shielded from the rains by the tall, overhanging stalks, lunging upward, striking each other, to cut the sky above them into star-encrusted blue-black shards.

There were pineapples growing in the wild among bamboo and shrubs, in what I first thought were areas of darkness but what I would discover in time were patches of soil, often in elevated mounds, thereby draining well, that received shafts of light at the time of day when the sun was high. They were red, these pineapples, with traces of the yellow and the green you know of pineapples but much more of an ocher red, blossoms of rust. And they were not the monstrous things you find in supermarkets here, but small, scarcely bigger than an orange, all the better for sneaking into the small spaces where the light made it to the earth. In later months, when I saw a pineapple shining in a cone of sunlight, I would pick my way through the undergrowth, come up beside it, and look up to see what the pineapple could see, to find the sun that found this fruit.

When I think of those pineapples now, I always think of a hand grenade. It is an image seen somewhere, almost certainly later, an image written over memories already laid down.*

I remember so much. There is a woman squatting at a fire, her sari pulled around her, and she is blowing through a piece of bamboo into the base of the fire. There was less oxygen in her breath, it occurs to me now, than in the air around her, since it was exhaled breath. But it was

---

*Used by the U.S. Army in the Second World War and the Vietnam War, the Mk2 defensive hand grenade was known as a "pineapple" because of the grooves cast into its shell, in order, it appears, to improve fragmentation while incidentally helping the grip.

flowing fast through the length of the bamboo and so the flames grew greater.

As an adolescent back in Britain, I believed that what I saw in boyhood was a representation of a beginning, a homeland without politics, that such memories built up a picture of a time and place, that these things I had seen, these things I had tasted and smelled, the stuff set down in the store of memory, that they were an ark from which a whole world could be re-created. But my belief in this idea waned as I grew. It was an ambitious idea to begin with, but even before the ambition perhaps it was simply wrong in its root, a false premise: to think it possible to re-create a world. Whatever the why, I lost faith in it as I came to construe the meaning of memories ever more narrowly. Some pineapples grow in the wild in one corner of a remote part of the world—remote from me.

I remember a joke about a mathematician, a physicist, and an engineer riding a train in Scotland. Looking out the window, the engineer sees something that catches his eye.

Look, he says, it's a black sheep! It seems the sheep in Scotland are black.

The physicist shakes his head. Nonsense, he says. All we know is that there are some black sheep in Scotland.

The mathematician looks at his two friends, sighs, and with all earnestness observes: All we can say is that there is at least one sheep in Scotland, one side of which is black.

At every stage, the world that breaks in through our senses struggles to find a footing in our brains. We might liken memories to the messages recorded on a tape, but we mistake the message for the medium, or the other way around, for memory is the tape itself. When I listen to my memories now, I believe that all they tell me are stories about themselves. All I know is that in a corner of Sylhet province in Bangladesh, moved first by the sight of pineapples, there was a little boy, one side of whom turned to face the sun.

As the tangle of forest gave out to an open space, there came into view a long, wide field with the orderly appearance of cultivation. At its far end it swept into a hillock, on which there squatted a low tree, with long branches reaching out like the wires of an umbrella.

Aubergines were, as I came to learn, grown in that field, and over the next four seasons, when they were chest-high, I would help to harvest them. To the side of the field, in a depression in the soil, which was otherwise unmarked, was the grave of my grandfather.

When King Fahd of Saudi Arabia died in 2005, he was buried the following day in an unmarked grave, in accordance with the austere practices of the dominant Wahhabi variety of Islam. Saudi Arabia did not declare a period of national mourning, the national flag was not lowered, and government offices did not close. The idea is that we return to God with nothing, each standing equal to others; Death, the great leveler, treats king and pauper alike. At the other end of the spectrum, let me add by the way, if you visit the Ottoman cemeteries in Istanbul, such as the vast grounds at Eyüp and Karacaahmet, not only will you see elaborately carved stelae marking the site of the Muslim dead, but you will also find many headstones topped with carvings of hats and headgear corresponding to the deceased's station in life: the pasha's fez, the janissary's börk, and the bashlyks of courtiers. Ottoman class was preserved in death, a heresy, presumably, in the eyes of Saudi Muslims.

The hillock at the end of the field belonged, as I would learn, to the family, but it was where, with my grandfather's blessing, the local Hindus would bring their cows to die, in a part of the world where, historically, varieties of religious practices, not just Hinduism, Buddhism, and Islam, but varieties within each, carried on side by side. In fact, many intermingled to form syncretic faiths, which is even apparent today in the practices of Muslim Sylhetis in London. My own parents, I remember, once attended a convention of some visiting Hindu guru or swami, held at Wembley Arena, and my mother used to visit Hindu fakirs in London to have her future foretold. All this is by the by and, indeed, I came to learn these facts only later, and only later still would I grasp the significance of such things in the war of 1971.

On emerging from the forest of bamboo, then, I saw to my left the field and hillock, as I say. To my right was the hamlet. My body sensed imminent relief, and I could feel the sinews of my legs begin to yield to their tiredness. I approached the cluster of mud huts and shacks that comprised the family homestead, my grandfather's and his sons'. Perhaps it was a kind of home. Something from infancy came down to me, not a memory but an echo heard many years later.

The moonlight threw a blue-white powder over the area, and I saw the moon itself glancing off the taut skin of the pond, bursting on the leaves of the coconut trees, transfiguring them into torches of velvet green. From time to time, I could hear the somersaults of fishes in the pond, while all around from everywhere and nowhere came the croon of crickets, geckos, and tree frogs, fused into a purring song.

A memory inside me was trying to wrestle its way through to consciousness. But to know that you once saw the same things, a landscape, a hamlet, and a house, in an altogether different way from how you see them now, and to know this without being able to recall the former memory itself, can cause a disembodying sensation. It is as if over time the self has divided in two, a mitosis of the man and his memory, that leaves the boy parting from his infant self, and later the adult from the youth, like the image of human evolution, from primate on all fours, through the savage half man, bent double, to the proud heir to earth, *Homo sapiens*, who walks tall, each man abandoning his predecessor, each stage only preparation for the next, and in the end childhood left behind, put away.

I saw, then, a form on the veranda of the main house, sitting on the step. I could make out a dash of long black hair, iridescent in the darkness, and the drape of a white sari over the bent form. The woman's head was nestled in her crossed arms, which braced her hunched-up knees. She has not seen me, I thought. I stood there taking in the gifts of my senses, crickets plucking the air, the forest rising behind the huts, the treetops knitting into the blue fabric of the night, one moon shimmering in the sky and another floating on the surface of the pond. I picked up a loose stone and tossed it into the pond to watch the water strike up in a vibrating luminosity, a remarkable geometric precision.

The woman was now standing a few steps off the veranda, the whites of her eyes catching the light, her hair shining. I tried to imagine how I must have looked to her, but I was so tired all I could see was my body crumpling.

We both walked and, when we met, we stood for a moment, each regarding the other. She was in her midtwenties in those days, slender and beautiful, and I do not think I will ever forget the tenderness in her eyes. She lifted her hand to cup my cheek and then curled it around the back of my head and pulled me into her breast, holding me tightly. My body gave way, and the exhaustion from the day folded over me. This is how I began the next four years of my life in a village in the northeast corner of Bangladesh. They were the happiest years of my life, but they began with tears.

4

Welcome Home or Mother of Exiles

Knowledge, and especially disagreeable knowledge, cannot by any art be totally excluded even from those who do not seek it. Wisdom, said Aeschylus long ago, comes to men whether they will or no. The house of delusions is cheap to build, but draughty to live in, and ready at any instant to fall; and it is surely truer prudence to move our furniture betimes into the open air than to stay indoors until our tenement tumbles about our ears. It is and it must in the long run be better for a man to see things as they are than to be ignorant of them.

—A. E. Housman

The picture of the human condition presented here is in many ways disturbing. This might be a reason for some people not to read the book—perhaps those who lack familiarity with the ways of philosophical discourse, for the young, the very sensitive, and for those who are liable to depression. I ask the prospective reader to bear this in mind.

—Saul Smilansky, philosopher, *Free Will and Illusion*, author's note

And I gave my heart to know wisdom, and to know madness and folly: I perceived that this also is vexation of spirit. For in much wisdom is much grief: and he that increaseth knowledge increaseth sorrow.

—Ecclesiastes 1:17–18 (KJV)

In the month that passed before Zafar first spoke about Emily, he and I settled easily into a pattern. I gave him his own set of keys to come and go as he pleased, and at my insistence he took up the mansard of our house, which was maintained as a virtually self-contained flat for visitors and consisted of a large bedroom, a bathroom, and a box room under a south-facing window, which served as a study-cum-lounge. There was even a kitchenette, though Zafar would take his meals with me and, at the beginning, with Meena, when she happened to be home in time.

Meena's firm, like several investment banks, was bearing the brunt of the downturn in equity and bond markets. Mine had taken some losses because of its substantial commitment to mortgage-backed securities and other lines of business linked to the subprime markets, but the losses had been limited because we'd identified a warning bell and took heed when it sounded. Yet however modest the losses, I was at the center of them.

I was not without supporters. Several partners, including some senior ones, had taken me aside, though only individually, to say they recognized that the whole firm had been squarely behind my project to build up the MBS business and that it was disingenuous now for anyone to suggest that I should take the fall for the collapse of that sector.

I spent less time at work, most of it helping the derivatives desk unwind our positions. And now, with the collapse of the mortgage derivatives business, what I am left with is more time of my own, more time—the irony is not lost on me—*at home*, that home, my home, the home where, but for Zafar's arrival, I would have wanted least to spend my time. To spend time? I knew what to do with money, how to sow and reap on the markets, but time? How do you spend time? And how might you learn to do so?

There was a time, not long ago, in fact, when work had complete hold over life, when I *was* my work, when I took such pleasure in it that work was the recuperation for work itself. But that is gone now. Everything is changed.

In that first month after Zafar's return, some of this new time I spent with Zafar, sometimes at home. But often we went for long walks, which we took in a variety of places, by the river, or on Hampstead Heath, or through the Georgian squares of Bloomsbury, after meeting at the British Museum or the British Library.

Though we did from time to time talk about my work and the financial markets generally, I was never keen to do so, and, besides, I wanted to know more about his life. My interest, it began to dawn on me, derived from that area of the soul into which circumstances can take us, where we feel compelled to reevaluate things, things taken as given, the most basic things—the role of love, the meaning of work, the progress of a day and a whole life, *the old dispensation*, as Zafar described it. The phrase *no longer at ease in the old dispensation* is something that Zafar had used often years ago and that today I know, having searched for it on the Internet, comes from a poem called "Journey of the Magi," by T. S. Eliot, who was born in St. Louis, Missouri, but made his home in England. Eliot's reference to the magus's unease with the old dispensation is understood to reflect his own unease, after his conversion to Anglo-Catholicism, with the atheism and perfunctory Christianity around him. I don't know how much of this Zafar had known in our college days, when he seemed to strike up those words at every opportunity. They seemed pompous on the lips of an undergraduate, although I was, of course, deaf to the reference. But I wonder now if it is possible that in comments here and there, comments such as that, one could perceive the tiny makings of all that was to unfold over the years. It is a natural-enough human tendency to search for early signposts of the present. One is scarcely able, for example, to hear oneself think today above the holler of economists and politicians claiming to have long seen the signs of financial and economic disaster, if not to have foretold its coming.

In an ill-lit Italian restaurant in Knightsbridge, Zafar spoke about Emily. He began not with the first occasion of meeting Emily but instead with the afternoon on which he met her family for the first time—her mother and brother. I see now, of course, that his relationship with Emily was never a relationship with one person, nor was it an engagement with only one family. But in this relationship with a particular family, I think, Zafar encountered a version of England, and even of the West (though he never presented his account in such grand terms)—a version that had haunted him. In that relationship he had been forced to confront his demons, as the expression goes. He would have suggested that this analysis was incomplete, and, it is fair to say, his own account did not frame the predicaments of his life in such stark simplicity.

Nothing I can say about my feelings in those early days after his reappearance can properly account for the depth of my wish to talk to him and to hear him. I had yet to understand it myself, or begin to do so. There were some obvious things, and I'll come to those, but they didn't explain the sense of urgency and commitment. But the foregoing paragraph brings into view something I had not seen clearly before, something that is one more piece of explanation.

In Zafar, I had always perceived a stance toward the *world*—that he had a stance, where others seemed to me to hold merely attitudes to the people they met. I know that in reality the contrast was not as sharp as I have put it, but I'm putting it in a way that makes the underlying point clear. I had never really considered my own stance, or whether I even had one—how I stood in relation to the world. If all this sounds vague, then so be it, at least for the time being.

What I knew of Emily and her family before a certain afternoon in the midnineties at the South Asia Society in New York, the day on which I once believed Zafar first met her, was acquired mainly from hearsay and reputation, although some details did come firsthand. Robin and Penelope Hampton-Wyvern had two children, Emily and James. James was the younger by a year. The parents divorced when Emily and James were in their teens, though even before their divorce there was talk about their unhappy marriage. The Hampton-Wyverns—Penelope (who retained her married name), Robin, and Robin's new wife, Anne—lived within the Kensington area and were all known in the more established social circles of that part of London.

I knew them through school. James was a gangly boy when I first met him, who stood in his clothes like a wire frame, with a mop of wavy hair that always gave the appearance of having been hacked into shape by a few strikes of the comb. The first time I saw him—at Eton, where we both boarded—was on a playing field on a cold day in a football match against Winchester, at which I was a reluctant spectator, one of the conscripts brought in for a show of support. James stood with his knees locked, his head swaying not with the tides of action on the field but to some remote force, looking as though he was anywhere but on a sports ground. I still had baseball in me, the legacy of the American years, and didn't much care for football—*soccer*, I maintained—with its kicking and bruising. Here, James and I found common cause. Though I was two years his senior, we came to be on good terms. He was regarded as something of a loner, who enjoyed fishing and shooting, and who avoided team sports as much as one could at school. The story was that he had been deeply affected by his parents' divorce and had drawn into himself. Boys being boys, and public school boys at that, this sort of observation was never made aloud, but the latent understanding among his peers was evident in the fact that when word filtered through that James's parents had divorced, the boys of his house showed him an unusual solicitousness, inviting him to all their activities and generally toning down the kind of joshing that marks growing up in such a school.

The father, Robin Hampton-Wyvern, was a High Court judge who'd made his name as a successful Queen's Counsel in the field of tax law, before being raised to the bench. Robin was a tall man, with sharp eyes somewhat tempered by a ruddy complexion; Somerset Maugham would have said he had a high color, if I've understood the phrase correctly. I hesitate to describe him as English because I have heard that there was quite a bit of the Scots in him, descendants of the Bruces, apparently, though this may be groundless talk. I don't suppose it matters. (There's also a story that an ancestor had changed his name, adding one or the other, Hampton or Wyvern, to distance himself from some rogue relative. There's pedigree in such a maneuver, of course; the Saxe-Coburg-Gothas come to mind.) The man was an amiable fellow who did not show the reluctance of other lawyers to assist friends and acquaintances with legal advice. My own parents had once asked him to recommend a lawyer to advise on setting up family trusts to hold funds sent by my grandparents in Pakistan. Robin insisted on dealing with the matter himself and refused to accept a fee. My grandfather had Harrods deliver him four cases of single malt. Zafar takes what I consider a rather cynical view of Robin's generosity, regarding it as a means by which Robin forged links of grateful indebtedness with others, which he could call on as and when need arose. There's no doubt that those he advised, friends and neighbors who belonged to the same social circle, were prominent people of influence in a variety of walks of life, but I am inclined to take a more generous view in the absence of firm evidence to the contrary. Zafar contends that people can be moved to act in certain circumstances not by conscious expectation of reciprocity but in accordance with conditioned motives of which they have little awareness. Put that way, that is to say in bland psychological terms of unconscious motives, it is hard to dispute, but I still hesitate to form a dim view of an act that does good (which Zafar would say does not make it a "good act") because of a tenuous belief that the motives behind the act might be impure. Still less am I inclined to discount a positive act where the actor has no knowledge of his unconscious selfish goals. I raise this now, perhaps belaboring the point, because these matters have proven to be something of a preoccupation of Zafar's, this question of the boundary between awareness and self-deception. He has talked about it himself, and his notebooks again and again return to it.

When Zafar met Emily, I did not know much about Penelope. If my parents ever talked about her, I was not present. It was of course known that Penelope's mother was Baroness Hardwick, who spoke in the House of Lords on social affairs, having been put there by Margaret Thatcher. In her time, the baroness had been a feature of the local press in the Royal Borough of Kensington and Chelsea, where she'd been a stalwart of the Conservative Party in the borough's politics, thumping tables, championing family values, and telling single mothers and delinquent fathers to shape up or ship out, after having done everything in her powers, it was said, to institute a new housing policy discouraging riffraff from settling in the area.

I have seen a picture of the baroness, a rather curious photograph hanging in the en suite bathroom attached to Emily's bedroom in her apartment—an odd place for it, I think. The baroness is photographed with the Dalai Lama, just the two of them standing together. The background suggests the photograph was probably taken in the House of Lords; I thought I recognized the room—I've been to the Lords for supper with a friend of my grandfather's. In the picture, the baroness is clearly straining to smile. She looks slightly lost, as if standing on unfamiliar ground. The Dalai Lama looks at home.

Zafar once described the Hampton-Wyverns as coming from the stock that populates the foothills of the aristocracy, a buffer zone, whose driven accomplishments lend the higher reaches a shield of legitimacy. Emily was a boarder at Wycombe Abbey, a leading English school for girls, which maintained links with Eton; the sisters of a number of Etonians attended the school. She had been awarded a scholarship—a reduction in fees—in recognition of her general tendency to excel at everything academic.

After the Hampton-Wyverns' divorce, my parents maintained a link of sorts with Penelope, in part because of another, older, indirect connection we had with the family—the second route of my acquaintanceship with them. Penelope was close to Aisha Marwan, a Pakistani socialite from a military family known to my parents. My grandfather and Aisha's father had both served in the armed forces, both been rapidly promoted into the vacuum created by the retreating British officer class in 1947. My parents would host Aisha for a few days in Oxford and even let her have the run of the apartment we retained in Kensington when she pitched up in the U.K. on an annual jaunt, "to take in the waters of civilization, darling." But my parents never quite warmed to her and accommodated her out of duty, accepting her as an entertaining diversion. She and her husband, a man whom she scarcely mentioned, maintained a stud farm on the outskirts of Lahore, where, as far as we could tell, she spent most of her time, riding horses and drinking Pimm's, when she wasn't attending lush parties in the city.

Aisha's purpose in life was to circulate information in society as if she were hemoglobin in the body. She talked about everything she had heard and seen, she gossiped about her closest friends and worst enemies, about acquaintances, and about people she had never met but who seemed vivid in her imagination. Her excited retelling evidenced to my mind an utter disregard for the distinction between first- and secondhand information, so it was never clear whether she had actually been present when, for instance, the former president of Pakistan, General Musharraf, had allegedly gotten so drunk at an officers' ball, she said, that he pissed in the basin of the ladies' bathroom while coming on to the wife of the Norwegian ambassador. I never got much out of the stories, and I think the titillation for my parents gradually wore thin. Notably, however, she said very little about Penelope.

When he talked to me about Emily and her family, and, for that matter, about much of everything else, there were moments when, I thought, he talked as if he might have been talking to a third party, someone who had never known anything at all. At the time, I had not yet read his notes; only later did I see that his narration drew heavily on his own writing, as if in part he were reciting. And there was the DVR and its talismanic presence in our conversations. Whenever I switched it on, Zafar never so much as nodded in acknowledgment, as if, I think now, he understood why I had taken to it. Between his spoken words and my act of putting it on the record, I would manifest my own confession. And when he seemed to be addressing a third party, perhaps that was a means of making me listen anew, afresh.

We think we have the measure of so many people, we have the sense of what they're about, what drives them in the world. How many do we think of in this way? We might count them. But when we begin to think of how many people we believe in turn have the measure of *us*, things fall apart. Who has the measure of us? Parents? When I was growing up, perhaps mine did. In my teens and even into college, my parents had a running commentary of life, but now I recognize that in fact what they were following was my growing up. They were, as Zafar might say, attending closely to the growth and temporal needs of the infant until maturity, when that creature sets off on his own, no differently from other primates. Somewhere along the way, imperceptibly, like passing through the midpoint of a tunnel, I emerged into adulthood and independence to find that my parents had retreated from my life, returning to their own again. They knew me, so to speak, within parameters.

And then my concerns briefly became *our* concerns, Meena's and mine, though that honeymoon of union, that unity of hopes, loves, and fears, was short-lived (though long enough for the pairing to have issued offspring, had there been a unity of purpose there). And now my concerns so resolutely belong to me and me alone that when I look upon those dreamy days with Meena, I wonder if they were not merely a haze of endocrine-driven delusion, a suspension of every sane faculty to clear the way for mating. There was passion. Lord knows there was passion. We believed that the passion was testimony to the depth of our mutual love, when in fact it exposed the intensity of the loneliness that had driven us toward each other, that had primed us for the intimacy of the act and the fantasy that fueled it all.

But that delusional urge is only one of the varieties of self-deception that encourage us to believe we know another human being and, for that matter, ourselves. This faith in having the measure of others really becomes unstuck when you begin to consider how many you'd acknowledge as having the measure of you. That number dwindles before your eyes.

My friend appears as several Zafars to me now. There is the Zafar in our college years, the Zafar who reappeared at my door, the Zafar revealed to me by his story, and a Zafar in the pages of his notebooks. Perhaps he had always been too various to be known, but it seems to me more likely—to paraphrase something from those notebooks—that the truth is finer and that the only answers each of us hears are to the questions we are capable of asking.

Yet it's one thing to be ignorant of everything in the years when he'd disappeared, and quite another to have seen nothing of what had been in front of me. I thought I'd introduced him to Emily, but I was wrong about even that, something you'd think you couldn't get wrong at all.

Soon after I proposed to Meena, all the parents met. My family drove up to Wolverhampton from Oxford. My grandfather was with us: On the phone from Pakistan he had insisted that my parents delay visiting Meena's parents by a week, so that he could fly over to London and come with us. I am his eldest grandchild, and I was going to be the first grandson to get married. I had met the parents before, and they seemed like lovely people. The father had a grocery store in a suburb of Wolverhampton, where they lived and where Meena was born. Her family was originally from the Punjab, as was my family. But unlike mine, her ancestors left the Punjab for Kenya in the swirling mass of migration for work in other parts of the British Empire. Her mother stayed at home, above the store, and raised Meena and her two older sisters, both now married and gone. Assembled in a living room crowded with sofas, we all spoke English, mainly for my benefit, though Meena admits that her Urdu only creaks along. But from time to time the gathering broke into Urdu, and it seemed at the time that there was an intimacy in the room because of the shared language and references. It was all very nice, I thought.

On the drive back, my parents said they'd had a pleasant time and that they thought Meena's parents were good people, but that really what mattered above all was whether Meena and I were suited. You must be the judge of that, said my mother. My father said very little, thereby allowing, it seemed to me, my mother to represent a corporate view. But at home, late in the evening, my grandfather took me aside in the library.

She's a lovely girl, bette, said my grandfather, and your mother is entirely right that the main concern is whether you like her, not whether we like her or them, which of course we do—they're good people. I'm not saying you'd be marrying beneath you if you married Meena. Such ideas are simply unacceptable in these modern times in which we live. We are above those things now.

He lowered himself into an armchair and set his whisky down. I took another seat.

But let's talk heart to heart, grandfather to grandson, na bette?

My grandfather addressed me as "bette," an Urdu term of endearment that I understood was reserved for sons. My own parents always addressed me by name, though occasionally my mother would call me "sweetheart" in English, which was naturally the language in which we communicated.

Of course, I said. You must know I have great respect for your opinions.

I hope I've earned it, bette. There's a lot of your father in you, you know? Yes, quite a lot. He has, mashallah, a great marriage, as you've seen, but I think this, in no small part, is due to a meeting of minds, a common cultural framework, you understand. They may seem very modern, and in fact your parents are very modern people, bette. But I think—and this is where you must decide for yourself—they've had it rather easy.

In what way?

My grandfather paused then, his eyes looking away.

They've been able to take for granted the shared values and social position they have, without perhaps reflecting on the role such things have played in their marriage—and, for that matter, in their lives.

Which is?

Again, there was a gap when his eyes did not meet mine, and I wondered suddenly if rather than reaching for the words, he was holding them off.

Common social position is a glue that binds people; it fixes you into a broader scheme of family and friends and like-minded persons.

My grandfather spoke diplomatically, but his message was clear enough. I was going to marry beneath me, and he thought that this could cause problems. I loved my grandfather, but as I looked at the old soldier sitting in the armchair, the titan of Pakistani industry, I saw a man whose homes were crawling with respectful servants, a man who couldn't bear "all this queuing one has to do in London and New York." He wasn't, in the end, very modern at all. I was able to console myself with the thought that modernity was perhaps not to be expected of men of his age, who had lived with ideas that had never needed defining, never drawn scrutiny.

Yet his suggestion that the success of my parents' marriage was founded on something like shared class status did trouble me. I knew that other families would rather a child marry outside, marry a Westerner—which always meant white—than marry a Pakistani of lower class or birth. But weren't they other families, not mine?

I had come to think of my father in a tender way as a bumbling academic, his head in his thoughts, and of my mother as the dynamic, pioneering, and assertive woman. They were two people with friends in varied circles looping around them, whose commitment to education and modern values was tangible in the things they expressed, with words, with subscriptions to *Amnesty*, *The New York Review of Books*, and the *New Statesman*. Surely they were free of my grandfather's class sensibility, just as I believed I was? The world, having moved on, had forced men like my grandfather to describe things once unspoken; being confronted with the vulgar mention of class, such men were straining the words available to them. Might not the moving world have carried my parents further, taken awareness to its breaking point, and unbound them altogether from old expectations?

But I remembered my parents' relative silence in the car on the way back from Wolverhampton and the few words uttered. There was my mother's remark: *They are good people*, my mother said, *but what matters is whether Meena and you are suited.* As my grandfather nursed his whisky, I thought of that "but" lodged in the middle of the sentence uttered by my mother, the pivot of meaning from which doubt now radiated in circles.

I married Meena for love. When I married her, she had a simplicity of taste and purpose, which I saw in that worn-out, stained backpack hanging off one shoulder, and I loved that pared directness about her. Now she has luggage. A Gucci bag she checks in and a leather carry-on with a chunky golden buckle whose Prada logo never stops glinting.

A decade and a half later, so much has changed. It is not contemptuous familiarity that I feel. Not the familiarity that, we're told, wears down relationships, the humdrum routine and dulling of senses at witnessing the same rituals, the same behaviors, day in, day out. Familiarity was not our ruin but rather change was. Zafar disagreed on this, saying that the change was already carried within me, a potential energy that was always there. Eventually, he said, I was bound to find Meena wanting. Every man, he said, carries his own pyre, which sounded like another one of his literary references. But I believe that Meena and I changed. Once I asked myself if I'd misunderstood something at the beginning, if I'd failed to read something, some sign, if I had shut my eyes when my heart was opening. But I have ceased to ask myself these questions. For a while we had walked together, and then somewhere along the path we each took our own way.

The prevailing state of affairs between us two could not have continued. We were to have that ritual of the most modern of marriages, the trial separation. On her return from a quick work trip abroad, instead of coming home she moved into one of the firm's serviced apartments in Knightsbridge. More change was bound to come. Yet I have to accept that Zafar's presence, my listening to his story, and letting into my life someone at once foreign and familiar, influenced the pace and even the direction of motion in my own affairs. To be precise, it—he—has influenced how I see things. Is that not direction? How one regards the past, how one sees the present—do these not show our way ahead? Or are we to side with the fund managers behind those absurd advertisements for investment funds, where they glorify their track record in bold while hiding in small print the reality that past performance is no guide to the future and that nothing's quite so insecure as a security? Can making half the print small save the whole thing from its inherent contradiction?

I was born in 1969 in the town of Princeton, New Jersey, where we lived a few streets from Library Place in a quiet, leafy part of town dotted with roomy two- and three-story colonial and Victorian houses, some painted in pastel colors, all with spacious yards.

There were other graduate students who were married, some with children, but unlike those families, who lived in apartments, my parents and I lived in a house that my father was able to buy outright because of my grandfather's generosity. I went to kindergarten and elementary school in Princeton, amid its serenely beautiful streets, in the kind of international neighborhood you find in certain university towns in the U.S. Most of my classmates were the children of academics—I'm hard-pushed, in fact, to recall any who weren't. I still maintain contact with some of the friends I made there and have gathered that many of our peers went on to respectable jobs, some to become academics themselves, others to become lawyers, bankers, and politicians. Two are members of the president's Council of Economic Advisers, which is a rather disproportionate representation for one American elementary school.

Through the parents, every corner of the world was represented in the school. The semesters were, to my memory, long successions of events marking religious festivals, new years, and obscure holidays from around the globe. In the 1970s, Princeton already had a number of academics and students from South Asia, mainly from India but also some from Pakistan. I knew a Pakistani boy and an Indian boy, but I never met them socially outside school. The South Asian children in Princeton played cricket, while every Saturday morning my father drove me out to Mercer County Park for Little League, and, in fact, I still have the first baseball mitt he bought me. At Eton, some years later, I tried to get a baseball group going, rallying the American contingent. Though how loyal to America were they who'd been sent to Eton for schooling? It never took off; I think the masters regarded it with suspicion while the boys probably saw it as an inferior version of cricket.

At home we spoke only English. My parents did not discuss Pakistani politics and they did not discuss Pakistan. The food we ate, however, was Pakistani—my mother was and still is a superb cook. I say that the food at home was Pakistani, but I should add that in Princeton my mother took to baking. To this day she bakes that most American of foods, apple pie, and she does it better than anyone else in the world.

And there was Crane, the Crane of my childhood, the boy who was my best friend at elementary school and who is to take a place in this story. Crane was in and out of our house all the time, his own being joyless, I think now, not so convivial, and ours filled with people coming and going, bustling with young academics in the spring of life, filled also with smells of alien cooking, blistering spices, and a father who was present. During the week, Crane's father lived in Manhattan, increasing his fortune in finance, raising the credit ratings agency he'd established that later put a noose around my neck. In the nineties, Forrester, the agency, would develop an expertise in rating collateralized debt obligations and mortgage-backed securities; on my own account, for business, I would have occasion to meet the man, Forrester senior, but I'm getting ahead. He and my parents had met at one of my grandfather's parties in New York. It turned out we all had homes in Princeton and so they became friends. His son and I went to the same summer camp in Vermont, and in Princeton I sometimes visited Crane at his home to play. When we left Princeton to move to Oxford, I continued to see Crane but less frequently: My parents still visited New York when my grandfather came from Pakistan on business.

I remember now a summer day at that Vermont camp, whose days strung together made up the long vacation in my American years, when Crane and I, out in the woods on a trek with the counselor, along with three other boys, aged eight, broke away from the rest, Crane diving into the undergrowth and I following, a follower even then, for an adventure, he said, though I could see it in his face that breaking away was the adventure itself.

Oh, look, I said, there's a hidebehind.

Where?

Right behind you.

Crane turned and of course he couldn't see it. My father had told me about the lesser spotted hidebehind, a bird with one wing, which therefore flew in clockwise circles around your back and was really, really hard to see, he said, so you had to be quick like a mongoose, which I knew had to be really, really quick, even if I didn't know what a mongoose was. My father laughed his face off as I spun on my heels trying to take the bird by surprise. The hidebehind carried on in my world for a while, because I wanted it to, even after my father gave the game away.

It's gone, I said. No wait, there it is again.

Hey, looky here, Crane said, stopping. He was peering over a patch of dirt.

I'm no fool, I thought, but coming closer I saw the object of his atten-tion, a chipmunk on its side, twitching, and I knew, as did Crane, that the creature was wounded or sick, that the animal was dying.

We should put it out of its misery, he said.

Even though I didn't know what that meant, there was a part of me that sensed the awfulness of it. It sounded like something a grown-up would say, and I looked at Crane with admiration.

Then Crane lifted his foot and placed it above the chipmunk's head, letting the sole hover in the air above it. My stomach felt bad. Slowly he brought his heel down, grinding it into the dirt is how I remember the sight, and I can hear now the skull cracking, like peanut brittle. When he removed his foot, the creature lay in a distorted shape, its head sunk into the earth, and, nestled in the dirt and fur, was the ball of an eye.

At the time, any onlooker might have concluded that I was being raised as an American. American is in fact what I was and what I continue to say I am if pressed on the matter. I have an American passport. This point, if I state it matter-of-factly, seems to close out the persistent ques-tions of Europeans.

I know, however, that when I say I'm American, I don't mean much more than that I hold an American passport. I'm entitled to a Pakistani passport because of my parents, and though I obtained a British passport in order to ease travel within Europe, I otherwise travel on the U.S. one. But such patriotism as there is in me really goes no further: I am not moved when I hear "The Star-Spangled Banner"; I do not feel the urge to leap to America's defense when I hear Europeans castigate the whole country (despite the obvious foolishness of regarding as homogeneous a continent that runs from California to New York and Montana to Texas—it was put well by a friend, a New Yorker born and bred, who lives there still, when he said that America was fine to visit but he wouldn't want to live there). Perhaps the closest I come to feeling myself American is when a U.S. immigration officer snaps the navy blue passport shut and hands it back with a smile and with the greeting "Welcome home." At that moment, I have felt to varying degrees the sensation of a breeze kissing the back of my neck, which might very well be called patriotism.

It might ultimately be rather trivial. But I know that such things, small as they might seem to me, are far from trivial to others.

In New York, all those years ago, in another conversation as we idled about in Greenwich Village, I mentioned to Zafar my experience on being handed back my passport at JFK the day before. His reaction startled me. Before I could ask what was going on, he had turned on the sidewalk, hailed a cab, and was climbing in. My friend directed the cabdriver to take us to lower Manhattan, where we caught the ferry to the Statue of Liberty. He said he wanted to show me something there, and since I had only ever seen the statue from Manhattan, I went along with his sudden impulsive turn.

As we pulled away from the port, the Twin Towers of the World Trade Center loomed up, and then, when the ferry heaved farther into the bay, with the Manhattan skyline receding in that picture postcard image of New York, I began to feel the combination of romance and longing that such a sight is, I think, bound to arouse in native and visitor alike. The sun was high and the city's glass skyline gave off specks of dazzling light. The water was calm and it seemed as if lower Manhattan were floating on the surface of the sea. At the stern of the ship, hoisted on a pole leaning toward the foamy wake, was the flag of the United States of America.

I felt no tie to America at that moment, as I might have done, nothing in the way of being at home, but instead I stood there as a witness to the overwhelming *idea* of America, as Zafar has described it.

On Liberty Island, Zafar showed me what he wanted me to see. Engraved on a plaque is the famous poem written by Emma Lazarus and donated to an auction to raise money for the construction of the statue's pedestal. Fragments of the poem were familiar enough, but when I stood beneath the statue of Lady Liberty, the embodiment of the hope of freedom, when I read its famous message in one unbroken whole, as if this were where it had first been written, I felt again the tingle I had felt the day before at JFK, and that I feel now from time to time, when an American immigration officer, a Hispanic American or Korean American immigration officer, says, "Welcome home."

"Keep, ancient lands, your storied pomp!" cries she
With silent lips. "Give me your tired, your poor,

Your huddled masses yearning to breathe free,
The wretched refuse of your teeming shore,
Send these, the homeless, tempest-tost to me,
I lift my lamp beside the golden door!"

I heard Zafar read those words, softly but just audibly enough above the shuffle and murmur of other visitors. When he finished, he looked at me and, in a voice that I am convinced bore a hint of accusation, he said: If an immigration officer at Heathrow had ever said "Welcome home" to me, I would have given my life for England, for my country, there and then. I could kill for an England like that.

Years later, I would understand what I had not understood then, that in those words there was not only reproof—that was obvious—but there was also a bitter plea. Embedded in his remark, there was a longing for being a part of something. The force of the statement came from the juxtaposition of two apparent extremes: what Zafar was prepared to sacrifice, on the one hand, and, on the other, what he would have sacrificed it for—the casual remark of an immigration official. Hyperbole perhaps, but only if hyperbole means the beating heart taking charge of tired words.

So now I ask myself this: Can it really be true that everything that was to follow might have been averted by one kind remark from an immigration official?

At Liberty Island, however, I found myself explaining to Zafar that the U.S. immigration official probably meant nothing very much and that the remark only demonstrated empty American friendliness. Even as I said this, I could hear the ludicrousness of my attempt to apologize—though quite what I was apologizing for, I can't say.

Zafar was silent for the next half hour. Back on the ferry, we stood side by side, watching the Statue of Liberty fall back against the New Jersey shoreline. The day was waning and the sun had lowered. Against it, my friend looked possessed of a simplicity unfamiliar to me. I had the feeling of wanting to help him, without any notion of what that meant and paying no heed to his limitless self-sufficiency.

Did you notice that Lazarus has the Lady herself speak out? he asked me. Remember the passages with quotes about them? It's the Madonna.

Is it?

"Mother of Exiles." There she is, said my friend, looking out eastward. She's pleading on behalf of the poor and the meek, for they shall inherit the New World if not the Old. Imagine Christians from Eastern Europe arriving by boat here. What did they think?

Didn't one of the exhibits say Lazarus was Jewish?

She was.

Weren't they mainly Jewish—the immigrants from Eastern Europe?

Jewish visibility says more about Jews than it does about migration patterns from Eastern Europe.

What do you mean?

There was a lull in the conversation as Zafar considered his answer.

I've read that in fishing communities throughout the world, the same story is apparently told about dolphins, the benign dolphin is how it's described, about a fisherman thrown overboard but saved by a playful dolphin that nudges him all the way back to land. But you have to ask: What if the dolphin is just playing, nudging away for fun but with no regard for the direction it's moving this bobbing creature, the stricken seaman? Who knows? There may be lost fishermen whom the incoming tide would have returned to safety but for the dolphin who playfully takes them off to the setting sun. The only fishermen we ever hear from are the ones brought back to shore. The rest perish at sea. Which is another way of saying we live in the world we notice and remember. Scientists call it the availability bias.

So I tend to think, I said, that most Eastern European migrants to America were Jews because I know more Jews who migrated here from Eastern Europe than I know non-Jews?

Or know of, said Zafar.

Yes, of course! There's Morgenstern, von Neumann, and Gödel, and all those other Eastern European intellectuals who escaped Nazism and landed up in Princeton. They were all Jews.*

---

*Oskar Morgenstern was an economist who, along with John von Neumann, founded game theory. Von Neumann was a formidable mathematician who made contributions in many fields. There is a story, in connection with Gödel, which says much about both Gödel and von Neumann. On October 7, 1930, on the third and last day at a conference in Königsberg, Germany, in the final graveyard question-and-answer session, Kurt Gödel announced his staggering theorem in one sentence, an off-the-cuff remark: *There are indeed propositions which are true but unprovable.* It went unnoticed by all but one;

Not Gödel.

No?

Lutheran. He said he was a theist and believed in a personal God. Einstein believed in an abstract God, the God of Spinoza, he said, who apparently reveals himself in the harmony of all that exists and not in a God who concerns himself with the fate and actions of men.

And Gödel did as well?

No. The two of them discussed God, or so it's thought; no one really knows what they talked about. No, Gödel, possibly the greatest logician who ever lived, believed in a personal God you could talk to, and he said so.

I was surprised to hear this and, I have to say, Gödel slipped a notch in my estimation. But what I find myself perceiving now is that although Zafar and I never discussed religion, other than in the terms of politics and society and never in the sense of a spiritual enterprise, my friend had evidenced a deeper interest in God, in the figure of Christ as I now know, than I understood then. In hindsight, I see now the pieces of the thread that had gone unnoticed.

Is your father a believer? Zafar asked me.

He seems to be. Goes to mosque on Fridays. Always has.

Do you think physicists make God in the image of science?

I don't know. Religion is something he *does*.

He drinks, doesn't he?

Yes. And likes his bacon crispy.

I have thought again of that day in New York, of darting to the tip of Manhattan and jumping on the ferry for Liberty Island. I remember it vividly. But I must wonder why I should have been quite as moved as I was by the words of Emma Lazarus, knowing that I had no claim to the poem's categories; tired and poor, deprived of freedom—I was never these things. Is there, I have asked myself, a part of me so disingenuous that I can be moved in this way? The thought of those who would have a much better claim, who would be better deserving, embarrasses me a

---

John von Neumann, visiting from the United States, buttonholed Gödel after the session. That is how Gödel's Incompleteness Theorem entered the world.

little. But at the end, as I reflect on Zafar's story, I am left to consider whether the quiet, answered longing I felt in the glow of those words did not evidence something deeper in all human nature, a receding cry in every human heart, when the promise of home peeks into view.

During their frequent visits to the U.S. from Pakistan, either my grandparents would come to Princeton or, more often, we would join them in New York, where they'd take up a suite of rooms at the Carlyle on the Upper East Side. My grandparents had extensive connections in New York society, in the diplomatic, banking, and business circles, and I remember the cocktail parties they hosted as dazzling affairs though the conversation always surprised me with its formality and accessibility. As a child I maintained the expectation that obscure and difficult things would be discussed. My parents circulated in the crowd and were always smiling or laughing, and I marvel now at their tremendous versatility; they were at home among academics and scholars but equally found pleasure in the company of businessmen and political types.

The women at those parties were very beautiful, and in New York my mother looked beautiful to me in a way I had not seen her before. She was a classical beauty in her day, tall, fair skinned, slim, with long black hair and green eyes. My mother was Punjabi, like my father, but over centuries the sweeping tides of people from Central Asia had left behind a mixed gene pool, the widely differing effects of which can be seen, in fact, in many Pakistanis. I can't remember exactly when, but at some party or other in New York my mother suddenly looked stunning and remote to me; it unnerved me, and I remember holding her tightly when later I kissed her good night.

In Princeton, my family had many friends. To my young ears and eyes, the variety of accents and national identities was a source of wonder. And my parents, perhaps inheriting my grandparents' talent for bringing people together, acted as a focus for social life. My mother's cooking was legendary, and I remember that quite a few wives sat in the kitchen, watching and learning, while my mother cooked. There was also Sergey. He was a riot. Sergey was a graduate student in chemistry. He was Russian and Israeli, explained my mother, and I remember adding "and American." My mother smiled, and I remember being rather pleased with myself for my correction. Sergey met my father at the university, I think, but soon he was around at our house all the time. His command of English was probably much better than he let on, but he constantly got things wrong, especially pronunciation, which to a seven- or eight-year-old child was highly amusing.

My favorite was his pronunciation of the *h* in words like *how* or *help*—he pronounced it like the *ch* in *loch*, a wet, rasping sound. I used to taunt him with my imitation: Chello, Sergey, chow can I chelp you? I would say.

Did you know, he asked me once, that there are eight ways of pronouncing *o-u-g-h* in the language of the English?

He proceeded to recite them, while counting each one off on his fingers.

Yes, he said, there is *tough, cough, through, though, bough, ought,* and, finally, there is *borough*—*borough* the way the British pronounce it.

I looked at his hands.

That's seven, not eight, I said.

Okay. Seven or eight, what does it matter?

Sergey loved my mother's cooking and wanted to learn how to cook "the Asian food," as he called it, even though in America in those days, and still today, "Asian" is used to refer to people from China, Japan, and other parts of East Asia. I often came home from school, one street away, to find him in our kitchen hovering about her, helping my mother prepare a meal, my father still at the physics department; inevitably she would be laughing. He described her cooking as "chemistry with flavor," though, in his pronunciation, *flavor* rhymed with *hour*, which mystified me until my mother explained that he was rhyming the British spelling, *flavour.* Why that was an adequate explanation to me attests to Sergey's eccentricity in my eyes.

When my mother teased him about his pronunciation, he would threaten to teach her "horrible Russian words and you would not know what you are saying." My mother had taken up learning Russian around this time—she's a superb linguist, fluent in French and German, as well as in South Asian languages, of course. Sergey would declaim in Russian— "unspeakable words"—with riveting melodrama. My mother's hand would jump to cover her mouth and, taking a step back, she would feign horror.

Sergey was also something of a handyman around the house. He put up shelves and even did a bit of plumbing, replacing the taps in the kitchen sink, as I recall. He helped me make a sled for the winter snow and hung a swing in the garden, a tire at the end of a rope tied to the branch of a tree. Then Sergey suddenly left. I remember asking my father if Sergey was going to bring back my bike, which he'd taken away to mend, to be told that he'd already left for a professorship somewhere. My father was cross that Sergey had failed to return the bike, but within minutes we set off to replace it, and, after my initial distress, I was rather pleased by the whole deal. The new bike was a lot better than the old one, and I remember that my father insisted we also buy a chain and lock for it.

In Princeton, our circle of friends included graduate students and professors, people from the four corners of the world, as I say, and our house was always an open and friendly place. But I see now that in the absence of all things Pakistani, an aspect of my parents' lives was kept at arm's length. For Friday prayers, my father did not attend a Pakistani mosque, as he does now on the Cowley Road in East Oxford, for there were none in Princeton, nor did he meet with other Pakistanis to pray. Instead, he would drive to Lawrence, outside Princeton, where a small Arab Muslim community would assemble in someone's home, an immigrant outpost clustered around one family.

There were rare episodes when I sensed what might be pictured as a tiny hollow space within me, along some inward edge, a sensation that I have struggled hard to describe in my own mind. To borrow language from my father's world of physics, a black hole might make its presence felt by its gravitational effects on something nearby. The black hole itself is by its nature incapable of being observed because nothing can leave it, not even light or any electromagnetic radiation. It is the feeling of missing something without conscious awareness of what it is you're missing, though even this, I think, rather overstates it. Perhaps that's what friendship can do: the presence of another indirectly giving us better access to the hidden parts of ourselves.

I remember an assembly at the beginning of the school year when I was seven or eight. The teacher explained that our grade was going to stand up on the stage, and one by one we were to say "Welcome" in our mother tongues. When the teacher asked me to speak in Pakistani, I certainly didn't know what to say. For that matter, I didn't even know to correct the teacher and say that Pakistanis might speak Urdu or another language but never Pakistani, just as Belgians might speak French or Flemish but not Belgian.

We left Princeton for the U.K. in 1981, and my parents slowly began to express again their Pakistani heritage. Then, entering my teens, I sensed their transition, while at the same time I grasped that during the years in Princeton my parents had shut something out. There was, I understood later, a reason for it all—for holding Pakistan at arm's length: We had been ostracized.

5

The Situation in Our Colonies

And what you thought you came for
Is only a shell, a husk of meaning
From which the purpose breaks only when it is fulfilled
If at all.   —T. S. Eliot, "Little Gidding"

Sometimes, Tom, we have to do a thing in order to find out the reason for it. Sometimes our actions are questions, not answers.
                                    —John le Carré, A Perfect Spy

Would you care for a Bath Oliver? said Penelope Hampton-Wyvern.

In a restaurant in Knightsbridge, Zafar related his first encounter with the Hampton-Wyverns—with Penelope and James.

I'm sorry? replied Zafar.

Would you like a biscuit? she asked.

You should try one, said James—that is, if you haven't had one before.

I took a biscuit from the plate. Very nice, I said.

A bite crumbled in my mouth.

They're made, said Mrs. Hampton-Wyvern, to the same recipe William Oliver of Bath confided to his coachman in 1750.

I've never had such an old cookie before, I replied.

Do you like the books? asked Mrs. Hampton-Wyvern.

I'm sorry?

You were looking at the books. Some marvelous first editions. Trollope, Thackeray, and Eliot among them.

T. S. Eliot?

No, George.

Yes, of course, I said weakly.

The conversation fell away, as if my error had marked a precipice. Of course it's *George* Eliot, I thought. You idiot. Those three were contemporaries. T. S. Eliot came later. And he wasn't even British—at his end maybe, but not at his beginning.

Have you read *Daniel Deronda*? I asked, breaking into the silence.

The tale of the Jew, replied Mrs. Hampton-Wyvern.

Only he discovers he's Jewish much later, chimed in James.

These days every man's discovering the Jew in himself, said Mrs. Hampton-Wyvern.

I liked it, said Emily.

I did not ask what Mrs. Hampton-Wyvern meant; I didn't want to risk finding out.

Wasn't he illegitimate? said James.

The Victorians, said Emily, were obsessed with illegitimacy. *Bleak House* and *Little Dorrit* and *The Woman in White* are all about that— illegitimate children with maids and fallen women. It was quite personal for some of these writers—some of them had illegitimate children themselves.

Oh, yes, now I remember. The Bastardy Laws, said James.

This drew a smile from everyone.

Illegitimate children inherited nothing, Emily said.

Emily sat with her knees pinched together, her hands resting on them, fingers interlaced, and her heels backing up against a foot of the couch. Her elbows were pulled in, almost touching.

They had no legal standing, continued Emily, unless the father made some specific provision for them.

Yes, but when he did, said James, it made for excellent drama at the reading of the will!

Don't forget, I interjected, the drama of someone trying to bridge the class divide.

I preferred *Middlemarch*, said Mrs. Hampton-Wyvern. It's always nice to learn a thing or two from a novel, don't you think?

The Great Reform Bill, which broadened the electoral franchise, said Emily.

The Act, not the Bill, Penelope pointed out.

But not to women, added James.

Even so, the Tories were quite resistant to the Bill, I interjected.

Yes. I suppose I should declare a family connection of sorts, said Mrs. Hampton-Wyvern. A great-uncle of mine, Lord Launceston, was one of the few Tories who supported it.

James snapped up from the sofa, plucked a book from the shelf, and handed it to me.

The hard cloth-bound cover fell open, like the lid of a cigar box. I drew the tips of my fingers over the coarse paper and let the pages leaf out until the title sheet appeared. *Middlemarch, A Study of Provincial Life, By George Eliot.*

It's lovely, I said.

Thank you, said Mrs. Hampton-Wyvern. It's rather a nice collection, if I say so myself. Took some time to put together. My grandfather was quite a bibliophile, you know.

Zafar is incredibly well-read, said Emily.

I was actually admiring the bookcase itself—I mean the furniture.

James grinned. Mrs. Hampton-Wyvern looked at me earnestly.

What do you like about it?

It has a good finish. Someone has taken care and I like that.

But it's nothing special. You don't think it's special, do you?

It's effective and sometimes that's enough to make something special. Neither ostentatious nor, nor—

Reticent?

Exactly. It has the right molding for the room, picks up the dado, and all the edges are properly chamfered so the eggshell won't chip or wear for a while yet. You can see, too, even at this distance, that the paint's been sanded between coats.

You're able to see that?

Bad paintwork shows a mile off, I replied, especially on MDF, since it absorbs so much paint. In fact, if you don't give MDF a heavy primer to begin with, I continued, you end up having to lay on five or more coats of emulsion, which in turn increases the risk of paint runs.

Mrs. Hampton-Wyvern was nodding agreement, as if already familiar with this. For the first time, but not for the last, I wondered if I was being manipulated.

You then have to take even greater care to sand between coats, I added.

As I talked to Mrs. Hampton-Wyvern, I noticed Emily's posture: her eyes fallen to the floor, her shoulders slumped.

It's a nice bookshelf, I added inanely.

How do you know it's made from MDF and not pine or a hardwood or even ply? asked Mrs. Hampton-Wyvern.

MDF, I replied, is a standard material for this sort of furniture. It's cheap—if it's going to be painted, it doesn't make sense to splash out on wood, so to speak. Bookcases and cabinets make good use of alcoves either side of a chimney breast. You can see, by the way, that the bookcase wasn't installed at the same time as the rest of the woodwork in the room, such as the architrave around the door and the dadoes, because its skirting doesn't precisely match the skirting boards where the walls meet the floor, although, very sensibly, the carpenter who built this didn't try to form a ninety-degree miter joint where the two skirting boards meet, which would simply have failed to key up, but instead scribed the skirting of the cabinets at the bottom of the bookcase over that of the wall.

I wanted to ask a question, but I knew that to do so would be to call attention to something potentially embarrassing. How does someone of her background—her social standing, which defines so many Brits— how does she know about MDF and ply? Brits are embarrassed—are required to be embarrassed—about showing they know about something that doesn't properly belong to their orbit in life. And here I knew it in my bones that there was some kind of embarrassment just around the corner. I don't know what tipped me off. I cannot point to anything specific that signaled the presence of a potential embarrassment in the room, but the presence was unmistakably there. It might have been the way Emily leaned forward in the same moment or the way James's eyes glanced upward or perhaps it was the ear recoiling from the dissonance between the rugged contraction "ply," instead of "plywood," and the rest of the honorable Mrs. Hampton-Wyvern's speech. I don't know. Embarrassment is possibly the paramount emotion of the English, and efforts to avoid it account for many of the small peculiarities of social life in England.

Mentioning "miter joints" and "scribing" should have called forth questions from Mrs. Hampton-Wyvern, if she had been unfamiliar with those terms of trade, if only to ask out of surprise how I knew about such things. People do that, they ask you how you come to know about something, whenever the conversation shows you know a thing or two about a field of which they themselves know nothing.

It is possible, looking back, that the fact that I hadn't hesitated to use such language—miter joints and scribing—might have suggested to her that I'd noticed she had a knowledge of the carpenter's vocabulary, that perhaps I had caught her reference to "ply" and caught her familiarity with things of which she *ought* to know nothing. It's possible she was sitting there wondering why I wasn't asking her how *she* knew about MDF.

Therein lies the heart of the matter: England and an English education, in which to carry knowledge was a social act, a statement of class and position. At Oxford, young men and women sat on oak benches in the wood-paneled dining hall, beneath large gilt-framed paintings of great men. Here were Adam Smith, Cardinal Manning, and Charles Algernon Swinburne peering down the lengths of their noses, knowingly. Over there were three prime ministers of Britain, there were writers, judges, and field marshals, and there were dukes and earls, enough to fill an entire legislature. One day Christopher Hitchens and Richard Dawkins, more recent old boys, may join them, but for now, beacons of the age of Empire illumined the great hall, their white flames of hair, their ermine, their cocked heads full of mission, their fucking belief and self-belief commanding obeisance. And beneath these paintings, beneath the vast vaulted ceiling, there sat men and women—boys and girls, many still in their teens, for God's sake—speaking as if their every utterance was borne aloft by God's grace, as if their opinions resonated reflection and scholarship, effortless superiority in the place of effort. They inflated what little they knew to fill the voids. Because everyone knew and accepted this—a prerequisite of being in denial—no one upset the precarious suspension of disbelief, everyone was complicit in a stage-managed pretense. This then, right here, against the stone and ivy, beneath leaded windows and time-beaten timbers, is where my hate began. In England, the root of true, rightly guided power, the essence of authority, was not learning but the veneer of knowledge, while projecting genuine ignorance of all that is vulgar. This applies to the new aristocracy as much as it ever did to the old, to the *neoaristocracy*, an international elite waving passports bloated with visas and residence permits, permanently everywhere, shielded from the vulgar by fast tracks and VIP lounges.

At Harvard, when I attended, it was different. Knowledge there, amid the innocence of the New World, was regarded differently. The people and their history was of another kind. Many were Jews and East Asians, many bearing the mark of outsider, for whom knowledge was never a citadel of power to be defended against the hordes but the object of assault, the prize to be fought for, so that when it was won, it was hard earned and, being wrested from those who would deny it them, it was opened up, the turrets blown apart by egalitarian rage. I did indeed expect it to be the same in Cambridge, Massachusetts, as in Oxford, England—power is power, isn't it?—but it wasn't. Maybe it will be one day, if power hardens over time, like water under pressure, as layers of snow turn to ice under the accreting burden of subsequent snowfalls. But that day has yet to come in America. That's why America frightens and seduces Brits, especially the British elite. It bears the forbidden fruit of egalitarian hope, and everyone, high and low, can shake the branches of that tree.

I believe that Zafar was rather naïve about his American experience, though not wholly unaware of it; why else say *when I attended*, a caveat to his description of Harvard that could only serve as an out? Why bulletproof the eulogy unless you thought it vulnerable?

Am I naïve? he continued. Am I wrong? Let me tell you about the High Court judge—Harrow and Trinity College, Cambridge—who interrupted counsel during a trial to ask who the Spice Girls were, when that girl band was at the peak of its popularity. Among the elite of Britain, education, which is to say the administration of knowledge and learning, at places like Eton, Harrow, Oxford, and Cambridge, is about ensuring ignorance of all the right things—or is that wrong things?—all about ensuring disdain toward them, or better still, blessed indifference.

But I'm getting ahead of myself. I was holding forth on the properties of medium-density fiberboard when Emily stood up.

Mother, I have to make a phone call, she said.

Without looking at her, she addressed her mother as "Mother," a formality unknown to me, and which seemed odder still when I heard James call her "Mummy." Is this how these people speak to each other?

If you must, darling, said Mrs. Hampton-Wyvern.

Emily's exit tilted the balance of gravitational forces in the room, as if

I had been a small satellite of hers. After all, I was in that room because of her.

She and I had been seeing each other for several months by then. I'm not sure you can call it a courtship; after exchanging emails and telephone calls, when I was still in New York, we began meeting up from time to time, when I came back to London. This went on for well over a year. An anthropologist will tell you that she was of a higher status than me. So I played hard to get and kept conversation on the level of ideas until one day outside a restaurant, where we'd had an excellent meal, she reached for my lapels and kissed me. I'm digressing. The point I want to make is that a few months of dating had been time enough for the ring of her cell phone—her use of it, the furtiveness—to condition me, condition my body, to respond with anxiety, but even so I persisted in telling myself that her furtiveness was only the impression left by a clumsy demonstration of good manners. She removed herself to make and take calls because she was polite, but she could do it better.

I understand you're also a lawyer, said James.

Just starting out, I replied.

Is it everything you expected it to be? asked Mrs. Hampton-Wyvern.

I didn't expect much. I hoped it would be challenging.

Is it?

It's still too soon to say, but the signs are good. Some things are a little confusing.

What are they?

This and that. I'm not really sure how to describe it.

Do try.

The social rules, I said.

Yes? she said, drawing me out.

It's another world, isn't it? The English bar, the Royal Courts of Justice, the Inns of Court. They're all very odd institutions, don't you think?

I'm not sure I follow.

It's so far from the world I knew growing up. For that matter, it's also a world away from Wall Street. I sense a lot of rules I don't know, rules of conduct, rules about what to say and how to say it and what not to say, rules that everyone knows, the lawyers and judges, though they don't seem to *know* that they know the rules, as if sensibility to the rules is seeded in the womb, an instinct coming before awareness. Those rules aren't, as far as I can tell, written down anywhere.

Isn't that true of every walk of life, every *world*, as you put it?

Mrs. Hampton-Wyvern knows, I thought, that I had worked on Wall Street; neither she nor James asked why I had referred to Wall Street. Why should it surprise me that Emily had spoken to them about me? But it did. Will they ask about *the world I knew growing up*? Aren't they even curious? What else had Emily said to them?

There's a question of degree. On Wall Street, for instance, the rules for traders like me were pretty straightforward: Make the firm money and you'll be fine.

And at the bar all you have to do is win cases, surely?

Even if both sides in a case are represented by the top two barristers in the country, one of them still has to lose.

You only have to do well, then.

I hope so. It's still early days. All I can say is that I have the impression there are things being said—and I mean even the stuff of idle banter in the corridors of chambers—things that mean more than the mere words being used to say them, and there are things that remain unsaid that possibly no words could convey.

From Mrs. Hampton-Wyvern's perspective, getting on in legal practice was of course only about winning cases. The rest of it was a given to her, something to which she could only have been oblivious. But my experience at the bar had already confirmed to me that I would never be granted that security.

At the end of the first quarter of the year of training, which is to say right near the beginning, I was made aware of the presence of overarching social rules, if not their content. Edmund Staughton, the chair of the pupilage committee, gave me the first-quarter performance review. I sat in his chambers on an armless wooden chair across a leather-topped oak desk, repro through and through, as he leaned back in his capacious seat.

Zafar, he said, might I give you a word of advice? Perhaps—and I trust you'll appreciate that this is meant well—perhaps you could conduct yourself with a little more reserve and even with a touch more deference toward senior barristers in and around chambers. That's all I wanted to say, and I don't think we need to dwell on the point any more than that.

I thought I saw embarrassment preventing him from elaborating; I hoped it was embarrassment. Of course there were certain things, particular moments, to which, I imagined, he might have been referring.

There was, I remembered, an awkward discussion with a senior barrister—or was it an exchange of monologues?—in the dining hall of one of the Inns of Court. There were a few other senior barristers in the group, and I happened to be there among them for a hot lunch late in an English autumn. A portly man, this barrister, but he had an oddly delicate touch as he made his way around the plate before him, knife and fork pinched between fingers, his movements gliding with improbable finesse over the heaped rubble of food.

So many of those lawyers look the same at that age, the late fifties. Quite a few sherries, g&ts, and more or less everything, so much consumption leaving a red hue in their faces, and the prospect of gout.

He explained that the other day he was reading a book and came across *BCE*. Have you come across *BCE*? he asked the table generally.

BCE, he continued, means *Before the Common Era*; that's before Christ to you and me. And instead of *AD*, this book referred to *CE*, *Common Era*. Now of course I know this political-correctness business is a trifle overstated, but don't you think *BCE* is stretching things somewhat? I mean, why can't they say *BC* and *AD*? Why not say that? It seems to me we're being forced to adopt a language just to accommodate overly developed sensitivities.

One of the other barristers muttered agreement and the others plowed on with their meals.

How are you being forced? I asked.

An atmosphere of politically correct intimidation, he replied. Of course, nobody's holding a gun to my head, but that's the beauty of it. Getting you to change the way you talk about things just by intimidation and all because certain words don't suit them. Blast! We should jolly well say what we mean and not pussyfoot about because someone's so preciously sensitive.

Another barrister glanced at me. My attention remained on my lunch.

Once the topic had edged off the table, I offered a comment on something that had made the press just that day, a report by a consulting firm on the economics of the bar and cost-effectiveness.

So, I said, the bar is anticompetitive, it seems, although I suppose that was never in doubt. Was it ever justified? Isn't that the question? The Bar Council's restriction on the supply of barristers is obviously anticompetitive. It's a closed shop like any trade union, I said, catching the eye of the portly senior barrister.

He winced. Was it because he'd been reduced to vulgar membership in a trade union?

And, I continued, the requirement to hire a barrister, an extra lawyer, before you can take a matter to court, that's just plain absurd. I'm sure American companies here must be baffled, to say the least. Some of them are probably asking themselves why they shouldn't let their contracts be governed by New York law and steer clear of England altogether.

The senior barrister, a man who made his livelihood in the comfort of the bar's protectionist rules, pressed his flubbery lips together but said nothing.

When Staughton and I met in his chambers, for my first performance review, and he told me things that he believed were self-evident, things that went, if not without saying, then without saying very much at all, I was troubled. What part of me was I being asked to give up?

I did have one question for him.

And how was my work these past three months? I asked.

Excellent, he replied.

Unless I'd misread him wildly, Staughton was oblivious to the point I had just made. I felt as if we were rehearsing a play but reading from entirely different scripts.

Of course, I mentioned none of this to Penelope Hampton-Wyvern; I shared none of my stories but kept my discussion to a few words about vague social rules.

I wonder if you might not be quite so confused after all, said Mrs. Hampton-Wyvern. You seem, if I may say so, rather thoughtful and I daresay you're coming to the bar with a much wider experience of the world than other barristers I know.

Might she be referring to her ex-husband, I thought, the High Court judge and former barrister; might that friendly remark have actually been a little dig elsewhere? James was grinning at me. Emily had not yet returned from her call.

Every part of life has its own ways, said Mrs. Hampton-Wyvern. Don't you think?

I suppose you're right.

Are you worried you might miss an important social rule and stumble?

It's possible, I replied.

Well, you'll just have to pick up the rules as you go along. And if you stumble, you'll have to pick yourself up, won't you? said Mrs. Hampton-Wyvern.

Yes, I will.

Mrs. Hampton-Wyvern addressed her son: I expect you need to be getting on with your packing?

Quite right, he said, standing up. I'm off grouse shooting in Scotland. Do you shoot?

I've never yet had occasion, I replied.

James again gave me a smile. It seemed to me a warm and generous smile, a boyish smile. But there was more in that smile, and though I could not know what exactly he had in his mind, I did believe then that his little grin acknowledged the distance I would have to cover to go from not shooting to shooting. Perhaps, I thought, it even acknowledged the distance I had covered to meet the Hampton-Wyverns. Not long afterward, however, I would learn that the Hampton-Wyverns had covered that distance already, going the other way.

James had barely stepped out of the room when Mrs. Hampton-Wyvern leaned forward in her seat.

You seem like an affable young man, she said. You may consider this out of turn but I must say it. Zafar, be careful with my daughter.

Of course, I said earnestly. It was exactly what a solicitous mother might say. In point of fact, I was flattered that she thought of my relationship with her daughter as serious, and I was also gratified to think that Emily must have represented it to her in such a way. I wanted to reassure Mrs. Hampton-Wyvern more, but Emily had appeared at the doorway. I could not immediately tell if she had heard anything of what her mother had said.

Zafar broke off there to make us both some coffee, but when he resumed his narrative, he did not pick up where he had stopped. At the time, I thought he was just veering off on another aside. Only later, when he talked about meeting Emily in Kabul, did it become apparent that what he framed in general terms was actually an observation drawn from very personal experience. He would return to the Hampton-Wyverns, but now he wanted to talk about Afghanistan and for that he was laying some groundwork.

Many years ago Zafar told me about a TV program he had seen in the junior common room at college. It was a time when liberals in the Church of England were condemning the brutality of Thatcher's economic project. The archbishop of York appeared on the show, and the presenter, Jonathan Dimbleby, said to him: *Your Grace, there is a great upsurge of the urge in people for certainty. Their charge is that you offer them not that kind of certainty but doubt.* The archbishop paused to reflect. With his hands clasped, as if in prayer, he replied: *Has it occurred to you that the lust for certainty may be a sin?* This memory comes back to me now as a sign that his more recent preoccupations have actually been some time in the making.

I have seen serious scientists and mathematicians give talks, said Zafar, and their faces and manner conveyed nothing of the politician's earnest certitude or confidence, no sign of gravity but of playful levity, as if—I have thought—as if they were a tad embarrassed, as if they didn't fully accept that anyone else could be interested in what they had to say, or as if they were vaguely uncomfortable with this business of dissemination, a task that is auxiliary to their true calling, which is the inquiry and discovery itself. But now I suspect that this outward appearance may be the natural state of anyone who is in proximity to the truth. The mathematician cannot rely on his authority as a mathematician to carry him one inch of the way. It is not some modesty in the character of the mathematician that tells him so but something in the nature of mathematics itself that reveals the irrelevance of his person. If his mathematics is correct, his written findings are immune to every assault. Authority in the form of experience, authority in the form of worldly wisdom or charisma, such kinds of authority are impotent. The politician's conviction is a stand-in: Men who want you to know that they are sure in their own minds seldom have the reasons to show on the page. This is what Einstein meant when he said that one author would have been enough.* But it doesn't stop there. The mathematician knows that nothing empirical, nothing which we are to perceive in this world, can undermine by so much as one whiff of doubt any mathematical claim, and because he knows this, he is free.

The irony is that scientists are much less certain about what they say than politicians, policy makers, and pundits. The certainty of the kind you see in the face of a politician declaiming on tax increases or hear in the voice of a commentator condemning or endorsing a foreign policy decision, or the certainty you detect in the words of an op-ed writer pontificating on one thing or another—I used to think that they arrived at their certainty after considering an issue in great depth and finding that the evidence fell overwhelmingly in favor of a specific position. You must think me naïve ever to have thought this way. But I did. I used to think that a good argument was the midwife to certainty. If, as I now believe, it is the wish that fathers the thought, then certainty is the lingering imprint of a wish on thoughts and arguments, like DNA retained in progeny, acting invisibly but with visible effects.

I don't know who it was that said that the three greatest feats of science in the twentieth century were Einstein's theory of relativity, Crick and Watson's discovery of the double helical structure of DNA, and Gödel's Incompleteness Theorem. Few can doubt the impact of Einstein's mass-energy equation, and if impact be the measure, then relativity gets a place on the podium. As for DNA and the double helix, we may be forgiven a little anthropocentrism, for nothing has ever so teased our lustful hubris as the power to understand and alter what we are. But what of Gödel's Incompleteness Theorem? *Time* magazine included Gödel on a list of its Twenty Greatest Thinkers and Scientists of the Twentieth Century, but the truth is that unlike relativity and DNA, the Incompleteness Theorem has no place in the popular imagination.

At the center of the mathematical enterprise stands this rather awkward

---

*Responding to the publication of the book *One Hundred Authors Against Einstein*, a work ostensibly directed at his physics, Albert Einstein said, "If I were wrong, then one would have been enough."

result, an extraordinary one that uses mathematics itself not to expound an irrefutable observation about circles or prime numbers or topological invariants and conformal mappings but to say something about the nature of mathematics itself. It is a theorem that denies certainty in the very realm where you might expect it most. Why should that matter? Mathematics is unique in all human endeavor. I might think that a violinist does or does not have a feel for music; perhaps I can have an opinion on that, for what it's worth, but that opinion is always vulnerable, can only be vulnerable, to one differing opinion. Nothing that is proven in mathematics, however, can be assailed or undermined. You may take it as granted. It is the parent, the lover, the friend you can rely on, imaginary if need be. Mathematics, which doesn't include the tawdry efforts of statistics or probability, pure mathematics, the product of the human mind turning to face itself, turning into itself, and finding in the realm of necessary consequences, where no contingent fact is to be seen or heard or smelled or tasted or touched—it discloses a beauty that exhausts human comprehension and a certainty the senses can never touch. No other effort in this world can deliver a thing of such exhilarating beauty that is also true in that way, *in that way*, I say, whose beginning and end are one and the same, which requires no venture beyond the cranial cage, no reliance on the perceptions that deceive or the memory that corrupts, no appeal to anything experienced. Christ in heaven! Can you bloody believe it?

Of course, I was moved by Zafar's passionate charge for mathematics. I had studied the subject in my own youth, so that what he described sounded echoes in the corridors of my memory. It's said of mathematicians that mathematics is their mistress, their first love, or the great love of their lives. It is a hackneyed metaphor and, come to think about it, one not uniquely applicable to mathematicians. But in my time, I've had enough of a feel for mathematics, have dipped in her shallows if not plumbed her depths, to vouch for the quality of intimacy.

Zafar moved on to an exposition of Gödel's Incompleteness Theorem, but this took us along yet another digression carrying us further afield. He did not, in fact, lose his thread, and, in due course, he returned to his story of meeting the Hampton-Wyverns and then the narrative of events in Afghanistan (in fact there was only ever just one thread, winding in ways that are now apparent). Even so, I am inclined to skip over the account concerning Gödel's Incompleteness Theorem, a digression too far, which should not be taken as an indication of anything other than my own need to keep a grip on the twisting and turning of Zafar's discussion, the ranging back and forth.

In 2000, how many people knew what subprime mortgages were? he asked me.

Hang on! How did we get to mortgages? I responded.

Zafar simply repeated the question.

Not many, I said, giving up and going along with him.

And before September 11, 2001, how many do you think had read Ahmed Rashid's book about Afghanistan?

Taliban?

Yes.

Your point is?

When a journalist asked Harold Macmillan what he feared most in politics, his reply was, *Events, dear boy, events.* The event defines everything, changes everything, not just afterward but also before. People can't bear the unexpected, they won't let it stand and they'll change their memories to make what was unexpected now expected. Just as nature abhors a vacuum, men abhor the vacuum in history, the discontinuity wrought by the unexpected, and they'll go back and fill it out, go back and try to figure out how it happened, try to identify what we didn't see before, that to which we once were blind but now can see. We go back and revise our understanding of the world, with the benefit of having experienced the event.

What event?

Unexpected events. Things we just didn't see coming. We plan our policies, making predictions every which way. But look at the past, even the written one. What is it but a chain of surprises?

9/11? The financial crisis?

External events, events that come out of the blue, said Zafar, changing lives all the time, every year, if not every day. Our choices are made, our will flexed, in the teeth of events that overwhelm and devour us.

As Churchill said, I added, history is just one bloody thing after another.

Was that Churchill? asked Zafar.

Isn't there a convention that if you don't know who the author is, you can always attribute it to Churchill?

I thought it was Edna St. Vincent Millay.

You can always attribute it to Edna St. Vincent Millay? I asked Zafar.

No. Millay said, It is not true that life is one damn thing after another; it's one damn thing over and over.

That's actually more interesting, I responded.

But I suppose you're right. In fact, as Churchill himself said, the false attribution of epigrams is the friend of letters and the enemy of history.

He said that?

No, replied Zafar.

Our conversation ended there for the day. It is from this point, I think, that his Afghan account took on a markedly darker hue. If I think now, as I am inclined to do, that this was the moment Zafar began setting out the case for his defense—defense of what happened in Afghanistan, of what he did there—then I am forced to accept that he was no less setting out a case for prosecution, a case to establish the culpability of others, and of me. This is what I think he meant by his references to 9/11 and the financial crisis, and in a narrower way a reference to why and how things changed between him and Emily. It is only once the dust from historic events has settled that people pick their way back across the battlefield to survey the damage, and then rewrite history. Alan Greenspan, that wily chairman of the Federal Reserve, was lauded once, not long ago, as possibly the greatest Fed chairman ever, a master of the markets, manipulating interest rates to perfection. Today, even in the eyes of former acolytes, Greenspan's reputation is in tatters. Too free and easy with money, they say, always was. Under him interest rates fell and money became so cheap that there was little to give investors and banks pause before putting more and more borrowed funds into riskier and riskier investments. Enter subprime mortgages, mortgages to those who couldn't really afford them, who would default in due course. But it is only after the event that the eyes of history look back. Who could know that in the hills of Central Asia, trouble was brewing that would spill from the skies of Manhattan? Yet afterward the eyes of the West, if not of the world, and all the thunder of its armory came down on Afghanistan. There are some words in one of Zafar's notebooks that appear to have been taken down at a museum in Copenhagen (if one is to go by the surrounding notes and observations on that city) and are attributed to Søren Kierkegaard: *Life can only be understood backward; the trouble is, it has to be lived forward.*

I met Mohammed and Sila Jalaluddin, said Zafar, in the summer of 2001 in Washington, D.C., where the husband had been a midranking World Bank official. Beginning in the autumn of 2001, Afghani-born professionals working in public policy or international development, numbering a few scattered across the globe, were drawn into the incipient reconstruction efforts after the American invasion of their mother country. Mohammed Jalaluddin's career had until then been trapped in the doldrums of D.C., in no small part due to his reputation as a difficult man, but it was now carried up on the wind radiating from the crashing Twin Towers that lifted everyone in his business. He, like so many of them, came from that breed of international development experts unsparing in its love for all humanity but having no interest in people. What else explains the implacable set of the lips? They peddle an august wisdom safe in the knowledge that it can never be proven false. They know that such advice, bought and paid for in good money and in the kind of honors and offices they crave, will only be tossed into the maelstrom of conflicting political demands and corrupt claims, in which their advice will lose its identity, so that disappointments and failed outcomes only exonerate them and justify each new contract for further service.

But no one works alone, not even the most curmudgeonly, not when a job has tasks to be delegated. On a day in June 2001, Penelope Hampton-Wyvern received a telephone call from an old paramour, one Rudiger Dornhoff, an ex-UN staffer, who had heard that a former colleague was looking for a junior consultant to hire. Emily had taken a degree in public administration from Harvard, but her grades fell some way short of the triple-A rating for the elite young professional program. So, like many aspirants to UN jobs before her, she sought a route in through the many unguarded passages known to insiders. Consultants under contract are never subject to the same degree of scrutiny.

I never met Dornhoff, continued Zafar. I know some facts, but I have speculated about the rest. He was retired, but, having no family to mind, he remained at his former employer's side, like an old sheepdog, and offered his services as a consultant on projects in which he had once been involved.

Dornhoff met Penelope Hampton-Wyvern at a bookshop near Campden Hill some forty years ago. Penelope was then a dark-haired twenty-three-year-old, already engaged to be married to Robin. A Swiss nobleman, of the rather pointless Swiss kind, Dornhoff was a graduate student in economics in London. He and Penelope met, he flattered her, she swooned, he made overtures, she blushed, this went on, he persisted, and then she told him she was already engaged. Over the years Dornhoff maintained with Penelope a largely one-sided correspondence of post-cards from his exotic UN postings. His hopes might have risen when word reached him of Penelope's divorce, but when he spoke to her next the optimism would have been deflated by the same cheery affection from her as a sister might bear for a younger brother. The point here is that Dornhoff had information from behind enemy lines, and Emily, now armed with a master's in public administration, was the soldier of beneficence in search of a just war.

I gave up the delusion, which lasted only as long as the notion of love between Emily and me was tenable, that goodness is what drove her. In its place was an older conviction, released from abeyance. I have an idea that much human misery can be traced to a tiny source, whose true identity remains hidden as it is time and again mistaken for something else. And the mistake is one that is easily made, for the source of misery is the source, too, of greatness, so that pride will not let a man regard the two faces at once. Is that not the Promethean fable, that the fire stolen from the gods will light men their way even while it burns their hands?

I do not trust a man who says he does not care what others think of him. I rather suspect there's little else he cares about. It's not just that a person's fabrications and the carefully woven stories he tells about himself are all begotten of the dark drive to elevate himself into a creature of significance. It's not just that he will lie through his teeth, as he convinces himself of his veracity, in order to enhance the esteem in which he is held. The root of mischief is that he will organize all his affairs and dedicate his every work to the advancement of his reputation and that this object alone will drive him on. When evil enters the world, do you think it comes with horns and cloven feet, billowing some foul stench?

What others think of him, his place in society, the regard of his peers, is the prime motive of a human being's every enterprise. Freud never made enough of this. Otto Rank called it the hero instinct, every man's craving to be a hero despite the universe that mocks him, as if in all its vast splendor it ever spared a thought for another paltry contingency.

Rudiger Dornhoff, having been informed by Penelope that Emily was looking for a job at the UN, had been keeping a faithful eye on the bulletin boards, and when a post was advertised for a temporary contract with a fellow with whom he'd worked on a few projects in Indonesia, a fellow who would no doubt find useful a testimonial for Emily from Dornhoff himself, the Swiss picked up the phone to her.

That was in June 2001, and the fellow looking for a temp was Mohammed Jalaluddin, who, by October, would become recognized as the most senior Afghani at the UN, World Bank, or IMF, and would find himself desired as never before. The future of *his* country—the U.S. passport didn't matter for these pressing purposes—would depend on him. The lives of twenty-five million would depend on him. But he couldn't do it all on his own, and there beside him would be Emily, so very reliable, bright, and, my goodness, never has there walked on the earth a woman so vulnerable to the father figure, a pilgrim from one shrine to another, in search of the ideal.

By March 2002, the United Nations Assistance Mission in Afghanistan was well established. Land Cruisers were roaring into Kabul; U.S. helicopters laden with UNAMA staff churned the dust at makeshift airfields in outlying districts; and, not least, up and running, pulling pints and pouring shots, was the UN bar in Kabul. Mohammed Jalaluddin, Emily Hampton-Wyvern, and a hundred important people were in place, housed in a compound adjoining that bar. The stage was set.

What had become of us by then was neither fish nor fowl but somewhere in between, skating the surface: Do fish think of the boundary between water and air as a surface, only coming at it from below? We had technically parted. Technically, too, we remained in love, insofar as one can ever know these things. Love was a garland strung with doubts and uncertainty. There were of course small matters, such as my never featuring in her conversations with anyone, something I had gathered over time, sometimes through the looks of sheer surprise in the faces of people who surely would have been bound to know. And there were other things, too, that had kept the relationship in a state of permanent beginning. In her dealings with me, Emily Hampton-Wyvern was the most unreliable person in the world. It confused me at first because in her professional life, by exasperating contrast, she was the pillar of reliability.

It is not the Bible's only splendid irony that it is to Peter to whom Christ says you will be the rock upon which I will found my Church, so that today the Church of Rome accords to Peter the status of its first pontiff. An irony, because this is the same Peter who, when approached by centurions in the garden of Gethsemane, denied Christ, not once, not twice, but three times before the cock crowed; the same Peter who had earlier insisted, three times, that he would do no such thing. I am reminded of the injunction that you should treat a man as you believe him capable and he will become that person—a ridiculous homily. It seems to me that the picture is somewhat different: not more complex, less so.

I know that even when I put down all that I have heard, I cannot complete the picture. Zafar, like everyone, I suppose, is to be pieced together out of the fragments that fall about us. I have set out and will set out what I know, but I know so little, in the end, and least of all causes, which my father's scientist in me longs for. It is no consolation to reflect that every cause itself is an effect, making the search for causes and reasons a fool's errand.

I am too much an imitator to be a true writer. But if I were writing a novel, rather than simply setting out the facts I know—those that I have been told, those that I have read, and those that come to me through my own experience—then I might have given a thought to hanging upon the bare facts the ornamentation of reasons. That kind of elaboration, on my reading of works of fiction, seems to be the fashion, to tell a story that begins at the beginning, in childhood, and trace out the trajectory of a life that is marked by its very beginnings. Is that psychoanalysis? Whatever its name, the story I would write, were I so inclined, would say something about how Zafar's childhood formed him; it would set forth incidents that account for the deep alienation he felt (an alienation I would, in the writing, confidently locate in him); it would explain how he came to know that he was two years younger than he had long ago been led to believe; and it would make more of the nature of his parentage, more than the few facts I have at my disposal, which don't even tell me how he came to know that his father, his true father, was a Pakistani soldier who raped his mother, and that this mother, his true mother, was the young sister of the man who raised him as his own son.

Which last fact really should get a banner headline rather than a buried aside in ruminations on the difficulties I face in writing. And yet what have I now but his notebooks? Notebooks that show an old and recurring interest in the subject of rape in war and rape in Bangladesh during the liberation struggle. Notebooks that record no more than bare sentences containing the facts I've mentioned. But think for a moment: Why would he have recorded anything more than that in his notebooks? Certainly not as an aide-mémoire. For how could you possibly forget anything of a conversation in which you learned the shocking truth of your origins?

In my possession there is only what I have learned. This fact alone constrains the story I can tell, the sense of a life, the forces that made it. Besides, I have to say, I do not set great store in the hydraulic conception of the human psyche that psychoanalysis presents, that a push here and a yank here, and out, over there, comes the consequence, or that holding in anger is like holding in a sneeze. Lacking authority here, I know I am speculating, but it seems to me that in the appropriate context, the psychoanalyst might say: You can see why the man doesn't get close to women; the boy was never close to his mother. But equally, the psychoanalyst might say of another man: You can see why he is always too eager and quick to get close to women; the boy was never close to his mother.

I don't know what story I would write to account for Zafar, to provide the buttresses of causes and effects that support the structure of a human life, as it could be described, as it might be understood. The job is not made easier by all the vacancies, the questions left unanswered and others thought of only later, like the witty riposte that arrives halfway up the staircase, too late to be of any use. Zafar spoke abundantly, as never before, but in the end all I can include is whatever I can draw from what he said or wrote. How then to span the piers?

My father is too generous a man to actually roll his eyes when he's invariably asked at dinner parties what his work is about. Give a sense, a flavor of what it's about, is what they ask him to do. Being a civil and courteous man, perhaps believing that it probably doesn't matter, a flavor is what he supplies—or at least what his dinner guests believe they've been given. And he will listen as well, smiling warmly, as a guest invokes—as a theoretical physicist's guest will do—Einstein's theory of relativity as metaphor for some proposition in the social sciences. Relativity, my father will hear, demonstrates such and such (in some field as far removed from science as everything but science). My father will remember but will never mention what Einstein came to wish after long suffering to hear the abuses to which the mere heading of his theory had been put, as if to invoke the name of the theory was to import all the authority of the ancient and timeless lambdas, epsilons, and deltas of a beautiful mathematical argument. Einstein wished to hell that he'd called it the theory of invariance, which is to say, he wished he'd given it a name whose meaning was exactly the opposite of *relativity* and which, he said, would have been just as accurate.

But our private conversations, between father and son, are free of the disingenuous concessions of dinner parties. Metaphors have their place, he says, but never as explanations, never as substitute for the thing itself, which is the only thing that can turn on the lights or leave us in the dark. His suspicion of metaphors recognizes that our proclivity toward them probably springs from our very nature, which is given to analogize, to link one thing with another, and to make whole the disparate. But exercising this instinct is not the same as giving an explanation.

His respect for my mother would keep him from saying so explicitly, but psychoanalysis is only a grand metaphor, he says. It is not even a work in progress but a stopgap until work has progressed on the real thing.

I see that I have gone far enough down one road and now I want to return. In the result, I cannot tell the story that is not a metaphor, the only story that is true. Perhaps it's as simple as this: I don't have it in me.

Zafar returned to his account. He had explained how Emily had come to be in Afghanistan, and on another occasion he had talked about a telephone call from her, asking him to join her. This raised the question of if and when he would meet her. But his narrative first picked up where he had left off. Suleiman had given him a tour of Kabul, taking in the view from a hill overlooking the city, after which they returned to AfDARI.

He and I, said Zafar, had not been standing long in the courtyard of AfDARI, under the dappled shade of a mature mulberry bush, before a young woman arrived at the main entrance. The gatekeeper drew open the iron gate, its hinges resisting with a shrill. I noticed that he did not acknowledge her, no smile, not even a nod. I put that down to deference toward her sex and perhaps her station. She was a white woman, a pasty, unhealthy white, and wore a pale gray shalwar kameez with a dark blue hijab on her head, curls of mousy hair peeking from underneath. From one shoulder hung a tan leather satchel unbuckled and stuffed with papers. The Afghans are racially diverse and even include men and women with eyes as blue as a Norwegian fjord, but the manner in which this woman carried herself, her confident stride, her unhesitating eye contact, instantly marked her as a Westerner.

Someone waved at her, and I tendered a perfunctory smile as she strode past toward the main building and climbed the steps before disappearing inside.

The director of AfDARI, explained Suleiman, is a married man. In France, he has a wife and two children, and in Afghanistan he keeps a photograph of them on the desk in his office. We can count our blessings that we are standing in the courtyard and not in the office adjoining his.

Why's that? I asked.

Because they do not have the shame even to hide the sound of what they are doing.

Suleiman drew his breath.

AfDARI needs new leadership, he said. The current director is a hold-over. He was appointed by donors during the Taliban days and AfDARI was a token gesture. This man is corrupt through and through. Forget his sexual morals; he's creaming off huge sums, and of course it will only get worse with all the money now pouring in. What can we expect? He's an outsider fitting out a nice second home on the French Riviera. The question is: Do you want the job?

Me?

Yes.

Suleiman, I'm flattered. But how do you know I'd be any better?

You *would* be better. You'd be much better.

It's very nice of you to say so, but I'm not sure it's my cup of tea. I'm not sure, for that matter, what it is I'd be better at. Besides, you only just met me, and I can no more take his job, my friend, than you can, if I may say so, offer it.

I'd been in Kabul not even forty-eight hours. I knew already that this was a time and a place where things could happen very quickly, where bureaucratic decisions were being taken in an instant by youngsters un-encumbered with history, where government departments were being run by foreign administrators barely old enough to run their own bath. Decision making here was unimpeded by the demand to consider and reflect on experience. Even so, what exactly was the basis of Suleiman's choice? He obviously took a liking to me. But was there more? Does Suleiman have his own career prospects in mind? Has he hit a glass ceiling for Afghans that might first be cracked by someone like me, halfway between insider and outsider?

Your reputation precedes you.

Your flattery is flattering, I replied.

I had no reputation, I thought—which, I suppose, is a reputation of a sort. Without any reason, I wondered if Suleiman was hinting at knowing the colonel.

I spoke to some of our elders this morning, he said. They are Afghans who are nominally consulted on major decisions taken by the executive director, a sort of advisory board. Of course they haven't met you, but what I said convinced them very quickly.

And what did you tell them? I asked.

I told them you're smart. I told them that you're a very intelligent man who is not an outsider.

Suleiman, do you think I'm one of you?

You are from a poor country like mine. You are a Muslim. And you've lived among them so you know them, you know how to press their buttons.

If I am not for them, I am against them?

Precisely.

My dear Suleiman, I think you might find you have more in common with George Walker Bush than you'd like to think.

How is that?

Tell me what your elders said.

A change is what we need here and they will support it.

If I have to give an answer now, I'll say no.

Then why don't you think about it?

An hour later I was standing in the entrance hall of AfDARI, a large room with high ceilings and a crisscross of black-and-white tiles. Three doorways opened onto the hall; one of them was wedged open and led into a long corridor. At one end of the hall, there was an improbably large mirror with an elaborate gilded frame. On the wall opposite the main doors, facing the arriving visitor, was an array of mounted displays, posters, and notices all showcasing AfDARI's good works.

Poster after poster boasted AfDARI's hand in a range of enterprises, from irrigation and drinking water projects to building schools and supplying teaching materials. No sight better expresses the politics of aid, the dynamic of the West and the developing countries, than the image of children, happy or in need. All the children in the pictures were boys. Established in the time of the Taliban, AfDARI had been the main clearinghouse for whatever crumbs of foreign aid fell from the table to a country of little interest to the United States, after the collapse of the Soviet Union.

A door in the hall opened. The woman whom I had seen arrive only half an hour ago stepped out, glanced at me, and then struck out across the tiles. I heard the main gates creak open and listened for their shutting but heard instead a growing sound of female voices. As they closed in on the building, I made out American accents, and among them an English one.

I considered removing my sunglasses; I was indoors, after all. I was wearing a suit and a smart shirt and polished shoes. The sunglasses would confirm the absurd picture of a pimp, or a drug dealer, or a Pakistani ISI officer with James Bond delusions.

The women entered the hall. One broke away and came toward me in long swinging strides, as her face flashed a bright beaming smile. She was rather beautiful, a soft face and eyelashes sprinkling above bright blue orbs. She had a delicate nose, thin and turning up ever so slightly at the end. Large noses, misshapen noses, asymmetric noses, such noses are noticed; a beautiful nose is never noticed but found, and it is the rest of the face that alerts the eye to look. A head scarf lay far back on her head, barely clinging to it, so that her rich brown hair topped a picture of vitality. A red down-filled knee-length jacket, cinched at the waist and lowering over a pair of jeans, failed to subdue the imagination from picturing the curves of her figure. As she approached me, she removed her hijab and opened her jacket.

Hello. My name is Nicky, Nicky Amory. Who are you?

She spoke in a crisp English accent. She was not wearing a ring.

Zafar, I said, removing my sunglasses.

Hello, Zafar. Do you work here?

I'm sorry, Nicky. I don't. But perhaps I can help anyway?

You're British.

Is it the accent or the good manners?

Oh, not the manners, she said, now quite earnest.

I mean you have excellent manners, of course, she added quickly, a little flustered.

Such good manners on your part to say so, I replied. If I may say so, I added.

No, no. The British aren't a . . . a well-mannered lot.

She hesitated, and I thought she was stopping herself from saying *good-mannered*.

All smiles they might seem, she continued, but they'll stab you in the back if it'll win them a square foot of land that doesn't belong to them. Dreadful place. Can't stand it. Left fifteen years ago and haven't looked back.

There are codes of conduct to curiosity. Most people say a little about themselves and their work, a transactional advance into the account to draw down when they ask you what you do. Westerners do this, that is. It's a payment for inquisitiveness. But South Asians in the main have no embarrassment about getting straight to their own curiosity. Yet Nicky, who was no South Asian, had none of the Westerner's indirectness.

Why are you here, Zafar? What do you do?

Not sure, I replied.

Oh, I see. Spying, are we?

What do you mean?

Kabul is full of spies. Turn your head and look—there's another mysterious type lurking in the shadows. Or not. They call themselves advisers here, by the way. Who do you spy for?

For myself, like everyone, I replied.

I see. We're all spies. Never the person we think we are.

Least of all to ourselves.

Oh, I like that. You must be the existential spy, she said.

Any point in issuing a denial?

None whatsoever, darling.

Nicky was disconcerting but in a pleasant way. A beautiful woman, seemingly not a day over thirty (though actually near forty, I would gather later), leading some kind of charge, sporting the combined personality of a campaigning journalist, Miss Moneypenny, and a determined nun. The name was fit for a porn star, completing the drama of this woman's persona. I think what pleased me most about her was the confusing impression I had—even very quickly—that although she could easily write off entire nations, she would be the last person to judge another human being.

The other women joined us. It appeared that this group of four was part of a larger contingent sent by a U.S. charitable foundation that organized exchange visits of professionals in American nonprofits with those in developing countries. Nicky was the deputy director of an international microfinance organization, an "initiative," she called it, which helped communities in "LDCs" (less-developed countries, she added politely) find ways to borrow small amounts of money for business purposes. Women were central to this initiative. Other organizations were also represented, the figurehead for all of which was Bianca Jagger.

Nicky turned to me and said, I've got a meeting with this chap, the executive director, eh . . .

Maurice Touvier?

I did not mention to Nicky the little I already knew about him. I knew that Emily had been impressed by young Monsieur Touvier's expertise with Excel spreadsheets. She had forwarded by email a budget drawn up by the gentleman, for my comment, she said, adding that she thought it rather impressive. It was a list of hardware for a new UN unit to direct reconstruction efforts: umpteen Land Cruisers, computers, satphones, and so on. Emily had asked for my impressions, but I didn't share them all with her: Monsieur Touvier had an excellent command of the coloring features of the software.

That's it, said Nicky. I have a meeting with him. Why don't you come along for the ride?

He's not expecting me.

Who knows what to expect in this country? Anyway, I've taken a fancy to you and won't hear no for an answer.

Excellent. When is your meeting?

Now.

Oh. I can't do now. In fact, I'm already late for something else.

What?

If I told you, I'd be a terrible spy.

We're all going for a drink tonight. Come with us?

Sounds good.

I lied about having another meeting. I just didn't want to meet Touvier. Barely two days in Kabul and already I felt the stir of revulsion, already I confronted the stain of hypocrisy. But it didn't come to me as a finding of fact, as a revelation in the behavior of others—it didn't feel like that. Rather, it was a conclusion, a deduction from what I had always known, as if I'd proceeded a small step from footings already laid, like a syllogistic argument, *All Cretans are liars, Epimenides is a Cretan*, and all that I had done, which I could have done anywhere but in fact was doing in Kabul, was to conclude that *Epimenides is a liar.*

In the evening, ten minutes after picking me up, our little convoy, a dozen women and me, pulled up at the gates of the UN compound, an area soaking in artificial floodlighting. Soldiers in blue berets milled about a flank of Humvees by the gates, lighting cigarettes as they laughed, machismo in their sweeping gestures but nervousness, too, in furtive looks to the side. We climbed out of the cars and filed into a prefabricated security booth, not dissimilar to the ticketing booths you might find at the entrance to a public attraction, a castle or the botanical gardens at Kew. Our passports were checked and we were frisked before being allowed to proceed through a narrow hallway into the compound. I have no doubt that my association with this group of Western women sanitized me, and I thought of how a man might feel when, on arriving at the door of a nightclub in New York with several women on his arms, he and his coterie are ushered in ahead of the long line.

From the right of the hallway there came a hubbub; that way, I assumed, lay the UN lounge and bar. But to the left, leading outside, was a door propped open with a brick. I slipped off toward it, separating myself from the women ahead of me, and came out onto the compound area under the night sky. There were soldiers wandering about beyond, spilling onto the road. An Afghani man was standing by the door smoking. We exchanged greetings and I asked him for a cigarette. I handed him my Bic lighter, telling him that it was extra, I had another. He explained he was waiting for a crate of wine for Mr. Maurice. It struck me as a trifle odd that he was waiting inside the main gates, but I didn't probe.

I was, by the way, dressed entirely inappropriately for Kabul. You see that I now wear cargo pants and the like, clothes better suited to travel in out-of-the-way places. But I had arrived in Kabul in a black suit and black shoes and a sky-blue cotton shirt; I had dispensed with the tie, which I kept folded in my pocket—silk ties make strong rope. Wearing a suit had become a habit in South Asia. It cut through a lot of questions. I had taken on the dress of a slightly older generation and projected a rather businesslike persona.

At Oxford, I never had money for decent clothes. But I was a student, so what did it matter? There's a funny thing about all those public school boys, the Paulines and Wykehamists: They were so scruffy.

Zafar made me smile. It was certainly true of me.

They seemed not to care in the slightest how they looked, he continued. Do you remember Stinky Flowers?

David Flowers, I said.

But everyone called him Stinky.

Because of his last name, I replied.

But there was in fact something stinky about him. He didn't wash; I'm sure of it. Is that what an education at a grand English public school gives you? Not self-confidence, but rather a lack of self-doubt, the certainty that the world will welcome you as you are, which is the cream of society, no matter what you look like.

Not everyone who goes to Eton is like that, I said to Zafar.

Did you know that there isn't a drug on earth that works on more than seventy percent of the population? A pharmaceutical drug.

And?

Not one drug. Pharma companies consider a drug a success if it's effective in a much smaller proportion of patients. You're not going to write off the drug, said Zafar, just because thirty percent of the population don't fit the pattern.

It's not the same.

Of course it's not the same. That's why it's an analogy. The point is that it's similar in a relevant respect. I'm not talking about the minority of public school boys. I'm not even talking about the majority necessarily. I'm only saying that there's this pattern in public school boys that you don't find in others to quite the same degree.

That they smell?

No. Their sense of entitlement, their attitude.

Zafar, I thought, was right about the attitude to clothes. I fell into the category of carefree dressers at college. It never seemed to matter very much. So long as you had appropriate gear for events—a suit, black tie, white tie, etc.—what did it matter what you wore around college otherwise?

I asked Zafar why he'd worn a suit in Afghanistan.

He explained that wearing a suit in South Asia had a normalizing effect.

A suit means business, he said. It shuts out certain kinds of irritating interactions that can undermine one's work. Bangladeshis, and for that matter South Asians generally, are an inquisitive lot, always probing to establish one's family ties. I had seen the instant slightly deflated, even crestfallen, look people gave when it transpired that I was not linked to any great family—quite the opposite, I was a social nonentity. It seemed to disappoint them: Suddenly their opportunities for gaining favors diminished before their eyes. How different it was, it is, in America. There I might answer curiosity with the information that my father was a waiter, my mother a seamstress, and the response would be utterly different. I know some would call this naïveté, but the persistence of the myth of the clean slate is itself the guarantor of an optimistic faith in human freedom, the capacity to break bonds and forge something new. Even this new president is himself a sign of the underlying spirit of a country that has the capacity to believe in change, unlike the Europe that so fears it.

But optimism, by its nature, is boundless, brooks no limits, knows no discouragement, keeps going, does not know when to stop. To go from America's founding belief that it can form an ever more perfect union to a belief that it can reconstruct another country in the image of its hopes for itself—to cover that distance—does not take long: A politician does it before he tells you that he approves this message. Yet this is not news. From pride to narcissism, the road was long ago marked out by corpses.

There I was, within the UN compound in the Shar-e-Naw district, the mansions district, under a black sky, and I wondered what devil had brought me to this place. What was my real motivation. I knew, of course, how I'd come there. I knew, too, who had asked me to go and what each of them had wanted of me. But in those moments, as I stood there puffing on a cigarette, on the brink each time of choking, I wondered again what my own motivation had been. And there was the thought of Emily; there was a good chance she would be there, inside.

This was the hub. Many UN staffers, as well as others, lived in the various houses scattered about the compound, all behind a wall guarded by soldiers. Everything in the space was accounted for, everything in the service of human beings. Everything lifeless but the priority to protect life. There was no sign of vegetation, neither a tree nor a bush, just stone and brick and whitewashed walls and dust. It was obvious that the building was never conceived as it stood but had metastasized over time, that it had grown here and there, pushed out on one side and later on another, so that the floodlights carved shadows from the corners of the houses, the sudden alcoves and jutting boxes. Above the buildings, condensing steam bubbled from a vent.

Some of the Afghani drivers of the cars parked beyond the gates had gathered together while their masters were socializing indoors. They smoked and talked, despite a soldier's hand-waving remonstrations to move away. I stepped around a corner of the building to recover a moment, a preparatory calm without demands on the senses, only to be met with new sounds, beating music and the jostling strains of raised voices. Laughter clambered out through an open window that released, too, the smoke from cigarettes and the vapors of sense-rattling alcohol. Kabul in the spring of 2002, when the West had barely arrived, yet again, and there was this bar, a den of warm merriment while drivers huddled in the cold outside and men in blue berets scowled at the locals.

6

Blood Telegram or Bill and Dave

The very fact that the totality of our sense experiences is such that by means of thinking . . . it can be put in order, this fact is one which leaves us in awe, but which we shall never understand. One may say "the eternal mystery of the world is its comprehensibility."

—Albert Einstein, "Physics and Reality"

The earth is home to a creature, a great ape he calls himself, that has taken on the task of explaining the universe, of accounting for all that there is, his world, his social world, his physical world, the fall of empires and apples alike. The creature is now wending his way along the corkscrew path of his evolution, inside a few splintered years hewn from a vast time line not of his own making, a time line that goes back to some soundless bang venting all the nuclear waste studding the voids of space, a time line that goes far forward, beyond the day when this creature's biological changes will make him as charming to his descendants as his artists' impressions of the first biped hominid are to him now—a time line that will long outlive the hour his planet perishes in the final blaze of a dying sun. Does it not strike him as disturbing that the explanations of the world he finds are intelligible to him? Has he not paused to consider that if he finds an answer, it is only to a question he is capable of asking? Until he learned better, he said that man was unique among creatures for having language, unique among creatures for having reason, unique for the gift of conscience, unique for conceiving other minds, unique it seemed in every way. The animal's hubris now persists in his idea that the truth beneath what he perceives, from the cosmic out there and forever to the mundane here and now, and even the man-made, that such ever-present truth as he believes there could be will not exceed his capacity to understand.

—attributed to Winston Churchill in Zafar's notebooks

The first time, said Zafar, that I visited her mother's home, Emily, her mother, her brother, and I sat in the drawing room nibbling at Bath Oliver biscuits, sipping dusty Earl Grey, and discussing nineteenth-century novels, apparently only the four of us in the house. At that moment I had no reason to think otherwise.

In a room that took up virtually the entire floor, we were settled into a sprawling arrangement of sofas, enough for us all to maintain a decent distance from one another. The furnishings of the room could have placed it at any time within a hundred years. The salmon and peach upholstery, the fireplace and its brass guard and magnificent stone surround, the pleated pelmet concealing the curtain rails above the mullioned sash windows, the shiny black Bösendorfer piano watching us silently, its fall board shut, its rack empty of sheet music, yet its great lid open pointlessly, like the unfurled sail of a boat on a windless sea. Everything in the room sounded the measures of inherited wealth. On one wall there was a small display of portraits of Emily and her brother as children, and of Fitzwilliam, the border terrier, all three portraits evincing the same weight of brushstroke, unadorned by color, the same regard for light and shade. There were side tables here and there. One beside me bore several stiff white cards, leaning against three vases, invitations to events with words printed in great swirling flourishes, the Lord and Lady So-and-so request the pleasure of the company of the Honorable Penelope Hampton-Wyvern, "At Home" on the next line. The dates for all, I noticed, were past. And there was another table that caught my eye, made of mahogany with an elaborate ivory inlay, which might have looked ostentatious, I thought, if much of its surface had not been covered by images. Beneath the cream shades of a table lamp cast in wrought iron and porcelain and another lathed from dark woods, there were photos in small gilt frames, some old and gray, some in sepia, and a few in color. I took in all the photographic images as one impressionist claim on my senses. Only months later, when I came closer to them, would I look upon one of these photos, a photo of Emily, with, well, nothing short of horror.

Apart from the lighting, the only other traces of modernity were tiny white speakers mounted on the wall above the white bespoke bookcase that was seamlessly merged into the wall, which was to become, as I've explained, the subject of conversation with Penelope. It was this bookcase itself that commanded my eye the longest, enough to register its form and to recall how I spent the summer vacation before college.

I began that vacation working at the same restaurant as my father, waiting tables alongside him. The plan was to earn a little money to help the family, as during the previous Christmas and Easter vacations, but on this occasion my father hinted that I might also get to keep a portion of the pay to supplement the bursary that was to see me through college. In those days, a means-tested award from the state meant that nothing, not one penny, would have to come out of my parents' pockets; tuition and maintenance expenses would be covered. But after one week at the restaurant, everything came to an end.

The staff referred to my father, who was the head waiter, as "the Major." Though my father was never, as far as I know, a major in any army, the proprietor, an old man who had fought for the British in Malaya, and whose son had served in the Indian army during the 1971 Indo-Pakistan War, had given my father a rank and title that fitted his sturdy frame and the authority of his voice.* I think that for the old man, as for all men

---

*The 1971 Indo-Pakistan War broke out when India intervened after nine months of the ongoing Bangladesh Liberation War, during which India was overwhelmed by refugees from the new nation. One somewhat underreported aspect of this under-reported war was American complicity. I repeat here a passage recorded in Zafar's notes, which is an excerpt from Christopher Hitchens's book *The Trial of Henry Kissinger*:

> By 1971, the word "genocide" was all too easily understood. It surfaced in a cable of protest from the United States consulate in what was then East Pakistan— the Bengali "wing" of the Muslim state of Pakistan, known to its restive nationalist inhabitants by the name Bangladesh. The cable was written on 6 April 1971 and its senior signatory, the Consul General in Dacca, was named Archer Blood. But it might have become known as the Blood Telegram in any case . . . It was not so much reporting on genocide as denouncing the complicity of the United States government in genocide. [Hitchens describes it as "the most public and the most strongly worded demarche from State Department servants to the State Department that has ever been recorded."] Its main section reads thus:
>
> > Our government has failed to denounce the suppression of democracy. Our government has failed to denounce atrocities. Our government has failed to take forceful measures to protect its citizens while at the

whose wars have made them, time pivoted on an hour when he was tested.

Down in the kitchens, at a small round table in a corner, against jute sacks of rice, drums of vegetable oil, and tubs of ghee, beneath a fluorescent tube, where staff took turns to grab a half hour for lunch, I sat with my father and the head chef, each of us with a plate of rice and the "staff curry" of mutton and stray vegetables, eating with our hands.

Between mouthfuls of food, with particles of rice trickling from his mouth, the head chef gave me some advice.

I hear you're going to university, he said.

Yes, I replied.

A good man, your father, he said. Not many of our people send their children to university.

He lifted another handful of rice and curry to his mouth before he continued.

They all want their boys to go into this dreadful restaurant trade, he said. But what good can come of it?

The chef had no children of his own.

I hear, he added, it will be expensive for your father. You must work hard to fulfill his hopes just as he is working hard to pay for your tuition.

My father did not say a word and neither did I. But later, after midnight, as we returned home, he suggested that I might want to think about doing something other than waiting tables that summer.

---

same time bending over backward to placate the West Pak[istan] dominated government and to lessen any deservedly negative international public relations impact against them. Our government has evidenced what many will consider moral bankruptcy, ironically at a time when the U.S.S.R. sent President Yahya Khan [martial law administrator, based in West Pakistan] a message defending democracy, condemning arrest of a leader of a democratically elected majority party, incidentally pro-West, and calling for end to repressive measures and bloodshed . . . But we have chosen not to intervene, even morally, on the grounds that the Awami conflict, in which unfortunately the overworked term genocide is applicable, is purely an internal matter of a sovereign state. Private Americans have expressed disgust. We, as professional civil servants, express our dissent with current policy and fervently hope that our true and lasting interests here can be defined and our policies redirected.

I did not express any emotion then, when my father made his suggestion. I simply did not feel anything I recognized as anger, and even if I had, I knew of nothing in him to appeal to. But when the head chef praised my father for an unearned credit that my father then failed to deny, I did feel something. I now know the meaning of the flash of tensing in the muscles across my chest, the name of the quickening of breath and pulse. I know also that the only anger I was aware of in those days was my father's, my mother's, too, as she goaded him on, and that I had always been holding back an anger—the anger I owned—that was only growing. For a long time, including the day I met Emily, I believed that decent people did not wish to cause suffering. This I now know not to be true. I know also that within me a rage was building, gathering mass and momentum from the varieties of injustice, with each humiliation— humiliations we shrug off because, we say, we're better than that, better than them. But how arrogant is it really to think we're above anger? Arrogant and incorrect. In fact, my true self always knew better. That self was acquiring the psychological means for wreaking utter violence. The fury, in fact, was never far away.

That night when my father suggested I look for work elsewhere, I accepted his suggestion without debate. And so it was that I came to work on the renovation of houses. In July 1987, on a day not nearly as warm as it was bright, I took a bus from Willesden Green to Kensington, uncertain what it was I hoped to find there, but like the economic migrant who travels to the West, I thought vaguely that opportunities abounded in the streets of the affluent royal borough. Besides, I wanted to see more of Kensington. I had been there once, that winter when I hitched a ride to go to my college interview in Oxford. Kensington, I had thought then, seemed a world away from Willesden.

When I arrived, I walked through the streets, through its many mews and lanes, and I saw scaffolding and boarding and Dumpsters in the roadside, mounting with the rubble of construction, so many that they might all have submerged themselves beneath my senses had I not been specifically looking. I saw numerous renovation projects, and so I knocked on doors and asked if there was any work. No, mate, and Nothing here, mate, came the reply over and over. And then I changed my tack. I'll work for you for nothing, I said, and if after a week you like my work, you can pay me whatever you think is right.

I joined Bill and Dave, carpenters—chippies, they called themselves—from opposite ends of Essex, two giants in tough canvas shorts, pockets full of tools, and leather belts studded with clasps for mallets, chisels, and screwdrivers. One wore a red Arsenal shirt. Bill and Dave were working on the renovation of a five-story Georgian house on a crescent-shaped terrace.

The building was legally protected by English Heritage, so any renovation work was subject to rigorous controls. Bill and Dave were highly skilled: Later, I'd see that the fact that their vans always looked spotless told you everything about their clients, the buildings they worked on, and the streets on which the vans would be parked.

Because the terrace of adjoining houses followed the curved contour of the street, the rooms in the house weren't entirely square, which presented certain difficulties in the construction of furniture fitted into corners. This fact became useful to me.

Bill and Dave had come in near the end of the renovation project to deal with various woodwork, such as bespoke furniture, skirting, dadoes, and picture rails, and to reconstruct four flights of stairs. The existing staircases, while sturdy, were irretrievably damaged by carpet adhesives and decades of tread. Moreover, since the carpet had been removed, successive repairs over time had left the stairs with a mishmash of materials, including a number of makeshift chipboard risers and treads. All the furniture—bookcases, cabinets, and wardrobes throughout the house—would be constructed on site, except for the kitchen cabinets, which the two men later confided to me were actually off the shelf. Nine times out of ten the owners can't draw, said Bill, and can't even describe what it is they want. They're bankers and lawyers, he said. Bill and Dave would then show them a catalog, just for ideas, and right as rain the owners would pick something out and say they wanted that, just that, and no they didn't want to buy it off the shelf but wanted it made to measure, tailored to their lovely house, so that it had that personal touch, the real thing, not something you could find in any house in the area. Exactly like that, they'd say, still pointing to the picture in the catalog.

They can't tell the difference, said Bill.

Can't tell their arses from their elbows, said Dave.

At first, all I did was clear up after these two men, fetch tools and materials, and maintain a steady supply of tea and custard cream biscuits, as Bill and Dave went about their diligent business of bringing wood and other materials to life, while plumbers, electricians, and painters came and went around us. When the day ended I'd pack the power tools into the two vans, and in the mornings I'd unload them again and set them out where they'd need them in the house.

I warmed to Bill and Dave quickly. I remember that both of them always said "thanks" or "cheers, mate," even to each other. Such words did not seem to figure in the vocabulary of Sylheti, a language in which, rather than saying thank you, one balanced the whole sentence on terms of deference to age or class. This had the effect, I had noticed, that those who were senior in age or higher in class weren't required by the language to indicate deference and were therefore saved from stooping for the tools to express gratitude.

My mother had always winced when I said please and thank you. Thank you, I'd say when she gave me a second helping of rice and curry. Or thank you when she handed me a lightbulb as I stood on a chair to change the ceiling light. Thank you was an English phrase that ruptured my spoken Sylheti. My mother would grimace and insist that I stop saying it. Because we never had that kind of relationship, I could never ask her why. I have thought that she couldn't bear to hear me say thank you because it signified how far away I'd moved from the culture and values she had inherited, even then. But over the years that have passed since boyhood, I have come to regard such explanations, where mere cultural difference is invoked at every turn, as facile and unilluminating. I now consider her distaste as having had a quality of depth I had not attributed to it before. I think the woman who had raised me, who had provided a family for me, however flawed that family was, was offended that I had turned the web of duties, which bound a family together, into the mere exchange of favors, thank you and please standing for reciprocation. In her mind, I believe, a network of duty and service, tightened under centuries of evolution, had been reduced by my thank you to the trading culture of the West. It was duty and obligation, not measured gains, that reinforced the bonds within the extended family to make something stronger than there would have been otherwise, strong enough and large enough to endure hardships. My understanding came much later, though.

But in the summer before college, when I heard Bill and Dave say please and thank you, occasioned at every turn and gesture, I was charmed.

Above all, I liked Bill and Dave because of the banter between them. The two of them talked incessantly about the work in a language that was new to me. A carpenter's world is steeped in a vocabulary of its own, and Bill and Dave were masters of that vocabulary. It was never just a hammer but a cross pein pin hammer, never just a plane but a rebate plane, never a mere clamp but a three-way edging clamp or a G or an F clamp. Each tool had a specific function, and Bill and Dave would never make do with one tool where another was better suited to the job. I fetched the tools as need arose, and very quickly I came to know each tool's name and function.

This isn't just a cross-head, or even a Phillips cross-head to be specific, explained Bill as he showed me a drill bit for screws. This, he said, is a Pozidriv bit. Look closely and you'll see that the Pozidriv bit has four additional points of contact with the screw.

I nodded.

It doesn't have the rounded corners that the Phillips cross-head bit has, he continued. Its chief advantage over the cross-head is that, provided the screw and the bit are in good condition, the bit won't cam out, which means you can apply greater torque. By the way, you may think knowing the names of tools and hardware is about identifying them, but if that's all you think then you'd be wrong. You see, calling things by their proper names is the beginning of wisdom. That's a Chinese proverb and they invented writing. The wisdom, in case you're wondering, is that when you get names right, you narrow the gap between you and the thing. The most important tool is your hand and you'd be in serious trouble if there were a gap between you and your hand. So names are important. Unless you're talking about roses, that is. But only roses.

I learned much simply by keeping one ear on the two men discussing the work as they went along, while I went about my own tasks. In fact, I think overhearing is quite possibly the only honest way to make the acquaintance of anyone. We may never know who someone is, but at least we have some sense of how he behaves with us, through our engagements with him. Eavesdropping is undoubtedly useful, where some or other information is sought, but the accidental eavesdrop, such as might be afforded on coming down the stairs in the morning in the home of a

friend one is visiting—this kind of domestic eavesdrop can be illuminating in another way. Standing there in midstep, one knee cocked, one
hand on the banister, while overhearing one's friend talking to his wife,
one gains an impression of something rare: how the friend relates to another in the world, in one's absence. That self is never apparent in any
direct conversation, for one cannot have a conversation without influenc-
ing the stance of one's interlocutor. In conversation, I only see the man as
he presents himself to me, as he responds within the present and history
that there is between him and me. We are not each one person but number at least as many as those whom we know. What one hears upon eavesdropping might shock or titillate, since it is always illicit, always a stolen
property, always guaranteed the character of the forbidden. Yet against
the light of day, what one has heard may emerge as little more than the
revelation of one's own self, the reality that discloses itself only when
regard for oneself and for how one is perceived is removed from the act of
listening or watching. How else to account for that disturbing sensation
of witnessing the independent existence of another human being whom
one knows only in direct engagement? And how else to make sense of
the disquiet than to confront the self-centeredness it exposes? If there is
indeed honesty in that moment of eavesdropping, doesn't it spring from
one's absence, which frees one to listen without the din of one's own ego?

On day three, as I came up the stairs with a tray bearing three mugs
of tea and a plate of custard creams, I heard Bill talking to Dave.

Paki-man is fitting in well. Gets stuck in, he said.

Nice boy, said Dave.

Speak of the devil, here's our Paki-man, said Bill, seeing me standing
in the doorway.

Now let's have that tea.

They downed their tools.

Dave made eye contact with me.

Bill, I don't think our new friend likes being called Paki-man.

No? Why's that, then? asked Bill, as he dunked a custard cream in
his tea.

I wasn't sure if he was asking Dave or me.

I suppose, said Dave, some people might construe it as derogatory,
offensive, even.

This was in 1987, before Salman Rushdie's novel *The Satanic Verses* was published, before people took to the streets to burn a book many had never read. My own father would say he refused to read a book that corrupted people with its filthy blasphemy.

So does that mean, responded Bill, that I should not use a word because someone might take offense?

Bill, said Dave, unless you were born yesterday, you must know "Paki" is rather a charged word. You don't need a PhD in sociology to know that, do you?

Do you know about the Redskins? asked Bill.

I don't suppose you mean the American football team?

Correct. I don't mean the American football team, which, by the way, could be called an American American football team. I mean the Redskins band, I mean the Redskins movement, I mean left-wing skinheads.* A skinhead today is linked with far-right extremism—at least in the public imagination. See a skinhead on the street, and if you're black—or brown like our friend here—you'd be shit scared, you'd feel threatened, maybe even insulted without a word being traded.

I see where you're going with this, said Dave.

Exactly. The Redskins couldn't be further from neo-Nazis politically, but by adopting the same appearance and dress as right-wing thugs, they undermine what skinhead means.

And, said Dave, completing Bill's line of argument, if more people become aware of this, then a skinhead walking down the street is less likely to cause others to feel threatened.

Exactly.

So a word can mean exactly what you want it to mean, said Dave.

Exactly, Alice.

But, I interjected, you've just shown the opposite, haven't you?

How's that? asked Bill.

Well, the real skinheads, the original ones, wanted it to mean one thing, but if the band is effective in redefining the meaning of *skinhead*, then the original skinheads can't have it their way. They can't have *skinhead* mean what they want it to mean.

---

*The Redskins were a 1980s skinhead band, whose members espoused left-wing anti-racist values.

The two men exchanged looks, as if each sought confirmation from the other.

So maybe words, I continued, can't mean exactly what you want them to mean. Not for long, anyway.

I suppose that's right, said Dave.

Are you offended? asked Bill.

I'm troubled—I *was* troubled. I wasn't sure where you were coming from, but I think that just watching where you were going with it has made me less troubled. Not troubled at all, in fact.

Not offended? asked Dave.

I didn't like what I was hearing, not at first, but now I don't mind at all, I said.

In fact, I couldn't help smiling. Perhaps I was too young, with too limited an experience of the world to fully grasp how unusual the scene before me was, but it had an inherent comedy about it, the very different registers between their work and their banter. The conversation between the two men carried on and I pitched in once or twice. It ranged from the question of banning the use of certain words and the degree to which one ought to consider other people's feelings, to questions of free speech and the cost of limiting one's vocabulary.

When the custard creams were finished, I gathered the mugs onto a tray.

Then, abruptly, Bill turned to me: Hang on a moment! How exactly should I pronounce your name?

Zafar, I said.

Zafar, where are you from?

Willesden, I said.

Of course you are, said Bill, smiling at me. As English as Admiral Lord bloody Nelson himself, the Duke of Bronté of the Kingdom of Sicily. But where were you born?

Bangladesh.

The two men looked at each other.

Bill, he's not a Paki, then, after all.

Indeed he is not, replied Bill. Zafar, our apologies are in order. A Paki comes from Pakistan. You, my boy, are from Bangladesh, and as anyone who watched George Harrison's 1971 Concert for Bangladesh will tell you, Bangladesh—or should I say East Pakistan, as it was then?—Bangladesh didn't fight a bloody war with Pakistan just to have the likes of us calling its good people Pakis. You, in short, are not a Paki-man.

I was shaking my head with disbelief. It was presumptuous of me, but I wondered how two carpenters from Essex could know the story of a small country on the other side of the planet, a place dismissed by Henry Kissinger as an "international basket case." They could not have known of the four happy years that I carried in me. I felt connected to these two men from the edge of London and to the world they inhabited because they knew about Bangladesh, knew even about its liberation war. Bill hadn't described it as a "civil war"; it was never an internal war. Whether it was deliberate or not, I could have hugged him for that tiny accuracy.

As I started toward the doorway, tray of empty mugs in hand, Bill called out.

I've got it!

He glanced at Dave and then looked at me again.

Anglo-Banglo, he said. That's what you are.

For five days, I listened to these two men working away, and in good spirits I did all the grunt work. I watched and learned.

Then luck came my way when Dave called in sick with flu. Summer flu, a right fuck, said Bill.

Mitered joints are all about trigonometry, especially in rooms whose corners aren't square. Of course Bill and Dave had some clever gadgets and measuring devices to take all the mathematics out of the work and speed things up, tools to get the proportions right, even a device for measuring lengths and angles. The measurement of internal lengths in an alcove with a standard metal tape is notoriously inaccurate because of the curl of the tape at the end; it's just not good enough for the high-end furniture Bill and Dave were making. But Dave was sick and the gauging devices were stored in his van outside London, on the other side of the city, at the other end of Essex from Bill's home.

Bill asked if I could help out by doing some of the cutting, while he tried to get the measurements right. But he was taking a long time, going back and forth, shaving off more and more of whatever piece he was trying to fit perfectly, and I stepped in.

Bill, I can do that for you, I said.

Do what?

Measure everything out. Do all the calculations, even get cracking on the measurements and calculations for the staircase. I can cut the risers and treads; I can work the sliding compound miter saw.

Yeah, mate, I'm sure you can, but we're already one man down and we need to finish up here by the end of next week.

I can do it faster, much faster, than you can.

Bill smiled. I felt I had taken a gamble, though perhaps I had taken no gamble at all and it was my own insecurity to think that I had. I like to think that at that moment, Bill saw a boy on the edge of becoming a man, a boy who was cocky all right but who had also just spent five days doing the most menial work without complaint and without pay, and had therefore earned the right to speak up.

We worked fast. I measured out everything, calculated angles and lengths, and measured out again: The carpenter's rule is measure twice, cut once. At the end of that day, Bill gave me twenty pounds, as he did on all the following days that summer, when the three of us worked on a number of projects mostly in and around Kensington. Twenty pounds seemed like an enormous amount of money to me; my bus fare to Kensington and back left sizable change from a pound.

When I sat there in the drawing room of Penelope Hampton-Wyvern's home, looking at the bespoke bookcase against one wall, I might have appeared composed and still, but my body felt reverberations from the memory of that summer working with the philosopher-carpenters. Of course, none of this would have been known to Penelope when she saw me looking at the bookcase and mistook it for an interest in the books.

I used to think, as I have said, that I introduced Emily to Zafar. In March 1995, I visited New York, where Zafar had already been some time established as a derivatives trader, while I, in my London base, was beginning to come into a sense of competence in my work. I invited Zafar to accompany me to the opening of an art exhibition at the South Asia Society of North America, which in those days was located in a rather eminent building on Vanderbilt, close to Park Avenue. My grandfather had been a patron of the society in the seventies, coming to its rescue when its hobbling finances threatened closure. It is, I assume, because of this that members of my extended family have always received invitations to receptions and openings. While this particular event was promoted as an exhibition of Afghan rugs, most of the rugs on display were made, as I recall having read in the catalog, by craftsmen from Uzbekistan and not Afghanistan. Such conflations reflected a lack of discrimination that changed altogether after September 11, 2001. Zafar has since explained to me that soon after the American intervention in Afghanistan, rug prices shot up as hordes of aid and development workers began cleaning up the rugs, so to speak, to send back to their homes in London, New York, and D.C., and to decorate their new houses in Kabul; property prices also rocketed. In fact, the new do-gooders contributed to massive inflation, distorting the local economy, said Zafar, so that engineers and doctors gave up their vital professions for quick money as drivers shuttling the officials of the UN and aid agencies from one meeting to the next. But I suppose, Zafar had added, there is a silver lining: The West now knows rather more about these rugs.

The opening of the exhibition was to be combined with a reception for the sponsor, an Afghanistan-born businessman of my grandfather's acquaintance. The man lived, or rather had set up domiciles, in Geneva and New York, and had apparently taken to calling himself an exile, despite having left Afghanistan long before the Soviet invasion, and even while, as more recent word had it, he'd cultivated a number of horticultural concerns in Afghanistan with the tacit permission of its Soviet-backed government.

I was of two minds about attending, not only because I would be jet-lagged by midevening, after flying into New York forty-eight hours before, but also because I wasn't particularly keen to meet the Afghan businessman, not for some lofty ethical reason but because inevitably I would be pumped for information about the extended family. Through my parents, I was sufficiently up to speed with its news to give a passable account, but I rather feared the Afghan might follow me about for the evening, hungry for news about my grandfather's businesses, even if I told him, as I had in the past, that I knew nothing.

For all my misgivings, I went to the reception, carried there by a sense of obligation to my grandfather, who had sent word, which I received that morning, that if any member of the family happened to be in New York at the time, he would appreciate a show of face at the reception. I owe the man a good deal but I also love him.

When Zafar and I arrived at the exhibition hall, it was dusk and the reception was already under way. I needed to go to the restroom and left Zafar to fend for himself. Some of the eccentricities that attach to the reputation of mathematicians did indeed attach to him, but those eccentricities never seemed to cripple him socially. They were actually apparent mainly in private one-on-one conversations when, for instance, in the course of discussing something he might suddenly stop in midsentence, disappear into himself for a few moments, before returning to pick up whatever it was he was saying. Sometimes, he simply walked off. He might, for instance, be so absorbed in something he was reading that, as I recall once, when coming to the college library to fetch him for lunch, I had to shake him quite violently before he stirred. In fact, I'd had to do so just that evening, before the reception, when I collected him from his trading desk, prizing him from an array of computer screens.

Still, I knew he was quite unafraid to approach people and make his own introductions. I have seen him stride up to people and say: Hello, my name is Zafar. What's yours? He would tilt his head and smile, and that was enough to strike up a conversation. But I returned to find Zafar standing alone with a glass of champagne in hand, looking at a map of South Asia.

A few paces from him stood a woman facing the adjoining exhibit. She looked vaguely familiar. Her face was powdery white and her eyelashes suggested mascara; she wore a black dress cut just above the knee, and her wavy hair was bunched up high at the back of her head. The breast of her jacket promised a curve, though later I would grasp the falsity of that soft curve when it gave up a padded bra. At the South Asia Society, standing by a hanging rug that evening, this figure maintained itself in a stillness that seemed to continue forever. She looked beautiful to me, and I was struck by a feeling of physical weakness, as I have always been on those occasions when feminine beauty aroused me.

I recognized the woman. Emily! I exclaimed, as I drew near. She smiled to see me and she then looked lovelier than I ever remembered her, lovelier than James's skinny older sister, lovelier than the reserved eighteen-year-old Oxford undergraduate I'd known, with little to say for herself; she had blossomed. Of course, I know that Zafar says he didn't find her quite so beautiful, but I don't buy it. I just don't.

I made introductions, and if there had been at that moment any indication of recognition on Zafar's part, or, for that matter, any sign of mutual attraction, then I failed to notice it. Perhaps I was distracted in my own way.

We exchanged information, where we were, what we were doing. I explained that I'd just joined the firm where Zafar was already a trader in the New York office. I was in New York for induction before going back to London. I explained to Zafar my connection with Emily through her brother and also through a mutual family friend. As I think of it now, I remember that Zafar said only a few words throughout this. Emily explained—but only after I'd pressed her on her connection with the event—that she'd come to the reception as a guest of Aisha Marwan, our mutual friend, the Pakistani socialite who was apparently in New York for a wedding. Aisha hadn't arrived yet (and would never show).

It was hard going getting anything out of Emily. Zafar has described her personality as secretive, and I now wonder if by this he meant something more than that she withheld information, if perhaps he was identifying some underlying character trait that caused her to withhold her *presence* before people. Even if I had not seen her in two or three years, I knew the reputation she had acquired, which was of a hugely ambitious person, dedicated to advancement. But it seems to me likely that such deprecatory remarks as have circulated from time to time might owe more than a little to the envy of other women. Nevertheless, the evident ambition suggests one line of analysis, which is that Emily saw her relationships and exchanges with people purely through the prism of function, so that unstructured social banter was foreign to her mental makeup.

Emily explained—not without some coaxing—that after Oxford she'd spent two years at Harvard studying public policy, which she was just finishing, and was thinking about going back to England to train as a lawyer, although at some point she wanted to work in international development.

After hearing out her answers, Zafar leaned forward.

You don't seem sure about it? he asked her.

What was the *it*? I thought.

I'm trying to decide.

The three of us hung loosely together, drifting back and forth. I introduced my friends to Hamid Karzai, now president of Afghanistan but at that time a rather shady figure involved in the oil business. We chatted pleasantries, Karzai expressing an embarrassingly effusive friendliness toward me, and he asked me to pass on his good wishes to my grandfathers, "both of them," he said with baffling emphasis.

Inevitably, I reluctantly encountered the Afghan businessman, but when he quite obviously took a shine to Emily I found my moment to slip away. Zafar had already wandered off.

I toured the exhibits, taking in the rugs and other items. From time to time, I looked over at Emily, who now had a little gathering around her, which included Karzai as well as a small, wiry figure whom I did not recognize but who seemed to be holding forth to the circle around him. This man, I would learn much later, was Mohammed Jalaluddin.

When I saw Zafar, I stopped to regard him and could not resist a grin; he was going from one vinyl wall panel to the next, reading the explanatory text without stopping to look at the rugs.

I think I was still grinning when I looked over at Emily—perhaps I had in mind to share the observation with a nod—but as I watched her, I saw that she was stealing glances at Zafar.

The following day, when Zafar thanked me for taking him along to the reception, I brought up a rather odd moment that I had wanted to ask him about. At a certain point in the evening, I had been standing with Karzai, Zafar, Emily, and the wiry fellow, along with two or three other men who said nothing and grinned inanely from time to time, after the fashion of hangers-on. Karzai praised my grandfather before the assembled group for some or other business decision. I thanked him for his kind words and was about to ease away when Karzai shot a forefinger into the air.

You must have my tickets. You're a cultured man, he said to me. I have two tickets for the New York City Ballet. You must have them.

Before I could respond, he had plucked them from his breast pocket and pushed them into my hands. Two seats. I hated ballet.

I'm sorry, I said, but I'm afraid I'm already fixed for that evening.

Then you must pass them on.

I handed them to Zafar.

I couldn't possibly accept. These are excellent seats, said Zafar, looking at the tickets.

But you must, said Karzai, smiling not at Zafar but at me. It is my gift.

I wished Zafar would just thank him so we could all move on.

All right, said Zafar, coming to my rescue. However, addressing Hamid Karzai, he added: But you have to tell me what your favorite charity is.

Hamid Karzai looked a little confused.

What is your favorite charity, Mr. Karzai?

I can't have been the only one wondering if Karzai might not have a favorite charity. Emily and I exchanged looks.

UNICEF, he said finally.

Excellent, said Zafar, pulling out his checkbook.

Zafar tapped my shoulder, I turned, and against my back he wrote out a check.

They're expensive tickets, Mr. Karzai, said Zafar, but then UNICEF is such a deserving cause, he added.

As he tore off the check, I saw that it was made out in the amount of three hundred dollars.

Would you like to send this to UNICEF, or shall I?

Why don't *you*? replied Karzai, whose smile was visibly forced.

As I say, the following day I asked Zafar why he'd written a check to UNICEF.

The man said it was his favorite charity, replied Zafar.

You know what I mean.

A man like Karzai doesn't give gifts, he exchanges favors.

You think ballet tickets put you in debt to him?

No, but it makes it just that much easier to call *you* and inquire how I enjoyed the ballet before asking you a favor. They trade on the stuff; this is how these people work.

Afghans?

Elites. Why should you, of all people, need tickets for the ballet?

Your grandfather could buy the whole First Ring faster than a Russian could say Mikhail Baryshnikov.

Maybe he was just being friendly, I said.

You don't believe that.

Zafar, I thought, was overanalyzing.

What in the world could he want from you? I asked.

I was introduced to him as *your* friend.

Which means I might have owed him something, not you.

Zafar had paid off Karzai, made a show of giving UNICEF, Karzai's favorite charity, an amount equal to the face value of the tickets, in order that I wouldn't be beholden to the man.

Wait a minute, I said. Does that mean I owe *you* a debt?

I suppose it does, replied Zafar. I might even call on it one day, he added with a grin.

I laughed.

What are you going to do with the tickets?

I've never been to a ballet.

You've got two tickets.

I considered the possibility, even without any good basis, that he might invite Emily. But Zafar said nothing.

I'm surprised Emily's going to become a lawyer, I said. I never pegged her for that.

But she didn't say she was becoming a lawyer.

She did. She said she's going to law school.

She said she's going to train as a lawyer.

Why go to law school if not to become a lawyer?

I don't know. But who says she's going to train as a lawyer? It's a means, not an end. Go to law school or go into the law, but *train as a lawyer*?

I hear she was very ambitious at school. She worked her tits off.

Was she in our year?

Year below, I replied.

What did she read?

English, I think.

Then the numbers don't add up. She said she's just finishing two years at Harvard.

Zafar always spotted things like this. I paused to do the arithmetic.

English was a three-year degree, and she was a year behind us. My friend was right. And, in fact, I later learned that after Oxford she spent a year studying art history in Florence and another year working for Sotheby's in London, though these facts are of no consequence.

I see what you mean. Two years are missing, I said.

Exactly. Do you think she's calculating? he asked.

You're the one doing the calculating.

No, I mean *calculating*.

Maybe she's indecisive. Some people just have to keep their options open. They don't know what they want—they can't help it.

Maybe both, he said.

That, then, was how I thought he met her: with my introduction. The truth of it was rather different and it leaves me uncomfortable. In another of our conversations, which took place in the week after he gave his account of meeting Penelope Hampton-Wyvern for the first time, Zafar told a story about Emily Hampton-Wyvern, something that happened some years before that evening at the South Asia Society, but in his usual way he approached the business apparently from a tangent, setting down another piece of the picture, a lemma. He said that he had always been drawn to people with interesting names, and he explained, quite matter-of-factly, that before he met Emily, he had fallen in love with her name, the whole of her name. But this was not, he went on, the first time he had fallen under such a spell.

Zafar reminded me that at Oxford he'd had a blazing affair with a Jewish Rhodes Scholar from New York. In those days, before cell phones and email, college porters took down telephone messages for students and pinned them onto a large corkboard in the post room by the lodge, small pieces of yellow paper, folded once, with the names of the recipients on the outsides. Porters came in every few minutes during the day to pin messages to the board, while students milled about checking for messages and mail. At night there were fewer calls, these from overseas, but the porters still came and posted the messages as they arrived. The college had a large number of international students.

In the freshers' week of his first year, explained Zafar, he was mesmerized by the post room. I once saw a notice, he said, admonishing students for scaling the scaffolding that had been erected in the front quad for renovation work taking place there. *Anyone caught climbing on the scaffolding will be hung thereon*, it read. I remember thinking that objects were *hung*, while people were *hanged*. The next day, someone had drawn a line through the warning, leaving the original text still legible, and had inserted underneath, *Anyone caught hung like scaffolding will be climbed upon*. Then the day after that, the notice, with its witty edit, had been moved to the locked glass-fronted case beside the main gate, ordinarily reserved for announcements for all the world to see of scholarships, academic honors, and more orthodox signals of the college's pool of talent.

The post room was the conduit for the whole of the outside world. Students came in with expectant faces or braced for disappointment. This is where messages were left, messages sent from far and wide, at all hours of the day. All this was long before Oxford received the newfangled Internet.

I would sneak in late at night, said Zafar, in order to read the messages pinned to the board. Not meant for me, but they were my view of other worlds. I would take down those messages and discover in them snapshots of other lives, how life might be elsewhere for others, through a simple message of love, perhaps, from a parent or an aunt. I would learn something of the people I saw walking across the garden quad in jeans and tattered T-shirts, clothes that said everything of the carefree optimism attached to lives unimpeded by need, for what could trouble someone, I thought then, who had family, parents who left messages saying only that they missed their son or daughter? These notes bore single lines from which my mind could draw backward a whole story. The message board was not inert to me, not cork and pin and pieces of yellow paper, but a thronging clamor of sound, some of it mere information, numbers and dates, but much of it the private communication of love.

When I returned a note to the board, I would take care to fold the yellow piece of paper along the existing crease and put the pin through the same hole in the paper. I was careful, listening for the sound of footsteps in the porter's lodge, on the other side of the internal door, or for the shuffle of feet on the gravel outside. But it was not enough to be careful.

One night, I took down a message for a student called Peter Brooke. The message read simply: *Am arranging Easter holiday in Bermuda. Will you join us? Let us know.* It came from someone who had evidently given his name as Lord Brooke and, even as I heard someone approaching from within the porter's lodge, I could not wrest myself from revulsion and envy: Why on earth did this person feel it necessary to establish his nobility with a porter?

It is remarkable that station is so important to such people. By then I knew, of course, of the complicity of the working classes. I had understood that rank was important to everyone, even the lowest on the social ladder. I remember Steven, the old man—he must have been in his late fifties by then, if not older—Steven the scout, who cleaned the rooms for students who evidently could not be asked to do it themselves, Steven who could never have been Stephen with a *ph*—how wrong does St. Steven look?—Steven who served lunch and dinner in Hall, too, and called every undergraduate boy *sir*. When I once asked him to call me Zafar, *Yes, sir*, came the reply.*

I was holding the note for Peter Brooke in my hand when I heard the door handle turn. I fumbled and dropped the pin. The door opened.

The porter looked at me, looked at my hands, and saw that I was holding a yellow note. The note could have been for me, I thought in my defense. But there were never any messages for me and he must have known that, in that small college of fewer than two hundred undergraduates. He pinned another note to the board and left the room, without making eye contact again.

The following day I received my first message on the notice board. It was a summons to the dean's rooms.

The dean explained that privacy was invaluable in keeping a community together. It was apparent, he said, that I had been reading a message meant for someone else: The porters had not taken any messages for me yesterday. I was rather touched, in fact, that he said "yesterday"; whichever porter had reported me would have told him, I'm sure, that I never received messages in order to establish why he, that porter, was so cer-

---

*Zafar's recollection of this incident differs from mine slightly, but in a key respect. I was present at the time, at the counter in the dining hall, standing two or three persons away from him. Zafar asked for a main course and Steven replied, Yes, sir. But contrary to his account, at that point Zafar didn't just ask Steven to call him "Zafar." He said: Steven, when you say "sir," I look for my father. Please call me Zafar.

I cannot imagine that Zafar ever addressed his father as "sir." I doubt he ever addressed him in English.

tain that the message he'd seen me holding could not have been meant for me.

I told the dean what I was doing and why. He did not seem surprised, still less angry, and I felt, as I have often felt in certain English circles, that the parties to the exchange were acting out roles, merely going through motions, while the real content was somewhere else, perhaps hovering in the air between.

As pleasant as it is to see you, he said, I'd prefer not to have you called to my rooms again. Do you understand?

I nodded and left, though I was not quite sure what he meant. Perhaps it was naïveté on my part—perhaps even a willful naïveté, to which I was blind—but I sincerely believed that while he was not endorsing what I had done, he knew, in the wisdom gained from years as dean, that simply forbidding me was not going to be enough, that if privacy could not be guaranteed, the next best thing would have to do—I must not be caught again. Then, as now, I believe that the English use language to hide what they mean.

One day I saw a message, a piece of folded paper pinned to the notice board, for one Rebecca Sonnenschein. The pin had been perfectly centered in the letter *o*, probably without conscious thought but perhaps guided by the porter's unconscious eye. I noted that none of the letters of the name hung below the imaginary line. There was no *y* or *g* or *p* or other such letter. I never took down that message in order to read it; her name was enough.

That name, Rebecca Sonnenschein, evoked in me a time and place of intense romance, of intellectual illumination. Sonnenschein spoke to my mind of learning and culture, of *Jewish* learning and culture, which consisted for me then, as it does today, of the higher sensibilities and the rejection of the baser trends found elsewhere in the European psyche. To me, Sonnenschein contained the distillation of all that was good and true of Europe, emerging in my mind from romantic shadows falling across ill-lit cobbled streets between rows of elegant houses with high ceilings and tall shutters, the sound of a piano and violin performing a duet over the cold air. For two days, I sat in the junior common room and I waited for a woman with a Jewish look, a stereotype, and the sound of an American accent—Rebecca Sonnenschein just had to be American.

There she was, ordering a jacket potato in the pantry. A week later she would take me out to lunch at Brown's. When I explained to her that my budget didn't extend to eating out of college, she said she would treat me. I was very poor in college. I didn't feel it as poverty. Supper in college was subsidized and, besides, there was always a particularly cheap Danish salami at the Co-Op supermarket, slices of fat with flecks of pink meat, hummus, and bread rolls. All this kept me clear of poverty, but when I reflect on what I didn't have and on what others must have had then—on what Emily had had—I see that my experience of college had been limited by a relative poverty. No college-organized reading weekends with other students in the hills outside Florence or in the Scottish Highlands. No holidays abroad, no skiing, no expensive restaurants—all restaurants were expensive.

At lunch, Rebecca recommended the chicken Caesar salad, at twelve pounds and ninety-five pence, I observed, enough Danish salami for two weeks. Rebecca Sonnenschein introduced me to many things: She made me unafraid of fierce debate; she made me feel that in my encounter with the world, it was within me to set many of the terms, if not all; she introduced me to sex, to mad, wild sex; she taught me that a gym can be fun and she put me onto salads; and through her I saw that some people have no use for the political borders of countries. But above all the things she did for me—and I'm quite serious—Rebecca Sonnenschein showed me that difficult questions can have simple answers. I once asked her why she loved me. It is an insecure question, even, I think, when we tell ourselves it is born of mere curiosity. We were sitting in my room, both reading, she on the bed and I in an armchair. What, I was ultimately asking myself, was this beautiful American Rhodes Scholar, a graduate student, doing with this homeless Bangladeshi?

She looked up from her book.

It's your money and your passport, sweetheart, she replied, flashing me a smile with her bright American teeth before returning to her book.

I listened to Zafar's narrative with a mix of feelings. Our conversation had taken us away from where he'd begun, his first meeting with Emily's family (although I was certain he'd return to this story). I had gained the impression of hearing one digression upon another. But despite the lack of design, which such an apparently haphazard account might suggest, I sensed that there was some underlying theme or movement. I came to see that his stories ran together, like the rivers of his boyhood coming from the mountains and forests and the plains, a long way from their sources but ultimately joined together in one song, a harmony of place and time.

I have never had much difficulty with feeling at home. The nearest I have ever come to an identity crisis was on reaching border controls at the airport, before a flight, to discover that I'd forgotten my passport. I have wondered why I had not spotted it before, why I had never grasped that the question of belonging governed the interior life of my friend. Certainly he never discussed it, but had he also restrained every sign? That is the context in which I see him standing in the post room, reading the messages on the board. The matter of where one belongs is something I had understood to be significant in the lives of others, but they were strangers, people I had read about. And yet here it was in someone not only familiar but who was to me, all those years ago, someone whom I had always thought of as my equal, even my better.

I don't think I can fault myself for not having seen where his searching might lead to, the fraying and unstitching of a human being—all that was too far away then, in our younger days. Perhaps I couldn't understand because in our youth we are condemned to see in others no one but ourselves.

It was of course mathematics that framed our first meeting as students. Both of us loved it—or *her*; Zafar used to say, "I've been with the mistress"—though for me there was never quite the same passion that there was for him. I remember once coming to him with a problem whose solution had eluded me. He did not instantly offer an answer but looked out the window and seemed to have turned far away. While my friend seemed to me to be struggling, I hit upon an idea that might have been, I thought, the beginnings of a proof.

I think I have the answer, I said.

Yes, he said. I have three solutions but I'm trying to work out which is the most illuminating.

For Zafar, mathematics was always about the journey and not the destination, the proof of the theorem, not merely its statement. After all, what does it mean to say that something is true if you can't show it to be so? I think that in the journey, Zafar found a home in mathematics, a sense of belonging, at least for a while; it is a world without borders, without time, in which everything exists everywhere forever, and I see now what power such a thing might have over the psyche of someone so rootless.

Meanwhile, an unsettling prospect was forming in my mind. I understood him to say that Emily Hampton-Wyvern's name might in a superficial way have drawn him to her, as did Rebecca Sonnenschein's, but his account offered no connection with Emily or, indeed, her name. Rebecca Sonnenschein's, yes, but how, I asked him, did Emily come into the picture?

One of the notes that I took down from the message board, replied Zafar, was addressed to you. Inside it was a message from Emily Hampton-Wyvern.

7

The Violin or Leipzig

I saw the hill and the vineyards and the watercourses and I realized
that this music wasn't the same as the stuff the band played, it
spoke of other things, it wasn't meant for Gaminella, nor the trees
beside the Belbo nor for us. But in the distance toward Canelli you
could see Il Nido against the outline of Salto, the fine red house, set
among the yellowing plane trees. And the music Irene played went
with the fine house, with the gentry at Canelli, it was meant for them.
—Cesare Pavese, *The Moon and the Bonfires*,
translated by Louise Sinclair

The first time ever I saw Emily, said Zafar, not just the name but Emily
herself, was an evening years before the encounter at the South Asia Society in New York, before my stint as a banker, and before, still, my time
at Harvard, which is to say, before I had been screened, vetted, sanitized
by associations, and made presentable. It was in November 1988, during
my second year at Oxford, at the University Church of St. Mary the
Virgin.

In those days, when I had no money for concert tickets, even for
concerts given by university ensembles, I would search the notice boards
for performances, and on the day before the first night, I'd go along to
the venue to see the final rehearsal, which in the normal course was an
uninterrupted run-through of the program and was usually scheduled
in the evening, presumably in order to avoid clashes with lectures and
tutorials.

On the evening I first saw Emily, I had made my way from college,
down Turl Street and onto the High, in fog-soaked November darkness,
and came up to the gate of the church, half expecting the doors to be
closed to the public. There were not many venues in Oxford for classical
music. Somewhat grander performances were held in the Sheldonian,

but otherwise Queen's College chapel, the Holywell Music Room, and the University Church were the main settings. I rather liked the Holywell Music Room, which I had read somewhere was the oldest purpose-built music hall in the world. It had struck me that the claim was the height of presumption—might there not be a music hall in the Middle East, in India, or somewhere else that was older?—until I was forced to concede my own presumption to think that the author of the claim had meant to say Europe and not the world. Most human disputes, one might speculate, ask us to choose not between arguments proceeding from empirical observations about the world but between competing sets of bare assumptions.

I knocked on the front gate of the University Church. If the vicar answered, he would let me in—he knew my face—but to anyone else I'd explain that I left my scarf on one of the pews somewhere. Once inside, I would go off to the side and the musicians would begin their business, quickly forgetting me.

I waited for an answer and then tried the door. It was unlocked. I found a seat not far from the stage, in the shadow of a stone column but with a clear view of the chancel, where the musicians would play.

If the musicians didn't arrive immediately, I thought, I could sit and consider again the figure whose body adorns the cross, this fellow who had fascinated me ever since the first encounter in the morning assembly of an Anglican primary school in central London, so that now, more than a decade later, I often came to this church, a short walk from college, to look at him, sometimes even to attend services. The vicar, a terribly nice man whose sermons were sprinkled with the phrase *in a very real sense*—as if there was any other sense—probably thought I was a lost sheep taking timid steps to return to the flock. Perhaps I underestimated his wisdom. But in those days, when I sat and looked at the crucifix, it was not love that burned in my heart but growing rage. What is the beginning of rage, the beginning of anger? Not dislike, but love. It is possible that rage was always there and that his lordship, Jesus Christ, was only the focus of my rage. That would be in keeping with the fellow's self-sacrificing character; he might have offered himself for anger, not love, for all the rage that came his way. Have you read Graham Greene's *The End of the Affair*?

No, but I've seen the movie.

Throughout the novel, the narrator, Greene's alter ego, Maurice Bendrix, is angry with God, even when he doesn't believe in him. His anger magnifies when it transpires that he's lost the woman he loved. There is a passage—near the beginning, I think—in which he says that love and hatred come from the same gland, that they can even produce the same actions. Well, that's a novel, a story, but it's worth a thought that anger is no less God-given than love. That's the appeal of Catholicism. They have a calculating honesty, the Catholics, marshaling the base resources, far from denying them; the Anglicans with their carrot cakes, their village fetes, raffles for the new church roof, and teas with the vicar—they have no respect for anger.

You're not a Christian, are you? I asked Zafar.

Do you mean: Have I been received into the Church of Rome?

Well?

I used to think, said Zafar, that Islam wasn't there for me when I needed God.

Zafar's answer was less than direct. Meena had remarked on this indirectness the day of his return into our lives. An air about him left one with the sense not to pry, an understanding that he would share only what he volunteered. It was the odd politeness-cum-formality that carried this off, which in our youth I mistook, I think, merely for an aspect of the charm he had and not as a device to keep the distance. Was it not the formality of those Oxford lawns, and the intimation of design, that warned you to keep off the grass?

But there was another dimension now, something different, edgier. I had witnessed episodes of aggression before, the skinheads on the walk near Portobello Road, for instance, but they were contextual, weren't they? What was new was the presence of something I won't try to capture in a single phrase—it was not the threat of aggression. But one sensed it about him even if one might have intuited it in the way of an unknowing creature.

The ritual, continued Zafar, the recitation of the Koran, the ignorance of the meaning of words, the choreography of standing, kneeling, and falling prostrate, its unthinkingness, all offended my mind, which demanded reasons and explanations. The only book my parents ever gave me was on Eid when I was sixteen. My mother must have picked it up in one of those shops in the East End, where they sell tapes of Koranic recitation, books about Islam, and varieties of calendars with images of the Kaaba, and where the doors to the shops are always left open so that, as you come up the street, you cannot avoid the electrically distorted caterwaul of a Pakistani mullah. The book was written in English and it was about how Islam predicted science. In fact, I think it was actually called *How Islam Predicted Science*. It was full of the most idiotic assertions.

But the gift did show that my parents had in one respect understood something, that I needed words. Do you know the story of Muhammad and Mount Jabal al-Nur?

No.

About the cave called Hira?

I know that. Broadly speaking.

Muhammad was a good man who would retreat to this cave to pray and meditate. And it was during one of these periods of isolation that he was visited by the archangel Gabriel, who commanded him to read from a document. *Read!* exhorted the angel. Muhammad was illiterate and, trembling before this supernatural apparition, he replied, *I do not know how to read.* Once again, the archangel commanded him *Read!* and again, Muhammad answered that he could not read. And the archangel, raising his voice, commanded: *Read in the name of your Lord who created, Created man from a clot of blood. Read!*

And Muhammad began to read. The first miracle of Islam was that an illiterate man came to read, so it would be wrong of me to say that Islam did not value the written word. But my God would be a God I could read, one to consider and in a language I understood. Wasn't meaning, I thought, thought once, the whole point of the divine? I believed that Islam's response to the pursuit of meaning was not to provide answers but to drill and drum men into forsaking meaning for ritual and habit. I believed such things when I thought that meaning counted for more than the rewards of ritual.

When people say that religion is only a crutch, I have to wonder what the *only* means, for I can't imagine anyone would dispute that a crutch allows us to carry on the business of living, half hobbling but better than without it, while taking the weight off the wound to aid the process of healing. I know that it is invoked only as a metaphor, but it seems to me that metaphors are never *only* anything.

When I eventually turned to religion, after the long draw, when I sought out a god, I did so because I needed practical help right away. Religion was never far from me, but it was the defects and deficiencies of my relationship with Emily that finally sent me reaching for the love of God. I found in him, because I wanted to find it in him, what I could not find in Emily, what I had not found in England, in my home there, but what I had known once as a child in my village in Sylhet. Love that is earned or deserved is always suspect; the great observation on which Christianity is founded is that the greatest love cannot be earned or deserved. That is not an ethical rule but an empirical observation, a scientifically testable proposition, and on that rock an entire religion has been built, a magnificent cathedral of hope.

But you say it was Emily that drove you to God?

Do you know what a tug-of-war is?

Of course I know what a tug-of-war is! We did it at school, I replied.

Do you have to hesitate every time you say school?

What do you mean?

Don't Etonians refer to school as college? he asked.

They call it school, just like everyone else, I replied.

Just like everyone else?

Come on. You were talking about coming to God, I said, ignoring the jibe.

Something rather puzzled me when I was a boy. On the title page or somewhere in the front matter of a book, they used to tell you a bit about the author. More often than not, included was the fact that the author went to this or that school. Mentioning university, I thought, was fair enough: In those days I had the notion that university was where education began and that school was disastrous. Today, mention of anything about an author seems to me to be an act of vanity or a concession to human curiosity. But to mention what school a child or an adolescent went to seemed very strange indeed. Take *Down and Out in Paris and London*. It says at the front that Eric Arthur Blair went to Eton. The man changed his name for the book cover, but you were told where he went to school.

I was very slow, continued Zafar. I don't think it was until I got to college—to Oxford—that I began to understand that those chaps who mentioned their school weren't talking about education in the sense I understood it, the stuff in books or the stuff you figure out yourself with pencil and paper and a pocketful of axioms. I got wind one day that some people thought I'd been a scholar at Winchester. When someone asked me directly, I remember the look of disappointment on his face when I said I hadn't, that I'd gone to a state school. Why was he disappointed? After all, I'd got to Oxford and he knew I was doing well there.

I did not offer Zafar an answer. Instead, perhaps out of embarrassment, I reminded him that we'd been talking about what turned him to God and before that about Emily.

In a tug-of-war, he said, two teams of men—teams of boys—pull on a rope against each other.

I know.

You know this, but let's fix the image. What you see is the whole assembly, a line of boys and rope, moving in one direction or the other. When you see the handkerchief, the red handkerchief, in the middle of the rope move in one direction, all you know is that the total pull is greater on that side than on the other. But what you can't tell is which of the boys on that side is pulling the hardest. You can't even tell if one or another of the boys is not doing a thing, is unnecessary. You can't tell whether the winning side would still be winning with one fewer boy.

My first instinct is to say Eton, I interjected, but that sounds like I'm calling attention to the school I went to, so I say school instead.

Understood. My point is that a given effect can be overdetermined by causes. A number of things all together sent me looking for religion and I can't parse them out.

But why Christianity and not Islam? Actually, I don't want you to lose your thread—I still want to hear about meeting Emily.

Did you know, asked Zafar, that relationship counselors advise that the time to work hard at a relationship is when the going is good? The time to work on the roof is the summer.

Paying into the bank now to draw down later?

Ah, the banker speaking.

Is that what Meena and I should have done? I asked.

I don't know the answer to that, replied Zafar. But I do know that I didn't make much of an effort to discover Islam. It would have been a huge effort, of course. For one thing, I'd have had to get past all the drivel that's published in those books that line the walls of East End shops selling Islamic materials, the shops adjoining mosques in London and elsewhere. Finding interlocutors who could actually speak in a language I understood, whose written word demonstrated a familiarity with the same questions I had, putting aside the matter of answers—that in itself would have required a great labor. Where were they? All this before 9/11. Nowadays, it's easier. People who know a thing or two about Islam but can also write in English—modern intermediaries—they're everywhere, and their books can be *found*, and the Internet makes it easier to find things out. But before 9/11, what did someone like me do? Which, by the way, raises the possibility that some of the young men and women now returning to Islam in droves might be doing so at least in part because Islam has become more accessible through better books and better speakers and not just, as everyone seems to maintain, because they've been politicized by the war on terror.

If you had your time again, you'd go deeper into Islam for answers?

If I had my time again, I'd believe in reincarnation.

I chuckled at that and so did Zafar. Religion has never preoccupied me, I have to say. My father's faith, as I said, was a private affair, my mother abhorred all religion, though she reserved a special venom for Islam, and while I attended Anglican services at Eton, in the end I grew up like many, I think, without acquiring the taste for religion, organized or otherwise. It is perhaps this business of God that I struggle hardest to measure in Zafar's story and that leaves me contemplating the prospect either that my aptitude for grasping such matters is lacking or, less pessimistically, that such matters as another man's God and perhaps another man's love inherently surpass understanding.

Zafar continued his account, returning to those days at Oxford, though not at first to that evening in the University Church of his first encounter with Emily.

He explained that in the beginning Christianity was convenient. At Oxford, he said, the Christian Union was organized, reliable, and always welcoming. I used to scan the Daily Information sheet on the college notice board for visiting speakers hosted by them, and I'd go along to some or other church or chapel to hear a Christian speaker. Yet for all the lectures I heard, what I took away was the simplicity of the Christian message of love. I was primed for it, of course—I knew that even at the time—for love had been in short order as I grew up and most of it compressed into a few years in a village in Bangladesh from a woman whose connection to me was denied until it was too late to be acknowledged, too late for the fact itself to give pleasure, not to mention the relief that could come from the explanation.

Christians have something, I thought, continued Zafar. Christianity, as I say, grasped a fundamental truth of love, namely, that love cannot be earned or deserved. This idea moved me terribly, this God who loved, a break against the lonely tides and the lurking anxiety of a whole life of homelessness. When I sat in those churches and looked up at Christ on the cross, I wondered, despite myself—however much the hallmark image might repel another instinct in me—I wondered whether somewhere ahead on the journey this man might join me; the thought of a companion in him reassured me, if he was indeed what he might yet be. Yet for all the power of this idea, I already knew how far I could not go. I could never believe I had a life *in* Christ, never think to love others *through* him. Even as I saw the virtue of forgiveness, I knew that to relinquish my passionate, undirected grievances would be to abandon myself. Whatever company he, He,* might offer, there were lines in the sand. Practical matters stood in the way. I could never, for instance, give myself over to the ritual of Holy Communion, of eating the body of Christ and drinking the blood of Christ, not because of some revulsion at the cannibalistic barbarism but because the metaphor was never convincing *even as metaphor.* Most of all, when I touched the oak pews and ran my fingers over the knitted covers of the cushions and kneelers, when I gazed at the stained-glass images of English saints, when I considered the words of the Nicene Creed, it was as apparent to me as the alienation that made me, that kept me at the edges of things, that here was a very local rendering of a religion that had come from a part of the world that the proud Englishman could only look down upon. The Christianity before me was English, white, with Sunday roasts and warm beer and translation into the English language. Even the Bible at its most beautiful, the King James version, was in a language that asserted and reas-

---

*Here I imagine that the second time Zafar used the pronoun, when he gave it emphasis, he was using it with an initial capital letter.

sured its readers of their power. Little wonder that schoolboys at Eton could sing of Jerusalem being builded here in this green and pleasant land. Such high praise: a pleasant land. The English Christ was of here and now, immanence on the village green, with barely a word or symbol in the liturgy and ritual transcending northwestern Europe, still less this world or universe, as partisan as the embedded journalist. He was an English God under an English heaven.

My friend Zafar, his face grave and intent, fell silent at this point, his thoughts carried to some remote region in his cavernous dark eyes. Between the criticisms of religious parochialism, I had the impression of another sentiment, one that isn't quite apparent in his words as I look over them now but that I felt nonetheless at the time. If his exposition had seemed, on its face, to consist of one rejection after another of Christianity, it also left the impression of a man possessed of strong, even violent feelings, which, one might speculate, is a sufficient basis for religious conversion. That is the Pauline story, is it not?

Tell me about that evening, I said to him, about the church and Emily.

There I was, he said, hidden in the shadow of a column, looking over the pews to the altar and beyond that the cross, contemplating this alien people clutching their God, when the door slammed shut and a shaft of ice-cold air struck me. The first musician had arrived. Violin case in hand, she walked through the aisle between the rows of pews.

I still retain a vivid impression of that young woman moving between the aisles, but I have wondered if it's an image I have transposed from subsequent memories, as if history has insisted on pushing outward at the beginning, for the fact is that she did not seem at all remarkable to me then. She was pretty, I thought, even beautiful in a way, but not . . . not arresting. Women change so much in those years between eighteen, when I first saw her at Oxford, and twenty-five, when I saw her next in New York. From this vantage, so many years later, it is possible to absorb that change, to regard it with a scientific eye; at eighteen, women move into the prime of their sexual attractiveness. The heroines depicted in nineteenth-century novels might well have been feisty and strongheaded well into their twenties—things, by the way, which if found in a man would scarcely get a mention—they might even have had a canny awareness of male motivations and even some guile, but they were nothing without the physical bloom of postadolescence that has always been lauded and craved everywhere. At eighteen, Emily possessed this; there was enough beauty for her youth to hold up but not, I think, so much as to endure the passing of it.

She pulled a chair from a low stack at the side of the small stage. Rather than carry it, she dragged it across the floor to center stage. I remember imagining the scuff marks being made on that stage, I remember wondering whether the chair legs had rubber tips, I remember wondering whether she had looked to see if they had rubber tips. And, perhaps, as I recall all this, if I am permitted to read anything into something so small, I might be inclined to think that in that tiny act of omission, of not carrying the chair but dragging it across the floor as she held up her head—so that I can now see she could not have noticed any scuffing or scratching of the floor—perhaps in that act there was contained the whole of her character.

She retrieved a music stand from a cluster in one corner. Her movements seemed to me strangely clumsy, as if I had expected something finer from a violinist. I have seen grace in her, though much later and in other places. I've seen her in the bath, for instance. I saw the grace with which she held a bar of soap in her hands, as if holding a dove, I thought tenderly, rousing it from sleep for release into the air. I can see it now. Or the grace in entering a restaurant and taking a seat, the unthinking ease, the movements so slight they barely mark the memory. But I understood only later that her grace was confined, circumscribed within the pattern of household habits, that it was the grace of a woman tended to by comforts, so that when she was taken out of her sphere of convenience by even one music stand with an unfamiliar mode of opening, its limitation was exposed. So much about those people looked like one thing but was actually another. Emily's grace was not physical grace; she was graceful when she powdered her face but without grace when she opened a car door. Grace, as I have seen it elsewhere often enough, comes from an understanding, which resides in the muscle, of the relationship between the body and the world; it not only recognizes the limitations of the body it inhabits but works with those limitations so that each act shows respect toward the physical world, respect for its dominance, and proceeds from an acknowledgment that the world will not simply do one's bidding. How easy it is now to read so much into each moment and every careless act.

On the stage, chair and music stand now assembled, she sat down, unzipped a flap in the violin case, pulled out some sheet music and placed it before her. The young woman looked about her and, seeing the piano, she walked over to it, violin in hand. She wedged the instrument under her chin and then, as she held the bow, she struck a key. When she tuned the violin braced in her neck, I noticed that her chin was very slight, disappearing no sooner than it had made its presence known.

She tuned efficiently, methodically, and yet her face gave no expression whatsoever, no furrows that might suggest an intensity of listening. Presently, she finished tuning, went back to her seat, turned a few pages and, returning the violin to her neck, she began playing.

Normally the first musician to arrive for rehearsal sets out a number of chairs and stands. That is what I had seen. Of course, this isn't true if the rehearsal is for an orchestral piece, but if the program is for chamber music and the stage isn't set, then the first musician usually gets started on putting out the chairs and the music stands. This young woman hadn't brought out any other chairs and music stands. And now she was playing a solo piece, which had me doubting that I'd got the program right; perhaps she was to be performing a solo recital.

She played and I recognized the piece. Bach's Chaconne. Do you know it?

I do.

One of the finest pieces of music written for the violin. Johannes Brahms wrote about Bach's Chaconne in a letter to Clara Schumann, saying that it captured every emotion possible in a few minutes and that if he, Brahms, had written it, he would surely have gone mad.*

How did you come to know it?

Mathematicians like Bach. You must know that.

---

*"The Chaconne," wrote Brahms, "is the most wonderful, unfathomable piece of music. On one stave, for a small instrument, the man writes a whole world of the deepest thoughts and most powerful feelings. If I imagined that I could have created, even conceived the piece, I am quite certain that the excess of excitement and earth-shattering experience would have driven me out of my mind."

Zafar was right in a sense. I read in one of my father's science journals about a study showing that a strangely disproportionate number of mathematicians rank Bach as their favorite composer.

Yes, but how did you first hear it?

I arrived for a tutorial with Professor Sylvester one day. There was classical music playing in her room. As I sat down, she went over to turn it off, but I asked her if we could listen for a minute. After the tutorial, she asked me if I wanted to borrow the cassette. That's how I found my first ninety minutes of Bach. The Chaconne was on that tape.

Emily, continued Zafar, played with technical mastery. The violin was in tune, the harmonies were in tune, there were no scratches of the bow, the music was straight and clean. I am not a musician, I have never learned to play a musical instrument, but I'd heard enough music to be able to tell these things at least. What I could not account for then was the emotion I had: I felt nothing. The music was lifeless.

I have heard musicians speak of phrasing and shaping, I know that they talk about articulation and interpretation, but I do not know what they mean when they use these terms, not precisely, and I knew less then. All I could say was that her music, music that was perfect in its notes, was cold to me, but I doubted my authority; I felt I could not pronounce on these things, that I would exceed my station.

These rehearsals were fraught with guilt for me but not because of the subterfuge involved. I tell you why I sneaked into those halls. I did not sneak in because these were rehearsals from which the public were excluded; in fact, many of them were open to the public, and there were rehearsals where I saw visitors come and go, sit and listen. I sneaked in because this music did not belong to me and I had no right in it. And because I had no right, there was guilt. I felt treacherous, but of what?

Of course you have a right! I said with an emphasis that surprised me.

But that was how I felt. It's not about passports or naturalization certificates.

Exactly. It belongs to everyone.

Do you know Bach's Prelude No. 1, *The Well-Tempered Clavier*?

Not by name.

You probably do know it. It's a beautiful piece and quite short. It has a lot in common, I think, with his first cello suite: a geometric simplicity and progression. I heard it once—the prelude—at one of those lunchtime concerts in Hall, and the student sitting next to me asked me what I made of it. I thought he was probably asking me about the performance rather than the composition, and I remember thinking it would be presumptuous to comment on the skill of the pianist when I knew nothing of playing the piano. It's a beautiful piece of music, I replied. The young man smiled and said that he'd always thought it a trifling thing, a practice piece for children.

That's ridiculous, I said to Zafar.

I now think he was wrong, continued Zafar. But it takes time to overcome another person's educated confidence. The feeling of entitlement is just that, it's just a feeling. Just as the feeling that one does not have an entitlement is nothing more than a feeling.

Isn't that a matter of choice?

Can you choose *not* to love a person?

Don't you mean: Can you *choose* to love a person?

Well, that would be more relevant to you, wouldn't it?

Bach's Chaconne, you were saying?

There might be ways to make it easier not to resent another person.

Chaconne.

We'll come back to it, said Zafar.

But again he seemed to disappear into his own thoughts.

Some years ago, in my first year at Oxford as I recall, a friend of my mother, an actress-turned-director, came to dinner in my parents' home. The director described tools an actor might use to convey intelligence. It seemed to me that certain character traits come off a person without words, that they just rise from the surface like moisture burned off by the sun, and intelligence, I thought, was just such a trait. I've met people whose intelligence is apparent, before sound waves can carry their words—not infrequently, they are a rather laconic sort. But how, I wondered to my mother's friend, does an actor convey the intelligence of a character, an Einstein or a Newton, whose intelligence might be greater than his own?* The director explained that one device is to have the character appear to drift off into his thoughts.

---

*In fact, the director's response was first to set the question in the broader problem of an actor trying to convey mental or emotional states generally. She mentioned the name of

Today I regard her thesis with a certain skepticism. There are many reasons why a person might wander off into his or her own thoughts, daydreams, and preoccupations. She might, for instance, be contemplating what color nail polish she should wear for the upcoming ball next weekend. He might be wondering if he switched off the gas on the stove and could be retracing his movements before leaving the house.

There I was, continued Zafar, sitting in a patch of shadow in the church, she oblivious of my presence, listening to this note-perfect rendering, technically accomplished even to my ear and yet hollow. It made a mark on me. A few years later, in 1991, at a dinner party in Cambridge, Massachusetts, I asked the German composer Nathanael Sandmann-Hoffmann, a visiting professor of musicology, if he had encountered this.

Encountered what?

I asked him if he'd ever heard a piece of music played perfectly, music that he knew was sublime, and yet had been completely unmoved by it. The professor's face broke into a wrinkled smile, and I thought he was remembering some moment or episode, perhaps once forgotten, that had amused him.

I have, he replied, setting down his glass of wine by the stem.

In the last year, explained the professor, there was in Berlin a concert, which was of course the year after the coming down of the wall, in fact. Many musicians from East Germany are now in West Germany, the doors to which have suddenly opened to them. A number of such musi-

---

Duchenne, a French neurologist of the nineteenth century, who had identified certain facial expressions exhibited by everyone, that, he concluded, were involuntary, including a particular smile, now known as a Duchenne smile, which cannot be created by a person but is the involuntary effect of an emotional state. The particular muscles involved in expressing this smile cannot be consciously willed into action; they're activated only when someone is genuinely very pleased. Before I could ask this actress-turned-director how she'd heard about this nineteenth-century French neurologist, she explained that Duchenne's work was of enormous interest to the Russian director Constantin Stanislavski, the father of method acting. The problem Stanislavski identified was how an actor could convey emotions whose corresponding facial expressions could not be willed.

When I asked Zafar, one day, why the photo of Emily in Penelope's house had horrified him, he replied that she'd had a Duchenne smile. Even children born deaf and dumb, he said, burst into luminous smiles. I'd never seen her smile like that at me.

cians are very good indeed. There was such a feeling of excitement in the German air, so much goodwill toward all men, with reunification now an imminent reality. The political mood added to one's excitement as a lover of music to hear all these musicians from the East. As I have mentioned to you, I attended a concert that included a performance of . . . it was Brahms's Piano Concerto No. 2 in B-flat major by a young German pianist from Leipzig, the city where Sebastian Bach was cantor at St. Thomas, as I expect you know.

The German people, continued the professor, can be rather earnest about their music, which is not in every instance to be taken for discernment. On this occasion, the whole audience leaned forward and furrowed their brows in the most severely concentrating manner. I felt exactly what you have described. I wanted, so to speak, to shout, *The emperor has no clothes!* The music was stillborn. It was really quite dead. But, you know, this sort of thing is very common in conservatories. I see it all the time in students. I have under my tutelage one student now, for example, who plays in this way. He is from the southern part of America, from Alabama, I believe, and, I gather, he comes from a devout Baptist Christian family. I have wanted to say to him that he should get out more, that he should live a little. He should get himself fucked, I have wanted to say, as the great Martha Graham said to her dancers, but of course the sexual correctness of the American university being what it is, I have never done so.

The professor laughed as he spoke.

Such ratifications as the professor's, they came later. Until, little by little, experience taught me otherwise, self-doubt permitted no judgment about great art, great music, and such things. If I was right and the young woman's music was indeed lifeless—if I was right, I wondered, can she herself not hear that her playing is lifeless? It seemed to me an unbearable state to play the violin that way, without emotion, without love and joy.

Maybe they *cannot* play with emotion, I suggested to Zafar.

But there's a simpler explanation still, which was: What the hell did I know? The wisdom of that German composer, the ratifying, the borrowed confidence, came only years later. What right, I thought, had I *to have* an opinion about this musical performance, to think it anything less than accomplished? It's their music, not mine, and they know what's what. I'd never touched a violin or piano, let alone learned to play either. It seemed an altogether neater explanation. I was ignorant and presumptuous and they weren't.

Explanation of what?

My doubts about my judgment. My doubts weren't really about the quality of her playing, not even at root about whether I was capable of forming a judgment—anyone can have a gut reaction, which may be as real as it gets—but my doubts were about whether I had a right. Who was I to think I knew good from bad?

Aren't you overthinking it? She'd learned how to play an instrument with skill but not how to play music with emotion, I said, rather pleased with my formulation.

But wouldn't you want to learn?

Maybe she can't. Maybe her emotions are hidden from her.

She stopped playing, said Zafar, the moment the rest of the ensemble, arriving as a group, entered the hall. I stayed while they rehearsed the Schubert string quintet. I have to say, I couldn't focus my listening; I was preoccupied.

At the end, after all the others packed away their instruments and went, the ensemble's leader and the young woman were left.

The leader of the ensemble, its first violin, was a tall, thin man, evidently several years older than the others. I supposed he was either a graduate student or a junior fellow. He spoke with an uncertain note in his voice.

Emily, he said, you play very well.

Thank you, she replied.

Those are the first two words I ever heard her say. *Thank you.* They are terms of politeness. But in all the time I was with Emily, I don't think I ever heard her say *sorry*. It bothers me, this does. I can't even think up the image of her doing so, the sound of her voice making that word. It is easy enough, don't you think, to imagine someone you know well saying words you imagine them saying. But why can't I imagine her saying that word, just saying *sorry*?

For a long time, I wondered if it was my own mind somehow suppressing every memory of her saying *sorry*, whether in fact she had said *sorry* but the apologies themselves had so wounded me that my mind had pushed them beyond the reach of the remembering self—an apology is, after all, an acknowledgment of a harm done.

Do you really doubt your judgment so much? I asked Zafar.

Not anymore. I did then, and that's the nub of it: the disaster it all wreaked not on my judgment but on my ability to rely on my judgment. I lost my bearings.

You were saying—

Yes. I had the impression the ensemble's leader was considering his words.

You're a very skillful violinist, he said, which puts you in a position to develop certain aspects of your playing others would have difficulty with.

Emily gave no response.

Yes, well, he continued, it might be useful to develop your expressive voice. Obviously this is something longer term. We'll be great for tomorrow.

As the young man spoke, Emily was entirely silent and perfectly still. It was impossible, for me at least, to discern her reaction, if there was any. The young man seemed increasingly awkward, and I thought of an adolescent shuffling his feet in embarrassment. Had there been a stone on the floor, he might idly have kicked it.

If you don't have plans this evening, we could talk about this over a quick supper.

The young woman smiled at him.

That would be nice, she replied.

Zafar's account left me with questions. I wanted, for instance, to ask him if he'd ever mentioned that evening to Emily when he met her years later, when he and Emily were seeing each other. As it turned out, he would later address this himself. Our conversation had brought us past the midnight mark, and I saw in his face that my friend was overcome with tiredness. Nevertheless, I could not but ask him, if only for a stop-gap until a full answer came, about that parenthetical remark, that he had finally turned to religion when he needed urgent help. What had prompted his appeal to religion? But his answer only raised in my mind more questions, which would have to wait.

Religious conversion, said my friend, is an act of destruction. Turning to God can save your life, but, in the process, it can annihilate your soul.

He rose from his seat and, wishing me a good night, he pulled the study door shut behind him. Left to my own devices, I faced the melancholy in the room, and I asked myself if it was his or mine.

8

Poggendorff and Purkyně

When I was a kid growing up in Far Rockaway, I had a friend named
Bernie Walker. We both had "labs" at home, and we would do various
"experiments." One time, we were discussing something—we must
have been eleven or twelve at the time—and I said, "But thinking is
nothing but talking to yourself inside."

"Oh, yeah?" Bernie said. "Do you know the crazy shape of the
crankshaft in a car?"

"Yeah, what of it?"

"Good. Now, tell me: How did you describe it when you were talking to yourself?"

So I learned from Bernie that thoughts can be visual as well as
verbal.   —Richard P. Feynman, *The Pleasure of Finding Things Out*

After passing through the lens, light traverses the main part of the
eye, which is filled with vitreous humor ["glassy liquid"], a clear,
gelatinous substance. After passing through the vitreous humor,
light falls on the retina, the interior lining of the back of the eye. In
the retina are located the photoreceptor cells numbering approximately 126 million. A feature of the retina is the optic disk, where
the long threadlike parts of the cells conveying visual information
gather together and leave the eye through the optic nerve. The optic
disk produces a blind spot because no receptors are located there.
It is a remarkable thing that in the very center of our field of vision
there is a blind spot, a disk of nothing, nothing seen, nothing registered, a region of darkness where we might least expect it, if we
ever notice its absence, which we do not.

—Neil R. Carlson, *Physiology of Behavior*

In 1896, from his observatory in Arizona, Percival Lowell discovered
a pattern of scarring on the surface of Venus. The arrangement of

lines resembled the spokes of a wheel radiating from a hub. Lowell believed he saw features of the terrain, "rock or sand weathered by aeons of exposure to the Sun." The spokes appeared "with a definiteness to convince the beholder of an objectiveness beyond the possibility of illusion." His research, including his findings of canals on Mars, fired the imagination of a generation. H. G. Wells cited Lowell's work as inspiration for *The War of the Worlds*.

Yet Lowell was alone in seeing these strange markings and, in time, with more advanced telescopes, his claims were discredited. But what did Lowell see? The problem was resolved a century later when an optometrist and amateur astronomer pointed out that Lowell had "stopped down" his telescope—reduced the exit aperture—to the point of unwittingly turning it into an ophthalmoscope. What Lowell actually saw was the network of blood vessels on his retina. Believing he'd found evidence that man was not alone, Percival Lowell had in fact been gazing into his own eye.

—attributed to Winston Churchill in Zafar's notebooks

As Zafar gave his account of tea with Penelope Hampton-Wyvern, I let him speak uninterrupted. But I could barely conceal my discomfort in those flashing moments when rage took hold of him. I could not recall having seen anything like it in him before. Even when, those years ago, he struck down the neo-Nazi in that cobbled mews in Notting Hill, his manner and conduct—the quiet, unassuming South Asian of his own description—had shown restraint and control which, while in its own way alarming, had evidenced no deep well of anger. But in the course of merely recounting tea with the Hampton-Wyverns, even where there was no prospect of physical violence, when he was talking to *me*, he seemed to be raging against some unseen enemy and spoke of such things as class, privilege, and networks with shocking ferocity.

A few days later, once the dust had seemed to settle, I tried to broach these subjects. We were sitting in a café in Bloomsbury, next to the window, looking onto the British Museum. I brought up his meeting Penelope, but the conversation didn't seem to be moving.

Do you see what the little girl is doing? he asked.

Zafar was watching a child sitting with her mother. The little girl was eating chocolate cake.

The girl's putting the spoon on her plate, he continued, then breaking off a small piece of cake and putting it on the spoon. Watch this—

The girl lifted the spoon, but when it was hovering in front of her face, instead of doing what you'd expect with the utensil, she picked off the crumbling piece of cake with her hand again and popped it into her mouth.

How cute is that? he asked.

Don't we choose to be victims? I asked.

A young waitress in a short skirt finally brought us our coffee. I moved the voice recorder away from the mugs. That device had quickly slipped into the rituals when we sat and talked, signifying a reassuring continuity, a means of keeping track, at a time when things were changing, things were breaking, when further changes looked certain to come.

The British class structure is terrible, isn't it? I added idiotically, like an incompetent chat show host, trying to provoke a guest.

Zafar was looking out across the road. High above the main entrance of the museum, the Union Jack fluttered from a pole. The door to the café opened and cold air blustered in behind an elderly couple complaining about the weather.

Aren't they all? asked Zafar.

What do you mean?

Aren't all class structures terrible?

Don't you think it's something we can fix? At least the way we deal with it.

We? Listen to you, the class warrior.

As individuals, I mean. I'm not talking about class war, I said.

No one does. The Cold War's over, socialists scattered to the winds and with them all talk of class.

Maybe you can't change the world, but at least you can change the way you look at things and how they affect you.

The world is what it is and our task is to see it rightly?

Exactly, I said.

What if you can't see things as they are? Zafar asked.

You learn. Isn't that what education is all about?

He said nothing.

I don't buy your take on it, I said.

What's my take?

Education isn't about gaining power. It's about opening our eyes and letting in the light.

He did not answer. I thought he was being deliberately obtuse.

In the street, a young man dashed across the road and, as he did so, dropped something, a phone perhaps. A car drove over it and carried on without stopping.

Zafar's gaze went out toward the British Museum, upward, through the leafless trees, toward the bright British flag beating against a gray December sky. His eyes looked still, as if time itself were lingering in the air above him, waiting for an opening. My father had a similar gaze when he was lost in thought, perhaps in some idea of physics or, equally likely I think, in something mundane. My mother used to say he was staring off into space-time.

Do you know why they fly flags at half-mast?

Because someone has died? I replied.

I mean where the tradition comes from.

No, but I bet you're going to tell me.

I bet you ten pieces of cake.

You want to eat ten pieces of cake? I asked him.

No. If I win, *you* have to eat ten pieces of cake.

Tell me why flags are flown at half-mast. You've actually got me quite curious now.

You've always been curious.

Very droll.

Pay attention. With the accession of James I in 1603, British ships flew two flags, the English cross and Scottish saltire. But there was another existing convention. When a battle or military exchange had taken place, the victor's flag was hung at the top with the loser's just below. The question of which flag should go on top, after a military victory, against the Spanish, say, was resolved by letting English ships fly the cross in the superior position and Scottish ships the saltire.

But why are flags flown at half-mast when someone dies?

Flying a flag at half-mast or, to be precise, not halfway down the pole but one flag shy of the top is to make room for the invisible flag of Death, the victor over all men.

I think Zafar and I both pondered the image for a few moments. Now I saw it differently.

Why, I asked, were two flags flown after James I became king?

James I of England was also James VI of Scotland.

Yes, of course.

Actually, I say *British* ships, but there was in fact no Britain to speak of. Given the historical enmity of the English and Scots, James went out of his way to appeal to the English, quite literally. When he traveled from Scotland to assume the throne in London, he stopped off at towns and villages throughout England, ingratiating himself with his new subjects. But here's the thing. What's called the Union of the Crowns did not actually mean the union of Scotland and England. There was still no Great Britain. That had to wait another hundred years. James was king of two separate sovereign states. So let me ask you this: If anyone can be described as English, surely the monarch of England is a good candidate?

Unless he's German, like the Windsors.

Ah, you may joke, but James also ruled Ireland. My question is, do you think today's patriotic Brit is likely to regard his queen as British or not?

Point taken.

And yet here was James, king of England, king of Ireland, and king of Scotland. He was an Englishman, an Irishman, and a Scot, and king of separate sovereign states. So when an English patriot asks if it's possible to be both British and Pakistani or British and Bangladeshi, it might be worth pointing out that for over a hundred years, the monarch of England had more than one national identity.

For a while, we sat in silence.

Do you know Poggendorff's illusion? asked my friend.

No. Tell me about Poggendorff's illusion, I said in sudden good spirits brought on by the instant recognition, a familiar sense, that Zafar wanted to play.

He pulled out a pen, took a napkin, and drew a straight vertical line before asking me if we should get another coffee.

I'll order them—I need the bathroom anyway. Finish your drawing, I said.

The voice recorder is a way of eavesdropping on yourself. It is the equivalent of a door, slightly ajar, letting you listen in on yourself at a time that is past. One of the surprises contained in the recordings are the tiny things I missed the first time around. Listening to the recording of that discussion in the café, for instance, I realized that with the pretext of wanting more coffee, Zafar might very well have engineered my removal from the table so that he could put together his diagram without giving the game away.

I returned from the bathroom and, as I settled back into my chair, my friend pushed the paper napkin toward me.

You're amused?

Give me the great illusion—I wait with bated breath, I said.

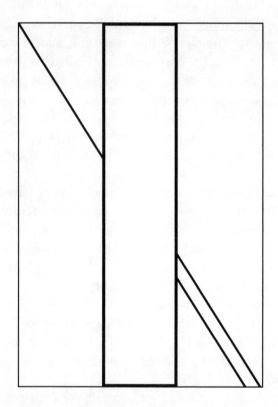

That's good, he said. Now let's begin with the obvious part, something we can agree on. This diagonal line on the left—which of the two diagonals on the right does it extend to?

The top one, I answered.

Of course it does, said Zafar. Now take this other napkin and line it up to check you're right. Humor me.

I should have seen it coming. As I brought the edge of the folded napkin against the diagonal in the top left of the diagram, it became apparent that this line extended downward not to the top diagonal, as I had said, but to the bottom one.*

This is Poggendorff's illusion, said Zafar. Johann Poggendorff, he continued, was a nineteenth-century German physicist and the creator of a number of measuring devices. Your father will probably have heard of him. There are countless optical illusions of a similar type—you probably know the Müller-Lyer illusion: two parallel lines with arrows at the end, arrows inverted on one of the lines; which line is longer?

I know that one, I said.

But it's Poggendorff's illusion I like the most, because it reminds me of the distinction between a reason for doing something and an incidental benefit of doing it. But I'll come to that. You say that once we know how the world actually is—once we see it correctly—we can fix things. Now that you *know* what the truth here is, let me ask you one more time: Which of these two diagonals on the right, the top one or the bottom, which of them looks—and I mean *looks*—like it's the extension of the diagonal on the left?

The same. Nothing's changed, I replied. It looks the same as before.

Knowing how things are doesn't make you see them correctly, doesn't stop you from seeing things incorrectly. Stare at the image as much as you like, it's all in vain. It will never surrender the truth, not to your naked eyes; you have to go in armed with a straightedge.

Yes, yes, I said, somewhat defensively—this was a human cognitive failing, everyone's shortcoming, but I couldn't help feeling that somehow I'd been shown up.

---

*I did not keep the napkin but have reproduced the diagram after consulting pages on the Internet. Of course, the diagram also appears in Zafar's notes, where beneath it are the words *Knowing doesn't fix things*. When he wrote those words, I have wondered, was he referring to a specific thing, something he came to know, which was an answer to a question but which never resolved things for him?

Do you know Harvard's motto? he asked.

Veritas.

And Yale's?

No, I don't.

Lux et veritas. Light and truth. Quite a distinction. Shining a light doesn't always reveal the truth of things. Jan Evangelista Purkyně said: *Illusions of the senses tell us the truth about perception.*[*] So the question is, he asked me: Do you trust your senses, your perception of the world?

Trust is a slippery word, I said. When I tell you that I trust someone or something, a newspaper or politician, say, I mean that his behavior agrees with my expectations of how he'll behave.

Do you trust your own perception of the world?

Optical illusions aside, I think the way the world behaves tends to agree with my expectations of what it will deliver.

Aren't you putting the cart before the horse?

How so?

Your expectations are formed by your perceptions in the first place. Then you use later perceptions to determine if your expectations have been met. What if your initial perceptions make you form stupid expectations? What if your own perceptions are rigging the game before it's started?

And we're all living in a matrix of illusion, like the movie?

I looked for a response, but he just smiled.

Maybe, I continued, not *trust* then but *believe*. Don't we have to believe in our perceptions? I asked. We have to have some faith. What's the alternative?

Do you have to believe in evolution if you reject creationism?

Doesn't it follow? What's the alternative?

Why not hold off having a belief? Why do you have to have a belief one way or the other?

I read somewhere about a survey, I said, showing that most people who said they believed in Darwinian evolution actually got its basic ideas completely wrong when they were quizzed about it.

---

[*] Zafar provided no reference, but I have been able to establish that the remark is attributed to Purkyně by Hans-Lukas Teuber in the rather alarmingly titled volume *Visual Field Defects After Penetrating Missile Wounds of the Brain* (1960).

Exactly. Those people, said Zafar, have rejected creationism and placed their faith in ideas that they mistakenly regard as Darwinian evolution. Aren't they better off suspending belief altogether rather than clinging to false gods? They don't even meet your test.

What test?

Why do they need Darwinian evolution in their lives—their warped notion of evolution, that is? Didn't you say you need to believe your perceptions—you *need* to believe something?

That day, I forgot to remind Zafar that he said he'd explain why he liked Poggendorff's illusion more than others. When I recently researched the illusion, I discovered something quite extraordinary, which I suspect he had probably had in mind even as he looked out the windows of the café at the Union Jack above the British Museum.

According to one authority, the British national flag was designed in such a way as to overcome the pitfall of Poggendorff's illusion, whose effect was known even before the German physicist formalized it. Here, some say it has to do with fimbriation and rules of heraldic design, and perhaps this is what Zafar was hinting at when he mentioned the distinction between a reason for doing something and an incidental benefit of doing it. In any event, the optical illusion is countered in the Union Jack by displacing the red saltire of St. Patrick slightly so that each spoke of the saltire can at least *look* aligned with its opposite spoke on the other side of the Cross of St. George. Along the length of each spoke of St. Patrick's Cross, only one half of the width (not length) of the spoke is included in the Union Jack.

The flag is surprising for another, related reason. I expect many people think, as I did, that the flag is symmetrical about the central vertical and horizontal axes: that the top half is a mirror image of the bottom and the left half of the right. In fact, this is not true. The lack of reflective symmetry is visible in the corners of the flag. At the top right corner, the red saltire of St. Patrick meets the northern edge of the flag. If the flag had reflective symmetry about the axis that runs from left to right through the middle, then the upper left arm of the red saltire of St. Patrick would also meet the edge of the flag on its northern side. But it doesn't; it meets the western edge. (The only symmetry the flag has is 180-degree rotational symmetry about its center.)

As I say, Zafar mentioned none of this business about the Union Jack. Instead, he proceeded, in his odd way, to where he was heading that day. I see that now.

Do you love her?

Meena?

Who else?

I'm not sure, I said.

Of course you don't. But it doesn't matter, right?

What do you mean I don't love her? I didn't say that; I said I'm not sure.

Does it matter?

Does what matter?

Does it matter whether you love her?

It might help.

So you don't love her, said Zafar.

I didn't say that.

I had always suspected him of a capacity for cruelty. I think I know why Zafar was attractive to women. I think I know how he drew them. He invaded their private spaces; he asked direct questions, questions just shy of inappropriate. For instance, he asked Eva—the young woman in Central Park—about her hair. That in itself should have scared women off. But Zafar was also manipulative. He invaded a woman's space, but he let her know—he helped her believe—that she was safe when he did so. There was the smile, but there was also the mere fact of asking a question. It gives the illusion of control to the person who can choose her answer. When I thought of Zafar like this, when I understood how his manipulation worked, it brought him down a peg; he didn't seem quite so charming. Maybe he didn't know what he was doing. Maybe it was just ingrown habit. But the fact that it's so well learned makes it no less manipulative. In fact, as I reflect on this, it seems to me that he and Emily had that in common; they were both highly manipulative. They had applied their skills in different directions, quite obviously, but whatever Zafar might ultimately have thought about the ways the two of them had been unsuited to each other, in this one regard—their respective capacities to manipulate—they had been perfectly matched.

You know what Erich Fromm said about love?

Who's Erich Fromm?

Jewish German American philosopher and psychoanalyst. He said that we must give up the notion that since love is a condition of the mind, its presence can be proven by a form of words. We give up this idea when we see that far from being a condition of the mind, love is an activity, a form of conduct.

Interesting, but so what?

She's away a lot, but you never call her.

Marriage isn't a transaction.

So she calls you, but you don't call her, he said.

What's going on?

I'm asking questions and you're uncomfortable. Relax. I can stop, said Zafar.

Of course he could stop and I could have stopped him. I can hear it when I listen to the recording. I could have said *Do stop*, but I said nothing. It's a difficult thing to admit, but Zafar's potential for cruelty has always pulled me in, binding me to him. Here he was, staying at my home, eating my food, availing himself of my hospitality. I wanted to tell him that I was the successful one here. But the ungenerous thought couldn't withstand the reality: My marriage was a disaster; my home, this retreat, was foreign soil, made bearable only by his arrival. And as I think about it now, even the huge house was a stucco-fronted lie made of bricks and mortar. I bought the house, as Zafar remarked, before I joined the firm, before my first paycheck. I've relied on my family in so many ways that can never be escaped. I used to think these were the bonds across generations.

I could have told Zafar I'd made something of my life, that I was still young and there was so much more I could do, but even then I knew the hollowness of it, the irrelevance of it. I had just been fired from the firm after a vote of the partnership, by people I had counted as friends, fired by an email asking me if I had a moment to spare for a chat, fired for taking risks whose payoffs funded their children's schooling ten times over; risks that they encouraged me to take; risks that the regulators and central bankers encouraged us to take; risks that homeowners and governments the world over encouraged us to take; risks that no one knew would come back like this. Who would have thought in the first quarter of 2008 that Lehman Brothers would go belly-up before the year was out? Who *actually thought* that the markets were going to sink into the worst crisis since the Great Depression? None of the absentminded rocket scientists on Wall Street did. I'm not one of them, but I worked with them, hired them, and respected them. They're smart people, very smart. Here was their golden opportunity to make a mint betting against the market—that's what you can do, bet against the market, and if they'd thought the market would tank, then they'd have been the first to bet against it. Sure, there were mavericks here and there already betting against the housing market, where it all started. But they never gave you convincing reasons for their view. They might have said the housing market was heading south, but nothing they said, at the time, given what we knew, at the time, given what the market expressed, at the time, none of their reasons, at the time, nothing they said was ever more worthy of our belief, my belief, than what everyone else—the overwhelming majority—was saying. What do you do when everyone believes things are going well except the few who aren't any more convincing?

And here was Zafar, opening the wounds, a friend coming at me from behind my back. Who did he think he was?

Do you remember what you said years ago in New York? Finance was a meritocracy, you said, and you liked that about it.

I remember, I said.

Well, was it?

By and large, I said. The *was* stung.

Why did that matter to you? Actually, hold that thought. I need the gents. Can't put it off any longer.

It was a fair question. After all, back then I couldn't very well have said that a meritocracy was likely to favor me. The evidence probably pointed the other way: I had gained only an upper second-class degree at Oxford and was able to stay on for a graduate program because I wasn't relying on a scholarship or research council grant. I suspect that the extent of self-financing in higher education, at that time and, as far as I know, even now, is not common knowledge, but there it is; those in the know, the paying students and the receiving university, didn't have much incentive to advertise the fact. And as for those who don't go on because they can't self-finance, they're never heard from again. But that is how the world is and it seems to me little use to fight it, especially when no one else seems to be doing so.

As I waited for Zafar, the absurd notion formed in my mind that he might have vanished. That while I had been looking out the window, he had slipped out the door and simply disappeared.

I overheard two young women sitting at an adjoining table.

My friends think I'm mad, said one. They're always saying, Cheryl, you're mad, you are. But I think it's all right, you know. It's like you got to be a bit crazy, otherwise you'd go mad.

Mayonnaise is just posh salad cream, innit?

I suppose so, replied the one.

It's American, right?

No, I think it's French.

Yeah, but why do they say, "Easy on the mayo," then?

On the telly?

Yeah.

Americans like French stuff.

You like it, don't you?

It's not as greasy.

You mean salad cream?

Greasier than mayo.

What's pastrami?

At another table, a young American was talking about his yoga class. He complained to his friend: It was like someone in the room was draining my green energy.

So why, Zafar asked after he returned, did the meritocracy matter to you back then? It's not as if you'd suffered because the world had failed to recognize your merits.

I expect you're going to tell me.

I think it's tougher for people like you. You guys make the right calls and things happen, whereas regular folks—*like me*, he said, shooting me a grin—regular people have grown up knowing full well the world is unfair. We don't expect anything different, and we're so battered by the unfairness that we don't even hope for anything better. The world is—and I'm not trying to use your words against you; or were they my words?—anyway, for most of us, the world is what it is. You guys are the idealists.

194 | ZIA HAIDER RAHMAN

Finance, I said, is by and large a meritocracy, and that's a good thing. You can't fault me for wanting to be a part of that. After all, you got something out of it, didn't you?

But you weren't really attracted to finance because of what it was but because of what it was *not*.

Here we go again, I said. I think I might have rolled my eyes.

Finance is not about connections, it's not about who you know but what you know, it isn't like your grandfather's world, with secret deals on golf courses and in country clubs, kickbacks and Swiss bank accounts.

You don't know him.

I don't have anything to protect by lying to myself.

I think Zafar was wrong, but the irony is that I so wish he'd been right. The fact is that my own early success in finance did owe something to connections, connections that have now come home to roost.

What's your point? I asked.

You could have tried for academe, but what if you'd failed? Or worse still, what if you'd ended up with a second-rate lectureship at a second-rate university somewhere? What would your father have thought? Ivy League or why bother? Now, finance, on the other hand, that was safer. At least you couldn't be compared to your father or grandfather.

Or maybe I just knew what I wanted, I replied.

The conversation now taking place did not feel like two friends trying to figure something out. It had none of that affection and trust of conversations on our walks everywhere else all those years ago. There was instead an earnest, impatient drive to get to the root of things, dispensing with the markers of friendship. More than once, he'd asked me, *Why does it matter to you?*, a mischievous question that he loved. But this time there were no accompanying smiles, no unspoken gentleness. If anything, his comments and questions seemed presumptuous; I hadn't seen him in years. One of those articles my father sent was about some studies that show that while every person thinks he himself has changed hugely over time, those close to him typically think he's changed very little. Was that it? Did he think that he knew me because he believed people didn't change?

Do you look down on Meena?

The question caught me by surprise, but that was Zafar's way.

You think I do.

You don't want children with *her*, do you?

Come on, Zafar.

Class isn't something you look at, it's not stuff around you. It *is* you, it's the eyes with which you see the world. And you have to look in the mirror to see your eyes. Do you know what Bertrand Russell said about mathematics?

I expect he said a lot about mathematics.

About why he liked mathematics?

No, but I bet you're going to tell me, I said, slightly irritated by the all-too-familiar didactic tone.

A hundred pounds?

Tell me.

Russell said he liked mathematics because it was not human and had nothing in particular to do with this planet or with the whole accidental universe—because, like Spinoza's God, it won't love us in return.

That may be true, but how is it relevant?

You know that Russell was a philosopher and a mathematician, but he was also the grandson of a prime minister and in fact he was an earl himself. Mathematics is as far removed as you can get from that background.

But there have always been aristocrats in mathematics.

Yes, there have, in the one field where station and position and authority don't matter a jot. Who you are counts for nothing. In 1900, at the second International Congress of Mathematicians in Paris, David Hilbert gave the keynote address and set out his famous ten problems, mathematical propositions that needed to be proven. Hilbert, as I'm sure you know, was the towering figure of mathematics in his day, a man of huge authority and unrivaled mathematical intuition. One of the problems was proving the consistency of arithmetic, and Hilbert believed the proof was close at hand.* But within thirty years of Hilbert's challenge, a young man by the name of Kurt Gödel, at the very outset of his career, a man with no record of achievement, let alone anything to rival Hilbert's,

---

*From a given set of axioms, using logical reasoning, mathematicians derive statements that are true. Hilbert believed that mathematics was consistent, i.e., that it is not possible to derive two different statements that contradict each other. That is what Hilbert's intuition told him, but he did not have a proof.

showed that the great master himself was wrong and that mathematics could not be proven to be consistent. And that was the end of that. Mathematics doesn't care about authority, it doesn't care about who you are, where you're from, what your eye color is, or who you're having supper with.

Zafar's conversation seemed that day to amble here and there, but as I come to consider it again, I find two strands joining together—the impossibility of correcting the misperception of optical illusions and the question of authority for truths. In his notebooks is this note: *In order to catch even a fleeting glimpse of the world, we must break with our familiar acceptance of it.* Is such a goal beyond our ability, beyond mine?

My parents were born in West Pakistan, one half of an improbable state established at the partition of India in 1947 amid the hurried retreat of the British Raj. Pakistan consisted of two regions separated by all of twelve hundred miles, the width of modern India. East Pakistan was to become Bangladesh, where Zafar was born. These were, as he described them, two wheels unconnected by an axle, two wheels that were bound, and not only in hindsight, to go their own ways. The peoples did not share a language, they did not share the same food, they did not even share the same religious attitudes.

In 1971, West Pakistan sought to suppress what it saw as rebellion in the East. My father and mother, then recently arrived in the U.S., opposed the militarism of the West Pakistani junta and made their feelings known to fellow Pakistanis in Princeton and farther afield.

All this had come out before I went to Oxford. At a certain point I started to ask and my father answered, at first with a trickle of information. When I returned with more questions, he and my mother spoke about it extensively, even when, I must say, to recall those days caused visible discomfort.

My father once asked Zafar where he was born. It was late in the spring of Zafar's final year at Oxford, and we had both been invited to supper at my parents' house. As I recall, the evening was unusually warm and so we sat in the garden, although every few minutes my mother asked whether we should move inside.

By that time, the years of my parents turning their backs on Pakistan had long ended. Talk of Pakistan and events there had been brought back into the home. When my father asked Zafar where in Bangladesh he was born, I saw that the past, Pakistan's past and his past, were not so distant, for it struck me that my father had never before asked Zafar what was an obvious and natural question, especially among South Asians. I had been foolishly slow about all this. The war of 1971 and the holocaust of West Pakistan's conduct in East Pakistan, his criticism of his homeland, the ostracism and then my parents' disengagement—all of this was a history of personal suffering that my father carried with him.

I had never connected the dots before, but when I considered at that moment my father's affection for Zafar, my friend who was born in Bangladesh, I could trace back the warmth of feeling to their very first encounter, and I saw that my father's attitude had always possessed an aspect of hope.

I was born in the northeast, in Sylhet, replied my friend.

I know Sylhet, said my father.

Your grandfather, said my mother, directing her comment to me, was stationed there briefly in 1943, in the dog days of the Raj. I believe it was a staging post for the British campaigns in Southeast Asia, she added. Sylhet was part of Assam in those days, I think, she said, turning to Zafar and my father for confirmation.

It was, said my friend. As a matter of fact, in 1947, two parts of British India were allowed referendums to decide whether or not to join Pakistan. One was North-West Frontier Province, whose Pakhtoon majority threw in their lot with Pakistan rather than neighboring Afghanistan. The second was Sylhet, which was cut out of Assam after the population decided to join Pakistan's eastern wing. But the referendum wasn't quite a resounding victory for accession to Pakistan; in fact, the part of Sylhet where I was born voted against joining Pakistan and for remaining within Assam and therefore within India.

This I did not know, said my father.

Loyalties were quite divided but in a way that was masked by outcomes.

That can't have helped the people there in 1971, said my father.

When East Pakistan seceded? I asked, keen to join the conversation.

Yes, said my father.

No, I expect it didn't help, said my friend.

Over the course of the evening, we talked about South Asia, about its troubled history, about my grandfather's service for the British during the Second World War, and about the 1971 Bangladesh Liberation War, which led to the Indo-Pakistan War at the end of that year.

My father explained that in 1971 he was a critic of West Pakistan's military suppression of East Pakistan. Although he himself had nothing to apologize for, there was a note of regret in his voice.

In the first few months of the war, he explained, he wrote a letter to *The New York Times*—we were in Princeton then—condemning West Pakistani aggression. To its credit, *The Times* published it. Why, he continued, should the editors have bothered? After all, this was a war in faraway lands of which they probably knew nothing and cared less. British necks, not American ones, carried the chain of colonial guilt, and America had nothing to do with Pakistan.

But the truth of the matter was somewhat different, as we now know, said my father. In 1971, while the butchery was in full swing, Pakistan was a conduit for secret negotiations with China. In July, Kissinger detoured to China in total secrecy while visiting Pakistan to clear the way for Nixon's visit. The Americans, you see, were relying on Pakistan as an intermediary, even as the slaughter was raging.

We all listened to him quietly.

On the morning of March 25, 1971, under plans drawn up on five sheets of paper by two majors in two days, the army put into action Operation Searchlight. Perhaps Zafar knows about this, said my father.

But Zafar said nothing. I'm not even sure that my father was expecting a response. My father was talking as if talking were necessary, and perhaps Zafar had understood this. I wondered how much my friend already knew about those events. I myself was ignorant of so much about Pakistan. That day I told myself I would set aside time to remedy this, but the years came and went and I never did. I'd made the same promise to myself before but never kept it. Only now, prompted by Zafar's return and the circumstances of work and marriage, not to mention the world's new interest in that region, have I gone back over the past and taken time to discover more.

Under Operation Searchlight, my father continued, every Hindu and every potential opposition element in Dhaka was to be killed. Journalists and lawyers were systematically hunted down. Doctors and engineers were killed, academics and other professionals.

You spoke out against this, didn't you? I interjected.

Many others also did. There were American diplomats who wanted their government to condemn Pakistan, but Nixon was playing Cold War games.

It must have been very difficult for you in the Pakistani community, said Zafar.

It's all past now, but yes, it was hard at the time. I'm afraid to say we were shunned by Pakistanis in Princeton and New York.

We received threatening letters, said my mother. But, she continued, your father knew he had to speak out.

My father poured us all some more tea. The garden air was perfectly still.

When India intervened in December, I was relieved. Of course, I was sad for my countrymen, sad for the poor soldiers, as ever fighting wars for idiotic leaders, but I believed that it would be over soon, which it was, and that Pakistan would emerge from it all, from its own moral reckoning, a wiser and less belligerent nation. It was naïve idealism.

My father stopped there and poured some milk into his tea. The rest of us were silent.

But you know, even two days before the final surrender, when Pakistan had no hope of victory, the army carried out one last operation in Dhaka, rooting out as many intellectuals as they could and killing them.

From her slight leaning toward him, you could tell that under the table my mother had taken my father's hand.

Well, the war ended, continued my father, but Pakistan's troubles were only to carry on in one shape or another. As for Bangladesh, with three million dead, hundreds of thousands of women raped, and an entire generation of its professionals, its engineers, its doctors, its thinkers and doers exterminated, that poor country was hobbling on its infant feet.

The estimates vary, said Zafar.

How, asked my father, does the expression go? Truth is the casualty of war, slaughtered by victors and vanquished alike. I know they'll argue till the cows come home about the numbers, but the estimates don't vary enough to alter the magnitude of the horror.

In the quiet, I became aware again of the garden. Late spring in Oxford, the first floral scents, the sound of the brook, and these things my father and Zafar discussed, they seemed to belong to another time and place. At the time, I knew nothing, of course, about the facts of Zafar's origins. Now, when I look back on that evening, I am a little disturbed by what I see was Zafar's enormous restraint. The discussion must have been close to the bone and yet he held back so much. It seems to me now that Zafar's conversation had a tendency to take on an academic tone when it hit something emotionally charged, by way perhaps of a defense mechanism. If that's not too facile.

I haven't read very much about this period, said Zafar, but one thing that did strike me when I read about India's intervention is that the Indian military leadership was an extraordinarily diverse group of people.

You mean Manekshaw and the rest? asked my father.

Who was Manekshaw? I asked.

Sam Manekshaw was the head of the army, my mother replied. He was a Parsee from Zoroastrian Iranians who migrated to India way back. And there was Jacob, of course. You meant Jacob also, didn't you? she asked, looking at Zafar.

My friend nodded.

Jacob was an Indian Jew, his family originally from Iraq, said my mother. He was second-in-command of Indian forces in the east. And there was Jagjit Singh Aurora, a Sikh, who accepted the Pakistani instrument of surrender. Yes, it was quite a diverse bunch at the top of the Indian military.

I wouldn't let that diversity deceive you, said my father, speaking to Zafar.

What do you mean? I asked.

They were all really the same, Hindu, Jew, Sikh, Zoroastrian. They were all educated in the same military college founded by the British, you know?

My father also studied with them, said my mother. Before the British left, she added.

As a matter of fact, continued my father, there's a fascinating letter you absolutely must read, from a Pakistani officer to his Indian counterpart on the eve of a conflict. The Pakistanis are under siege, they've suffered huge casualties, and their cause is lost, but despite this the Pakistani officer is goading the Indian officer to join battle. The language is superb. It's in English, of course—it's pure Victorian Rajput English. He writes to the Indian officer as if they both went to the same public school.* They're all from the same social group. I've heard this before and, if you don't mind my saying so, Zafar, everyone makes so much of this diversity in the Indian army, when really they are focusing far too much on religion and race and not seeing the reality, which is that these officers come from the same class. Good Lord, all the generals, even the Pakistani ones, went to military college together, under the British. In the most important respect of all, they weren't remotely diverse.

Some of the Indians and Pakistani generals had earlier fought side by side in the Second World War. Manekshaw fought alongside those formidable Gurkhas, now part of the British army.

Manekshaw, my mother interjected, said that any soldier who says he's not afraid of dying is a liar or a Gurkha. Anyway, all this will come out, my mother concluded. It's only two decades since the war, but it will

---

*I tracked down the letter he was referring to. It is from Pakistani Lieutenant Colonel Sultan Ahmed to Brigadier Hardit Singh Kler of the Indian army:

> *Dear Brig,*
> *Hope this finds you in high spirits. Your letter asking us to surrender has been received. I want to tell you that the fighting you have seen so far is very little, in fact the fighting has not even started. So let us stop negotiating and start the fight.*
> *40 sorties, I may point out, are inadequate. Ask for many more.*
> *Your point about treating your messenger well was superfluous. It shows how you under-estimate my boys. I hope he liked his tea.*
> *Give my love to the Muktis [Bangladeshi resistance fighters allied with the Indians]. Let me see you with a Sten in your hand next time instead of the pen you seem to have such mastery over,*
> *Now get on and fight.*
> *Yours sincerely*
> *Commander Jamalpur Fortress.*
> *(Lt. Colonel Sultan Ahmed)*

Lt. Colonel Sultan Ahmed and his men were overrun shortly after this letter was received.

all come out, including the American role in it. They have a thirty-year rule, don't they? I mean their official documents are released after thirty years, no?

She looked around for confirmation, but no one seemed to know.

So, she continued, American shenanigans in Pakistan will come out in 2001 and 2002 and then questions will be asked. These days no one needs Pakistan as an intermediary for anything.

9

Dressage and the Common Touch

My wife and I knew Captain and Mrs. Ashburnham as well as it was possible to know anybody, and yet, in another sense, we knew nothing at all about them. This is, I believe, a state of things only possible with English people of whom, till today, when I sit down to puzzle out what I know of this sad affair, I knew nothing whatever. Six months ago I had never been to England, and, certainly, I had never sounded the depths of an English heart. I had known the shallows.
—Ford Madox Ford, *The Good Soldier*

Anyone thus compelled to act continually in accordance with precepts which are not the expression of his instinctual inclinations, is living, psychologically speaking, beyond his means, and may objectively be described as a hypocrite, whether he is clearly aware of the incongruity or not.
—Sigmund Freud, "Thoughts for the Times on War and Death"

Sometimes people carry to such perfection the mask they have assumed that in due course they actually become the person they seem. —W. Somerset Maugham, *The Moon and Sixpence*

The conversation that day in the drawing room in the home of Penelope Hampton-Wyvern went on and on. Which is not to say that it dragged on; quite the contrary, when I consider how much *felt* communicated, I marvel at how scarcely two hours could have contained it. Perhaps the elites run to a different beat of time.

When Emily came back into the room after her phone call, she said, Mother dear, Zafar won the Patrick Hastings scholarship.

I was surprised by Emily's apparent pleasure. When I informed her the week before that I'd been awarded the scholarship, a scholarship for which she, too, had applied, her face had turned white. Emily had offered no congratulations, and without a word she had walked away, and the following week she winced when she saw my name in the announcements at the back of *The Times*, near the crossword. I had thought then: What could she possibly envy? This was a woman who had had all the blessings of life, who had been born to wealth and privilege, had gone to the finest schools in the world, a tall and slender lady possessed of a sufficient beauty and the quietly confident charm of upper-class women. Beside her, others seemed shrill.

But my understanding changed. I think that in Emily's eyes, her proudest achievements had been tainted by the same social favoritism that cleared her path to those achievements, nepotism and favoritism, which give with one hand and take with the other. The esteem to which she felt she was entitled, by virtue of her talents, was always sullied, either because others saw only the privilege and access that aided her successes or because, even when they didn't see those links, she did.

Emily sought absolution and found in me a confessor, an outsider to whom to depose the truth of her tainted advantage, renouncing the lie without giving up its gains. She told me, for instance, that the panel that awarded her a scholarship to Harvard had included a family friend. I heard from her about the barrister tasked with deciding on her admission to chambers, a man who was at the time seeking promotion to the rank of Queen's Counsel, a status that commands huge fees and on whose behalf Emily's father was writing a testimonial. Did she think her confession necessary? Did conscience compel her to disclose the professional conflict (even at the cost of disclosing her father's own indiscretion in telling *her* that he was writing a letter on behalf of her boss)? Was she driven to present the Emily she despised so that the better Emily could be loved? Loved by me?

Sitting in the gaze of the three-way mirror on her dresser, Emily Hampton-Wyvern, I imagine now, saw herself as three Emilys, one who longed to be loved, respected, and admired for her notional self; another, a less-reflective Emily, who seized every advantage given to her and took others that weren't; and a third Emily, one I shudder to think of, one whose existence I think even she could acknowledge only glancingly, one capable of cruelty darker than you or I can imagine.

Righteous indignation might have been enough motivation on that particular afternoon for Emily to advertise her new beau's successes, independent and hard earned. Perhaps mine might have sanctified hers, by association. Nevertheless, something else was at play. Emily had a visceral drive to attack her mother. I know how we indict our parents for heinous crimes long before we see them as flawed human beings. And of course it's easier to bring wisdom, the best of it borrowed, to account for the lives of others than to apply the same in the measure of one's own. But I think Emily held her mother at fault for everything because she blamed her for her parents' divorce, so that in all things her mother drew Emily's ire. The privilege that robbed Emily of quiet enjoyment in her successes, while clearing her way to them, did after all come from birth, and the woman she called "Mother" was certainly responsible for that.

So I've heard, said Mrs. Hampton-Wyvern. Did you know that Emily's father won the award? Some years ago, of course.

No, I did not, I said, glancing at Emily.

Congratulations, said Mrs. Hampton-Wyvern. Shouldn't we crack open some bubbly?

Not at all—these things are random, I replied.

Do you think five Court of Appeal judges would make random decisions?

Mrs. Hampton-Wyvern, I thought, knew quite a bit about it already, more, in fact, than I'd told Emily. On the other hand, perhaps the award was judged in her husband's day as it was in mine. The English bar is hardly famous for changing fast.

Maybe their lordships felt pressured to spread these awards around a little, I replied.

She meant to flatter me and I think, in retrospect, I might have been more gracious.

What the dickens can you mean by that? she asked.

Mother, you of all people can't deny these awards always go to the same people, said Emily.

I don't. They go to those who deserve them.

They go to the well connected, said Emily.

That's plainly not true, since Zafar was awarded one, answered her mother.

Isn't that the point? said Emily. Things are changing. How many deserving students can there be in Kensington?

Here were the makings of the dainty champion of the downtrodden, the oppressed. Not just deserving students from outside Kensington but also the black races, I thought, or the poor or even the third world might get a shout.

Britain can't carry on protecting the privileged, continued Emily.

I began then to perceive the complexity of Emily's relationship with privilege, her hostility toward it not merely at an intellectual level, hostility that was not even a purely emotional blow against injustice but a force that gathered in the depths of rebellion.

It took six months before she invited me to go with her to a party. Six months of excuses while she went on her own. What? She thought I didn't know? She never told me but she needn't have: A day later I might see a party dress hanging on a chair, a pair of high heels outside the wardrobe, lying askew, waiting for the weekly housekeeper, and, on the dresser, lipstick uncapped. Is it prying if I don't actually look for signs but can't help noticing them? I'm a pattern seeker, and breaks in patterns scream for attention.

So what *did* we do? We might have seen a movie or a play or gone out for dinner. Most of all we stayed in the bedroom. Or sat in the lounge, she working and I reading something. We went to her mother's for supper every week. I arranged dinners with some of my acquaintances, but after she made her last-minute excuses twice and then failed to show on the third, I stopped doing so. We did things together but never with others.

Maybe she feared what lay in wait for us. When the day arrived, the words came as a casual suggestion, muttered while her face was hidden behind the open door of the refrigerator, as if something sitting in the fridge had caused her to remember: *Fiona's having a party. Would you like to come?*

What I should have said was, Who the hell is Fiona? And how can you be so casual about it, just drop an invitation like that after six months of avoiding taking me to a single thing?

And yet what do I do but agree meekly? I used to think that I was giving her the benefit of the doubt, when in fact there was nothing to give. My insecurity had destroyed the certainty I should have had in what was plain to see.

Let's go, I said.

Before the party, I imagined that word must have got around that Emily was seeing someone, but no, not at all. None of her peers seemed to know. Or did they know something? Had they caught the waft of rumors? And did they think, because there was only gossip and never confirmation, that the relationship wasn't serious? *Maybe it's just a passing fancy, a little exotica, a bit of rough (no surprise there—like mother, like daughter). After all, she hasn't brought him out until now, has she?*

Fiona threw the party in a vast private room at a restaurant off Sloane Square. From the doors to the roof terrace, eddies of cool air softened the blows of perfume and cigarette smoke. They drank Bellinis as the waiting staff tiptoed about them daring to interrupt with canapés, and the young ladies shriveled their noses. Now what might that be? cried Gemma. A barely straightened forefinger seemed poised to motion the food away. Gemma worked in public relations and knew Fiona from Wycombe Abbey. Gemma wore jeans and an engagement ring with a rock the size of a minor African state, and she lived in a house she'd just bought in Fulham, *around the corner from Brasserie Émile*, she said, with a glance to see if I knew the place. A test? *Oh, yes*, I lied.

It was all about networks, though they would never have said it themselves. Like apes knuckling down to a forest clearing to groom each other, they thronged to the drinks parties and dinner parties, the art openings and first nights. I could never feel myself present.

I heard a confident male voice say, I should introduce you to my friend Richard Pembridge at the Foreign Office. He's at the embassy in D.C., but I think he's taking up an ambassadorship. Some hardship post in Asia. Pakistan or Bangladesh, I think. I glanced over and saw a young man, tall and handsome, speaking to Emily. His unkempt blond hair fell and rose in bluffs across his forehead, improbably fluttering over his brow. The flirting was transparent: the broad chest and robust chin pushed out, hands open, arms wide, inflated to make the beast appear bigger, never covering the body, the broken glances reattached, and the incessant rhythmic smiling. That subtle play of gestures to mark in-group familiarity; beneath it, the thrust of sexual advance.

And to think that at the beginning I imagined *me* showing off *her*. I daydreamed about it, sitting on the bus going somewhere, I daydreamed about going to dinner parties with her. Have you met my girlfriend? I'd say. Who am I kidding? Have you met my wife? That's what I said. And I watched as I grew in the estimation of the men and women. I saw myself swelling before them. What I didn't count on was that my new milieu would consist of people who weren't just familiar with Emily's pedigree and status but were drawn from the same stock, and whose very association with her was part of that status, so that rather than finding myself in a position to brag about her, the question any idiot must have been asking—the question I was asking—was: What the dickens was she doing with him? It took me much longer even to begin asking myself what the dickens I was doing staying with her.

I met a man called Hugh at the party. He was wearing a rugby shirt and in one hand he clenched two bottles of beer by their necks. Every party has a Hugh at the edges. His right arm craned up and down, over and over, so that his fat hand could parry away the inevitable locks of wavy hair that came tumbling over his forehead. Hugh and I exchanged names, and when he asked me whom I knew, I said that the host, Fiona, was a friend of my girlfriend.

Where are you from, if you don't mind my asking?

I live in Brixton, I said.

He let out a guffaw, gently nudging me on the shoulder, relishing what his drunken imagination took for mutual amusement. I acquiesced with a grin.

No, I mean really, Zephyr. Where are you from?

When I was eight years old or so, the local authority's social services had taken an interest in our family, and one summer at their suggestion and expense we took our first vacation, in Clacton-on-Sea. At the holiday camp, there were talent contests, games for children, darts tournaments for men, and a pub. I expect there were plenty of things to do besides, but I spent most of my time away from my parents playing pool by myself. I remember being fascinated by the motion of the balls on the table. My mother cooked pungent Bangladeshi food in the chalet—that's what they called those terraces of two-room self-catering units—and the smell pervaded the entire camp.

I made friends with Charlie, an eight-year-old from Manchester with a thick accent. Can I play, too? he asked, and that was enough to begin a friendship, my first. Charlie didn't seem to show any hint of the wariness of the children at the virtually all-white school I attended in London. At the end of our first game, after maintaining a running commentary of every ball either of us played, and cheering me on with an enthusiasm that I instantly saw was genuine, he asked me my name.

I don't know why but I said it was *George*. George. George? How much more English can you get? I still don't know why I did that. I can think of possible reasons, but I don't know which one is most relevant. Shame? Or just that I didn't want this boy who was nice to me to get my name wrong.

One day, after I returned from practicing on the pool table by myself, my mother said, as she set down a plate of food in front of me, that three "white people," a boy and his parents, had come by asking for George.

Oh? I said. But I did not look up to meet her eye and we never spoke about it further. After that I was too ashamed to play with Charlie again and avoided him for the remaining few days of the vacation.

I let Hugh's mispronunciation drop.

I was born, I said, in Bangladesh, on the eastern side of India.

Marvelous. Do you go back often?

I've spent some years there.

But your family's moved here, has it?

Yes.

Political reasons? Let me guess—father's a diplomat but the new regime was no longer friendly. Am I right?

Politics is everywhere, I said, making as much sense as a drunk could stomach.

Love India, said Hugh. Marvelous place. And I simply love curry. I'd curry everything if I could.

Everything?

Everything!

Curry favor, too?

What?

Curry's flavorful.

Exactly!

He exclaimed this as if I'd shared some terrific insight.

What do you do here?

I'm a lawyer.

Immigration lawyer?

I hesitated as a wicked thought tempted me.

Yes, I said.* As a matter of fact, I'm back in India next week to give master classes on how to beat U.K. immigration controls. I don't just do immigration, though. No, in two weeks, I'll be in the High Court resisting an application from the Algerian government for the extradition of alleged terrorists from the U.K. Blew up a children's hospital in Paris before bolting for Blighty. Guilty as sin, as far as I can tell. But we're British, old chap, and they deserve a fair trial, don't you think? Should be a lot of fun.

Hugh looked shocked.

More champagne, I said to him, raising my empty glass, and I walked off leaving him open-mouthed.

For a while I stood against the bar, sipping my drink while viewing the crowd. More people arrived and I watched the women turn, almost as one, a ruffle across the room, to look at the newcomers. They only glanced at the males, but as they looked over the new females joining the herd, their eyes screwed into points and their brows tightened, each touching her own hair. Nothing bears as much severity, as much unsparing regard, as one woman's appraisal of another.

The man standing next to me at the bar turned to face me. It was the tall blond who had promised to introduce Emily to his friend at the Foreign Office.

Funny, isn't it? he said.

What is? I replied.

The way they size each other up. They can't help it.

Human, don't you think?

He extended his hand. The name's Toby.

Zafar.

We shook.

What do you do, Zafar?

I looked at him and wondered how this might go. He'd pronounced the name correctly.

---

*Actually, as I understood it, Zafar was developing a practice in banking regulation.

Have a guess.

He looked me up and down but returned to my face and lingered on it.

A writer?

A good guess, I said.

Somehow I was flattered. It was pleasant to be regarded as a writer, and, I thought, something of an improvement on lawyer.

Your turn, he said.

Toby was wearing jeans, a white shirt with double cuffs, brown moccasins, and an expensive watch.

I have no idea.

You can do better than that.

You don't do anything.

Toby laughed.

That's not far off the mark, he said.

Then quickly changing the subject he said, You noticed the women?

Don't they want to be noticed?

Again Toby chuckled.

No, he continued, I meant you saw how they all looked at the women coming in.

I was warming to Toby.

Except one, he added.

Oh, yes?

Yes, that woman over there. He motioned with his head. She didn't turn at all.

He took a sip of his drink, a martini.

Spoke to her earlier. She's Emily Hampton-Wyvern, you know.

Ah, I said. Apparently it was a name one was supposed to know.

Huge flirt.

Really?

Yes, kept staring me in the eye. Funny she didn't look at the other women.

Why's that?

Well, you'd expect a flirt like that to size up the competition, wouldn't you?

Apparently, I thought, I was bound to know her name but not know her in person. Was I merely *among* them but not *of* them?

I was conscious of race but as an awareness of difference, sometimes uneasiness, sometimes an irritation with others for their failure to see beyond it. In social situations, though, the ruling emotions had nothing to do with race and everything to do with things these people might not have noticed at all, but for those signs I leaked from every pore, the betrayal of my own doing. Race never undermined me from within; it was rather the invisible things coalescing that brought on a private humiliation. The invisible possessed my heart with shame.

For a long time, I didn't want to believe it to be true; I couldn't bear the thought that it might have some objective reality, that there was something in the essence of my self that divided me from them. Either I was imagining it or I was behaving in a way that caused it—and of course, I thought, I could change my behavior, I *will* change my behavior. It wasn't the lack of Jermyn Street shirts or the wrong haircut or anything so superficial that put the distance between me and them, I thought, but it was rather something else they saw. They saw the way my eyes moved, my eyes watched, they saw through the scholarship boy who's always afraid he's going to trip up so he grabs every piece of information around him, every gesture, and reads every sign—because reading is what he does. They saw that none of it came naturally to me but was arranged by an effective mind, and because it was arranged and considered, measured and oblique, they saw the workings of design, the sweat of labor, and not the effortless charm of superior origins.

I listened to Zafar attentively without interrupting him, much as I wanted to. I had no clear question but only a vague uneasiness with this unfamiliar face—or, rather, faces—this fluctuation from crystal clarity of exposition to a barely restrained fury. Anger is not an emotion I've had much truck with, not in family life and not even at work, where, contrary to the popular image, the trader and banker is more egghead than hothead. Anger makes me uncomfortable; anger, when it shakes off the authority of a human being and breaks out, is disturbing. And that is what the anger of my friend felt like to me, a man whom I had thought the model of self-possession. I had seen him angry, properly angry, only once before. We were riding the subway in New York, the uptown number 2 train, standing in the aisle. Zafar was looking down at a young man, dressed like a corporate lawyer or banker, who was reading from a wad of papers. Seated next to him was a young black man in baggy jeans and a loose-fitting bomber jacket. His frame stretched across two seats, though for all his sprawling recumbence he looked uncomfortable. Zafar was peering down at the papers of the lawyer type: the words *Innocence Initiative* were printed at the top of the page and below them *Case Evaluation*. Even I knew that Innocence Initiative was a nonprofit that took up cases of miscarriages of justice.

Is that what I think it is? Zafar smiled at the man.

The young man nodded and smiled back at Zafar.

But Zafar's face turned nasty.

What the hell do you think you're doing reading this in public, in full view of people on this train?

Zafar was shouting and the whole carriage was looking.

You shouldn't be reading it here, you goddamn idiot. Do you know who I am? I'm a partner in a law firm* and you better hope my date this evening goes well because that's just about the only thing that'll make me forget to call your boss and have your silly little ass tomorrow. Do you understand?

The poor man was visibly shaking.

Now get off the train, said Zafar.

The ferocity of the attack was frightening and, rather foolishly, I thought I might be next in the firing line.

So who's the date? I asked, attempting humor.

Zafar gave me a look of disappointment.

I admire your respect for confidentiality, I added meekly.

You really think that's what gets me, breach of fucking confidentiality?

Isn't it?

I tell you who that guy is. He's some new associate at a corporate law firm who gets to jack off from doing a bit of pro bono work. If he'd been sitting there reviewing merger docs for Citibank, I wouldn't have said a thing. But he wouldn't have read Citibank docs in public. The case files of convicts, that's different. He thinks so little of those sad bastards that he doesn't care tuppence about their confidentiality and he thinks no one else does. That's what gets me. Want to sit down?

*He was not even a lawyer back then.

Zafar installed himself in the newly vacated seat. The young man in baggy jeans had shrunk to one space, freeing up another for me.

I looked at him now, discussing a party that sounded like any of a number of parties in West London I've attended over the years, agreeable enough though ultimately inconsequential, and I began to understand another Zafar, older than the one I had known, someone who had been emergent all the while.

You were at that party, by the way, he remarked. You came in shortly before I left and introduced me to Crane Morton Forrester.

Of course. Crane came in that morning, I said.

I remembered it fairly well. I had thought that Crane would like Zafar, though had I been asked why, at the time, I might not have answered very convincingly. The two men, Zafar and Crane, had little obviously in common. But knowing what I now know, I wonder whether I had unconsciously perceived something that they both shared. Crane became a soldier, and a soldier, like my grandfather, is a man of violence, socialized and conditioned to be aggressive, but in his heart a man who might have been first in his tribe to venture onto the plains to hunt and first to defend the tribe at home. Though I might not have been able to put it into words, it seems likely that I sensed both men's inclination toward survival.

Crane joined the Marines, I said, remembering a conversation I had had with his father before he did so.

He died in Afghanistan, I added. It was in the news—his father's a senator.

I know, said Zafar. I know.

In her mother's drawing room, Emily was championing me because she knew the West London set intimately, she knew its ways, its connections, and she knew how it gathered into itself its own, sprinkling them with the blessings of privilege. And she knew how it could be otherwise. A year in Cambridge, Massachusetts, had opened her eyes, she said in not so many words. How could it not? How could anyone so British remain unaffected by the encounter with people who ate, drank, breathed, and swam in ideas. People did not flow to that city in some continuum of unthinking tradition—Eton and Oxford—but answered the summons of ideas and learning, a call to prayer for the honest, people who showed no deference to breeding, manners, or detachment. They didn't care for detachment. Ideas and learning should excite, should make you angry or elated, and why not show that?

Of course she was going to champion me. How many deserving stars can there be in Kensington? she had asked. She couldn't do otherwise. And of course her mother would resist. Is that what you mean? her mother had asked me. Is that what I'd meant when I said the judges were probably spreading the awards around these days? But how to respond, how to answer a direct question that is obviously unwanted? Uncompromising honesty or diplomacy? They are beautiful, these people, when they speak. Their conversation is a landscape of byways forking at every step, this choice between the direct and the delicate, between what is meant and what is polite, and they are beautiful because they can go the polite way but to the discerning ear make themselves understood.

The same choice—how to respond, to fight or play, defuse or discharge—such a choice had confronted me at the interview, before Court of Appeal judges, for the very award Mrs. Hampton-Wyvern was now discussing.

The interview had begun on a light note. I had arrived at the Inn of Court with only a minute to spare and was led straight to the interview rooms, without even time to leave my things at reception. The door was opened and I stepped into a large room with five judges sitting behind a long oak table, all white males. I clutched under my elbows a newspaper, my satchel, and a bottle of water.

The chairman, with a blazon of white hair and a kindly face, waved me in.

Do come in, he said, do come in. And do bring in your things, including that bottle of water—at least, I trust it's water.

Whatever it is, I replied, it's purely for medicinal purposes.

A ripple of laughter went through the panel of judges; the joke had an ingredient judges like, a reference to the outside world but incorporated as inside information, an in-joke, something breaking into the windowless courtrooms.

That was how it began, and the interview skipped along from there. I fielded question after question, including a couple about my academic background. The chairman mentioned that he knew two Court of Appeal judges who had studied mathematics as undergraduates, and I remember thinking it was splendid of this judge to say so. I believe this good man wanted me to understand that he wouldn't let an unconventional background stop me and nor should I.

But one judge remained silent through all this until near the end. This man leaned forward, looking vaguely distressed or perhaps only confused.

I'd like to ask you a question or two, if I may.

I nodded.

I see here that you live in Brixton. My son says he goes to Brixton from time to time, and he tells me that on every street corner there are young men, black men, I might say, but that's beside the point, many of them selling marijuana. He says it goes on all the time and that it's part of the culture. It does sound dreadful to me. Now what do you say about that? How does one, in fact, respond to that?

There are other ways he might have framed his question. He might, for instance, have asked me about policing policy and whether a so-called light-touch approach could be justified. Should the police turn a blind eye and concentrate on greater crimes, or is marijuana a gateway drug and its sale therefore to be checked?

But he didn't ask me that. Instead, speaking with a distaste that I was sure the other judges had noticed, he told me about his son's experience, he told me how black men sold drugs on the street, a part of their culture—did he sneer?—and he asked me how one responds to that.

It's difficult—isn't it?—to know exactly how to respond to that, I said.

The air had frozen, as if all the human muscles in that room had tightened, save those of the judge who'd asked the question. The one beside him had turned his head toward him, but he had also tilted away, lifting his chin, as if to a put a distance between the two of them. I looked at each member of the panel, one by one.

As illuminating as an anecdote might be, I said, there's no substitute for evidence. I'd need a lot more facts before I could even begin to tackle the question of how one might respond.

A moment passed in total silence, just long enough for the chairman to recognize an opportunity and jump in. Excellent, he said. Absolutely right.

In the drawing room of Penelope Hampton-Wyvern's home, everything—the lines of every piece of furniture, the ironwork and porcelain of every lamp, the fabric of the curtains, the stately presence of the Bösendorfer, the carved frames of the pictures and photos, even the Bath Oliver biscuits—spoke of an observance of unwritten rules. The presence of these things may appear to bespeak the expression of conscious taste, of desires and choices, but look closely at the preferences. What autonomy of choice do you have if your preferences are so obviously conditioned by your social milieu? Where is your autonomy if what you choose is what you are bound to have chosen?

I have always felt that choice is a rarity in life, that it lies in wait in the crevices of time, to surprise us when we seem to have the least room to maneuver. The grand architecture of our time on earth bears no choice at all, no trace of will, free or otherwise. Without our will we are born and against it we die. We do not choose our mothers, any more than they choose the children they bear. We do not choose the circumstances of our parents, the home and inheritance, the unearned talents, or the circumstances of our formative infant years when our brains congeal into a steady state and the neural pathways set us on the course of our lives. Most of the time, we heed unwritten rules. They may be rules of culture and conditioning, patterns imprinted on the tender firmament of youth, or they may be the rules knotted into our brains, woven with DNA by our biological parents, but they are all still rules by which we live, by which we are governed. That notion of choice as we move through the world, the free will that we claim so proudly, is only the reflection of the body's foregone direction, an image in the distorting mirror of ego, a trick of the light.

To answer Penelope honestly or to do so diplomatically, that was the question, the choice, before me. My mischievous casual remark—*maybe their lordships felt pressured to spread these awards around a little*—had now assumed proportions much greater than I'd intended. I was regretting it and was searching for an escape route, a form of words that would draw a line without embarrassing anyone.

These days, I said, there's a lot of talk about political correctness, and there are people who say they feel pressured into saying and doing what's politically correct. It would be presumptuous of me to imagine that the judges would be immune to the pressures that others are complaining about.

Anyhow, I continued, it's just an obscure award in a tiny corner of the world—although I'd be lying if I said I wasn't pleased to get it.

I maintained my stupid smile throughout. Mrs. Hampton-Wyvern smiled, too, but Emily did not.

We had been sitting for the better part of an hour when there came from the hall the shuffle of feet, the tinkle of keys, and the click of the front door shutting. Until that moment, I had assumed, as I think I mentioned, that there was no one else in the house. The sounds from the hall were undoubtedly audible to everyone, yet no one responded, no one acknowledged my puzzlement let alone offered an explanation.

If I were to trace my concerns at the time about Emily to any particular moment, I could point to a number of earlier episodes that had already seeded a disquiet, but tea that day had the distinction of throwing a new light on her.

I had at the very beginning taken Emily's reserve as English feminine modesty. I had already seen something of the way certain English women understated their intelligence, especially where it might show them to be better than or the equal of the men around them, as if such exhibition were lacking in grace. But this, my first mistake, was replaced by another when I began to wonder if perhaps there was something *I* was saying or doing, or not saying or not doing, that caused Emily to be so unforthcoming about herself and accounted for her furtive absences. From time to time I have thought that somehow I might be responsible for hurtful behavior on the part of those to whom I have given a hold on my heart. It makes one wary.

That afternoon, however, it dawned on me that Emily's secretiveness might be a trait that attached to the whole family, so engrained as seldom to surface into conscious choice, a secretiveness that skirted the field of vision of the family itself. They appeared suddenly as people who had sealed something in a long-forgotten vault, and I remembered an afternoon some years earlier, before I met Emily, when, as a tourist, I visited a castle in Niedersachsen. Specifically, I remembered the swell of emotion, which was to subdue me for the remainder of the day, as I came upon a blue braided velvet rope hung between brass stanchions, cordoning off the part of the castle retained in use by the incumbent aristocrat, his children, and his grandchildren. I stood in the vast hall, by the chrome pillars, my fingertips touching the rope. On the other side there was a huge wooden door slightly ajar. The rope kept visitors within the public precincts of this stately home, but it also rendered those same public areas public, not private, not *home*. The thought aroused compassion. The selfsame rope, it seemed to me, cordoned off a family, a privileged one perhaps but a family nonetheless, and now these people went about their lives in one corner of the house slowly forgetting—or hoping to forget— the home they had known.

I wonder now if, in their six stories and endless space, Emily's family had not cordoned off parts of themselves. Doors opening and closing; the liminal presence of unspoken affairs; the air of good manners in which honest interest in the truth of people seemed vulgar; and above all the exquisite handling of information, its measured withholding and release, like an inch on the reins of a dressage horse—all these things were of the essence to the conduct of their lives, and into this milieu and its ways I was admitted and even welcomed.

10

In the Time of the Breaking of Nations

The spreading of the Gospel, regardless of the motives or the integrity or the heroism of some of the missionaries, was an absolutely indispensable justification for the planting of the flag. Priests and nuns and schoolteachers helped to protect and sanctify the power that was so ruthlessly being used by people who were indeed seeking a city, but not one in the heavens, and one to be made, very definitely, by captive hands. —James Baldwin, *The Fire Next Time*

He didn't even hear what I said; he was absorbed already in the dilemmas of democracy and the responsibilities of the West; he was determined—I learned that very soon—to do good, not to any individual person, but to a country, a continent, a world.

—Graham Greene, *The Quiet American*

Zafar is standing outside the UN compound in Kabul. With a pinched flick from his fingers, he sends a cigarette butt flying into the night air, and when it grazes the ground he watches it release flecks and sparks of red. I watched the cigarette disintegrate, said Zafar, embers scattering over the courtyard, as I gathered confidence to take on the main building. The doors opened into a wide lounge area, a very large room with sofas and armchairs arranged in clusters, brightly lit with fluorescent tubes on the ceiling and floor lamps around the edges. I counted five large television screens hanging high on the walls. All set to CNN, they were streaming images of destruction—volume turned down, closed captions on. The place was buzzing with people. There was grave discussion, drinking, too, of course, but the main activity was talk: serious faces leaning forward. Nicky Amory and the group I came with were not in this room. The bar she'd mentioned must be elsewhere, through the archway in the corner, from which music blared, rhythm and blues, or was it hip-hop?

And in between the beats an African American voice, a black man's voice, the only black man in the room, a disembodied black man amid white faces and white forearms, a white mass.

Which is when I saw Emily. She was sitting in a square arrangement of sofas and armchairs around a sprawling coffee table, every seat occupied by an admirer, each with a drink in front of him. Even though she was facing the main door, she would not have seen me, for Emily's attention never strayed from the narrow cone of her own field of vision. It is a strange thing, but such little details, knowledge of how another person perceives the world—you pick them up when you spend time with a person. They are inferences, of course, and they could be wrong, but you go with them not because you need to but because you cannot but do so. She was talking, and talking narrowed her perspective even more. I stepped to one side, suddenly conscious of obstructing the doorway. She was explaining something, holding court, her body as still as a village green on a summer's evening. When Emily spoke she never hurried, never that ripple of urgency a voice has when a speaker knows that others are waiting to speak. On the coffee table in front of her lay her notepad with her lists of things to cover—Emily, the consummate list ticker, every advance marked off, progress by bullet points. We are a species in love with lists. We even live our lives by the lists of others, the orderings of our days: the Ten Commandments, the Five Pillars of Islam, the Four Noble Truths, the Seven Habits of Highly Successful People. Everything is made simple by lists, made digestible, parceled into manageable units, reducing the complexity of the world into the simplicity of a line. The triumph of possibility, of finding our feet by looking for them, looking downward—the victory of modest means over the terror of a world lying beyond reach, surpassing human understanding.

And now those slender fingers, fingers that seemed graceless on the strut of a violin, now they pick off the arguments as she makes them to the ring of men. Her face, the picture of seriousness, bears the gravity of the matters at hand. It was a face with a job to do. Where in the world could confidence be demanded more than in the private chambers of their hearts, these white males doing the Lord's work, liberals with the mission of development, on the side of the angels even as their way to work was cleared by the devil himself? It was 2002 and reports were being written, fact-finding missions were finding facts, and plans were being laid. No effort was spared to make these plans, the plans of the United Nations Assistance Mission in Afghanistan, the plans of the provisional government, the plans of NGOs, great plans for the poor Afghanis, the poor bastards—all the world had plans, plans to be implemented for that beleaguered people whom history had dealt such a dreadful hand, don't you know?

I see her now, holding forth in her quiet, feminine, and very British way, those men hanging on her every word, her authority in part borrowed from Mohammed Jalaluddin; she represents him, his chef de cabinet in a cabinet of two, and he the most senior Afghani in the international development community. Where is he now? At a meeting with the UN representative Lakhdar Brahimi or perhaps he's with Hamid Karzai. She is his absent voice and she can be relied on to stay on message as surely as a list can be trusted to hold its course. There she is offering a smile to a fellow, and it is that superb smile of the Empire's benevolence, an insincere smile though she does not know it. Everyone is now playing the game, and this is the board, this room a square on the board, and because they do not see the rules that they have internalized, because a Hercules aircraft brought them from Spangdahlem, Ramstein, or Brize Norton, because they are all part of history here, in the making, making it, because they are so humbled by the great task at hand of building a nation, of helping Afghanis rebuild their nation, because so many have died—what can be more real? They're playing the game as it's always been played: the game of Empire and Ego. See? It sounds like a board game already.

One or two are jotting down notes. One man takes a sip from a tumbler with ice—whisky, I think to myself, whisky in Kabul—and accidentally dribbles a little onto his shirt. He glances at Emily—first and only at Emily—to see if she's noticed. He is embarrassed. But has he any shame about drinking whisky in Kabul? Do these people believe it was only Talibs who held to the faith of their fathers? Were the Afghanis merely oppressed townsfolk and they the cavalry? These fucking people. By what right?

They are the offspring of civilizations that have promoted individual rights, the rights of the self, yet establishing the limits of the private sphere not at the line where skin meets air but outside the body, not at the point where the fist and another's nose are separated by a breath of air, not even before the thumping vibrations of the air meet the ears of the natives, thrusting one man's private sphere, his black man's music, into the native's, whose private sphere is his tribe, which, unlike his European liberal counterpart, is more than himself. That's what my liberal friends have done. And I see them sitting there now. Their repugnance at the unequal treatment of women, their repugnance at the treatment of homosexuals, these could not be accepted as just that: repugnance. They cannot abide *Let them be* but fight their wars of reconstruction to the banner of *Let him be* or *Let her be*. They have built this monument to the European enlightenment, the West's enlightenment, and they call it *human* rights, and on that rock they have founded their new humanity, and in its name they act with clear conscience. Bush and the neocons— God bless them—might have wanted their natural resources and strategic positioning, but the liberals were always after their souls.

I knew Zafar could be very animated. I had seen it when he talked mathematics. But I'd never known him to have any strong opinions on politics, or at least I'd never heard him express such. Yet now he seemed possessed. I still cannot quite say why, but I wanted to interrupt him, perhaps to break his stride, pull him back, keep him from going off the rails. Or perhaps to save myself from becoming too uncomfortable.

Are you uncomfortable? he asked me, breaking off from his flow.

Why should I be?

I meant, in your seat. You're fidgeting.

No. I'm fine. I'm fine. Please, go on.

Zafar leaned back, looking unconvinced.

And now these heroes, he continued, they want to refashion the world in their image. They can do this only as long as the world that they are on the very cusp of changing is seen as a reliquary of humanity. This is the Orient they need to imagine. They paint pictures of intense color and beauty without depth. They charm us, but they charm themselves first. The fluttering kites, a caravan under a vermilion sky, and the night train over a chasm, children with eyes of moon, silk roads, and the derring-do of Burtons and Lawrences. Their coin is the ecstasy of beauty, and with it they buy their right in the world.

Everything seen by the West is seen through the West. The Western reader, who is already the most adventurous person in the world, is afraid, for he has been taught to fear the Orient. This state—a mix of charm, mystique, and danger: the ingredients of riotously good sex—is the guarantor and license of military, economic, and cultural enterprises that reduce the Orient. It is the basis for creating fear.

When I was a child, our first home in England was a squat in Marylebone, in a part of London that is now rather chic. We lived in a condemned building, which no one could be bothered to demolish. We lived in two rooms—a kitchen and the other room—in the basement with an outside lavatory. I can remember the place vividly, everything about it, the rubble in the yard, through which we picked our way to the lavatory, the single room almost wholly taken up with two beds. But while I can remember the kitchen, the two-ring electric hob and the secondhand fridge that alternately rattled and gurgled, while I remember that side of the room where our food was prepared, a few square feet, I can recall nothing of the other half. Yet my memory has not failed me. I have no visual memory of the side below the small window at the far end—*far* for a boy—because whenever I entered the kitchen I kept my eyes away from it; I never looked that way. There is nothing for my eyes to remember. From time to time, I might catch a scuffling sound, or from a scurry or scratch I would see a gray thread, a spark of static, at the perimeter of my vision. If I was in the bedroom, I might hear my mother now and again going at the rats with a broom. I was terrified of them, and the only response was not to look. This is how fear works. It transforms our perceptual field. It changes how we allow ourselves to experience the world—in order to circumvent the fear.

Zafar's mysterious East was, if I understood him correctly, a conjured enchantment of the West. But I found it hard to follow him. Even so, I wonder now if in fact Zafar had undertaken his own enchantment, if he'd endowed Emily with this same charm, mystique, and danger, had given her qualities that had no more real presence than as the bare bones upon which to hang a fantasy. From what I knew of her, growing up in overlapping social circles, she was if not ordinary then unexceptional, other than perhaps in having an academic aptitude. What took me by surprise was the note of jealousy entering Zafar's narrative; I would never have put him down as the jealous sort. Listening to him discuss

Emily, listening to the account of Kabul, of him standing in that room with a view of Emily, I wondered whether he had in fact loved her.

I see Emily, continued Zafar, but she does not notice me, and she won't unless I do something. To my right is a pile of magazines—*The Economist*, *The Atlantic Monthly*, and others. I pick up the nearest and walk right up behind the chair opposite her, outside the circle of chairs and sofa, this ring with Emily its leader. I open the magazine and look her way and catch her eye as she looks up, and I look away. Why do I look away? Emily will not leap up and come to me. I know that. Emily will not exclaim "Zafar!" at her sheer surprise to see me there. I was in Kabul, she knew, staying at AfDARI, she possibly knew, but what was I doing here at the UN bar? There will be a break, a pause, a hesitation, maybe not so small in fact, and the men will look up, too, because they will follow her eyes. You know that we can't help that? It's a physical response that is virtually impossible to suppress. But because I look away before they look up, I retain anonymity and they cannot identify me as the man whom Emily then ignores. I look away to save myself that little shame.

I walk to the archway, toward the funnel of noise from the bar. Her eyes won't follow me, because that would signal to her ring of admirers the cause of her momentary distraction. But she'll come, in her own time. She'll come and find me.

I had started my journey a week earlier. In 2002, the UN rapporteur on human rights in Afghanistan was a chap called Dr. Hassan Kabir, who was based in Dhaka, Bangladesh. The "Doctor" honorific and his name were inseparable. In South Asian circles, his career and history commanded awe: sometime fellow of All Souls, once a partner in a giant international law firm, and in his day instrumental in the founding of the modern state of Bangladesh as an author of its constitution. Of the eight or so who put their pens to the document, all but Kabir were to perish over the years in various coups and assassinations. Wit and cunning, they say. I could never utter his name without thinking of that other doctor, Henry Kissinger, which is the best irony since Kissinger spared little effort to thwart the emergence of the new nation. Perhaps I think of Kissinger because political divides are thinner than others, social ones, for instance. National interests don't vary, only nations do.

What happened in the bar? I asked, interrupting Zafar.

I'm telling you what happened. What do you think I'm doing?

Zafar got up and walked over to the drinks cabinet and pulled out a bottle of whisky and two glasses. He set them down in front of us, poured himself a drink, and pushed the bottle toward me. I didn't pour.

Two weeks before Kabul, in Dhaka, Dr. Hassan Kabir asked me if I'd consider accompanying him on a visit to Afghanistan; he needed someone to take notes and generally undertake tasks while there. I said I'd consider it, and he asked me to give him an answer in two days. But the following morning I received a call from his office, informing me that Dr. Kabir had been called to Geneva and New York and would be unable to make the trip to Afghanistan; also a visa had been arranged for me through the offices of the Afghani ambassador in Geneva and that arrangements for flights to Kabul had also been made. Given how keen Dr. Kabir seemed to be that I should go, I felt a refusal would have marred my relationship with him. Influential people seem to think that helping them would be an honor.

I thought you went to Afghanistan because of Emily. Didn't you say she called you?

The call from her came the following day, but I didn't let on that I was already set to go to Kabul for the UN rapporteur. I didn't want to give her an excuse not to come through on her claims that there was work for me to do. I wanted to see what she would organize, what kind of introductions she'd make, if she thought I'd come to Kabul at her behest.

But why did you feel you needed to test her like this?

If she thought that I'd come to Kabul because she had wanted my help and I arrived to find there was nothing for me to do, then I'd know that she had asked me to come because she wanted to see me. How perverse is that? The idea that I could rely on her unreliability and see in it the intimation of love. Since when was unreliability a virtue? When did it ever do any good?

On the PIA connecting flight from Dubai to Islamabad, as I settled into my seat, pressed in against the window, a young man sat down beside me, tall and rather burly. Unavoidably his forearms extended over my own armrests. Mohsin Khalid introduced himself to me, *at your service*, in a thick Pakistani accent, and beamed from under a Red Sox cap.

Do you like flying? he asked.

Not particularly, I replied.

I hate it, he continued. Which is funny, to say the least.

I looked at him.

I climb mountains, you see. I don't mind heights at all. But only if I can look down. Funny, isn't it?

I smiled back at him. Would you like the window seat?

Oh, no. I need the space of an aisle seat. Besides, it's not the same, looking out a window and looking down the side of a mountain.

I suppose it isn't.

I climb mainly in the Karakoram, but I've done others. Everest, also. Always impresses the Westerners when I say that. But the idiots don't know Everest is easy compared to K2, a climber's mountain. You know of course that the *K* in K2 means *Karakoram*?

I do know that, as it happens.

Of course you do. K2 is a fucker of a mountain, bhai sahib, oh, yes. Everest is bigger, but K2 is much tougher, a savage mountain any road up. But to the Western mind, big is all that counts, and the bigger the better. Americans especially. That's all they want to know.

Did you go up from the Chinese side?

Very good. You know your geography.

I like maps.

As a matter of fact, I have climbed it from both.

Is it hard for a Pakistani to get into China—so close to the border, I mean?

In life, all things are possible. Did you know that we mountaineers have smaller amygdalae than most people and therefore have a smaller fear response?

Really?

So you know what the amygdala is, then? he asked.

Something like broccoli but in the brain, right?

I have no idea, but I think you might be right.

How do you know this about mountaineers? I asked him.

About the amygdala?

I nodded.

I read it. In one of those, those . . . what do they call them?

Books?

Precisely! I read it in a book. Although, as far as I can tell, everything and his uncle seems to be put at the door of the amygdala.

'Twas ever thus.

So where are you traveling to? he asked.

Same as you. Islamabad, I replied.

Of course, he chuckled. I'm sorry, I meant what is your final destination?

Kabul.

Afghanistan, the biggest mountain of all. Good luck. For whom do you work?

I trained as a lawyer.

They need lawyers?

I laughed.

I'm sorry, he said. I didn't mean to be impertinent.

Not at all, I reassured him. You know the joke? What do you call five hundred lawyers at the bottom of a lake?

I don't know, he replied.

A good start.

He laughed, and we passed the flight in amiable conversation. He discussed various aspects of mountaineering. I asked questions and he obliged with answers. When I asked him how he made a living at it, he explained that he didn't.

From time to time, he said, I will guide parties on climbing expeditions. That brings in a little.

So what do you do?

I take them up. They have money and egos but no sense—

I mean, what do you do when you're not rappelling the north face?

Ah. By day, I work in the family import-export business.

What do you import and export?

Anything. That's the nature of the business. If we focused on one thing, we'd get caught up in someone's supply chain and inevitably we'd get taken for a ride, and we don't want to be held hostage, do we? So we import and export as requirements dictate.

Before we disembarked, Khalid expressed his pleasure at meeting me and gave me his business card. That might have been the last I saw of him, but half an hour later, as I emerged from the airport terminal onto a bustling outdoor concourse, where the overwhelming light had me reaching for my sunglasses, there was Khalid waving to me from the road-side. He offered me a ride to my hotel. When I explained that I had not made any reservations, he exclaimed, Oh, well! It's settled, then. You will be my guest.

We arrived at a large house in the diplomatic enclave, below the Marghalla Hills. Mature climbers covered the walls of the building and rain had smeared the white stucco, leaving black patches and vertical runs of gray. There was nothing of the modern ostentation of houses in afflu-ent neighborhoods in South Asia, none of the ornate iron gates or wide jutting terraces above the ground floor. Instead, the two stories of the house, its tall windows, and its aspect onto the road were all arranged, I thought, with such simplicity as to suggest that the house must once have stood in larger grounds.

The driveway took us under an archway of overhanging trees, down an incline, and around the back. The car had barely come to a stop when the door opened and an orderly addressed me. Please, sahib, he said, ges-turing the way into the house. I was led through a spacious hall—it had a wide stairway—and was shown into a long, airy lounge. I saw no one else. There was an arrangement of sofas and side tables, all in cane, and some rugs, and a coffee table with a small pile of chess books. I looked for the open chess set. Tucked away in the far corner of the room, which was open to light on two sides, between two opposing chairs, was a table giving off the dull gray of cast iron. Something at the center of that table was covered in a piece of cloth embroidered with golden stitching. There was no lamp on the table, nor any nearby, and the words *chess by daylight* came to my mind, and the words seemed curious to me, carrying some incalculable significance.

Here and there were rugs. In the corner of one, I noticed—because I was looking for it—the tiny white square of nylon that bears washing instructions.

The walls were adorned with framed photographs, mainly of military personnel, some taken outdoors, others against a studio background. One picture in particular caught my eye, squat and wide angled, reminding me of matriculation photographs. When I drew up close enough, I saw that it was exactly so, a photograph from Exeter College, Oxford, class of 1964. Next to it was a photograph of soldiers, taken, according to the caption, at Sandhurst, the British army's officer training center, where the future senior ranks of the armies of the colonies and postcolonies were sent, and are sometimes still sent to this day.

There was one dark face in the Oxford photograph, floating among rows of white faces, and, true enough, this face was also in the second photograph. I then heard a voice.

You're an Oxford man, aren't you?

I turned. Before me was the man in the photograph, much older, but the same man.

I studied there, I replied.

But you're not an Oxford man?

His furrowed brow emphasized the question but gave no suggestion of genuine puzzlement. He had the fallen shoulders of old age that made me think of young men who stand tall, as if to exceed their own height. A sheer forehead rose above fulsome gray eyebrows before crashing into thick white hair, swept back, probably with the Brylcreem that is so popular in South Asia. An immaculate mustache framed the judgmental tilt to a robust jaw. He wore a gray Nehru suit and dark leather sandals.

If going there to study makes me an Oxford man, then that I am, I replied.

But in spite of all temptations, to belong to other nations, he remains an Englishman!

You know your Gilbert and Sullivan.

It's not mine. In the army, the officers used to play bridge, you know? Mad about the game. They used to ask me: Mushtaq, old chap, why aren't you a bridge man? I'm a chess man, I'd say. So are you an Oxford man?

Is a man who climbs mountains a mountaineer or a mountain man? I replied.

Quite. Hello, Zafar, old boy—may I call you Zafar?

Of course, I replied.

Pleased to make your acquaintance. Colonel Sikander Ali Mushtaq, retired.

How do you do? I said, taking his extended hand.

Your mountaineer friend—my nephew, by the way—has gone off on some business of his own, but he may join us for supper. Do you play?

Chess?

I learned the game as a boy from a friend, he said. He played very slowly and seemed ever calm and composed in the face of all the trials that came his way. He had a hard life. Father was a bastard. Chess teaches patience. Every game is different. A game can be deeply unsatisfying, dissatisfying, even as it delivers your triumph. Making victory alone your goal is to make failure of the worst kind a foregone conclusion.

How so? I asked.

It is an obtuse notion that a given game of chess stands alone and apart, that it is free of past and future, an egoistic notion that the game at hand is the one game that matters. Only arrogance can allow such a view. What matters is the beat and rhythm, the heave and ho of game after game, so that the cumulative history shows one the texture of what might be, of what is inherent in the thirty-two pieces and the sixty-four squares and, most of all, the board. Some people think chess is about the pieces. It is always about the board. One begins with the board half covered and half open, and as one progresses, one reveals its mysteries. But only game after game. Mark my words, Zafar. Only game after game. Do please take a seat. I shall have a whisky. May I pour you one?

Thank you.

He opened the door and called out for two whiskys, and with the door open I could hear the hum of servants.

Interesting photos, don't you think? Oxford and Sandhurst, continued the colonel, emblems of Empire, and there we were, the former colonial subjects, sitting at the feet of dons who trained the colonial administrators. In 1835, Lord Macaulay, as I expect you know, wrote in his famous paper to the British Parliament about the superiority of the Western canon. In it, Macaulay writes a passage that I have never forgotten since I first set eyes upon it: *We must at present do our best to form a class who may be interpreters between us and the millions whom we govern—a class of persons, Indian in blood and color, but English in tastes, in opinions, in morals, and in intellect.*

The colonel paused, presumably to let the quotation take effect.

We have never overcome the sense of inferiority, he continued. Our elites study at their universities in their language. Marx called Macaulay the systematic falsifier of history. Do you know what I studied at Oxford? History. But whose bloody history? Theirs. We bought their values wholesale in exchange for our dignity, grafted their subject-ruler mentality onto our own so that these countries of ours are incapable of anything like democracy. Millions go starving while the rich and powerful in Pakistan, India, and Bangladesh lord over them, disdaining them and denying them. We mimic the Westerners though we hate them.

Even as his language conveyed emotion, there was a deliberate care in his tone. His speech was the sound of a mind at work, but there was also a stillness behind it, like the calm that broods over an island before a storm.

I had taken to this fellow—with caution, of course—and in the polite way one gives a confirming opinion in amiable company, I offered a thought.

When a jihadi, I ventured—holding the word for a moment to allow its weight to fall—calls a Westerner a devil, it seems to me that he acknowledges the power of the West, for the devil is a mighty figure, a fallen angel but an angel all the same.

Indeed, said the colonel, holding my eyes with a curiosity that lasted forever.

But, my dear fellow, he said, breaking the sudden intervening stillness, your metaphor demonstrates the point in a way you might not have intended, for you know your Christian, er, Christian divinities better than your Islamic ones.

Fallen jinn, I said, remembering something I had read somewhere.*

Quite. Humans and the jinn have free will; angels do not—they are

---

*Christianity and Islam share much theologically. They have the same prophets. Jesus occupies an esteemed position, as the Messiah who will return at the end of days—in Islamic theology. But the devil in Islam is a fallen jinn; the jinns were beings of "smokeless flame," a race of supernatural beings with special powers, distinct from angels, created alongside man but invisible to men. Apparently, the English word *genie* has common roots with the Arabic *jinni*, as do the words *gene* and *genius*. In Zafar's notebooks are these lines: *What would etymology have looked like to the speakers of Old French, late Middle English, Latin, or Ancient Greek, had there been records to draw on? Would we today still think of European languages as having been born in Europe?*

only instruments of God's will. But the jinn also embody power, so your point stands, mutatis mutandis.

I'm obliged, I said with a smile. Macaulay's Minute, I continued, was first and foremost an argument for English as the language of instruction in schools in British India. It's about extending the writ of an official language.

Language indeed, said the colonel, glancing at me.

The reference was not lost on the colonel, said Zafar, that language was ever an instrument of oppression, and that he needn't go back a hundred years or a continent away to understand this.*

My dear boy, said the colonel at length, you have a sensitivity to history

---

*I came across the following material in Zafar's notebooks, which, judging by the surrounding matter, was written long before Zafar's conversation with the colonel. I assume it's of Zafar's own composition; there is no attribution. It's no surprise that behind anything any of us says there may stand a whole catalog of things unsaid. But what I find unsettling about this extract is that it provides a window into how much Zafar restrained himself when he talked, a glimpse at that catalog of things unsaid:

If in 1947 the partition of India created two new nations, the smaller could only have been conceived in the madness of those times, a bird of two wings and no body. And if West Pakistan and East Pakistan were two regions united by a common faith, then they were also two peoples divided by different languages. Even the name of the new nation, the most loyal expression of a people's language, its label, was an act of exclusion and subordination. The prefabrication of one Choudhary Rahmat Ali: *P*, Punjab, *A*, Afghania, *K*, Kashmir, and the -stan, the annex of land, land of the PAK, with an anaptyxic epenthetic *i*, don't you know, just to root the acronym in the land, all of which made a neat little pun, Land of the Pure, the Muslims, while it brought together its constituent peoples. Only it didn't. Where were the Bengalis? Where was the *B*? One thousand miles of India between them. Surely not left out merely because the pun wouldn't work but never conceived as a piece of the country, a part of the main. Next, in 1948, the West made Urdu the sole official language of the two parts. Imagine that, making Urdu—alien in speech and script—the only official language of the Eastern part, whose people were among the most attached of any to their mother tongue. They rebelled against it, and on February 21, 1952, things came to a head in clashes between the West Pakistani military and students at Dhaka University. Many died. This is even before things fell apart, before the war of liberation in 1971. To this day, Bangladesh marks the date, known as Language Martyrs Day, as a public holiday. In fact, that is admirable but does not come without a cost. I fought in 1971. I don't propose to insult you by rehearsing the debate about numbers killed and so on. Nor would I dare to suggest that all that is by the by, for nothing falls by the by that we do not make it do so. It is not enough simply to say that we made mistakes. That can never be enough. But where does that leave us?

There was silence, broken only by the arrival of whisky.

Let me speak, continued the colonel, about Reagan's mad dog Colonel Gaddafi. In his heyday, the old Libyan rogue was leader of anti-Western sentiment, the champion of the third world, but look at how he dressed, how his own army was fitted out. Why is it we all wear Western military uniforms? We hate the bastards and would bayonet them given half the chance, but we button up in their shirts and tie our laces in their boots. You studied—

Mathematics, I said. But as I did so, I had the impression that rather than answering a question, I had preempted him.

---

in 2000, UNESCO made that date, February 21, International Mother Language Day. Who noticed? Who cared?

Over the years I have had the same dealing with Pakistani cabdrivers. There I am, riding in a cab in London or New York, and because I am interested in the migrations of cabdrivers, these people, themselves so often migrants, whose job it is to take others from one place to another, I ask the driver where he's from. Or perhaps I ask because I want the fight. The Pakistani driver answers, and after a quick look in the rearview mirror he asks me the same. From Bangladesh, I say, adding that I spent half my life in the West. We are from the same country! We are brother Muslims! exclaims the Pakistani driver in the last English he thinks he'll be using with this customer before breaking into Urdu. I have to interrupt him to say that I don't understand a word of that language, though I do, and I ask him if he speaks Bengali. No, they say, laughing. No, they say with a horrible laugh, as if the idea were ridiculous to all. Why is it that they laugh? Then they'll tell me that I should learn to speak Urdu. Should you, I retort, speak Bengali? They laugh. You do know, I say, that Bengali is the fifth most commonly spoken language in the world? You do know that wars are fought over language, wars in which millions die? They shut up for the rest of the journey.

At least, this is what I imagine saying.

A splendid subject, an education in thinking, without the encumbrance of knowledge. Tell me, Zafar, my boy, what takes you to Kabul?

I thought you'd never ask, I said.

Now that, young man, is the first untruth you've told me.

Looking back, I am better able to see the change in Zafar's exposition, particularly as he started on those turbulent times with Emily. But despite my growing impression that there was something he was not talking about, something he was skirting around, I could not but be struck by how much about himself he was also sharing. At first, I saw it as an enormous change in the man I knew, but that notion did not survive reflection. What presumption is involved in attributing change to him when all that can be said is that I had come to know something about him that I had not known before? One ventures, therefore, that what one takes to be a change in another person is in fact only an improvement of one's own understanding of that person, or that what we thought we knew is shown to be a false presumption of our own making. It might even be the object's perception of a change in the subject, *the observed's* perception of a change in *the observer*, that permits *the observed* to behave in a way that had hitherto been suppressed—did Zafar feel I could now listen when he had before felt I couldn't? Might the only real change to have taken place be a change in myself? If such a possibility is disconcerting, one must ask: Why?

I need to go to bed, Zafar said.

He looked exhausted.

But there are so many questions. Who was this colonel? What did you say to him? Did you stay there that night?

Yes, that evening I stayed as a guest of the colonel. He was hosting a dinner party, to which he invited me. As if he thought he was addressing my concerns, the colonel said that his guests were house-trained and would refrain from asking me why I was there or where I was going, though they might ask where I was coming from. Very un-American, the colonel had remarked.

And the UN? I asked Zafar.

We'll come to all that tomorrow. I must sleep.

At that, Zafar stood, picked up his glass, and downed the rest of his whisky.

I listened to his slow steps receding up the stairs. It was early December, and in the few months he'd been staying with me, I'd grown accustomed to the presence of another person in the house. When Meena had been here, she'd been away so much, at work late, at work on the weekends, that the house had felt unoccupied. One's own presence was confirmation of emptiness. I liked having my friend around.

He occupied the space as if it were his own, and that pleased me so deeply I was afraid of it ending. He would come and go, sometimes disappearing for days, but he was a grown man and didn't need to be asked where he'd been. I did not want him to feel I was poking my nose in his business; he would tell me if he wanted me to know. But once, after an absence of a few days, I did ask him, and his glance showed his surprise at my asking.

I was in Wales, he said.

We were sitting in my study. I had heard him entering the house, then his steps going up the stairs—taking his bag to his room, I thought—his steps coming down, and then the tinkle of glass in the kitchen. Zafar had ordered a crate of champagne the week he arrived. He came into the study, bottle of champagne and two flutes in hand, where I had been sitting in the armchair, leafing through the *FT*, finding nothing more to read. I took my feet off the ottoman.

After opening the bottle, pouring two drinks, and handing me one, he parked himself at the desk and pulled a coaster onto the green tooled leather surface.

Cheers! I said.

To life! he replied.

I never heard him say that in other company. I suppose he might have done so when I wasn't around, but I like to think not. One takes such tokens of affection as one can find.

What's in Wales? I asked.

Happy days. Good times.

You went there with Emily?

Yes, he said, looking away.

At the beginning?

Yes.

And did you get what you went for? I mean this time.

I wanted to see what effect returning would have, what I might feel.

I'm sorry, Zafar.

No. It's quite all right. I stayed in the same cozy little inn, in the same room above the inn's wood-paneled drawing room, and I lay on the same endless bed, surrounded by the fireplace, the tasseled rug, and a Queen Anne dresser, where she sat and fixed herself in the morning. I felt nothing. It was as if someone else had been there. Not me.

Zafar was quiet again. And again, the question came back to me: Did he love her? Was it difficult for him to face—to face what? He was sad; it was in his eyes and mouth, which now looked unfamiliar, as if he'd pulled on a mask or pulled one off. The muscles around the face were slack, which is when perhaps emotion in its retreat lets go the reins.

There's a line, he said, in Graham Greene's *Travels with My Aunt*: *It is well to have a few memories of extravagance in store for hard times.*

Was Wales an extravagance?

He was wrong, you know?

Who?

Greene.

How's that? I asked.

It's the memory of extravagance that makes other times hard.

Are these hard times?

Do you remember those bops in college?

The ones you never went to?

The ones where half the men stood around watching everyone else dance.

Which means you were watching the men watching, I said.

What can I say? I like to watch.

Creep.

They always played the same tunes.

"Tainted Love" by Soft Cell and lots of Morrissey, I said.

And that tune, "Sit Down," wasn't it? Rather ironic for a dance song. By James.

Yes, of course, he said. What's so funny?

I was chuckling.

How do you know about stuff like that?

Zafar didn't respond, and I suppose that was fair enough.

There was a line in that song, he said presently, that comes back to me: *If I hadn't seen such riches I could live with being poor.*

Yes, if only you didn't know that the Joneses next door just got a top-of-the-line lawn mower.

Something like that.

11

Twenty Questions or Failing to Credit Risk

House prices have risen by nearly 25 percent over the past two years. Although speculative activity has increased in some areas, at a national level these price increases largely reflect strong economic fundamentals, including robust growth in jobs and incomes [and] low mortgage rates . . .

> —Ben Bernanke, chairman, President's Council of Economic Advisers, *Testimony Before the Joint Economic Committee of Congress,* October 20, 2005

I know that most men, including those at ease with problems of the greatest complexity, can seldom accept even the simplest and most obvious truth if it be such as would oblige them to admit the falsity of conclusions which they have delighted in explaining to colleagues, which they have proudly taught to others, and which they have woven, thread by thread, into the fabric of their lives.

> —Leo Tolstoy, *What Is Art?*

Overambitious projects may be objectionable in many fields, but not in literature. Literature remains alive only if we set ourselves immeasurable goals, far beyond all hope of achievement. Only if poets and writers set themselves tasks that no one else dares imagine will literature continue to have a function. Since science has begun to distrust general explanations and solutions that are not sectorial and specialized, the grand challenge for literature is to be capable of weaving together the various branches of knowledge, the various "codes," into a manifold and multifaceted vision of the world.   —Italo Calvino, "Multiplicity," translated by Patrick Creagh

My father loves playing board games. Most of all, he loves Chutes and Ladders, an utterly pointless game. I've never considered the matter before, but it occurs to me now that he would first have come across the game in Pakistan. In his boyhood there, if he had called it by an English name, then he would have known it as Snakes and Ladders. But there's the possibility he might have known it by an Urdu name, since the game, as I've discovered on looking it up, is actually ancient Indian in origin. My father and I first played it together in Princeton and so it is that we have always called it by its American name. I wonder these days about such small things, and wonder whether they mean anything or nothing at all. The best I can come up with is that their meaning might lie only in being noticed, in being allowed to be remembered.

Chutes and Ladders was for the home; on road trips, we used to play Twenty Questions, a word game known everywhere, I think. We played it in Princeton, as far back as I can remember, in the car on Saturday mornings on the way out to the baseball field. I would have twenty questions to figure out what he was; I could ask him if he was an animal or if he was a plant or if he was a sportsman or a scientist. Later, to the list of categories were added theorem and formula, my father taking care to distinguish the two. Twenty yes-or-no questions to work out who or what he was and then it would be his turn to ask the questions. I remember that it would take me a long time, before the game even started, just to decide who I was going to be, so many possibilities yet none coming to me, but my father always waited patiently.

I think of those Saturday drives often now, when I'm in the car, because of something he taught me on one of them. My father was a physical formula that day, which I ultimately failed to identify in twenty questions. It is a fundamental formula of classical physics that every schoolboy is taught: The kinetic energy of an object in motion is equal to half its mass multiplied by the square of its velocity. The mass of a thing, explained my father, was the same as its weight on earth. My father asked me what the energy of a car traveling at 30 miles per hour was, and I replied that I didn't know how much a car weighed. He said: Good point. I remember his affirmation, of course. Assume it's m, just m, he said. Half of m times 30 squared, which is half m times 900, which is 450 multiplied by m. Now tell me what the energy of a car traveling at 40 miles per hour is.

I worked it out, slowly, and I replied that it was 800 multiplied by m.

That's nearly twice the energy of the car traveling at 30 miles per hour, he said.

800 is *almost* twice 450, I said.

Correct. And it's energy that kills you, that's what does the damage, not the speed alone.

What do you mean?

A bit of dust that hits you at forty miles an hour will just bounce off. Now I read something yesterday that said the chances of a child dying after being hit by a car traveling at forty miles an hour are about eighty-five percent, but if the car's traveling at thirty miles an hour the chances are forty-five percent. How can there be such a big difference? After all, the speed increase is only one-third. You got it. It's because the energy is almost doubled.

I never thought of it as a lesson but as something my father found fascinating and wanted to share with me, and I now think of it every time I drive, if only in the moment it takes to move from third gear into fourth.

One day, when I could not have been more than fifteen—I had already gone up to Eton, so it must have been on short leave one weekend—I poked my head around the open door of his study. He was in his chair, turned toward the window, his back to his desk, with his feet up on the sill. He was looking out at the evening light. Even then I admired him for his work. Thinking is what he does, and he could do that facing a darkening sky.

Hey, buddy, he said with his back to me.

My father does not have a Pakistani accent, nor an American one. His voice, he says, is each accent inflected by the other, and because there aren't many Americans who settle in Pakistan and learn to speak Urdu as well as the natives, we can't know, he says, but maybe their accents land up somewhere next to his, even if geographically he himself is going the other way. His voice has a rich enveloping warmth, without the means ever to rise in anger. I suppose you might describe it as having the softness of cashmere silk, *Kashmir* silk, but I think now of Zafar and hold back: I think he would laugh at such description, and fair enough, I suppose.

I sat down on the ottoman—the same ottoman after which Zafar would ask on that very first day of his return into my life, and which he, of course, would later repair—my father's ottoman, which the dear man gave me years later when I set up home on my own. It was where I had sat as a little boy and where, at the age of fifteen and probably too big for it, I sat as he turned in his chair to face me with a bright smile.

We remember the things that in their time had a presence. There is no sensory faculty for the perception of voids, only clues by which to infer their existence, making them harder still to remember than to perceive.

On my visits home, my father never asked me on my first day back how school was going. Maybe on the second day, as that day was, or the third, if there was one, but never on the first day back. I see that now but never noticed it then.

I asked him what he was doing. He explained he was working on the spin of subatomic particles.

Which is, by the way, the sort of remark that's a real conversation stopper at dinner parties, causing my mother to roll her eyes for the benefit of guests, even if it was followed by a gesture of affection for my father.

What's that? I asked.

The spin?

I nodded.

It's a property of the particle. Just as people have properties, like compassion, mercy, love, and anger, particles have all sorts of properties. Electrical charge, mass, even color. And spin is another property. Except it isn't anything like the spin of a ball.

Then why call it spin?

Good question. I think the names physicists give correspond to things we can imagine in order to talk about something we can't imagine.

How do you know it's there, this spin?

That's the strangest part of it. It isn't there. In fact, spin comes into being only when we look for it. Until we do, it's not there.

I was puzzled. I must have looked puzzled.

Nature is mischievous. She plays tricks, explained my father. Remember our game of Twenty Questions?

Yes.

When we take measurements of a particle, it's as if we're asking the particle a question about what it is. Imagine the particle playing the game. Every time we ask a question—take a measurement or reading—the particle gives us an answer, yes or no, so that over twenty questions or twenty thousand we get a picture of what this thing is. Make sense?

I wasn't convinced.

Me neither, he added, but that's how I've been thinking about it.

Have you really been thinking about Twenty Questions?

As a matter of fact, I have.

My father chuckled. Let me tell you something about how I used to play the game, he said, not how I play it now, but how I played it back in Princeton. You used to take a long time deciding what you were before I could start asking questions.

I remember.

But I never did. I didn't take a moment. I cheated.

How?

I made it a rule to always answer your first three questions with a yes, a no, and a yes.

You mean you hadn't decided on what you were when you started your round?

I had no idea.

Are you serious?

I used to dress it up, of course, he continued. I'd umm and ahh just to give the right impression, but I didn't have a clue. But by the fourth question I had to think up what I might be, subject to the conditions set by my answers—yes, no, and yes—to your first three questions. It made it easier to get the game going and made it a little more interesting for me.

That sounds like fun.

Now imagine playing the game but answering every question randomly and then at the end, and only then, trying to figure out what you are.

But that could be impossible. What if your answers don't match anything in the world?

Maybe, he continued, but that's actually rather like what these subatomic particles do. We observe them, they give their answers, and we figure out their spin, even when all along they never had any such thing.

I didn't really grasp what all this meant—the physics eluded me—but I don't think my father expected me to understand. In fact, I think he wanted to convey how baffling these ideas were even to him, even as he lived to wrestle with them.

After supper that evening, my mother headed out to her class; she was ever diligent about her retraining as a psychotherapist and never missed a lesson, even when I was home during vacations. My father and I loaded the dishwasher and again sat down at the dining table with some ice cream.

Chutes and Ladders?

Sure, I said.

We often played after supper, though I understand—and understood even sometime in my boyhood—that men seek out excuses to ease conversation.

Let's play Twenty Questions also.

Twenty Questions first? I asked.

Let's play them at the same time.

I smiled at my father. It was my turn to play it as he once did: He might be asking the questions, twenty questions, but with this new version of the game, I would be the one working out who I was.

We played the two games slowly, switching from one to the other and with so many digressions as we played, conversations about this and that. We talked a little about my studies. I was doing well enough, I'd say, and mention my grades—I always did well enough, never more, and he might remark on the surprises that come from pushing oneself, remarks delivered with an abstraction that at once directed them nowhere or to himself but were shared for my benefit. I know that this quality about my father, the keenness of eye, for instance, for the links between things—the digressiveness was something that Zafar had as well. I know there was a similarity between them that must have drawn me to Zafar. There were wild differences, of course. My father was deeply interested in the politics of the world; in his beliefs he was a liberal through and through. But Zafar back then had little to say on such matters. Yet for all the differences, their similarities—the digressions, the wandering searches, the discernment of links—they were all comfortingly familiar to me the first time I talked to Zafar in the Junior Common Room of our college at Oxford.

In science, my father said, nothing is worth a dime that doesn't accord with our observations of the world. There's really only one field in all of human endeavor where no observation can undermine the authority of a statement.

Mathematics?

Yes. Are you an animal?

No. Why didn't you become a mathematician?

1, 2, 3, 4. I wasn't good enough, he replied.

It was the first time I'd heard that tone in my father's voice; an expression of a deficit and longing and—at the risk of putting it a touch too high—of a wound.

In Zafar's notes, I came across a scrawled entry that I think reflects the sentiment. I don't know whom Zafar was writing about or if it is a quotation from somewhere, but the note says, *His personal tragedy was the tragedy of all men, that they cannot shake off the lives that might have been, the unlived lives that follow them.*

Do you know what St. Francis of Assisi said about proselytizing? asked my father.

What?

Evangelize by all means and, if necessary, use words.

That's great.

Are you an abstract noun?

Yes, I replied and rolled the die.

I've never been inclined to give you instruction on how to live. I'm not sure I'd know where to begin. Besides, the most useful lessons your mother and I could teach you are the ones we've taught unwittingly through our actions. Don't they say that the best lessons have no teacher, only a student?

But you want to say something now?

He rolled the die. Are you a scientific concept? I'm not sure it's as much a lesson as something to consider.

Tricky. Probably not in the sense you're thinking, I replied.

You know that theoretical physicists rather enjoy trying to find metaphors from everyday life to elucidate physics—why call it spin?—but it seems to me we could go the other way and use physics as a metaphor for life. I have been thinking about our game of Twenty Questions in the context of quantum mechanics, but it occurred to me a while ago that it is also a metaphor for living. The task is always to try to figure out who you are. Are you an emotion?

Yes, I answered.

I had a friend at Princeton, a Russian graduate student. He had a cute message on his answering machine, delivered in his thick Russian accent: *Who are you and what do you want? Some people spend a lifetime trying to answer these questions. You, however, have thirty seconds.*

My father and I chuckled.

What happened to him?

Gone. My point is that you could think of the people you meet in your life as questions, there to help you figure out who you are, what you're made of, and what you want. In life, as in our new version of the game, you start off not knowing the answer. It's only when the particles rub against each other that we figure out their properties. It's the strangest thing, this idea in quantum physics, and yet somehow unsurprising when you consider it as a metaphor. It's when the thing interacts that its properties are revealed, even resolved.

I moved my game piece along, landing at the bottom of a ladder.

That's it really, he added. That's all I wanted to say.

All that was then, over two decades ago, and if I were required to provide a reason why that occasion comes to mind, it may be that I am thinking now also of a rather more recent day in September 2008, just before Zafar's reappearance, when I visited my father with an ill-formed hope that he might have words of advice—however much the grown man in me might have resisted putting it in those terms. I drove up to Oxford on that same road I've driven so often before, but on this day with a heart weighted down by worries. I cannot say that I had the purpose of going through them with him, for I had not properly articulated anything in my own mind in the nature of a question. Granted, there was the question of whether and what to disclose to the financial regulator— I had yet to receive the formal invitation to appear before a congressional committee—but what I carried in my breast was, rather, a vague disenchantment and directionless sense of being. There was also the state of my marriage, the drift of which was, by then, too long and wide to be accommodated as the passing consequence of our respective and collective commitment to work. The road to Oxford was sure enough, but the course of my mind was lost in byways. Rather than by any resolve, I think now, I was drawn home because it was the first place of security.

It is, in the end, Zafar's lack of home, to paraphrase his notes, the unmooring of his body, which leads to and results from the unmooring of his soul, in one of those incalculable feedback loops that rule us beyond our limited wit. I have been fortunate in many respects; life has been unsparing in its blessings. But I have come, early or late (I don't know), to understand that what has made me in my own eyes at times, and I suspect in others', a rather unadventurous and even boring human being has also saved me from greater woes; that my greatest asset was the stable love of parents I admired.

The plan that day was to join my parents for a dinner they were hosting. A social event was not what I had had in mind, but my father suggested it might be diverting—not a banker in sight—and I could stay on through Sunday.

He was not there when I arrived. He had been in Trieste for a conference and was supposed to be on a flight back that morning, but, my mother explained, he'd got the departure time wrong when he booked his tickets. My mother could have sent me a message before I set off for Oxford, letting me know, but I suppose she had been looking forward to seeing me.

Except for my father, the party was complete when I arrived. There was Oswyn Hapgood, a middle-aged classics professor at All Souls, and his wife, Maud, the two of them standing in the drawing room, drinks in hand, sweet sherries the both of them, I'm sure. Of the two, Maud was the connection; she and my mother were fast friends—my mother explained from where but I cannot recall. I'm not sure now, in fact, if my father really liked Hapgood (perhaps that's why he didn't just ditch the ticket in hand and catch an earlier flight). Also invited was one of my father's doctoral students, Nathan Littwack, a Rhodes Scholar originally from Philadelphia, ten years younger than I, who was, I learned, set to take up a professorship at Caltech only a few months later. He was very clever, and the terms my father had used when speaking of him suggested a friendship across the generational divide. Nathan was laying the table and seemed to know his way about the place.

With Nathan was Lauren. I say *with*, although that wasn't immediately apparent. Lauren had the ease of so many Americans I've met, an air of familiarity with whatever environment they were placed in that some Europeans take for pushiness or even a sign of entitlement. I think it was a *Hey, hon* between them—from whom to whom I don't remember—that tipped me off. It would be disingenuous of me not to confess that what was most striking about Lauren were her breasts. I would have bet my bottom dollar it was a push-up bra that made for the flawless curves.

My mother made introductions quickly before returning to the kitchen, where she was putting the finishing touches to dinner. She was assisted by Rehana, a Pakistani woman from Cowley, whom my parents retained as a housekeeper.

I set about helping Nathan. But when I couldn't find what we called the *nice cutlery* in the drawer where it had always been kept, Nathan suggested I try the drawer on the other side of the hutch dresser. He was right. I can't be the first visiting son or daughter to find unsettling the small ways home changes once the children have vacated the nest, even setting aside the agency of parents in instigating those changes. The nice cutlery had been in the drawer on the right for as long as we'd lived there. But that was the point. *We* no longer lived there, I reminded myself, but only *they*, and *they* could make their home in such image as suited them.

You're in banking, I hear, said Oswyn Hapgood, his head leaning back. I could see his nostril hairs. His high forehead was fringed by a mat of tightly coiled silver hair and below, some way below, by two of the bushiest eyebrows ever to crawl the earth. Some people are said to have a face for radio, so the quip goes; Hapgood had a cranial arrangement for academe.

I am, I replied, and left it there.

Inserting herself into the pause I'd opened, my mother explained that I was a partner in the firm. At the time, she knew less than my father did about my work and certainly had no idea about the mounting difficulties I was facing at the firm. But I was surprised by the hint of pride in her voice. When I was growing up, my parents were never the sort to brag about their son, but in more recent years, I've noticed, there has come through something of the proud parent in them both, and in my mother particularly.

Who would think there'd be such drama in banking? added the professor.

His manner, his every gesture, suspended him on the brink of super-ciliousness, and I wondered if there was simply some shy man inside whose timidity had isolated him from the norms of acceptable social behavior. My mother refers to academia as "the Asylum."

But gauche though he was, Hapgood was right. In the preceding twelve months, the British bank Northern Rock had been nationalized, mortgage lender Bradford & Bingley was wobbling precipitously, the stock markets had suffered their largest fall since September 11, 2001, and the European Central Bank had raised interest rates by twenty-five basis points. Even in that September of 2008, there had been more drama than I had seen in all my time in finance. American investment bank Bear Stearns, on its knees with huge liabilities, was bought for a paltry $2 a share by JPMorgan Chase. The giant U.S. mortgage lenders, Freddie Mac and Fannie Mae, were taken over by the government after the dis-closure of $5 trillion in liabilities they couldn't meet. Lehman Brothers—good God, Lehman Brothers—filed for bankruptcy protection. AIG, one of the largest companies in the world, was bailed out by the govern-ment, and in the meantime Treasury Secretary Henry Paulson proposed a massive taxpayer-funded rescue plan for the financial services industry: the Troubled Assets Relief Program. Less than forty-eight hours before I visited my parents, Washington Mutual went into receivership, making it the largest bank failure in U.S. history.

I'm in *investment* banking, I said to Hapgood. The trouble is in com-mercial banking—in lending. We don't provide mortgages.

The distinction might seem disingenuous, but it was the one partners had been encouraged to draw where circumstances allowed it. And it might have been enough of an answer for Hapgood, but not, I see now, for anyone with a sharp intelligence.

In September 2008, I was still a partner of the firm, and the firm's interests were mine and mine the firm's. That, more or less, was what partnership meant, a united front of common interests. The first rule of the firm was not to do any interviews and to keep the firm out of the public view. Most people don't really know what investment banking involves, and because of that ignorance, and because a mob is in too much of a hurry to bother with evidence or reason, it was best simply to stay out of the public eye. But the financial crisis was changing things. The firm had mobilized a PR machine, and the posture adopted in the face of public criticism was that the firm needed to do a better job explaining to people what it actually did, something the firm, head bowed and cap in hand, admitted it hadn't been good at doing. It is what politicians do when confronting a hostile public: an expression of regret for failing to explain choices and decisions—which is no apology at all.

What I don't understand, continued Hapgood, is how it is that so many banks could do so badly and yet pay their staff such large bonuses.

Some banks are doing well, I replied.

How did yours do?

It's doing well, I said, although *not too badly* would have been closer to the mark.

And why is that?

Foresight, I think.

Come now. There has to be more to the explanation.

Hapgood wanted detail, and I could not see how to escape obliging him.

Let's say you own a house. You've bought it with the help of a large mortgage, but you also have other debts. A personal loan to finance a car, perhaps. And, crucially, debts on your credit cards. Let's say you're currently meeting the minimum repayments on the cards, but you're stretched, and if your repayment obligations were to rise you'd be in trouble. What do you do if interest rates rise and you can't meet all your obligations?

You'd fail to meet them, said Hapgood.

We did some research and formed the view that most people would want to hold on to their homes as long as they could; they would rather default on other things—first and foremost on credit card debt—than fall behind on mortgage repayments. So we kept an eye on credit card repayments, and when we saw a marked increase in defaults on credit card debt, we saw that mortgages were not far behind and so we pulled out of that market.

What do you mean by "pulled out of that market"?

I mean we eliminated our exposure to mortgages.

You weren't holding on to mortgages?

Exactly. Make sense?

Was it really that simple?

It was really that simple.

Why didn't other firms do this?

A few did. My firm, Goldman Sachs, and a couple of others.

Hapgood seemed to digest all this, but he wasn't done. I should have known.

Do you think bankers are paid too much?

Oswyn! Oswyn's wife, Maud, interjected.

Oh, dear, I'm sorry, he said.

Oswyn Hapgood, the classics professor, looked ridiculous. My father had dubbed him Oswyn Hapless. Of the two and for the two, Maud was evidently the social compass, if she intervened in time.

No, no, I said. It's a perfectly reasonable question. Not all finance professionals are paid big bonuses, I said, addressing Hapgood, but when my firm does pay those bonuses, it does so because those bankers would otherwise run off to other firms.

Do we really need all this financial wizardry?

Finance does a lot of good—

Yes, but does there really have to be so much of it?

Some people ask how much we need classics professors and how many we need. I happen to think we need them a lot. But that's not much help when you're trying to figure out how much to pay professors, and it certainly doesn't tell us what we have to pay to keep them from heading off to American universities.

Nathan Littwack had been silent until then.

How do we know that? he asked.

How do we know that we don't know how much to pay professors?

No. How do we know that we have to pay bankers the bonuses we pay them in order to keep them at their firms?

When we don't pay them enough, I replied a little wearily, we see them leave. It happens quite often.

When I joined the firm in July 1993 as an associate in sales in the fixed-income division, I believed—and I still believe this, notwithstanding what Zafar says—that I was hired because Zafar put in a good word for me. He had already been with the firm for some time, joining them in their headquarters in New York not long after Harvard, when I was beginning to look into finance while finishing my master's thesis. I had other friends in the industry already, two of them from Eton, but they were all in European investment banks—the Eton boys at very staid English ones, not one of which, as it happens, would survive the 1990s American onslaught in the financial services sector, the aggressiveness of the U.S. banks and their innovativeness. It seemed to me in those days, as it still does today, that the most exciting names in finance were American: my firm, Goldman Sachs, Morgan Stanley, and the rest. So I sent Zafar an email. He suggested I write to Doug Hendricks in Structured Products, a rising star whose group, he said, was talking about some intriguing new ideas. Doug replied that he needed to hire more people in London and that he was going to be there the following week. I was called in for "just a couple of interviews," but I faced a barrage of bankers over five hours, partners and senior professionals, before I met Doug.

A few days later, I asked Zafar if he'd heard anything. I called him from London, and I can now picture him, as he must have been, sitting there at work, leaning back in his seat, facing an array of screens, with his headset on, the microphone hanging by the side of his mouth. He explained that Doug had come over to him that morning and had asked him what he, Zafar, thought of me.

What did you say?

I said I wouldn't recommend the work to you if I didn't think you'd take to it.

What did he say?

I'll tell you what he said: If that's what you think, then it's good enough for me.

Wow. They must think highly of you.

He'd already decided to hire you. He was just banking a favor from me.

That's a bit cynical, don't you think?

He's a banker. It's a free option.

If he was at your desk, everyone could have heard him.

He's a smart guy. He doesn't want people to think he can't judge a good hire from a bad one and has to rely on a relatively new recruit.

Exactly. So why say it?

Because he knows that everyone else knows what he really means; everyone knows how stupid it would be to rely so much on the word of a newbie, and a friend of the applicant to boot. He wants me to think he's doing me a favor. And he thinks I'm naïve enough to buy that or smart enough not to show I'm offended because I don't.

You make the place sound like some kind of psychological theater.

Know a place that isn't, do you? Anyhow, you got the job because he wants you.

Thanks.

Don't thank me. I get a thousand dollars from the firm because I introduced a successful applicant.

Two weeks later, when I arrived in New York for orientation (before returning to join the London office), Zafar and I had supper in the West Village, around the corner from his apartment, at an Italian restaurant where he seemed to be known to the waitress. Once he'd answered a few questions I had about the firm, a silence opened up between us. Zafar seemed to drift off, his eyes apparently settling on the waitress, who smiled at him. But when he failed to return her smile, I perceived that he was somewhere else altogether.

How about you?

How about me?

How did you get into it?

Interview, like you.

But what was the process like? What put you on to it?

Call from a headhunter in the final year at Harvard, interview with a banker, and a job offer.

Interview with a banker? Doug Hendricks?

Zafar seemed to consider his response.

Not Hendricks. A huge man—he'd been a linebacker in college—this huge man strode into the office, fell back into the sofa, and looked at me for an eternity without saying a word. I've seen your résumé, he said, and you can do this shit. Question is, do you have the fight in you? Do you?

What did you say? I asked.

I have more fight than anyone needs for any job, I said. I've come a long way, from a mud hut in the rainy season in a part of the world you only know as a basket case of misery. I spent a year of childhood in the basement of a derelict house in two rooms and an outside lavatory, and when I try to remember the kitchen, I can only picture the half that didn't have rats. I've grown up in some of the worst projects in London. I've been kicked and spat at because of my race, I've had teachers send me to remedial classes because they thought I was stupid when I was just silent, I've been beaten black and blue my whole short life and I've made it here. Have I got the fight? You tell me.

I was astonished. Once again, I felt, as I have often felt in his company, a strange feeling of envy. It doesn't make sense to envy another human being for his hardships, but envy is what it was. I can find nothing heroic in my own story.

Did you seriously say that? I asked.

Zafar was smiling.

No.

What did you actually say? I asked.

Well, he didn't actually ask me much. Instead he wanted to show me some things about his work, so we talked finance for a couple of hours.

A two-hour interview?

More like a tutorial.

You mean he was trying to sell it to you?

Not really; he was testing to see if I could pick up the stuff.

Within three years, Zafar left the bank and returned to Britain, in order, he explained, to practice law. He had made up his mind, even if it meant training for the English bar. I admired that in him, the speed with which he made and executed life decisions.

Oswyn Hapgood was certainly tiresome, to put it mildly. A year earlier, I would happily have discussed the question of bankers' pay without the slightest discomfort. But this was the end of September 2008, the markets were in turmoil, and the effects of the financial crisis were spreading into the economy. My firm, though by no means the worst affected, had suffered some losses, and not just in the United States. As was the case at a number of American firms, almost all European business was dealt with through London. It was London, in fact, that picked up most of the work outside the Americas and Asia, and all that added up. The U.K. had witnessed significant bank failures and, in ways I could never have predicted, much of the distress came back to my desk and the group I headed, though by then only nominally; effective control had passed, against my protests, to the head of the division, to the firm's chief financial officer and the firm's risk officers.

There are at least two questions here, explained Nathan Littwack.

When not speaking, he sat perfectly still, his elbows resting on the table, his hands clasped together and, it appeared, his thumbs pressed, nail-side, against his lips. I did not know this young man, but I knew already certain things about him. When Nathan Littwack listened, you knew that he was listening to your every word. When Nathan Littwack spoke, his words were inseparable from his body language. And when he articulated something that he had obviously considered carefully, I saw what others in that room would have seen—the precision of a certain kind of academic, one like my father.

The first, he said, is whether any given bank needs to pay what it pays in order to keep its staff. We have the answer to that, he said, nodding my way. I might be wrong, but it seems to me that that's not the right question, he continued, not when governments are looking to increase regulation.

What is the right question?

Does the *industry* need to pay its staff what it currently pays them in order to keep them from leaving the *industry*?

But, Nathan, I said, it's not the industry that pays staff but firms.

So what about a tax on firms, said Nathan, dependent on what the firm pays out in salaries? A flat rate. Wouldn't that push down bankers' pay across firms?

Lauren came in here.

Have you seen those graphs of bankers' pay and average pay in the rest of the economy? The NBER, I think, or was it Shiller?

Not Shiller, Nathan corrected her.

NBER? said Hapgood.

National Bureau of Economic Research, explained Nathan.

Where the hell would bankers go? she asked me. Bankers' pay was always higher than pay in the rest of the economy, she continued, but not by much until the eighties, when it started to climb steeply. Not coincidentally, median average income in the U.S. is less now than in 2000. Less! The majority make three hundred dollars less now than in 1980, and all the gains in the last thirty years—all the gains!—went to the top zero point one percent. That's zero point one percent. The top one percent own forty percent of the wealth of America! Today, you'd have to cut bankers' pay by eighty percent before their jobs were remotely comparable to other jobs. Can you think of an industry where all those bankers can get paid anything like what they get in finance?

Hapgood, less hapless now and more emboldened by the Americans, piped in.

Does it not stand to reason, he asked, that the financial industry should foot the bill for getting us into this fine mess?

That's a horse of another color, said Nathan.

Hapgood's bushy eyebrows leaped up like startled rodents, but I couldn't tell if this was because he was unfamiliar with the idiom or because he understood that he'd just been told that what he was saying was irrelevant.

The conversation carried on in this vein for part of the evening, and I am forced to admit that my responses weren't the most robust. Bankers generally, I think, are not given to considering the wider context of things, just as, I'm sure, most busy doctors do not give much thought to the national state of health care and the problems of insuring a whole society. People by and large go about their work, and where hard work is called for, they go about that work to the exclusion of concerns that do not, in the final analysis, further the work at hand.

Nathan was a very smart young man who evidently had the nous to figure things out for himself, but I daresay he was following the financial news rather more carefully than did most people outside finance. What he was talking about were the same things being reported in the financial press, including a tax on banks to create a reserve for bailouts, a tax on certain financial transactions, and a tax linked to salaries and bonuses but paid by banks. Each of these had its own rationale. All of them drew ultimate justification, however, from the cascading failures of those financial instruments that had come to dominate the financial world.

These instruments are not understood by most people and, in fact, they are so widely *misunderstood* that the first thing a journalist writes about them is that they're widely misunderstood. I can't be alone in noticing that until recently, even the august *Financial Times* gave the derivatives and bond markets little more than a passing mention, always regarding it necessary to point out that most trivial fact: that the price and yield of a bond move in opposite directions. Nobody outside the business—and not everyone inside—could get their heads around the new products.

As I think about this lack of understanding, I am reminded of something Zafar said concerning the teaching of mathematics in schools; it was an obvious point, so obvious I was left wondering why it had never occurred to me, who had also studied mathematics. One bad maths teacher, he explained, can wreak havoc. A bad history teacher, when you're twelve years old, say, might mean you don't acquire a very good grasp of the First World War or the Potsdam Conference. It leaves a hole in your education. The next year, you manage. The early deficiency doesn't hinder you very much when you later study the Russian Revolution, not in those years when you're not studying any of these things in any great depth anyway. But mathematics is different. If you fail to digest the material prescribed for that year, then everything that follows, in every subsequent year, is next to impossible to take in. Right from the beginning, mathematics education is accretive, a pyramid, each layer of brickwork building up carefully on the last. You can't understand trigonometry if you haven't grasped the idea of similar triangles. You can't grasp calculus if you haven't understood areas and velocities. And you can't understand anything at all if your basic algebra is poor. It's why mathematics professors have such a hard time explaining their work to the public. The great majority of students are vulnerable to one bad teacher. It isn't enough for a child's mathematics teachers as a whole to be generally just as bad and just as good as his history teachers. In fact, even if mathematics teachers were generally, which is to say as a group, better than history teachers, the presence of one bad maths teacher early on hampers him mathematically if it doesn't doom the child to mathematical ignorance.*

General incomprehension of derivatives, from the bus driver and waiter to the classics professor and newspaper editor, is understandable: Any decent exposition requires a fair bit of mathematics. My father tells a story about Richard Feynman, who'd been dubbed the Great Explainer because of his talent for explaining theoretical physics. When a journalist asked him to describe in three minutes what he'd won the Nobel Prize for, Feynman replied that if he could explain it in three minutes, it wouldn't be worth a Nobel Prize. Feynman, I think, is making the wider

---

*In an article in *Science* magazine in 2000—one of those links emailed to me by my father—the novelist David Foster Wallace writes:

> Modern math is like a pyramid, and the broad fundament is often not fun. It is at the higher and apical levels of geometry, topology, analysis, number theory, and mathematical logic that the fun and profundity start, when the calculators and contextless formulae fall away and all that's left are pencil & paper and what gets called "genius," viz. the particular blend of reason and ecstatic creativity that characterizes what is best about the human mind. Those who've been privileged (or forced) to study it understand that the practice of higher mathematics is, in fact, an "art" and that it depends no less than other arts on inspiration, courage, toil, etc. . . . but with the added stricture that the "truths" the art of math tries to express are deductive, necessary, *a priori* truths, capable of both derivation and demonstration by logical proof.

Where Wallace describes mathematics as an "art," he adds a footnote quoting from a book by the Cambridge mathematician G. H. Hardy (who famously discovered the self-taught Indian mathematical genius Ramanujan). The book, *A Mathematician's Apology*, was given to me by Zafar as a present many years ago, on my graduation. It is a moving exploration of the joys and sorrows of mathematics. Quoted by Wallace, Hardy writes:

> The mathematician's patterns, like the painter's or poet's, must be beautiful; the ideas, like the colors or the words, must fit together in a harmonious way. Beauty is the first test; there is no permanent place in the world for ugly mathematics.

Wallace's footnote is especially affecting when one considers that Hardy took his own life, not long after finishing the book, and that Wallace did so as well, a fact the *Financial Times* found room to record despite the festooning ticker tape of corporate failures in September 2008.

point that an explanation of something by reducing it and simplifying it over and over, until all that's left is some familiar metaphor that is actually without content, helps no one's understanding of the thing itself and is only the repetition of a familiar image.

Even the basic elements of financial derivatives are mathematical. But quite apart from the mathematical content, the other problem is that to understand derivatives requires, I think, an understanding of other more basic ideas in finance, whether or not they in turn have some mathematical content. It's accretive, to use Zafar's language. Perhaps this is not exclusive to finance. As far as I can tell, medicine is just the same, as well as the law.

Reading over all this, it sounds like the beginnings of a kind of defense. And that it might be. I know that my own lawyers will draft something to submit to the congressional committee and that this should form the basis of my oral submissions. They'll also groom me in fielding questions. And the firm will doubtless make available its own lawyers, even to a former employee, but on them, needless to say, I won't be relying. There is defending to be done, I know. But the attack, more than likely, will take the form of that imprecise populist haranguing that politicians excel in. Lynching has a civilized form. But while there's plenty to apologize for, apologizing wholesale for some vague offense of "getting us into the mess we're in" can't be one of them. It doesn't stand up. Back in September 2008, at supper in my parents' home, I was already quite defensive. These days I'm even more so. I have a dialogue going on in my head, a defense I'm crafting in pieces.

In the midnineties Zafar left the industry for law but I remained in banking, joining the Structured Products group in London. The group had been newly established to explore opportunities for the firm in a field where others had taken the lead, notably a team at JPMorgan headed by Bill Demchak and Peter Hancock. In late 1994, I had been asked to look at a deal JPMorgan had recently closed with the European Bank for Reconstruction and Development. The deal had created a buzz, but there's no doubting that as much as the deal, it was the glamorous and spunky deal maker at the center of it who had set tongues wagging.

The background was an environmental disaster five years earlier. In 1989, the oil tanker *Exxon Valdez* ran aground off the Alaskan coast, releasing a massive oil slick. In a class action suit four years later, Exxon was fined $5 billion. It's true that on appeal in 2008, the U.S. Supreme Court would cap the oil company's liability at $500 million, one-tenth of the jury's award back in 1994, but at the time Exxon faced the prospect of making a massive payout. It turned to its banker, JPMorgan, for a credit line to draw on as need arose. But providing such a large credit line would have hefty implications for JPMorgan.

Every time a bank makes a loan, it runs the risk of the borrower not paying back. Moreover, a bank relies on loan repayments in order to run its own business, to repay depositors who want their money and even to make payments to its own creditors. So the risk of a borrower defaulting entails a risk to the bank, its customers, depositors, and creditors and, if the bank is big, a risk to the financial services sector. Regulators, who, in theory at least, are looking out for customers and the industry, step in here and require a bank to set aside capital every time it lends—just put it in a reserve account where the bank can't touch it. With this reserve, barring the catastrophic default of a large number of its borrowers, the bank ought to be able to take a few knocks without going down and damaging the sector in the process.

If JPMorgan ran a credit line to Exxon, it would be huge, and JPMorgan would have to reserve a huge amount of capital, capital which could not be put to any use, not even to earn interest. Of course, banks don't like this; they want their money to be making money. That's where Payne came in.

I met Meena, as I've mentioned, on the training program in New York, fell in love, courted her, and wooed her. I remember I even cooked for her—or tried to, balls of spinach and pine nuts or something, which fell apart in my hands and had me stabbing the phone with my forefinger in search of a decent restaurant near Wall Street that would deliver in half an hour. With training over, Meena and I returned to London. More and more, I stayed over at her small apartment, even as week by week the contents of her wardrobe migrated to my house, where they garlanded the furniture. On a very cold night in December, when I'd persuaded her to come for a walk on the Albert Bridge to see its famous Christmas lights that didn't exist, I proposed. Two weeks later, on a bright Monday

morning in January, I saw Payne, for the first time, in a breakfast semi-
nar at the Guildhall in London, sitting on a panel with two men. When
it came her turn to speak, Payne sprang to her feet, this slim, beautiful
woman, her chair taking the force of the recoil, and in a dozen bold
strides, with legs that went, as they say, all the way to the ground, she
crossed the stage to the lectern. She wore knee-high boots, black leg-
gings, and a tartan skirt, her hands free of any notes. Payne had bright
blue eyes—*with flecks of gray*, she would insist—and long blond hair,
sometimes tied up in a bun. Descended from an old Boston family of
jurists and commercial men—two ancestors, I learned, had sat on the
state Supreme Court and another, one Josiah Edgerton, a business associate of John Quincy Adams, had boasted the largest agricultural holding
in the Commonwealth of Massachusetts—Payne was as blue-blooded as
they come in America, and yet she had little to show of the genteel manners you'd imagine would come with high birth. For one thing, having
the certain knowledge of what she wanted, with not one sinew of self-
restraint or inhibition in that body to hold her back, she did not hide her
intention to get it, and for another, as financial journalists have noted,
she swore like a trooper. In the world of finance she had acquired the
sobriquet House of Payne. I think she took pride in it.

The European Bank for Reconstruction and Development was established in London in 1991. Its stated mission, Payne explained, was to
invest in market economies in the formerly Communist countries of Europe. In 1994, it had considerable credit, which it was looking to extend
to the right borrower. JPMorgan—which meant *she*—grabbed an opportunity and negotiated a deal with EBRD under the terms of which
EBRD would cover JPMorgan in the event that Exxon failed to meet any
repayments once Exxon began drawing on the credit line. EBRD would
effectively insure JPMorgan against the credit risk posed by Exxon, and
in return JPMorgan would pay EBRD a modest annual premium. The
deal was the first, or the first to garner attention. Because of the European aspect of the deal and the prospective business it had opened up,
Payne moved to JPMorgan's London office, after receiving promotions
so fast even the rubberneckers got whiplash.

With this arrangement in hand (it had recently been given a name:
credit default swap), Payne went to the SEC and successfully argued
that JPMorgan had effectively removed the credit risk exposure incurred

by extending a credit line to Exxon and should therefore be excused from having to set aside vast amounts of capital to cover default by Exxon.

When my firm asked me to find out about these credit default swaps, I jumped at the opportunity. There's a lot of money to be made as a market innovator, but the number two position also has its benefits. Number one takes on the costs of developing a bold idea and the risk it might fall flat, while number two can avoid number one's mistakes. After all, it's the second mouse that gets the cheese.

After the presentation, I dropped Payne an email suggesting we meet over coffee to discuss her ideas. She agreed, and we met at a bistro near the Bank of England. She wore a figure-hugging black skirt stopping above her knees, with a matching jacket, which she slipped off before sitting down. Beneath this she wore a white cotton shirt, with upturned collars, fitted to her figure, tapering down to a narrow waist and cinched into her skirt. The shirt was unbuttoned down to her cleavage. It seems appropriate to mention these matters in order to set the scene.

What Payne told me over coffee changed my life. The scheme is easy enough to explain because, once I got to grips with it in my own time, it came to form the basis of pretty much everything I did for more than a decade.

In a securitization, a so-called sponsor takes mortgages or corporate loans, things that promise a stream of cash flows, and synthesizes securities out of them. Like any bright idea, it was really startlingly simple, once someone had it. You create a special company, somewhere offshore for perfectly legal tax reasons, and then have that company buy a pool of mortgages, say, so that it stands to receive mortgage repayments. The company then offers to sell to investors a security of its own creation that promises a series of payments funded by the pool of mortgage repayments. When I say pool of mortgage repayments, I mean repayments from upward of tens of thousands of mortgages. That was part of the point: Investors who might be interested in buying these synthetic securities, pension funds and hedge funds, for instance, had no interest in an anemic dribble from a few mortgages.

As I gather my thoughts here in order to get to the point, I am reminded of a joke Zafar made when he was still in banking. I say joke, but Zafar was always rather serious about banking and often talked about accountability, as he called it. This stuff is so esoteric, he once said, that the only people who understand it are in the business. What about regulators? I asked. Regulators, he replied, have one eye on the revolving door. Academics make money teaching traders their latest research, and politicians don't know their arses from their elbows. Can you imagine the people on a march against finance? The guy on a megaphone shouting: *What do we want?* And everyone answering: Specific curbs on short selling in certain circumstances. *When do we want it?* In phases and at appropriate times.

That's the joke. It was funny at the time.

However important the details of securitization may be, the important thing here is what I took away from my conversation with Payne.*

---

*The synthetic securities we wanted to sell had to be fashioned in such a way that it was relatively certain that investors would receive payments. Here came the clever idea: Create a type of security, A, which would be the first to draw down from the aggregate of mortgage repayments received and pay investors who had bought that security. The point of this was that although the pool of mortgages is supposed to receive a total of, say, $10 million every month in repayments by homeowners, all securities of type A will pay investors a total of, say, $2 million (assuming an appropriate number of type A securities are sold). That way, even if a large number of homeowners default on payments, so that the pool only receives, say, $7 million, the type A securities, being the first to draw from the pool, will nevertheless still be able to pay out $2 million to investors (with $5 million left over).

But there's no reason to stop there—at least there didn't seem to be then. Why not create security B, which pays out but only after payments under A have been made? You could sell another $2 million of those securities. The idea is that payments are owed first to investors in A and thereafter to investors in B. The special company would have to pay out a total of $4 million every month to investors in A and B. The risk to investors in B was the risk of so many homeowners defaulting that the pool of mortgages held by the special company brought in not the $10 million (that would come in if no homeowner defaulted) but less even than $4 million, say, $3 million. The first $2 million would go to investors in security A. But after that there would be just $1 million left in the pool to pay investors in security B. Security B is therefore a little riskier than A but not a whole lot riskier. After all, payments to investors in security B are threatened only if more than 60 percent of households fail in a given month to make their mortgage repayments. Nevertheless, because B was theoretically riskier than A, it would fetch a lower price than would A.

Bankers have names for all these things, of course. For instance, the offshore companies created to receive the mortgage repayments are called special purpose vehicles or special investment vehicles. Securities like A and B are known as collateralized debt obligations, or CDOs, and A and B are referred to as different tranches of the security,

The synthetic securities we offered to investors had to be assessed for risk. Potential investors needed to know how likely it was that the mortgage repayments behind the securities would dry up. Rating agencies have the job of assessing the risk in a security before it's offered for sale and of giving it a credit rating, as if its being a separate company from the ones arranging the creation of the securities guaranteed independence! Not so much arm's length as shoulder to shoulder. Securities with triple-A ratings, the same ratings enjoyed by U.S. government bonds, are considered the safest. And the ratings go down the list, all the way down to subinvestment grade, the ratings given to so-called junk bonds or distressed debt (or where there's no rating at all). The triple-A rating is the one that's prized, the one investors in CDOs were looking for.

At our meeting, Payne described the difficulties she'd been having persuading ratings agencies to give the securities a high rating.

I'm sure you can be very persuasive, I said.

Yellow-bellied, spineless chickenshits. Ask what's bugging them and they can't say. If they weren't so gutless, they'd be making money as traders and not working nine to five as actuaries in ratings agencies. Fucking salarymen.

How do they rate the securities?

They haven't yet.

I mean, what's the methodology?

Can't get their heads around them. We asked them to work with us. Moody's, S&P, they'll work with you on a consultancy basis. But they're just so damn slow. We're going round the fucking houses with them. We need one of them to bite, and the others will climb aboard. They actually stand to make a fuckload of money in fees.

What about Forrester?

No.

Might be worth a try.

If the big ones won't touch it—

A the senior tranche and B the mezzanine (there might be yet another tranche lower down and riskier, and therefore cheaper, which would be called the junior tranche). But the language is unimportant, as is even much of the detail, except perhaps in preserving the mystique of the priesthood.

Not being the biggest might mean they're hungry.

Maybe.

What happens to the lowest tranche? That has to be a hard sell, I said. I had a few technical questions about what she'd told me. And, besides, I rather enjoyed trying to test her.

The sponsor holds on to the equity tranche; shows the sponsor's got some skin in the game.

How do you deal with the risk?

What do you mean?

What if the mortgage market goes belly-up?

Really?

Humor me.

Well . . . you can use a credit derivative, a credit default swap—you could even use it just to enhance the credit of the securities.

Who writes those credit default swaps?

Anyone could. Insurance companies have the stomach. AIG will want a piece of the pie.

Here's a question for you. What's to stop the sponsor taking the equity tranche—you called it equity tranche presumably because it behaves more like equity than a bond?

Right.

What's to stop the sponsor taking the equity tranche, funding it, and getting it off their books?

Using it as collateral to borrow against?

Yup.

The market wouldn't like that. Potential investors will get jittery about the sponsor's valuations. Then there's the fact the sponsor will still be on the hook for services to the SPV, so that means investors will want the sponsor to keep a dog in the fight.

But what's to stop my bank helping the sponsor fund the equity tranche, once the securities are issued?

Nothing. Just bad risk management. Why would a bank want to take on that risk? Especially a bank advising on the issue. Anyhow, you like it, don't you?

Very attractive. Incredible it's not been snapped up already.

The ratings agencies are a bottleneck, for one thing. It's new, and new always scares the accountants.

All this must be keeping you busy.

Keeps me off the streets.

Can't leave you much time for other things?

If I wanted a part-time job, I'd run for office or shine trophies for the Red Sox.

What I understood from Payne was that getting one ratings agency onside was the next step. I knew that putting the structure together and gaining the market's interest would take some time, but, of course, I was already thinking of Forrester.

Just when I thought the whole thing was a wash, Payne Cutler surprised me.

You wanna get a cocktail tomorrow night?

Sure.

I'll call you when I leave the office.

Sounds good.

I stayed late at the office, but I didn't hear from her until a half hour before midnight.

It's Payne, she said. Heading out now. See you at the Soho Tavern in fifteen.

By the time my father arrived, the evening had ended and the guests had left. We were tired and after a nightcap we all turned in. The next morning, the three of us had a long breakfast of bacon, eggs, and French toast, after which my mother left for the Sunday farmers' market.

Zafar once told me that his parents had never asked him if anything was troubling him, never asked what the matter was. He had wondered in later life if that was because *he* had never let on or because *they* had never picked up on anything, or because, despite picking up on something, they could not bring themselves to ask. I found this last proposition difficult to grasp, when it seemed to me that the natural instinct of parents—biological or otherwise—was to respond to the faintest distress of those they rear. That basic level of sensitivity and solicitousness is something one finds even in good friends.

It was noon already, and my father suggested we go to the pub. If we stay there long enough, he said, your mother can join us and we can all have a Sunday roast together.

We drove out to the Trout in Wolvercote, north of Oxford, right on the water. My father came back to the table with two pints of bitter and a broad smile. The man doesn't like bitter, but when I pointed it out, his reply was that he likes having bitter in an English pub: when in Rome.

Quite the Englishman, I quipped.

Look out the window, he replied.

And?

I didn't grow up with this, you know.

With what?

What do you see?

The river.

He smiled.

I'm not mocking you, he said. But your answer is funny.

I should see electrons and photons and so on?

That you could do, but I see something else, the river, yes, and also a cold blue sky, autumn leaves, the episodic retreat of life, the willows mourning over the water.

Quite the poet this morning.

If you are not familiar with it, you notice the weir in the brook or the brook in the weir. I have no idea what the words are for such things. God bless them, they have these Anglo-Saxon words that show up nowhere but in places like this. I've read T. S. Eliot, a lot of Rudyard Kipling, and something of Thomas Gray, and so I see England in the manner of a foreigner, a place forever defending the past, doing quiet battle with the future, and in its very own way a country of charm. But if all that you see is what you saw in your youth, the prospect of Eton an unnoticed backdrop of an adolescent boy, the antique towers that crown the watery glade, as Gray said, then you see something else. Like breathing air, English air. What do you see?

I see a river, I said, smiling at him.

Tell me what you wanted to talk about.

How do you know I've got something to talk about?

When you don't have something to talk about, you don't avoid talking.

He gave me a wink and took a sip of his beer.

I began by telling him what had been happening in the world of finance, giving him some detail, most of which I had the impression he knew because he had been following the news carefully, not for his own sake, I think, since he'd never paid much attention to finance before, but because of what the turmoil might mean for me and Meena. When I got to telling him that I thought the firm was about to let me go and would possibly even try to hang me out to dry, my father did not make reassuring sounds, did not contradict me with the groundless optimism of someone reassuring himself as much as another—that was never his way. He simply listened. (Some years ago, he explained to me his belief that that kind of hollow consolation was disrespectful because it presumed that the person being consoled wouldn't see or care about the absence of reason. The thing to do first and foremost, he believed, was not to talk but to listen, and listening, like anything difficult, is easier said than done.) I talked for some time, finding more and more details to tell him. Even things I hadn't consciously thought much about I brought up, understanding then how much they had actually been weighing on my mind. I set out my analysis and explained that I'd spoken to a couple of friends also in finance, and they couldn't fault my reasoning. Congressional subcommittees, now sprouting like weeds, were identifying witnesses to call to hearings. They know two things. Of all the people closest to structured products, mortgages, and securitization in my firm, I was the most senior; and my firm would cut me loose faster than I could say scapegoat. If the firm saw even the slightest benefit for them in front of Congress, they'd pin everything on me. That's the point of blaming a rogue trader: It's the trader that's rogue, not the bank's checks and balances, not the bank.

At a certain point I stopped talking. I felt I'd poured out everything, everything I'd been holding in, even when I didn't know I'd been doing so.

What does Meena think? he asked me.

My reply did not come immediately. I had not mentioned Meena once. My omission must have been as obvious to him as it now was to me.

As you must know, things aren't going well there either.

I'm sorry to hear that. We'd love to see her.

She spends a lot of time away right now.

How is your health?

Fine.

That's good. I'm glad. So at least you have your health.

He smiled. Dear me, don't lose your sense of humor!

I forced a grin.

I'd appreciate any advice, I said.

Eat more vegetables. And whole grains.

My father, who had been sitting opposite me, got up and took the chair beside me, at a right angle to mine. It was how my mother liked to sit. There's something less confrontational this way, she'd said. This way you see the person's good side.

The view is different from here, he said, taking another sip of his beer as he looked out over the river. He took his time, collecting his thoughts, it seemed, before resuming.

There is a funny little story about Charles II and the Royal Society, said my father. The king was regarded as rather pompous and obscurantist, an idiot, really, and one not to be duly impressed by members of the esteemed society. At a dinner to mark the founding of the society, he put a question to them that quite confounded the great scientists. Why, he asked, does a dead fish weigh more than a live one? Despite their great and learned efforts, the members failed to arrive at a compelling answer, when finally someone pointed out that they did not in fact have different weights. Perhaps the king was a buffoon, or perhaps he wasn't quite so dumb after all.

It is possible, continued my father, that we accept premises more readily than we should. False dichotomies are the stock of politicians only because too many are ready to accept the premises as given. Anyhow, that is by the by. Before I make good the point I'm groping to make, which really, after all, is not an especially significant one, let me say that I don't presume your woes can be resolved by recourse to reason alone or even with reason in the mix at all. Everyone knows in the intimacy of his self, if not his reason, that when the soul is under siege reason is not up to the fight.

What's going on?

What do you mean?

Why do you sound like a classics professor?

A bit stuffy?

You said it, not me.

Maybe I'm not sure of what I'm saying. I don't think I'm unsure. Am I unsure?

He chuckled.

Philosophers talk about solving problems, continued my father, but also about *dissolving* them. Wittgenstein, for example. Sometimes, when properly regarded, the problem in front of us is understood to be no problem at all, or at least not of the kind we believe it to be. We tend to favor the status quo. It seems to me we see every adverse situation as a challenge to restore ourselves to the status quo ante. You know the refrain: I just want to go back to how things were. This seems short-sighted. How things were might well have led you to the way things have woefully become.

Are you doing any theoretical physics these days, or are you just reading cognitive science papers?

As physics goes, I'm past my prime. Besides, one must play to avoid Jack's fate. If I were setting out on the academic road today, I'd go into cognitive science. Don't get me wrong. I love theoretical physics, but right now, meaning at this point in human history, we've finally got to working on the brain using those precious scientific methods that we've been using to work on everything but, and cognitive science is where . . . is where it's *at*, as you Americans would say. You laugh, and maybe I set too much store in science, but I do believe cognitive science really is where it's at. Granted, some of these chaps claim more for their science than their science has earned. But it's still early days, and in the excitement of finding something new, one has to expect a degree of overreaching. Look at the Internet: Not so long ago everyone thought it was the beginning of a new kind of economy, but now one can quite legitimately doubt this is true. Nevertheless, the Internet has brought about great changes. If we give the new cognitive sciences a little time, it seems very likely, to me, at any rate, that their ideas will also translate into applications in daily life. There's a cognitive scientist here in Oxford who told me that he and his wife now spend much less money on *things* and prefer to spend on *experiences*, such as interesting holidays, because, he says, research has established that it's the experiences that have an enduring effect. Material things appear to be swallowed up by the hedonic beast in us and all too soon lose whatever power they had—or we believed they had—to give us pleasure. He and his wife have changed the way they live.

Do you really need cognitive science to reach that conclusion?

Well, that's a whole other ball game.

Couldn't he have come to the same conclusion in therapy?

Now what possible reason would he have to go to therapy? Do you know something I don't? Let's not deviate too much. I have a question for you. You know what the most dangerous thing in the world is?

What? I asked.

A story, replied my father. I'm not kidding. Stories are dangerous. And I don't mean stories whose messages are capable of endangering. I mean that the form itself is dangerous, not the content. You know what a metaphor is? A story sent through the super distillation of imagination. You know what a story is? An extended metaphor. We live in them. We live in this swirling mass of stories written by scribes hidden in some forgotten room up there in the towers. The day someone thought of calling pigeons flying rats was the day the fate of pigeons was sealed. Does anyone who hears them called flying rats stop to ask if pigeons actually carry disease? Or Plato's cave. If a fellow knows nothing else about the man, he knows something about a cave and shadows. You've heard that good fences make good neighbors, but did you know that when Robert Frost wrote those words he meant the opposite of what that phrase has come to stand for? Frost was being ironic; he was talking about the things that divide us. But the image contained in the bare words *Good fences make good neighbors*—that image is so good, so vibrant, that in our minds, in the minds of so many, it's broken free of its unspoken ironies.

My father paused.

My mother told me, some years ago, that when she first met my father she was charmed by the way this young physicist treated everything in such an ethereal, abstract way. But quite soon she came to find it annoying, especially when she wanted to talk to him about things that couples talk about, *private things*, she said to me. As my mother saw it, either he was not taking things seriously or he was not inhabiting the moment; he was somehow not only abstracting whatever they were discussing but also abstracting *himself* out of it. But I came to see, she said, that it was precisely his tireless distancing and questioning that brought him, for instance, to a view of Pakistan's behavior in 1971 that cost him—cost us—his friends and much of his family. At the time, I must tell you, I thought him rather too quick to judge our country so adversely, even though he would have told you he thought himself slow. I thought him rather selfish as well. In the end, I was the slow one; it took me a little longer to shed from my eyes the scales of a rather phony patriotism. I came to understand that your father was not in fact a disembodied mind, which can be charming in the way they are whose heads float in the clouds. Thinking for him was purposive because it clarified the root of action.

These, my mother's words, insofar as I remember them, come back not infrequently when I talk to my father. At times, I have caught myself expecting the kind of conversation I might have with intimate friends or colleagues—caught myself, I say, because I become aware of the expectation when it confronts and is defeated by that curious mix of distancing and intimacy that is the essence of my father's language. And yet, more often than not I have found some kind of solace in what he says.

You are faced with certain choices, continued my father. Or so you think. But you have other choices also, choices you might have overlooked. You have an overabundance of choice.

And now I remember Zafar's words from a long time ago. For most men, he said, the choices they make are determined by their constraints, but for the very rich, their constraints are determined by the choices they make. As I think of my father and recall those words of my friend, it is little wonder that I grew so fond of Zafar so quickly—and perhaps little wonder also that I often found him infuriating.

Don't you chaps think choice is an illusion?

You chaps? said my father.

Scientists. Free will is an illusion and all that.

The word *choice* means different things, said my father. There's a fork in the road whether or not the traveler has any choice about which to take. I've always been a little puzzled by this popular notion that scientists reject free will.

It's a break in causation, I interjected.

A break in causation indeed. But physicists have been happy with breaks in causation ever since quantum mechanics entered the scene.

Yes, but quantum mechanics is pretty esoteric, don't you think?

There was an article in *Scientific American* in 2001 in which the author stated that quantum mechanics underpins thirty percent of U.S. gross national product, from semiconductors to lasers and magnetic resonance imaging. I'm not sure how he came to that figure, I have to say. In fact, I wrote to the fellow to ask him about it but got a most unsatisfactory reply. He couldn't remember where he'd found the figure. In any case, when quantum physics conceived particles ruled by uncertainty and indeterminism, that was the day science called a truce and breaks in causation reentered its domain. Yet people still think free will an unscientific concept because it involves such a break. I think this misconception is related to another misconception about science, one I often come across in arts and humanities scholars, which is that they think we deal with certainties and definite knowledge. That's wrong in fourteen different ways, but at the very least it demonstrates a lack of understanding of what scientists actually do. They work at the frontier of science, which is where the fun is, and which is also where there is anything but certainty. It is about adventure, even for theoretical physicists like me. Which neatly leads me to ask you if you've thought about taking risks.

That's what my job involves, I replied.

You're only taking a risk if there's really something at stake. Why not set off on a completely different angle?

You mean quit finance?

There's a great study Daniel Kahneman talks about in his Nobel lecture. Patients are more likely to agree to a treatment if its effectiveness is described in terms of survival rates rather than in terms of mortality rates, even though the two are the same thing, in the end—so to speak. Actually, it turns out that even doctors are more likely to recommend the treatment if it's described in terms of survival rates. And you'd think they'd know better. If you call it quitting your job, it doesn't sound so good. How about striking out on a new adventure?

You think *striking out* sounds better? Tell that to the last batter at the bottom of the ninth, with bases loaded, I said.

See? Language matters.

Whatever you want to call it. I'm not finding all this very helpful, I have to say.

Have you considered writing things down?

For what purpose?

I find mind maps quite useful.

You think I need to draw mind maps?

A common mistake about religion is that belief comes before practice.

Why would you practice if you didn't have belief?

Here's a little experiment. Make a sad face. Actually, it works better when you're on your own. Try making a sad face.

I did as he suggested.

Now imagine you're very happy.

Again, I did as he suggested.

It's difficult, no?

Okay. But so what?

There's a great study in which subjects were shown slapstick cartoons and asked to rate how funny they were. One cohort was asked to hold a pencil in their mouths, sideways between their teeth, while watching. That group reported the cartoons as being funnier than the other group did.

Why should holding a pencil in your mouth make a difference?

Exactly. Why should it? The speculation—a perfectly sensible speculation, it seems to me—is that holding the pencil that way puts your face in something like the smiling configuration. Matter over mind, you see. How you behave affects how you feel. Religious people who value praxis, rituals, and performance, they understand this. Buddhists have long known the benefits of meditation and, by the way, that's one religion not overburdened with beliefs. I think writing can be a meditation, a praxis, a mode of prayer. Sometimes the discipline of putting things down on paper can help you overcome constraints just a little, and a little might be all you need. You could write in prose or draw a table. Even thinking about column headings could be useful.

Mind maps and matrices, I said.

It might help. You don't know until you've tried it.

Right, I said. I'm sure I looked unconvinced.

I'm sorry, he said. Another beer?

My father got up to go but, taking another look at me, he sat back down. He gave me a huge smile.

It may surprise you to learn, he said, but I have in the past wondered whether I should be more worried than I was about you and your future. I even wondered if my failure to worry made me a bad father.

Really?

Yes, he said, apparently pondering it, but added: In the last century, 1986, I think it was. I forget the day.

You've never worried about me?

No, not really. I used to think it was because of our advantages. There's not much to worry about, I suppose, if you know that short of nuclear devastation or worldwide Communist revolution, your son will live comfortably. But that wasn't it. After all, your mother worried and she also grew up with every advantage. In fact, isn't it understood that the lot of parents is to worry? It's part of the job description.

So why didn't you?

I don't know. Disposition, probably. People are different. Maybe when you have children, you won't worry either. Don't misunderstand me. I appreciate things are tough now, but I believe you are equal to the challenges.

Why have neither of you ever encouraged me and Meena to have children?

Because we only had one child. You have enough expectations to carry around.

What expectations?

Inevitable ones. Your mother and I don't have to do anything for you to form your notions of what we expect.

I should leave finance, you think?

Your grandfather talks about his foundation. You could go and knock that into shape.

That's not the kind of thing I'm into.

Perhaps you could make it the kind of thing you're into. Why not? I'm not suggesting you should, mind, but just wondering aloud. You know, I may be stuck on this question, but I can't tell where you chaps in finance actually take on risk. I mean you all seem to stay in the business even when you don't make your firms big bucks. Even when you do lose your job in one place, a friend hires you into some other firm. You've told me so yourself. It rather tickles me that this business that involves gambling—socially useful gambling, I daresay, but gambling nonetheless—this business doesn't require its participants themselves to take on very much risk.

You don't approve of finance, do you?

On the contrary. If you wanted, say, to make the world a better place—and don't for a moment think that I think you should, but it's impossible to say some things without suggesting an ethical stance—if you wanted to make the world a better place, then I rather suspect the best thing you could do is stay in finance, make even more money, and give it to good causes. Given the choice between becoming an aid worker or funding a hundred of them—it's a no-brainer. But I'm approaching the question rather less altruistically. I think the best way you can get through this is to redefine what you think your situation is. I don't think finance will give you the chance to take a risk, the chance for *you* to take a risk and *learn* to face uncertainty. Gambling with chits is fine—is it chits or chips?

Chips.

Gambling with chips is fine, said my father, but maybe you could try putting yourself on the table. If I were you, I'd talk to Meena and let it take you where it takes you. And when you don't know what to say, say you don't know what to say. But of course, I'm not you.

I've never known you to be prescriptive, but what I'm hearing is that I should change my life completely.

I hope I'm not being prescriptive. Change your life by all means, but only if that's what you want to do. Half the gain is in just wanting change. You know what the problem with politicians is?

What?

They're the kind of people who want to be politicians.

It's easier said than done, I said.

Of course it is. Everything is easier said than done.

Quite.

Except talking, he added.

Sorry?

Talking isn't easier said than done, he said, smiling at me.

But don't they say talk is cheap? I replied.

And worth every penny. Talk to Meena, he said.

Speaking of talking, I said, acknowledging that he'd deftly brought it back to Meena.

The thing about talking, he said, is it makes you thirsty.

Now you're talking.

This conversation took place last year. If I were to put my finger on what it is about it that makes it significant in my mind, I would have to declare that I don't readily know. At the time, my experience of it was lined with a sense of frustration, which gave way to a feeling of disappointment. Yet it is a conversation that I continue to circle back to, so that I am left to suspect that the significance of a conversation is contained in how it is remembered and that only time can disclose the measure of its effect.

12

Henna Tattoo or Redundant and/or Superfluous

A novel was something made up; that was almost its definition. At the same time it was expected to be true, to be drawn from life; so that part of the point of a novel came from half rejecting the fiction, or looking through it to a reality.

Later, when I had begun to identify my material and had begun to be a writer, working more or less intuitively, this ambiguity ceased to worry me. In 1955, the year of this breakthrough, I was able to understand Evelyn Waugh's definition of fiction (in the dedication to *Officers and Gentlemen*, published that year) as "experience totally transformed"; I wouldn't have understood or believed the words the year before. —V. S. Naipaul, *Reading & Writing: A Personal Account*

But isn't one's pain quotient shocking enough without fictional amplification, without giving things an intensity that is ephemeral in life and sometimes even unseen? Not for some. For some very, very few that amplification, evolving uncertainly out of nothing, constitutes their only assurance, and the unlived, the surmise, fully drawn in print on paper, is the life whose meaning comes to matter most. —Philip Roth, *Exit Ghost*

Thus I rediscovered what writers have always known (and have told us again and again): books always speak of other books, and every story tells a story that has already been told.

—Umberto Eco, *The Name of the Rose*,
postscript, translated by William Weaver

You should write a book.

About what? replied Zafar.

A memoir. An autobiography.

Why?

Put your story down on paper.

Books tend to involve paper. Still.

People read memoirs, I said.

So everyone should write memoirs?

Not everyone can write. You *can*. You can stay here and write.

How do you know I can write? he asked.

How do you know you can't? You don't know until you've tried, I said.

I can pick my nose in front of the pope. Doesn't mean I *should*.

You don't like memoirs?

If I like reading them, then I should want to write one, too. Right?

No, I said, exasperated. If you *don't* like reading them, I continued, that's an argument for not writing one.

One should never do anything one doesn't like.

No. One should probably not write a memoir if one doesn't like memoirs. Why not write a novel? I asked, opting for another tack.

All novels are autobiographical.

That's not true. All novels are fictional.

Philip Roth didn't write about colonial Europeans traveling up the Congo river into the heart of Africa, Conrad didn't write about an Indo-Trinidadian settling postcolonial England and Naipaul certainly didn't write about immigrant Jews in the northeast of America.

What do you have against memoirs?

Memoirs are stories of redemption, said Zafar, half of them about a tragic childhood finally overcome, the rest about fleeing the working treadmill for the romantic Tuscan hills or the countryside of Provence and finally discovering what life is actually all about. Look at what I've survived, or see how I've changed: I've taken risks and now I know what's really important. I have nothing against memoirs, but what if there's no redemption to speak of? A manual on failure and dissatisfaction, how to be unhappy, the secret to unhappiness—now that I could write.

You're unhappy?

I exaggerate. But I'm only exaggerating. Or how to lose one's faith. I could write that.

What faith?

How many memoirs do you know where the reader likes the memoirist less at the end than at the beginning?

Maybe, I suggested, it's what happens when you listen to someone's story long enough—you become sympathetic. Did you know that the more information juries are given about the felon, the shorter the sentence they recommend? Apparently, even telling the jury where the criminal lives—doesn't matter where—reduces the sentence.

Is a memoir a case for the defense?

Maybe it's the writing itself that brings what you call redemption. Isn't it cathartic just to figure things out, on the page, laid out in front of your eyes?

You've read a lot of memoirs?

No. Can't say I have.

Even if you had, you still wouldn't know.

Know what?

Know whether writing a memoir is cathartic. What about all those memoirs you don't get to read because they don't get finished? Started with all the hope in the world but abandoned halfway through because the author realized that writing it was dragging him down or because writing it killed him or just drove him insane. Spare a thought for those half-finished memoirs lying in drawers, like bloody daggers, memoirs that, far from delivering catharsis and closure, opened up old wounds.

I'm talking about *writing*, not hara-kiri.

The pen is mightier than the sword.

What about those notebooks?

Emily used to urge me to write. About what? I'd ask. About anything, she'd say. But one day when I suggested it might be interesting to write about us, about her and me, even to write about her family, she gave me a look of horror. There might even have been contempt in there.

I'm not surprised. They're a secretive lot, that family.

Meaning you think they have secrets?

Maybe secretive isn't the right word. Paranoid.

What if they have secrets to keep?

Wouldn't be a secret if I knew the answer to that.

Can't call them paranoid if you don't.

They just don't talk straight.

I suppose they might be paranoid in wanting to hide something of no interest to the rest of the world.

Aren't you overthinking this? I said, my frustration returning.

When I was a boy, said Zafar, my parents told me that my birthday wasn't what was shown on any official documents. I didn't have a birth certificate—certificates weren't a priority in rural Bangladesh. My parents told me it was on a different day, a different month and year from the official British records, different from what they'd filled in on application forms for welfare benefits and school enrollment and library membership. But the next day, they told me not to tell anyone my real birthday, never to mention it to a teacher. My father explained that if the authorities got wind of it, we'd all be sent back to Bangladesh. I was very young, and for some years I thought that we were frauds in Britain, that our very presence in the country was based on a lie. Do you think my father was being paranoid?

Coming from Bangladesh, I replied, your father would have had little idea what the authorities would or wouldn't care about. That's not paranoia; that's prudence. But what about staying here and writing something?

Why are you banging on about this writing?

You could stay and write a book. The flat at the top of the house is there to be used. Why not?

I'm touched.

Don't be facetious.

No, really. I'm touched.

Why not write about your father? You could write about Bangladesh, you could teach people about a part of the world they know little about.

Of course, replied Zafar. Yes, it's very important that people learn about that, very important. Never mind the financial crisis, the wars in Iraq and Afghanistan, never mind global warming and the imminent peak oil crisis. Did I miss anything?

That's not all they're thinking about.

You're right. What the world needs now is answers to all its questions about Bangladeshi history. And it especially needs to hear these answers from me, an alien in his native land and interloper among his hosts, because I know so much about Bangladesh, I'm a bloody authority, that's what I am, a leading international luminary on the history of Bangladesh.

Calm down, dear.

Many people do know quite a lot about Bangladesh. They happen to be living in the region. I don't think Indians and Pakistanis are quite as ignorant about Bangladesh as the people you have in mind, and they make up a fifth of the world.

What about writing for a Western audience? I asked.

Bridging two cultures?

Why not?

You know what Naipaul said about Indian literature?

Tell me what Naipaul said about Indian literature.

Indian literature written in English is astonishing because nowhere in history has a literature been produced that is written by one people about the same people but for another people to read, a literature sustained by a market abroad, the book readers of the West. Naipaul may lament this, but it is only a natural step from what came before to conscript now a generation of native intermediaries. Travel books were always written by the outsider, even if that outsider had a piss-poor command of language and customs. How well will a book about modern India sell to a Western audience, a nonfiction book about this shocking economic trend-bucking phenomenon, if it were written by an Indian? You have to wonder whether these writers Naipaul's talking about, whether they end up playing to Western stereotypes. The fact that they get good reviews, that some of the writing is regarded as excellent, the fact that characters are said to be well drawn—*so accurate, so true to life*, how would they know?—none of that is actually evidence of the contrary and could actually be evidence of the same.

You could write against that, with one foot in the East and the other in the West.

Yes. There's a good market for that, isn't there? A thick book with a lovely cover, a silhouette of a minaret and dome, a view of the hills. Lace the edges with the pattern of a henna tattoo or a sari border. Very nice.

Markets don't lie, I said, ignoring his facetiousness.

Do you know what an axolotl is? asked Zafar.

At this point, I'm certain I merely rolled my eyes.

An axolotl is a kind of salamander. Salamanders start off as one thing but at a certain stage in development they metamorphose into another, rather like toads from tadpoles, very much like them, in fact. The interesting thing about the axolotl is that somewhere along its evolution it decided it wasn't having any truck with this change thing and it remained at that tadpole-like stage before metamorphosis. It doesn't have to metamorphose even to reproduce.

So how is it a kind of salamander if it can't do that?

Do what?

Metamorphose. If it can't metamorphose, then it's just like everything else that can't.

Ah, well, here's the interesting thing. If you inject an axolotl with a solution of iodine and a thyroid-stimulating hormone, and you shouldn't try this at home, then the axolotl does in fact metamorphose; it goes through a radical transformation in hours or days and turns into something very much like a tiger salamander. The other thing I know about the axolotl, which is also amazing, is how extensively it can regenerate itself. It can regrow entire lost limbs. It can even regrow parts of its brain. Ain't that a kick in the head?

Now that's an experiment not worth thinking about, I said.

But once an axolotl is induced into metamorphosis, its life span shortens and it can never go back to what it was.

Thank you for the primer on axolotls. When you said you'd considered writing about Emily's family, what did she say?

She said she was a very private person.

How did you respond? To her?

Exactly, I said. No one can tell their own story, is what I said. They're the most untrue stories of all, the stories we write ourselves, by our own hand and in the first person, where our own dishonesty is hidden from us. Everyone has a region of privacy, things they keep from the world, but that region is only a protective layer behind which are the things they themselves cannot see, a layer shielding them from themselves.

You said this to her?

Something like it, but I don't think she was listening. I think she was anxious about the prospect of me writing about her family.

Sounds about right, I said to Zafar.

She did, however, say I was expecting too much of writing. On the contrary, I said. I don't expect very much of it at all. You should write your own story, she said. Which is not your story? I asked. No, she replied. Is no part of your story my story? I asked her. I'm a private person, she repeated. Do you have a copy of *Brideshead Revisited*? Zafar asked me.

I think I do, somewhere, I replied.

On the title page are the words: *Brideshead Revisited: The Sacred and Profane Memories of Captain Charles Ryder: A Novel.* But if you look on the reverse, the page with the copyright statement, there's an odd note, almost invisible, signed with Waugh's initials. It says: *I am not I: thou art not he or she: they are not they.* Everyone knows that Waugh's inspiration for his story was the Lygon family. But the question remains: Why did he write this? Why write that epigraphic disclaimer?

Libel?

As if merely saying that it's not about them would save it from amounting to libel, like announcing that a fictional American president from Texas, whose father was president, too, is a lying son of a bitch. There has to be more to it. And besides, it's a novel. The names are all different, not to mention the facts are bent out of shape. The oddest thing about it is the *thou: thou art not he.* Waugh is addressing someone specific, which only calls attention to the very question.

What question?

Whether it is in fact about the Lygons.

Maybe in his head, it wasn't fiction. Maybe it was all very real.

Isn't that true of all novels and their authors? Or the good ones at any rate. That they're very real to the author?

Maybe he wanted to make the distinction clear to readers?

Then why bury it in the title verso page under the technicalities of copyright dates and publishing house?

Why do *you* think he did it?

I don't know, replied Zafar.

When did she say this?

Say what?

No part of her story was yours.

A year or so into the relationship.

It must have hurt.

I wondered. I asked myself if we could ever be married, if our stories could ever combine.

Bridging cultures, then.

Zafar seemed to ponder this for a while, and I chastised myself for reminding him of something painful. I wasn't there, but it seemed to me that had those been her words, they would have put a great distance between the two of them.

Presently Zafar picked up his thread.

Bridging two cultures, he said. That might be worth writing about.

That's precisely what I'm saying. So you *have* thought about it.

What do you know about the Ponte Vecchio?

Cross off axo . . . axo—

Axolotls, he said.

That's easy for you to say.

Practice a little but often.

And now Florentine bridges.

What do you know about it?

It's a big bridge with buildings on it. Jewelry and souvenir shops. Mainly a tourist trap when I went there, but then Italy's one big tourist trap.

Bridges are fragile things. A bridge belongs to nothing, to nowhere. The mind settles on the emptiness between its ends, a region of suspended animation.

But you can walk that bridge. That's what you can write about.

The two cultures I had in mind were the sciences and the arts or the sciences and the humanities or the sciences and literature or whatever name it goes by.

C. P. Snow?

But I don't know how to write about that.

Why would you want to?

Sometimes I think it matters, said Zafar. Sometimes I think I see a gulf and I think it matters very much. And sometimes I wonder if I'm seeing a gulf that isn't really there. Maybe it just matters to me and it doesn't really matter otherwise. You ask any of your nonscientific friends to list the Ten Commandments and they might struggle after seven or eight, but seven or eight isn't bad. If, on the other hand, you ask them for the Second Law of Thermodynamics or Newton's First Law of Motion, they look at you as if you're a social buffoon.

Science is so very specialized, I said. I don't think my father knows the first thing about genetics. How can anyone other than a scientist know anything of substance about science?

But still it doesn't get me past the nagging thought that there's something wrong in an entire establishment, all the opinion formers, all the policy wonks, and everyone who's anyone in the public life of Western societies—there's something not quite right about them being scientifically illiterate when it's science that's changed the lives of human beings in postindustrial societies more than anything else, and science that will do the same in the years to come.

That's a bit presumptuous, don't you think?

What? That science changed more than—

No. That the entire establishment—whatever that is—is scientifically illiterate.

All right. Not everybody.

Write about it.

I don't know where to begin. It's just too big. Anyhow, I'm not sure it's even there, this gulf. And even if it is, maybe it doesn't matter.

My true motivation for encouraging Zafar to write was to have him stay. Although the thought did not preoccupy me, I knew from the day he reappeared that before long he would leave. Even many weeks in, Zafar kept his possessions in his own two bags; he lived out of them, and they were never more than one item short of ready to go.

What about the conversations on the DVR? There must be some interesting conversations on it if you recorded them. Were they interviews?

Zafar didn't respond.

There aren't any conversations on it?

I think you'll find that there are.

But they're not interesting?

You should be the judge of that.

It was only later that I realized why Zafar was being so shifty. He must have been smiling to himself inwardly, for he would have known, so careful had he been in his choice of words, that he had actually only suggested that I listen to the conversations on the DVR. When I finally did and took the DVR back to its first recording, I discovered that there was nothing on it apart from the conversations between the two of us. As I say, I only figured out all this later. When I confronted his oddly shifty responses, I moved on and tried a different tack.

What about your notebooks? Why not make something of them?

They don't cover the half of it.

Don't let the perfect become the enemy of the good and all that. Glass half full.

Do things by halves?

Can't they be organized into something?

Do you know Robert Oppenheimer's words from the Bhagavad Gita?

You're all over the place. More than I remember you being.

Do you? he repeated.

After he saw the first atom bomb explode? Yes, I said.

Now I am become Death, said Oppenheimer, *the destroyer of worlds*. Apparently, he was a decent Sanskrit scholar, you know? Not half bad.

Oppenheimer the physicist?

Scientist and Sanskritist, now there's a bridge. He said he translated it himself. So you have to wonder why he got it wrong. Apparently, a better translation is: *I am Time, who has come forth to annihilate the worlds*. So much more powerful, don't you think? The Song of the Lord. And not a tautology. More meaningful.

Tautologies mean nothing.

More resonant.

A tautology is nothing more than a tautology.

I got the joke the first time. Maybe the original doesn't have quite the resonance in the shadow of the mushroom cloud. My notebooks are just notes. When I read them, they call up memories. Without the memories intact, the notes are like queer ciphers. And memories are completely unreliable. Time destroys memory.

But memories are all we have, aren't they?

How little, replied Zafar.

And how precious. Have you seen *Blade Runner*? I asked him.

Zafar nodded.

Near the end, when Roy the android—

Rutger Hauer.

Yes. Roy the android is defeated by Deckard, and as he prepares to die he says something like: I've seen things you people wouldn't believe. I've seen attack ships off the shoulder of Orion and something about the Tannhauser Gate, et cetera—I can't remember the rest.* Did you know that Rutger Hauer extemporized those words?

Zafar shook his head.

The point is that in his dying moments the things he describes are things he remembers. They don't mean anything to you and me, but they're the things Roy remembers. For my money, the movie's about what makes an android human. Where's the dividing line? But then that comes down to the question: What makes a human being human? The answer in *Blade Runner* is memory. However flawed and faulty, however much you get your wires mixed up, the memories are what make you you. Don't we have to hold on to them?

Writing is what you do when you don't want to forget.

Exactly. There are ideas in those notebooks of yours, I said. I don't know how much of it makes any sense, but there's got to be something there, a thread, questions that preoccupy you. Isn't that what they're about?

Read them, he told me. I don't feel the compulsion to write a book, but maybe you'll be moved to write something, something about yourself.

No one can tell his own story. Didn't you say that?

But you disagree. Prove me wrong. Or invent someone to tell your story. Spectators see more of the game than players do.

Why don't *you* invent someone? I asked.

Look, said Zafar. It was he who now showed exasperation. I don't know how to get anywhere close to my own life, he said. My drama, like everyone's, goes on upstairs, in the head. And I don't think you can write the drama of the mind. All you have are the things people do. It's always about what they do, and yet the mind is where the battles take place, the tragedies and comedies that rule the day. So we fall back on metaphors, accounts of stuff that happens in flesh between people, the movement of limbs, the actor curling the lips, the vibrations of vocal cords, the rush of air, a painter in a rage flinging paint at the canvas— it's always the kinetics that steal the show while the governing drama,

---

* "I've seen things you people wouldn't believe. Attack ships on fire off the shoulder of Orion. I watched C-Beams glitter in the dark near the Tannhauser Gate. All those moments will be lost in time, like tears in rain. Time to die."

the theater of the mind, plays out behind the curtain. Shadows in the cave.

Have you read *The Moon and Sixpence* by Somerset Maugham?

No, Zafar replied.

It's modeled on the life of the painter Paul Gauguin. The whole novel stands in the shadow of the protagonist's inscrutable decision to abandon his wife and children, abandon his life as a stockbroker, and disappear first to Paris and then to the South Seas to . . . to paint.

You sound like a revision aid.

I read it at school. Maugham can't give a half-decent explanation for this decision and falls back on speculation. And when the painter himself is pressed, he is, as Maugham says, too lacking in self-awareness, whatever that means, to be able to explain it himself.

There you go, then. Some things just don't see the light of day.

But it's not a bad book, not at all. You don't knock a tiger for not having wings.

I'm not saying it isn't and I'm not saying there isn't a book to be written—you can have a go. What I'm saying is that the thing I want to write I can't write; maybe it can't be written. You talk about inexplicable decisions, but what about actions that do not proceed from anything that can be called a decision? How can it ever be enough to speak of blind rage? The unspeakable does not bear utterance. And even if the words were there for the discovering, how much pain would I have to overcome to hold the pen steady for long enough? I remember a famous passage in *Daniel Deronda*: *There is a great deal of unmapped country within us which would have to be taken into account in an explanation of our gusts and storms.**

That's where imagination comes in, I said. Writers use their imaginations. It's a gift human beings have, and a writer uses it to go to those

---

*Zafar's notebooks record several passages from *Daniel Deronda*, including:

> How trace the why and wherefore in a mind reduced to the barrenness of a fastidious egoism, in which all direct desires are dulled, and have dwindled from motives into a vacillating expectation of motives: a mind made up of moods, where a fitful impulse springs here and there conspicuously rank amid the general weediness? 'Tis a condition apt to befall a life too much at large, unmoulded by the pressure of obligation.

places hard to reach, those unmapped countries within us. Imagination is a compass—a compass from God, if you will.

Your English teacher must have been very good. Maybe he'd want *you* to write.

Now you're condescending.

Zafar gave me a disarming smile.

My dear fellow, he said pompously, I should be very surprised if your mind, such as it is, did not consider me condescending.

Whatever.

You know V. S. Naipaul's famous advice to the young Paul Theroux? *You have to tell the truth.* We think we know what he means and in fact we probably do, but only because we know vaguely what Naipaul must think vaguely. He's saying more than merely that a novel is an experiment in life, which is what George Eliot said; after all, other than metaphorically, it isn't that at all. A metaphor is useful only for transforming what happens, *enriching* it in some way. It *never* tells you what actually happened, how it happened, or why it happened. A fleeting thought might be compared to a ship on the horizon, but surely it's saying something that a ship on the horizon is never compared to a fleeting thought? When a football manager speaking about the range of talents in his team says sagaciously that when you make wine, great wine, the very best wine, not all the grapes are the same, you know he is speaking metaphorically—unless he happens to have a gig running a vineyard on the side. But what he is actually talking about—the right way to compose a football team—remains unproven, remains untouched by the metaphor. If metaphors increase our understanding, they do so only because they take us back to a familiar vantage, which is to say that a metaphor cannot bring anything nearer. Everything new is on the rim of our view, in the darkness, below the horizon, so that nothing new is visible but in the light of what we know.

Listening to Zafar, I could not help thinking that perhaps Emily was right. Far from expecting too little of writing, Zafar expected too much, but only because he expected too much of human thought. His language sounded somehow constructed, even more so than it had done all those years ago. I see now, of course, that what he was talking about were things that had long preoccupied him, some old, some more recent, some that happened in 2002, six years earlier, and that they had preoccupied him with good reason. It is little wonder, for instance, that he was concerned with human motivation for action, which he went on to discuss, since the very thing he asked of himself had to do with his own motivation for the actions he came to take.

If the province of science is *how?*, continued Zafar, then the rigor of life, the predicament of living in the world, is contained in the question *why?* Wittgenstein said that when all the questions of science have been answered, all the problems of life will still remain. That may be, but it is equally true that when all the work of art is finished, when we have been blinded by every metaphor under the sun, not one question of *how?* or *why?* will have been touched. Tell the truth: First you have to find the truth, and there's no guarantee that you can. But it's even worse than that. What science is now making plain, in a way we once dimly suspected but could never say for sure or to what extent, is that we don't know the half of our own minds. It seems the least reliable thing a person can say about any of his actions are the motivations that he himself ascribes to them. Naipaul's advice cannot be dismissed, but the best to be said for it, which is the best that Theroux can do—because he's human—is that it enjoins Theroux to root out any conscious dishonesties, and if he's lucky a few unconscious ones will come out in the tangle. Peanuts.

Why not think of a book in the same way you think of a map or a translation? It's not perfect, far from it, but it's something.

A ringing endorsement. I had a friend who used to see a therapist, and she said something about the experience that's stayed with me. Just being able to speak about some dreadful things, she said, and seeing that the therapist wasn't falling apart from hearing them was helpful. What struck me was that I could imagine someone else saying that being able to speak about dreadful things and seeing that the therapist *did* break down in tears was helpful. It seems to me that this is the big difference between writing and talking. When you talk, you get to see the effect, and maybe it's witnessing the effect that matters to you and not just framing your thoughts in words. We learn about the weight of things by seeing how they affect others. Why would you want to leave a broken person alone with a pen?

I'm running out of arguments, I said to him, and frankly I'm not sure it's worth forcing this. I don't agree with most of what you say. I don't think your position is quite as reasoned as you seem to think it is—

For fuck's sake, what's with this writing nonsense?

Zafar's face changed. We were in a restaurant, in Holland Park, where no one shouts unless it's at a waiter.

Has it occurred to you that I might not want to write, that I might actually want to talk. I'm not telling you to read. All you have to do is listen.

You misunderstand. Of course we'll talk—

Has it occurred to you that you might actually be the person to whom I have to say what I'm saying? Maybe you don't want to find out why I'm telling you. You have a role, you know, center stage, I'd say. I could equally ask you if you don't want to listen.

Of course I'm listening—

And what the fuck makes you think I want to sit down and write and stew myself in all this shit? Putting things on paper makes things real, hardens them, makes them unchangeable, even before things have made sense. Since when did books ever solve anything? They only raise more questions than they answer, otherwise they're just fucking entertainment, and I'm not here to fucking entertain you.

Zafar stopped there. He fidgeted in his seat before picking up cubes of sugar and adding them to his coffee, one after another. The restaurant was empty. The lighting had been turned down.

I'm just saying . . . I'm just saying that your reasons seem like dressings for wounds.

Nice, he replied.

I don't remember you being so bleak in college.

I wasn't as untrusting. I had faith in the goodness of people, the perfection of love.

What happened?

Everything ends. And it's how they end that leaves the lasting effect.

That's another argument for writing: making something that outlasts you.

And there I was thinking that's what children were about.

Zafar had been speaking about the past, but I knew nothing of where he was in the present. There remained also the question: Why had he come here, to the U.K., to my home? And what was he doing these days? No sooner had this last question presented itself to me than it seemed out of place.

It seemed to me that asking him what he was doing these days, let alone asking why he had come to my home, was to reduce our history of friendship, or reduce the intimacy that had evolved in the days since he reappeared, as he and I talked in a way we had never done before. It was inappropriate. There remained instead a sense of the present held in abeyance, left at the door, to enter later perhaps. For now, the past had spread through this house, crisscrossing the walls of the kitchen with Zafar's stories and mine, redecorating a home in the colors of childhood and families and memory.

There is an observation in Zafar's notebooks: In our twenties, when a friend tells us his relationship has ended, we ask, *Who ended it?* In our thirties, we simply say, *I'm sorry.*

In that shift is, I think, a change in our attitude to causation, from a belief that causation can be understood to a recognition that at certain times it is useless. Causation is about how things were necessarily true, because this led to that. In our conversations in those wintry days, there was always a quality of longing about them, particularly when they reached far back. Longing for what? When Zafar spoke about the past, I felt the presence of many pasts, the one that was spoken, but also other unlived lives, the lives uncaused, yet imagined. There is not one past but many, and every memory carries the spirit of all.

After a few days of reading from the bag of notebooks, I raised again, tentatively and for the last time, the idea of him writing a book.

You must be short of cash. A book could give you an income.

We were in the kitchen. Maria, the housekeeper, had left some pasta marinara for supper.

Zafar gave me a glancing look, as if to acknowledge my cheek in raising the matter again.

I have enough, he said. I had more, until last year when my parents nearly lost their house. Northern Rock collapsed at the same time as they came out of the fixed-rate period on their mortgage. They were hammered by the rates at the same time the bank was tightening up on risky loans. I have a little equity in a company that was doing well. Some of the dividend now goes to them to help make mortgage repayments. But I have enough. I don't spend much.

What company? I asked.

I am embarrassed now for failing to express appropriate commiseration for his parents' difficulties. The small remark about them should have struck me in a number of ways. Yet all my curiosity fixed on the surprising news that Zafar had invested in shares, for Zafar had never seemed to me to have an interest in owning anything, in assets, not even a house. And the remark about his parents was also the first mention of anything recent in his life. Of course, it didn't tell me where in the world he'd been living, it didn't tell me what he'd been doing, but I did not take the opportunity in front of me .

I remember a lawyer friend of mine—actually a friend of Meena's— explaining to me that in a criminal trial in which the defendant has prior convictions, the prosecution cannot, other than in exceptions, raise those convictions in court. But, the lawyer friend explained, if the defendant in any way claims he has a good character, then those convictions can be raised by the prosecution to rebut the defendant's claim.

I don't mean to liken Zafar to a criminal, but there has always been a certain mystery about him, and it was moments like this one, when he volunteered some information, that opened the door to inquiry. I could have asked him about his parents. I could have asked him when exactly he had heard they were in trouble and how he had heard. I could have asked him where he was at the time. But I didn't. Instead I asked him what company he'd invested in.

What company?

Zafar then told me a remarkable story, which again underlined how little I had really known. In 1994, he explained, he met an extraordinary woman at JFK airport.

I remember, he said, that the Dow had closed above four thousand just a few days earlier, the first time it had ever done so. There was an exuberance on the Street that was exciting and scary—think of extreme sports. Every banker was charging every meal and cab ride to his expense account, and firms were turning a blind eye. You can tell a firm's hit a downturn when the row of private cabs waiting outside the building shortens. A couple of months earlier, I'd received my first bonus—which wasn't as large as you think; I never fought hard enough. I took my first vacation since that week long ago at a holiday camp on the English seaside, arranged by concerned social workers. I spent a week in Panama.

With this woman?

I went alone. I met Marcy Feuerstein in the airport lounge, where she was trying to calm her three-year-old daughter. The girl took one look at me and was silenced. She was fascinated by me for some inexplicable reason in the way maybe only children can be. I sat near them and smiled at the child, who smiled back. That was the beginning of our conversation.

Marcy, it transpired, had just left Microsoft and was starting up her own business, as well as raising Josie by herself. She lived in California but had just finished three days of meetings in New York and was on her way back. She talked eagerly about the pitches she'd made to potential investors, and what she said intrigued me. It seemed to me a remarkable, exciting thing, this field she was entering. Even then I knew that my excitement was not really to do with making money. Marcy was attractive—she was beautiful—and there was some flirtation in our conversation, but even that was not at the root of my interest; I don't think it was. Marcy was starting a business in wireless technologies for corporations, to provide the hardware and software to enable companies to network their firm-wide resources wirelessly. Such technology was almost unimaginable; it was 1994.

When I was a boy, I was intrigued to read about the properties of light. I read that what we call light is only the visible part of a spectrum of radiation. I learned why the sky is blue and how a rainbow is formed. And then I read about how light is both wave and particle, and I saw a diagram somewhere of the double-slit experiment. I thought about light, and it occurred to me that we cannot see light rays going across our field of vision. I know now that even when we see rays of sunlight shining through the window of a chapel on a winter's afternoon, we do not see even one single ray of light that makes it to the ground because every ray we think we see is in fact no ray at all but the impression left by streams of light reflected off dust particles and fortuitously sent in the direction of our eyes. The image of shafts of light with dancing motes, so common in words and photographs, remains an illusion, you see. The conclusion of this is that if we look on a ray of light from the side, and the air is free of dust, then the light will in fact be invisible.

Wireless links, connections without material ties, without constraints that hold you in place, ethereal vines that reach out to you, tethers for the rootless. I didn't really know how to think about Marcy's business idea itself; she seemed to have barrels of energy and a riot of ideas, but over the years I've come to suspect that the true source of her vitality and drive was a fear of being accused of failing her daughter. I can't know for sure, because I did not know Marcy before Josie, nor, for that matter, do I know the Marcy in another universe who never had Josie. It was, in any event, the magic of these invisible wires tying people together that thrilled me, as I sat there in the lounge, watching Marcy stroke her daughter's hair unconsciously while discussing all the issues involved, how to make wireless secure, how to make it stable, the problems of interference, establishing connectivity across different platforms. On the strength of my wonder, I invested in her business and came to receive a small investor's dividend each year, although now paid from shares in the large tech company that eventually bought her out with its own stock. The dividend is enough for me.

You never told me, I said. I was annoyed that he hadn't mentioned any of this to me.

What for?

Maybe I would have invested?

Most British universities weren't even hooked up to the Internet. Would you have invested in corporate wireless networking systems?

I ask myself now if Zafar had always thought of me as lacking courage. I remember seeing him once after he returned from a weekend parachuting. He jumped tandem, he said—it was his first time and perhaps he hasn't jumped again. He loved it and described it as something like swimming. You're so high up in the air, he said, the ground seemingly unchanging, that you really can't tell you're falling. Seconds that seem like hours pass before the first small chute bursts open, pulling out the main chute, and you feel yourself yanked like a rag doll. I listened to Zafar waxing lyrical, and of course the thought passed through my mind that he hadn't asked me to come along with him. If I had asked him why, he would have answered—as I knew—with the same question: Would I have come? I suppose I didn't ask in order to avoid an exchange that would only diminish me.

During that conversation, I continued to push him just a little further on the business of writing. Eventually, after a pause, Zafar began telling me something that I did not immediately recognize as a story.

Alessandro Moisi Iacoboni was born in 1942 in a village four hours by mule from the town of M——, in a part of Italy where the spoken language is neither Italian nor German but shows the influences of both. Alessandro's birth came nine months and two weeks after a day in June when an ill-disciplined division of Heeresgruppe C of the German Wehrmacht swept through the village, an incursion that caused a degree of embarrassment in those quarters of Italian society, which had enthusiastically supported Mussolini's alliance with Germany.

Who cares about this? I asked, but Zafar merely continued.

Alessandro's mother died three days after what was by all accounts a terrible labor. It was this mother who might have kindled in little Alessi the fire of the Jewish faith but, as it was, her death cleared the way for the Catholic nuns of Our Lady of Modena, in the village school, whose influence found no resis—

What about writing your own story?

I interrupted Zafar and, as I listen to the recording again, I am rather ashamed that I did so. Listening is hard, as my friend once said, because you run the risk of having to change the way you see the world. I can admit something now, which this interruption only evidenced: I have been inclined to force the people around me into boxes. It's a subtle thing, but to hear someone talk without imposing one's own expectations, one's own categories—I've never been very good at it. Of course, only the wearer knows where the shoe pinches, but listening well is—to stay with the metaphor—the only way to walk a few steps in his shoes. How does someone fail to grasp that, something so absurdly obvious?

It *is* my story. It's the story I want to tell, said Zafar.

Zafar never finished telling it, but I found it later in his notebooks, where, he'd said, I could read it if I wanted. I don't know what to make of it.

I have rather regretted interrupting him. For one thing, it would have been another kind of story to hear it from his own lips, though I'm inclined to think his memory would not have conjured all its detail. But

I have assuaged my regret with the thought that if I do not consider the story a piece of the highest sentimentalism, then perhaps it is because in the end it went unsaid, unspoken, as if it were something that remained where it ought to have remained, as if its proper home was the privacy of that recess where decent men tend lost love.

I think now that he was right: He said that it was *his* story and it was the story *he* wanted to tell. It seems obvious to me now that every story belongs to its teller. So I include the passages from the relevant notebook here and let them speak for themselves.

13

Alessandro Moisi Iacoboni

If there is any substitute for love, it's memory. To memorize, then, is to restore intimacy.

—Joseph Brodsky, "Nadezhda Mandelstam: An Obituary"

Great is this power of memory, exceedingly great, O my God, a spreading limitless room within me. Who can reach its uttermost depth? Yet it is a faculty of my soul and belongs to my nature. In fact I cannot grasp all that I am. Thus the mind is not large enough to contain itself: but where can that part of it be which it does not contain? Is it outside itself and not within? How can it not contain itself? As this question struck me, I was overcome with wonder and almost stupor. Here are men going afar to marvel at the heights of mountains, the mighty waves of the sea, the long courses of great rivers, the vastness of the ocean, the movement of the stars, yet leaving themselves unnoticed.

—Saint Augustine, *Confessions*, Book X, "Memory,"
translated into German by Romano Guardini and
from the German into English by Elinor Briefs

Perhaps everybody has a garden of Eden, I don't know; but they have scarcely seen their garden before they see the flaming sword. Then, perhaps, life only offers the choice of remembering the garden or forgetting it. Either, or: it takes strength to remember, it takes another kind of strength to forget, it takes a hero to do both. People who remember court madness through pain, the pain of the perpetually recurring death of their innocence; people who forget court another kind of madness, the madness of the denial of pain and the hatred of innocence; and the world is mostly divided between madmen who remember and madmen who forget.

—James Baldwin, *Giovanni's Room*

Alessandro Moisi Iacoboni was born in 1942 in a village four hours by mule from the town of M——, in a part of Italy where the spoken language is neither Italian nor German but shows the influences of both. Alessandro's birth came nine months and two weeks after a day in June when an ill-disciplined division of Heeresgruppe C of the German Wehrmacht swept through the village, an incursion that caused a degree of embarrassment in those quarters of Italian society which had enthusiastically supported Mussolini's alliance with Germany.

Alessandro's mother died three days after what was by all accounts a terrible labor. It was this mother who might have kindled in little Alessi the fire of the Jewish faith but, as it was, her death cleared the way for the Catholic nuns of Our Lady of Modena, in the village school, whose influence found no resistance in the decreased Iacoboni household. The boy's father, having barely tolerated his wife's superstitions and now embittered by the cruelties of war, believed that the God of Abraham, far from deserving of Jacob's esteem, warranted a good hiding. He would leave Alessi in the care of the good sisters of the Savior, while the villagers attended Sunday mass, and he would make the journey to M—— in order to replenish the stock. Signor Iacoboni was the village grocer.

Young Alessandro might have fallen by the wayside but for that propitious combination of wit and good luck that furnishes as good an account of how a life came to be, such as it was, as is likely ever to be found. At root, an inquisitive nature directed the boy to make capital of his schooling, despite the torments of children (blame for whose racial animosities must be laid at the doors of their parents). His humiliations do not bear repetition, and Alessandro himself, with no mother to soothe him, consigned each episode to the vaults of memory no sooner than they had occurred, throwing the key away, so to speak. In so doing, he grew to believe himself possessed of unusual mastery over his memory.

Away from the classroom, Alessandro helped his father in the shop, but his persistent questions drove his father to distraction. *Why, Father, do we have snow shovels in the summer and why are they on show outside? So that when the snow comes, no one will say that we've hiked the prices in winter. Why do you bring back so much copper sulfate with you every time you go to M——? Don't we have a lot in the back already? So that when the time comes there will be enough. When the time comes for what, Father? They use it on the vineyards to protect the grapes. Protect them from fungus and disease.*

What's fungus? And so it went on, questions of all kinds. *Why do so many animals have four legs? Why not three? Old Nico says the moon can move the ocean. Do you agree, Papa?*

His father would inevitably tire, sending Alessi out, which rather suited Alessi, who spent many a happy hour under the hazels, in the vineyards and terraces, under the lime blossom or in the bracken or the reed beds around the watercourses, reading or making up stories, stories of every kind, stories told to a woman he imagined, whom he called *My Mama*, and when he picked apart plants, to her he described everything he saw. He spied on the peasants and watched old Nico tending his vegetable garden and he learned. In books, too, he found plants, books he came upon at school or books lent to him by the village mayor, a Communist, who, between arranging favors for kinsmen and party faithful, felt moved, it is not hard to imagine, to assist the least of the village (who happened also to own the grocery). Alessi learned how to graft, and there was once an apricot tree that stood for three decades that the child Alessi himself had grafted onto the plum. He saw a picture of a mango in a book, was puzzled to read that mangoes do not grow true to themselves, and looked anew with astonishment at this earth that sprouted such varied fruits.

Word of this peculiar boy circulated, and one day, in Alessi's twelfth year, his father received a visitor from the household of the Contessa Sylvia di Cossano, the lights of whose eponymous hamlet Alessi had seen through the aspens on clear nights as a nest of stars on the black hills. The emissary explained that her ladyship kindly requested to meet the boy so that his future might be considered. The conclusion was foregone. Alessi was installed in a boarding school in M——, where he would see his father on the grocer's weekly visit. The boy had not yet the maturity to see that his father's unhesitating acceptance of the contessa's proposition marked only what the man had long known: The road leading out of the village had been beckoning his child from the boy's first utterances. In due course, Alessandro earned a scholarship to study medicine in the university in Bologna. Three days after arriving in the grand city, the young man received word that his father had died.

Although it is true that in the life of Iacoboni, we have few sources upon which to draw, something may be said of it nonetheless, and here the opportunity arises to make a point of more general application.

Autobiography, we know, is flawed from the moment the nib of the pen touches the parchment, flawed because it begins and ends with an unfinished work, and flawed because its author himself is the victim of the most cunning deceptions. (It may be argued that the only lives to follow a form with meaning are those of suicides.) But we may go further, for there is a wisdom abroad holding that the records of a life, as drawn on in the course of a biographer's work, for instance, can illuminate the whole of it, as if the penumbras of light shed by each fragment overlap to cover the entirety, when no reservation is made for the possibility, only too real, that episodes in the course of a life there may be, whose bearing, in the final analysis, far exceeds the barely traceable mark, if any, which they might leave on even the most extensive record. It may even be the case that the bearing of such episodes escaped the sensibilities of the subject himself. Rescue from stalling altogether before the darkness comes only when we accept that we may enter into the void a counsel of honest speculation, brokered by goodwill and the search for the truth. We can only imagine and, with an attitude of respect, are entitled to do so.

At the age of twenty-three, just two weeks after taking his final exams and before the results were known, Alessandro read a story in an unremarkable student literary journal. In the years to come, had Alessandro been asked to proffer an interpretation, he would have replied that there was nothing of note in the tale; he might have tendered only vague impressions, he might have mentioned that it had a maudlin turn, that it suffered, perhaps, from the overwriting of impatient youth, but as for its details Alessandro would have been able to relate almost nothing. That he would remember the story at all can be put down to a single phrase, a phrase in its opening passage, which, having been laid within him like some spirit, would be born again and again in the months and years to follow, though with his own name substituted for the long-forgotten and finally insignificant original one: *In the hour of his death, Alessandro Moisi Iacoboni would cry out for his mother.* When he read the tale, one May morning in the library of the university, he could not have foreseen that this phrase, this ordered collection of words, was to command his life in ways he could not have expected, that he would be seized by the fear of yet another substitution, another name, though not for his own. Nor could he know that in the years to follow, the meaning of the phrase, ringing in his ears, would itself be changed by his life.

In 1967, Alessandro's career as a physician and scientist began apace, full of promise, and it was blessed in its very first years by a chance scientific discovery made possible by his diligence, for Fate, as Louis Pasteur, another notable physician but of an earlier age, remarked, favors the prepared mind. In those days, Alessandro received several minor awards, which marked him out for future reference. Alessandro made the world his home, he traveled widely, and he steeped himself in the culture of each new place, coming even to dream in its native tongue. Alessandro made friends easily, though some might have said not very deeply.

His scientific and medical reputation grew. He kept meticulous notes of all his consultations, regarding each patient, to use a current phrasing, as a human being first but also as the potential hope for others through what might be learned from his or her ailments. He was considered reliable so that more and more he came to be relied upon.

Then Alessandro fell in love. In March of 1972, he attended an academic symposium in the heart of Vienna, not far from the Staatsoper, at which symposium he delivered a creditable paper and impressively fielded an array of questions, but from which he quietly slipped away before the conclusion of the day's proceedings, being somewhat worse for wear, having arrived in the city only that morning by overnight train from Paris. Alessandro wandered across the Opernring and into the Kunsthistorisches Museum, with only the modest expectation of emptying his mind in preparation for the effort of the symposium dinner.

He idled through its halls, and while he barely took in any of the museum's considerable collection of masterpieces, he nonetheless gained an advantage from the restorative effect of the ambience. He was searching for a sign showing the way out, when he turned a corner and was brought to a standing stop by what he saw. The painting was by the Italian late-Baroque painter Luca Giordano, and, as Alessandro would observe after emerging from his stunned regard, its subject was precisely as its title attested: *The Expulsion of Lucifer from Heaven.*

Facing the image of Lucifer, Alessandro was overcome by sadness. As if before Alessi alone in the hall, the archangel Michael, Lucifer's own brother but instrument of God's will, thrust Lucifer down, casting him (whose name signifies light itself) from the illumination of heaven into the darkness of exile. Notwithstanding an epic assembly of detail, including, for example, demons and devils scattering and falling, it was the face of Lucifer that arrested Alessandro's eye, the exile's upturned head, the arched muscles of the neck straining like a drawn bow, the jugular taut as wire. Above all were those eyes, knives of blue, Lucifer pleading with St. Michael, begging for the mercy of a God whose mercy was spent.

It is tempting to think that in those moments Alessandro remembered the story of Joseph that he learned at the nuns' feet, Joseph, whose brothers drove him into the desert but who was restored to the fold and whose father rejoiced to see him again. Might Lucifer one day be reconciled with his father in heaven? The Lucifer whom Giordano presented to Alessandro bore no hubris but only the anguish of leaving home and losing love. Was this how evil entered the world? If it was pride that exiled Lucifer from heaven, then surely it is sorrow that fired his hatred.

Stumbling out into the gardens of the museum, Alessandro came upon a secluded café, where, beneath the linden trees, setting down his hat and uncoiling his scarf, he took off his glasses, and, leaning his elbows on the table, buried his face in his hands and wept. If there had been anyone watching at the time—and there was—such witness might have supposed he was merely massaging his eyes, for Alessandro did not let out a sound, nor did he shake, but instead his tears pooled in the interstices between his eyes and palms. It is observed parenthetically that although Alessandro was never prone to cry, it is a fact that within the week he would cry once more.

Duly, which is to say centuries later, he recovered himself, ordered an espresso from the waiter, and put on his glasses. As his coffee was set before him, Alessandro caught the gaze of a woman at the next table. She was, in his instant conviction, unapproachably beautiful, but, having perhaps been shaken free by his crying of some of those social restraints in himself, which he reviled, Alessandro offered to the woman, with such alacrity as to deny the possibility that the utterance was an act of courage, these words issued with measure and poise: *The daffodils are early this spring.* The woman laughed with pleasure.

Alessi was overcome with longing of a kind he had never felt before. An account of the outward appearance of this woman might be considered appropriate here, a mention of porcelain or roseblush skin, for instance, but a moment's reflection is enough to remind us that the evocation of the sublime to one man might to another stand merely as the image of plain beauty. Indeed, let us take direction from language: The (Italian) word *vago* means vague, but an appropriately remote meaning connotes beauty and grace. It is wisdom itself, therefore, to refrain from describing the woman and to let the imagination, which is the true and only expert in this field, do its work. Alessi, who had never considered himself courageous, watched his own body rise from its seat, the cup of coffee, scarf, and hat in his hands, and walk to the woman. For him, it is not too fanciful to suggest, this sequence of acts amounted to a private heroism.

The two lovers spent a week in Vienna, most of it in the room of a hotel (or, to dispense with all vestige of delicacy, in the bed of their hotel room), where the elegance of its appointment was exceeded only by the cultivated discretions of the staff in the face of their guests' private lives. How is it possible, Alessi asked himself, that another human being's body can so convincingly seem an extension of one's own? As she lay there in the mornings, Alessi watched patches of dawn's searching light find her form. Alessi noted the stark absence of reason in the room, the bond without explanation, the inadequacy of all he knew to account for this, and as he watched her rub her eyes and smile at him, he understood that his life now contained two domains, science and love; that the two domains were divided not by reason, for even science makes claims about love, but were divided because suddenly subjectivity had borne in on him and he would not ever care for the science of love. When he had never before considered if science was necessary, never posed the question, here and now the answer came; here and now he believed that in this it was not.

Vienna sang in a whirling haze about the two lovers. They visited Stephansdom, and were each charmed, above all else, by the sound of the other's footsteps on the stone floor. They bought the most expensive tickets at the Staatsoper—the only ones still available—where they had scarcely heard the overture to . . . well, it does not matter, for they slipped away at the interval and hastened to their room. Alessandro felt an urgent charge running through him, a positive need to be inside her, to make love over and over.

In the evenings, they stepped out for dinner and to walk under the soft lights of the city, while a cool breeze circled them. They entered a lingerie store, at her girlish urging, her arms extended and her two hands pulling on his. As she lifted various paltry items into the air about her, he felt not only lust drive through him but also what seemed like an equal yet opposite force of tenderness.

One evening they passed a concert hall. The poster declared that P—— would be performing Mozart. As the strings in the orchestra finished tuning against the piano, Alessi felt her hand grip his. He looked at her, but her eyes were fixed straight ahead. Presently a hush fell over the hall and then, emerging from the canopy of silence, a single oboe broke through, "Gran Partita." As the oboe made its lofty way through the air, Alessandro's soul was so moved it went seeking something to cry for. Later, he would not remember having cried. She squeezed his hand again, and this time she was looking at him. She rose from the seat and, despite the reproachful Viennese faces, the two hunched figures squeezed past the knees of their neighbors. At the hotel she made love to him and afterward, holding him in her arms, she kissed his lips as Helen might have kissed Achilles' heel.

To eavesdrop on lovers or to recount their words of tenderness is unquestionably ill-mannered, but it is also foolish to expect words exchanged in a mood of tenderness to bear up to the unforgiving regard of an age as cynical as love's language is naïve. To describe their exchange, our beautiful Italian does not in only two syllables afford the same nuances as the English word *mawkish*. But to describe it thus is to accept defeat against the cynicism.

"You think that I am drawn to your weakness," she said. "This is not true at all. Let me tell you something you may not know. The world is inhabited by three kinds of men. There are the weak, who are only that. There are the strong, who are nothing more. And there are men like you. Moisi, my love, you carry a deep well of strength that is yours, that will always be there. Your tears are the surface of that well."

Alessandro had never known such happiness as was his in Vienna. He would never know it again. After a week, the two parted, having laid plans to meet again a week thence in another city of Europe. They exchanged telephone numbers and agreed to speak the next day. The next day, Alessi waited by the phone but no call came, and when he dialed the number, her telephone was always engaged. After a week of trying the same number over and over, Alessi put down the phone. Alessi remembered how she had remained silent about herself and how he had done the same and, for this small mercy, he believed he ought to be grateful, as if seeking to persuade himself that she had carried away no part of him.

The months passed and then the years, and although Alessi never forgot that week in Vienna, although he never forgot the intensity of feeling in those seven days, although he never forgot the woman, he did continue with life. In his outward form, one might say even that he flourished, for professionally he grew and grew and his scientific inquiries yielded greater and greater insights.

But here is the unaccountable fact. At a point in time that cannot be located exactly, Alessandro became possessed of a fear, an irrational and unscientific fear, which took hold of his sleeping hours. In a perversion of the original story, Alessandro Moisi Iacoboni came to believe that in the hour of his death he would cry out the name of his lost love.

He railed against his dreams, for what should it matter what trifling thoughts seize a man in his final hour? What should it matter to the present, to the life in hand, that it might end with a vision of loss? Isn't a life worth more than that? And here Alessi reminded himself of the people he had helped, the patients who had survived because of his skill, and the physicians and pharmacologists whose understanding he had increased. Was that, he asked, not enough to dismiss all thought—all the dark dreams!—all the absurd fear of the closing mutterings of a dying man in his worn-out brain? Why, he asked above all else, should such an ending be the worst fate he could imagine awaiting him? For that was what it was: the terror of a meaningless end that unravels everything. Such fear and such dreams remained with him to fill out the hollows of his heart.

Alessandro therefore came to believe that he had to trick this end, must wrong-foot his apparent destiny, that he would have to take matters into his own hands. That was the thought, the contemplation of design, that was to carry him through many years.

In 1990, Alessandro accepted a chair at the Johns Hopkins Medical School in Maryland. Alessi was delighted by America, fascinated by this world within the world, and threw himself into all things American. He watched baseball and football, he bought season tickets, he was crazy for burgers and hot wings with blue cheese dip. He took to wearing a Baltimore Orioles cap on his rounds at the hospital and at the lectures he gave in the medical school. He loved the absurd game shows on television, where ignorance seemed to be celebrated. Five years after arriving, he became an American citizen. For a decade, Alessandro lived in what was apparently a blizzard of good humor, and the truth of it was that America had indeed infused his days with a simple joy. But it was a joy whose greatest achievement was to make bearable certain dark nights in which the old fear revisited him.

In September of 2001, Alessandro Moisi Iacoboni settled into window seat 12A, next to an elderly gentleman, on a fully booked Boeing 727 at Boston's Logan Airport. Still percolating in his thoughts were the discussions he'd had at Harvard Medical School in a meeting with collaborators on a research project. In New York he was scheduled to give a lecture at the Albert Einstein College of Medicine, before traveling back to Maryland. Shortly after the plane had reached its cruising altitude of thirty-one thousand feet, Alessandro felt a mighty ache in his upper abdomen. He curled over in his seat grabbing his chest. Alessandro knew what it was.

As he lay dying, Alessandro forgot his chosen fear. He did not think of the woman he had loved in Vienna, he did not utter her name, he did not pine for that loss. Nor, contrary to what some might imagine of men at their end, did he recall childhood, its accumulated tiny humiliations, the wounds that could not heal; he did not remember the taunting of the children, he did not remember the hatred in their eyes, or the occasion he threw his arms around a teacher, who only pushed him away with a look of disgust. He did not remember the nuns, who had shown nothing of the tenderness of Christian love. Such memories, when they come, do not come back vaguely but with the detail of a knife unsheathed. Yet to him then they did not come at all. Instead, Alessandro thought of the postage stamps in his wallet, stamps he had purchased in the various places he had lived, stamps unused, left over, stamps that signified letters and postcards unsent, the words he had never spoken and the people to whom those words had not been said. He thought of those wasted stamps. If you had been watching Alessandro at that moment, as he lay in the aisle of the airplane surrounded by flight attendants, you might have seen a curious smile spread across his face, you might have heard the muffled sound of a muttered word, and if you had been familiar with the accents and dialects of a corner of Italy, you might have recognized the voice of a child born only four hours by mule from the town of M——, for in the hour of his death Alessandro Moisi Iacoboni, like all men, cried out for his mother.

14

The Colonel, the General, the Nuclear Physicist, the Spymaster, and the Novice

Bring over a poem's ideas and images, and you will lose its manner; imitate prosodic effects, and you sacrifice its matter. Get the letter and you miss the spirit, which is everything in poetry; or get the spirit and you miss the letter, which is everything in poetry. But these are false dilemmas . . . Verse translation at its best generates a wholly new utterance in the second language.

    —John Felstiner, *Translating Neruda: The Way to Macchu Picchu*

When I find myself in the company of scientists, I feel like a shabby curate who has strayed by mistake into a drawing-room full of dukes.

    —W. H. Auden, "The Poet and the City"

I can remember at one official function [in West Pakistan] where there was a group of women, wives of members of the elite, and I overheard one laughing to the others, "What does it matter if women in Bengal are being raped by our soldiers? At least the next generation of Bengalis will be better looking." That was the kind of attitude you found here in 1971, and it is still around today.

    —Patrick French, *Liberty or Death*

Tell me about the UN bar. Did you meet Emily?

I did, replied Zafar.

And what happened?

I should tell you first about the supper I had with the colonel and his guests.

Before you went to Kabul?

You should know what I'd been hearing in Islamabad.

And then you'll pick up the story in Kabul?

Then I'll pick up the story in Kabul.

Listening to Zafar, I was like a child hearing a story at bedtime, interrupting and impatient to hear all its mysteries impossibly revealed at once.

A member of his staff showed me upstairs, continued Zafar, to a well-appointed bedroom at the back of the house, with its own bathroom off to one side.

I took a nap—though perhaps I didn't actually sleep—and I got up refreshed and ready. After washing and putting on a clean shirt, I stood in front of the mirror and considered whether to wear my tie. The colonel had been dressed in traditional Pakistani costume, so I decided a tie would be inappropriate. I thought of the custom in Iran, where men wear Western suits and shirts but do not wear ties, ties being regarded as the ultimate symbol of Westernization. Such a fine distinction seemed to me comical at that moment when of course I had in my mind the colonel's observation concerning Gaddafi's Western military uniform. Forswearing ties looked like a petty and childish act of defiance, and yet there it was, imbued with enormous meaning. I left the tie in my jacket pocket.

Before opening the doors to the dining room, a uniformed soldier sheepishly asked for permission to frisk me. When he patted a pocket, I took out my digital voice recorder and, responding to his quizzical look, I said it was a phone. These days phones do everything, but in 2002 cell phone technology was just getting going—and this was Pakistan. The soldier rolled his head from side to side, maintaining an inane grin on his face. I moved toward the dining room when he stopped me. *Please, sir*, he said and disappeared behind a door. He returned carrying a tin, holding its lid open. *Please, sir, we will keep phone safe only.*

The guests were gathered in a large dining room, standing about with drinks in hand. They were all men, all older and gray haired, from a generation before mine, more than one generation yet not quite two. The room was made out in an English Victorian mode, but the furniture was all repro, nothing worn or scuffed about the wood, a little too even in tone. On the walls were unremarkable paintings, landscapes was my impression. Dominating the room was a large painting on the far wall: a ship caught in a storm, a galleon tossed upon cloudy seas, below an improbably large moon. The painting was positioned between two vast windows, whose curtains weren't drawn even though daylight was fast fading. This room was an unloved space, and I could not imagine the colonel dining there alone.

Ah, Zafar, exclaimed the colonel. Come, come, my boy.

The colonel was dressed in a dark gray suit, no Nehru collar this time but a double-breasted English cut and a shirt with a high collar. There was no tie but instead an ostentatious crimson cravat.

We took our seats at the oval table, the colonel directing me to a seat opposite his. There were three other guests.

Let me make introductions, Zafar. The rest of us know each other. This here is General Firdous Khan, said the colonel, indicating the man on my right, a richly mustachioed gentleman in khaki uniform with immensely broad shoulders and signs of a healthy appetite. I thought of a tank.

Most pleased to make your acquaintance, said the general.

Firdous, continued the colonel—and you may call him General Khan—Firdous is a splendid fellow, despite his utter lack of cultural sensibility, which of course does his Pakhtoon brethren proud. He's actually a three-star general, only three stars, a lieutenant general, you see, but they like to be addressed as *General*. He will have much to tell you—what is it you know, Firdous? he asked, turning to the general. Anyway, continued the colonel, he can talk to you about something or other, provided we keep him stocked with food and drink.

Mohammed Ahmed Hassan, said the colonel, gesturing toward the man on my left, who was smoking a cigarette (and would stop only to eat), is with ISI.* He's a spy and he looks it, don't you think? Hassan-bhai, welcome, we don't judge you. Unlike everyone else.

And finally, let me introduce you to the least among us, a chap on whom you needn't waste too much time since he's barely sober, I daresay, though sobriety would, in his case, hardly guarantee lucid conversation. Dr. Reza Mehrani is a distinctly shifty sort. No, not because of his Irani ancestry—we are modern people here—but because he's a scientist of some description concerning himself with atoms and suchlike. They call him the god of small things. Rumor has it he's also a first-class bridge player, but since we play only chess in this house, I've no idea why he's

---

*Inter-Services Intelligence, whose senior officers are drawn from the military.

here. How is the lovely wife? And remind us what in God's name she sees in you.

Ricky, said General Khan, pass the bloody whisky.

Khan outranked the colonel by a notch, but rank gave way here to a leveling informality. Ricky, evidently, was the colonel's nickname among friends. The men obviously had a shared ancient history. In fact—and I'm getting ahead a little—over the course of the conversation they slipped into Urdu here and there, and when they did, they used the very informal second person form of *you*. English has lost something of value, I think. It's still there in German, in the informal *du*, in the French *tu*, and in the Spanish *tú*. English used to have it in *thou*, and it remains in the Lord's Prayer: thy will be done, thine is the Kingdom.*

Even before I said anything, I became rather self-conscious. There was of course the unfamiliarity of my circumstances—the middle of 2002 in a staging post for a war to avenge the destruction of the towering icons of America, and I am in Islamabad, the guest of a Pakistani colonel—but this in itself was not the cause. I might, instead, have been uncomfortable to be in the presence of the Pakistani military, men of an age to have sullied their hands in 1971. But even that was not on my mind. It was a rather trivial matter, now that I consider it. These men had rather thick Pakistani accents and I was conscious of my own voice, its decidedly educated English sound. To my mind's ear—I had barely spoken—it already sounded out of place, even false and presumptuous.

Before bringing in the food, an orderly went around the table with a jug of water and a large bowl, and every man washed his hands. The meal was a surprisingly simple affair of two meat curries and dhal with a platter of rotis and a bowl of rice, and the men were oddly restrained in the portions they served themselves, even the general, his girth notwithstanding. I thought of the Bangladeshis and Pakistanis in Britain, among whom it is apparently a matter of statistical record that the incidence of heart disease and diabetes significantly exceeds the British national aver-

---

*I don't claim to be an authority on the Urdu language—far from it—but I do know that in Urdu, as in other South Asian languages, there is yet another informal second person, one that connotes an even greater degree of informality, in the main reserved for addressing children and servants, but also used by people who've known each other for a great length of time. This is what Zafar is referring to, I'm sure.

age. I met a doctor once who worked at the Royal London Hospital in the East End and who explained to me that there was a growing consensus that Bangladeshis and Pakistanis in Britain were eating too much and eating the wrong kinds of food, too many fats and sugars.

As I watched these men eat, while I myself ate, I thought of animals driven by the instinct to survive. You may speculate that this attitude—seeing animals—came from some kind of alienation, a rupture with society. My own understanding was more prosaic. The news wasn't making sense to me. Which is to say, I had difficulty following the arguments. One argument, underpinning so much then, ran as follows: The Taliban had harbored Bin Laden, Bin Laden headed Al Qaeda, and Al Qaeda had executed the attacks. But there were matters of proof, not necessarily conclusive proof, but a requirement that these steps be borne out in evidence. Bin Laden's proud owning of responsibility was to come two years later, for instance. And even if the evidence was there, even if such evidence was to be found, there remained the question of whether it all amounted to an ethical justification for the actions now being undertaken. However, if I were to tell you that in the very first month I opposed the war, then I'd be every bit a liar as the liars who take us into wars. My emotions ran high when I recalled the collapse of the towers. America had my heart and she had been wounded. Geologists apparently call our geological era the Anthropocene, the Age of Man. It made more sense to me to think of the private goals of beasts, each alpha male, from the Blairs and Bushes to the Cheneys and Rumsfelds, consolidating his power and securing his personal material future with the unthinking frightened herds following. I had no time for conspiracy theories.

The men ate quickly, as soldiers might, tearing off chunks of bread and mopping up sauces. They didn't touch the rice, and I speculated that it might have been put out for my benefit; I was Bangladeshi, after all, from a people who ate rice—I'd never seen roti in my village—and whose land was a checkerboard of rice fields. I served myself a scoop.

All the men ate with their hands, save the colonel, who used a spoon. It wobbled a little as he raised it, his fingers no longer obeying him to the letter. Perhaps my eye lingered on this a moment too long, for the general commented: If you play chess with Ricky, he'll get you to move his pieces.

I smiled embarrassedly and engaged my food. Only much, much later did I perceive the art in the general's remark.

The conversation moved in desultory fashion through family matters, births, deaths, and marriages, the business ventures of some or other child and the educational achievements of a grandchild. It was all, I later understood, a deferral of the real topic, the U.S.-led intervention in Afghanistan. In those days, that must have been the only talk of the town.

Afterward, we washed our hands and, carrying the idle conversation with us, moved to the lounge, where the colonel had received me earlier. We settled into armchairs and sofas. I noticed that the pieces on the chessboard, on the table in the corner of the room, had moved, a defeated few now standing at the edge of the board. A game had been played, though at my distance it was not possible to tell if it had resulted in a victor.

You've been very silent, Reza-bhai, said the general. What is ticktocking in that cranium?

Mehrani looked around the room.

Drones, he said, letting the one word hang melodramatically.

Mohammed Hassan, the ISI official, exhaled a plume of smoke that drifted across Mehrani's face. I wanted to laugh, and for a few moments my whole being was dedicated to restraining the muscles around my mouth and my eyes.

That's it? asked the general. You say nothing and then expect one word to suffice?

The Americans cannot stomach casualties, said Reza Mehrani. When the body bags are airlifted by the dozen to their Dover air base, that's when they pack up and leave their wars. So this time, they will be using drones. The technology is ready for it.

You are a very scary fellow, said the general. Don't misunderstand me. It's not what you say but how say it. You could order a chapati and I would be scared.

He's right, said Hassan, the man from the ISI.

See, said the general. Even the spymaster thinks you're scary.

They will use drones on a massive scale, added Hassan.

You think science and technology are just instruments of war, said Mehrani, directing his remarks to the general and the colonel, but science and technology actually change the game.

How will it change the game, dear boy? asked the general. The Americans have always fought their wars by proxy. Drone attacks are simply a variant.

If they so much as launch one drone attack in Pakistan, I'll personally put my boot in the American ambassador's behind, said Hassan.

What nonsense! You wear soft slippers. You want to tickle the good ambassador? said the general.

They want their wars but they don't want to shed American blood.

You think Kissinger cared about American blood in Vietnam?

In the American Civil War it was possible to buy your way out of serving in the Union Army for three hundred dollars. A commutation fee, they called it. All legal and aboveboard.

The price of patriotism.

The poor who have nothing else to sell, they are the ones who become soldiers. They are the organ donors.

The military contractors are already coming in.

They were there *ahead* of everyone.

Bhai, mercenaries have been fighting wars since before the pharaohs.

I don't see American elites joining the U.S. Army. So tell me, where is the loyalty in the West?

Come now. Since time immemorial, soldiers the world over have never lifted a finger for country. Everyone knows that a soldier fights for his comrades.

You mean to say that our boys will do America's bidding simply because a soldier will fight for his regiment?

For his platoon. I'm saying that at the sharp point of battle that is why they fight. Whether it comes to the point of battle is another matter.

That is *my* point.

They'd sooner desert than fight their kin.

Why have you agreed to U.S. bases on Pakistani soil? I asked, speaking for the first time.

I'm sorry, I quickly added. That was meant as a question and not an accusation.

I said the same thing to that American lackey *Busharraf*, said Dr. Mehrani, and I most certainly meant it as an accusation.

Tell the boy what the man said, said the colonel.

These things are more complex than the Western press would have you think, added Mehrani.

It's important that the boy should have a complete picture, said the colonel. Tell him what Musharraf said.

He said, *Go fuck a dog*, interjected the general, and turning to Mehrani added: A direct order from your commander in chief.

We are in a bind, explained Hassan. If we say no to America, they'll fight their war anyway—they're straining at the leash—but they'll fight from bases in India. And that way lies ruination for Pakistan. Not only would we lose the support of America, but we would be entering the nightmare vision of an India allied militarily to America. And later, with Afghanistan conquered, we would have no strategic depth.

Zafar, do you know what he's talking about? the colonel asked me.

Because if you do, perhaps you'd care to explain it to us, said the general.

Strategic depth? I replied.

Do you really think they can conquer Afghanistan? the general asked Hassan.

Conquer, perhaps not, not in any comprehensive sense, replied Hassan. But if you think they'll leave the country altogether, if you think for a moment they won't maintain permanent bases, right in the thick of it, a slingshot's distance from Central Asian oil wells, and on the border with Iran, then, my friends, you've been taking too much Afghani opium.

Strategic depth, said the colonel, addressing me, is the very idea of Afghanistan, in particular the border country, providing a hospitable environment for our troops should we need to regroup after an Indian military advance, so that India would never rest easy if, God forbid, it ever mounted a serious foray into Pakistan. The Indians merely knowing that we have such depth is enough.

That's one way to describe strategic depth, said Mehrani.

What's yours?

It's an aspect of the lunatic obsession we have with India, he replied. India doesn't care about us. We spend so much time talking about India. It's the staple of our cocktail parties. But do you think for a moment they talk about us quite so much in Delhi? Their military budget is seven times ours. Are they remotely afraid of us? asked Mehrani.

You think we should spend more?

We should spend less. Look at our country. It's a total disaster. Sixty percent of our children are born significantly stunted, physically stunted!

Male illiteracy is at forty-one percent, female at seventy percent. Virtually no health care for the poor. Tax collection is at ten percent, the lowest in the subcontinent, lower than that of Bangladesh, for heaven's sake.

Reza-bhai likes statistics. He's a scientist, said the general.

Here's a statistic for you, Reza-bhai, said Hassan. Come to think of it, Zafar, you'll also like this. It's rather mathematical. Pakistan may be what you say, but she has a very low Gini coefficient.

You have read the *Dawn* editorial, said the general.

Was that a slip, I asked myself, or had the ISI officer intended to unnerve me by indicating that he knew I'd studied mathematics?

The Gini coefficient is the work of no less auspicious an institution than the United Nations Development Program. It measures national income inequality, the ratio of the income of the bottom ten percent to the income of the top ten percent. Pakistan's Gini coefficient is lower than India's, lower than America's, lower than Nigeria's, lower in fact than that of forty other countries.

I haven't heard of the Gini coefficient, so I don't know, I said, but I think you mean the other way around.

What?

Ratio of *top* ten percent to *bottom* ten percent—if your point is that Pakistan has lower income inequality, I explained.

Each of them considered this and a few moments passed as the four men stared into space while their brains turned over. Then in unison, they said, *You're right*, before breaking into laughter.

How is that possible? How can income inequality be relatively low? I asked.

Indeed, replied the ISI official. Here, he continued, we have the heart of the matter. That which is the source of so many of our woes is also the source of strengths. Kinship and patronage.

As in Bangladesh.

As in India.

But even more so here, continued Hassan. Kinship and patronage. The two work together to make this country. Westerners never tire to point to our corruption; they never tire to highlight our moral failings. We are lawless, they say, and if you listened to them you would think we haven't a shred of integrity. But that is the opposite of the case. You see, my boy, in Pakistan there are very powerful moral obligations at work, those of kinship. Loyalties to one's family, to one's clan, tribe, religion, and extended kinship networks—such loyalties override anything our elites bring in the form of laws. Our laws are largely inherited from the British and are no more the expression of the people's voice than the laws imposed by a colonial power. But the loyalties that bind people together, these flow in the blood of Pakistanis.

How the blazes does that explain a low Gini coefficient? Now that you've let the Gini out of the bottle, I think you should explain that, said the general, quite evidently enjoying his pun.

The looting of the state is seldom for the sole benefit of an individual. That is very rare—

As in military contracts, added Dr. Mehrani mischievously, though none of the others seemed to take the bait. He was the only civilian among them.

When a man, a politician or a bureaucrat, takes a sum, a commission, or a payment, he is taking it into trust for the benefit of a wider group. He will pay servants, gunmen, supporters, political transport for supporters, political hospitality, and then he will share the rest among his relatives. Unlike countries such as Nigeria where a few plunder the treasury, siphoning off proceeds from oil that ought to benefit the nation and stashing them in Western bank accounts, in Pakistan the moneys get spread around. Therefore, income inequality remains relatively low. As for the military, the good doctor knows very well that the military is the only island of sanity in an ocean of madness, said Hassan.

Well put, said the general.

The army is industrious, it is efficient, and it gets the job done. Why else do you think Pakistanis have turned to the army time and again? For God's sake, even elected governments seek our help. In '99, Sharif* put the military in charge of water and power in order to restore order and enforce fee payment. And you know what else? asked Hassan, looking at me. The military is a meritocracy, he said, as if this was the clincher. No one can deny that. Do you know who's going to head the ISI next? The director general of military operations, General Ashfaq Kayani, the son

---

*Nawaz Sharif was the democratically elected prime minister of Pakistan, 1990–93 and 1997–99.

of an NCO, a lowly sergeant. And look at Musharraf, he's the son of a Mohajir.*

What is it Voltaire said of Frederick the Great's Prussia? Where some states have an army, the Prussian army has a state, said Mehrani.

The Americans know nothing about the realities, the basic facts of this part of the world, the general added, ignoring Mehrani's barbed comment.

The British are no better, said Hassan. The British are delusional. Just the other day, the British ambassador was complaining to me: If only the American soldier would behave half as well as his British counterpart. In what way? I asked him. We hand out sweets to the children, he said, we respect local customs, and we don't go charging in all guns blazing. I almost throttled him. Respect customs at the barrel of a loaded rifle? They still regard themselves as the benevolent imperialists, but in Afghanistan the duplicitous shit heads are hated even more than the Americans. Do they think we in this part of the world don't know history? They tried fucking us up the Khyber Pass every chance they got but still they think they're nobility. Fuckers.

Calm down, bhai, said Mehrani.

Pour me some whisky.

The educated classes know something; give them some credit, said the colonel.

Don't fool yourself. I was in Washington last month, said the general, with Sattar† at a meeting with Colin Powell. The chap sat opposite us and for fifteen minutes he spoke of Pakhtoon and Taliban interchangeably—he said *Pashtun*, of course. It became unbearable, and even Kurshid,‡ a Punjabi, was agitated enough to point out that two senior officials with him were Pakhtoons but decidedly not Taliban. I wondered to myself if Powell might even need it explained to him that there were Pakhtoons in both Afghanistan and Pakistan. At the very least, you

---

* *Mohajir* is an Arabic word commonly used by Pakistanis to describe Muslim immigrants from other areas of South Asia who migrated to the new state of Pakistan (mainly to the Western half) on partition. In the early days of the new nation, there was in some parts of the established native population an ambivalence toward these newcomers.

† Abdul Sattar, foreign minister of Pakistan, 1999–2002.

‡ I have not been able to identify this person. It's possible that Zafar has the wrong name.

would think he'd been briefed about *us*. One should always know whom one's meeting.

Hassan, the ISI official, smiled at me.

But what about their Great Unwashed? It is by their license that their armies are waging war. They know nothing. What does "tribal area" mean to them? What does Swat mean to them, other than gunslingers in an American TV drama?

The masses defer to the educated classes, as they do everywhere.

Have some more whisky, said the general.

I'm fine, said Hassan.

Have some more whisky.

Okay.

Let's talk about these educated classes. Zafar, said the colonel, you will have some insight here. When you are in the West and you are discussing Bangladesh with one of your educated friends—or let's say you are discussing some aspect of your family life—tell me, do you feel the conversation has a different quality if you are speaking to a Bangladeshi, or a subcontinental, for that matter, from what it feels like if you are speaking to a Westerner? Don't you feel you have to explain less?

Feel, feel, feel. How did bloody feelings come into the picture? What are you talking about now? asked the general.

Even when your Western friend is a child of Enlightenment liberalism? asked Reza.

Yes, even when your Western friend is a child of Enlightenment liberalism, added the colonel.

Tell us about your feelings, said the general.

Let the boy answer, said the colonel.

There *is* indeed a difference, I said. Talking to diasporic South Asians—

Diasporic? Must you? said Hassan.

Let him finish, insisted the colonel.

Talking to expatriate South Asians about South Asian things is usually a lot easier than talking to others. Not always, though. I've met South Asians, men usually, who shrink from conversation that has a South Asian turn.

Ah, yes, the babu, said the general.

I'm sorry?

A coconut. The South Asian who has become white in all but skin color, replied the general.

But I wonder if the events of September 11 have changed that, I said.

Certainly we hear of young British Muslims becoming radicalized in the face of the West losing its collective wits, said Reza.

But short of that radicalization, I continued, I think expatriate Pakistanis and Bangladeshis—the babus, as you call them—they can no longer keep their distance. And there's a deep pleasure in talking to someone who knows where you're coming from right away, who knows what you're talking about and can even finish your sentences. Nothing really beats that familiarity, that feeling of being swept into a vortex of mutual understanding. You all must know this. But equally I find it troubling. Is everybody so pleased to find a shared experience that their emotions rule the content? Not always but sometimes, sometimes as I walk away from the conversation, I wonder if it was a conversation framed by common defensiveness, a sense of unity by exclusion, which makes me uneasy because those kinds of conversations also exclude things that could challenge or test whatever's being said. It's true of everyday life, people not just talking but seeking common ground on the most mundane things—it's the problem of clubs—except that the impulse gets magnified, I think, when there's a defensiveness framing the conversation.

Silence.

You're one of us, dear boy. You're one of us. Welcome home.

Because I'm not one of them?

You're not in favor of the American war?

I knew two people who worked in the World Trade Center.

Surely one's position should be independent of whether one knew a victim of the nefarious miscreants. Otherwise one falls into the danger you mentioned—of letting emotions rule one's judgment.

You're one of us because you are a Muslim. Do you know the Shahadah? asked Reza.

You just called him a Muslim and yet you ask him if he knows the Shahadah, said the colonel.

Do you know it in English?

I'm no authority, but I don't think the English translation qualifies as a declaration of faith, I said.

Humor me.

There is no God but Allah and Muhammad is his messenger, I said.

Exactly.

He qualifies, does he? asked the colonel.

Exactly wrong, said Reza. This is what we teach our children. Why? I'll tell you why. It's because we use their translation, their bloody translation, which is just plain wrong.

Reza-bhai, why the blazes would we teach them the *English* translation? asked the general.

Your boys went to Aitchison! he snapped back. Now there's another thing. Our best schools are *English* medium. Do you know what Arab Christians call God? he asked, turning back to me. All those Palestinian Christians and Coptic Christians, those fellows like Edward Said and Boutros-Ghali. Arab Christians speak Arabic, and what do they call God?

If I didn't know, I could now guess, but it would have been impolite to steal his thunder. Tell me, I said.

Actually, for that matter, do you know what virtually every Maltese calls God?

Maltese? asked the colonel.

People from Malta. I believe they're called Maltese.

They don't speak Arabic, surely? asked the colonel.

They speak a Semitic language, Ricky. And they're Roman Catholics and they also call God Allah, because that's what Allah means.

Aren't you making too much of a translation?

Aren't you making too little? Why do we keep seeing this over and over, this bogus translation of the Shahadah? It loses the meaning entirely and instead leaves the impression we worship some foreign god called Allah, when in fact the Shahadah is a beautiful creed of monotheism. It has nothing to do with the name of God. If you want a name, Islam offers ninety-nine names for God, precisely because he has no name. So tell me now. What is the Shahadah in English?

There is no God but God and Muhammad is his messenger.

Exactly right. You're one of us because you are a Muslim and you are from here, said Reza.

I'm Bangladeshi.

The great wound from which we will never recover is the betrayal of East Pakistan, said the general.

Whose betrayal?

The conversation came to a standing stop.

Not to change the subject but—

Indeed.

Speaking of which, surely the culprit here, the root of the matter, is Saudi Arabia. The hypocrites won't do anything about the Saudis, said the general.

Has anyone been following the cricket?

The Saudis are overmaligned, protested Mehrani.

You have a conflict of interest, O God of small things.

The Christians have their bomb. And the Jews. Must the Muslims be denied? asked Mehrani.

Be that as it may, Saudi finance makes you biased. No, the Saudis are undermaligned. Did you know that the Saudis still don't provide advance manifests for flights going to the U.S.? How is this possible when every one of our Pakistani boys is being pulled over to have some *gora* shove his hand up his backside? In fact, right up to September 11, Saudis who applied for U.S. entry visas were not required to attend an interview at the U.S. embassy. Visa Express they called it. Travel agents arranged it all, Saudi travel agents acting for the U.S. State Department! What madness!

Not every country, he continued, has the utter lack of accountability the Saudi rulers enjoy. The Saudis spend preposterous sums on arms even though they have not fought a war in over sixty years and despite the fact that their external defense needs are totally met by the U.S., by U.S. carrier groups and F-15s permanently patrolling the Persian Gulf. So you have to ask, why do they spend this money? Much of it makes its way into the pockets of Saudi princes, but an equally large amount funds a military dedicated to protecting the Saudi royal family. Those royals are so hated by their own people that they live in fortresses defended by the National Guard, the best trained, best equipped, best paid, and most expensive bodyguard organization in the world, in human history, in fact. With this, they can oppress their people at will. You know what the locals call the venue for public executions in Riyadh? They call it Chop-Chop Square.

You say the Saudis are to blame, but it is the Americans who permit all this, said Mehrani.

They are co-conspirators, said the general. You think a thug is exonerated because a bigger thug is standing behind him? Yes, of course oil is at the root. Oil and business. I was reading the *Petroleum Intelligence Weekly*—

Sounds like a barrel of laughs, said Mehrani.

Very droll, said Hassan.

On September 12, 2001, the Saudis pumped out—oh, I see! Barrel of laughs. Very good.

Thank you, said Mehrani.

The general looked helpless; he seemed to have lost his thread.

September 12.

Indeed. On September 12, 2001, the Saudis pumped out an extra nine million barrels of oil, most of it for the American markets. Oil prices barely moved after the worst terrorist attacks in American history. Saudi Arabia has half of the world's surplus production capacity. What does that mean? It means that Saudi Arabia, unlike any other nation in the world, can move oil prices to suit its whim, but in exchange for U.S. protection the Saudi king keeps them stable.

Now he's going to tell you that the destruction of the Twin Towers was a Jewish conspiracy.

You laugh, but some of these conspiracy theories . . . I'll tell you this much—

Conspiracy theories are not what they seem? interjected the colonel mischievously.

Exactly so, replied the general, altogether blind to the colonel's joke.

What do you make of these conspiracy theories, my boy?

The colonel took me by surprise.

Yes, you. What do you make of them?

Generally?

Or specifically.

I think conspiracy theories are lies.

Well said, replied the colonel, though not taking his eyes off me.

Lies, I continued, propagated by a shadowy international force.

The general was the only one not laughing.

I'm not talking about conspiracy theories, he said.

What exactly are you talking about? asked the colonel.

That would actually undermine my argument.

Which is? I must say, I'm losing your thread.

The Saudi royal family keeps oil prices low. Americans may complain about the high price of oil, but a democratic Saudi Arabia or an unfriendly one would hike prices and gouge the world markets for what they're worth. Why do they keep it low? Because they've earned protection or a blind eye from America, as the royal family's needs dictate. Washington has been paid off, defense contractors are kept in fine fettle, and the U.S. Navy takes care of Saudi national defense to boot. It works like a tax on Americans. Who, after all, pays for the American aircraft carriers and fighter jets that protect Saudi Arabia? Who pays for the oil but the U.S. citizen? One in five dollars earned from oil-hungry Americans buys off Washington and defense contractors.

But Americans are better off. They get low oil prices, as you say.

Yes. Everyone is happy. Except. Except ordinary Saudis. We talk about income inequality, but ordinary Saudis live in a country that won't even keep relevant data and doesn't want to know or let it be known; everyone is happy except ordinary Muslims who see the Hejaz overrun by foreigners. What did Osama bin Laden say right after the September 11 attacks? What was the first thing he posted on the Internet? He called for the expulsion of the infidel from Arabia. The Muslim world watches the hypocrisy with righteous indignation.

The Americans are not alone.

Of course not. Britain has become a poodle and Blair is a bastard of the highest magnitude. And now these bastards justify their invasion of Afghanistan with platitudes about freedom and liberating the Afghani people. You can't turn on the news without seeing some Western political sage quoting surveys showing that Afghanis just want to lead their lives in peace and security. You know what? When I hear that, I want to reach for my gun. Afghanis, the pundit says, are no different from the people of Britain or America. Does he mean to say that the British and Americans don't want anything more? The way of life of a nation is more than merely living in peace. If people don't have peace and security, of course that's all they want. When they have that, the other wants come into play. They then want a certain kind of society and certain kind of life. And our idea of a good life is not the same as theirs. Neo-imperialists, all of them. They cannot abandon their imperialist mentality, every utterance steeped in orientalist bullshit. And back they come for the same, over and over. The British diplomatic service is overrun by them; though they may think they're above it all. Take that chap who went for a long walk. I hear his book is coming out soon, something about Afghanistan. Yet he traveled across half of Asia, you know. Orientalist to the bone but with enough romanticism to stave off the disappointment that awaits the rest.

That's a little unfair, I interjected.

What do you mean?

He's orientalist *because* he traveled across half of Asia? You haven't advanced anything approaching an argument, unless you're saying that everyone who writes a book should describe all his experiences. Is that right? I asked him, a little facetiously.

You like him? the colonel asked me, intervening. Of course you do. You have a soft spot for Etonians. What is the American expression? *Get over it.*

He then did something that caught me totally off guard. He winked at me. The wink did more than take the edge off the admonishment contained in *Get over it*; it acknowledged my embarrassment—the general was on the mark—but it also made me feel that my embarrassment was safe with him.

Bloody British. Bloody perfidious Albion, said Hassan, now quite hammered. One swallow does not a summer make, I tell you.

Definitely more whisky, said the general.

No two ways about it, added the colonel.

The following morning, I was taken to the airport for my flight to Kabul. We drove in a Land Cruiser with dark windows, the colonel and I sitting together in the back.

You're staying at AfDARI, aren't you? the colonel asked.

I don't know where but I believe the UN rapporteur has made arrangements.

I'll have you picked up at the airport. In Kabul, I mean. And in future, when you come to Pakistan, I'll have you picked up at the airport here also. As a matter of fact, fly PIA and use your credit card. We'll have you reimbursed.

Thank you, but that won't be necessary.

Nonsense, he replied.

You know that I have an employer, I pointed out.

Keep it that way. It is your company I enjoy.

I think you may be mistaking me for someone else.

Not at all. That, I think, is what you're doing.

I know you're in the Pakistani army, someone senior, and I suspect with a little more authority than your rank confers.

I mean that you are mistaking yourself for someone else.

I see. You're a Zen Buddhist after all.

I think you are a little secretive.

Not very effectively. You and your friends seem to know enough.

What is strange to me is that although I know a fair deal about you, I'm still puzzled as to who you really are.

Anonymity is my middle name.

The colonel chuckled. I should have liked a son like you, he said.

Do you think I'm involved in some kind of subterfuge? A masquerade?

No, no, no! You're not a pretender. You're much further on. No, my boy, you are so unsure of your bearings that you wonder if you're pretending to be the person you actually are. How can I tell? I see it in your face. I see the searching assessment, which you hide well but unsuccessfully, at least to me. You have never had doors opened for you, and so you learned how to pick locks, as did I. I have survived every administration. We are a dangerous breed, you and I. We are lock pickers. We are dangerous to others and to ourselves. It is always a great risk to open a door if you don't know what's behind it. You didn't talk much last night.

Should I have spoken more?

We also have that in common.

What?

We both like to watch.

Only you make a living from it.

Everyone who watches has their living made from it.

There's the Zen again.

Your anger is misdirected.

What anger?

Hate them. You're angry with them.

Now you sound like Darth Vader.

328 | ZIA HAIDER RAHMAN

Excellent films. What? You thought the reference would elude me? We get films here, too. As far as I could see, those films were about gun-slinging Americans. That man Harrison Ford looked like a cowboy.

Hate isn't healthy, I said.

Don't tell me: Hate the sin but love the sinner. I believe that if hate doesn't find its rightful place, there's only one place left for it to go.

Where's that?

Inward.

At the airport, the colonel was brisk with his valediction. When a plane roared overhead, he leaned forward and spoke.

Find out what's in the envelopes. And be careful with Crane, he said.

What envelopes? I replied. I had no idea what he was referring to.

The colonel glanced at the driver.

You don't *have to* share it, he said. Find out and then decide.

As I walked into the building, I realized that he had used the sound of the jet engines for cover.

15

Where Credit Is Due

Rating agencies continue to create and [*sic*] even bigger monster—
the CDO market. Let's hope we are all wealthy and retired by the
time this house of cards falters. :o)
   —Senior S&P executive Chris Meyer, email to colleagues Nicole
   Billick and Belinda Ghetti, December 15, 2006

SHAH: btw [by the way]: that deal is ridiculous.
MOONEY: I know, right . . . model def [definition] does not capture
   half of the risk.
SHAH: We should not be rating it.
MOONEY: We rate every deal. It could be structured by cows and we
   would rate it.
                     —S&P analysts Rahul Dilip Shah and Shannon Mooney, IM
                     conversation, April 5, 2007

One common misperception is that Moody's credit ratings are
statements of fact or solely the output of mathematical models.
This is not the case. The process is, importantly, subjective in
nature and involves the exercise of independent judgment by the
participating analysts . . . Importantly, the rating reflects Moody's
opinion and not an individual analyst's opinion of the relative creditworthiness of the issuer or obligation.
   —Raymond W. McDaniel, chairman and chief executive officer,
   Moody's Corporation, *Testimony Before the U.S. House Committee
   on Oversight and Government Reform*, October 22, 2008

Probabilistic propositions constitute a little world unto themselves.
What is stated in probabilistic terms can be interpreted only in
probabilistic terms. If you do not already think in probabilistic terms,
predictions emerging out of the probabilistic world seem vacuous.

Can one imagine the Sphinx foretelling that Oedipus will probably
kill his father and marry his mother? Can one imagine Jesus saying
that he will probably come again?

—J. M. Coetzee, *Diary of a Bad Year*

I don't think Crane ever considered going into his father's business.
There was too much of the outward-bound about him, certainly in the
boy I knew. The fact that he attended law school is, I can only imagine,
down to some sort of coercion from his father, the kind of man who
would try to mold his son into the image of his legacy.

In 1998 Forrester senior (in fact Forrester II), was a United States
senator and a member of the Senate Armed Services Committee. As I've
mentioned, I met him first when my parents and I lived in Princeton
when I was a boy. The Forresters had a home there, where he, then a
prominent figure in New York's financial community, had installed his
family, at safe remove from the mad metropolis.

As any reference to him in the press was bound to include in those
days, Forrester had built a fortune in the eponymous ratings agency he
founded. In more recent times, the business diversified into other sectors
of finance, attracting concerns in some quarters about potential conflicts
of interest, but the core of the business remains providing credit ratings
for financial instruments before issue.

In the spring of 1996, at his invitation, I met Forrester for lunch at
the Yale Club in New York. Forrester was a Yalie, said to be a member of
Skull and Bones, the Yale secret society, and was a patron of the club in
New York, where, I understood, he often stayed when visiting that city.
A lifelong Democrat in the patrician mold, Forrester had gained the office of senator from New Jersey. It was a matter of public record that he
had spent more of his own money on financing his first election campaign than had any other politician in any election, *east of the Mississippi*,
I'd read, though I expect that that rather hackneyed qualification was in
this case superfluous.

I'd known the Forresters for many years, but though I counted Crane,
the junior, among my closest friends, that closeness owed more, I'll concede, to the special quality of friendships forged in childhood than to
any coincidence of spirit. Nevertheless, I was surprised to receive an

email from the father, whom I hadn't seen since my wedding, asking me to lunch when I was next in New York or Washington. Crane had been talking with his friends about joining the Marines, which apparently the father was opposed to, and having otherwise no notion what might have prompted the surprise invitation, I rather wondered if the father was hoping to enlist me in a campaign to dissuade his son.

When did you get in? asked Forrester.

I flew in yesterday.

How are you? How is Meena?

All going well, I replied. Of course Forrester remembered my wife's name. It rolled off his tongue with the familiarity that belongs to the shrewd politician. She's fine, I said. Thank you for asking. How is D.C.?

The waiter appeared, and Forrester, taking charge, ordered a bottle of white wine, pausing briefly to let me nod my assent. The Roof Dining Room, set out in rather feminine elegance, evidently attracted an older generation of silver-haired suited men and a smattering of young men, bankers and lawyers seeking to impress clients, no doubt. The round tables were elaborately laid, cutlery placed perfectly as if marking the hours on a clockface, opulent flower arrangements, and plenty of space on and between tables. There was a certain New England charm in its aesthetics, unself-conscious and without irony. Americans know what they like, more so than most of humanity, which leaves me skeptical of the claim, made usually by Europeans, that the American is insecure in the face of European history. It may be that at some time, as the story goes, Yale did age the appearance of certain of its buildings by spraying the exteriors with acid. But the fact that such a thing would be done when it could hardly escape public knowledge shows, in my view, the readiness of America to go it alone. I imagine now what Zafar, to whom America meant so much, might say to this and I'm minded to think he would agree. America is not short on energy, and its citizens believe quite heroically that things can be made to happen quickly, as only the freedom of the market permits. And history for the American is but one such thing. It, too, can be accelerated to meet demand.

D.C., replied Forrester, is D.C., a cesspit of egos and small minds. Not enough good people. Have you thought of politics?

Not for me, I replied quickly.

You should, said Forrester, but without much conviction.

As a matter of fact, I think Crane ought to think about going into politics, he added.

Here it is, I thought, what he really wanted to discuss: his son's future, which men like Forrester believe to be their own. Forrester was near enough to my father's age, but his body seemed to have been reduced to an instrument of iron will. When later he rose to visit the bathroom, I could not but regard his physique. His slim figure seemed conditioned to bring out the best in a perfectly tailored suit, while my father held off the worst of a good appetite with a weekly game of squash. Forrester's hair, combed back with a dash of some glistening product, had turned white and silver, and his face, ravaged by years of tough business, must now bear, I thought, the blows of American politics. His fortune might have secured him a degree of independence, but in the byways of Capitol Hill, the lobbyists and potential funders also peddled access, influence, and prefab constituencies, without which no American politician has any more voice than a mumbling vagrant on the street.

I suppose you know Crane's talking about the Marines.

I nodded.

What do *you* think about that? he asked.

I don't imagine Crane's short of advice. He'll make an informed decision.

Forrester smiled at me.

Something you learn pretty damn quick on the Hill, he explained, is that journalists don't care a dime if you do or don't answer their question. What they want is for you to kick the other side and, added Forrester, fixing my eye, they only come knocking on your door when they think you'll deliver that. As a matter of fact, they want you to make it personal.

Sounds unpleasant, I said, but immediately regretting that I might appear to be passing judgment on him for taking part in it.

It's not about pleasant or unpleasant. Business teaches you that. It doesn't matter a hoot what you think of what the customers want or what you think of the customers, for that matter. The only thing that counts is delivery. You got to deliver.

The senator leaned forward. I think Crane's a damn fool.

Has he signed up?

Not yet. I want you to talk to him. He'll listen to you. He likes you—I like you—we go back a long way.

I'm not sure my advice would count for much.

Forrester glanced at me.

Let's order lunch, he suggested.

What's good?

Our focus shifted. Forrester made some recommendations, and, with the waiter dispatched, resumed talking.

I have a great deal of admiration for your grandfather. That man was born for business. And I mean real business, manufacturing, oil refining, shipping, not finance, like mine—you know what I mean. No, he actually made things. He must be getting on?

In his eighties but still works a full day.

I'd have been surprised to hear anything else. Your grandfather made me a lot of money once.

He's a good businessman.

A great businessman. And he knows a thing or two. BCCI is before your time.

I've read about BCCI. The Arab bank that collapsed.

I had money in it. Your grandfather advised me to get out before it fell apart.

And how did he make you money?

Saving money is the same as making money. That piece of sound advice was worth a pretty penny.

I didn't ask if my grandfather had been paid for it. I did, however, think of Payne and JPMorgan's reserve capital that was now freed up thanks to EBRD's credit default swap. To save money is to make money.

Don't get me wrong. I have no fear for my boy's safety. Crane can't think they'll treat him like the rest. He's the son of a goddamn United States senator and one who's on the Senate Armed Services Committee, for Christ's sake. Do you think we'd ever go to war if the boys we sent out to fight for us were the sons of Wall Street or Capitol Hill? Hell no! No amount of Kuwaiti oil would be enough. Crane's going to be molly-coddled in some backwater of intelligence or given a military attaché position in Bermuda so that he can drink rum on the beach and hammer the ambassador's pretty second wife.

What is your concern, if I may ask?

The senator grinned at me.

I want Crane to get on. He's had a fine education and he's got a decent head on him. He needs to make a go of things. We're not put on this earth to fuck around. We have to make something of our lives. Crane's had all the privileges, and it's time he used those privileges to good effect.

What do you have in mind? I asked.

He could do anything he wants. He could go to Wall Street, Christ knows there are more than a few bankers who owe me, or he could try his hand in politics. There's plenty of governorships he could aim for. Heck, the boy's got an Ivy League degree and a JD; why doesn't he do something with that head of his? I'd fund his campaign if he wanted to run for office in New York. Attorney general, why not? Or if he wanted to go back to New Jersey, I've got enough leverage with both the Democrats and the Republicans to get him appointed AG. He's got all these options and he wants to throw them away for some half-assed idea of . . . I don't know what.

I can talk to Crane, but as you say, he's not stupid and I can only—

Talk to him about all the options he has. I know the boy respects you. I've been following your career, and I think you're on to something with these collateralized debt obligations. You have a talent. You know, the ratings agencies are still trying to figure out how to rate these things. I believe in you. And if you apply yourself, you can get Crane to hold off signing up and instead spend a couple of years on Wall Street or the Hill. He can get a job as counsel to one of the Senate committees. Just try something first. Jesus wept, he's fresh out of law school and he's thinking of going into the Marines. What a waste!

I'll see what I can do.

That's all I can ask. Now tell me about these CDOs I keep hearing about.

Forrester's direct manner gave the impression of a man following items on a mental agenda for the conversation. For my part, when I accepted his invitation to lunch, I did not have in mind to discuss the CDO business. Until then, my team had been focused on getting one of the larger and longer-established ratings agencies on our side. But right there in the Yale Club it hit me that maybe Forrester and his agency had more to gain. Mentioning that my grandfather once helped him out was a nice touch, as if to suggest he was now going to take a hit in order to repay a favor, when the truth was that, if anything, any ratings agency that agreed to rate my CDOs stood to make more than a tidy sum. They'd get their fee, and if there was more business in the pipeline, they'd be milking a new cash cow. It was merely a question of getting them over their initial wariness.

As Forrester and I moved on to coffee, he listened attentively while I described the products we'd developed. From time to time, he interjected with technical questions, testing the limits of my own understanding. The man had done his homework. If it was hard to *price* these things accurately—which is to say price them relative to other securities—then it was no less difficult to assess their creditworthiness, and to assess the credit rating they should be given by the likes of Forrester's agency.

You do know I don't have anything to do with the agency anymore? asked Forrester.

I came here at your invitation, I reminded him.

The business is now at arm's length from me. I'm in the Senate and a man can't serve two masters. I got to tell you, I don't even have a seat on the board. But if the agency has a sense of how you're pricing these things, I'm sure it'd help them get a handle on the credit.

In the month following my conversation with Forrester, Crane held off joining the military (though only for a year). In the same month, the senior tranche of the new CDOs, my CDOs, received a triple-A investment-grade credit rating from the agency Crane Morton Forrester II had established, as did the tranche of CDOs immediately below that. As simple as that. Business moves fast. So much for conflicts of interest. Let me point out, if it isn't obvious already, that there's some irony in the term *conflict of interest*: In practice there is seldom a conflict but rather a confluence, a mutually rewarding arrangement. I think that to Zafar it might have been the ugliest thing in the world, though I expect he would have added that it's simply inevitable.

16

A Modest Proposal

Lorem ipsum dolor sit amet, consectetur adipisicing elit, sed do eiusmod tempor incididunt ut labore et dolore magna aliqua.
—Meaningless placeholding text, loosely derived from parts of Cicero's *De finibus bonorum et malorum* and used by printers since the 1500s in order to direct attention to typesetting style rather than to content

And the Gileadites took the passages of Jordan before the Ephraimites: and it was so, that when those Ephraimites which were escaped said, Let me go over; that the men of Gilead said unto him, Art thou an Ephraimite? If he said, Nay; Then said they unto him, Say now Shibboleth: and he said Sibboleth: for he could not frame to pronounce it right. Then they took him, and slew him at the passages of Jordan: and there fell at that time of the Ephraimites forty and two thousand.   —Judges 12:5–6 [KJV]

I have already explained that the first time Zafar saw Emily was when she was practicing her violin in the University Church at Oxford. He did not speak to her then and, by his account, she did not notice his presence. The second time he saw her, which was the first time they met, was that evening at the South Asia Society in New York in 1995. I recalled it vividly, and I brought it up with him. I told him I remembered Emily stealing glances at him, though he himself did not recall registering this, and I remembered Hamid Karzai and an Afghan businessman I couldn't avoid.

He explained that it began there. A week after that evening, he said, I received a call at work from Emily. I hadn't given her my number, but she remembered I worked in the same place as you. Emily reminded me of our meeting, of your introduction, as if I needed reminding. I *did* recognize her that evening; she was the same young woman I had seen playing the violin all those years earlier, but I would never mention that fact.

She asked if I might be able to help in a small way. I remember that she didn't at all use my name. In fact, it was only several months later that she began to say it, after I told her that if she mispronounced it, the worst thing that could happen was that I'd let her know.

I have a friend, she said, who's interested in banking, in derivatives trading. That's what you do, isn't it?

Yes.

He's graduating from business school, and I wondered if you might be able to have a word with him, a sort of careers advice or chat about what you do. He can talk by phone, if you prefer, or he'll meet you wherever you want, or in Wall Street, I'm sure.

Do you think he needs help?

There was a silence.

He doesn't know if derivatives trading is right for him.

I do fixed-income derivatives. I don't know anything about equities.

What's that?

Equities or fixed-income derivatives?

Both, she answered.

Fixed-income derivatives are things like options on bonds, swaps, caps, floors, interest-rate derivatives. Equity derivatives are to do with stocks and shares. Banks run these things out of separate divisions, I said. I thought that perhaps it was not *help* that her friend wanted but a stepping-stone to an interview.

I'm not sure what he wants to do—and I don't think he is. Perhaps you could talk to him about fixed-income derivatives?

How much mathematics has he studied?

I'm not sure.

You're not sure or you don't know?

I don't know.

What was his degree in?

He's doing an MBA.

His first degree?

History.

I don't know any history graduates in fixed-income derivatives trading, not in this firm. Did he go to an American university?

For business school?

For undergrad.

Why does that matter?

If he did, he might have picked up enough mathematics in his minor.

Oh, I see. No, he went to Oxford.

There are plenty of jobs in banking that don't require much mathematics—just none in fixed-income derivatives trading. I'm not sure I can help other than to repeat that he'd probably find the work very difficult. It's not impossible, but if his classes at business school didn't leave him with a working knowledge of the mathematics of derivatives, then he'll first have to find the enthusiasm for a lot of hard work just to get up to speed, only after which he can figure out if he'd like the work. Perhaps you could explain this to him. Give him my number if he still wants to talk.

Again, there was that silence.

This all sounds rather fascinating, she said.

Finance? I asked.

Yes.

Again, the silence.

I'd like to learn more about it, she added.

This time I was silent. I thought of recommending a book on finance.

Perhaps we could meet for coffee? she asked.

The business school student never called me.

But the beginning proper was in the following year in London: One day, no more than two months into the affair, when we stepped out of a restaurant in Brixton, I asked her to marry me. It is astonishing to think now that I asked her so soon, knowing not very much about her, really, and yet at the time I was of course convinced in the uttermost depths of my heart that this was what I wanted. Only later was I able to interrogate that conviction and trace the source of the certainty. I have always believed—and believed it so clearly that I should say that I have always *known*—that certainty is a subjective state, and no less so the certainty about other subjective states, so that when one is asked whether one is sure about anything, one can only answer: *Yes, but I might be wrong.* One could even go so far as to say that one is absolutely sure but that there always remains the qualification that one might be wrong, for, if nothing else, between the subjective state of certainty and the world presented to us there is the mediation of this laughably fallible perception.

And yet in those days I carried a conviction on which I could have sworn my whole life, sworn the lives of others, and so it seemed the most natural thing in the world to ask her to marry me. In those days, which seem so much longer ago than these ten years, I believed I loved her.

Do you mean you now think you didn't love her? I asked.

Zafar didn't reply.

It's an odd qualification, I explained to Zafar, to *believe* that you loved someone rather than just stating that you did. It suggests you've changed your mind—you now think you didn't actually love her.

And what, responded Zafar, is really the distinction? Perhaps I should simply say that I loved her. After all, I wouldn't say that I *believe* this fruit tastes bitter or that I *believe* this milk smells sour. Isn't love the same, simply the gift of the senses, an affect received by them, and in fact only a state in ourselves, one that we perceive? Like the knowledge we have of where, at any given moment, our limbs are, through the sense of proprioception. Yet therein is the mischief, for how much do our senses fail us, mislead us?

I can't get my head around this thing, he continued. We say *love* and somehow absolve ourselves of the question *why?* at the very moment of its greatest importance. If, when you say love, you refer to those physical signs in the presence of the beloved, if you mean the shortness of breath, the quickening of pulse, the dilation of pupils, and all the rest of it, then what use at all is it to say you *love* a person if any number of things— things that don't make the beloved—can make you feel that ache for someone you really don't know from Adam or Eve? If it springs from what you know about him or her, you know so little that in any other realm you would be a fool to form a judgment on such a flimsy premise, and yet you can fall in love with much less. All the same, I cannot deny that love and our conceit are everything.

It seems impossible to escape the conclusion that I'm entitled to say only that I believed I was in love. I expect you'll remember what Virginia Woolf famously said about love and self-deception: Of course love is the only thing that matters to us; just think of all the delusions we maintain in order to preserve it.*

That day, before I asked her, Emily and I had had a pleasant lunch in an Italian restaurant. I'd ordered a bowl of carbonara and she a Florentine pizza. Emily left food on her plate; she always did. I have never been able to rid myself of the compulsion to eat everything, even long after the needs of the body are met, letting nothing go to waste.

Emily and I were in Brixton, not New York, and, if anything, the portion sizes were on the small side. Nevertheless, Emily was leaving a good deal of food on her plate, setting pieces aside, and as I continued to watch her I realized that she was leaving all the parts of the pizza that came into contact with her hands. Emily never ate food she had touched. Often when she and I ate together I would think of all the meals I ate with my hands as a boy. At first I wondered why she never went to wash her hands before eating; it was my habit—the habit of someone who grew up eating with his hands—and when I mention that I'm doing so, it often encourages others to follow suit. I say this because, over time, I noticed that she never, not once, went into any bathroom away from home, though she did use bathrooms in hotels. When I thought about it, I imagined she'd never cleaned a bathroom in her life.

Nor have I. You don't hold that against me, do you?

Do you remember Gandhi cleaned the latrines in his ashram? Zafar asked.

In the movie?

I don't know why it bothers me so much, but I keep thinking about those fingers of hers. I've even imagined that Emily's attitude toward

---

*I expect you'll remember, he'd said. I wasn't even sure how many o's there were in Woolf until I looked her up. Zafar's recollection (of his own notes, if not the original, as it transpired) was close but not exactly right. The exact words are from *Night and Day* by Woolf:

> But love—don't we all talk a great deal of nonsense about it? What does one mean? . . . It's only a story one makes up in one's mind about another person, and one knows all the time it isn't true. Of course one knows; why, one's always taking care not to destroy the illusion.

what she'd touched was the attitude of women who in another age would have worn thin silk gloves. And I think of all the decent food, food that had done no wrong, that she left behind. Childhood poverty looms over one's whole life. Its effect is felt even as the effect is separated from the cause, despite all the intervening events, even wealth and success. Growing up poor primes every emotion for a certain key.

I remember, I said to Zafar, when we went out for supper in Manhattan back in the day. You used to get the leftovers to go, and when you passed a homeless guy, you'd hand it to him. You know what used to get me about that?

What?

That you noticed the homeless guy. Time and again, we'd be walking and talking, and yet you'd notice the homeless guy.

The portions are so big in America.

It was good of you.

Just as eating everything on the plate is good?

Yes. It *is* good.

It isn't. I wanted to rid myself of the need to eat everything on the plate, because the compulsion served no useful purpose; in fact, quite the opposite. Where there is plenty, eating more than you need at that moment is gluttony. The food is going to waste either in the landfills or in your own body. You're damned either way, so why not just give it up and be done with the guilt and torment? I never chose to see the homeless man; I just did, and I did because however much I tried—however much I might have made the prospect impossible by acquiring degrees and getting paid stupid amounts of money in jobs that promised security—I could never shake off the certain belief that I was only one small misstep away from the same destitution. It's stupid, but only if you think that it's a rational thought or a conclusion to some kind of reasoning, which it isn't. It's just the way it is, among those things you carry forward into your life from childhood. Fighting it isn't any good.

Why would you want to rid yourself of that?

What? The sheer terror of poverty? Why would anyone want to leave that?

Zafar's sarcasm took me by surprise.

Only someone who doesn't have it could ask that, he added.

No, I meant the sensibility to the homeless.

Listen. I'm talking about *why* I noticed the homeless guy. You can't understand it because you don't know what it's like.

Why are you having a go at me? All I'm saying is that when you see a homeless guy and give him food, that's a commendable act of charity.

You said it yourself. I always noticed them. I noticed them because I couldn't help it. Only from the inside can you know what it's like from the inside. Understanding isn't just knowing or learning what it is but knowing what it's *like*.

Do you think you might be confused a little?

I think I might be confused a lot.

You say love is about actions, and all I'm saying is that your actions were quite loving.

What? Giving some sod on the street the leftovers that would have gone in the bin?

Yes.

Think about Emily's brother, James, said Zafar. The Hampton-Wyverns had their Christmas shindig during the day but, on Christmas Eve, James—or so Emily told me—helped out at a soup kitchen at a homeless shelter in West London. He must have served more meals in one evening than I've handed over doggy bags of scraps in all my time in Manhattan. That's the kind of relationship I want with poverty—something that doesn't bite me every time I see affluence or misery.

Zafar's account of the beginning of his relationship with Emily revealed aspects of him that I had never properly appreciated. I listened to him and steadily I formed an impression that was so starkly at odds with the understanding I had had of him that I began to call into question my own judgment. I cannot help but wonder now, as I consider this point, whether Zafar might have intended this, or at least have been conscious that his narrative might have that effect. I had sensed a background of adversity, but the man I'd met at Oxford seemed to be so comfortable in his skin, so much above me, so terribly clever to begin and end with, so sure in his dealings with others, that no one could reasonably have contemplated the vicious tempest that churned below the surface. In Zafar's notebooks, there is a line from Somerset Maugham, whom I admire, as I say, a line I have already used as an epigraph to an earlier chapter, but that bears repetition. *Sometimes people carry to such perfection the mask they have assumed that in due course they actually become the person they seem.*

You asked her to marry you. You never told me.

It was autumn 1997, said Zafar. Autumn in England, even in the metropolis, even in Brixton, he said, can surprise you with its melancholy beauty, every time. Outside the restaurant we stopped in the square to collect ourselves and take our bearings for the walk to my flat. The evening's failing light picked out the edges of leaves on the tops of the trees. The blustery wind scattered debris along the street, and I was in love with the world. I took Emily's hand.

We neared a road, stopping for the cars streaming past. I looked right and made out an oncoming gap. When I looked left, I saw Emily's face, a picture which in that instant elicited unfathomable tenderness, and in an act of folly, in a moment that seemed to have no root in conscious planning, as the bulk of my weight listed from the back foot onto the front, as I held her eyes so that I would have no doubt that she heard the conviction in my voice, I asked Emily Hampton-Wyvern a question I would never ask her again.

She let out a little laugh, a perfectly formed ladylike laugh. Just enough. And I said nothing more.

Afterward, I told myself that this laugh was the reason why I could never ask her again. But the truth is that this so-called reason was a cover I gave myself, a refuge from inclement facts—but while not wholly ineffective, it could not forever hold off the reality. Reality seeps through the cracks. She would never marry me. It wasn't going to happen. Even after the engagement, I still believed this. In fact, even if we'd got married, I knew I would still believe that she wouldn't marry me and I don't think I would have been wrong. I don't think I would ever have occupied the space set aside in the romantic vision of the girl whose formation was in another country, a land that shared not even one border with mine, no border of race or nationality of course, but still less any border of class. I've said it before: Race, or as everyone now likes to say, *ethnicity*, was never so much a source of anxiety as class. In point of fact, racial difference was part of the attraction for both of us, I am sure, an aspect of the fierce sexual love binding us, central to it.

This was 1997. Five years later, when *she* in turn asked *me*, all my own laughter had left me.

She asked *you?* I asked.

She did, though really she asked under duress.

How do you force someone to ask you to marry her?

The duress didn't come from me, said Zafar. We were going to break up. That much was pretty certain. Asking me was her last-ditch attempt to rescue things, even when, I think, she had no wish to rescue the future but only the present, as it was.

I'm sorry, Zafar, but I'm not sure I understand what happened. Of course I want to ask you what went wrong, but I can't help thinking that something about it must also have been right. Otherwise, you wouldn't have stayed in it. I know a lot of it was long-distance and you don't need to explain to me how things can just keep ticking over if you're apart for big stretches. But there must have been something you liked about her?

Can you fall in love with someone you don't like?

Who? Me?

Can a person fall in love with someone he doesn't like?

I suppose some kind of attachment is possible, but I don't know if I'd call it love.

Because, asked Zafar, you fall in love with the *person*, the person you don't know?

Because *like* is an aspect of *love*.

In the following summer, not so long after the proposal and laughter but long enough for memory to find an accommodation, we went to Tuscany. Villa Fontana, which belonged to Emily's grandmother, whom I had yet to meet, sat on a hillside not far from Lucca. A steep tarmac road, under a bright blue sky, curled around the hill overlooking olive groves. To my unaccustomed eyes, the bark of those trees looked as dry as kindling. In our hired car, we inched toward a huddle of cyclists, each one dressed the part: cycling shorts and streamlining sunglasses.

There was a sense, even when we had climbed only a hundred yards, that the view higher up would be spectacular. I remember the sound of the car, its agonies as the incline fought us, a shrill plea for mercy. I glanced at the gear lever.

It's at times like these, I said, you wish you had another gear between neutral and first.

Yes, she replied.

A second passed before she shifted the gears down to first and overtook the cyclists.

When we pulled up outside Villa Fontana, I was surprised to see that it was no more than forty yards from the side of the road. I had been expecting—I don't know why—something set deep within much larger grounds. My first instinct was to look for the fountains, but there were none, which fact I interpreted as a sign of the age of the place.

At that time, everything basked in a favorable light. A colonnade of conifers lined a path to a two-story house with tall windows, their shutters open flat against the exterior walls. The house had an unkempt outer appearance. I remembered a story I'd heard about the Englischer Garten in Munich. My guide, an American friend I was visiting, who had taken up a year-long fellowship at the Max Planck Institute, explained to me that the English Garden, a large park in the center of Munich, was so-called because it was organized along principles that in parts of mainland Europe were known as the English style, disorganized, unkempt, and overgrown, rather like areas of Hampstead Heath, I suppose. Standing in front of the villa in Tuscany, I remembered the corollary my friend had added: Apparently, this kind of natural disorder requires a lot of work—more than any other kind of garden.

We spent a week there, eating, reading, making love, and floating on wide inflatables in the pool. Emily never liked walking very much. If she visited a tourist spot, a thing to see, she might have been compelled by a sense of obligation, but walking for its own sake never held anything for her. So I went on walks by myself whenever she chose to read or take a nap or simply lounge by the pool. We did walk together once, up the road we came on, up around the house and to the top of the hill, and when we came over the crest, the view opened onto a wide vista of a deep valley carved from the earth leading west to a dwindling sun. I read somewhere of a particular view that is found in paintings across cultures and across time. It is apparently a universal aesthetic, and it consists of a valley, of hills directing the eye to the center, of trees and shrubbery of

varying colors of green, and a path, either explicit or implicit in the con-
tours of the land, that winds through the valley to an expanse of water
in the near distance, a lake. Evolutionary biologists have speculated that
a view with such elements is ubiquitous in our art because it was engrained in the psyche during man's formative evolutionary period, for it
is the view of a land that is hospitable to human habitation, a welcome
sight to early humans in search of new beginnings. Nature maketh man
to lie down in green pastures and leadeth him beside the still waters.
And it was the very view from the hill that Emily and I stood on. Behind us was a church, its walls crumbling, its paintwork mottled by
moss and rain, because in the end the earth takes back everything and
all God's work. Beside it, under the evening sky, and on an incline that
made the act unfamiliar and new, Emily and I made love, and it was
every bit as romantic and tender and urgent as any two human bodies
have ever willed.

The sex was extraordinary. For me, I mean. Generally speaking. At
other times, I mean. By that I don't mean it was full of gymnastics or
contorted geometries. Sure, there was spontaneous sex in unlikely places.
There was enough of the drama, but what I mean is that it was powerful.
It was almost always fucking, animal-like, but fucking in the head for
me. It was not so much that she was good at sex but rather that the idea
of Emily never failed to arouse me. I felt moved to greater and greater
efforts and attentions. I learned more and more about the workings of
her body, the pathways of stimulus and response. Sex was the realm in
which I could take control of her being, the only place where I could approach understanding, so that sometimes—quite often, in fact—her body
became an extension of mine. The scents of my own body came to remind me of her. You know, I hesitate to use the word *control*. I don't recall any explicit evidence of a desire to control her, to control her actions
or her thoughts. But in the end, *control* is the right word, because I
wanted to control the Emily in my head, which was the Emily that was
more and more in control of *me*, of my mental composure, of my waking
thoughts, more and more the source of anxiety. A wise man once said to
me—a psychiatrist, but to say more would be to get ahead of myself—
that I had placed too much faith in trying to understand her. I was trying
to understand her because . . . well, because understanding is what we set
so much store in, understanding others, ourselves, understanding the

world; because of that, but also because understanding is a mode of control, it subdues the unruliness of people in one's head, it brings order and confers control where it is most sought, in that theater in the mind in which the avatars of people we know stand as actors resisting direction.

Tomaso visited on day six. Something happened that morning, before he arrived. I was perusing the villa's bookshelves again, hoping against hope that another search would give up something overlooked, in the same way a man might open the fridge several times in an hour, half hoping the contents have miraculously changed. Only, that's never what we really hope for, is it? What we won't admit to ourselves is that we're hoping our preferences might change, that the cheese and the tomatoes might suddenly appeal, or that the book we passed over before might somehow now catch our interest.

Emily came up beside me.

Found anything?

Not yet, I replied.

Look here, she said, pulling out a book. Have you read this?

She was holding *Erewhon* by Samuel Butler.

See. The title spells *nowhere* backward, she said.

I looked again at the title.

No, it doesn't, I said. Though I'm no man of letters, I added.

Yes, it does, she replied.

I looked again.

Prove it, I said.

She took a closer look.

You're right, she said.

I tell you what *is* cute though, I said. *Nowhere* can also be read as *Now-here*, which means exactly the opposite.

She wasn't listening. She looked crestfallen, perhaps even defeated, but I tell you I did not have it in mind to defeat her. Hers seemed to me an easy enough mistake to make, and I think now of our human tendency—her tendency, my tendency—to see only what we wish to be true.

She gave me a look that was not easy to read, as if I was being held responsible for something.

It's certainly an anagram of *nowhere*, I said.

I'm going to sit by the pool, she said.

Tomaso was a friend of hers, from the same college at Oxford, an Italian with a crop of tousled brown hair and shoulders permanently pulled back after the fashion of proud men who are seldom the tallest in their company. He was educated at Lancing, Emily explained—Evelyn Waugh's public school, I thought—but when I met him, I saw that his accent was nevertheless very Italian. She told me that he was a business journalist with Reuters, stationed in Turkey, though I later learned— don't ask me how—that he had also established a fledgling gambling business online, in which Emily had been an investor. These gambling dot-coms, as you know, ran into difficulties with American regulators a few years ago.

Emily explained that he'd returned to Italy that week with his girl-friend, to his mother's home, somewhere not far away. He and his girlfriend, a slim English girl with perfectly unblemished skin and dark eyes—whose name I can't for the life of me remember—came to Villa Fontana for lunch.

From the beginning, Tomaso seemed to be sizing me up, and I specu-lated about whether he and Emily had once been an item, whether, at any rate, some embers of his love their fire retained—to quote that black Russian Pushkin. Did you know Pushkin was black, African black, had African blood?

I did not, I replied.

You can see it in photographs. He was very proud of it. Anyway, con-tinued Zafar, she hadn't mentioned anything about a past romance, and after Tomaso arrived there wasn't a moment when I could ask. But then, I would never have done so anyway.

You were at Oxford? Tomaso asked me.

The four of us were in the kitchen preparing lunch. I was making up a salad, standing at the kitchen table. He was standing on the other side of the table, holding a glass of red wine, while Emily was fetching things from the fridge.

Yes, I was, I replied, thinking that perhaps he thought this was some-thing we all had in common.

I was at Magdalen, he said.

Were you happy there? I asked.

Yes. I suppose I was. Did you meet Emily at Oxford?

This marked out a boundary in his relationship with Emily. Clearly, she had not said much about me to him. Moreover, he could not have known her so well at Oxford that he could assume, therefore, that if she had known me there, she would have mentioned me to him. Yet the moment this thought passed through my mind, I realized its error: Emily was, as you put it, so secretive. Who knows what she would have told anyone?

We met in New York, I replied.

New York?

New York.

You were in New York?

I was working there.

I was in business school there, at Columbia. What were you doing?

I was a banker.

What kind of banking?

I traded derivatives, I replied.

So you were a trader and not a banker?

It struck me as a little pedantic and even a touch too assertive to make a point of the distinction.

I've never seen a coin with the image of a tail on it, but that doesn't stop people from saying *Heads or tails?* when they toss a coin.

He looked puzzled by my remark.

I'm not sure what it means myself, I said.

Emily was now standing behind Tomaso, outside his field of vision, at a counter laying out antipasti on a platter. She turned to glance at me. Her face bore no expression.

A trader, then?

True, I replied. I rather hoped he would leave the point there.

Why New York?

I was already in the U.S. before I got the job.

Doing what?

Law school.

Where?

Harvard.

He seemed puzzled by this.

But how do you go from law to trading derivatives? Isn't it very technical?

Law?

No. Derivatives.

You think the law isn't technical?

No, I mean derivatives. They're very mathematical, aren't they?

I studied mathematics before law school.

Oh, he said. He seemed to consider this.

A few moments later, he left the kitchen to return with a bottle in hand.

I brought this for you, he said, presenting it to Emily.

He had not said *we* brought this. His girlfriend looked down.

Emily took the bottle and, as she turned it in her hands, I noticed the label.

Hey, I said, that's the olive oil they sell in that shop we went to. Marchmain's, wasn't it? Near Harrods, on Beauchamp Place.

I put some effort into pronouncing *Beauchamp*, trying to capture the French accent fluttering over the word.

Tomaso's family produce it, she explained. It's pronounced *Beecham*, she added.

She did not look at me.

Of course it is, I replied.

One way or another, I thought, the English will get you, even if it's with their French. I had been put in my place: That'll teach me not to question the ordering of letters.

Thank you, Tomaso, she said. We'll use it in the dressing.

Tell me, Zafar. Are you Indian? he asked, as if making a prediction, the brow leaning forward, the eyebrows raised expectantly, the tone of voice willing ratification.

I could forgive him the interrogation thus far and perhaps even further. We're all quick to take whatever measure we can of whomever we meet. What is that strange sensation when we feel we have the person in the hand? We're so eager to know the station given to a man by birth and curious to learn about the one he's acquired through his own deeds, and when we have this pair we lean back and swell with the satisfaction of having got the sense of what he's about. And for the preservation of that satisfaction, we will protect our expectations of him from subversive reality by means of blinkers that come down like some hysterical blindness. Is that the root of class? A simple system.

I was born in Bangladesh, I answered.

I have been asked that question—Are you Indian?—umpteen times, and my reply has always been the same: I was born in Bangladesh. In the U.S., in order to account for my accent, I might add that I grew up in the U.K. But then, in the U.S. I'm more likely to be asked if I'm British. The British accent trumps skin color, certainly in New York, and even after September 11, 2001.

The point I want to make is that when I'm specifically asked if I was born in *India*, my reply—that I was born in Bangladesh—generally meets one of three reactions. The first is the look of recognition, evidence of knowing where Bangladesh is. The second is the look a person gives when he stands corrected but without enough information to grasp the correction. Bangladesh, I say by way of further explanation, is east of India—it used to be East Pakistan; it's between India and Burma and south of Nepal and Bhutan. In some cases, this is enough to draw a nod of recognition, but in most the irresistible evidence of their faces is that their confusion is only magnified; if they could not quite place Bangladesh, then more likely than not they struggle with Bhutan and Burma. But some of the blessedly baffled have sufficient education to suspect that they ought to know better, and they might feign, entirely uselessly, a look of recognition.

The third reaction is by far the most interesting. It was Tomaso's response. For years, I believed I had no understanding of it. Now I think that most likely I have always had some inkling, but I didn't want to confront it.

The third is the look someone gives you when he believes your response ratifies what he said. The eyelids close, the head nods, and a smile hovers at the edges of the mouth. It bespeaks satisfaction, as if nothing in their expectations or understanding of the world has been disturbed— on the contrary, it just received confirmation. All this I saw in Tomaso's face. He could have left it there. Nothing more was necessary.

Which used to be India, right?

Correct, I replied.

The head continued nodding, just enough to be sure of being noticed while I was cutting tomatoes with a kitchen knife. My guess, borne of more verified guesses than I'd ever wish for, was that in Tomaso's mind the boundary between India and Bangladesh, however it might be drawn politically, was not sufficiently hard in culture, in the imagination, in rightly guided imagination, to warrant note.

I looked at the tomatoes I was cutting.

What's this I hear, Emily? Tomaso asked. Apparently, you're going to work at the UN.

Emily smiled at Tomaso. Her smile was engineered, machined into her countenance, an embossed symbol rather than an emotion. To Emily, that smile was somehow enough of an answer to all manner of questions, even when it was no answer at all. It earned her time. But when, more often than not, no further comment came from her, you did not press her. Somehow, to do so felt inappropriate.

I used to marvel at the skill of it, until it dawned on me that what I saw was not the exercise of skill but the expression of a character habituated by the behaviors of a family that threw the cloak of secrecy over everything it did, an act of prudence, as if to smother every trace of some pestilence threatening to escape. She behaved as a body conditioned to respond to a certain stimulus of the senses.

When do you leave? he asked Emily.

He glanced back and forth from me to Emily. He was probably a good journalist, I thought. He did not ask me what he must have wanted to ask. Or was that my own insecurity? And what would I have told him, if he had? That she would go to the UN, cross the Atlantic, with my blessing, for I never wanted anyone else to think that I had held back a woman, I never wanted anyone to house me any deeper in the pigeonhole of a South Asian male?

There are a few hurdles yet, she replied to him.

Tomaso sat down and, turning to me, asked, Do they make olive oil in India?

I'm sorry. Where?

In India.

I believe they do, I replied. I turned to Emily and reached for the bottle. Let's use Tomato's olive oil, I said.

Tomaso's, said Emily, correcting me.

It must have seemed an easy mistake to make; I was cutting tomatoes, after all.

Tell me. Is it true that Indians believe the earth sits on a giant turtle?

Time came to a brief halt.

Are you asking *me*?

Yes.

In some cultures, a rainbow is a symbol for the refraction of light.

Now what does that mean?

And Reno is west of L.A., Rome is north of New York, but do you speak African?

I beg your pardon?

Beg all you like. You're not getting it.

Excuse me?

Yes?

Tomaso shook his head. He looked exasperated.

So?

So, what?

So, is it true? In India, do they believe the earth sits on a giant turtle?

Do you know which country has the largest Muslim population in the world?

I do know. Indonesia.

Indonesia is the largest officially Muslim state, but the country with the largest Muslim population is India, which is a secular state.

Right. But you haven't answered my question.*

Are you a Catholic?

I am.

So you believe in the transubstantiation of a wafer?

Well, I'm not sure I subscribe to the whole theology.

---

*Zafar is wrong on key points: Indonesia is not and was never an officially Muslim state; furthermore, while India's Muslim population is vast, it is Indonesia's that is the largest. What makes the exchange between Zafar and Tomaso intriguing, however, is that my friend must have known that what he was saying was not true. Of course, I don't mean that Zafar was infallible, but given the subject matter of the specific statements he made, asserting them so confidently, I cannot accept that he didn't know the facts. Yet why lie? My friend was a slippery son of a gun. Looking over the dialogue, I wonder if he was testing the shallowness of Tomaso's knowledge, as well as setting a trap. When Zafar "corrected" him, Tomaso responded with *Right*, when my friend must have known his correction was wrong. This is a side of Zafar I never liked: If he was pulling a fast one, you wouldn't see it coming and, worse still, not even see it when it was right there.

Likewise, I don't know if all Hindus, or even some, believe that the earth rests on a giant turtle.

Then why are you talking about Muslims?

I can safely say that two hundred million Muslims in India—if they are Muslims in more than name—don't believe that the earth rests on a giant turtle. Muslim ontology is not so far from Christian and Jewish ontologies. So to answer your question, there are many *they* in India who do not maintain that the earth rides on the back of a turtle.

I see, he said. He seemed to consider this.

I returned to the salad I was preparing.

Do you go back often? he asked.

Sorry, are you talking to *me*?

Yes. Do you go back to India often?

I've been there a couple of times, I said, pouring olive oil into a jar.

It must be very hard.

Why?

They're so poor.

Yes, Tomato, the poor have it hard.

I shook the jar of olive oil and balsamic vinegar. This time there was no doubt. It wasn't a slip of the tongue. I wasn't making a mistake with his name.

Why are you so British? he asked. The man stood up. In his hand was the glass of red wine. Why can't you be more Indian? he continued. You have such a fine tradition and culture and history but you've become an Englishman.

Now you're insulting the whole of England.

The name's Tomaso.

You say potato.

You're nothing like my Indian friend at Oxford.

How many times a day do you forgive someone his ignorance?

Is that an apology?

I'm sorry, Tomato.

And at that, Tomaso emptied his glass over my shirt. He thrust it in my direction and the wine came flying out. A few drops made it to my face.

That was unnecessary, I said.

You asked for it, he replied.

I wish I could tell you I had a witty comeback. The ones I formulated came too late and they weren't so witty after all. I suppose I could have tried to justify myself, but where to begin? And why bother?

I looked down at my shirt, looked at Tomaso, looked at Emily. Somewhere in the room must have been Tomaso's girlfriend.

Silly me. I've spilled wine on my shirt, I said and left the room. When I returned, the two of them had gone.

If Zafar's story had meant to convey what it was he liked about Emily, I didn't get it. Searching now for clues, I find myself asking if he had meant to suggest that there was a certain romance about being with her, the Tuscan hills, making love under the stars, the remove from his childhood, a certain glamour in a certain life. It sounds shallow to me, too shallow for my friend, I would have thought, but my instincts settle there. Perhaps he himself saw a shallowness in that, and that is why his little aside never meets the mark of answering my question. I did in fact press him on the point, though his answer seemed to me a touch disingenuous, which only returns me to my own conclusion.

Good times, he said, are interesting times.

By such a standard, the incident with Tomaso, I said, must have been a great time.

His answers were unsatisfactory, but I left it there. And then there was the sex. Of course, I was uncomfortable listening to this—for reasons I'll come to very soon—but what struck me above all else as he discussed the sex was that he was prepared to do so. Men don't talk like that, not the men I know. And perhaps because of that, I had the thought that Zafar would not be staying very much longer. I had the thought that such openness evidenced a disconnection with the regular world, that he had abandoned the cultivation of a self to suit the society of his fellow men. I looked at him and saw that he would never have a job again, never return to the treadmill, never pay a mortgage and make a home and raise a family. He had slipped off the wheel.

17

My Brother's Keeper or Betrayal

It is easier to forgive an enemy than to forgive a friend.
—William Blake

Whenever he related his experience with Emily, Zafar's demeanor changed and a darkness gathered about him, so that age and weariness showed in the features of his face. More or less everything he told me about his time with her was news to me. Sometime in 1997, we began to meet less and less frequently and, since the period coincided with a substantial increase in work for me—business in the mortgage market spiked, and the prospect of making partner quickly loomed in sight—our friendship waned. Time then seemed to move so quickly that I did not gauge the absence of friendships very well. Meena was also busy; having found her feet in finance, she'd set off at a sprint. I believed our relationship was content and strong and we could draw on that contentment to sustain us through the long working days of separation.

And so it was that a year passed without our meeting, Zafar and I, and then another. Such regrets as I have are few; I am not an old man, but even if there had been time enough to accumulate regrets, I do not think my constitution works that way. My circumstances have also helped, I daresay, for I don't think I ever faced the prospect others face of regretting bad decisions that took them down the road to financial burden or ruin, lives ruled by mortgage repayments and school fees, that seem to be the lot of so many people. True enough, I've not been immune to financial difficulties. But they were—they *are*—the difficulties of someone with good fortune.

However, I do now have regrets about that time of my life. I'm not so presumptuous as to imagine that if I'd remained a presence in his life, he might not have declined as he evidently did in that time. What is the word for it? I say *declined*, but what was it? A descent? Collapse? Unraveling, unstitching, falling apart, breaking down?

I want to give an explanation, but there is no reason. I told myself afterward that perhaps I was consoling Emily, but her demeanor did not warrant such a view. There was no obvious distress in want of relief. Where there is nothing that can amount to an explanation, I am left only with the possibility of stating what happened. By that, I do not mean what Zafar would have meant, for to him, it must be apparent, what happens is as much in the mind as in the exercise of the body and its limbs. Our thoughts and feelings, the emotions and instincts that drive us on, these were to Zafar no less the stuff of the drama we enact than our actions that are easily described if not explained.

Zafar spoke of the will, disparaging its purported freedom. And though I reject his rejection of the will, I understand the simplicity of his point: Only without invoking the idea of will can we properly speak of causes. If you want to know why a man made a choice, it won't do to say that he simply chose. Zafar's exposition therefore stands as an account of causes: the center line in a tug-of-war moves because men pull on the rope. But when we take the will out of the picture, should we not turn then to passions and instincts and drives in finding our causes? In his notebooks, Zafar records a passage from the philosopher David Hume's *A Treatise of Human Nature*, a well-worn passage, I know: *We speak not strictly and philosophically when we talk of the combat of passion and of reason. Reason is, and ought only to be, the slave of the passions, and can never pretend to any other office than to serve and obey them.* I cannot pretend that I have reasons or justifications.

I remember the date because it was my father's birthday, a Saturday in April 2000, and I was driving up to Oxford to visit him for lunch. The roads were uncluttered at ten in the morning, and the skies were clear and blue enough to drive with the cover down. My thoughts drifted in and out of matters of work. We had just completed a string of almost identical transactions on which the firm had made substantial profits, and I was thinking about how the structure might potentially be replicated with other clients and about ways it might have to be tailored. As I drew into Oxford, slowing to the pace of traffic, my phone rang.

Hello, it's Emily Hampton-Wyvern.

Hello, Emily. How lovely to hear from you, I shouted over a passing truck. It's been ages.

Where are you? What's all the racket?

I'm sorry. I'm on the road, I replied. Something was wrong, I thought. Why, after all, would she call?

Zafar's in hospital.

Good God. What's the matter?

He's in a psychiatric hospital.

I said nothing.

He's in a psychiatric hospital, she repeated.

I was shocked by the news. It's quite a thing to be hospitalized that way, isn't it? It's what doctors do *to* you, because you don't know better, your mind can't know better. But shock wasn't the whole of what I felt. Zafar was undeniably someone I cared about. Someone I admired and in some ways envied. Yet there it was: I was shocked, and yet another part of me was not surprised. Which is not to say that I could see it coming. There was the mystery that surrounded Zafar, that was part of his attraction. I knew nothing really of his childhood, of his formation. What I did know—my brief encounter with his parents—only fed a thesis: He'd seemed self-made, came from nothing, but how far can that go? How feasible is it? Was he a working-class boy who had overreached? Lived beyond his psychic means?—to take some words from his notebooks.

That's awful. What's wrong?

Emily did not answer. I assumed she hadn't heard me. I thought of pulling over, but the road had suddenly become clear.

What happened?

Still there was no answer. It struck me that perhaps she didn't know.

How is he?

Before she could reply, I added: That's a stupid question; he's in hospital.

Are you free this evening? she asked me.

Shall I come over?

Would you?

I'll be there at eight.

18

The Blood-Dimmed Tide

Mathematics, as applied logic, which nevertheless stays within pure and lofty abstraction, holds a curious intermediate position between the humanistic and realistic sciences; and from the descriptions Adrian shared in conversation of the delight it gave him, it became evident that at the same time he experienced this intermediateness as something elevated, dominating, universal, or as he put it, "the true." It was a great joy to hear him call something "true"; it was an anchor, a stay—one no longer asked oneself quite in vain about the "main thing."

—Thomas Mann, *Doctor Faustus*, translated by John E. Woods

Zafar returned to his account of events in Kabul, to Emily and the UN lounge. But if it appears that some time passed before he did so, it is largely the effect of my own reconstruction of our conversations. I did, after all—for reasons I've already given—bring forward the Afghan story. And, as I look over what I've put down so far, I see that much of the intervening material concerns me and my own life. Yet it's equally true that my friend didn't tell the Afghan story from beginning to end without deviation. That's just not Zafar. He had taken me back to Islamabad in order, I understand, to set the context for his involvement in what happened in Kabul, when he met Crane. But now he took up the scene in the UN bar again, after making his presence known to Emily in the lounge.

He left her with her circle of admiring men, he explained, men ever gravitating toward her, as ripe apples to the soft earth, he said. She now knew that I was here, in the compound, in Kabul. Passing through a low arch, I came into the bar, a cavernous room with plenty of sofas and armchairs, as in the lounge, but with furniture and people packed in and pressed together, and the lighting dimmer. Yet what attacked my senses were the smell and the noise. In several months of working in South Asia, I had not smelled that pungent admixture of alcohol and human bodily odor. It came from another world. The music was loud, the soles of my feet tingling with the vibrations, a volume to muffle the clamor of sexual gambits unbuckling over the scene. It was a scene of horror. This is the freedom for which war is waged, in the venerable name of which the West sends its working-class heroes to fight and die. If the Afghanis had been asked, would they have allowed this blight on their home? Is this what Emily was fighting for?

Men are social animals, we are told, the evidence all around us. I went to Glyndebourne once with Emily and her mother, all of us dressed to the nines. The music was good enough, some or other opera, but it seemed to me that Glyndebourne was as much as anything else a social occasion: picnic hampers bulging with booty from Fortnum & Mason and Harrods, jams, Gentleman's Relish, and strawberries. Champagne bubbled over the sound of corks popping. A scene from what? An impressionist painting perhaps? Yet what do I know about their art? It was a beautiful summer's day. Penelope said hello to friends and acquaintances—the brush of cheek against cheek—and so did Emily. I saw two other South Asian faces and wondered if, after years of passing off, I now looked even half as much at ease as they did.

If Glyndebourne was a harmless social venue, which is no small *if*, the UN bar in Kabul was the antithesis. What the people in the bar were doing wasn't *just* getting together for a few drinks in a familiar setting. It wasn't *just* hip-hop in the background, the press of bodies, the lingering stares, the offers to buy a drink disguising and disclosing other intentions; it wasn't even what I overheard in every snatch of conversation, that human drive to seek out agreement, to approve and concur, that craving for the fellow feeling of a shared view of the world that might actually come from nothing more than wanting to be liked.

A beautiful young woman—and I mean *beautiful*—stood with a drink in hand. In the clouds of smoke, her lips seemed to tremble. She had poise and grace and legs all the way to Tuesday or Christ Almighty or the ground, whichever is the longest. You could have taken this woman, this almost imaginary creature, for one of the models gliding about Union Square in New York, a lingerie model, not the brittle-boned, concave clothes hangers of catwalks. Such women frightened me off: Imagined women can satisfy only the imagination. Behind her was a man talking to another woman, though he kept glancing her way. As for the man actually talking to the model, who might or might not have had her attention, he looked uneasy in the company he was keeping, as if his jacket was a size too small. The model, I thought, was the kind of woman Emily would be careful not to be seen beside, a woman who could reduce her.

I looked for the group I came with. Nicky was on the other side of the room, curled into a sofa, talking to Sandra, a middle-aged Korean American woman I'd been introduced to in the Land Cruiser.

Zafar! We thought we'd lost you. Sandra had you pegged as the disappearing sort, without so much as a goodbye, but I said you were a proper gentleman.

Putting on a cockney accent, I said: A proper gentleman.

Nicky had a wonderful smile, bursting with true pleasure, a bright, uncomplicated smile, a smile that sang affection, as any fool could tell. Emily never smiled at me like that. Yes, I think there was genuine tenderness in Nicky's smile. And yes, she flirted with me, but it was bounded flirtation. She had told me not long after we met—forty-eight hours in Kabul contained so much time—about her wonderful husband, a jazz musician, and her two little boys, a house ruled by wild men.

I think few women can pull it off. It requires a particular skill. Of course, there's no skill in laying down a boundary; on the contrary, I would have thought a married woman with two children would have to work hard if she wants to avoid mentioning family in response to any question that so much as touches on the personal. But Nicky had the skill to build the wall true and strong without putting the flirting in the shade.

Sandra's leaving the U.S. because of Bush.

Canada? I said, turning to Sandra.

Vietnam. Our youngest is adopted—he's Vietnamese—and we're thinking we might take him back there, you know, his roots and so on.

She knocked back the last of her drink.

How the Star-Spangled Banner did George come between you and Uncle Sam?

Sandra grinned at me and got up.

What are you drinking? she asked. Evidently, she thought my question was rhetorical.

No, no. Let me, I said.

Stop that! What are you having?

I think the drinks are subsidized, said Nicky.

They are when I'm paying, said Sandra.

Whisky, I said.

Nicky?

I'm okay, replied Nicky. She was holding a glass of white wine, still half full.

Sandra disappeared into the thicket of people. Nicky lowered her voice.

What did you find?

What do you mean? I asked.

Oh, come on. You disappeared.

I smiled at her.

Do you wonder what we're doing here? I asked.

I *know* what the Americans are doing here. They want blood. Somebody has to pay.

I mean all this development and reconstruction. What's it really about?

I met you only this afternoon and I know this about you: You think people never say what they mean. The truth is, nine times out of ten what they say is all they mean.

What's it really about?

It's about development and reconstruction.

Nicky was on a fact-finding mission with a women's microfinance NGO, lending small amounts to women who want to organize themselves into small enterprises.

We can do some good here, she continued. This is a miserable country, Zafar. I don't need to explain that to you. It needs help. Isn't it that simple?

Is anything that simple?

I sat down beside her on the arm of the sofa. She seemed absorbed, and I wondered if she was thinking what I was thinking, if she was going back over her own words and considering them again, their meagerness, their vagueness, and that the exculpation was always that the country needs the help that people like her were ready to provide.

It was then that I noticed Emily approaching us. What did Emily see? She saw me with an attractive woman.

Nicky greeted her with that boundless smile.

I'm Nicky, and this is Zafar.

Emily extended her hand to offer that limp handshake I had seen before, and I could now feel Nicky's confident grip closing around it.

Emily turned to me and I think we both said hello at the same time. If Nicky was observant, she would have noticed that Emily didn't extend her hand to me. But when I thought about it later, it occurred to me that even if Nicky had noticed, she might have assumed Emily didn't want to embarrass this South Asian man, a pious Muslim for all anyone knew, who might not shake hands with women.

I still don't know what to make of that bizarre moment, what possessed us to pretend we had never met before, what thought or calculation had passed through her head or through mine, which would have had to have been unconscious in me, for I did what seemed to be ordained, without premeditation, reflection, or design, as if here in Kabul, Afghanistan, I was in a new world, one far away, and we had all taken on new clothes, in order to become unrecognizable, in order to discard our former selves and reinvent the people we were, in a land where people were not people, not even actors, but pieces on a game board.

You know, Richard Feynman likened research in physics to watching a curious game unfold on an eight-by-eight board of alternating black and white squares, trying to figure out its rules—but watching it, he explained, under odd constraints so that you can only view one corner of the board, and there notice things and try to discover the rules behind them. You might notice, for example, that a bishop—a tall wooden piece that evokes the image of a bishop—only stays on the same-colored squares, but then later suddenly grasp that the bishop can move along diagonals only, which is a deeper rule and one that explains the earlier observation, too—and so it goes on, this scratching away at the corner, unearthing rule after rule, trying to discern the patterns and rules of the game.

Afghanistan, too, had become a game, but it wasn't chess, not as we know it, not even the game of chess that is played in Asia, with its differences that confound you (the king, or rajah, that does more than stupidly wait) and similarities that deceive you, but an altogether different game in which the players fight to set down the very rules. It is possible that in that moment, when Emily looked at me and said hello, when her hand remained hanging limply from her arm, having shaken or been shaken by Nicky's hand, when the smile I wore was as much for myself as it was for her—it is quite possible that in those moments I had some premonition of violence, of the only thing that could disturb the polite games, of what I was capable of doing. Before I looked it up, I thought the origins of the phrase *turning the tables* lay in Christ's fit of rage in the Temple, at the house of prayer being made into a den of thieves. But apparently it owes more to board games. Either way, it would be apt.

What do you do here? asked Nicky.

I'm with the Assistance Mission, replied Emily. She didn't give her name.

You must work with AfDARI, said Nicky with an intonation that sought confirmation.

When I first met Emily, I thought it charming the way she didn't respond or engage in conversation in the way everyone else did. Most people would have said, *Yes, I work with AfDARI from time to time.* Perhaps even, *Do you know Maurice Touvier?* Most people would move the conversation along, but Emily did not. Sometimes, when talking to her, just for the fun of it, I used to hold back from saying something to keep the conversation going, just to see what would happen. Silence entered and the whole world stopped turning on its axis, and the conversation would not move along, and when the moon yanked the earth back into motion she might introduce another subject altogether or go and do something else. She rarely asked me anything. And there was seldom any idle banter, as if there's anything idle in the banter between lovers.

Those eyes, they just stared. They used to baffle me. How, I asked myself, could she not break eye contact like the rest of us? Until, that is, you think about it differently, until you begin to see that the experience of looking someone in the eye isn't the same for everyone, and that maybe for Emily locking eye contact and staring just didn't give rise to the compulsive demand from a denuded self to look away, to break it off—she wasn't overcoming anything by staring. She interacted differently. There wasn't, I began to suspect, the same engagement, the same experience of wave after wave of information and meaning hitting her retina, when she stared at you. Like the mountaineers we think of as courageous. That they may be. But if their amygdalae—parts of the brain central to the operation of the flight instinct—are smaller than those of the rest of us, as research suggests—as Mohsin Khalid mentioned!—then their *experience* of threats and dangers is different. There's a popular notion that liars can't look you in the eyes. But it's not true. They actually do the opposite even if they might not know they're doing it. They stare at the person they're lying to because they need to know if the lies they're telling are working, if they're being believed, so that they can better tailor their lies or augment them, even as they speak. So why do we fall for eye contact and take it to confirm honesty, when in fact it could be evidence of duplicity? Does Mother Nature think that a lie believed is a secret kept and that thereby is social harmony preserved?

I have a meeting at AfDARI tomorrow, said Nicky. With Maurice Touvier.

Why? asked Emily.

I'm with Microfinance for Women.

Emily did not acknowledge recognition—which meant nothing.

On a fact finder, continued Nicky, just scoping out what's going on and how we can do something positive.

Emily held that expression, the air of not being entirely present, even as she looked you in the eyes, and with the suggestion of a smile, faint enough to confuse you and thereby hold you off from asking her if she was listening. It is, I'm inclined to think, the look unskilled diplomats give when they talk to someone they regard as inconsequential.

Where are you staying? asked Nicky.

I'm here on the compound.

That sounds nice.

When did you arrive? asked Emily, turning to me.

About half an hour ago.

When did you arrive in Afghanistan?

Yesterday.

Her smile disappeared.

Where are you staying?

At AfDARI, I answered.

And what brings you here? she asked.

Same thing as Nicky. Fact-finding. Apparently, Afghanistan's the land of lost facts.

You're so cagey, said Nicky to me.

I think he's a spy, she added for Emily.

Yes, I'm with the BS.

What's that? asked Nicky.

The Bangladeshi Secret Service.

Shouldn't that be BSS? asked Nicky.

If I say BS, I mean BS!

Emily grinned.

It was nice to meet you, she said to Nicky.

She turned to me, maintained her smile, and left.

Sandra returned with the whisky.

Wasn't that Emily Hampton-Wyvern? asked Sandra.

I thought her name was Melissa, said Nicky.

Emily, said Sandra.

Are you sure? asked Nicky.

Maybe it's just Melissa's rumor, I said.

There's that public school wit, said Nicky.

Remember what Ermintrude said?

Sandra was speaking to Nicky.

Is anyone really called Ermintrude? I asked.

Why not? replied Sandra.

I mean apart from cartoon cows.

Are you calling my friend a cow?

Are you calling her Ermintrude?

Fair enough. Our friend at Reuters—Ermintrude—says she gets around.

Who?

Emily, replied Sandra.

Didn't waste any time hitting on *you*, added Nicky.

Thanks, Sandra, I said, raising the glass she'd just handed me.

Apparently, she's a spy, said Sandra.

For whom? I asked.

For *whom*? Where's your smoking jacket? asked Sandra.

British intelligence, said Nicky.

I heard CIA, replied Sandra.

How do you know? I asked.

Everyone says so, replied Nicky.

So then what does that mean? I asked.

It means she can't be, said Nicky, sounding uncertain, as if she were expecting me to mark her answer.

It means, said Sandra, she can't be the kind of spy who relies on people not suspecting she's a spy.

Or, I said, the kind of spy who relies on no one thinking that others suspect her of being a spy.

What kind of spy is that? asked Sandra.

I don't know. Maybe there's no such kind.

Nicky, you do pick up the strangest men, said Sandra.

The Queen, I said, raising my glass again.

We stayed a little longer before Nicky reminded us of the curfew. There wasn't enough time to drop me off first, so I went back with Nicky, Sandra, and the group.

The women were staying in a house maintained by Bernice Miller, a vivacious human rights campaigner. Bernice had a beacon of long blond hair and, by all accounts, an irrepressible passion for throwing parties. She'd parachuted into Afghanistan, quite possibly literally, right after the Americans liberated it, and having barely hit the ground she set about publicizing the plight of civilian victims of American aerial bombardment.

She was hosting the group of women in a large house, but for some reason—perhaps to do with security—all of them, upward of twenty by my reckoning, were to sleep in two large adjoining rooms on a tessellation of mattresses and makeshift cots. I was shown a corner, and a middle-aged Afghani man brought me a couple of blankets. The generator was going to be turned off soon, but everyone looked like they'd had a long day behind them and were ready for bed. I didn't undress.

In the morning, I got up and picked my way across the slumbering bodies. As I pulled the door shut behind me, a woman emerged from the bathroom across the landing. She was wearing a bathrobe. Before I could look away, she gave me a wink, as if I'd just been caught in the act. I pulled the door shut.

Downstairs, there was coffee. Through the windows lay a vast open space where there might once have been buildings but that now lay flattened without trees or brush and on whose far side the new day's sun was simmering in the cold air. The previous night, we'd driven past the fortress of the American consulate and come to a stop not far from it. I supposed neighboring areas had been cleared, perhaps for expansion, perhaps as a buffer.

I finished the coffee, pulled out my notebook, tore out a page, and left a note by the coffee machine addressed to Nicky, mischievously thanking her for *a memorable night*. I stepped out into the courtyard and asked a guard if somebody could arrange a ride to AfDARI.

When I arrived half an hour later, Suaif, the gatekeeper, let me in.

Miss Emily, he explained, she came to find you. We told her we did not know where you are.

From the courtyard, I could see that a window to my room had been broken.

Is she here?

She has paid for the window to be fixed.

Suleiman appeared across the courtyard.

I heard you were out on the town last night, he said.

I went to the UN bar.

Which one?

What do you mean *which one*?

Kabul now proudly boasts dozens of bars.

Already?

At least two run by the UN.

How do locals feel about that?

The rich love it; the poor are disgusted.

Inside my room, we stood side by side looking at the broken window.

I'd kept the curtains drawn on the east side of the room facing onto the courtyard, in order to keep my luggage out of sight. The window on the south side had no curtains. Anyone could have looked in from there. If Emily had asked the gatekeeper to look for me, the man would have known to go around the side of the building and, standing by the black tree, look in through that window.

I hear there was some drama this morning, said Suleiman.

Sorry about the window.

Why did she break it?

I don't know. I can't call her. My cell doesn't work here, I replied.

That's the private sector for you. The UN brought in a multinational and it hasn't set up roaming, so you have to get a dedicated phone to work on its local network. There's a phone in the office.

Had she really come in, I asked myself, knocked on the door and, failing to get a response, smashed a window before asking anyone? Had she really left a roll of Afs to cover the costs? I thought of Suaif, this middle-aged engineering professor reduced to guarding a gate; this proud man who slept in a corner of a room in the AfDARI compound set aside for menial staff; this man in his home away from home, who watches helplessly as a Western woman enters and, by the power vested in her by the UN, ISAF, NATO, the West, and her white skin, smashes in a window without even asking him if there was some other way to get in or look in; this man who then stands stripped of his own authority, what feeble authority it ever was, as she hands him cash—did she bother to count?—to cover the costs and keep him sweet.

What was she looking for? Looking for me? Did she fear I'd been abducted? This was Kabul, after all. Or was it Nicky she had feared? Whatever the motive for breaking in, was it not the act of omission that was reprehensible, the disregard for the gatekeeper in his native land? Did it really not even occur to her to ask him for help?

I turned to Suaif and shook my head and prayed he'd understand that I wanted then to apologize for everything, for everything that had been done and was going to be done.

She left you a message, said Suleiman, fishing something out of his trouser pocket.

He handed me a note in a sealed envelope: *Come to supper at the UN compound. 7:30. Please come. I want to show you off.*

By noon, the windowpane was fixed with a square of wooden board, and I was in my room, writing in my notebook, when there came a knock on the door.

I heard you were in town. Remember me?

Hello, Crane, I replied. Good to see you again. How are you?

Crane Morton Forrester looked much the same as when you introduced him to me at that party a few years earlier, the same brutal mass, a giant slab of ham that obscured the whole doorway behind him. He wore military fatigues and boots, but covering his chest and shoulders was a great wool jumper, blue and plain. Something about Crane threatened clumsiness.

What brings you to this neck of the woods? I asked.

I could ask the same of you, he replied.

Tourism, I said. I hear they have superb beaches and the girls are to die for.

You Brits kill me. Crane laughed.

And you? I asked.

Just quit the Marines; signed up a couple of years ago.

Before September 11?

Yup.

You were in Operation Enduring Freedom?

Fuckers had me in the embassy. No action. Haven't seen squat.

So you quit?

Military contracting, that's where the money's at. I'm with Blackstar.

I nodded.

First learn the ropes, then start my own outfit.

Sounds like a plan.

Sure is. Two words, my man: plausible deniability. That's the beauty of private military contractors. Gives Washington plausible deniability.

He gave me a beaming smile with a knowing look, as if he'd shared a clever yet simple insight.

There was movement by the door. From behind Crane's form, Suleiman appeared. Suleiman himself had to duck in doorways, but next to the huge American with his wide receiving arms, the young Afghani looked narrow and vulnerable.

There you are, buddy, exclaimed Crane.

He patted Suleiman on the back, though he might as well have patted him on the head.

You've met Sully? Crane asked me.

I nodded without engaging Suleiman's eye.

Suleiman handed Crane an envelope. Crane took it but gave not a word of explanation.

Sully's a Red Sox fan, aren't you, Sully? Think you got a shot this season?

Suleiman glanced at me. Was he telling me something? I thought, of course, of the colonel and his request: *Find out what's in the envelopes. And be careful with Crane.*

Baseball can break your heart, Mr. Crane. It's a game of surprises.

He's a philosopher, our Sully, a man with an impossible dream.

Crane turned back to me.

Listen, I've gotta get going. How about grabbing a beer sometime?

Sure, I replied.

How long you here?

A while.

Great. I'll show you around. There's a lot of action if you know where to look.

Crane then actually gave me a wink. The second wink I'd received in twenty-four hours.

Sully knows how to get hold of me, he added.

After he left, Suleiman pulled the curtain ajar. Crane's massive frame lumbered across the courtyard.

That man is disgusting.

Why was he here? I asked.

He collects mail here. Always envelopes.

Where are they from?

They're local, dropped off by jeep.

UN jeeps?

Unmarked jeeps. Can't make out anything. Normally the director takes receipt and holds them for him.

But they trust you with them?

Not completely. The jeep was just here, and I don't know if you noticed, but it didn't leave until Crane stepped out into the courtyard with the envelope in his hands, and Crane always steps out as soon as I give him the envelope.

Why do you say he's disgusting?

I met Crane several months ago, said Suleiman. He was some flunky in the embassy; I got the impression he was an errand boy in Kabul. One day I was here late and curfew was minutes away. Crane happened to be stopping by—to collect an envelope—and he offered to drop me home in his Land Cruiser. It had military markings—the curfew doesn't apply to them. Crane has been here since the beginning but never far from Kabul. I think his father's a senator.

He's on the Armed Services Committee.

That's right. So we're in Crane's air-conditioned Land Cruiser and I think he's been drinking. The air stinks of alcohol. And he starts to talk.

He tells me, and forgive me for repeating such words, about this girl he knows just outside Kabul, out west, and how tight she is, how much he likes that young pussy and her tight ass—I am telling you what he said, and believe me, I cannot bring myself to tell you it all in detail. He tells me he loves Afghan pussy. He swears that one time he fainted—dear God, forgive me—he swears he fainted, he came so hard in her ass. He tells me he tries to make it up there every week. The girl's father knows what's going on all right, he explains, but they don't care so long as he sweetens the deal. The father stays away and the mother takes the kids out and he gets the girl and the little Afghan house all to himself. You know, Sully, he says, there's nothing tighter than thirteen-year-old Afghan ass. I am sitting silently in the Land Cruiser. He goes on Fridays, he says, and stops by the dogfight on his way back. I don't know what the driver is thinking. He must speak English if he works for the embassy. For all I know, this might be the driver who takes him to the girl. He asks me what I think. And I didn't say anything, but I will tell you now that my very thought was: Should I kill this son of a pig? What I say to him is that he must be a very happy man. You bet your ass, he says, and laughs. So now you see. It is not enough to destroy the country; they rape our girls and they humiliate our men.

Of course, I'm disturbed by what Suleiman—

It's simply not true! I exclaimed, interrupting Zafar. I've known Crane since . . . since fuck. He can be a shit—*could* be a shit—but this. I don't believe it. There's no evidence for it, I said.

Zafar didn't respond.

Is there any evidence? I asked him.

Why don't I just tell you what happened?

I nodded and Zafar continued.

I listened to Suleiman without interrupting him, listening for what it is he wants to volunteer to me.

There are bad people in the world, I said to him presently.

There is bad and there is evil, he replied, and there is only one thing to be done with evil.

I didn't respond immediately.

Do you have a Dictaphone? I asked him.

There's one in the office.

Can you record Crane talking about this?

Suleiman grinned but just as quickly lost his smile.

Will I get into trouble?

I can't promise you you won't, but I believe you won't.

What did you have in mind?

Have you looked inside the envelopes?

They're sealed.

His face showed again, briefly but unmistakably, those shadows of fear I had seen when I first met him.

What are you afraid of? I asked.

I am not afraid.

I regretted my question. Young men do not bear their fears well. Moreover, I saw that Suleiman might still be smarting from Crane's patronizing gesture, Crane patting him on the back, on the head, as if he were a child.

What do you think is inside them? I asked him.

Money. You?

I'm not sure. How thick are they?

Maybe a centimeter thick. Not even that, he replied, gesturing with forefinger and thumb.

How many pages would you say?

I don't know.

Guess.

Ten or twenty, I don't know.

When do they come, the envelopes?

Mondays and Thursdays.

Only those days?

Always Mondays and Thursdays.

When?

Noon. Like just now.

Always?

Always around that time.

Never later or earlier?

Give or take fifteen minutes.

Are the envelopes brown?

Sometimes brown, sometimes white.

Always the same size?

No. Different sizes.

Always different?

Not always. Mostly large.

We need to find you two minutes. Can you get your hands on a digital camera?

His eyes widened; I think he only sensed what I was getting at and it occurred to me that his fear might have prevented him from seeing it for himself.

What are you thinking? he asked.

Get a camera and I'll explain.

I saw Suleiman again later that day. He asked me if I'd given any thought to the post of executive director. I hadn't. He asked if I could, and we left it at that. Clearly, Suleiman and—if he was to be believed—the Afghani trustees thought Monsieur Touvier wasn't up to the job, or something worse.

I first came across Maurice's name a month earlier, when I was in Bangladesh. Emily had sent me an email—not long before her plea by telephone to come and save twenty-five million lives, give or take—with an attachment she asked me to comment on: *Your strategic thinking would be hugely appreciated*. It was an Excel spreadsheet setting out a budget for a new outfit within the UN, she explained, to coordinate donor aid, which she'd drawn up with someone's help. That last fact, that she'd been helped, had to be said, I thought. She didn't know her way around spreadsheets, she knew I knew that, and she wouldn't want me to think she was passing it off as her own work. It was *really rather clever*, she said. I wondered if she actually believed that.

There were tables of budget items and costs, including Land Cruisers, property rental, electric generators, backup generators, computers, printers, office furniture, budgets for staff—local and international (the salaries were wildly different)—all the way down to stationery. What the thundering fuck was *clever* about it? This was a budget, a simple list of things they thought they needed or things they wanted, *they* wanted. What could I know of their needs? What could she imagine I might know? I was in Bangladesh applying my legal training to fight corruption in government, in the police, against the rackets in education, the massive government contracts for schoolbooks to primary schools, in a country that had an established civil society with many NGOs and aid agencies, the largest recipient of British aid after India. But she couldn't know that, could she? She couldn't know that Bangladesh had the world's largest NGO, that in fact within a few years that NGO—a Bangladeshi NGO—would be running development programs in Afghanistan, that it already did so in other countries, alongside the likes of Oxfam. She was no expert herself, armed with just a graduate degree in economics from Harvard, legal training, and then a year working for Jalaluddin developing training programs for UN staff, flowcharts, brainstorming sessions, and role playing. What *could* she know? Not long enough for a budding doctor to get in the same room as a patient.

But then there was a line near the end of the email, after saying she wanted to hear from me, a throwaway all-important line, a casual remark that had all the weight of the comment that isn't measured but delivered direct from the unconscious. Not an error, for there's nothing else that some part of her wanted to say; not a Freudian slip, not when you mean one thing but say your mother. *I'm curious to know what it's like to go back home.* That is what she'd said.

At the root of it, was it that? An idea that I'd know about these things because I was going back, like Jalaluddin, the Afghani who lived in New York and D.C., and worked his whole adult life in the U.S., straight out of graduate school, married an American, had American children, and yet came *back home* to Afghanistan, the authoritative voice with credibility, with legitimacy, because that's where he came from, so he must know a thing or two, and could be relied upon because he was educated at an American university, from that buffer class of native informants. Was that it? I must know because I was back home, too, in the same part of the world, also at the brink of the British Empire.

So when she says that, writes that, thinks that, does she think I'm not British? Or am I both British and Bangladeshi, the favored two-step of the dancing liberal? You can be both. Who's to decide what you are? You can decide. And that liberal never for a moment imagines himself to be dancing the same dance of the bigot, the dance of language and labels and names because everything's in a name—that's what he decides.

I listened to Zafar without interrupting him, noting the change in his tone and demeanor. He had delivered the story of Suleiman, Crane, and the envelopes calmly, even, I might say, without drama, however horrific that business about Crane might have been. Yet now, as he talked about Emily, he seemed agitated.

This ruck between the liberal and his antithesis, continued Zafar, never touches the thing that the liberal and bigot take for granted, which is the feeling of belonging, his own feeling of belonging and another's lack of such feeling, which is a question not of what ought to be but of what is, an epistemological question, a hard question, no doubt, but isn't that the beginning of wisdom, to see how it is?

Is that what Emily thought, that in going to Bangladesh I had made a romantic journey home? But what then had she made of everything I'd told her? What did it mean to her when I told her one rainy afternoon as we lay in bed after making love—I can't remember how it came about—that I spoke another language from the language they spoke in the capital, Dhaka? I said *the capital, Dhaka* in case she didn't know, not to save her the embarrassment but to save me the embarrassment. What did she understand then, when I told her that the corner of the country I was born in was once so unsure of joining the rest that it almost didn't, that I came from a corner *of that corner* that actually voted against joining the rest? What did she make of that?

What could I conceivably have to say about the budget, the spreadsheet? Or was that request just tacked on as an excuse to write to me, now that we had broken up, now that we were no longer in the same country, no longer flesh within flesh but only, merely, still stuck in each other's heads? Just an excuse to talk, itself a means to be spoken to, to be regarded and not set aside.

I stared at the spreadsheet, I searched its cells for formulas, of which there were none but the obvious subtotaling and totaling. I right-clicked the document icon and pulled up its properties file and saw that its author was one Maurice Touvier, a name I didn't know. Who was this Maurice? I looked for what I couldn't see, but the only thing I could imagine she might think *clever* about it was that it was colorful. It had pretty colors. And I thought of another spreadsheet, one I had put together a year earlier, to stress-test dates.

There was the possibility that it was for her own sick entertainment. It wouldn't have been the first time. There was the chance that because of that jealousy of hers she was playing a little game. So much about power. I asked her mother once if she thought Emily might have a tendency toward jealousy. Penelope laughed. In fact, she shrieked—I'd never seen this ladylike woman ever do that. Emily's mother, the woman who'd watched her little girl, her eldest child, grow amid the chaos of her parents' marriage falling apart, as her own sense of guilt expanded. That motherly guilt was so deep that she had come to accede to everything her daughter asked for—every allowance, every dispensation—so that she had come to accept the bitterness with which Emily addressed her as "Mother," even in a conversation void of hostility, unlike James, who called her "Mummy," so that Penelope knew the power of a word more powerful than any other, more powerful than "Father." Emily's mother, the woman who had stood by and watched her daughter twisting and warping into a machine that shut off any regard for its own motives, a machine that retained a pipeline from motive to action but never, one could begin to conclude, a means for going back to motive and asserting control over it. What, after all, was her own mother's motive for her actions all those years ago?

She could only remember her own jealousy when she learned of that woman, of Robin, her former husband, and that woman, that woman who now shared her name, which was his name; she could only feel now the jealous knife that cut into her bone—and cut into Emily's, too, as she told me the story—when the sales assistant at Harvey Nicks, where Penelope had left a pearl-drop earring that had needed repair, had produced instead a diamond necklace for Mrs. Hampton-Wyvern, the new Mrs. Hampton-Wyvern, just one bloody month after Robin and that woman had married. Oh, yes, Penelope knew all about her daughter's jealousy.

That should have been the beginning and the end of it, but of course it was not. Not for me, who is every bit a part of an age, a West, that identifies pathology in the strong emotions, in jealousy, hatred, and rage. Could she really be jealous? This gentle English flower, this model of restraint, the very embodiment of moderation and measure, projecting an image of calm judgment and good sense, never adding emphasis, never making a dramatic gesture with the hands, never raising her voice. Emily was a woman without strong opinions on anything unless a strong opinion would further her professional interests. How could she be jealous of me? What on earth did she fear (as if fear might prompt it)? She had men falling about her like fruit from a tree, no, from an orchard of trees, an orchard in an earthquake, all there for her picking. But she'd wanted me and I was so flattered—couldn't she see I was flattered? Wasn't that enough to head off her jealousy?

Suleiman had one of the AfDARI cars drop me off at the UN compound. He didn't ask me how I'd be getting back, and I think now that he must have assumed that before the curfew I'd be offered a ride back by my hosts or that I'd be staying with them overnight. For my part, I gave it no thought.

I asked for Emily at the main gates, and one of the guards went inside. The sounds of the bar spilled out onto the road, everything starting a little earlier, everything moved forward in the day because of curfew or maybe because the morning light here is intensely bright. Seven in the evening and there are cars parked outside, not all with UN markings, and the drivers are gathered again, smoking cigarettes. A few minutes later Emily appeared, coming from across the courtyard, her image outlined by the floodlights behind her. As she drew closer, she came into clearer view, but as she passed the bar exit, just at that moment when she might have made eye contact with me, she looked back, as she would have done, I thought, if someone had called out from behind her. I heard nothing. Her half-turned figure stood motionless for all of a moment; she was wearing a fitted shirt, narrowing below her shoulders and cinching her waist. What disturbed me was a sarong she wore below that, tightly wrapped around her, so snug against her body. Its deep red and amber colors reminded me of a summer dress I had bought her, a flimsy thing that bared as much as a summer dress can do—like a good essay, I remember a teacher once explaining, large enough to cover the important areas but small enough to be interesting. How I imagined her in that dress, glancing back at me over her shoulder. Imagined, I say, because she could not have carried out, let alone carried off, that simple gesture, for there was no levity, no play, in her. A summer dress for the woman who otherwise dressed conservatively, who dressed to make her indistinguishable from the career-driven, besuited, independent modern woman.

But that sarong in those circumstances, holding her body, in that country, at that time, it offended me as much as a summer dress had delighted me in Hyde Park and on the stairs to her bedroom. I was mortified. Once again, and not for the last time, I felt I wanted to apologize to someone, to the Afghanis here and there, the drivers waiting by the gates, the attendants, the cleaners and cooks, the staff, the servant class.

But even as my indignation grew, my feelings pulled me in another direction. I felt the same sweeping tenderness for Emily that I'd felt the day she first wore the summer dress I'd bought for her, when we took a turn in the park in the glow of a warm evening in London.

That perhaps is the sum of it all, so far as that woman went—goes—that I always felt besieged by inconsistencies, not in her but in me, in my feelings for her, that those feelings split me asunder to leave me partitioned into people who hated each other, and to side with one was to scorn the other. You ask if I loved her and I tell you that I did but that I hated her, too. Paul Auster quotes the *Memoirs of Chateaubriand* in *The Book of Illusions*—in fact, the protagonist, Zimmer (from A to Z, Zimmer's an alter ego of Auster), translates the work—and in the passage that Auster himself translates, the French nobleman writes: *Man has not one and the same life. He has many lives, placed end to end, and that is the cause of his misery.* Does Auster mean that a man's lives run consecutively or concurrently, that he is condemned to live again and again, or that he is many and that his sentences run concurrently, alongside each other, *placed end to end*? In which sense? In the sense that each life within him rises as the last one falls, or in the sense of a man going forward as many selves contained in the same, standing shoulder to shoulder? I have thought it was the latter. I thought, as I still do, like the long-forgotten rabbi, that it is the tension between half brute and half angel that is the cause of a man's misery. I hated Emily for the same reasons I loved her; the two feelings sprang from one well, so that a dress brought forth love and a sarong hatred. I hated myself, too, for loving her, for loving her for that which I hated about her. It is because of this continuing state of civil war that every act of love by one part of you is an act of betrayal to another part, and so it was, it had to be, that I was destroying myself by simply being with her and therefore having to take sides against myself.

In the compound, there was no kiss, no gesture of affection. Why should there have been? After all, we'd broken up, hadn't we? I'd gone to Bangladesh and she'd already gone to New York. And this was a place of work. A year ago in New York, at the UN, the same. Meeting me downstairs before the security checks, not so much as a peck. Nothing to undermine the professionalism. Or was it because her colleagues thought she was single, available? I hated suspecting and hated even more to see myself as someone even a little suspecting.

The preservation of professionalism. Now that is something I could understand. Even to believe, as I am certain she did, that given the sexual politics of the workplace, an ambitious woman must appear unattached—even this I could understand, I could respect, even if I didn't agree or disagree with it. It is a rare character, the kind Nicky Amory had, that is able to assert and mobilize her sexuality while deftly enforcing in that same professional space the clarity of her commitment to her husband or her lover, the light touch that moves in two ways. It is a character that instantly wins my undying loyalty. It is self-restraint that applies itself before there's anything to restrain. Emily just did not have that character. One must not expect too much of others.

Joanna and Philip will be there, as will Maurice, she said.

I didn't know Joanna and Philip, I'd never heard of them, and as for Maurice, perhaps that was the same Maurice who headed AfDARI. Perhaps she thought I'd know the name from there. But if it was that same Maurice, I didn't say what I guessed: Maurice was unlikely to show. In the UN bar the night before, Nicky had said that Maurice had cut short her meeting that day and that they'd rescheduled for the next. I'd expected Nicky to drop by when she came for her meeting and, if I wasn't there, leave a message. She was obviously reliable, just that sort of person. But when I left AfDARI for the UN compound only half an hour earlier, there'd been no message from her. Her meeting with Maurice must have been scheduled for the evening.

What's for supper? I said instead.

I don't know, she replied.

So who are they?

Philip went to Winchester, she said.

He's not here?

The school.

I'm missing the point again, aren't I?

Maurice was at the Sorbonne.

He's over fifty?

What makes you think that?

Since 1968, other than an administrative entity, there has been no such thing as *the Sorbonne.*

He's our age.

Anything else I should know about them, so I don't put my foot in it?

What do you mean?

You know, Philip and Joanna are married. But not to each other.

He's divorced.

Children?

I think so.

Good friends of yours, then? Not the children, I mean.

Yes.

Nice to have good friends possibly with children.

Zafar, sometimes you say the funniest things.

Well, I'm here all week and don't forget to tip your waitress.

We were halfway across the courtyard when there was a shout from behind us: *Emily!*

It was Crane. He was staggering out of the side exit from the lounge, propped up by someone else. It wasn't even eight o'clock. He pressed his arms against a wall and crouched over. I heard him vomit. Beyond him, on the other side of the gates, the drivers stood silently, watching.

He's rather loud, said Emily.

A loud American. Who would have thought? I said under my breath.

Sorry?

What do you want to do?

Let's get inside, she said.

I hated this place. I hated it through and through. What was I really doing here? Hassan Kabir had asked me to come, but one day in and still I had no message from him or from the staff at Bagram. What am I doing here? As I stepped forward against the contrary impulse within me, I wondered if I had asked the question aloud. Emily was giving me a puzzled look.

From the direction of Crane, out of the darkness emerged the figure of a man, the one, I assumed, who'd struggled to bring Crane out. Crane was now gone, or at least his voice was.

Hello, Emily.

In the half-light, I could see him well enough. But he moved in the shadow cast by the floodlights behind me, my shadow, not Emily's. When he came close enough, he strained to make out my face. My black hair, dark skin, and dark suit would have made it difficult for this man, I thought—and for Crane, for that matter—to see me. He was blond and handsome, his hair cut short, stubble roughening the edges of his youthful complexion. His khaki jacket was open and its collar was up-turned. The pockets of the breast and waist were buttoned down, all four. There is method there, I thought. It was a jacket design with pedigree, tested and proven: Even the clothes have a colonial descent. His shirt collar was open, two, maybe even three buttons, so that a twist of jewelry in the nape of the neck, a gold chain perhaps, caught traces of light. He couldn't have been more than thirty. Few expat men and women with families would do these development jobs, Hassan Kabir had explained to me back in Bangladesh. Marriages don't survive the strain. What strain? Let's be precise about this. The strain of infidelities within a band of danger junkies charged up every hour of the day with power, horny at the threat from dark alien powers, ancient and obscure, and aroused by the power they themselves command, which they could never wield back home in their established democracies.

Zafar, this is Maurice.

Emily introduced me.

I noticed the order because the usual pattern in social situations is for the new arrival to be greeted and then introduced to present company: *Hello, Maurice. This is Zafar.* But I could make nothing of it. Sometimes, a phallic object is just a phallic object.

Hello, Zafar. Pleased to meet you.

We shook hands, his firm and decisive, mine its usual rather feeble thing. Though I cannot know, I think I have never felt present at the moment a male sizes me up. I am only observing. Which is not to say that it is an unimportant moment. Quite the reverse. When a handshake has a sure and steady grip, it's filled with the significance of how some-one wants to be read, how he wishes to be regarded, even if it comes in the form of ingrained habit.

I'm sorry for the disturbance, he said in an accent that rolled the *r* into the beginning of a gargle at the back of the throat. Bloody Americans, he added.

He motioned his head in the direction of the gates. Crane was no longer there. Maurice held a bottle of champagne by its neck. Had he just bought it at the UN bar or had he brought it from elsewhere, unbagged, unveiled? In New York, liquor sold off the premises has to be packaged in a brown paper bag, but not here, far from the puritans.

I suppose that's the price of having a bar, he added, referring to Crane's behavior.

But who pays? I asked under my breath.

Pardon?

Indeed.

We continued toward one of the residential buildings.

Where are you staying, Zafar?

If Maurice had seen me at AfDARI, he certainly did not recognize me. If he'd been notified of my stay, perhaps he didn't recognize the name.

I'm staying at AfDARI, I said, in one of the guest rooms.

His brow furrowed and there passed over him a look that lacked a precise definition. It contained puzzlement but also included recognition, a troubled element, identification, and even deduction. Something to do with me being at AfDARI? Was the crux of the anxiety to do with Crane or with Emily or with something else altogether? And in the midst of those fusing facial expressions, I wondered if I had perceived in him a question, too, *What did I know?*, though nothing of what I perceived could be relied upon, so complete was the confusion, his perhaps but mine certainly.

Barely had we entered the apartment and Emily completed the introductions to Joanna and Philip, when Maurice excused himself.

I'm afraid I cannot stay. The French ambassador, he has called me away and ... well ... you know. But I wanted to make you a small gesture.

He handed over the bottle.

There was the expression of regrets all round, and he took his leave. When he shook my hand, he made no eye contact.

The room was large enough for two beds, a small sofa, two chairs, and a table to one side, covered in files and papers. A naked lightbulb hung from the ceiling, and a large Afghani rug lay in the center. There isn't anything remotely interesting to say about Joanna and Philip. I'm sure they are nice enough people, but I found myself in no mood to chat, no mood for conversation, either honest or polite. Philip was an earnest man in his late forties with the squat physique of a wrestler. He was thinning on top, and on his face lay a moist sheen that didn't quite coalesce into sweat. He tried his civil best to get the conversation going, but I'm afraid to say I didn't help. Technically, it was a dinner party, for there was dinner.

I asked them both what their work involved and how they'd got into the development business, and if I don't go into that now, it's because it bored me then to hear it. Joanna and Philip didn't ask me what had brought me to Kabul. Had they detected my lack of interest? Or did they not ask because Emily had given them an explanation—did she represent me as her ex-boyfriend or her boyfriend?—or was it because she'd told them that she'd asked me to come—were they that close to her?—or was it because she'd told them that the UN rapporteur on human rights in Afghanistan had asked me to come—but how would she know that?—or was it because there were already numberless new arrivals in Kabul, would-be development wonks, skulking about the city waiting for a Western development agency to throw some meat their way, and they, like all hyenas, needed no explanation when the smell was in the air? In those days, where else could anyone want to be?

Joanna wanted to know more about what I was doing in Bangladesh. That I was living there, Emily must have told her. I said that I was working on reforming the Bureau of NGO Affairs.

That can't win you any friends, said Joanna.

Luckily, I'm rather antisocial, I replied.

I probably should have been more gracious. Probably I should have smiled.

What does the Bureau of NGO Affairs do? asked Philip.

NGOs have to be registered with the bureau, and foreign donors can only send money to NGOs in Bangladesh with the bureau's blessing. So bureau officials hold up the process and demand bribes. There are activists in Bangladesh trying to push through reforms that would change the processes and eliminate some of the opportunities for corruption.

Who are you talking to?

Quite a lot of people in government and in Parliament want to see change, but they can't speak out easily—they'd be fired of course, and then they'd have no influence whatsoever. The Bangladeshi constitution actually entitles a party leader to expel her own MPs from Parliament without cause, something you don't see in most parliamentary democracies.

Is that true?

I don't know. It's what I've been told over and over and what I've read in the constitution. There's a curious provision originally put there at a time when coalition governments were hugely unstable because of the large number of political parties. A single MP could cause havoc simply by threatening to switch to another party. The point of the constitutional provision was to stop self-serving, wayward MPs before they destabilized government and forced elections every ten days. When the provision was adopted, I don't imagine anyone had given thought to perverse consequences down the road.

Why don't they change it now?

It's a constitutional provision, which means it's hard to change, and for obvious reasons party leaders love it.

But you say some of these people will talk to you?

Yes. Some civil servants and politicians, braver than most, though not in public yet.

And what kind of changes are you talking about?

Nothing that hasn't been thought of before.

Such as?

I'm sure this can't be all that interesting to you.

No, it is. Go on, said Joanna.

Emily said nothing but just stared at me. She always fixed her stare on me if I was party to the conversation. I used to feel rather flattered by it, at the beginning taking it for admiration, as a man might do, but I soon began to wonder if she stared at me out of a curiosity, even a variety of perverse delight. Emily never said a controversial thing in her life, always the voice of moderation and good temper, politic and circumspect to perfection, and it occurred to me that her staring was evidence of some lascivious pleasure in the ever-present threat, whenever I was talking, that I'd drive a bulldozer over social norms.

If a donor wants to send a hundred thousand dollars to a Bangladeshi NGO, they have to submit paperwork to the bureau before they can do so. The bureau then goes through a rather mechanical process to make sure everything's in order, ostensibly, for example, to make sure the money's not going to fund some terrorist outfit and so on. What happens in practice is that some or other official holds up everything. The donors or NGOs know that a bribe smoothes things out. A simple piece of legislation could make quite a change, a bill introducing a deeming provision in the statute books, to be precise. If the bureau doesn't inform the donor in, say, three months of any concerns it has, then the relevant paperwork would be deemed by law, the new law, to have been processed and the donor can go ahead and send the money in the safe knowledge that they're in compliance.

But won't the corrupt bureau official just say that he informed the donor that there were problems with the application and that the donor and NGO went ahead despite being notified?

That's where technology comes in. Everything's online and transparent so that anyone can log on and see what's happening to a donor application for bureau clearance. If the bureau raises any queries, it would be required to specify those on the Internet file for that application. Again, if no queries are listed there, then the legal provision would deem there to be no queries at all. The key point is that the whole thing would be transparent to everyone and everyone would be involved in policing it. Actually, I think the donors rather than the government might be more uneasy about it.

Why?

Because everyone's so fixed in a mind-set of secrecy. Even if there's nothing underhanded going on, secrecy is the culture. I sometimes wonder if secrecy is an end in itself for all these people, donors, NGOs, the UN, the development community at large, if it confers some kind of reward on the human psyche. Perhaps secrets are power not because of their content but because only the select know. The bureau, by the way, could do a lot more positive things. Making the pool of information it gathers transparent and open to all, for instance, could help disseminate lessons learned from NGO projects, save the reinvention of wheels, and ultimately coordinate efforts for maximum impact.

It would need funding.

Possibly, but not necessarily a lot, and it would probably save many times its cost. Small but key changes in a system can have a huge impact. On the other hand, it might not work.

Too many obstacles?

No, it might not work even if we did get there. My reasoning could be wrong and my estimates of numbers might be wide of the mark. More than that, it's the unknown unknowns that bother me even if I have no clue what they are—because I have no clue what they are.

Joanna and Philip chuckled. Donald Rumsfeld was loathed in Kabul, and his comically philosophical maxims were the butt of many jokes, but still I had to admit that his distinctions between known knowns, known unknowns, and unknown unknowns were insightful and useful.

Hindsight makes it hard to see what was predictable and what wasn't. What worries me is that there might be questions out there that I haven't thought to ask. Isn't that the history of international development and Western beneficence: unknown unknowns invoked to legitimize excuses for what comes to pass when their preponderance should be a restraint on intervention in the future? I'll tell you this, I added. One question I don't know the answer to is what the hell I'm doing here in Kabul.

Isn't there a lot to be done? Afghanistan needs good people, said Philip.

I looked at Emily.

I'm flattered, but it's not my war. It's dreadful, I said.

The war itself is over. The Taliban are ousted.

The war has only started.

And the country should be left to rot?

The white man's burden. How far will he go in the name of helping his inferiors? The country should be left *alone*.

Philip might have taken offense, but he had the self-restraint not to show it.

You're in a better position to help than most.

How's that?

Well, as a Bangladeshi and a Muslim you have a lot more credibility here, a lot more authority.

I don't know where to begin with that one.

Begin where you like, he replied.

That—his tone—was, I thought, the first show of male aggression, the first display of antlers. He'd held out for quite some time (and much longer than me). This is why men of his class of Britisher make such fine diplomats.

Credibility with whom?

With the Afghans.

Because the new colonials care very deeply what the Afghanis think.

Philip didn't seem to register my irony.

As for helping the people of Afghanistan, I'm not a missionary, I don't have the faith in my own ability that you do in yours, faith to do good, faith in the rightness of your cause and the truth of your methods.

Missionaries were at the vanguard of the British Empire, many of them genuinely believing they were doing God's work and never questioning their role in sanctifying the exploitative project. You will know what Archbishop Desmond Tutu said: *When the missionaries first came to Africa, they had the Bible and we had the land. They said "Let us pray." We closed our eyes. When we opened them, we had the Bible and they had the land.*

We should get out, I added, and steer clear. I have no place here.

The room became silent. Joanna, sitting on the sofa, had parked her eyes on her knees. Emily was looking at Joanna, perhaps, I thought, to apologize. Philip, the thoroughgoing Englishman, pretended that nothing had happened, and for that I was grateful. I had become carried away. Even in my agitated state it was evident to me that anger was taking over my bearing, and it alarmed me. Something was gathering in me, as if armies had been summoned from all corners and the ground bore the first tremors of their approach. Now I might call them armies of injustice, humiliation, and defeat, but at the time I felt them as only the beginning of a kind of end.

I should be getting back to AfDARI, I said, glancing at my watch.

Good grief, said Philip. You'd better get going.

Take something for your driver—we should have sent him something to eat, said Joanna.

I don't have a driver.

You haven't come by car?

One of the AfDARI cars dropped me off.

I thought he'd go back with Maurice, said Emily.

Joanna and Philip looked at each other.

You won't make curfew, said Joanna.

Really? asked Emily.

You'll have to stay here, continued Joanna. We'll make a bed of sorts.

I'm sorry, I said feebly. I rather thought I might get a lift back from one of the cars parked outside.

The drivers will be gone now, said Philip.

I am sorry.

Not to worry, piped Joanna cheerily, plenty of room here.

I stayed the night in that very room. Philip left for his quarters in another building on the compound. Made up for me was a bed of sofa cushions on the floor, next to Emily's bed. Joanna had the other single bed. We all went about things quietly.

I prayed to fall asleep quickly. I couldn't bear the thought of lying awake in this space, after an awkward conversation like that, and with Emily only an arm's reach away. When Joanna pulled the sofa cushions onto the floor, had she been guided by some intuition to set them close to Emily's bed? I was tired and sleep came quickly. It wasn't a heavy sleep but a familiar shallow slumber, as if a reluctance held me from wading into the depths of unconscious life. Dreams came, vague forms, actions and actors, all with insufficient density to be remembered. And then the loneliness. That can easily be remembered in the dream state, a feeling of loneliness and a distance from everything I could ever hope to long for. You ask me if I loved her. And I tell you so many things but never answer the question because I cannot see how the category applies and still less because that word is—what is it Shelley said?—too often profaned. But this I can tell you: That night a purity of feeling came from time to time, the feeling that was there whenever a moment closed around us, a suspended moment in which I could sustain the belief that we were alone, that our attention was fully given to each other. I reached up to Emily in the darkness. This hand that is mine, that mediates so much of what goes on between me and the world, coiled under her blankets and, after first touching her back, came to rest on her waist, from where it moved along a short arc and when it reached her hips, it gently pulled at her.

She, whom I had known always to fall asleep quickly and deeply, was still there, still there with me, as if we two were standing on the shores of sleep, a long, wide beach of white sand. She turned to face me, bringing herself closer by rolling over, and raised her hand to my cheek.

There was no darkness. Flimsy sheets for drapes bled light from the floodlit compound and slivers of illumination formed geometric shapes on the walls and high ceiling of the room. The eyes needed no adjustment in order to see.

I have thought of Zafar as a generous human being, and though that opinion has not fundamentally changed, what I perceived then was another side to him. In his dealings with people in Kabul, on his own account, there was belligerence and willful obtuseness. I rather think, for instance, that this chap Philip had meant that Afghans would regard him as Bangladeshi and that this very fact would put Zafar at an advantage. Which had been suggested, after all, in Zafar's own description of his exchanges with Suleiman. It seems to me that in Kabul he was spoiling for a fight. When Emily mentioned that Philip went to Winchester, Zafar's willful misinterpretation—*He's not here?*—is telling. It seems quite plausible to me that Emily had perceived Zafar's interest in people's backgrounds, which, again, is borne out by his own account. Did not the Pakistani general tell him to get over his infatuation with English public schools?

In the morning, when I arrived at AfDARI, I buttonholed Suaif at the gate.

Do you think you could ask Suleiman if he has a moment to speak to me in my room?

A few minutes later Suleiman appeared. I had packed my bag.

Can you get me on a flight out of here?

Suleiman glanced at my carry-on. He beckoned to me.

Where do you need to go?

Islamabad or U.A.E.

You're ready to go now?

Yes. We can talk later.

Give me ten minutes.

Twenty minutes later, he returned.

There's a Pakistani army flight for Islamabad in half an hour. You have a seat on it. Let's go.

19

Requiem for the Unlived Life

CARDINAL PANDULPH: You hold too heinous a respect of grief.
CONSTANCE: He talks to me that never had a son.
—William Shakespeare, *King John*, Act III, scene 4

God, what a woman! and it's come to this,
A man can't speak of his own child that's dead.
—Robert Frost, "Home Burial"

All of us, grave or light, get our thoughts entangled in metaphors,
and act fatally on the strength of them.
—George Eliot, *Middlemarch*

On the first night in the hospital I slept as soundly as if Death had cradled me. Even in my sleep, I vaguely perceived an unfamiliar quality, as if I were weightless, as if I might even have acquired an immaterial form. I might have come there of my own volition, but now that I was there I felt I couldn't leave, and for a while, in fact, I wouldn't be permitted to do so. I had holed myself up, strangely comforted by the knowledge that human influence on my consciousness would be curtailed: I wouldn't see anyone whom I didn't want to see. I felt protected from others and, I think, because of that I felt protected from myself.

That Zafar had been in hospital was not news to me, of course. In an earlier conversation, Zafar had said, *I was once the patient of a psychiatric hospital.* Now, when Zafar began to talk about his experience in hospital, I wondered if that earlier mention, however parenthetical, had been deliberate—the parentheses there precisely to hide the design. I had expressed no surprise, no shock or concern. Had I thereby confirmed something to him? Was his intention to see my reaction and from it draw conclusions about what I knew, had known? If I had anxieties about what Zafar knew (or didn't know), they were soon to give way to the discovery that it was I who knew so little and he who had figured out even more than I knew.

On the morning of the fourth day, the consultant came to visit, continued Zafar. Until then I'd been seen by a junior doctor, whose only function appeared to be to check that I was taking my medication, something the nurse could have done. The consultant, Dr. Villier, was a tall, slim Englishman, with soft blue eyes. If his smile was insincere, I certainly could not tell; the man was the embodiment of doctorly bedside manners. I'd first met Villier a month before, in his offices on Harley Street, when I learned that, as well as practicing as a consultant psychiatrist, he had a practice as a psychoanalyst, the combination of which made him interesting in my eyes. On his rounds in the hospital, Villier was accompanied by a junior doctor, a plump and balding South Asian man—Indian, I thought—with round features, a bulbous nose, and earlobes that sagged as if weights were clipped to them. Gold-rimmed spectacles circumscribed the tiny black points of his eyes. Whenever those eyes weren't focused on Dr. Villier, they darted suspiciously about my room, moving from one to another of my few possessions. I laughed at my own suspicion.

You've met Dr. Mirchandani, of course.

I nodded.

How are we feeling today? Villier asked.

I could not but grin.

Villier was smiling. I'm sorry, he said, but what's the joke?

Your use of *we* . . . in a psychiatric hospital. *We* are well.

I see, he said. He allowed a chuckle that settled back into a smile.

It can't have been, I thought, the first time this had been pointed out to him. I've been sleeping very well, I said irrelevantly.

I'm glad to hear that. As I expect you know, we gave you something to help with the sleep.

Mirchandani looked at a clipboard and, in what I took to be a Punjabi accent, read off the prescription for Dr. Villier's benefit. Mirchandani sounded unconfident and Villier thereby became yet more elevated in my estimation. The South Asian doctor stood rigid, his knees locked. Villier's body, however, was that tiny bit removed from stillness that is the mark of a kind of Englishness. As he sat on the edge of the bed and spoke, his hands and lower arms moved in small circling gestures. The senior physician appeared to occupy more of the room, and I sensed that the two men didn't have an entirely easy relationship. Mirchandani will know, I thought, that I'd met Villier before I arrived here, and that Villier and I therefore had the narrowest but altogether important history that he, Mirchandani, did not have with this patient. Mirchandani's only conversation alone with me, by the way, would take place in my second week, when, leaning forward, as if to take me into some confidence, he would ask me if I was sure I needed to be here, if I knew what kind of people came here, and if I was aware how much it cost. If this was his way of winning me over, it not only failed but allowed me to write him off altogether.

How have the days been? asked Villier.

I've been reading and writing.

I noticed the books by your bedside. Dante's *Inferno*. And this, he said as he picked up the other: *Go for Gold: Five Steps to Super-Success*.

Gifts, I said.

An interesting choice.

Christmas past and Christmas future.

Which one's which? he asked, again smiling.

You tell me.

May I ask why you brought *these* particular books with you?

I didn't. They arrived yesterday. They're gifts from Emily, I said. Express mail, you know, because there's no time to lose.

Villier's eyebrows shot up.

What do you make of that? I asked.

That *is* interesting, he replied.

You can do better than that.

It's *very* interesting, he answered, still looking surprised.

Are you always quite so surprised to find a thing interesting?

Villier said nothing. I'm not sure he heard me.

You can assume there is no irony in it, I said. She has, in fact, no sense of irony—none for making ironic jokes, anyhow, I added.

Had we been alone, I thought, he might have engaged me more easily. I didn't have the gauge of the men's relationship to one another, but I wondered if Villier needed to appear more in control in front of Mirchandani.

I'm sorry, I said. I'm feeling a little grumpy.

The truth was that I'd never felt better, not in months or even years. I had slept soundly with clear, simple dreams, deeply and long. And I had awoken unaided and early enough to witness the growing light of a new day. I put my good spirits down to that happy sequence.

Villier was Penelope's psychiatrist, and she had arranged the initial consultation, even coming along with me.

At the time, I had moved out of my apartment in Brixton into a bedsit in Hackney. I had left work, having taken unpaid leave, my cases handed over to others, but not before a disastrous quarterly review. I was spending waking hours watching television. I lived on one meal a day, either pizza, which I ordered in, or fast food, for which I ventured out into the world under cover of evening. At night, unable to sleep, I lay in bed reading, never taking in much and rereading paragraphs without effect, the words on the page coalescing into alien forms.

I resisted the argument. It was a long time, the interval between that first consultation and the days in hospital, before I stopped fighting, if not fully yet accepting, the psychiatrist's statement, what might have been a casual remark but for his fixing on my eyes, but for the silence he maintained after delivering it, but for the studied regard for my response. I could not accept that I was there because of Emily, however much his point was separated from moral responsibility. How does one person cause another to fall ill?

His words seemed so casual that first time, in his office. On the windowsill behind him were photographs. I made out the deck and rigging of a sailboat in one. There was a very fat edition of Boswell's *Life of Johnson* next to it. The room gave no sign of its medical use. But then, what exactly is the sign of a psychiatrist or psychoanalyst? What is the sign of the space between mind and brain?

The brain can be traumatized by stressful events, said Villier. It can be wounded by circumstances. Soldiers are the obvious example. But war is not the only venue for that kind of stress. There are other battlefields. Perhaps you think you must have been vulnerable in some way. And perhaps that's true, but that doesn't mean you caused your depression any more than an old man's arthritis caused a tread on the stairs to break. Certainly the man's injuries are made worse by arthritis. Had he been younger and fitter, perhaps he could have caught his own fall, but the step broke because it was weakened by termites. The broken tread on the stairs is the cause of his fall.

Penelope was in the room sitting in a chair next to mine. Villier glanced at her, a searching look on his face, confirming what I'd thought I'd seen through the corner of my own eye. Her head had sunk forward and she was staring at the clasped hands on her lap.

She stood up and turned to me.

I ought to leave you alone with the doctor. I'll wait outside with Emily.

I don't mind you staying, I said.

In fact, I really didn't care. The whole thing was already quite bizarre. But Penelope insisted. Later, after hearing everything Villier had to say, I understood that her purpose had been fulfilled by being present when he made the statement: *You're here because of Emily.* Penelope was there in the room so that Villier could say that in front of her and so that I would know that what he was to go on to tell me, now with her sitting outside, would be divulged with her assent.

Villier's demeanor appeared to relax after she left.

I've known the Hampton-Wyverns for a long time. I first saw Penelope as a patient, he said.

His voice had dropped, but that might only have been my perception because there was now no one else in the room. His formulation raised questions. *I first saw Penelope as a patient.* Did he mean to say that he knew her now as a friend? And, in that case, could he be trusted to speak impartially, or as impartially as a client has a right to expect of his lawyer or as a patient has of his doctor?

Let me share something with you, he said. Eighteen years ago, Penelope was in hospital with severe depression. In a terrible state, she won't mind my saying. By the way, she's happy for me to discuss this with you.

I nodded, though it wasn't asked for, perhaps to acknowledge the implication of an ethical constraint that would apply to any questions I might have. *Eighteen years ago,* he had said. Eighteen is a very specific number; not fifteen, not twenty, but eighteen. Had he consulted his files to refresh his memory? Or had Penelope reminded him? If so, why was she so closely keeping count of the years since then? Eighteen years. Emily would have been eleven, possibly ten, James a year younger.

She had been in hospital for three days, continued Villier, before she finally received a visit from her husband.

The children had always had a live-in nanny, I thought, so her husband wouldn't have been troubled to find a babysitter.

I was present at the time, continued Villier. I was curious to know more about their relationship, so when I was informed that her husband had appeared, I went to her room. In these kinds of hospitals, patient visits are carefully controlled.

What, I wondered, did he mean by *these kinds of hospitals*? Psychiatric hospitals or private hospitals?

Do you know her husband—her ex-husband—Robin?

I've met him, I replied.

Yes, of course you have. Robin—how shall I say this?—Robin was very cold toward her. One could not fail to be struck by the lack of physical affection. He did not once touch her. Now, I don't suppose that this is entirely surprising in the ordinary course of things. I can say this to you because I think you'll understand, but the English—in the Hampton-Wyverns' seam of society especially—they can be a somewhat reserved lot. I'm English myself, of course, but I rather think we could learn a thing or two from other cultures about the salutary effects of physical contact.

Villier held my eye as if expecting a look of recognition from me. I gave him it.

Robin brought the two children with him, he continued, and the nanny was also there. Penelope was really very demonstrative with the children. James, as I recall, was quite teary. The nanny brought him in, holding his hand, and then quite sensibly left the room, but that made no difference to Robin. There was no show of affection at all, nothing physical. I was standing outside through all this, off to one side, you see. I daresay it comes across as rather devious, but experience has taught me the tremendous value of a few snapshots with a candid camera, so to speak, eavesdropping, as it were. Nothing illegal, I might add—for your lawyerly sensibility.

Villier flashed me a smile before continuing.

I saw them as a group only two or three times during Penelope's stay in hospital—I mean her first stay. Later, when she came as an outpatient, we arranged a session or two with the family together, while that was still possible.

For whose benefit was his qualification? I asked myself. *I mean her first stay*, he had said. It added nothing from my vantage point; if he had paused to think about it, he would have seen that. It was a correction to his own internal monologue. Penelope, it seemed, had been in hospital more than once. Furthermore, from what he said, it was unlikely that during her later stay he met them all together, *as a group*. Presumably, then, the second stay happened after the divorce. Perhaps, I thought, it was precipitated by the divorce.

What has all this to do with me? you may ask, continued Villier. The reason you are where you are now is that Emily put you in this position.

Do you mean in this room? I asked.

If what Penelope tells me is accurate, you're not firing on all cylinders, are you? But you know that. You wouldn't have come here otherwise.

I've seen better days, I conceded.

I've met Emily on a number of occasions, and I also have the benefit of what Penelope has shared over the years. Emily seems to have much of her father's character in her.

That may be, I replied, but . . .

Do please go on. You can speak in confidence.

It's difficult to believe that another person can be responsible for my depression. I don't mind admitting I carry plenty of baggage of my own.

I'm interested to hear you say you're depressed. But first to address the point you make, I myself am rather loathe to use the language of responsibility, which is an ethical matter. I much prefer to think in terms of causation, which is not. You're a bright fellow. Given your background, you didn't come as far as you did without wit. Do you follow?

Questions about my background Villier didn't ask, not one. Penelope has shared a good deal with him, I thought—*given your background*—but since I really hadn't said much to her about my background, she must have formed her own ideas. She must have read between the lines of things. Evidently, Emily had also relayed to Penelope things I'd said, things that were said without any expectation of confidentiality, I should add. By then I'd known them for over three years.

If mood is like the weather, I said to Villier, I don't quite see how another human being could affect my mood any more than she could influence the weather.

It's a useful analogy, said Villier, this likening of mood to weather. But one has to recognize its limitations. It conveys the idea that at any given moment one has limited command over one's mood, but I don't think it captures the sense of what I'm saying here.

Villier went on to describe further the plight of soldiers, the trauma that affects their emotional well-being. He'd already talked about the old man with arthritis who trips on a broken tread and falls down the stairs. But in fact he was just getting going. He went on to talk about a farmer who fails to lock up a chicken coop at night and loses a hen to a fox: The farmer might have some responsibility, but the fox caused the loss. He talked for a while in this vein. He was possibly used to meeting resistance when he gave a diagnosis of mental illness, but with me I rather think he was pushing against an open door.

I don't know if you were wondering, by the way, but in my view Penelope didn't bring you here in the expectation I would talk you into breaking it off with her daughter. In fact, my impression is that she's quite fond of you.

Emily?

Penelope.

The two are not inconsistent.

I'm sorry?

She could be fond of me and want me to break it off with her daughter. In fact, she could want me to break it off *because* she's fond of me.

Let me ask you why *you* think she brought you here.

Don't you mean what do I think you think is the reason she brought me here?

As good a place to start as any.

Guilt?

I think so.

So do I.

She's awfully worried about you, that you might do yourself harm. Is that a possibility?

I don't want to be difficult, I replied, but . . . but I can't help it. I don't want to be difficult, but since we seem to have gone down the road of exactness, I have to say that I can't answer that question, and I say that knowing you might interpret it as a plea for help, although I don't believe that that's my motive. At any rate, anything that can be imagined must be possible, and most people have pretty vivid imaginations, don't you think?

If you feel the need, or even if you don't—for whatever reason, you can go to the Rectory clinic. I'm going to give you the address and contact information, he said.

He reached into a drawer at his desk, pulled out a piece of notepaper.

Just show up, he continued, at any time, day or night. They'll admit you straightaway. Penelope wants this to be available to you so you needn't be concerned with practical matters.

His eyes dropped. He was talking about money, I thought. Villier was being English. His coyness halved his age.

You'd be under my care. You can stay there as long as you need. You'll have your own room, of course, and it's all set in beautiful countryside. I just wanted to put all that before you. Is that all right?

Thank you, I said. I took the note, folded it, and slipped it into my pocket.

Now that we've dealt with that, do you mind if I ask you a few questions? I wouldn't be doing my job if I didn't at least go through the motions.

Villier's manner was sublimely English, down to the self-deprecation. I sometimes wonder if the English elites, the upper classes, actually believe themselves when they say these things, their genteel formulations, the qualifications they make at every turn. Their kind of self-belief seems essential to survive what would otherwise assail them as wave after wave of cognitive dissonance, statements of one thing while knowing the opposite, the expression of bare competence while sitting in the leather seat of his clinic on the premier private medical street in Britain, possibly in the world. Surely the dissonance would drive them mad so that the only way through it all is for them actually to believe what they say. But I might be wrong. After all, sallying forth with empire on the brain is a sublimely confident venture.

Villier asked me a variety of questions in a way that nearly concealed the workings of a checklist. I answered them as accurately as I could. But I knew the diagnosis. There are those who say that depression is a Western malady of affluence. That it may be. But when you are as deeply unhappy as I was . . . Let's be precise—when your human functioning has been reduced first to wretched indifference and then to worse, when the thoughts that gather around you, that are your own, have all the tenderness of an audience to a bare-knuckle alley fight, such lofty cultural opinions offer no relief. There is a person and there is suffering.

And yet, insofar as I knew, I had not come seeking help. I had agreed to Penelope's request because I thought it would relieve the boredom, even if temporarily. This boredom is something I'd never known and I've thought about it quite a lot since. My thoughts and sense experience used to hop from one thing to another, as if the world was just coming at me with meaningless stimuli, one after another. I couldn't latch on to a thought and then be carried by it as it moved into new territory. To do that, I think you need a narrative self inside you connecting you with experience, telling you how you fit into the subjective encounter with what you're seeing and attaching whatever significance it might hold for you. In those days, it was as if this narrative self had decided to go on vacation, leaving me without continuity of thought and feeling.

A few weeks after that visit with Villier, as I was sitting in my bedsit, I saw the dishes mounting in the sink. On the counter next to them was a knife. I glanced at the knife and the glance lengthened into a gaze. When the awareness of what I was doing took hold, I set about picking up a few things from the floor and stuffing them into a canvas bag. I'm surprised I had enough presence of mind to pack some toiletries and my toothbrush. I took a train out of town and from the station a cab to the hospital.

As I listened to Zafar talk about his time in a psychiatric institution, my thoughts did not stray, as they might have done, to what had happened outside, with Emily, but remained with him. He did not seem the least bit embarrassed to talk about it, and at the time I was rather flattered that he felt comfortable enough with me to discuss the matter. I see now, however, that it was I who was in fact uncomfortable, even embarrassed, about such a thing as going into a psychiatric hospital. This fact, here and now as I write, appalls me. I cannot imagine being so hospitalized without having such an overwhelming feeling of failure, catastrophic failure, that I could not possibly talk about it. For Zafar, there was no discomfort because I think there was no accompanying sense of failure. And herein I find myself confronted by that odd envy he has often evoked in me. The Zafar I know, from first to last, has lived life, taking its bare-knuckle blows, if not on the chin then in his long stride. Even going into a hospital, a nuthouse, a mental institution, a loony bin—in him I saw it as just a part of a life that journeyed out into all its corners. These thoughts come to me now, but when I listened to him talk, I thought of what a stage he and I had now reached that we could talk like this, the years passed, life turning up its disappointments, and how much he must feel at ease with me to open up this way.

I used to be skeptical of medication, he said, afraid I would lose myself, lose what is me. Yet what is this self that we so fear to lose? It's never there. The instant we try to reach for it, it slips away. This self *seems* nearest when I force my consciousness inward, when I compel it to focus, and then it rises like an apparition. But if it is at its most material when I'm conscious, then that self can never sustain a continuous being because any stretch of consciousness, of awareness of self, is cut short by the intervention of all that needs doing in a minute, let alone a day, curtailed by the steady beat of demands that render us unconscious of self and commit our body to this or that task at hand, to prepare supper or calculate a price for an exotic derivative instrument or pay a bill or do the laundry or draft a legal memo or tend a crying infant. Can medication rob us of something whose existence is tentative at best? Is it possible that the self is not an object, not a noun, but the verb characterizing the search for the object? And even as I talk about this self, even as I try to discuss it as if it were a thing apart, as if I were discussing the sweetness of pineapples that grow in the wild, I feel it is not I who am speaking but someone else through me.

I felt better with the medication; I compared the man whose body was mine with the man who was there the day before, and this man felt much, much better than his predecessor did. When I was skeptical, whenever I'd considered the prospect of taking medication, I had not been comparing the deeply, dangerously depressed person I was with the healthier and more even person I could be helped to be. Rather, I was imagining that the medication would make it impossible for me to be fully the person I believed I could *conceivably* be, that it would irreparably blunt me somehow.

The mistake did not lie in thinking this true. The mistake was to think that it was remotely relevant. It is irrelevant simply because the imaginary ideal human being, the one I believed I could conceivably be, is an unreachable person whom I could only *wish* to be, unreachable in any circumstance. The real me was always the me I was at any given moment, and not the unattainable me I could fancifully call from my imagination.

And tell me what could be more humbling than to be lying in bed at two in the afternoon, without a shower in twelve days; to look across the room you live in and see in the corner a pile of pizza boxes; to be afraid of undrawing the curtains and opening the window, so removed from people so as not even to wonder who would care if you did or you didn't do this or that; and to find that the day's only scintilla of hope flickers in the moment you reach for the television remote control.

After five weeks I left the hospital. I stayed in Penelope's home, in a spare bedroom at the top of the house. Emily joined me there. She herself had decided to move house and had sold her apartment. I never asked her if her decision had had something to do with me. You see, we never discussed anything that involved projecting ourselves into the future further than a week or two. While she was looking for something larger in Notting Hill, in an even more prestigious address—did she think I couldn't see the endless aspiration?—she moved in with her mother.

Of course, by this stage I knew about the curious domestic arrangement in Penelope's house. Penelope Hampton-Wyvern met Dudley Grange years ago, when she was still married to Robin, when Dudley's building company had been contracted to undertake a renovation of her home. Before breaking out on his own, he'd been a site foreman for a large building conglomerate. Dudley explained to me once, rather proudly, that he'd worked on the construction of what was in its time the tallest building in London, the NatWest Tower—now called Tower 42 after its address, he pointed out—and described how the building was the first of its kind: It had a huge core of reinforced concrete, one piece of concrete poured in situ in a massive operation requiring a fleet of cement trucks running to the site continuously over many weeks, so that as the lower levels hardened, concrete for the next level would be piped up and poured into the shuttered forms that also went up at the same time. From this single solid backbone of concrete, the floors fan out on cantilevers, and, from above, he explained, his eyes widening, the building's profile is three hexagonal chevrons arranged to resemble the logo of the NatWest

Bank. Construction was only the beginning; my genuine interest in his field of expertise seemed to open the doors for Dudley to hold forth on plenty else. Dudley, by the way, was in the house that day when first I met Penelope Hampton-Wyvern. They were his steps I heard coming from the hallway, before the sound of a door being shut as quietly as a sturdy Banham lock would allow.

He seemed an unlikely consort to Penelope, shorter than her by an inch and far from the full six feet of Robin. He was a chain-smoker, and the stale odor of burned tobacco was always on him. Spiderwebs of broken blood vessels clung to each cheek.

I never grasped the sequence of events involving Dudley and the Hampton-Wyverns but learned only vaguely that certain things happened within a space of a few years: the demise of a marriage; the separation, before which the beginning of an affair between Penelope and her builder; Penelope's hospitalization with depression; Robin, too, sneaking about with the woman who would become his second wife; and a divorce. All these things I learned but never with precise dates attached to them—why would anyone take care with dates? Or with conflicting dates attached, so that the events spoken of coalesced in my mind on a formless period sometime in Emily's early teens when her family life, I understood, was a tempest of dishonesty and infidelities.

When Penelope once broached with me the topic of her divorce— a very short conversation that took on the character of confession, with its underlying intimation of guilt for the impact on her children—she described the new wife as the woman for whom Robin had left her. But when Dr. Villier described the same episode to me, later, he did not give me to believe that it was Robin who had initiated the breakup, but instead I gathered that Penelope's relationship with Dudley was in full swing before Robin's departure. It is remarkable to me, by the way, that Villier was prepared to discuss as much as he did. There were moments of hesitation, when circumspection seemed to give his eyes the look of someone editing himself, but in the end he shared so much that I must wonder, as I imagine did Villier, if Penelope had understood the scope of the license she had granted him.

I do know one story that has a date to it, related to me by Emily herself. It was her first year at Oxford, when she received word that her father was to marry again. Apparently, on the day of the wedding, she came down to London and staged a protest with her brother outside the Chelsea Register Office, raising a banner they'd both made bearing the words DON'T DO IT, DADDY. When Emily told me this story, the image moved me. We were lying in bed, we had made love, and we were exchanging affectionate chatter in the drowsy moments when people come closest to intimacy, never very much intensity in the conversation and perhaps that's the nature of the thing, the reassurance of one mate to another that offspring will be tended together, which might also go some way toward explaining why Emily chose that moment to relate the story of her protest against her father's remarrying and why, for that matter, I myself wondered if she was making a statement to me, too, a plea for reassurance. I'm not nearly as skeptical as some people are of psychoanalysis, but I certainly don't need to wake up Freud for help—there's nothing I detected that wasn't visible on the surface. And perhaps this was Emily's governing fear, I have thought: the fear of abandonment.

And yet—and yet, I ask again whether in fact there was also a manipulativeness about it. You might remember a TV commercial for *The Guardian* newspaper, in the nineties, I think it was, in which a young skinhead in bomber jacket, jeans, and Doc Martens boots is seen running full tilt toward an elderly man standing on the street. The skinhead was an icon of Britain in those years. The scene projects imminent violence; at least that's what we're lured into seeing. But the camera pulls back and the frame widens, bringing into view what is going on above the elderly man. As I recall, a pallet of bricks is tied by rope to scaffolding. But the rope is fraying, its threads unraveling, and the pallet of bricks, now sagging, threatens to come crashing down on the old fellow, who is oblivious of the danger looming overhead. It was rather a mischievous commercial, since the left-leaning *Guardian* reader, who sees the skinhead running toward the old man, is likely to fall for the misdirection—the viewer's own misdirection—before the final reveal.

I *do* remember it, I said. Zafar was describing one of a series of commercials that all ran to the same theme: Things are not as they first appear, and you need to get the bigger picture in order to understand what's going on—you need, presumably, to read *The Guardian*.

It was a neat little commercial, he continued, rather good for its time, but quite aside from its political statement, it illustrates something about human motivation and action. In fact, it actually relies on the observation that the same action can be produced by different motivations, even opposite ones. You're rather fond of Graham Greene?

I am, as a matter of fact, I replied.

Years ago, at Oxford, when I asked you who your favorite authors were, you said Somerset Maugham, Graham Greene, and F. Scott Fitzgerald. An interesting group. Do you remember?

Indeed they are—my favorite authors, I replied. I didn't tell Zafar that I had no recollection of his having asked me. Nor did I share with him the fact that I'd actually read only one or two of each of their books; nor, to make my confession here complete, did I share the fact that I'd read so little fiction since my youth that my favorites, such as they were, had remained the same.

In *The End of the Affair*, continued Zafar, Graham Greene writes: *Hatred seems to operate the same glands as love: it even produces the same actions. If we had not been taught how to interpret the story of the Passion, would we have been able to say from their actions alone whether it was the jealous Judas or the cowardly Peter who loved Christ?*[*]

I think now, at the end, that Emily was not manipulative, not in a Shakespearean way, not like Iago, even if her actions were the same actions as those of a manipulative person. A different kind of motivation or disposition can produce the same actions, just as different situations can produce the same action. I think she told me about the protest because it would elicit sympathy and deepen the bond.

What's wrong with that? I asked him, although I was unsure whether he was exonerating her or accusing her.

Zafar fell silent. He seemed distracted. What motivation did he have in mind? If I am truthful, I must admit that I wasn't quite following him. And then the description of those authors was irksome. What did he mean when he said they were an interesting group? I had always suspected a condescension toward me in literary matters.

Why are they an interesting group? I asked.

Zafar smiled at me.

If those writers put themselves in their stories, they do so invisibly.

---

[*] I don't think I had ever grasped it before, but I saw it then. Zafar's eyes seemed to withdraw as if he were reading off a mental page on which those words were written. I found them, of course, later, in one of his notebooks.

That character, a narrator who's in the story but not really *of* it, that's an interesting character for you, no? I wonder if you like them because you know what it's like to stand on the sidelines.

I had not read all of their works, but as far as what I'd read went, Zafar was right about the presence of a narrator—*in* the story but not *of* it, as he put it.

I might like those writers for other reasons, I responded; they might just all happen to have that feature.

Perhaps you like them because those stories bring you close to your own experience of experiencing the world. They don't really get involved, people like Carraway, not just in the sense that the plot doesn't turn on them but because they resist forming profound attachments to anyone and only stand silently and watch. They are not the authors of their own lives, so to speak. Carraway takes his detachment a step further by giving it a name. He calls it reserving judgment, but he fails completely. To reserve judgment is to maintain an infinite distance. But nothing is visible at that remove. Is it an act of kindness, which is an act of engagement, that calls forth tenderness, when there is presented before us a human being with all his flaws?

I did not follow what Zafar was getting at then and, to be honest, I cannot be absolutely sure that I've grasped it now. But I've had a chance to think. Writing this has helped, this effort of looking in while looking out. That is what it is to consider the life of another, someone who made an impression, and in the course of writing discover—no, not *discover*, not quite, not even *learn* or *understand*, but simply sit and listen and fully embrace the risk of disrupting one's precious outlook on the world that such listening entails. Zafar was right. Every story belongs to the teller, and the teller's lesson to himself lies in the very way he tells the story. Writing has helped in many ways, helped me to think about a lot of things, to do with work, to do with Meena and family, and to do with Zafar also. I don't know now, for instance, if Zafar was quite as lost as I have thought him to be, quite as lost as at times he seemed even before he met Emily; perhaps I was the one who'd never really had much sense of bearings. It could all be just a midlife crisis: People who do the studies and run the statistics, they say that the so-called midlife crisis actually happens to men when they're in their late thirties, earlier than convention has it, which would make mine right on time or even a touch overdue. But it's more than that, or just different. It's true that I've lived as someone who

stands aside, choices determined by the sweep of ease and opportunity—
and the corollary of standing by is not participating. At the very beginning of *The Great Gatsby*, the narrator, Nick Carraway, tells the reader
about his father's advice to keep in mind that others never had the advantages he had. Reserving judgment, be it heroically difficult, is what
he should do. It becomes an ironic point, as one reads on, for the people
Carraway meets who are most deserving of adverse judgment are, I
think, people who had every advantage Carraway had—and then some.
But as I again consider that opening statement, having just retrieved the
book from my shelves and reread the passage, but with Zafar's remarks
in my mind, I see something else in it, which is that Carraway's attitude
keeps him one step removed. It keeps him one step removed from the
play, in the mind of the reader—in mine, in any event—but it also keeps
the man himself separated from the mess of life. In this light, his father's
advice actually reads like a statement of disqualification. I never studied
literature, so there's likely little store to be set in what I say about these
things. But that is what the opening now says to me. And though I surprise myself not to have thought so before, for now it seems obvious, I
wonder if our experience of a novel is enriched by our experience of life.

One thing I do question is whether Zafar was correct to include *The
End of the Affair*. In fact, that book seems rather obviously—bizarrely
so—out of step with his thesis. True enough, Bendrix, the narrator, is a
writer like Greene, but he is not some sterile bystander, for who could be
more caught in the plot than the man who consorts with an adulteress?

You were saying you moved into Penelope Hampton-Wyvern's house
when you came out of hospital. How long did you stay with her?

You and I had lost contact by then, two years or so before I went into
hospital.

That long?

What did Emily tell you? Zafar asked me.

When?

She told me she spoke to you when I was in hospital.

When did she tell you that?

Six months and seven days after I came out of hospital. Which is
when—and why—I began to wonder.

That's very precise.

My notebooks.

Is it important, then?

It turns out everything hangs on precise mathematics. Not complex but simple and precise. Funny really that it came down to simple arithmetic.

Go on.

When she told me—six months after I'd come out, as I say—that she'd spoken to you while I was in hospital, it struck me that you never called me when I was there, never left a message or sent word. Something had happened when you met Emily that discouraged you from calling then or later, not once in six months, seven including my stay in hospital, seven and counting. What could that have been?

Zafar's question sounded rhetorical, as if the answer was obvious, and that is what I hid behind in order to avoid answering, when a part of me wanted to tell him everything. But what was that *everything*? It now seemed like nothing of consequence, meaningless, nothing to speak of. Yet I felt like the pupil who understands that his teacher is *not* disappointed in him only because she never expected any better.

Why did she tell you that she'd spoken to me? I asked Zafar. She must have wanted to tell you something, I said.

But even as I said this, I wondered how much Emily had told him.

Should she not have done so? he asked.

I mean, what prompted her to tell you?

I asked her one day if she'd heard anything from you. Her reply was that she'd not spoken to you since I came out of hospital.

That's true, I said, with a plea in my voice that alarmed me, as if to say, *That was the only time. It was a one-off.* How absurd. Next thing I'd be saying is *It didn't mean anything to me. She meant nothing.*

And you, Zafar continued, hadn't contacted me in all that time, when you knew I'd been in hospital: *came out of hospital*, she'd said. For all you knew, I must have still been in hospital. Or, to be precise, as far as you knew, *I* thought *you* thought that I was still in hospital. There must have been a reason for not calling me. As for her wanting to tell me something, I'm not so sure she actually did.

Not sure she told you?

Not sure she wanted to.

Then why did she tell you? I asked Zafar, but it was the question I wanted to ask Emily right then. I would have demanded an answer from her.

She was looking for her powder kit.

Excuse me?

In the old days, they used to call them vanity bags. I like that. Do you know what cognitive load is?

As a matter of fact, I do. You know, that's another thing you and my father have in common. You both have this weird fascination with experimental psychology, I said.

I wanted to change the subject. It was clumsy.

Your father's explained it to you?

His weird fascination? I replied.

Cognitive load.

I *do* read, you know.

You mentioned your father.

As I understand it, cognitive load is when you give someone a task to occupy his cognitive functions and then ask him questions while he's performing the task.

It's a way of getting past conscious censors. When I asked Emily about you, she was rummaging for her compact in her handbag. We were in a cab nearing our destination, a restaurant.

That was the cognitive load?

The rummaging. Emily was such a shifty thing, so secretive and unforthcoming—as you yourself say—that I had to find my own sneaky ways of eliciting information from her. Funny thing is, I don't even think I was conscious of my own scheming, not at the beginning. Only later, on reflecting, did I realize what I was doing: asking Emily questions when her conscious attention was taken up elsewhere. And when I looked back over other occasions, I recognized that I'd been doing it. We end up doing things we're unaware of because of another's behavior. So much for autonomy.

This tendency—can you call it a strategy when to begin with I wasn't fully aware of it? This tendency was really only useful when the question required a yes or no answer and didn't require conscious effort on her own part to figure out the answer, a question about where or when something did or did not happen, for instance. Of course, sometimes the cognitive load was too much, and she wouldn't hear the question or would just wave it off for later.

If she'd been sufficiently distracted, continued Zafar, then later she wouldn't even remember I'd asked her a question. That was another incidental effect of a question posed at an opportune moment. But you're so busy worrying about where this conversation is going, you're not asking the obvious question.

I'm sorry?

Why did I think I might not get a clear or truthful answer if I just asked her straight out? Well, I suppose there's the fact that she was shifty. But that's general; there was something specific, too, although I don't think I could tell you what. I've thought about it, of course, but I can't put my finger on it. Intuition, a sense that something had been kept unsaid. Remember, it was six months since I was in hospital. When I went in, whom would she have called who knew me? Not my parents, certainly. If she'd called anyone, she would have called you. Maybe, in those six months, she'd acted evasively whenever your name was mentioned, but I don't remember you coming up in conversation. All I knew— however I knew it—was that I had to ask her when she wasn't *listening*.

Conversation with Zafar was, from time to time, rather peculiar, but here it had taken a decidedly bizarre turn. We were talking about everything but the thing we were talking about.

Why are we talking about this? I asked him.

I asked her if she'd spoken to you and she replied that she hadn't, not since I was in hospital.

When I left the hospital, I stayed at Penelope's house, as I've said, with Emily there, too. I was feeling much better, and everything seemed so much slower, somehow more manageable. Most days, the house was empty. One day in that first week, Penelope asked me if I would mind dropping off her car at the service center on Thursday afternoon. On Thursday evening, when she came into the house, she said she'd seen the car outside and wondered if I'd not had a chance to take it in for servicing. I said I thought she'd said Thursday. *It is Thursday*, she replied. I'd lost account of the passage of time, lost the feeling for it. I used to sit on a bench in the garden watching the hydrangea and dahlias shriveling and the leaves browning on the sycamore and apple trees. I took to writing things down in my notebooks, not just the usual things but the more mundane, too, and it is because of them that I can now put timings to certain matters. Later, when I tried to figure out how I could have overlooked the obvious, matters that I now see *were* obvious—not just an error of calculation but rather a basic failure to see—I trace the cause to the untethering from time. If I had retained a sense, not on paper but in my mind, of the proportions of an hour, a day, a week, and a month, then perhaps I would not have been so foolish.

I was sitting in the garden when Emily appeared, her jacket unbuttoned and open, wafting her way through an overgrown path. She sat down beside me. She pinched her lips together and through those pinched lips she forced herself to speak.

I have always wanted children, said Zafar to me, going back even to my early twenties. I used to think there was something wrong with me. Young men, men in their twenties, they're not supposed to want children, they're not supposed to daydream about raising children, are they? If anything, the male role in childbearing—well, there is no role. It's not his body that houses and feeds the baby, it's not his belly that blows up and weighs him down, and it's not from his body that the child is torn at birth. We might protect and provide for our mate, but that's all. We're supposed to want to play the field and sow our oats and have a good time and all the rest of it. But wanting children? That comes later, right? Yet that's exactly what I wanted. Thirty years old and what I wanted most in the world was children. Maybe I wanted a child in order to repair my own childhood; maybe the desire was to fix something in me. But I don't think so. This is what I think. Some things are random to our eyes because they are buried in our makeup, like the quantum mechanical randomness of the moment of a particle's emission from the nucleus of an atom. The randomness might be real or only the projection of our inability to grasp what's going on. I have the impression that women of our generation, the ones who have given so much to their professional lives, they think they can have children as late as forty. But it's random.

What is?

Some women can have children later and some women cease to be fertile much earlier, at thirty-two even. So a lot of women get caught out because they leave it too late.

Emily was which?

She could have children then, at thirty, but my point is that some *men* develop the desire to have children at forty-five and some earlier. Maybe it was just that: my instincts, my drives, wired up to trigger a wish for children from the moment of my maturity. That's not a purely random thing, but nor is it an explanation based on neurosis, on a desire to fix the past. After all, the same cause—a troubled childhood—could equally have left me not at all wanting children of my own.

Emily said she was pregnant?

I'd been in hospital five weeks and we'd last made love two weeks before I went in, two weeks in which I was unraveling and she was so very busy at work, so that when she told me about her pregnancy and I carefully pieced all this together—a herculean effort back then—I was able to work out that she was between six weeks and five days and seven weeks pregnant.

I can't tell you how happy I was, how deep the pleasure I felt as I sat on the bench and listened. Even as she looked afraid, I was smiling. If there was any sign of doubt in her face, I didn't see it but saw instead only the fear that I took to be the lot of women. Can the word *tearing* ever be as vivid? But I was smiling at myself, smiling at my own reaction, which came over me completely. I was smiling because this is what I had always wanted, because I was completely ready for it, because I had always wanted kids and I thought I wanted them with Emily, and all this was in me there on the bench in the garden and so I was smiling.

When I asked her if we could tell others, she replied that she wanted to wait a little, as people did, and do the telling herself, when she was ready, and I said I understood that. I was so understanding, you see, so bloody understanding.

And one day I started talking about names. There are places in the world where infants aren't named for weeks after they're born, even months, where infant mortality is so high that parents don't name children because they don't want to get too attached. I think the naming thing was a big mistake, but she didn't just go along with it, she was right there by me. I might have turned the key in the ignition, but she put her foot on the pedal; she talked about it again and again.

Jasper, she said. She looked at me closely. Was I going to suggest something a little more in keeping with the child's father's heritage? Something Bangladeshi? Something Muslim?

Or Charlotte, if it's a girl, I said.

I like Charlotte. Phoebe's also nice, she added, still looking closely. Wouldn't I make even a nod eastward, even sound out one of those transcontinental names like Jasmine or Sara? Or go exotic with Scheherazade or Salomé? But wait. Was she thinking about the last name, the surname, the family name? Was she assuming the child would get my last name, so that the first name could come from the West, the first name hers to choose? I hadn't thought about marriage, not since she'd laughed when I proposed, but was this now on the cards?

There aren't many Hampton-Wyverns left, she said, just my brother and me.

And your parents and your stepmother.

She's my father's wife, not my stepmother, she snapped back.

The point Emily was not going to make, because it involved a disagreeable idea, is that her father's wife couldn't have children and therefore couldn't have children who would also carry the Hampton-Wyvern name—the disagreeable idea being that her father might have wanted children with his new wife, the younger Mrs. Hampton-Wyvern. Emily had told me that the woman was infertile—another instance of postcoital intimacy—but that only raises the question, how did Emily know this? I didn't ask then because, when she was forthcoming, rarely enough, I didn't dare interrupt, for I was ever curious to know what it was that she, of her own unprompted volition, wanted to say. But the question remains: In what kind of conversation does this arise? *Daddy, are you going to have more children?* And the father reassures his daughter, bending his new wife's personal tragedy into the service of placating his children and easing his relations with them, *Darling, we're not having any other children. We can't.*

I wonder, she said, if we might not give it my last name?

That's fine. I don't care either way, I said.

Which was a lie. How could that be the truth? The truth was that all those years ago, I had been charmed by her name. I had seen it first in a message for you on the notice board at college. I had seen it again on a flyer for a concert in the University Church, at the rehearsal for which I saw her for the first time, where she didn't see me, and which encounter I never mentioned to her. What would I say? I was spying on you?

The truth was that names meant something to me and her name meant everything. People surrender judgment for much less. Did you know that there are two ways to change your name in England? The first is by deed poll, an official document by which you announce your new name to the world. The second is when you're baptized, when you announce your new name to God, and the law of the land bows to divine law. Giving my child her family name was an act of *cleansing* to me. However distasteful that now sounds, that is what it meant. It was a means of overcoming the bonds with bastardy, with my parents, overcoming bondage.

In the first few weeks after leaving hospital, which were spent in Penelope Hampton-Wyvern's house, I passed the days reading, sitting in the garden, or tinkling on the piano. Penelope was out most days.

For seven weeks after Emily told me, we talked about the baby. We talked about names, I marveled at the technology of strollers, descendants of lunar modules, and we stopped in front of Baby Gap, where I pointed at the clothes and said how ridiculous it was to spend that kind of money on clothes for a baby but had to admit that the clothes were just too cute and the baby would look adorable in them and why not? We talked about cribs and I said I'd like to make one, and she gave me a curious look. We talked about how we would tell others when the time came. She would tell her mother first, she said, in reply to my direct question, then her father, and then we could set about telling others. But we never talked about marriage, apart from that one time, when her laughter had hurt, and even though, by the time of the pregnancy, I'd found an accommodation for it, so that the sting had all but passed, some vestige of pride or self-preservation had walled off the subject. Perhaps marriage didn't matter to her, I thought. After all, were we not an unlikely couple? Weren't we forged in the furnace of modernity, two people sprung from their respective traditions? We were something else. Marriage was feudal, and she and I were the new republic.

That was the story I told myself, but she asked me once if I'd thought about schools.

I've been once. You think I should go again?

For the child.

I thought we might skip all that and raise the kid as a feral animal. Could be a neat experiment on language acquisition. What do you say?

Do you have any objections to private schools?

The penny dropped. The formula alone, *private schools*, said it all. Of course she knew I needed no translation—we'd had enough conversations in which *public* schools had figured, so why say *private* schools now? But wait. In those conversations where she'd mentioned someone's schooling, she'd never needed to use that formula *public school*. After all, you don't refer to *Eton, the public school*, do you? Everyone knows Eton, everyone knows Winchester, knows Harrow. She never needed to identify Harrow, *the public school*. Had schooling become a potentially divisive issue, now that a choice was to be made? Did she think that the phrase *public schools* drew attention to the inherent irony, that there was nothing public about them? Did she feel she couldn't speak of *public schools* to me, who was educated, for want of a better word, at state schools, who must have come out thinking public schools were the devil's own, the class divider, the fork in the road? Did she really think I would object? Did she not grasp how much I wanted to be rid of my history, not how little it mattered to me, but how much it mattered not to see my child walk any part of the road I'd traveled? It was no concession but a relief. The new republic would not be struck on the anvil of revolution, not if it meant such sacrifice.

None at all, I replied. Nothing in the world matters to me more than to give the kid the best start in life that I can.

She said nothing but somehow looked uneasy. There was a silence. I waited for a response.

Have I misunderstood? Do *you* have objections to private schooling? I asked her.

No, I don't, she said, and she smiled, a smile to herself it was.

I don't know where that conversation was going. Her mother was at the front door, so it ended. And because something about it had made me uncomfortable, I didn't raise the matter again.

At fifteen weeks, it is fifteen centimeters long. Its sex is predictable with almost 100 percent accuracy. The *it* has become a he or she in progress. He or she can make his or her own independent movements. He or she is, in short, so easy to imagine that only with conscious effort can you not do so, and even then you will only be telling yourself not to think about something. Information paints a vivid picture, and that is why those who would limit a woman's choice work first to have a woman *informed*, denying the right of a human being to choose how to be informed or to choose not to be informed. But what of the couple that decides to have a child? Who would deny them their daydreaming, his daydreaming and hers, the visions of a future human being?

There were signs, but I didn't notice them. She had, as I mentioned, sold her apartment while I was in hospital and was looking for another, staying with me at her mother's place. I was barely involved in the process, visiting only one property with her, an apartment much the same, I thought, as the one she'd left, differentiated only perhaps by its better address, something I would never have understood but for my fast education on entering her world. In those seven weeks we never talked about where we—we three—might live.

I did not perceive the signs because I was in love in an altogether new way. How does one talk about such love? I loved the baby before it was born, before God made the heavens and the earth, you know, before the idea of nations, before any plant had found the memory of its flower. I would pester Emily in bed to let me listen, and I would announce at the slightest tremor, certainly imagined, that the child was a kicker. *This one's a kicker.* I thought of how I would play with the baby and the toddler and the boy. I imagined making wooden toys, a doll's house, a tree house, a rocking horse. I drew sketches. I considered kinds of wood. No plywood; the edges might splinter. I fantasized about answering the child's questions. I liked doing that the most, Jasper asking questions, why after why, and I would give an answer and wait for the next why or say that I didn't know but that we could find out, and we go to the library and look things up or sit at the computer, Jasper on my lap, and call up pictures of butterflies and dragons, and I tell him never to mistake the names of things for the things themselves, still less for an understanding of what they are, and I say this knowing it will pain me to watch him learn, for I know the cruel fact awaiting him, that understanding is not what this life has given us. And I lie in bed with him between us, Emily sleeping, her body that had so often coiled into a question mark now echoing the fetal position; she is asleep but not I, too afraid we might roll onto him, onto Jasper, and I whisper into the curl of his ear, *Your father loves you all the way to infinity*, adding under my breath, whose force terrifies me, *and don't you ever underestimate infinity*. And I learn that when you hold seven or eight pounds of new human being in your arms, those seven or eight pounds teach you for the first time, against all the laws of science, how a thing can weigh so little and weigh so much. At another age I teach him chess and we start with a simple version of the game, each side with only a king, a queen, and a pawn, a new and familiar game, and I promise to play with one hand only, and he giggles and he moves the pieces helter-skelter and I move all three of my pieces onto one square and he giggles again because—it pleases me to believe—something in him understands something in me.

There were other signs. There was a moment when I thought it would all come out. Emily, Penelope, and I were standing in the kitchen, Penelope making tea. She took a carton of milk from the fridge, and as the door moved on its hinges she paused, as if time had come to a halt, as if perhaps she had noticed the luster of her daughter's skin or the softness of its edges.

You look really rather well, darling, she said to her daughter.

But I do not think Penelope considered any clearer notion than that. If the thought had traversed her mind, it had appeared so low on the horizon as to be barely visible. She might have shaken her head; I cannot say. Her daughter remained silent, and if I now remember Emily glancing my way, it seems equally likely that she studiously avoided my eyes.

One day, seven weeks after I came out of hospital and only a few days after that incident in Penelope's kitchen, Emily called me from work. I was sitting at an oak bureau in the office.

I'm sorry, my love, she said. I'm sorry but I'm not ready. I want to have the child, but we're not ready. Right now, you have to come first. We've got to get you better.

I said nothing. If you know me at all, then you won't ask why I acceded but why I said nothing. When I began to think about why, my answer first came in stages of error, approximating something hard to find, something obscured by layers of emotion. It seems the answer is, finally, rather prosaic. I believed that she needed me, that this bright and beautiful woman, who might possibly have no reason to love me, needed me now.

I can't do this on my own, sweetheart, she said. I don't have the strength. Come with me. Will you hold my hand?

When I try to remember the day itself, all I can assemble before my eyes are mere fragments, as if the sun that day fell in patches. We know or we believe that as well as taking the form of a wave, light has a quantum form of discrete packets. And, defying intuition, these two forms exist together, at the same time, if they exist at all. It is the simultaneity of opposites in one that pleases me, the coterminous existence of contradicting states. I never studied quantum mechanics or relativity; I was too much a pure mathematician in my youth. But now I'm glad I have only sketchy notions of such things, those notions that make their way into the popular consciousness, for the fuzziness around the fringes allows me to piece them together in such form as to make something consoling. I am reminded of what Einstein said on the death of his friend: *He has departed from this strange world a little ahead of me. That means nothing. For us believing physicists, the distinction between past, present and future is only a stubborn illusion.*

Late in the afternoon, even as dusk was coming in, we went south of the river, to a place where these things happen discreetly, privately, and conveniently, during hours that require no absence from work and no excuses. In the waiting room, I sat with her, holding her hand. I avoided eye contact with others, some couples and a few women who were there alone. I pitied the women on their own, and I sensed the couples clenching each other's hands. Perhaps, I thought, this is a kind of death, numbness brought on by the vulgar reality of shame. I did not like that room.

In the weeks and months to come, this particular day would return to me, not some uncertain date of an unfinished birth but this particular day with its uncompromising certainty. In the hour I waited, I grasped the nature of my own need. I needed to believe that what she had carried had mattered to her, maybe not as much as it had to me, but that it had mattered to her in some way. It would not be enough to hear it; I had to feel it in the muscle of my heart.

Inside the cab I reached for her hand. What exactly had happened? I did not know. Does this mean, I asked myself, that back in the surgery, somewhere in that surgery, in some plastic bag or some disposal bin, imprinted with words like *organic matter*, is that where something is, something that isn't a child but was the focus of a vision of the future, my vision, that had already acquired my love, not earned it, not deserved it, a love that went back through me, through generations upon generations of evolution? Can I ask what they did to you? I said to her.

I had an ultrasound, she replied, and then they gave me a pill and I have to take another one in two days.

Another ultrasound?

Another pill.

The road headed back north, and as we crossed the river I looked out onto the ribbons of silver twisting across the water, and I felt I was witnessing a time I would remember. But as the city's murmur rose about us, her hand slipped away. Her hand slipped away, and I knew that this child would follow me all the days of my life.

Am I not entitled to grieve? Am I not entitled to my emotions? Are we to be held responsible for the deepest feelings over which we have no dominion? In any civilized criminal law, our state of mind alone is never enough to condemn us: There has to be an act. But does morality judge us for our feelings?

You don't have to justify anything to me, Zafar.

This is what I was asking myself. And by not saying anything before, I believed I had lost the right to speak afterward, the right merely to express my feelings, which were not about regret but were in the nature of mourning.

Do you know what a period is made of? Actually, do you know what a tree is made of?

A tree?

To be precise, do you know where the stuff a tree is made of—where that stuff comes from?

Is this a trick question?

There's nothing misleading in the question.

It gets its nutrients from the ground, I said.

A tree is mostly made of wood and wood is mostly carbon, which is why it's burned for fire. Where does that carbon come from? Trees take in carbon dioxide from the atmosphere and breathe out oxygen. Photosynthesis strips out the oxygen—the dioxide—in carbon dioxide and releases it into the atmosphere, but what about the carbon? The carbon remains in the tree and the tree grows. In other words, trees grow out of the air.

I did not know that.

I read a story somewhere in which a woman said that when she was an adolescent coming into puberty, her mother, Boston Irish, explained to her that a period was the body crying because a child was not being born.

That's horrible.

Do you know what a woman's period is? What the stuff is?

Isn't it the placenta?

It's the endometrium. The placenta is formed only when a woman is pregnant. The endometrium is a membrane lining the uterus. It keeps the walls of the uterus from sticking together.

Well, there's something else I didn't know.

Nor did I, but six months after the termination I did some research. I told you that I asked Emily if she'd heard from you. We were in a cab. We were on our way to a restaurant, and while rooting about for her powder kit, she let slip she hadn't spoken to you since I was in hospital. Let me tell you what happened in the restaurant.

Near the end of the meal, Emily's phone rang and, as always, she stepped away to take the call. I sat sipping the coffee, with an eye out for the waiter to ask for the check. At the next table were two women, in their midthirties I guessed, though I didn't see them face on. They were sitting not opposite each other but at an intimate right angle, with me behind them. I overheard only a snippet, when one woman said with urgency in her voice: *You know you have to decide soon. You can't take the pill after nine weeks. They just don't let you, and after that things get a lot more complicated.*

Because of overhearing that, I did some research and some arithmetic. It came down to knowing how to count and knowing where to begin counting.

Emily had had a medical abortion. She said it herself, that's what it means to have an ultrasound and a pill one day and another pill two days later, and there was no reason for her to lie about that. And I was there when the cramping started, when she holed herself up in the bathroom. I've thought about why she didn't lie at that moment, when I asked her what had happened in the clinic, and it seems plausible enough to me that she was preoccupied when I asked, too preoccupied to think through the ramifications of what she was sharing. And perhaps she was implicitly relying on a man's ignorance of the workings of a woman's body, not to mention the ins and outs of such medication.

When she told me she was pregnant, I calculated she must have been seven or eight weeks into the pregnancy, and by that reckoning she would have been fifteen weeks pregnant when she had the termination. But in the U.K. in 2000, doctors couldn't prescribe the abortion pill for pregnancies over nine weeks. So she was lying to me about the gestation.

Couldn't she have simply been mistaken?

Only if she was mistaken when she told me but not mistaken when she spoke to the doctor. Even if she was only mistaken, the question arises why she didn't correct my misapprehension on any of the many occasions it was manifest.

Of course. I see.

The next question is: Why would she be lying about the gestation? First, she couldn't have got pregnant after I came out of hospital. For one thing, one week after I came out she told me she was pregnant. That's almost certainly not long enough to get pregnant *and* miss a period in order to find out you're pregnant. You see, the window of fertility is roughly speaking a six- or seven-day interval centered on the fourteen-day mark.

What fourteen-day mark? I'm not as smart as you; you'll have to go slowly.

You're smart, all right. You just haven't given it as much attention as I have. Fourteen days after LMP.

LMP?

The first day of a woman's last menstrual period.

Okay. I'm lost, I said.

If she missed her period, continued Zafar, took a pregnancy test, and told me she was pregnant all on the very same day, she would have had to have become pregnant at least ten days before that day. But I was in hospital until seven days before she told me. Put another way, if she and I had had sex the day I came out of hospital *and* she got pregnant as a result, she couldn't know for at least ten days, at the earliest, that she was pregnant, which means she wouldn't have known for at least a further three days after she actually told me. Do you see?

I assume you've worked the numbers.

Actually, that's exactly what I did. I put together a spreadsheet to stress-test the numbers.

Are you serious?

I'd be stupid not to. I had to be sure.

So you got her pregnant before you went into hospital?

We had sex two weeks before I went into hospital. I was in hospital for five weeks. She had the termination eight weeks after I came out. That's a total of fifteen weeks. She had a medical abortion which, as I say, means that she could not have been more than nine weeks pregnant when she had the termination. In other words, I couldn't have got her pregnant before I went into hospital and in fact no one could, not before I went into hospital. But we can narrow down the interval even more. Remember, she carried the baby for seven weeks after she told me she was pregnant, and it was one week after I came out of hospital that she told me she was pregnant. Which means she must have missed one period before then—if she'd missed two, she'd have been at least six weeks pregnant when she told me and she wouldn't have been given a medical abortion four weeks later. If you do the arithmetic, making sure to take account of the fact that she'd missed one period but not two when she told me, and the fact that the clock on a pregnancy formally starts on the LMP, then the conclusion is that she conceived at some time during the second week I was in hospital, give or take a few days. I know what you're thinking.

Did Zafar know what I was thinking? Yes, I saw Emily in that interval. Yes, I did more than just see her. Years had passed, but I remembered exactly when I visited her. That Saturday, my father's birthday, I remembered Emily telling me that Zafar had gone into hospital on Tuesday the week before. *Last Tuesday?* I'd asked her. *No, the week before,* she'd replied. *And you waited this long to tell me,* I'd thought. And later I'd considered the meaning of Tuesday. Tuesday, a grim day, his father's day off from work, Zafar had once said to me, though it was no explanation at all, I thought then.

You're wondering, continued Zafar, how I know what her cycle length was. Ninety percent of women have cycle lengths between twenty-one and thirty-five days. But what's to say her cycle length wasn't outside that? Twenty-one days or thirty-five? The beauty is, I don't need to know; the conclusion is the same. That's what stress-testing the numbers shows. Though for what it's worth, I happen to know that it was pretty much twenty-eight days.

I should say sorry, shouldn't I?

Zafar didn't respond.

I feel I need to explain myself.

I spent six months grieving for a loss . . . a loss that . . . How can an explanation of *your* actions touch anything . . . touch the grief, touch the consequences of . . . the consequences? I didn't know until more than *eight* months afterward. I was in hospital when . . . In hospital.

I owe you an explanation.

You can't say sorry *and* offer an explanation, said Zafar. What's an explanation supposed to do, other than make *you* feel better? If an explanation is a justification, then why say sorry? And if it isn't a justification, then it's a confession in search of absolution. *Explanation?*

But I shouldn't have . . . I shouldn't . . .

We sat silently, Zafar and I. The kitchen still smelled of the Thai take-out we'd had the night before. The housekeeper was scheduled to come the next day. I thought of all the pain Zafar had felt, the pain at the loss of a child, which it so obviously was to him. As he wrote in one notebook, *We carry people in our heads, which is where their deaths take place.* He had invested so much in the idea of the infant, much more than most men, perhaps. People vary. He'd talked about distributions, bell curves, the randomness that sets you down somewhere on the curve, most people bunched up in the middle, most people, I think, not so invested, some even looking back without one pang of regret or lament, and others, like him, wholly given over. He knew that the child had mattered to him—and wasn't that what he wanted of Emily? To know that the child had mattered to her. He knew that the child had mattered to him for reasons that gathered from every corner of his identity. If that was the wrong premise upon which to bring a human being into the world, to regard it as anything other than a new and independent human being, then it seems to me to be an argument entirely irrelevant to the pain. Feelings, the very heart of what a man is—they deserve our respect even if they never need to earn it.

How do you feel about it now? I asked him.

Zafar didn't answer, not right away.

We think of memory as if it were a hard drive, he said, and in some ways that's what it's like, but it's like something altogether different, too. It's a stage *and* a director, and over time the play changes, the characters are changed, but it's a funny play because we lose sight of what those characters once were to us. Memory is not static but a thing in motion, and because we are passengers without a frame of reference, the motion is imperceptible, so that at any given point in time, all we have is a set of memories, a thing of the instantaneous present and not of the past. I read somewhere, some researcher explaining that every time we recall something, our future memory of it changes, as if we rewrite or overwrite the memory with a new memory after each use in an ongoing palimpsest. Which, it strikes me, must make it hard to lose the memory of something whose memory you dearly wish to lose, which is to say that if memory serves us well, sometimes some things are blessedly forgotten. Do you have any cigarettes?

Listening to Zafar, I felt more sorry, more regretful, than I had already. Is that what he was doing, waiting to forget?

I think I have some cigars in the study, I said.

Cigars? Well, why not? Now is as good an occasion as any.

I returned from the study with cigars and also with cigarettes, having remembered seeing a packet on a bookshelf.

The cigarettes might be stale, I said, setting the packet down on the table. I held out a cigar but Zafar declined. He was not looking at me and I realized we had not made eye contact in some time. The realization saddened me.

He lit a cigarette, inhaled deeply, and let the smoke seep out of his mouth. I had asked him how he felt about it all now. Presently, he picked up his thread.

I ask myself, he said, what am I allowed to hope for?

I saw his eyes take on a look, the dusk of solitude, to borrow my friend's words from another context, and with the passage of time I watched those eyes retreat deeper into shadow.

I know, he said, that every memory is just a work in progress. But someday, if I make it to that rocking chair on the porch, I hope that all this, the love and loss, that it will all come back as little more than something somewhere long ago.

20

The Gospel of St. Thomas

The more I think about language, the more it amazes me that people ever understand each other at all.   —Kurt Gödel

Wouldn't we all do better not trying to understand, accepting the fact that no human being will ever understand another, not a wife a husband, a lover a mistress, nor a parent a child? Perhaps that's why men have invented God—a being capable of understanding.

—Graham Greene, *The Quiet American*

And if it worries and torments you to think of your childhood and of the simplicity and quiet that goes with it, because you cannot any more believe in God, who appears everywhere in it, then ask yourself, dear Mr. Kappus, whether you really have lost God? Is it not, rather, that you have never yet possessed him? For when should that have been? Do you believe that a child can hold him, him whom men bear only with effort and whose weight compresses the old? Do you believe that anyone who really has him could lose him like a little stone, or do you not think rather that whoever had him could only be lost by him? But if you know he was not in your childhood, and not before that, if you suspect that Christ was deluded by his longing and Mohammed betrayed by his pride—and if you are terrified to feel that even now he is not, in this hour when we speak of him—what then justifies you in missing him, who never was, like one who has passed away, and in seeking him as though he had been lost?   —Rainer Maria Rilke, *Letters to a Young Poet*, translated by M. D. Herter Norton

In Islamabad, when I emerged from the airport onto the outside concourse, I was met by a middle-aged man in an ill-fitting suit holding up a placard with my name on it.

From Kabul, sir? asked the man.

Yes.

This is a courtesy car. I am to take you wherever you wish to go.

A hotel. Anywhere but the Marriott.

I'd read that the Marriott was teeming with the world's media and the visiting senior officials of multilateral organizations, NGOs, and donor agencies. The rooftop was, as pictures already showed, a crowd of satellite dishes.

Very good, sir.

At my hotel, I left my bag in my room and went back downstairs to the business center, where I logged on to email. I drafted a message to Hassan Kabir explaining that after three days in Kabul, I had the impression that ISAF and UNAMA were too busy to be dealing with small fry like me. I clicked Send, and when my screen refreshed I saw that I had an email from Emily.

Where are you?

In Islamabad, I wrote.

I fired off my short reply and then tried to book a ticket to Dubai. There were no direct flights from Islamabad to Dhaka, or to Delhi, for that matter—I think planes going out of Pakistan were not allowed over Indian airspace. I took down the contact numbers for telephone bookings for Emirates and PIA and checked my email again.

There was another message from Emily.

Where in Islamabad?

It was difficult to answer her. Even then, in those dying days, despite the disgust and horror and the tides of anger, I wanted to tell her where I was, where I could be found, so that she could get on the next flight, I imagined, rush to my hotel in Islamabad, pay the concierge a bribe for the room number—for a surprise, she'd tell him (and was that really why I wanted a hotel other than the security-infested Marriott?). Or maybe she'd ask for the telephone number for the room—to call from a phone in the lounge, she'd say, but instead read off the last four digits and head for the elevator and knock timidly on my door and, when I open it, smile widely, a smile of reflex, and declare her love and so on and so forth. It was the most undignified, reprehensible part of me. And yet the part of me that didn't want to tell her where I was staying was equally complicit in betraying me, for reducing me in my own eyes, for it didn't want to tell her not because it wanted nothing more to do with her but because it couldn't bear the wait, the not knowing if she would come or not. What a tangle of negatives, double and triple. We were finished, weren't we? Months ago, made good and final when I left for Dhaka, Bangladesh, for who would ever go there other than to put distance between one thing and another, the old and the new, an end and a beginning? But then the planes brought down the towers and everything was fucked-up, clocks unsprung and compass needles sent flying, and who knew where or when they were. I have read that in the weeks afterward, there was a spike in the number of couples getting engaged. I have read that after 9/11, there was a big jump in the number of people deciding to drive rather than take a plane, to get from D.C. to Boston, from New York to Chicago, and apparently more people died in the resulting increase in car accidents in the six months after 9/11, in the increase alone, than in the attacks themselves. The whole thing is irrational, of course, the response to the attacks, the individual human responses and the collective political responses. Emily and I were all but finished, a final finish subverted by 9/11 breaking open the ambiguous days at the end of an affair. What is that line in Larkin's poem? *Specious stuff that says no rational being can fear a thing it will not feel.* And here I was wondering how I would respond to her question, what I would write, staring at the screen but feeling the suspension of my fingers above the keyboard.

You ask if I loved her, and I tell you that I did and I didn't. I've been here over three months, and how often have you spoken of Meena and yet how is it that I know that you wish to be near her? I know because our actions don't tell the whole story, they never do. It is not that thought is hidden behind the actions but that all the omissions and silences, the evidence of things not seen, must be accounted for if you're to see anything. Emily stood for something, she rescued me and condemned me in the same gesture. You may say that that is not love, and I would laugh at you for presuming to know what another's love isn't and what his love is. Emily was England, home, belonging, the untethering of me from a past

428 | ZIA HAIDER RAHMAN

I did not want, the promise through children of a future that was rooted, bound to something treated altogether better by the world than my mother, the girl who loved me.

I wrote back telling her where I was, giving her the name of the hotel, and no sooner had I clicked Send than I felt the onset of waiting. I had to buy a plane ticket, a ticket to Dubai, from where I could catch a flight back to Dhaka. I called the airline and booked a seat on a flight the following afternoon, enough time for Emily to get out here—if that is what she had in mind. But the waiting was terrible. It was as if time had changed, no more arrow in flight but a smiling Buddha sitting before me, a figure of marvel, with the patience to withstand an eternity of staring.

It was late in the afternoon. I had not eaten all day. At a restaurant I ordered a plate of kebabs that came with bread as long as my arm. I ordered a salad to go with it, but before it arrived I was full with meat and bread. In my hotel room, I turned on the television, but after two minutes of CNN, I switched it off and went back downstairs to the guests' business center to check my email. She hadn't written. Back in my room, I took a sleeping tablet and turned in for the night.

The following morning, I went downstairs and logged on. There was a reply from Hassan Kabir: I regret to have troubled you so. Note that I plan to be in Kabul next Wednesday and trust you will be able to join me there. If you stand in need of additional travel documents, visas, or letters to facilitate entry, let my staff know.

After a light breakfast in the hotel restaurant, I returned to my room, where I tried to work on some legal papers. I was in a buoyant mood. Even if I did not admit it to myself then, I can tell you now that some part of me was holding out the hope that Emily would show.

At four thirty, there was a knock on the door.

Hello?

It's me.

Door's open, I said.

It was Emily.

We made love.

Shall we call your mother and tell her?

Emily did not answer immediately. Was that calculation I saw, the same calculation I had seen before, time and again? She had asked me to marry her and I had said yes, so that perhaps all I had seen in that look was the doubt to which everyone is entitled at the moment they impose their will on the course of their lives. That must be it—that is what I wanted it to be.

Yes, let's, she said.

She spoke first. Zafar and I are getting engaged.

Getting engaged? I thought. Was there some ceremony involved? It occurred to me for the first time that I really didn't know the ins and outs of the process, not just the process that Emily must have grown up with, girls of her station, her place in English society, but the process of engagement and marriage, and what happens in between. The engagement as an abstract noun, the wedding invitations as embossed cards, that was about all I knew. There was a wedding ceremony, of course, a white wedding dress and a reception afterward.

We're in Islamabad now. We'll be coming to London.

Will we? I had no reason to argue with her. If I had become giddy with delight, however briefly, it wasn't because of the prospect of marriage but because Emily seemed to me for the first time to be acting with resolution about me, with a clear commitment to me. This even though I knew that the only thing left, the only thing to convey the requisite level of emotional commitment, was to ask me to marry her. Perhaps, too, I was just glad for the forward movement, the change in itself, the escape from the toing and froing, the ambiguities and vacillations, and the uncertainties of feeling loved one day and disregarded the next. There is always enough ground for self-deception, its possibilities endless. It is because I knew this then, because I felt the presence of these ideas, that I must wonder now if I had been going along with a game, calling her bluff, forcing her to play this card.

Emily handed me the phone.

Is it true? asked Penelope, her voice severe and direct.

Should I laugh at myself now for not being in the least surprised by Penelope's question? For in fact realizing that I'd expected the question and expected it to be meant genuinely, as it was?

It's true, I said.

There was silence.

I am *so* glad. Congratulations. This is marvelous.

Penelope went on in that vein for quite a while before asking for contact information. She took down the number for the hotel and I returned the phone to Emily.

Not yet, said Emily.

Evidently, she was answering a question, and I have wondered what that question might have been. *Have you told your father yet?* Or she might have asked Emily if I'd given her a ring—she wouldn't have known then that Emily had done the asking, that Emily had proposed to me, and not the other way around. But I think that this shrewd woman, mother to a daughter who had judged her deficient, who addressed her as "Mother" in a blunt, toneless voice and had not forgiven her for the failure of her marriage—was that all it was?—I think this shrewd woman had most likely asked her daughter if she could go ahead and announce the engagement. *Not yet*, Emily had said. The same reply she'd given me when really not so very long before I had asked her if we could tell people she was pregnant.

But after the call Emily became animated. She appeared to be quite taken by the idea of marriage, a wedding. Her manner assumed a jollity, and she might even have skipped and clapped her hands, had her character been that way disposed. But yes! I have seen her skip, maybe even clap her hands, I've seen the enchanting, gleeful skipping of a girl as I entered the house and down she came, down the stairs, happy to see me, reaching out and resting her hands on my chest. There were plenty of moments like that—I wasn't entirely mad.

I suggested that we call the airline and get her a seat on my flight. She took the airline's phone number from me but didn't call then—she had to go to the bathroom, she said.

In bed later that evening, she talked about the wedding.

If we have the wedding in Italy, at my grandmother's villa, then I think we should do something nice for our long-suffering friends and fly them over.

I suppose we could, I said, musing to myself how "our friends" so differs from "our respective friends." "Long-suffering," I thought, was there only to justify the extravagance.

I could not offer any more than that lame answer, *I suppose we could*. I think it's fair to say that there are women for whom the wedding is itself an object of and for perfection, the embodiment of an idealization that begins in childhood, in girlhood, and gains mass through adolescence and into womanhood. Emily was such a woman. On the other hand, I myself had only ever harbored dread of the wedding day, whomever I might marry in the end. I'd always known that I wouldn't have an arranged marriage; I'd always known that it was unlikely I'd marry a woman my parents considered suitable, a Muslim woman from the Sylhet province in Bangladesh; I'd always known that educated women with that kind of background and with a Western sensibility were few. There are many more now, but they are too young for me, of course—too late for me. I just didn't meet any people like that. The worst part of it for my parents must have been the fact that their social status never brought them near families with educated children. They were peasants in the sense that connotes nothing pejorative. They came from peasants and they knew that they themselves, that their class, was the obstacle to fulfilling their own ambitions for me, to make good their shame.

In any event, I now had little to do with them. My visits to their home in London were separated by months and sometimes years. In fact, I saw more of them in the one month when they needed help with their mortgage than in all the rest of time since I left their home for university. We seldom spoke on the phone. Once, three years passed without contact. When Emily had asked me if she could meet my parents—three months after I'd been introduced to Robin and four after Penelope— I explained things but afterward offered, *of course*, to take her to my parents' home.

But if they won't let you in, I said, or if they say they don't want to speak to you, there's nothing I can do about that.

They wouldn't?

I don't want to discourage you—you should know how it is—but if you're asking me, then I have to tell you what I believe. I think they won't let you in. But I might be wrong.

Emily didn't press the issue, and I didn't tell her that I'd already spoken to them about her and they'd said they didn't want anything to do with her and didn't want me mentioning her name in their presence again.

Because of this, I knew that I'd marry outside and that therefore my parents would never come to my wedding, so that when Emily started talking about flying people over to an Italian villa, when Emily talked about the little church high on a hillside overlooking a valley, a venue for

432 | ZIA HAIDER RAHMAN

the ceremony, and outside which, once, on a lush slope of grass—holy profanity!—we'd made love, when Emily broached matters of the wedding day, dancing like a girl, all I could think about were the implications of my parents' not being there.

And, in fact, I did not want them there. To have wanted them there would only have made sense if I'd wanted them to enjoy it, if I'd wanted them to give their blessing, but I knew that that was a wish too far. I'd have to wish first that some part of them could rejoice. And there was also a fear of embarrassment. It wasn't the fear of a banal embarrassment, of parents retelling compromising stories of childhood, as if my father or mother could make a wedding speech in English, but a fear of embarrassment at the evident rupture between them and me. Why should that cause embarrassment? I don't know. What I know is that when I consider that rupture, when I consider the various ways I am separated from my parents, the ways they seem alien to me and I to them, I fear that others might consider the same and that they, too, will conclude that I am an unfeasible human being, so that the embarrassment I fear is not just the universal child's embarrassment—Daddy, stop that, you're embarrassing me—but a deeper anxiety about who I am.

So when Emily spoke of chartering a plane, of a wedding in a Tuscan church sitting pretty at the top of a hill, I thought of how my half would not live up to her fantasy, to the ambitions of an ambitious woman. I imagined a wedding in which one half came incomplete, with an absence that pointed only to deficiency, a hole that everyone would be wary to avoid stepping into, whatever clever and moving words I might spin in the groom's speech.

In the morning, after a breakfast in bed, Emily made a curious suggestion.

Let's go and see a priest.

To get married now?

No, silly! To talk about getting married. It's what you do, go and see a priest.

Aren't we going to England?

We can see one here anyway. Don't you think it would be fun?

Talking to a priest?

Emily was enchanted by the practical matters of the process. She was like a girl playing with new dolls. I knew it was the prospect of losing me finally that had brought things to a head, but I wondered how much of the new mood was sustainable when the claims of work, of a professional life, came back in. That room was an enclave, separated from all the world, all the business of reconstruction and development, a piece of the world that had its own weather system, its own motion of time, an island populated only by two people.

On my way to the hotel two days earlier, I'd seen a great golden cross flashing in the bright sun, rising above a line of trees, as high as a minaret. A short walk down a wide avenue, whose fast-moving traffic made it an exhilarating peril to cross, and we came to St. Thomas's Roman Catholic Church in the Diocese of Islamabad-Rawalpindi, Pastor Anwar Daniel, M.A.

I knocked and we waited.

Any guess which St. Thomas this is named for? I asked Emily.

The Apostle Thomas?

Now that would be an irony.

Why?

St. Thomas went east, while the other apostles remained in the Mediterranean. Thomas landed up in India and founded a church there.

Really?

Indians practiced Christianity for fifteen centuries before Western missionaries came along and forced them to convert to the Church of Rome. There were Nazranis, for instance, part of the Jewish diaspora long settled in the south of India, who converted to the church of St. Thomas well before Vasco da Gama or Ferdinand Magellan set foot there. The Portuguese rooted them out because they were deemed heretics from the true faith. The unforgivable crime of Indian Christians was to disturb the European's understanding of himself, and the only proper response was to kill such people. Vanity of vanities. All is vanity. I know what you're thinking.

What am I thinking?

You're wondering, why the irony, though? Here is a Roman Catholic church bearing the name of the saint who founded the church that was destroyed by Rome.

How do you know about all this? Emily asked me.

You don't?

No.

Since I wasn't there at the time and I don't know anyone who was, I can only assume it must be from books.

A bolt opened behind the church door. Greeting us was a squat, rather well-fed South Asian man wearing a shalwar kameez and, strikingly, a clerical collar. He addressed Emily.

Good morning. What can I do for you?

We're getting married and we wanted to talk to a vicar, she said.

The priest looked surprised.

I am happy to talk to you, he said.

He stepped out, pulled the door shut, and led us to a small building next to the church. Inside, in his private chambers, we sat down and he offered us tea, which we declined.

We are a Catholic church, which means that I'm not a vicar but a priest. Are you Catholics? he asked, looking at me.

He had an odd verbal tic, flashing his tongue out between phrases, pursing his lips, calling to mind a dog lapping at water.

Anglicans, said Emily, stepping in. But we'd be very happy to talk to you, if you don't mind helping us.

I was wondering what in heaven's name there was to talk about. What were we doing here? Emily never showed a religious disposition. But of course! It was all ceremony and ritual. There was a process, a procession, of things to do.

If you don't mind helping us, she had said. A nice piece of manipulation at work. But how, really, could a priest help? It was, from my perspective, a decidedly odd thing to do, to reach for a priest, but everything Emily suggested seemed to come naturally to her, as if it were taken from an order of ceremonies.

And it tickled me to be in a church in Pakistan, a nation founded for the Muslims of India. I knew there were churches in Islamabad, I knew that there was one in particular that expat Christians attended, and I thought that perhaps this one might be it. It was in the right neighborhood. But counting against that possibility was, I thought, the fact that the priest was Pakistani.

If there was anything that needed discussing, any pastoral steer to give, this priest offered little. He was far too curious about us, as individuals and as a couple.

Where are you from?

We're British, said Emily.

And you? he asked turning to me.

I was born in Bangladesh.

Ah, Bangladeshi. I see.

What is bringing you to Pakistan?

I'm working in Afghanistan, said Emily.

Oh, really? You have the work cut out.

He chuckled.

You wish to be married here?

No, she replied, we'll be married in Italy.

In Italy? He looked confused.

Yes, my grandmother has a house there.

Your grandmother, she is Italian?

No.

He looked even more confused. He then turned to me.

What is your job?

I'm a lawyer.

Excellent.

Apart from addressing the priest's curiosities, the conversation didn't seem to be going anywhere. I could hardly blame him, two people outside his congregation appearing at his doorstep, asking for what exactly?

When he seemed to have satisfied himself that he had his bearings, he asked Emily if he could see me alone.

I'll wait outside, she replied. Perhaps I can look around the church?

The door is unlocked, he said.

When she left, the man turned to me and gave me a broad smile.

I have to ask you this and you can tell me the truth in confidence. Why do you want to marry her?

I didn't know quite where to begin and he must have seen that.

Do you love her?

Yes, I said.

But, he said, this love thing is a tricky business, don't you agree?

Again, I didn't know how to respond, and he did seem to want some kind of response, if only to let him progress along some route he had in mind.

You must be honest. Are you marrying her for the passport?

No.

Are you quite sure about this? The devil always helps us deceive ourselves.

I'm quite sure, I said.

Where will you live?

I don't know, I said, as I remembered a trite homily I'd read somewhere: A bird and a fish can fall in love, but where will they make a home? Unlikely, I thought. They only meet when the bird has the fish in its claws. Fall in love?

I was holding back information, and I saw that if I left it too late, he would feel insulted that I hadn't shared it sooner.

Perhaps I can help—I have a British passport.

Oh, I see! he said. He fell silent for a moment, lapping his tongue away, as if gathering his thoughts.

I think this lady is from a moneyed family. Am I right?

They're well-off.

May I ask—are you from a moneyed family?

No, I'm not.

I see.

Again, the pause and lapping.

Then you must think hard before taking this step.

He glanced at his watch. I would very much like to see you again, he added. I'm sorry, but I'm late already for a pressing matter.

Outside, we joined Emily and again he repeated his request to meet again. I had the impression it was me he wanted to see. We made promises, which I think we knew would not be kept.

What did he ask you?

So much for the privilege of confession, I replied.

Come on, said Emily.

He wondered if you were marrying me for my passport or my money, I said. Of course, it was the memory of what Rebecca Sonnenschein had once said, long ago, returning now to inform my reply.

Really?

More or less, I said with a smile.

We had lunch in the hotel restaurant.

I asked her if she'd booked a ticket on the same flight as me for that afternoon, knowing I hadn't actually told her which flight I was booked on. But before she could answer, her phone rang. How I hated that phone. It rang, she answered hello and then set off away from the table to take the call. She'd come back, I thought, and not say a word about the call. What right, I used to tell myself, did I have to know who she was talking to? None. But why it troubled me, every time, had nothing to do with rights. One expects it of anyone, if a call interrupts a conversation or a meal, an explanation will be given, however cursory—*that was so and so, had to take it, sorry*, or even, simply, *just work*. Is it not how people are supposed to behave?

She came back and resumed her meal.

Are you coming with me this afternoon? I asked, again, even though her doing so should already have been implicit in everything that had happened in the past twenty-four hours. The very act of asking, against that background, evidenced my doubts, signaled that I knew things weren't quite right and that she wasn't being entirely straight. And the fact that I wasn't making any more of this than to ask a question the answer to which had no *reason* to change, the fact that I wasn't confrontational, only added to the abasement. I was so careless of the dignity that every man must guard so that he can face himself each day. That I count chief among my regrets, the relegation of dignity.

To Dubai? she asked.

To Dubai, for London?

I'll get another flight.

Have your plans changed in the last fifteen minutes? I asked.

No.

She was looking me in the eye as she said all this, that gaze I've told you about, that look that studies the effect of what she's saying, that adapts and adjusts for what she sees, as if the purpose was to hold reality steady at the level of words that are spoken, as if that could ever be so.

We passed the rest of lunch in silence. When I suggested coffee, she spoke again.

I have to go to a meeting.

In Kabul?

No, here.

Did you know about the meeting before coming to Islamabad?

I came to see you.

Do you plan to get on the flight tomorrow? Should I wait?

I have to go to Kabul for another meeting.

Tomorrow?

Yes.

In development and reconstruction, it already seemed to me, people were paid not by the hour but by the meeting. Meeting was work, and the work was coordination, and coordination requires a meeting of minds, and so meetings are required in meeting rooms, so that things can be discussed and consensus reached and minutes taken, so work can get done.

Should I wait?

No answer from her. It was infuriating.

What did you imagine I would *do*?

She said nothing.

Do you know if Ariana's running flights from Kabul to Dubai? I asked.

I don't think so.

See if you can get yourself to Dubai tomorrow evening. We can catch a flight to London together, probably the day after. There's a flight at four in the afternoon.

There is a study that comes to my mind now, said Zafar. Patients—

Really? Another study? I interjected.

Do you really think you're in a position to tease me?

Go on, I said.

The study addressed the failure of patients to show up for appointments, no-shows, something that has always been a problem at doctors' surgeries. One surgery introduced a system of asking patients to repeat back to the receptionist the time of the appointment they just booked. Apparently, just getting patients to say the time of their appointment resulted in no-shows dropping by fifty percent or something astonishing.

It's one thing to ask a patient in a surgery to repeat something back— you're providing a service, after all—but it's another to do this with a friend, and another altogether to do it with your lover. What ruse can you apply and what price do you pay for applying a ruse to one so dear? I had no ruse.

I explained to Emily that I needed to book flights, or my flight, at any rate, at least a couple of hours beforehand. If I didn't do so, then I'd have to stay at a hotel in Dubai. Not cheap. Bear that in mind, I said.

Oh, the indignity! There I am asking her to get to Dubai tomorrow but telling her when the last flight to London is on the day after that. Some part of me implicitly conceding, suggesting that she could come later—isn't that what it was?—giving her an out to every request I made. That was the sum of it, this feeling of being broken into parts. I must have known something wasn't quite right when she appeared in the room. Her luggage was too small. Did she not count on me saying yes when she asked me to marry her? A carry-on wouldn't have been enough for her, not if she thought she might be going to London. And yet I shut out the wisdom of my own eyes. One part of me fighting with another.

I should get going soon if I'm going to catch my flight. Can I drop you off somewhere? I asked.

No, that's fine. I'm going to stay here for a bit; I have a little work to do before my meeting. You should go.

I settled the account, asked at the reception for a taxi to the airport, and went to fetch our bags.

Emily and I kissed outside the hotel and I got into the car and watched her go back inside.

To the airport, sir?

Yes, please. But can you first go to the end of the road, around the roundabout, and come back this way?

Certainly, sir.

As we drove past the hotel, I saw Emily getting into a car that had the livery of a cab company.

Thank you, driver. Let's go to the airport.

The car I was in was a Land Cruiser, not the Corolla or Nissan one might expect of a taxi. On arriving at the airport, I was not surprised to discover the colonel waiting there.

Hello, Zafar, he said, stretching out his hands and gripping me by my arms.

I'm sorry your visit to Kabul was so short. I trust you'll be returning soon?

It's possible.

I would like you to know that I'm here to help—we're there to help. I don't suppose you need help, but I want you to know that it is there. I trust you had a pleasant flight with our air force?

It was fine. Thank you for the car, by the way.

My pleasure. It will be here, as will a place for you to stay. Just let me know.

Do I need to?

He chuckled.

How are you? I asked.

I'm well, my boy. Very well. The sun is shining. What more can one hope for? You're on the PIA flight for Dubai.

Is that a question?

If you need it, you have a room at the Hyatt. In Dubai.

Thank you.

Let's get you checked in.

A plane roared over us, and under the thundering noise, as before, the colonel leaned forward and spoke into my ear: When you come back, I want to hear what you make of this Crane boy. The Americans want him out of the way.

I thought the colonel was baiting my curiosity. I said nothing.

In Dubai, I checked into the Jumeirah Beach Hotel and began the waiting. In twenty-four hours, she would either be here or not and a decision would be made. What do we so often do when a decision is hard to make? We do nothing. We do not even wait for time to make the decision for us—waiting requires awareness and focus—and we would rather push the matter outside our attention. The word *decision* has roots in the Latin *decidere*, which means to cut off or kill off. You can see it in the word *homicide*, for instance, *to kill a man*. A decision, you see, amounts to cutting off all the options but one. And it is not because the decision is inherently complex that we allow time to step in and take charge of making the decision but because addressing ourselves to the decision to be made fills us with anxieties or distress. When we make a good decision we may enjoy the satisfaction of having made a good decision, or at least the satisfaction of having made a decision at all. But when we let time make the decision for us, we are denied such satisfactions. Instead what we feel is relief, and if we stand to consider this feeling, we see that it is the relief that comes from knowing that we are now freed from having ever to endure the anxiety of confronting that decision. It is only relief. That is what time does to us all. It kills all the lives we might have had, destroys all the worlds we might have known. And that is why a man may commit suicide and never take his own life.

There was nothing to do in Dubai but shop and there was nothing I needed that could be shopped for. The hotel had been an extravagance, which I'd sprung for only with a view to Emily joining me there, a night together in a vast building in the shape of a long sailboat, looking out over the Arabian Gulf. Opposite it, on a man-made island, was what was described as the only seven-star hotel in the world, Burj Al Arab, Tower of the Arabs, its image always in the pages of the in-flight magazine of every airline that went through the Gulf. It was a towering giant, joined to the mainland by an elevated causeway, its front adorned by a fleet of Rolls-Royces, each with only two doors. The roof had a helipad, of course, and I have seen in a magazine the aerial shot of a solitary man striking a golf ball there, if it was not a pose, sending the ball into the blue abandon of the Arabian Gulf.

I went back to my room, pulled out my laptop, and went down to one of the restaurants to do some work. Legal work can be distracting—I liked arguments and reasoning, and from time to time a case could throw up an absorbing puzzle, perhaps not as often as you might imagine if television shows were anything to go by, but the occasional puzzle there was. My work in Bangladesh mainly focused on combating corruption, some of it litigation but much of it not really legal at all. It was what they called advocacy or even activism, trying to bring about the reform of institutions. I also took on commercial cases and had one such at the time, representing a consortium of bridge builders who, contrary to the contractual schedule, had not yet been paid by the government of Bangladesh. I tried to be careful about the cases I took on, avoiding any that might bring me into conflict with my anticorruption work, and on Hassan Kabir's suggestion I informed prospective clients that I reserved the right to cease representing them without explanation. Despite this—probably on Hassan's recommendation—some clients came to me. Some of those, by the way, did not actually want me to represent them but went around Dhaka getting consultations from lawyers who would thereby be conflicted from representing adversaries. You see the same sort of thing going on in D.C. sometimes, especially if there is a relatively small number of lawyers specializing in a narrow field.

The case at hand was a simple enough breach of contract: The consortium's claim looked watertight and I didn't detect anything untoward. Besides, I took a liking to the senior executives, who flew over from the Netherlands and South Korea. When I learned about the particular stretches of river where the consortium had built their three bridges, when the maps were laid out to give me some background, I remembered that I had crossed that same river not far from where these new bridges now stood. And I remembered that as a boy all those years ago, a quarter of a century it was now, I had made my way across that river, and I thought of that other boy, the boy on the train. I expect the executives were too engrossed in their explanations to notice any shift in my countenance.

But I couldn't focus on the work. Was she really going to join me? The ability, from childhood, to exclude the cares around me, to ignore the fact of the threatening presence of my mother and father in the flat, the power to stay all things but that which was right in front of me, my books or a math problem or a legal brief, that ability I had so relied upon slipped away again.

It was only in those periods of concentration, when the self is abnegated and the mind and the subject are fused and all thought is governed by the matter at hand, determined by it, as if it is not you that engages the subject, the work, but the work itself requisitioning the tools of your mind for its inherent purpose—it was during those periods that ironically I felt most in control, that gave the whole of time—before, after, and during—an aspect of will.

I sometimes wonder if I'm missing out on something, if the days would end better, I would sleep better, I would dream better, if I turned in each night having behind me a day when I built something with my hands, tilled the soil, farmed the land, like my father, like the people in the village where I spent those boyhood years. Outside in Dubai, beneath the blur of sun, on construction sites studding this edge of sand and sea, there were thousands of men, most of them South Asian, many my age, working with their hands, pulling heavy loads, a dozen dying in the assembly of each new skyscraper, crushed by concrete or sliced by high-tension wire.

And with every strain to wrest myself from the wandering thoughts, thoughts that took me into still-darker places, with every effort to bring myself back to the table, to the screen, and to focus on the work at hand, the work that required only so much as lifting the fingers, with every exercise of mental will, there came the sense of failure.

In this state, the hours went by. I was there from late afternoon until the evening brought a surge of diners and the sight of so many cheerful people forced me out. In my room, I tried to sleep, failed, watched television, drank a whisky, watched CNN, drank another whisky, got dressed, went downstairs, and stepped outside. Dubai at night in the spring is cold. I went back inside and asked the concierge if he could lend me a coat so I could take a walk. He showed no surprise. I set off without direction, and I walked and walked in a place where there's no walking to be done, where air-conditioned cars link air-conditioned buildings, illuminated by the fiercest streetlights in the world. And I think of the whole of the city, the people who inhabit its halls, who sleep now and breathe its recycled air and whose activities by day animate this strip of land on the rim of the desert, and I remember—because this thought is always a memory—that they will all one day be gone, that every one of them will be taken outside and pushed into the sand, that in a hundred years, or two hundred years, to be certain, every human being here, every lover and loser, every captain of industry and every hotel cleaner, every mother and father and every child will be no more and that these buildings will stand, not all of them, but enough will persevere without *them*. It is a thought that stills me, that brings a moment of calm. And I walk and walk, and amid the concrete, steel, and glass, under lights burning brighter than the noonday sun, it is the knot of anxiety, always tightening and turning, for which, above all else, I resent her. There is nothing so enfeebling, so degrading, as that state of fretfulness, of helpless agitation. And I'm wondering if those whiskys I had, those whiskys now percolating in me, now short-circuiting frayed neural connections, if those whiskys should be augmented by another and then another, even though I've never been prone to drink, not even the little that is enough to unsteady me; I'm wondering now if that might bring calm, if it might give me relief. Is this how people end up on drugs and alcohol, not out of despair but because of anxiety, the anxiety that dismantles the apparatus of thought? And amid all this, not for the first time, the time after time, the time and again, because I wished it, and because mathematics remains a refuge, I thought of Gödel's Incompleteness Theorem, a theorem so enchanting and disturbing, like love, a theorem that illuminates itself all the while it casts a shadow over mathematics, the queen of the sciences, the queen because she stands aloof, so resolutely disavowing the methods of sciences, so unstintingly disparaging of what we feel, what we touch, what we taste. I first came across it in a book in the library, a lovely little volume called *What Is Mathematics?*, which I came to understand was the perfect title for the book.

In the midst of this, in the long, cold, and illuminated Dubai night, I hear the *azan* streaming out over the city. It might only be the drawl found in the Arabian Peninsula, its music drained of its color, a victim of Salafi asceticism, but there remains enough beauty to reverberate against my memory, and its timing is perfect. *Allah-hu-Akbar, Allah-hu-Akbar,* a long pause, and then piercing through the silence of expectation, a second couplet, the same words but this time drawn out forever. *Allaaaah.* And in the voice I hear sorrow and understand how close humility and sorrow are, and if my heart spoke then, it said: Lord, here I am.

Zafar fell silent and I wondered if he might cry. Many men are, of course, uncomfortable with crying, uncomfortable with their own and still more so with the crying of other men. But I felt no discomfort with the thought that he might be holding back tears because, for no reason I can properly identify, I myself felt teary. He was not looking at me but at some spot on the wall, far away, and would not have noticed my brushing away a tear or two before he emerged again from his silence.

I am on my knees, he continued, on an empty night street, in a bright city between the desert and the sea, and I remember a story I read somewhere, barely more than a paragraph, a story of uncertain authorship, appropriately enough. No, not *remember*, but *call to mind*, because sometimes we draw on what we know—a song, a memory, a poem, an image, or a story—to augment what we feel, to make exquisite our moment of private suffering and perfect it. The story is saccharine, as hokey as a cross-stitched proverb in a square of embroidery hung on the wall of a suburban home. But it reduces me to tears every time, and in the privacy of hurting, the ego and vanity borne back, I call the story to mind. A man is walking with God along a beach and, looking back, he sees two sets of footprints, as is to be expected. But he notices that in places there is only one set of footprints, and he realizes that those places coincide with the most difficult times of his life. Turning to God, he says: Lord, you said you would always be with me, but in my moments of greatest need there is only one set of prints. God replies: My dear child, I have never forsaken you, for where you see only one set of footprints, that is where I carried you.

There are churches in the eastern tradition where they say a version of the Nicene Creed that differs from the one that you hear in an English-speaking Anglican or Roman Catholic church. They do not say *We believe.* They do not even say *I believe.* Rather, they say *I trust.* I've heard that the use of the word *believe* in the English creed only reflects a failure to find an effective translation. At any rate, I cannot talk of believing. I cannot say that I believe in the god whose name shall not be uttered or whose prophet died on the cross or whose archangel commanded an illiterate man to read. I cannot even say that I believe in the one true god. But in that Dubai night, on my knees, not for the first time and most likely not for the last, I wanted to put my trust in Him. The thing of greatest worth that we can give another is our trust. Abraham's offering was not Isaac; it was trust.

At four on the following day, when we both should have been at Dubai airport checking in for a flight to London, I got an email from Emily. I'd been sitting at the computer half expecting this—half expecting nothing and not expecting her to show but nevertheless hoping she would.

I'll be there tomorrow afternoon.

Nothing more, no mention of when in the afternoon, no acknowledgment even to say that she had tried to figure out a precise time but that she couldn't confirm, no acknowledgment that it might matter to me practically—should I book tickets on the six o'clock flight to London? Will she be there in time for check-in?—no mention of when *her* flight would depart from Kabul, let alone arrive.

I stared at the message. Could there really be such lack of regard? For she had not even asked the obvious questions: which hotel I was staying in or where to meet me. Had she just assumed that I'd let her know where I was staying, or had she not given it any thought? It is a truism—is it not?—that you can say much about a person's attitude to you by the questions he or she asks you. And yet she had asked me that important question, one of the most important we can ever ask: *Will you marry me?* That is a question and not a request, not like saying to someone at a dinner party: Could you pass the salt? What if they only said yes and did nothing but continue their meal and conversation with their neighbor on the other side? *Will you marry me?* is a question because the answer is a statement about the answerer's own vision of the future, of the future *the answerer* wants, something the questioner cannot divine.

And then when tomorrow morning came, I bought an airline ticket. I had told myself and I had implied to her that I'd head back east if she didn't show that day—Good God! I'd specified the day before that—and here I was reneging on the deal I made with myself, for the ticket I bought was for a flight to London. But what if she'd had cold feet? Or would have cold feet in the next few hours? Were there not signs that her feet were cooling?—if I may take the feet image a step further.

At three in the afternoon, just two hours before my flight, at the last moment an email could have reached me, I found a message from her.

I'll leave for London tomorrow, she wrote.

And I wondered, as I often did, how else the note might have been written: *I'm leaving for London tomorrow.*

I used to fantasize about a conversation we never had in which she said: Darling, I'm overstretched and this is what my work diary looks like, and these are the uncertainties I have to factor in. Would you mind if we kept our plans tentative? I'll let you know as soon as I know I can't make it. The dream I imagined would fill me with love. In the daydream, I felt wanted, cared about, I felt thought of. Once I met Marcy for lunch in London—this was before I started seeing Emily. Marcy was visiting on business. She had brought Josie with her, who was four at the time, and in fact I had arranged a babysitter so that Marcy could go to her meetings. I arrived with a present for Josie, a toy giraffe, giraffes being something of an obsession of hers. When she took the toy, this child of four said, with her soft brown eyes looking straight into mine and in a voice containing a tiny element of surprise that almost broke my heart, You thought of me. The daydream I used to have was one in which I felt thought of by Emily. Life is short, as the old saw goes, and there is so little time on this earth, none of it, not one minute, ever to be recovered, the years of the locust restored not here if anywhere, lost time never to be found, time so dear that the respect for another's time must be the very beginning of respect, so that if a lover can't give you that first respect, then . . . well. And even though she failed to show, I caught a flight to London. Perhaps, now that I think about it, I had already coupled my indignity to the indignity of the Afghanis. Though what the hell does that really mean?

I arrived in the evening and had accepted Penelope's invitation to stay with her. From there, I called Emily's father. Penelope had informed him of the engagement, and I half expected an invitation to lunch or drinks, but when none came I asked him if we could meet. The man suggested lunch with him the next day. Because that day would be a Saturday, I expected his wife, the other Mrs. Hampton-Wyvern, to be present, not so much because most people aren't at work on weekends, but because Mrs. Hampton-Wyvern, Robin's second wife, had no occupation to speak of, so one would have thought she'd arrange her week so that she could spend time with her husband on the weekend. Is it a stretch to imagine that that's what people in happy marriages do? But when I arrived the lady was out, taking Joseph for a haircut, explained Robin, as he led me down the stairs into the kitchen on the lower ground floor. Joseph was their dog. Until then I had never met Robin without Emily there, too. The dog's haircut appointment must have been scheduled in advance, I thought. Or not.

We ate in the kitchen at a small round table by the window, where, I imagined, the two of them had their meals, in silence, with little to discuss other than Joseph, adored by the new and childless Mrs. Hampton-Wyvern. We sat at an angle to each other, facing the window onto the well of light outside. The house was like many of the houses in Kensington, the ones I had worked on with Bill and Dave, a five-story stucco building, stairs with half landings. At the back was a private communal garden, shared with the great and the good, the right sort of people. Robin's house looked like it hadn't seen a makeover since the 1970s or '80s. There was Formica in the kitchen and melamine worktops, and the paintwork on the banisters had the encrusted history of one eggshell finish on top of another, every few years, without the care to sand down first, so that the detail of the molding had disappeared under the thickening paint, brushed from memory. I don't think Robin and his wife entertained people here much; even when I went with Emily, we might all have an aperitif at the house, but we'd saunter over to one of the many fine restaurants in the neighborhood for a meal afterward. Robin wasn't short of a few bob, as Dave would have said, so that one was left with the impression that the house had never enjoyed a share of whatever love might have moved within it. Perhaps there was not enough to spare.

I pushed myself across a plate bearing two sausages in dire need of medical attention and where, divided by an expanse of porcelain, lay helpless pieces of carrot and potato boiled out of their brains. Conversation hadn't yet caught on, but there were diversions in the room to hold the eye. I thought of the summer with Dave and Bill, and I remembered the accoutrements of the English public school that I came across in those houses, the class photographs of children away at boarding school. Here, too, in the kitchen, there were some photographs of Emily and James, and, looking at the pictures on the wall, I thought of how Emily always found a way to mention someone's schooling.

As you know, I said to Robin, I went to a rather ordinary state school, but I've been thinking about these public schools. Could you explain to me how you think they differ? There was mischief in my question. I wanted to see if and how he might temper his answer in deference to my state schooling. Of course, I would not have the counterfactual to compare with—I'd never know what he might have said to someone who had in fact gone to a public school—but there might nonetheless be clues.

Robin popped some more food into his mouth, which gave him a moment to consider his response.

When his answer came, it was evident that he'd misunderstood me, but the misunderstanding itself was so telling I refrained from stepping in to correct him. What I had meant was the distinction between state schools and English public schools. But what Robin had understood by my question was how public schools differed *among themselves*.

My father told me a story once, said Robin, and I don't know if it's true but it's rather amusing. After the war, there sprang up a number of new public schools to cater to a growing middle class, and rather quickly these schools turned out very able students who went on to Oxbridge. At that time, the headmasters of the old public schools formed a headmasters' association in order, it would seem, to formulate a response to the new competition. They met, the story has it, in one of the better clubs in London—

Where they eat well?

Precisely.

And everyone's a seal pup?

I beg your pardon?

Clubbable?

Indeed.

In the course of their conversation, continued Robin, the question arose as to what the public schools were for. What did their schools prepare their pupils for? The headmasters of Eton, Westminster, Winchester, and other schools were there, as was the headmaster of Ampleforth, a Benedictine monk, since Ampleforth is run by an abbey and is, as you know, unusual for being Roman Catholic.

Surely it's not unusual for Ampleforth to be Roman Catholic? I asked.

Quite, said Robin, glossing over my second foolish witticism before continuing with the anecdote.

The headmaster of Winchester stated that he prepared his boys for lives of scholarship; the headmaster of Eton said he prepared his pupils for government; the headmaster of Westminster said he prepared them for the armed forces; and when it came his turn, the headmaster of Ampleforth said he prepared his boys for death.

I smiled appropriately and wondered if a state school head teacher would ever admit to preparing his or her students for disappointment.

I don't suppose you have any idea why I asked to see you?

Robin never responded quickly, always deliberately, as if the sentences were formed first, in the manner of trial lawyers of an older generation, so that to begin with I did not notice a new edge in his voice.

I might but I wouldn't presume, he answered.

I suppose Penelope has told you that Emily and I are now engaged.

She has.

Something in Robin's tone troubled me. Then I had that kind of flash of insight that comes suddenly and must be the product of a brain processing information received from the eyes and ears but without conscious register.

Robin, should I have asked you for your daughter's hand in marriage?

Robin did not hesitate.

Well, as a matter of fact, I rather think so. I know that might sound rather old-fashioned these days, but there it is.

Should I now?

The horse has bolted, don't you think?

Even if I didn't feel I had done anything wrong, I apologized to Robin. It is a habit, isn't it? To apologize in the face of someone's grievance, in order to assuage him perhaps or merely to smooth over relations but not with any genuine remorse. It may be that those are the only apologies that work.

May I ask you a question? I asked him.

Please do.

What kind of man did you imagine Emily would marry?

Again, there was mischief in the question. How much would class or, for that matter, race be part of the kind of man he had imagined for his daughter?

Robin again seemed to consider his response.

There's a way this might sound rather crass, but I think you'll know what I mean when I say it. I'd rather thought Emily would do well to marry a Scottish laird sort of man. I think she needs someone to rein her in. She needs firmness.

I reflected that I was as far from the Scottish laird as could be. But I felt revulsion, too. I thought of the Asian women I knew of in parts of London, the people of my parents' acquaintance, housebound and subservient, and even if my mother was not such a woman, there was always the fact that my father controlled the credit cards and bank accounts.

I had never sought to rein in Emily, and here it was being described as my failing. Of course, it was directed at me. What I had regarded as virtue was represented as weakness. To issue an ultimatum to Emily, as Penelope had once urged me to do, was, I explained then, an act of aggression, though I do not believe that now. An ultimatum, properly conceived and formulated, is not coercion, since, outside marriage, at any rate, no one has a right to another human being's loving conduct: We have the right to issue an ultimatum just as we have the right not to abide by it. I consider Robin's words now in another light. If he had meant positive actions to rein her in, then I was not the man. But I could at least have set out my terms, the conditions for love, and that would have been within my rights and within hers to accept or reject.

What do you think are the key ingredients to a successful marriage? I asked Robin.

I'm hardly in a position to advise on that, he replied.

Why?

I'm divorced.

And married again.

It would be somewhat presumptuous, he said.

Only if I hadn't asked you. I once asked my professor at Oxford what made a good mathematician. She said she wasn't sure she was in a position to answer. I told her that now that we'd got the English disclaimer of modesty out of the way, she could tell me what she actually thought. Good mathematicians, she believed, try not only to correct their mistakes but to understand *why* they made them. I asked her if she was also assuming that good mathematicians made mistakes. Everyone makes mistakes, she replied.

Robin gave his answer.

Trust and respect, he said.

He would have been content to leave it there, but I wanted to hear more.

Please go on.

Look, I'll tell you this, but on the understanding that it must not get back to Emily.

He looked at me for confirmation.

I don't know what you're going to say, I said.

I don't trust her one bit. I don't trust my own daughter. She has a lot of her mother in her, you know.

I did not say it to Robin but remembered that Penelope had said the opposite to me, that Emily had much of her *father* in her. And Penelope's psychiatrist had said the same.

She's my daughter and of course I love her and all the rest of it, but there's no beating about the bush: She is a thoroughly untrustworthy young woman.

And respect. You said trust and respect.

Yes, respect, he said, seemingly remembering the question I had first asked. Respect is vital.

After lunch I returned to Penelope's house. Penelope had obviously been waiting: She wanted to know how it had gone with Robin. I said it had been pleasant and that I'd had lunch with him. She asked if Robin's new wife had been there and I told her that Robin and I had had a nice chat alone, adding that it was good to get to know him a little better. I was unforthcoming, because if I'd learned anything from the good Dr. Villier it was not to become entangled in Penelope's relationship with her ex-husband. When she saw that there wasn't much more to get out of me, she moved the conversation on.

I told some friends about the engagement, she said.

Oh, really?

I told Agatha and she was over the moon.

Agatha was Emily's godmother.

I also told Aisha.

How did she take it?

What a funny way to put it!

What?

How did she take it?

Well, how did she respond?

Zafar, you're no fool, are you? Not the least bit wet behind the ears, I'll say. As a matter of fact, when I told her, her first words were to ask me how I felt about it.

And how do you feel about that?

I'm overjoyed, of course. Absolutely delighted.

I'm glad and thank you, but I meant how did you feel about Aisha asking you how you felt about Emily and me getting engaged? But now that I spell it out, it seems a bit of a mad question.

Come now. Let's not be coy. Aisha is a snob and that's all there is to it. I told Emily's grandmother the news. She was delighted. You've not met her, have you?

No, I have not.

I have to say that it does seem odd. Emily's very close to her grandmother.

There had been an adjustment in Penelope's attitude toward me. It was the slightest thing, really, no marked change in her behavior, but I felt an openness that had not been there before. I liked the new feeling. It was unfamiliar, but I believe it was in its elements akin to the feeling of family. And perhaps because of that feeling, I shared with Penelope something that Emily had told me, which though Emily had not asked me to keep in confidence I had recognized then as something Emily would not want me to pass on.

I told Penelope that I had once asked Emily why she would not introduce me to her grandmother. You speak of her often, I said to Emily, but we've never met and you see her frequently. Obviously, there's no *obligation* to introduce me, but it's hard to believe it's just slipped your mind.

What did Emily say? asked Penelope.

She said something that unnerved me a little, if I'm honest.

What did she say?

She said that she was afraid her grandmother was a bit racist.

Oh, for heaven's sake! cried Penelope. We're going to see her right away. Emily?

No, her grandmother. Actually, Emily as well. She'll be here this evening.

You spoke to her?

Just before you came in.

We'll all see her grandmother tomorrow. I'll arrange it now.

Penelope had no need to hear anything more and left the room. I heard her climb the stairs. She preferred to make telephone calls from the study.

Late in the evening, Penelope and I drove out to RAF Brize Norton. Emily was apparently hitching a ride on a military transport plane. It was already late and we were both tired, so we did not talk much on the drive.

I felt a familiar anxiety about seeing Emily again, the fear of seeing her disposition changed, the fear that she would do or say something that would make me question her sincerity. I want to be able to say that there was another source of anxiety, something more noble for its concern with matters outside myself, but that would be a lie on every front. When I sat in the car in silence, my mind did indeed wander in a way that on its face had little to do with the thing between Emily and me, but only on its face. Love and politics had been some time in the convergence.

Emily was not an instrument of the military intervention, not a stated one, that is, not there in the service of the military aims of the invading forces. So what then to think of her hopping a ride on an RAF plane? Yet what is military intervention without the promise of reconstruction? What do we make of taking with one hand if there's a promise that the other is readying to give? And then who is in the service of whom?

When we arrived at Brize Norton, a soldier at the gate directed us to the Control of Entry building. There I explained to another soldier that I did not have my passport or my driver's license with me, hoping to avoid the ignominies of security checking that I imagined attended going beyond this point. He said I could remain on the air base and wait in that room but I would have to undergo a search first. I was led away into another room, where an official in civilian clothes searched me, more methodically than I've been searched at civilian airports, I might add. I returned to the waiting room, where Penelope was still in her seat. I didn't ask if she'd been searched, too.

Emily walked in, smiling at us both. Her shoulders rose as she raised her arms and wrapped them around my neck.

The following day, the Sunday, we visited her grandmother.

We should tell her about the engagement before she hears from someone else, said Penelope.

Of course, Mother.

We'll go now.

Shouldn't we arrange a time? Not appear unannounced, I mean.

She's your grandmother, dear, not the Lord Chancellor.

Will she not be at church?

Evidently Penelope had not told her that she'd already shared the news with her grandmother. I felt a little uncomfortable about being conscripted into the pretense, however benign Penelope might think it was.

She's not going to church today, darling. Now let's get a move on.

Emily was silent on the drive and again I felt a gulf opening up.

Congratulations. I'm delighted to hear the wonderful news, said the good baroness, not letting on that she already knew.

If she had a formidable reputation as a stalwart of Conservative politicians, if she had merited the sobriquet "the Dragon," then all that was for a persona outside her home, as far as I could tell. With me she was the model of a charming grandmother, pleased by the news of her granddaughter's engagement. There was nothing in her bearing toward me but good manners and apparent friendliness. What more can we ask for? It was a damn sight more, I thought, than my parents would show to Emily.

Her husband, Emily's grandfather, sat in an armchair, staring at us with a broad smile. I'd met him once before, soon after Emily and I started seeing other. He'd dropped in on Penelope on his own. Then he had been lucid, if a little bit the image of an old man most comfortable in the memories of his youth. But in a few years, he had deteriorated sharply, dementia plundering his brain, leaving him in this state of passive marvel. He said nothing other than to ask if I'd come by car. When he asked the third time, I smiled and I suppose everyone else took my smile for a sign of sympathy. I confess that I was smiling because the thought crossed my mind of giving him a different answer.

I don't suppose you've set a date yet, the baroness asked, looking at Emily and me.

There are a few obstacles still, I replied.

The moment I said it, I thought it a rather churlish thing to say and wanted to take it back.

Obstacles are meant to be overcome, she said cheerfully. She offered tea.

That evening, as I lay in bed with Emily, in those few moments of stillness before we fall asleep, when a double bed might widen and the sudden loneliness accommodate our private thoughts, I remembered that Robin had never congratulated me. He had mentioned trust and respect, but had he meant to share an observation? Did he intend to mean something specific, that I did not trust Emily and that Emily did not respect me? I looked at Emily next to me, already fast asleep.

She wanted to go back to Kabul in two days, and she wanted me to come with her, to show off her new fiancé, she'd said. And again, there was something about her of the girl who'd looked forward to engagement and wedding and all the ritual. Yet even as I regarded her, with infinite tenderness—my fiancée, my wife-to-be—part of me suspected I would have to wait some time for her to make it down the length of the aisle. I had waited for Emily so many times, waited for her to show up, waited for an explanation of why she was late, waited and waited. The easy analysis is that all of it had really been waiting to get married, but I think now that what I had been waiting for was for Emily to change. Does respect require us to take our lovers as they are? Take them or leave them?

Might Robin have been right after all, not in the thesis that what Emily as a person needed was someone to rein her in—a Scottish laird—but that if she was to have a *successful* marriage, it would have to be with someone who did so rein her in? It seems, though, that for many of our age a successful marriage is not the highest priority. Don't you think?

21

On Formally Undecidable Propositions or Waiting

Rape of woman or man.

[1] It is an offence for a man to rape a woman or another man.

[2] A man commits rape if—

   (a) he has sexual intercourse with a person (whether vaginal or anal) who at the time of the intercourse does not consent to it; and

   (b) at the time he knows that the person does not consent to the intercourse or is reckless as to whether that person consents to it.

   —Section 1 of the Sexual Offences Act 1956, England

I seem to have loved you in numberless forms, numberless
   times . . .
In life after life, in age after age forever.
                         —Rabindranath Tagore, "Unending Love,"
                              translated by William Radice

To be rooted is perhaps the most important and least recognized need of the human soul. It is one of the hardest to define.
   —Simone Weil, *The Need for Roots*, translated by Arthur Wills

The story of Bangladesh was unique in one respect. For the first time in history the rape of women in war, and the complex aftermath of mass assault, received serious international attention. The desperate need of Sheik Mujibur Rahman's government for international sympathy and financial aid was part of the reason; a new feminist consciousness that encompassed rape as a political issue and a growing, practical acceptance of abortion as a solution to unwanted pregnancy were contributing factors of critical importance. And so an obscure war in an obscure corner of the globe, to

Western eyes, provided the setting for an examination of the "unspeakable" crime. For once, the particular terror of unarmed women facing armed men had a full hearing.
—Susan Brownmiller, *Against Our Will: Men, Women and Rape*

If I now regard much of Zafar's story as a kind of defense, this understanding came only after I'd heard him through, and, even then, only after I turned it all over in my mind. Unlike the courtroom trial, where a charge is laid out in the beginning, it seems to me that Zafar held off for as long as he could what exactly this defense was for. But of course the moment had to come eventually.

As for judging the effectiveness of his case, I do not feel equal to the task, not because we all live in glass houses, but because I am implicated. Indeed, it may be that the reason I view our conversations as a search for absolution, an invitation to a reckoning, is that I have a hand in it all, and I find *myself* asking: How far into the consequences of an act can one be held responsible? How much do other causes relieve one of one's part? Or am I, as Zafar might say, the cellist who tries to hide his error behind the violinist's?

The news reports of Crane's death were not as extensive as those coming two years later, in 2004, of the death of Pat Tillman, who, after 9/11, left a career in professional football to join the U.S. Army.

According to the army's official version in the immediate aftermath, Tillman was killed in an ambush outside of the village of Sperah about twenty-five miles southwest of Khost, near the Pakistan border. It later emerged that Tillman had actually been killed by so-called friendly fire, a fact that U.S. officials had knowingly suppressed.

Some time before his own death, Crane had left the Marines—that much I'd gathered from the reports. But what the newspapers did not explain was what he was doing in Afghanistan. It turns out that Crane, by his own word, as reported by Zafar, had joined a private military contractor and was even working toward starting his own outfit. The Crane I knew certainly had the character for that sort of business, but what Zafar has told me about the circumstances leading to Crane's death leaves me unsure of what Crane was actually doing. Moreover, even after taking in the whole of Zafar's story, I still have doubts about what Zafar's role had been.

Before returning to Kabul, Zafar first flew to Islamabad with Emily. When they emerged from customs, he explained, Emily went off to talk to a UN official stationed inside the airport about UN flights to Kabul. In the few minutes she stepped away, said Zafar, Mohsin Khalid, the colonel's nephew and K2 mountaineer, appeared by my side, as if materializing from nowhere.

Should you need to stay in Islamabad, explained Khalid, the colonel would be delighted to host you again. Otherwise, if you wish, we can arrange for you to take a seat on one of the daily military flights to Kabul. There's one in two hours. You'll be in Kabul by one p.m.

Before I could thank him for the offer of help, Khalid had turned and left.

When Emily returned, she told me that there was only one seat on the UN flight and that the next scheduled flight was for the following day. Our plan—which was Emily's plan, since she had insisted on it— was to arrive in Kabul together and for her to introduce me to the people she worked with as her fiancé. But at Islamabad airport, after taking a few calls, she evidently resolved to get to Kabul quickly and so take the only seat. She suggested I take the following day's plane.

At Bagram air base,* I was met on the tarmac by an American soldier who said he had orders to take me to AfDARI.

From whom? I asked.

Pardon me, sir?

Who gave you the orders?

My superior, sir.

Do you take orders from anyone else?

I'm sorry, sir?

Do you know who I am?

No, sir.

Let's go.

---

* Zafar did not say if he had taken the Pakistani military flight that day or the UN flight on the following, but from his subsequent exposition, it can be concluded that he flew the same day.

It was just as well the soldier and I passed the journey without exchanging another word. The soldier needed all the focus he could get his hands on: Military personnel had orders to avoid slowing at road junctions and never to stop. The driving was crazy.

At AfDARI, the soldier barely let me step out before speeding off.

Inside I was greeted by Suaif. I asked after his family, in particular his boy, before being pointed toward the old room in the guesthouse.

Suleiman was already there.

How have you been? I asked.

I'm fine. I have the camera. You have a plan, don't you?

I'm fine, too, I said, picking the edge of the curtain to look out the window. Let's go for a walk, I added. I like walking.

Outside the gates, Suleiman walked briskly. He led the way. We crossed the road, reached the end of the block, and turned the corner before speaking again.

Suleiman was agitated. He spoke about his country, his *beloved country*, how it was being ruined and there was no way forward for people like him. He spoke with such animation and energy, and with such apparent disregard for maintaining a continuity of exposition, that I even asked myself if his mental faculties had not somehow been bent. When I recalled the Suleiman I had left scarcely one week earlier, the voice of the young man before me seemed to belong to another. Yet even so, I believed I had the impression of catching a glance—if that is the right way to describe the fleeting detection of certain sounds and gestures—of how that young man might have been transformed. I did not follow everything he said, but I had the sense of someone who was in the throes of seeing the world in a new way, one who might once have made observations, drily, without emotion, with cold disregard for meaning, but who having now surveyed the amassed data was forced into certain conclusions, raging conclusions that could not be ignored, discounted, or minimized.

Was an envelope delivered today? I interjected.

You mean for Crane?

I do.

No.

The jeep didn't come?

No.

Are you sure you didn't miss it?

It didn't come—or it hasn't come yet. It's two hours overdue.

That's unusual, right?

Right.

And Crane?

He's not been here.

Tell me something. Does the jeep come from the same direction?

I don't know where it comes from.

Does it come from the east or the west? When it stops outside the gate, which way does it point?

It points in the direction away from Suaif's sentry box.

Always?

Always.

And Crane's car?

Land Cruiser.

Where does he park?

By the gate.

Right outside?

A little farther on.

Even farther away from the sentry box?

Yes.

Always?

Yes.

Pointing away from Suaif's sentry box?

Yes.

Always?

Yes.

Good.

Why do you always ask this question? You did it last time also.

What question?

Always?

Always what?

Why do you always ask *always*?

I'm trying to figure out what can we rely on.

I see, he said.

But Suleiman didn't look like he'd understood.

Epistemology without whisky is like a fish without a bicycle, I added.

Excuse me?

Is Maurice here?

You mean right now?

I nodded.

He's out but he'll be back later this afternoon.

Good. Where's the driver?

Mr. Maurice's driver, he's with Mr. Maurice.

But I saw a car in the courtyard?

AfDARI has three.

Is there anyone else who drives?

There's another driver.

He's here?

Yes.

Good.

Suleiman listened carefully as I explained how we would get him a few minutes to see and, if possible, photograph the documents in the next delivery for Crane. Suleiman had mentioned that sometimes the men in the jeep handed him the parcel but only when they saw that Crane was already there at AfDARI. The plan involved getting the men to see Crane but preventing Crane from seeing the jeep, and then counting on the men handing the documents to Suleiman. The gate was central to all this, and Suleiman would have to get a driver to move toward it at a critical moment in order to force the jeep to move aside and out of view of Crane. If the jeep moved forward, however, the driver would still be able to see Crane side on, provided I managed to get Crane to come with me to the guesthouse. Crane, however, wouldn't be able to see them without turning around. Timing was everything.

When I finished, so as to confirm we were on the same page, I had Suleiman explain everything back to me.

I waited for Crane on the veranda outside the AfDARI office. The plan might not work if Maurice arrived before Crane; it wouldn't work if Crane arrived at the same time as the jeep; in fact, there were umpteen ways it wouldn't work and only one way it would. I looked at my watch before opening the copy of Graham Greene's *The Quiet American* I had brought with me and settled in for the wait.

Fourteen minutes later, Crane's voice—*Let me in, old man!*—came booming across the courtyard over the sound of traffic behind him. The gate gave out a screech as it was opened and shut.

From the steps of the veranda, I beckoned Crane to come over.

Hello, big Z. How are you? Crane looked genuinely pleased to see me.

Just fine. And you?

His handshake nearly ripped my arm off.

Spiffing. Isn't that what you Brits say? Hey, Sully buddy!

Crane gave Suleiman a thumping pat on the back.

Do you think we could get some tea? I asked Suleiman, who'd appeared on cue.

And, turning to Crane, Unless you want a beer?

You guys have *beer*? Crane asked Suleiman.

We don't, replied Suleiman.

Forgive my faux pas, I said to Suleiman. Tea's fine.

Suleiman left.

We Brits, I added for Crane, are known to drink a cup of tea from time to time.

There's that British humor again. You guys kill me.

Crane, there's a rather serious matter I need to discuss with you.

Oh, yes?

Why don't we sit down? I suggested.

Tell me what you know about Bagram, I said to him.

Why? What are you hearing?

I'm supposed to meet up with the UN rapporteur in a couple of days, and I still haven't got any word from them about when I can visit.

What I didn't tell Crane was that since the last time I was in Kabul I hadn't made any further effort to contact them. I needed to keep Crane waiting.

There's nothing to tell—I mean as far as I know. Sure, there's some kind of detention facility, but that's about all I've heard. That's an open secret, he said.

I probed Crane for a few minutes before Suleiman reappeared.

We've run out of tea. I'm just going to buy some, okay?

Fine, I said.

I understood that the jeep had just come, a little too soon after Crane's arrival, and that Suleiman was improvising a sign for me to get Crane to the guesthouse, since there would not be time now for even a sip before the next stage. A few moments later, the AfDARI car in the courtyard fired up and the gate let out its shrill sound.

Crane, let's go to the guesthouse, I said, motioning my head in the direction of the door to the office as if to suggest the veranda wasn't private enough. An unplanned bonus: Crane will assume Maurice is here, and that he would take delivery of the letter.

I hear you, said Crane.

I glanced toward the gate. I was counting on not being able to see the jeep from the steps of the veranda. The AfDARI car was waiting as the gate opened. Suleiman did not appear to be in it. The jeep must have reversed to let the car pass and, in so doing, had moved out of view behind the wall. I had to keep Crane from looking that way but make sure anyone in the jeep could see him from the back.

I've been talking to Colonel Mushtaq.

It's strange: I can remember that Crane didn't react right away. Some part of me must have registered that. I realized only later that the delay ought to have puzzled me. At the time, my focus was on keeping his attention away from the gate.

Sikander Ali Mushtaq, I said. Do you know him?

I know *of* him, of course.

Of course?

He's high up in military intelligence. Have to do your homework in a place like this, buddy.

What kind of place would that be? I asked.

We were nearing the guesthouse.

Goddamn war zone, he replied.

After you, I said, making sure to stop on the side of him away from the road so that as he looked at me he would not see the jeep. I saw the door of the sentry box open. Suleiman would be going to collect the envelope.

Inside my room, I walked over to the door at the back, taking out a packet of cigarettes.

Do you smoke, Crane?

That stuff'll kill you.

When in a war zone, I said. Mind if *I* do?

Go ahead.

Let's go out back. I sleep in here and don't like the smoke, I said, opening the back door.

We stepped outside and I pulled the door shut.

Crane was squeezed between me and the dead black tree. He moved around the bush to where there was more space. I stepped nearer to the wall. If Crane moved too far over, he might catch a glimpse of the jeep. I needed him closer to the wall and to me. Lowering my voice, I said: Mushtaq had something interesting to say.

Excuse me? replied Crane, obligingly moving closer to me, closer to the wall, well away from the line of sight to the jeep.

Mushtaq seems to think you're up to something and asked me if I'd find out.

And what did you say?

So you *are* up to something.

We're all up to something, Zafar. Everybody here is up to something. I could ask you the same question. Why are you here? Why not wait until the UN rapporteur gets here, why not come here with him and then go to Bagram? You know they'll let you all in then.

Why do you think they haven't responded?

Maybe they don't trust you. Maybe they think you might be working for the enemy. Heck! Maybe you are.

Now which enemy would that be, Crane?

What exactly did you want to ask me, Zafar?

As a matter of fact, I didn't want to ask you anything. I wanted to tell you something. That's all. I wanted to share something with you. Nothing I don't know is any of my business, but what I know is what I know and I just wanted to tell you what I know. You do with it what you will. That's your business.

That *sounded* like English—

You understand I'm not asking you anything?

Go on.

You weren't born yesterday, Crane. You know your reputation. I rather suspect you even cultivate it—or part of it, at any rate. I think you like being thought of as a cad, a noisy, rambunctious cad.

Boy, you're straight out of the nineteenth century, aren't you?

But there's a rumor, something you'll want to hear.

Crane looked at me intently and I let time draw out over us, cocoon us from what was going on in the guesthouse.

You do plan to tell me, don't you? he asked presently.

Apparently, you've been driving north to C—— every week, I said, and stopped there.

Again I let time draw out.

Driving is a crime?

Funny you mention crime. I never practiced extradition law, but, if I remember it correctly, there's a principle you might be interested to hear about.

Not if it means you don't get to the point.

Oh, I'm getting to the point. In fact, all of this is the point. In a way I've arrived at the point. In general, a man can't be extradited from country A to country B if the crime he's accused of committing in country B is not a crime in country A.

I went to law school, interjected Crane.

Excuse me, Crane. Did you study extradition law?

No.

Then I'll carry on, if I may. So if, for example, he's accused of drinking alcohol in public in Saudi Arabia, say, where doing so is an offense, then when he's in Germany, say, he can't be extradited back to Saudi Arabia, because drinking alcohol in public is not an offense in Germany. Of course, this parallelism shouldn't be taken too far. You asked if driving was a crime. Driving on the left side of the road in the States is indeed an offense, whereas in good old Blighty it isn't. Quite the opposite: It's mandatory. But that doesn't mean you won't get extradited from Britain to the U.S. simply because the alleged offense isn't an offense in Britain. The allegation has to be properly characterized, you see. What about the Foreign Corrupt Practices Act? Not quite about extradition but still a good question. There the United States is claiming extraterritorial jurisdiction. As an American citizen, in certain matters one has to behave overseas. You can see what a fine thing the FCPA has been when you consider that corruption has been all but rooted out of American oil and arms companies. But extraterritorial jurisdiction has nothing to do with whether country A is obliged to hand over someone to country B. What matters is whether what's alleged by B to have happened in B would, mutatis mutandis, constitute an offense in A.

What the hell is going on here?

I'm getting to it.

Zafar, if I'm not being accused of committing a crime on U.S. territory, then all this shit about extradition is irrelevant.

That's a good point.

Are you? he asked.

Am I what?

Are you accusing me of some crime?

In the United States? I responded.

Yes.

No, I replied.

Well, why the hell are we talking about this?

You're right, Crane. I'm prevaricating. Fact is, I'm uncomfortable.

Just say it. What's my reputation? Don't imagine I haven't heard it all.

Thank you, Crane. You're quite right. I'm sure there's nothing to it. Are you going to dogfights?

Crane looked at me, apparently quite genuinely puzzled.

Are you fucking serious?

You're not? I asked.

You're out of your mind, he responded.

You're not going to dogfights? I asked.

Is that what you wanted to tell me? That Colonel Mushtaq said I was going to dogfights? I haven't got time for this. *You* haven't got time for this.

Crane took a step toward the back door of the guesthouse.

And the girl? I asked.

Crane stopped. He was now right next to me.

What are you talking about?

I told you, Crane. I'm just talking about rumors, doubtless untrue, but you should know or at least you might want to know. We have a mutual friend, Crane. You could say I'm doing this as a favor to him. Do you want me to stop talking?

Go on.

Let's go inside, I said stubbing out the cigarette on the ground.

We were both inside, the back door shut behind us, when I resumed.

This is, as you put it, a war zone, and what happens in Kabul stays in Kabul, but only if you're discreet. The fact that others know could mean trouble.

What others?

I started to make as if I were pacing, as if I were avoiding the question. I moved toward the door, the one that led into the small hallway that went out into the courtyard.

Others, Crane, I said. I turned and paced again.

Fuck this.

Crane, you need friends here. You don't care what the Afghanis think. I can get that. But you can't afford to become a liability to the Americans, to your own.

Why the fuck should I care about stupid rumors?

What if it's more than rumors? What if there's evidence?

There was a knock.

I went to the door and opened it.

Yes! I shouted.

My back was to Crane. He might have caught at most Suleiman's face but would at least have heard Suleiman's voice.

I'm very sorry to disturb but there's a letter—

Thanks! I shouted and grabbed the envelope with both hands. With my back to him still, Crane would have heard an envelope being ripped open.

Suleiman exclaimed, No, sir! It's for Mr. Crane!

Thank you, Suleiman, I said, shutting the door.

I turned and walked toward Crane, handing him the torn envelope.

Excuse me. Where was I, Crane?

I've no idea, he replied.

Look. Here's the deal. Too many people know about the girl. If it gets out any further, at best they'll force you out of the country. At worst . . .

At worst what?

There's a war on, Crane; there's too much to lose. A lot of people need the Americans to stay here—can you imagine how much money's at stake? Actually, you probably can. These people don't need the scandal of a U.S. senator's son screwing an Afghani girl. The line between deniable asset and bloody liability is convenience. Your death is nothing to them. Nothing. I hate to say it, but from where they stand it's the neatest solution. Clean, upright, square-jawed all-American boy fighting for his country.

Are you really looking out for me? Crane asked.

He smiled. He seemed genuinely tickled by the thought.

We have a mutual friend, don't we? Call it loyalty.

Crane extended his hand and took a step toward me.

How long are you here? he asked.

As long as it takes.

Listen, I've got to go now, but can we hook up in the next day or two? I want to talk to you about something.

A girl? I asked, half joking.

No! No! No! I'll tell you later. So long.

Yes. So long, I replied.

Through the window I saw Crane walk across the courtyard to the AfDARI office.

God! You gave me a fright.

Suleiman had appeared from nowhere, announcing his presence with a tap on my shoulder.

Documents? I asked him.

Yes.

Did you take the pictures?

Yes.

The DVR? Where's the recording of Crane?

Suleiman pulled a flash drive out of his pocket, handed it to me, and was out the door.

A minute later, through the window, I saw Crane emerge from the office and I stepped out into the courtyard. Crane came over to me.

Why don't we meet for coffee tomorrow morning at ten? he said.

I saw something decent in Crane at that moment. I think it was a wish, even a need, to be on good terms with people.

I don't know if I've offended you, I said. I'm sorry if I have.

Hell, no! You Brits and your apologies.

How about Café Europa?

You've found the expat joints pretty quick, he said.

I pick things up.

See you tomorrow.

Listen, you're not going to the UN bar tonight? I asked him.

No. Why?

I thought I might go for a drink.

Me and my boys over at the American embassy are watching last night's big game. God bless the VCR. As a matter of fact, I'm heading there now. We'll get some beers in before the game. Say, you don't—

No thanks. Not my thing.

Not your cup of tea, eh? Cricket's the game for you chaps. Well, cheerio, then! said Crane, giving me a big smile as he walked off. I thought of a large, happy dog. That is how I remember Crane now.

Suleiman was standing on the porch and would have heard everything.

At nine forty-five the following morning, I was about to set off when the boy whose job it was to clean the rooms appeared at the door. He handed me a telephone message from Emily: *I'm coming over in just a minute.* I remained in my room. I asked the boy if there was a way to get a message to Café Europa—to Crane—saying I'd be late. The boy didn't understand.

And then the waiting began. Just a minute, she said. I have to tell you about the waiting, because if there is a proximate cause, it was the waiting. But how can *waiting*, which is no action, which is the definition of nothing happening, only the interval between things, between two waves of the sea—how can nothing beget something? When I had last left Kabul, only the previous week, I made my way to Dubai, where I received an email from her saying: *I'll be there tomorrow afternoon.* That was all. No other information, leaving me in suspended animation. But which flight? Kabul to Islamabad first? Or flying direct to the U.A.E.? But don't the direct flights come in at Sharjah and not Dubai? But that adds more time because you have to drive to Dubai. So little information to go on, and perhaps that was the point, not to engage any further, to avoid explanations in order to avoid anything that might approach an apology, because to apologize, and accordingly to explain, would be to acknowledge that she was letting me down. It was never a *refusal* to apologize, for a refusal or anything that appeared to be a refusal implied, let me repeat, a recognition that there was something that arguably required an apology or even an explanation. No refusal but, rather, behaving as if there were nothing to explain, not one word required. Did my failure to confront this make me complicit? An enabler, they call him, the friend who invites his buddy the recovering alcoholic to the pub. I remembered the first time, so long ago now, when she arrived at the Inns of Court, at the library, to meet me for lunch. Two hours late but not a word of apology or explanation. And I made the excuses to myself, not for the lateness but for the failure to explain, for I told myself that *she* must believe that *she* is not important enough to *me* that something even approximating punctuality would matter to me. A contortion to box out the reality, the only self-respecting conclusion, which was the reverse, namely, that I was not important enough to her to be given an apology, let alone to be punctual for. And again and again it happened, in one way or another. Did I do the same to her? I began to ask. After all, I know that there is a wall around me and that I, too, am seldom confronted, rarely taken to task. Did my memory spare me awareness of my own failures to abide by undertakings I had given? Was I also leaving in my wake a litter of broken promises? So it was that my notebooks became diaries, too, recording not just broken commitments but also every representation made by each of us, upon which the other might reasonably rely. For all the tedious familiarity with her unreliability and for all my own deluded accommodations of it, there was hurt and there was anger, as there must be to be disregarded by someone you loved, who you believed loved you, who previous indications—engagement!—suggested loved you. And then there was the other waiting, the waiting I had loved, the seven weeks from the day she told me she was pregnant. It was an active waiting, not limbo but a time for the imagination to take up materials from the landscape of memory and set to work. And at the end of that waiting, nothing. Nothing to justify the waiting. No conversation, no talking, only nothing.

It's easy to keep a clear head when thinking about something whose existence is outside you, easy to think clearly about mathematics, for instance. But what can be more important to think about than something that is so overwhelmed by emotions that the act of thinking becomes hard? Yet how do you look at something that clouds your vision? I have been full of anger my whole life, and if I've seemed to you or anyone as having been as calm as the kind of thinking that mathematics demands, then it is only because the anger had yet to find expression. The lexicographer is always behind the progress of language, his account by definition in arrears.

In that AfDARI guesthouse, I thought of all the waiting I had done and felt something rising in me. Most people have no need to break free of their inheritance. But those who need to break free of their past and have the means to do so will not escape the requirement of violence.

At ten thirty, I walked over to the gate. The driver and Suaif were standing about, talking. I wanted to be driven to Café Europa, but first I asked them if they'd seen Suleiman.

Suleiman has not come into work, replied Suaif.

Yes, but have you seen him?

He did not come in today, sir. There is a message for you.

What is it?

Your meeting this morning was postponed.

When did he give you this message?

He is not working today.

All right. When did you plan to tell me about this message?

Sir, I was told to give it to you only when you came into the courtyard and not to disturb you with it before.

Did he tell you why he wasn't coming to work?

No, sir.

I asked the driver to take me to Café Europa.

Suaif interjected: There has been an IED incident in Shar-e-Naw. Americans were killed. A few soldiers. It is difficult to go there now.

Only American soldiers?

And civilians.

Anyone injured?

Five Afghanis. No one else, sir, he added.

Café Europa, is it in Shar-e-Naw? I asked.

Yes.

I want to go there.

It is very difficult, said Suaif.

I insisted and got into the car.

As we approached Shar-e-Naw, we were stopped at a checkpoint and told we couldn't take the car any farther. I took directions from the driver, asked him to wait, and set off on foot.

First came the sound. People crying, not women but men, a wailing, the sound of cries for God, *Hai-Allah*, groans, and American voices on megaphones. Afghanis and ISAF soldiers scrambling. Then I turned a corner. If Crane was in that café, there was no way he could have survived. There was destruction everywhere, rubble and dust, boulders of concrete and a crater in front of the wrecked façade of a building, the Café Europa signage still hanging from a corner. I continue to remember that sign, a square of sheet metal with hand-painted text in blue and gold, and have wondered if our eyes are compelled to fix on something incongruous, seeking an emblem of the totality of what we see, of the shattered image that we cannot assimilate. We orient ourselves by metaphor, like that ghostly building left standing after Hiroshima, all of eternity in a grain of sand. This is how we avoid talking about blood and bones, and the shredded ends of limbs, and the head with open eyes, and crying men, grown men, my father's age, men with beards, lifting wreckage to find the dead. I felt sick, my gut convulsing like a caught fish. But what I remember most vividly is a sensation behind my eyes, an extraordinary pressure pushing my eyeballs out, as if they were no longer mine, as if my body were rejecting them. Did I want to cry or did I want to keep myself from crying? I wanted both.

I've heard it said that a sign a person is in shock is that he or she fixates on something trivial. The woman who's just heard her husband was caught up in a fatal traffic accident becomes obsessed with the lack of milk in the house, even when the police officer has said he takes his coffee black. I cannot claim I was in shock: I was too possessed of my faculties of reason for that, too much already concerned with precisely when various things had happened. Besides, to claim shock would be too cheap and easy an excuse for what was to come. Certainly, if I had been a better man, I would have been thinking then of Crane, making more of an effort to find him, I would have looked upon the carnage and reflected on man's inhumanity to man and all the rest of it. But instead, shock or no shock, my mind had fixed on a problem of timing. Could it really be that I had escaped certain death, perhaps by a matter of minutes, simply because I had waited for Emily, and Emily had been late? She knew I was already in Kabul. Flights in and out were infrequent, and when she left me in Islamabad, I was, as far as she knew, getting the next day's flight. How did she know I was already here? And did she know more? Did she . . . did she know about the bomb? How could she? Or was it just her tardiness that had saved me? The very thing that I had detested, the quality of her character that caused me so much anguish, the plain disrespect in missing the appointed time, time and time again, and without a word of explanation let alone apology. I always hated myself for waiting, hated myself for not making something of having waited. Until then, it had left me feeling sullied, ashamed instead of being angry with her. And now I was not prepared to accept that she had dillydallied and therefore I had lived. Not prepared to accept that a combination of her lack of respect and my self-demeaning waiting could have saved my life. At that moment, I would sooner have accepted that she'd had some conscious hand in it all. And because my mind had fixed on her responsibility, it had grasped that timing, as in all things, was of the essence. What took place and when? Who knew what when? A chain of events leading back to what?

I approached a soldier to ask what time the bombing had happened, but he didn't seem to understand.

Get back! he replied, an American. He added something in fragmentary Pashto before repeating the English slowly.

My friend is in there, I shouted.

I don't care if your mother is in there. Get back! he yelled, this time gesturing with his assault rifle.

Back at AfDARI, I asked Suaif if anyone had asked for me or if anyone had left a message with him.

Miss Emily? asked Suaif.

Anyone.

No, replied Suaif.

She didn't show up?

Please?

She didn't come here?

No, he replied.

Suaif's answer had me wondering if perhaps Emily had had no intention of showing up. Could it be that all she'd wanted by sending me the message was to delay my going to the café? And there, once more, I was making allowances for her. Even then.

Is there a phone in the office? I asked.

Maybe she called, he responded.

Is there a phone in the office?

Yes.

Is there another phone here in AfDARI?

No.

I crossed the courtyard and entered the AfDARI building. The door to Maurice's office was shut. I knocked but there was no answer. I walked in to find Maurice and the woman he'd been screwing. She was putting on her coat.

Do you mind? snapped Maurice.

No, I don't. Is this your handwriting? I asked him, showing him the note about Emily coming over.

I beg your pardon.

Is this your handwriting? I repeated. I was furious with this man, to a degree that cannot be explained by the little that I knew of him. What I was after was whether there was anything else in the exchange between him and Emily that wasn't written down, anything that could help me figure out what had happened, and how it was that I'd managed to evade the bombing by minutes.

Get out, shouted the Frenchman, raising his hand and pointing to the door.

I gripped the man's hand and pushed it back on the wrist. My fingers interlocked with his, and even in those circumstances, or because of them, it felt strangely intimate. Maurice let out a yelp and his knees buckled as I pushed his hand back past his shoulder and with my free hand pulled his elbow toward me. With his other hand he gripped the edge of the desk to stop himself from going over altogether.

I pulled open a drawer, rummaged about, took out a notebook, opened it, and held it at an angle to the light from the window. The message from Emily was written on the same notebook.

Who called? I asked Maurice.

The woman made to move for the door.

Did you expect me? I asked, turning to her.

I repeated, Did you expect me?

No, she replied meekly.

Are you expecting the man standing outside?

The woman shook her head but otherwise didn't move. She wasn't going anywhere now.

I asked Maurice: Who called you?

Emily, he replied.

On your own line?

We have only one line.

Cell phone?

The local network is disabled for everyone except UNAMA staff.

Satphone?

We don't have one.

What did she say?

Exactly what I wrote.

Do I seem like someone who's going to wait while you piss about? What did she say?

I pushed his hand. He let out a squeal of pain. Maurice, this feeble man, had become the object of my anger. Isn't that the way—our emotions from one thing attach to the next? Think of those pop-science articles in magazines, where the journalist first tells you about the scientist as a child, the irresistibly endearing little boy or girl, so that a page later you find yourself first rooting for the adult and then, irrelevantly, his or her ideas. I was angry all right, but in the end perhaps Maurice's only mistake was to be present. I was not prepared to accept that any part of everything that had happened was accident or without someone's design. Remember that Maurice had sometimes taken receipt of parcels and envelopes meant for Crane. Or so Suleiman had told me. Remember, too, that there was only one phone at AfDARI, as Suaif had told me, and that it was in Maurice's office. So what had Emily and he exchanged on the phone when she left her message? Something that might shed the smallest light on what had happened? Most important of all, I wanted to hear something that would confirm that it wasn't Emily's mere lateness, regular, predictable Emily tardiness, that had saved my life. It had to be something more than that, surely. Not the cause of the revulsion I felt toward myself for having endured all the disrespect.

I told you what she said, he replied.

When did you take the message?

I don't know. Nine thirty, maybe a little later. I had the boy take it over to you right away.

How, I asked myself, did Emily know I was already in Kabul? As far as she knew, I thought, I wasn't due until the afternoon, when the UN flight would come in. And why did she ask me to wait for her? Did she know I was going out, going somewhere in particular, even? Or was she asking me to wait there only in case I had plans to leave Kabul?

What do you know about the explosion this morning? I asked Maurice.

What do you mean?

What time did it happen?

I don't know. Sometime this morning.

I picked up the picture of his wife and child and tossed it at his chest. I left, satisfied that Maurice was only an idiot ruled by his groin.

Back at the gate, I asked Suaif what time he'd heard about the explosion in the city center.

This morning.

Can you be more precise? I set off at ten forty-five. You told me about it then.

I'm not sure.

Who told you about the explosion?

Ahmed across the road.

Why?

He was complaining about the traffic. He was late for work.

He came to you?

Yes.

When?

He comes at ten a.m., but today he was delayed. He came to see me before you came, sir.

Just before ten thirty?

Is that when you came, sir?

Yes.

Then yes, sir.

Why?

Please?

Why did he come over?

His boss had not arrived and he could not get into the shop. Maybe his boss was delayed by the explosion or traffic.

But why did he come over?

He came to pass time with me.

But he knew about the explosion?

He heard from someone. We hear news very fast in Kabul.

You saw Suleiman before this man Ahmed came?

Yes.

What time?

I don't remember.

What time did you arrive for work?

Seven a.m.

I left Suaif. I did not trust him entirely. I returned to my room to collect my bag. I could barely contain my anxiety. The hours of the clock were running through my mind, when, what, who, and intention washing back and forth, crashing on the walls of the cranium. There was calculation and there was fury.

Back outside, I climbed into the car and gave the driver Emily's address. When we set off, I had only the intention of confronting Emily. Part of me wanted to believe—wanted confirmation—that she had *knowingly* kept me from going to Café Europa, because I could not abide the thought that her tardiness had saved me. And because I could not bear that idea, I was furious, even before I knew one way or the other, and the rage was itself so all-encompassing that it ultimately did not care for confirmation. Perhaps it is not so strange, after all, for how are we to feel contingent anger, how can we hold the state of readiness to be blind with rage, provided something turns out to be the case? We can't. We are just angry, and if our anger does not take over we might stand down if it turns out that the anger was unjustified.

I arrived at the UN compound, continued Zafar, where I asked the driver to wait for me. I presented myself at the sentry box and was told to wait while a soldier went off in the direction of Emily's accommodations. A few minutes later a soldier explained that Emily Hampton-Wyvern had just left for the palace. I tried my phone, hoping that, by some miracle, roaming now worked on it. It didn't. I explained to the soldier that I was having trouble getting a connection—must be because of the bombing this morning—and persuaded him to send a message through to her by phone: *Urgent, for the attention of Emily Hampton-Wyvern. I am at the UN compound but leave for my flight in twenty minutes. I can't wait a minute longer.*

How self-abasing? Not I *won't*, but I *can't*. I can't wait a minute longer, as if to say it's outside my control, which is to imply that if it were within my control, you could still be late. Thirty minutes later an ISAF jeep pulled up outside the compound gates. Emily climbed out. Neither of us was smiling.

Inside Emily's room, detached from the life of the city, its hubbub, its fracturing of the mind's focus, I became the instrument of my fury. I had never felt such rage as I did then, such consuming vicious anger, and of course I was keyed up: I'd just witnessed a bomb site. I had yet to fully understand what precisely had happened, and, although I see now that I must already have begun putting things together, at the time, my body seemed entirely given over to imminent action, every nerve in the service of instincts, every sinew twitching with readiness. Do you know what a scientist would have called my state? Arousal. How primitive is this body, that it cannot reflect gross distinctions, let alone fine ones? Perhaps you think I should have been grateful to her: She had been tardy and that is what had saved my life. But you will have missed the point completely. I had been waiting for her all my life and never once had she waited for me, never a moment when she was on time. Had she even shown up earlier? Did she visit me in hospital? Had she even waited while I was there? The only future with her was short-lived. When a future had opened up, a vision of family came before my eyes, of love and affection and renewal and purpose, but she chose to shut that future out, and then, because of uncompromising mathematical reasoning, I understood—not learned, because she never told me—that the child could not have been mine. Don't tell me it wasn't yet alive. Don't tell me it was not yet something. I might have fallen in love with an idea, *but I fell in love with an idea*, and what is greater?

I was wrong. I had no control over the Emily in my head, no power; we have no more control over the people in our heads than we do over ourselves. What does an optical illusion tell you? It tells you that you have no direct access to reality. How do you begin to control a world you cannot see, a world that includes you? How much of what we do is driven by the vanity of gaining dominion over others, not to own them but with the purpose of shielding our beliefs from evidence that would contradict them? Reality has no way to force itself on us, and we can, in fact, alter what we think we perceive in order to suit what we want to believe. Listening to people is hard because you run the risk of having to change the way you see the world. We'd sooner destroy them.

At the airport, I tried to get a seat on a flight, any flight, out of Kabul, out of the country. I went everywhere looking for some or other official who could oblige.

Zafar had skipped over something. He had gone from Emily's room straight to the airport, quite obviously passing over what had happened in that room. So obviously that I think he wanted me to press him on it, to encourage him, to give him the courage to talk about it. I would raise it with him, I thought, but I would wait until there was nothing else left for him to say, nowhere else to go.

I had cash for a ticket, continued Zafar, U.S. dollars, but it seemed everyone else had also been willing to pay whatever extortionate amount was being sought in order to knock some hapless NGO worker off a flight.

When I had all but given up hope, a man appeared by my side, short, plump, and bald but with thick eyebrows and a thick mustache.

Hello, sir. You are having difficulty?

I'm trying to get on a plane out of here.

Do you play chess, sir?

I'm sorry?

Are you a chess player?

I play chess.

Some people think that chess is about the pieces, he said, echoing Colonel Mushtaq.

I looked again at this man, a positively odd-looking fellow, and I was sure that whenever his face took on an expression, those eyebrows and that mustache would have magnified the effect.

In fact, I replied, it's about the board. And you learn only from playing game after game.

Of course, during the flight I reflected on what had happened with Emily, but my thoughts were interrupted by ideas surfacing from my unconscious mind, popping into my head unbidden, about all that had passed in the twenty-four hours leading up to the destruction of Café Europa and Crane's death. What is it about a puzzle, a logical puzzle, that so grips us that we can't shake it off until we've solved it? You know the kind of thing: Six people have to cross a river in a boat that fits three, but the vicar can't be left alone with the cannibal and so on. Stuff like that. Even when you think you've set it aside in order to get on with whatever else has to be done, the brain carries on, and in the middle of making a cup of tea, when you're wondering how they make the edges of sugar cubes so sharp, out of nowhere the key to the puzzle hits you: You take the vicar over *and* bring him back. Images of faces kept coming back to me—Suleiman, the colonel, Crane—faces I had already read, but now, on rereading them in my mind's eye, I began to suspect my earlier impressions.

Whose side were they each on? The question only makes sense if there are sides to speak of. The West does not care to be reminded, over and over, that the Americans supported jihadis in the war against Soviet occupation. But if my enemy's enemy is my friend, what is the quality of a friendship founded on common hatred? What have we each learned about the other, when all we need to know is that we share a hatred? Think of two people who don't know each other very well, when their conversation chances upon a book, a rich and expansive book they both love. They become animated and bear a sudden goodwill toward each other, as if each is thinking, *You see the world the way I do.* Yet no two people ever feel the same way when stumbling on a book they both dislike. The conversation soon moves on.

In the mess of Central Asia there are as many sides as there are opportunities to steal a march. There are no sides to tell us who is doing what, for whom, and why. There are only exigencies, strategies, short-term objectives, at the level of governments, regions, clans, families, and individuals: fractals of interests, overlapping here, mutually exclusive there, and sometimes coinciding. No sides. Which should not surprise us. After all, we both know that good people do bad things, that friends will hurt you, and that everyone is from first to last on his own side.

By the end of the flight, a theory of what had happened had formed in my mind, but it was only after meeting the colonel again that its features would be confirmed.

It's a pleasure to see you again, my boy. How are you?

Good afternoon, Colonel.

The colonel was there at Islamabad airport. During the flight, I'd plugged Suleiman's flash drive into my laptop and discovered, as I expected, that it was blank.

I trust the flight was agreeable, he said.

Fine. Those envelopes. They didn't contain money, did they? I asked him right away.

Correct.

Military plans?

Close.

Bogus plans intended to draw Taliban action somewhere specific. You're going to set a trap, I said.

Well done, responded the colonel, as if awarding marks in an exam.

Suleiman works for the Taliban? I asked.

For the opposition.

How did you come to know Suleiman was working for this *opposition*?

Suleiman worked for us. He believed we had no knowledge of where his true allegiances lay. The question is, how did *you* know Suleiman was working for the opposition?

The colonel hadn't answered my question: too much information to share.

I didn't know for sure, I replied. But because he would have sent me to Café Europa, I suspected he wasn't everything he seemed. He also gave me what he wanted me to believe was a recording of Crane incriminating himself, but it was blank. And then there's the fact that he didn't show up this morning. In the wind, I imagine. What exactly did your message to Emily say?

The colonel did not bat an eyelid. On the flight, I had come to the suspicion that he had had a message sent to Emily, which in turn prompted her to contact me and tell me to wait for her. He seemed not the least surprised by my question, and I had the impression he was ready to say whatever he was able to say.

Simply that you were in Kabul, replied the colonel, and getting on a flight in one hour.

Why didn't you just leave a message for me at AfDARI but in Emily's name?

Because she might have learned by other means that you were already in Kabul and left you her own message. Then there would be two messages, potentially inconsistent ones.

What if she hadn't contacted me right away? Or what if she had and I still decided not to wait for her but went to Café Europa instead?

There were other ways to keep you away. You received the message held for you at the gate, did you not?

That was from you?

From us.

Of course, I said. I remembered my exchange with the gatekeeper at AfDARI. Suaif had not actually said that the message was from Suleiman. I had been asking him about Suleiman and Suaif had been talking about a message that said my meeting was delayed. Between my agitation at having again to wait for Emily and Suaif's erratic command of English, I had only assumed that the message had come from Suaif. Why didn't you have the message sent to me right away? I asked. Why have it held at the gate?

The message from Emily was the wicketkeeper; the one at the gate was a long stop.

You left the long stop, as you call it, waiting at the gate because if you'd had the message brought directly to me, I might have contacted Crane to postpone or cancel, in which case Crane might not have gone to Café Europa. Is that right?

You would have been kept away in any event, replied the colonel.

I don't know if I'm appalled or touched, I said. Tell me: Is Crane alive?

Regrettably not.

But you could have stopped that?

The colonel didn't answer. There was an obvious question: Why had the colonel wanted Crane to go to Café Europa? It was obviously also a question the colonel would not answer.

Was Crane really a pedophile?

That's what Suleiman told you?

In graphic detail.

Why do you doubt it?

Because when I suggested to Crane that someone had evidence of his pedophilia, he didn't seem interested. He must have known that there couldn't be any such evidence. Yet, curiously, he didn't react to the very idea that he was being accused of pedophilia.

What does that tell you? asked the colonel.

The colonel's Socratic method reinforced the idea that I already had much of the information in my possession and needed only to piece it together. Everything I knew about Crane's venality I had learned from Suleiman. This is not mathematics, in which content stands and falls by itself, but the world, in which authority and motive matter. Yet some claims are so horrific, so unrelentingly repulsive, we seem unable to stop and think whether the claims are true. The merest suggestion can destroy a career, a life. And if we cannot think about whether they are true, how can we think about them at all, when they are?

Surely you know? I asked the colonel.

Old soldiers have a tendency toward arrogance, not omniscience. Tell me what you think, and, if I can, I'll set you straight.

Crane actually did give Suleiman the impression that he was a pedophile. But it was just a fabrication to get Suleiman to hate him so that he would be only too eager to steal those documents that were being mysteriously sent to him. The ISAF jeep delivering them only enhanced the idea that the papers contained military plans. As for Maurice, he was unimportant, a bit player simply handing on parcels from time to time, without any knowledge.

So far so good.

What's not clear is who this opposition is that Suleiman was working for. Aside from Suleiman's role in Crane's death, there's no evidence that Suleiman was actually working for the insurgents rather than the Americans.

Why would the Americans want Crane dead? the colonel asked.

I'm not ruling out that there might be some reason I don't know, I said.

Suleiman was working for the insurgents and Crane for the Americans, explained the colonel.

Why kill Crane, though? I don't mean he didn't have a motive; he thought Crane was a nasty piece of work. But it's a lot of trouble to go to, mounting a bomb attack in Kabul with ISAF all over the city.

My belief is that he was most likely targeting you. He got Crane into the bargain for free.

Not the other way?

Possibly, but in the final analysis I do not think much turns on it.

Why would he want me dead?

Suleiman?

He didn't stop me from going to Café Europa. You did.

It's rather reassuring, in fact, that he wanted you dead. It confirms that he believes he has acquired valuable intelligence. Killing you would have prevented you from informing someone of what happened.

But I'm not dead. He must know that.

Maybe, maybe not. But who would you tell? Suleiman is not stupid. He knows you couldn't tell anyone without attracting suspicion, if, that is, you managed not to incriminate yourself. How would you explain that you knew Suleiman had acquired the documents? Killing you would have been neater, but it would not have added much.

I could tell *you*. Doesn't he know that?

He's not worried about you telling me. That's fine, because he thinks we wanted him to acquire the documents.

And he is right about that.

Yes. But he doesn't know that we're working with the Americans on this, at least as of one hour from now. The Americans had been trying for a month to set this trap, but Suleiman had neither the balls nor the ingenuity to copy the documents unnoticed. In fairness to them, if they'd made it too easy for him, it would have aroused his suspicions.

And Crane was part of all that.

We decided to step in—

Without telling the Americans?

They will know soon enough.

And Crane didn't know the Pakistanis were involved.

You say Pakistanis, but really it was a more limited operation.

And Crane wasn't in on that.

No.

Won't the Americans want to know why you didn't tip them off before Crane was killed?

My dear boy. The only way we learned anything was when a confidential informant, whose identity cannot be disclosed, came to me and told me, and it was too late for Crane then. But the Americans don't even need to know that.

What informant?

The colonel smiled. He was referring to me.

Did Crane seem like a monster to you? asked the colonel.

Yes and no.

The trouble with Crane, said the colonel, is that he was unable to fully inhabit a new persona—as you've just demonstrated. No, our boy Crane is a casualty of war.

Why did you not step in and save Crane?

When you play chess, does it matter whether you were black or white in a previous game? In one game, you are white, in another black.

You believe you need to stay onside with the Americans.

You can be more precise than that.

You, Colonel Mushtaq, retired, want the Americans to believe that you are onside with them. But you, Colonel Mushtaq, also want to see the war end as soon as possible. How is that for precision?

Good enough.

If the object of the exercise was to pique Suleiman's interest in the documents, why was Crane supposed to maintain the impression he might be a pedophile?

So that Suleiman would have a grudge against him. Politics and religion will motivate the mass, but if you want one man to act, then personal animus is so much more reliable. We needed Suleiman to risk getting at the contents of the envelope.

But that grudge went further than you expected?

The colonel frowned but didn't respond.

The jeep was later than usual that day, I said.

Yes. That was a difficult decision. You see, if we didn't deliver that day, albeit a little later, we couldn't be sure you'd stay in Kabul long enough for the next drop-off.

But it could raise suspicions. It was always on time.

Possibly. But Suleiman went ahead, didn't he? And after all that trouble, and the fact that he can't come back, he's now invested in the idea that the loot is worth something. He himself will be the best advocate for the reliability of those plans.

How did you know it had all played out as you expected?

The torn envelope.

I didn't imagine the colonel had actually seen the envelope but had heard about it. I thought of Crane. What was it Crane had said when, before we parted, I declined his invitation to watch American football with him? *Not your cup of tea, eh?* I don't know if he'd made a conscious connection and I can't imagine why he'd want to hint anything to me, but still I wondered now if Crane had noticed that Suleiman's promised tea never materialized.

Suleiman said he wanted me to become the director at AfDARI, I said to the colonel.

He seemed to be waiting for me to finish.

He said the trustees also wanted to see a change at the top. What was that for?

What do *you* think?

Flattery?

Perhaps, although I'm not sure you present yourself as someone easily flattered. I rather think the purpose was somewhat more subtle. It was misdirection. He was intimating that he himself was anchored to Af-DARI, to Kabul, and to the life he was ostensibly leading. He wanted you to take his frame of reference as the narrow one of careerism.

Sounds plausible.

The colonel was looking at me as if considering whether to tell me something.

That evening, said the colonel, after you had dinner with us, the general asked me if I was trying to flatter you with the attention of such top brass.

What did you say?

I didn't say anything. Why should I? Of course, if flattery worked, then so be it. But I was counting on something else. You have a character trait you must watch out for. I know because I used to have it. If you can rein it in, you'd be very effective indeed.

The colonel paused there, waiting for me to ask.

And what would that be?

You're not a trusting fellow, but you very much *want* to trust, and in the right conditions you will do so.

What conditions are those?

When you believe you are taking principled action.

The outside concourse was in the shade, but there was sunlight beyond, over the cars and buses. Islamabad already felt quite removed and the world far away—a feeling that I knew was quite false, but I hadn't the stomach to deny even an illusory sense of relief.

So what now? I asked the colonel.

Now I have to ask you to spend three weeks as my guest, he replied.

Only three?

Thank you, my boy. It will truly be my pleasure.

But in three weeks there will be interesting news. The Taliban ambushed somewhere?

Come now, said the colonel, brushing off my question. There will be time for such a word. You do know that you will be safe?

You could have let me go to the café.

Precisely. I really do enjoy your company, you know.

And it's so hard to get good help these days, I said.

Quite so.

We climbed into the Land Cruiser.

I think we'll have a bite to eat and play chess.

In the corner? I asked.

In the corner.

You have me cornered.

Only literally, my boy.

What I never broached with the colonel, of course, was how he'd known what was going to happen at Café Europa. For his part, the colonel had the good grace never to ask me anything about Emily, and I wondered how much he already knew.

I must tell you the truth, Zafar would come to say, in a phrase whose weight is borne by the word *truth*, a word that seems to claim the whole of a sentence wherever it appears. Truth is the thing that's sought, is it not? Remember Gödel's Incompleteness Theorem, which tells us truth is not there always to be found and that we cannot know ahead of the search whether the truth itself is of a kind that can be uncovered. Little wonder, then, that when it is truth that is promised, our ears will prick up, as did mine. Yet as I write now, reflecting again on that phrase after the passage of time, I find myself thinking not of *truth* but of *must*. I have read somewhere that we should look to our second thoughts for the deepest wisdom. As I now read Zafar's phrase, I hear a different stress. Why does a man feel he *must* speak?

I read Coleridge's *The Rime of the Ancient Mariner* when I was at Eton. Part of the English literary canon, it is the kind of poem that is precisely within the writ of a decent English education. I remember the English master, Mr. Humphries, asking us to consider the premise of the poem. A young mariner collars a fellow on his way to a wedding. Against his initial protest, the wedding guest is forced to hear the young mariner's story. Humphries, I recall, was so vexed by the mariner's compulsion to tell his story to someone that to the boys in the classroom his interest verged, I think, on the comical. The room failed to take up the question of why the compulsion, so that Humphries, resorting to random selection, singled out me.

It's made up, isn't it, sir? It doesn't really matter.

The poem doesn't matter?

No, sir. It's not really important, the compulsion you talk about. It's just a way to get the story out.

But doesn't that beg the question?

Sorry, sir?

Why does he feel he has to get the story out?

I don't know, sir.

I am afraid that the nuances of poetry, of the ancient mariner, did not strike land that day. It is only now that I can venture the thought, setting the mariner aside for a moment, that what we boys saw in that classroom was something Humphries had brought there with him, a personal preoccupation. We talk about taking work home and can fail to see, as an unformed boy might, that, conversely, into everything we do we bring ourselves and, as Zafar might say, our histories. It was, I'm now quite sure, a personal matter for Humphries, and I cannot now know what it was that made the question of the mariner's urgency Humphries's own.

The mariner who slays an albatross, thereby bringing calamity upon the crew, is possessed by the spirit of confession. Then I was too young to understand the redemption that comes from giving voice to what the brain seeks to hide from oneself. Only age reveals our drive, our compulsion to say something. Youth has nothing to declare.

All of which is to say that I think that on the question of why it was that Zafar was talking, even about the circumstances of that last day in Kabul and the events of the final hours, in particular the confrontation with Emily (if *confrontation* is the right word), the root of any explanation must be that very human urge to speak and tell, the impulse that brings the religious to the confessional box and others to the therapist's couch; even when the urge to tell has competition, including a drive, for instance, to withhold the self-incriminating; and even though there is a reason why we refer to horrors as unspeakable.

Is there something you don't want to say, something you've glossed over? You don't have to tell me, I said.

As he related the events in Kabul and Islamabad, Zafar had seemed agitated, shifting in his seat, leaning forward, leaning back, a picture of fevered animation. But now a strange calm descended over him. He did not look me in the eye but acquired that faraway look he sometimes had, evidence of a mind considering its memories, perhaps considering what to say, and I felt no urge to breach the silence stretching out over us.

When I came to the last of Zafar's numbered notebooks and to the final page of writing, I found two entries. Their juxtaposition was disturbing. Each on its own did not have any great effect, but seeing them obviously written at the same time, next to each other—that was unsettling. They are the first two epigraphs to this chapter.

Perhaps as much to temper the effect of the first two as for any other reason, I have included two more, the Simone Weil and the Susan Brownmiller, both taken from an earlier notebook. Zafar would have known that in due course I would come to his final entries. I cannot say if that is why he hesitated to talk at the critical moment, why he moved on so quickly to Islamabad and the final meeting with the colonel. Perhaps he knew those entries alone would speak volumes. But in the end he himself did speak, and he did return to that room in Kabul. In fact, he may never have left it.

In that closed room, Emily looked frightened. No, she *was* frightened. When you are the cause of someone's fear, she does not merely *look* afraid to you. What you see is what you get.

When someone is scared, we say she's scared stiff, she's frozen with fear, she's petrified, turned to stone. The woman with Maurice must have been somewhat afraid, but she had the presence of mind to make for the door. Emily did not move. She could not move, as if her mind no longer possessed her. And in that fact alone, I felt an engulfing sense of control. She was terrified, and I must tell you the truth: It was exhilarating, and I felt a unity with her. Can you imagine? A unity, the synthesis of threat and fear. Not threat but *violence becoming*.

I have said enough. I wanted to tell you something, I thought I would be explicit, make it clear what I did, leave no room to hide, but now I know I can't. I came this far, down the long river, visiting spurs and detouring to tributaries along the way, but here at the brink of the cliff, where the river meets the sea, I don't know how to speak the unspeakable. Our actions are always questions, not answers. If it is true that our will is free, how is it that we do things we regret? I know that our day is littered with actions that alter its course, as thick on the ground as all the irrational numbers on the line, and that only in fiction can a single act change a whole life. But how do we do that which in lucidity we would surely conclude could only bring about a fall from grace, a fall from which no penance could raise us?

22

Our Scattered Leaves

In that part of the book of my memory before which is little that can be read, there is a rubric, saying, *Incipit Vita Nova* [Here begins the new life]. Under such rubric I find written many things; and among them the words which I purpose to copy into this little book; if not all of them, at least their substance.

—Dante Alighieri, *Vita Nuova*, translated by Dante Gabriel Rossetti

All mankind is of one author, and is one volume; when one man dies, one chapter is not torn out of the book, but translated into a better language; and every chapter must be so translated; God employs several translators; some pieces are translated by age, some by sickness, some by war, some by justice; but God's hand is in every translation, and his hand shall bind up all our scattered leaves again for that library where every book shall lie open to one another.

—John Donne, *Meditation 17*

In the first daylight hour of a morning in February 2009, as I lay awake after a restless night and Kensington lay still asleep, I heard the low and heavy sound of the front door closing. With my one ear against the pillow, my other followed the fading metronome of steps outside. I did not run downstairs or even go to the window to call out, for I already knew that this is what would happen and I already understood that no response from me is what he would want. I would miss my friend, of course, and in the weeks that followed I missed him rather more, in fact, than at first I thought I would. He had chosen, for the time being at least, a life of few attachments, without such ties as bind a man to place or person, and it was a choice made in a lucidity that was his own. I smile now at my use of that word *choice*, for how much would he have questioned that? I myself cannot accept that we are without choice. Our choices may be limited by what is handed down, but within the frame of our circumstances, of our fortunes, good or ill, within a perimeter drawn by inheritance and accident, I believe we choose how to live. If Zafar is right, that belief may be an illusion allowed us by God, or the Fates, or natural selection, looking down on us as parents might look kindly upon the naïveté of a child. But I can let him have that, for who would deny that we are ever more than children in the face of existence?

Outside, the London sky was slow in accepting the morning sunlight. The traffic was scarcely a trickle. The days, not yet long, were getting longer. The house will be quiet today, I thought, as I lay in my bed, not that Zafar had brought any noise with him. His presence had slipped easily into the sparse workings of my home and the rhythms of my life. What I will not hear now is that beat of one's own heart audible only in the presence of human affection. His absence will be felt.

Three months were to pass before I received word from him again, on the only occasion I've heard from him since he left. I received a postcard, a card bearing no images. There was my address in Kensington, London, but there was no return address. The postage stamp was Jordanian, and it contained the image of a man's head and shoulders, something that might have been extracted from something greater. When I searched Jordanian stamps on the Internet, I discovered that the image was of Avicenna, a Persian mathematician and philosopher of the tenth century, a name I remembered vaguely from years ago. And when I looked him up and read about his work, I found that Avicenna had considered ontological arguments for the existence of God some time before St. Anselm had.

On the reverse side of the postcard, there was a URL, written in his hand, a universal resource locator, a Web page address, one of those tiny abridging URLs that disclose none of the information the true address contains. That was all there was on the card. I typed it into the browser on my computer, and when I pressed Return, the URL called up a photograph.

There are many maps in my father's house, and they all hang on one wall in the room we call the family room. Now that appellation, *family room*, seems a touch ambitious. A brother or a sister, one sibling, I think, would have made the name appropriate, brought the name home. I re-member Zafar gazing at one map and, on another visit home, without Zafar, I spared a few moments to look at it. The map showed the far northeast corner of India under the Raj, the part of the world that today includes Bangladesh and the neighboring states of India, as well as strips of Bhutan and Burma. I imagine him now focused on a corner of that corner of the world—if a corner can have a corner. I imagine him enlarg-ing in his mind's eye the place of his birth. I know of course that he had lived in Dhaka in 2001 and 2002, but a remote village and the capital city are worlds apart. And though I have no hard ground on which to base my speculation, the thought pleases me that at some time in those years he disappeared, my friend might have paid a visit to that area of the world, to the place where he had been happiest, as he once said, to the woman who had loved him.

Zafar did not say anything about what he had been doing in those years, the years after he left Afghanistan and before reappearing at my door, so that I am ashamed to see that all that I have learned is what I could already have known, had I made the effort to reach out. I never, for instance, called him or sent a note when he was in hospital, nor went to see him when he came out. It hurts to say *for instance*.

My friend once told me something his friend Marcy, mother of Josie, had said to him. He had asked her, rather foolishly, he said, if it was hard bringing up Josie on her own. Marcy had replied that it would have been harder with Josie's father around. It is what Marcy said next, as reported by Zafar, that now comes to my mind. What was hard, she explained, was not having someone to talk to about Josie, not having someone to make decisions with. Don't get me wrong, she said (or something like that), I think on the whole I've made the right decisions and I'm pretty sure we would have come to the same decisions if I'd made them with someone else. And yet it's not enough to know that. There's something about doing it with someone else, she said, something in just talking about it, something about how it leaves you feeling afterward. Decisions seem lighter; everything is lighter.

There are those who do not talk because they have no one to talk to. And there are those who do not talk because they have nothing to say. To learn that I have been neither, that I held my own hand to my mouth, has been hard. Talking, as my father said to me, is easier said than done. I have been uncertain of so many things, but I never seized the uncertainty as the source of joy that I now believe it to be. I never owned my marriage, never owned my friendships, never owned my relationship to my mother, never owned any of those things that cannot be bought.

It is hard to grasp Gödel's Incompleteness Theorem, I think. I never have, not really. I know this because although I have followed the proof—the one I found in the literature that on its face seemed most accessible—at the end I never had, to use Zafar's words, that sensation of ecstatic relief, of turning a corner and seeing the mountains open up and the valley shine under a golden sky, when heaven lowers a ladder of angels to receive you. That, I think, is what some people have known, at least once: divinity for men.

This, however, I know about the theorem: that it takes us—to use words not all my own—to the point at which two roads diverge, that we have to choose and the choice is not a happy one. Both roads take us into mathematical realms of simple language stripped bare of human conceit. Down one road is unbearable inconsistency, a world in which black is white and white is black and there is no way to tell them apart, in which—without a hint of exaggeration, with not so much as a touch of hyperbole or melodrama—one equals zero. This leaves us looking down the other road, one no less daunting and hard but that has the merit if not of leading us to the mercy of understanding then at least of delivering us from the torment of contradictions. Along this other way lies another world, also one of simple language. But it is a twilight world, for in its manifold embrace are things that are true, crystal blue propositions, which are as true as a man could ever hope to feel something to be true, yet which things—irony of ironies—the man will never *know* to be true, not because they merely lie beyond the wit of the creature but because mathematics herself condemns men to ignorance. This is the strangest thing: mathematical truths for which there can never be proof. Zafar's notes record the descent of hope, having once clung to a childlike dream; I know he knew that mathematics would never answer all or any

of the questions of human life and suffering, but the dream was that in her own land, in her own fertile crescent, mathematics would at least yield answers to her own questions and never, instead, mock the traveler with barren wells, never deny him the proof of how those crystalline truths are true at all.

Zafar had set himself to the pursuit of knowledge, and it is apparent to me now, in a way it was not before, that he had done so not in order to "better himself," as the expression goes, but in order to lay ground for his feet to stand upon; in order, that is, to go home, somewhere, and take root. I believe that he had failed in this mission and had come to see, as he himself said in so many words, that understanding is not what this life has given us, that answers can only beget questions, that honesty commands a declaration not of faith but of ignorance, and that the only mission available to us, one laid to our charge, if any hand was in it, is to let unfold the questions, to take to the river knowing not if it runs to the sea, and accept our place as servants of life.

The image my friend linked me to—thereby linking me to him, since he saw it also, like that moon which we all see—is of Kurt Gödel and Albert Einstein. The two men are walking in Princeton, New Jersey, on the path from Fuld Hall to Olden Farm. The photograph catches them some way off, two exiles in an alien land. It is a blustery day, the wind tugging at their coats, and we see only the backs of the figures, so that without further information we cannot tell which is the figure of Gödel and which of his friend.

The picture means much to me. Of course it reminds me of my childhood in Princeton, releasing time from the deep eddies of memory. Those were happy years. But it is the austerity of the image that is most affecting, the simplicity of its content. When I look at this picture, I see two people undeterred by time, walking and talking, bumping against each other, as they discuss the things that matter to them and why they matter.

Acknowledgments

I am indebted to Eric Chinski and Gabriella Doob at Farrar, Straus and Giroux; Paul Baggaley, Kris Doyle, and Kate Harvey at Picador; and Charles Buchan, Sarah Chalfant, Andrew Wylie, and Alba Ziegler-Bailey at the Wylie Agency. To Eric, Kris, Kate, Sarah, and Andrew, I owe a special debt. Discussions with Eric were vital. My thanks to Ivan Birks, Şeyda Emek, Ruth Franklin, Anja König, Lauren Marks-Nino, Sanjay Reddy, Amy Rosenberg, and Melinda Stege-Arsouze. Amy made fine comments on the manuscript. I am grateful to a physician for her clear responses to my questions. I would like to thank the staff and benefactors of the British Library, the New York Public Library, and the Saratoga Springs Public Library. It is a pleasure to record my gratitude to Elaina Richardson, Candace Wait, and the Corporation of Yaddo.